MW01675240

James M. Le Moine

Maple Leaves

A budget of legendary, historical, critical, and sporting intelligence. First Series. Second Series. Third Series.

SALZWASSER
VERLAG

James M. Le Moine

Maple Leaves

A budget of legendary, historical, critical, and sporting intelligence. First Series. Second Series. Third Series.

Reprint of the original, first published in 1863, 1864, 1865.

1st Edition 2022 | ISBN: 978-3-37500-595-5

Verlag (Publisher): Salzwasser Verlag GmbH, Zeilweg 44, 60439 Frankfurt, Deutschland
Vertretungsberechtigt (Authorized to represent): E. Roepke, Zeilweg 44, 60439 Frankfurt, Deutschland
Druck (Print): Books on Demand GmbH, In de Tarpen 42, 22848 Norderstedt, Deutschland

MAPLE LEAVES:

A BUDGET OF

LEGENDARY, HISTORICAL, CRITICAL,

AND SPORTING INTELLIGENCE.

BY J. M. LEMOINE. ESQ.

(Copyright Secured.)

QUEBEC:

1863.

TABLE TO CHAPTERS.

TO MY ENGLISH READERS.

A YOUTHFUL poet, L. H. Frechette, assumes in the preface of his charming little volume, "Mes Loisirs," that every book ought to have something of a preface, were it only a note of interrogation—?

Without admitting or denying this proposition, I have a word to say to my readers (if I have any), not precisely to tell them that the modest *Maple Wreath*, I now lay before them, is worthy of their approbation,—as it must stand or fall on it own merits,— but merely to ask on one point a little forbearance.

Just let some of them imagine they have to write a book in French. Would not the bare idea make them feel as nervous as a fish out of water? Such is the feeling which comes over me in inditing one in English. This litte volume may, perhaps, add another to the many proofs that no man can write well two languages. What remains to be done? Nothing, I fear, except to mend my ways and my English, should I ever repeat the attempt. A portion of the historical, legendary and sporting intelligence herein contained is scattered through many old books and memoirs, not of easy access to the generality of readers. In collecting it in one small budget, neither ponderous in form nor in substance, have I succeeded to furnish a manual of light reading for tourists, sportsmen and others? Time alone will tell. This bantling has taken up, pleasantly enough, many a leisure hour during long winter evenings, when my "Household Gods" were wrapt in balmy sleep, and when no sound invaded my study but the whistling of the northern blast through my old oaks and snow-clad pines.

To say it cost me neither trouble nor research, would be untrue. Dealing becomingly with some feudal topics, I found very difficult, notwithstanding the pains I took, to handle them gingerly. I have thrown in several light anecdotes to enliven the subject. It has, likewise, frequently been my lot to speak of the living and the dead, also of current events: severely at times; unjustly, I hope, never. Without ignoring the merits of other nations and other countries, I never shrank from standing up for my own, and I hope never will. Without forgetting the claims of ancestry; to whom we owe civil and religious freedom, and their exponent, representative institutions (even though our government be but a pale copy of a good original) one thing will frequently shew itself in these pages—that is,—the love of country. In the words of Scotia's bard:

> " Breathes there a man with soul so dead
> Who never to himself hath said,
> This is my own, my native land ? "

Or else in those of our own national poet :*

> " Sol Canadien, terre cherie !
> Par des braves tu fus peuplé ;

* Isidore Bedard. This gifted Quebecer was a brother of the late Hon. Mr. Justice Elzear Bedard. He represented in Parliament, the County of Saguenay, and died in Paris, in 1833.

Ils cherchaient loin de leur patrie,
Une terre de liberté.

Qu'elles sont belles nos campagnes !
En Canada qu'on vit content !
Salut, O ! sublimes montagnes,
Bords' du superbe St. Laurent.
Habitant de cette contrée,
Que nature sait embellir
Tu peux marcher tête levée,
Ton pays doit t'enorgueillir.

Si d'Albion la main chérie
Cesse un jour de te protéger
Soutiens-toi seule, ô ma patrie !
Méprise un secours étranger.
Nos pères sortis de la France
Etaient l' 'él te des guerriers,
Et leurs enfants, de leur vaillance
Ne flettriront pas les lauriers."

SPENCER WOOD GRANGE,
20th August, 1863.

ERRATA.

Page 14—Read " by-word" instead of " bye-word."
" 28—Instead of " about Governor Hincks," read " absent Governor H."
" 36—The note—leave out " Quebec."—" Backwoodsmen " instead of " backwoodmen."
" 50—Read " Capitaine de vaisseau " instead of " vesseau."
" 52—Read " 1725 " instead of " 1755."
" 55—Read " thirty-six millions."
" 61—Read " quotations " instead of " quations."
" 66—Instead of " Counts and barons dancing La Salammbo," read " countesses, &c., dressed à la Salammbo."
" 66—The note—Read instead of " he formed part," " the chevallier Lacorne formed part of the distinguished Canadians who offered their services to Major Preston."

MAPLE LEAVES.

The Grave of Cadieux.

CHAPTER I.

"Utawa's tide! this trembling moon
Shall see us float over thy surges soon.
Saint of this green isle! hear our prayers,
Oh! grant us cool heavens and favouring airs.
Blow, breezes, blow, the stream runs fast,
The Rapids are near, and the daylight's past."
Moore.

EVERY country has its legends, its wild stories of love or revenge; its traditional accounts of heroes; of battles won or lost; of brave men saved from certain death by some unaccountable superhuman agency; of wicked ones summarily punished. Poets, chroniclers, and historians mould these memories into more or less attractive form, throw light or shade on the picture, surround it with the halo of their genius, or leave it a dreary record of the past. It were strange, indeed, if our own inland seas, our wild lakes, our romantic forests—which for more than one century resounded with the tread or echoed the warhoop of the innumerable Indian tribes bent on exterminating one another, and equally hostile to the white man—should be an exception to the general rule. There is an ample harvest awaiting the future Walter Scotts, the Washington Irvings, or the Coopers, which Canada may produce; and towering amongst contemporary writers, we do know two whom elegance of style and intimate acquaintance with the historical and legendary lore of Canada, seem to designate as eminently qualified to collect the traditions of former days, to breathe in them the spirit of life: these men are the author of "Charles Guerin," and the writer of *Les Forestiers et Voyageurs.*

It is one of those ancient traditions, carefully collected, and divested of many of its marvellous episodes, we shall now try and lay before the reader.

Amongst the numerous stories or songs which old *Voyageurs* and *Northwesters* were in the habit of relating or singing a few years ago, after the toil of the day was over, and when the aroma of the weed rose in circles round the camp-fire, few had a wider range of celebrity than one generally known as the "Complainte de Cadieux;" it portrayed in simple but vivid language the singular fate of an educated and roving Frenchman, of the name of Cadieux, on the banks of the Ottawa River, close to *Portage du Fort*. But I fancy I hear an inquisitive lady friend ask: "Who was Cadieux? What brought him out to Canada? Was it to escape a *lettre de cachet*, or was it a *blasé*, Court *roué*, or a disappointed lover, seeking oblivion or concealment in the fastnesses of a Canadian forest, like the old Hermit of the Island of St. Barnabé?" Lady fair, I cannot say; I can only translate for you the history of the solitary tomb, which you can visit any day you like, near *Portage du Fort*, as Dr. Taché has related it.

Evidently, Cadieux must have united to bravery, and a romantic mind, a poetical genius: he finds his place amongst that resolute band of intelligent pioneers, the Marsollets, the Coutures, the Nicolets, etc., who were sometimes employed by government, sometimes by the missionaries, to interpret the various Indian dialects. Dr. Taché, to whom we are indebted for the narrative of Cadieux in his *Forestiers et Voyageurs*, tells us that he himself had frequently, in the course of his extended travels in the back-woods of Canada, heard detached stanzas of this mysterious wail of suffering and death, but until recently, the singular tradition, as embodied in poetry, had, as a whole, constantly eluded his grasp. Nor was he alone in his efforts to rescue it from oblivion; an old and indefatigable searcher of the past, the venerable Abbé Ferland, had diligently set to work, making enquiry in every quarter, writing even to the Red River settlement for information. To the pleasing writer of *Les Forrestiers et Voyageurs*, was reserved the satisfaction of graphically recording the old tradition. Audubon himself, when he discovered the magnificent eagle to which he gave the name of the Bird of Washington, did not experience keener pleasure than Dr. Taché on receiving from the lips of his old Indian guide, Morache, the whole *complainte* or song of Cadieux.

" In ascending," says he, " the great River Ottawa, one has to stop at the rock of the high mountain, situate in the middle of the *portage* of the seven *chutes*, at the foot of the island of the *Grand Calumet*: it is there that lies Cadieux's tomb, surrounded to this day by a wooden railing. Each time the Company's canoes pass the little rock, an old *voyageur* relates to his younger companions the fate of the brave interpreter.

" Cadieux was a roving interpreter, who had married a young Algonquin girl: he generally spent the summer hunting, and in winter he would purchase furs for the traders. After a winter thus passed by Cadieux at the *portage*, where he and the other families had their wigwams, it had been decided in May to wait for other Indian tribes who had furs for sale, and then all were to come down to Montreal. Profound peace existed in the settlement, when one day a young Indian, who had been roaming about, close to the rapids lower down than the *portage*, rushed back out of breath and shouted amongst the affrighted occupants of the huts: Nattaoué! Nattaoué!! The Iroquois! the Iroquois!!

" There was in reality at that moment, lower than the rapids of the Seven Falls, a party of Iroquois warriors, waiting to pounce upon the canoes, who generally descended at that season loaded with skins: one only chance of escape remained, that was to attempt to bring the canoes through the rapids—a hopeless project, it had ever been considered. This was not all: it would be necessary to station some parties in the woods in order, by firing, to draw off the attention of the Iroquois from the desperate attempt which would be made to go through the rapids and prevent pursuit. Cadieux, being the ablest and most resolute of the tribe, choose a young Algonquin warrior to accompany him in this perilous service: it was settled that once the interpreter and his comrade should have succeeded to inveigle the Iroquois in the woods, they would try a circuitous route, and attempt to join their own friends who were to send after them, should they be too long absent.

" Preparations being made for a start, it was settled that Cadieux and the Algonquin warrior, well armed, would go towards the Iroquois encampment, and that the sign for the canoes to break cover and start on their fearful race, would be the firing of their guns. Soon the report of a fire-arm was heard in the distance; it was followed by three or four others in quick succession; on went the frail birch canoes, amidst the foam and rocks, flying like sea birds, over the boiling caldron; it was a race for dear life, the extraordinary and superhuman skill of the red skins alone, under Providence, saving them from death in a thousand shapes."

"'I saw nothing during our passage over the rapids,' said Cadieux's wife, a pious woman, 'but the form of a *tall lady in white* hovering over the canoes and showing us the way.' They had invoked Ste. Anne, the patron saint of the mariner.

"The canoes escaped and safely arrived at the Lake of Two Mountains; but Cadieux and his devoted follower—what had become of them? This was ascertained some time after by the party sent to their rescue, and from the Iroquois themselves.

"Cadieux had quietly watched for the Iroquois at the *portage*, placing himself about an acre from his colleague, allowing the Iroquois scouts to penetrate to the centre of the *portage*, he waited for the death yell of one of them, shot by his helpmate, and then fired with unerring aim: the war whoop resounds, and the Iroquois fancying that they are attacked by a large party of the enemy, separate and charge in different directions. It is supposed that the young Algonquin fell here in attempting to join Cadieux, as was agreed on. For three days the blood-thirsty aborigines scoured the woods to find out traces of the encampment, never thinking for a moment that the enemy had been fool-hardy enough to attempt descending through the rapids. For three days and nights they searched for Cadieux, and these were sleepless nights for the white man! Foiled in their object, they retraced their steps and returned to their canoes. Several days had elapsed, and as no tidings of Cadieux came, a party was formed and sent to scour the woods; traces of the Iroquois were unmistakeable, and indications also of the presence of Cadieux in the vicinity. At the *Portage des Sept Chutes*, they noticed a small hut of branches which, apparently, had been abandoned; they passed it without much search and continued their route, thinking that perhaps Cadieux might have been compelled to ascend the Ottawa and take refuge with the Indians of the island. Two days later—it was the thirteenth day after the skirmish—they noticed, with surprise, on their return, on repassing what had previously appeared to them an abandoned hut, a small cross. It stood at the head of a fresh grave, on the surface ; in it, was deposited the corpse, still fresh, of Cadieux, half covered with green branches. His hands were clasped over his chest on which rested a large sheet of birch bark. The general opinion was, on reading the writing scribbled on the bark, and from other circumstances, that exhaustion, hunger, and anxiety had produced on the unfortunate interpreter that kind of mental excitement or hallucination which the French Canadians call *la folie des bois*, one of its peculiarities being the propensity its victims have in the woods of walking, unintentionally, in a circle and without making any progress. Cadieux had, doubtless, lived on wild fruit, never daring to light a fire, for fear of betraying his place of concealment to his merciless foes. He had grown weaker and weaker daily ; when the relief party had passed the hut two days previously, he had recognized them as friends, but the sudden joy at the prospect of a speedy deliverance was so great that it made him speechless and inanimate ; that when they passed him, seeing the last hope vanish, and feeling his strength fail, he had scribbled his adieux to the living and then prepared his last resting place ; this done, and the cross erected, he laid himself down to sleep the long slumber of death, covering his body as best he could with spruce boughs. Cadieux was a *voyageur*, a poet, and a warrior. What he had written on the bark was his dirge, his funeral chaunt. Before lying himself down to rest, he, whose imagination revelled in nature's grand scenery, and who could write *songs for voyageurs*, feeling a return of the sacred fire, embodied in verse his own dirge.

"This *chaunt*, by its simplicity, is very attractive ; it is much in the style of the old Norman ballads imported in the colony by the first settlers. The dying bard addresses himself to the objects which surround him, telling them of his regret for quitting life ; then, physical pain wrings from him a groan of anguish which is followed by a sorrowful thought at the loss of those nearest and dearest to his heart. He then next expresses his apprehension on witnessing smoke rise from his hut not far distant—then tells of the intense joy he experienced on recognizing the features of friends in the party sent out to rescue him—of his utter inability to shout out where he is—and of the pang which their final departure cost him. Cadieux next sees a wolf and a raven prowling round his emaciated frame ; the ardor of the hunter and of the backwoodsman fires his eye for a second, he threatens to shoot one; to the other he cries avaunt! go and feast on the bodies of the Iroquois I have slain near by. He next charges the song sparrow (the Rossignol) to convey his adieux to his wife and his 'well-beloved children,' then winds up by an invocation to the Virgin Mary. The piece of bark on which Cadieux's death song was written was brought to the post of the Lake of Two Mountains. The *voyageurs* have set it to a plaintive melody, well suited to a lay intended to portray the arduous life of a hunter and Indian warrior. It runs thus :—

"Petit rocher de la Haute montagne,
Je viens finir ici cette campagne!
Ah! doux échos, entendez mes soupirs;
En languissant je vais bientôt mourir.

Petits oiseaux, vos douces harmonies,
Quand vous chantèz, me rattachent à la vie:
Ah! si j'avais des ailes comme vous,
Je s'rais heureux avant qu'il fut deux jours!

Seul en ces bois, que j'ai eu de soucis!
Pensant toujours à mes si chers amis;
Je demandais: Hélas! sont-ils noyés?
Les Iroquois les auraient-ils tués?

Un de ces jours que m'étant éloigné,
En revenant je vis une fumée;
Je me suis dit: Ah! grand Dieu, qu'est ceci?
Les Iroquois m'ont-ils pris mon logis?

Je me suis mis un peu à l'embassade,
Afin de voir si c'était embuscade;
Alors je vis trois visages français,
M'ont mis le cœur d'une trop grande joie!

Mes genoux plient, ma faible voix s'arrête;
Je tombe. . . . . Hélas! à partir ils s'apprêtent:
Je reste seul. . . . . Pas un qui me console,
Quand la mort vient par un si grand désole!

Un loup hurlant vient près de ma cabane,
Voir si mon feu n'avait plus de boucane;
Je lui ai dit: Retire-toi d'ici;
Car, par ma foi, je percerai ton habit!

Un noir corbeau, volant à l'aventure,
Vient se percher tout près de ma toiture;
Je lui ai dit: Mangeur de chaire humaine,
Va-t'en chercher autre viande que mienne;

Va-t'en là-bas, dans ces bois et marais,
Tu trouveras plusieurs corps Iroquois:
Tu trouveras des chairs, aussi des os;
Va-t'en plus loin, laisse-moi en repos!

Rossignolet, va dire à ma maîtresse,*
A mes enfants qu'un adieu je leur laisse,
Que j'ai gardé mon amour et ma foi,
Et désormais faut renoncer à moi!

C'est donc ici que le mond' m'abandonne,
Mais j'ai secours en vous, Sauveur des hommes!
Très-Sainte Vierge, ah! m'abandonnez pas,
Permettez-moi d'mourir entre vos bras!' "

* This word, in old Canadian songs, is used for wife or betrothed.

A Visit to Chateau-Bigot.

4th June, 1863.

CHAPTER II.

"Selma, thy halls are desolate!"

Ossian.

"Ensconced 'mid trees this chateau stood—
'Mid flowers each aisle and porch;
At eve soft music charmed the ear—
High blazed the festive torch.

But, ah! a sad and mournful tale
Was her's who so enjoyed
The transient bliss of these fair shades—
By youth and love decoyed.

Her lord was true—yet he was false,
False—false—as sin and hell—
To former plights and vows he gave
To one that loved him well."

The Hermitage.

FROM time immemorial an antique and massive ruin, standing in solitary loneliness, in the centre of a clearing at the foot of the Charlesbourg mountain, some five miles from Quebec, has been visited by the young and the curious. The lofty mountain to the north-west of it is called *La Montagne des Ormes,* and the Charlesbourg peasantry designate the ruin as *La Maison de la Montagne.* The English of Quebec have christened it *The Hermitage,* whilst to the French portion of the population it is known as Chateau-Bigot, or Beaumanoir; and truly, were it not on account of the associations which surround the time worn pile, few indeed would take the trouble to go and look at the dreary object.

The land on which it stands was formerly included in the *Fief de la Trinité,* granted between 1640 and 1650 to Bishop Denis. This seigniory was subsequently sold to Monseigneur de Laval, a descendant of the Montmorency's, who founded in 1663 the Seminary of Quebec, and one of the most illustrious prelates in New France: the portion towards the mountain was dismembered. When the Intendant Talon formed his Baronie Des Islets,* he annexed to it certain lands of the *Fief de la Trinité*, amongst others that part on which now stand the remains of the old chateau, of which he seems to have been the builder, but which he subsequently sold. Bigot, having acquired it long after, enlarged and improved it very much. He was a luxurious French gentleman who, some hundred years ago, held the exalted post of Intendant or Administrator under the French Crown, in Canada.† In

* May, 1675, Louis the XIV and Colbert granted to Monsieur le Comte Talon, Intendant, the Seigniory des Ilets, "together with those neighboring villages to us belonging, the first called Bourg Royal, the second Bourg la Reine, the third, Bourg Talon, subsequently changed into the Barony of Orsainville."

† Hawkin's Picture of Quebec will give us an idea of the splendour in which the Intendant lived in his town residence:

"Immediately through Palace Gate, turning towards the left, and in front of the Ordinance buildings and store-houses, once stood an edifice of great extent, surrounded by a spacious garden looking towards the River St. Charles, and as to its interior decorations, far more splendid than the Castle of St. Lewis. It was the Palace of the Intendant, so called, because the sittings of the Sovereign Council were held there, after the establishment of the Royal Government in New France. A small district adjoining is still called *Le Palais* by the old inhabitants, and the name of the gate, and of the well-proportioned street which leads to it, are derived from the same origin.

"The Intendant's Palace was described by La Potherie, in 1698, as consisting of eighty *toises*, or four hundred and eighty feet of buildings, so that it appeared a little town in itself. The King's stores were kept there. Its situation does not at the present time appear advantageous, but the aspect of the River St. Charles was widely different in those days. The property in the neighborhood belonged to the Government, or to the Jesuits; large meadows and flowery pastures adorned the banks of the River, and reached the base of the rock; and as late as the time of Charlevoix, in 1720, that quarter of the city is spoken of as being the most beautiful. The entrance was into a court, through a large gateway, the ruins of which, in St. Vallier Street, still remain.

"The buildings formed nearly a square; in front of the river were spacious gardens, and on the sides the King's store-houses. Beyond the Palace, towards the west, were the pleasing grounds of the Jesuits, and of the General Hospital. This building, like most of the public establishments of Quebec, went through the ordeal of fire, and was afterwards rebuilt with greater attention to comfort and embellishment. In September, 1712, M. Bégon arrived as Intendant, with a splendid equipage, rich furniture, plate and apparel, befitting his rank. He was accompanied by his wife, a young lady lately married, whose valuable jewels were the general admiration. A fire, which it was found impossible to extinguish, broke out in the night of the 5th January, 1713, and burned so rapidly, that the Intendant and his lady, with difficulty escaped in their *robes de chambres*. The loss of the Intendant was stated at forty thousand crowns. The Palace was afterwards rebuilt in a splendid style by M. Bégon, at the King's expense. The following is its description, given by Charlevoix, in 1720, a few years afterwards. 'The Intendant's house is called the Palace, because the Superior Council assembles in it. This is a large pavilion, the two extremities of which project some feet; and to which you ascend by a double flight of stairs. The garden front which faces the little river, which is very nearly on a level with it, is much more agreeable than that by which you enter. The King's magazine faces the court on the right side, and behind that is the prison. The gate by which you enter is hid by the mountain on which the Upper Town stands, and which on this side affords no prospect, except that of a steep rock.'

"The Intendant's Palace was neglected as a place of official residence after the conquest in 1759. In 1775, it was occupied by a detachment of the American invading army, and destroyed by the fire of the garrison. The only remains at present are a private house, the gateway alluded to above, and several stores belonging to Government, formed by repairing some of the old French buildings. The whole is now known by the name of the King's woodyard." Since this has been written, extensive wharves have been constructed by the Corporation of Quebec. The reader is also reminded not to confound the Intendant Bégon with his successor, Bigot.

those days the forests which skirted the city were abundantly stocked with game: deer of several varieties, bears, foxes, perhaps even that noble and lordly animal, now extinct in Lower Canada, the Canadian stag, or Wapiti, roamed in herds over the Laurentian chain of mountains and were shot within a few miles of the Château St. Louis. This may have been one of the chief reasons why the French Lucullus erected the old castle, which to this day bears his name—a resting place for himself and friends after the chase. The profound seclusion of the spot, combined with its beautiful scenery, would have rendered it attractive during the summer months, even without the sweet repose it had in store for a tired hunter. Tradition ascribes to it other purposes, and amusements less permissible than those of the chase. A tragical occurrence enshrines the old building with a tinge of mystery, which only awaits the pen of a novelist to weave out of it a thrilling romance.

François Bigot, thirteenth and last Intendant of the Kings of France in Canada, was born in the province of Guienne, and descended of a family distinguished by professional eminence at the French bar. He had previously filled the post of Intendant in Louisianna, and also at Louisbourg. The disaffection and revolt which his rapacity caused in that city, were mainly instrumental in producing its downfall and surrender to the English commander, Pepperell, in 1744. Living at a time when tainted morals and official corruption flourished at court, he seems to have taken his standard of morality from the mother country: his malversations in office, his gigantic frauds on the treasury, his colossal speculations in provisions and commissariat supplies furnished by the French government to the colonists during a famine; his dissolute conduct and final downfall, are fruitful themes wherefrom the historian can draw wholesome lessons for his generation. Whether his Charlesbourg (then called Bourg Royal) castle was used as the receptacle of some of his most valuable booty, or whether it was a kind of Lilliputian *Parc au Cerfs*, such as his royal master had, tradition does not say. It would appear, however, that it was built and kept up by the plunder wrung from sorrowing colonists, and that the large profits he made by pairings from the scanty pittance the French government allowed the starving residents, were here lavished in gambling, riot and luxury.

In May, 1757, the population of Quebec was reduced to subsist on four ounces of bread per diem, one lb. of beef, HORSE-FLESH or COD

FISH; and in April of the following year, this miserable allowance was reduced to one-half. "At this time," remarks our historian, Mr. Garneau, "famished men were seen sinking to the earth in the streets from exhaustion."

Such were the times during which * Louis the XV.'s minion would retire to his Sardanapalion retreat, to revel at leisure on the life-blood of the Canadian people, whose welfare he had sworn to watch over! Such were the doings in the colony in the days of La Pompadour The results of this misrule were soon apparent: *the British lion quietly and firmly placed his paw on the coveted morsel.* The loss of Canada was viewed in France with indifference, and to use the terms of one of Her Majesty's ministers, when its fate and possible loss were canvassed one century later in the British Parliament, "without apprehension or regret." Voltaire gave his friends a banquet at Ferney, in commemoration of the event; the court favorite congratulated majesty, that since he had got rid of these "fifteen hundred leagues of frozen country," he had now a chance of sleeping in peace; the minister Choiseul urged Louis the XV. to sign the final treaty of 1763, saying that Canada would be *un embarras* to the English, and that if they were wise they would have nothing to do with it. In the meantime the red cross of St. George was waiving over the battlements on which the lily-spangled banner of Louis XV.† had proudly sat with but one interruption for one hundred and fifty-years, and the infamous Bigot was provisionally consigned to a dungeon in the Bastille—subsequently tried and exiled to Bordeaux; his property was confiscated, whilst his confederates and abettors, such as Varin, Bréard, Maurin, Corpron, Martel, Estèbe and others, were also tried and punished with fine, imprisonment and confiscation: one Penisseault, a government clerk (a butcher's son by birth), who had

* Those were times in which royalty did not shine forth in a peculiarly bright effulgence. On one side of the English Channel loomed out the handsome but effeminate figure of the French Sultan, Louis XV., revelling undisturbed in the scented bowers of his harem, the *Parc aux Cerfs*, *La Pompadour* and *La Dubarry* managing state matters; on the other, a Brunswicker, one who, we are told, "had neither dignity, learning, morals, nor wit—who tainted a great society by a bad example; who, in youth, manhood, old age, was gross, low and sensual:"—although Mr. Porteus (afterwards My Lord Bishop Porteus) says the earth was not good enough for him, and that his only place was heaven!—whose closing speech to his dying, loving, true-hearted Queen is thus related by Thackeray: "With the film of death over her eyes, writhing in intolerable pain, she yet had a livid smile and a gentle word for her master. You have read the wonderful history of that death-bed? How she bade him marry again, and the reply the old King blubbered out, '*Non, non, j'aurai des mâitresses.*' There never was such a ghastly farce."—(*The Four Georges.*)

† In 1629, when Quebec surrendered to Kertk.

married in the colony, but whose pretty wife accompanied the Chevalier de Levis on his return to France, seems to have fared better than the rest.

But to revert to the château walls, as I saw them on the 4th of June, 1863 After a ramble with some friends through the woods, which gave us an opportunity of providing ourselves with wild flowers to strew over the tomb of "Fair Rosamond," such as the marsh marygold, clintonia uvularia, the starflower, veronica, kalmia, trillium, and Canadian violets, we unexpectedly struck on the old ruin. One of the first things which attracted notice was the singularly corroding effect the easterly wind has on stone and mortar in Canada: the east gable being indented and much more eaten away than that exposed to the western blast. Of the original structure nothing is now standing but the two gables and the division walls; they are all three of immense thickness, and certainly no modern house is built in the manner this seems to have been; it must have had two stories high, with rooms in the attic and a deep cellar: a communication existed from one cellar to the other through the division wall There is also visible a very small door cut through the cellar wall of the west gable; it leads to a vaulted apartment of some eight feet square: the small mound of masonry which covered it might have originally been effectually hidden from view by a plantation of trees over it. What could this have been built for? Was it intended to secure some of the Intendant's plate or other portion of his ill-gotten treasures? Or else as the Abbé Ferland suggests:* "Was it to store the

* I am indebted to my old friend the Abbé Ferland for the following remark: "I visited Chateau-Bigot during the summer of 1834. It was in the state described by Mr. Papineau. In the interior, the walls were still partly papered. It must not be forgotten that about the beginning of this century, a club of *Bons-vivants* used to meet frequently in the Chateau." [Three celebrated clubs flourished here long before the Stadacona and St. James' Club were thought of. The first was formed in Quebec, about the beginning of this century. It was originally called, says Lambert, the Beef Steak Club, which name it soon changed for that of the Barons Club. It consisted of twenty-one members, "who are chiefly the principal merchants in the colony, and are styled barons. As the members drop off, their places are supplied by knights elect, who are not installed as barons until there is a sufficient number to pay for the entertainment which is given on that occasion." J. Lambert, during the winter of 1807, attended one of the banquets of installation, which was given in the Union Hotel (now the public Offices, facing the Place d'Armes.) The Hon. Mr. Dunn, the President of the Province, and Administrator, during the absence of Sir Robert Milnes, attended as the oldest baron. The Chief Justice and all the principal officers of the government, civil and military, were present. This entertainment cost 250 guineas. The other club went under the appropriate name of "Sober Club"—*lucus a non lucendo* perhaps: it flourished about 1811; we believe one of the By-laws enacted that the members were expected to get *tight* at least once a year, and be content with appearing sober, and use *silent spirit* the rest of the time. It seems to me more than likely that it was the Club of Barons, and not the Sober Club, who caroused under the romantic walls of the Hermitage. The third Club flourished at Montreal; it took the name of the Beaver Club, and was, I believe, composed of old *Northwesters*.]

fruity old Port and sparkling Moselle of the club of the barons, who held jovial meetings there about the beginning of this century?" Was it his mistresses' secret and subterranean *boudoir* when the Intendant's lady visited the château? *Quien sabe?* Who can unravel the mystery? It may have served for the foundation of the tower which existed when Mr. Papineau visited and described the place thirty-two years ago. The heavy cedar rafters, more than one hundred years old, are to this day sound: one has been broken by the fall, probably, of some heavy stones. There are several indentures in the walls for fire-places, which are built with cut masonry; from the angle of one a song sparrow flew out, uttering its anxious note. We searched and discovered the bird's nest, with five spotted, dusky eggs in it; how strange! in the midst of ruin and decay, the sweet emblems of hope, love and harmony! What cared the child of song if her innocent offspring were reared amidst these mouldering relics of the past, mayhap a guilty past? She could teach them to warble sweetly, even from the roof which echoed the dying sigh of the Algonquin maid. Red alder trees grew rank and vigorous amongst the disjointed masonry, which had crumbled from the walls to the cellar; no trace existed of the wooden staircase mentioned by Mr. Papineau; the timber of the roof had rotted away or been used for camp-fires by those who frequent and fish the elfish stream which winds its way over a pebbly bottom towards Beauport—well stocked with small trout, which seem to breed in great numbers in the dam near the château.

Those who wish to visit the Hermitage, are strongly advised to take the cart-road which leads from the Charlesbourg church, turning up near the house of a man named Charles Paquet. Pedestrians will prefer the other route; they can, in this case, leave their vehicle at Mrs. Huot's boarding-house, — a little higher than the church of Charlesbourg, — and then walk through the fields skirting, during greater part of the road, the beautiful brook I have previously mentioned; but by all means *let them take a guide* with them. I shall now translate and condense, from the interesting narrative of a visit paid to the Hermitage in 1831, by Mr. Amédée Papineau and his talented father, the Hon. L. J. Papineau, the legend which attaches to it:

THE LEGEND.

"We drove," says Mr. Papineau, jun., "with our vehicle to the very foot of the mountain. and there took a foot-path which led us through a dense wood; we encountered and crossed a rivulet, and then ascended a plateau cleared of wood, a most enchanting place; behind us and on our right was a thick forest; on our left the eye rested on boundless green fields, diversified* with golden harvests and with the neat white cottages† of the peasantry; in the distance was visible the broad and placid St. Lawrence, at the foot of the citadel of Quebec, and also the shining cupolas and tin roofs of the city houses; in front of us a confused mass of ruins, crenelated walls embedded in moss and rank grass, together with a tower half destroyed, beams, and the mouldering remains of a roof. After viewing the *tout ensemble*, we attentively examined each portion in detail—every fragment was interesting to us; we with difficulty made our way over the wall, ascending the upper stories by a staircase which creaked and trembled under our weight. With the assistance of a lighted candle we penetrated into the damp and cavernous cellars, carefully exploring every nook and corner, listening to the sound of our footsteps, and occasionally startled by the rustling of bats which we disturbed in their dismal retreat. I was young, and consequently very impressionable. I had just left college; these extraordinary sounds and objects would at times make me feel very uneasy. I pressed close to my father, and dared scarcely breathe; the remembrance of this subterranean exploration will not easily be forgotten. What were my sensations when I saw a tombstone! the reader can imagine. 'Here we are, at

* If the unrivalled scenery and happy peasantry of the Quebec district gladdened the heart of Mr. Papineau in 1831, how much more pleased he would be to witness the rapid strides in worldly wealth of the same peasantry since that date. One of those "neat white cottages," whose trim appearance struck him thirty years ago, now shelters under its roof the Rothschild of Canadian *habitants*, Monsieur Alexis Derousselle, who has succeeded in accumulating some £300,000, invested—*not* in stock of bogus banks—*not* in railroad shares, *nor* in bonds of cities brought into Chancery, but in substantial seven and eight per cent. *Bailleurs de Fonds*, in Montreal *Banque du Peuple* and *Banque Nationale* shares. M. Derousselle began life as a servant—he is entirely uneducated. Three hundred thousand pounds for a Lower Canada *habitant!* why this will do. Scores of peasants, who sport their simple *etoffe du pays* coats, are worth their £15,000; but who knows? who, perhaps, cares? Is it not customary to make the *habitant* a bye-word for abuse? Pray how many dozen rich western farmers could old Derousselle purchase?

† It is painful to watch the successive inroads perpetrated by sportsmen and idlers on the old Chateau. In 1819, an old Quebecer, Mr. Wyse, visited it; doors, verandah, windows and everything else was complete. He, too, lost his way in the woods, but found it again without the help of an Indian beauty. It was then known as the haunted house, supposed to contain a deal of French treasure, and called *La Maison du Bourg Royal*.

last!' exclaimed my father, and echo repeated his words. Carefully did we view this monument; presently we detected the letter 'C,' nearly obliterated by the action of time; after remaining there a few moments, to my unspeakable delight we made our exit from this chamber of death, and, stepping over the ruins, we again alighted on the green sward; evidently where we stood had formerly been a garden: we could still make out the avenues, the walks and plots, over which plum, lilac and apple trees grew wild.

"I had not yet uttered a word, but my curiosity getting the better of my fear, I demanded an explanation of this mysterious tombstone. My father beckoned me towards a shady old maple; we both sat on the turf, and he then spoke as follows:—You have, no doubt, my son, heard of a French Intendant, of the name of Bigot, who had charge of the public funds in Canada somewhere about the year 175—; you have also read how he squandered these moneys and how his Christian Majesty had him sent to the Bastille when he returned to France, and had his property confiscated. All this you know. I shall now tell you what, probably, you do not know. This Intendant attempted to lead in Canada the same dissolute life which the old *noblesse* led in France before the French Revolution had *levelled* all classes. He it was who built this country seat, of which you now contemplate the ruins. Here he came to seek relaxation from the cares of office; here he prepared entertainments to which the rank and fashion of Quebec, including its Governor General, eagerly flocked: nothing was wanting to complete the *éclat* of this *little* Versailles. Hunting was a favorite pastime of our ancestors, and Bigot was a mighty hunter. As active as a chamois, as daring as a lion was this indefatigable Nimrod, in the pursuit of bears and moose.

"On one occasion, when tracking with some sporting friends an old bear whom he had wounded, he was led over mountainous ridges and ravines, very far from the castle. Nothing could restrain him; on he went in advance of every one, until the bloody trail brought him on the wounded animal, which he soon despatched.

"During the chase the sun had gradually sunk over the western hills; the shades of evening were fast descending: how was the lord of the manor to find his way back? He was alone in a thick forest: in this emergency his heart did not fail him,—he hoped by the light of the moon to be able to find his way to his stray companions. Wearily he walked on, ascending once or twice a high tree, in order to see further but all in vain: soon the unpleasant conviction dawned on him that like others in similar cases, he had been walking round a circle. Worn out and exhausted with fatigue and hunger, he sat down to ponder on what course he should adopt. The Queen of Night, at that moment shedding her silvery rays around, only helped to show the hunter how hopeless was his present position. Amidst these mournful reflections, his ear was startled by the sound of footsteps close by: his spirits rose at the prospect of help being at hand; soon he perceived the outlines of a moving white object. Was it a phantom which his disordered imagination had conjured up? Terrified, he seized his trusty gun and was in the act of firing, when the apparition, rapidly advancing towards him, assumed quite a human form: a light figure stood before him with eyes as black as night, and raven tresses flowing to the night wind; a spotless garment enveloped in its ample folds this airy and graceful spectre. Was it a sylph, the spirit of the wilderness? Was it Diana, the goddess of the chase, favoring one of her most ardent votaries with a glimpse of her form divine? It was neither: it was an Algonquin beauty, one of those ideal types whose white skin betray their hybrid origin—a mixture of European blood with that of the aboriginal race. It was Caroline, a child of love borne on the shores of the great Ottawa river: a French officer was her sire, and the powerful Algonquin tribe of the Beaver claimed her mother.

"The Canadian Nimrod, struck at the sight of such extraordinary beauty, asked her name, and after relating his adventure, he begged of her to show him the way to the castle in the neighborhood, as she must be familiar with every path of the forest. Such is the story told of the first meeting between the Indian beauty and the Canadian Minister of Finance and Feudai Judge in the year 175—

"The Intendent was a *married man: his lady resided in the Capital of Canada; she seldom accompanied her husband on his hunting excursions, but soon it was whispered that something more than the pursuit of wild animals attracted him to his country seat: an intrigue with a beautiful creole was hinted at. These discreditable rumors came to the ears of her ladyship: she made several visits to the castle in hopes of verifying her worst fears: jealousy is a watchful sentinel.

* Error—he was a bachelor.

"The Intendant's dormitory was on the ground floor of the building: it is supposed the Indian beauty occupied a secret apartment on the flat above; that her boudoir was reached through a long and narrow passage, ending with a secret staircase opening on the large room which overlooked the garden.

"Let us now see what took place on this identical spot on the 2nd July, 175–. It is night; the hall clock has just struck eleven; the silvery murmur of the neighboring brook, gently wafted on the night wind, is scarcely audible: the *song sparrow has nearly finished his evening hymn, while the †*Sweet Canada* bird, from the top of an old pine, merrily peels forth his shrill clarion; silence the most profound pervades the whole castle; every light is extinguished; the pale rays of the moon slumber softly on the oak floor, reflected as they are through the gothic windows; every inmate is wrapped in sleep, even fair Rosamond who has just retired. Suddenly her door is violently opened; a masked person, with one bound, rushes to her bed-side, and without saying a word, plunges a dagger to the hilt in her heart: uttering a piercing shriek, the victim falls heavily on the floor. The Intendant, hearing the noise, hurries up stairs, when the unhappy girl has just time to tell how she has been murdered, points to the fatal weapon, still in the wound, and then falls in his arms a lifeless corpse. The whole household are soon on foot; search is made for the murderer, but no clue is discovered. Some of the inmates fancied they had seen the figure of a woman rush down the secret stair and disappear in the woods about the time the murder took place. A variety of stories got in circulation; some pretend to trace the crime to the Intendant's wife, whilst others allege that the avenging mother of the creole is the assassin; some again said that Caroline's father had attempted to wipe off the stain on the honor of his tribe, by himself despatching his erring child. A profound mystery to this day surrounds the whole transaction. Caroline was buried in the cellar of the castle, and the letter 'C' engraved on her tombstone, which, my son, you have just seen."

I now visit this spot several years after the period mentioned in this narrative I search in vain for several of the leading characteristics on which Mr. Papineau descants so eloquently: time, the great des-

* Melospiza melodia.
† Zonotrichia albicollis.

troyer, has obliterated many traces. Nothing meets my view but mouldering walls, over which green moss and rank weeds cluster profusely. Unmistakable indications of a former garden there certainly are, such as the outlines of walks over which French cherry, apple and gooseberry trees grow in wild luxuriance. I take home from the ruins a piece of bone; this decayed piece of mortality may have formed part of Caroline's big toe, for aught I can establish to the contrary; Chateau-Bigot brings back to my mind other remembrances of the past. I recollect reading that pending the panic consequent on the surrender of Quebec in 1759, the non-combatants of the city crowded within its walls; this time not to ruralize, but to seek concealment until Mars had inscribed another victory on the British flag. I would not be prepared to swear that later, when Arnold and Montgomery had possession of the environs of Quebec, during the greater portion of the winter of 1775–6, some of those prudent English merchants (Adam Lymburner at their head), who awaited at Charlesbourg and Beauport the issue of the contest, did not take a quiet drive to Chateau-Bigot, were it only to indulge in a philosophical disquisition on the mutability of human events; nor must I forget the jolly pic-nics the barons held there some sixty years ago.*

On quitting these silent halls, from which the light of other days has departed, and from whence the voice of revelry seems to have fled for ever, I recrossed the little brook, already mentioned, musing on the past. The solitude which surrounds the dwelling and the tomb of the dark-haired child of the wilderness, involuntarily brought to mind that beautiful passage of Ossian,† relating to the daughter of Reuthamir, the "white bosomed" Moina:—"I have seen the walls of Balclutha, but they were desolate. The fire had resounded in the halls: and the voice of the people is heard no more. The thistle shook there its lonely head; the moss whistled to the wind. The fox looked out from the windows, the rank grass of the wall waved round its head. Desolate is the dwelling of Moina, silence is in the house. ...... Raise the song of mourning, O bards! over the land of strangers. They have but fallen before us: for one day we must fall."

* The Hon. Mr. Dunn, Administrator of the Province in 1807, was the senior baron; Hons. Mathew Bell, John Stewart, Messrs. Muir, Irvine, McNaught, Grey Stewart, Munro, Finlay, Lymburner, Paynter; these names were doubtless also to be found amongst the Canadian barons; the Hon. Chas. De Lanaudiere, a general in the Hungarian service, was the only French Canadian member.

† Book of Carthon.

Crumbs of Comfort for Lawyers.

CHAPTER III.

AMONGST the innumerable feudal burthens and medieval cobwebs which time or legislation have successively swept away in European communities, there was a seigniorial privilege which, to say the least, was of rather doubtful propriety. It was one of those rights which one would be more apt to look for under the heading of *Droits Honorifiques*, than under that of *Droit Utiles*. French writers designate it as *Droit de Jambage, Prélibation*, &c., and as I do not care to be too explicit in describing it, it will suffice to say that it had for its object, as many pretend, to confer on the lord of the manor the same right which some royal lotharios in France claimed in those marriage contracts "où le Roi a signé." No data have yet been found whereby to establish that it ever existed in the colony: the chances are, that in such cases the Canadian seigneur would have fared as badly as those Piedmontese nobles, who, for a like attempt were, according to Guyot,* summarily hooted out of the kingdom. That this right—high prerogative, if you prefer—which might have suited old King Solomon, appears in charters and grants, there can be no doubt: and although we do not see that the Seigniorial Tenure Commissioners paid much attention to it, when they recently sifted the matter, taking in consideration the manner in which existing rights have been dealt with, we may make ourselves quite easy that, if it did exist, the $800,000 provided in the budget of 1862, to indemnify seigniorial rights will be properly applied and distributed.

This right, it has been pretended, is inserted in the land patent of the representatives of a very illustrious Canadian house; I

* Guyot goes on to say that in times gone by, the clergy claimed an indemnity for commuting this feudal custom. Despeisses also mentions a singular case. If we accept their authority, how thankful we must feel to know that feudalism is dead and buried for ever. What a scandal it would be through the civilized world, if even the bare possibility could exist that the Archbishop of Canterbury, for instance, might claim so many "fat capons" at Michaelmas for refusing to avail himself of such a right!

firmly believe, however, that never, even in his palmiest days, did this seigneur think of availing himself of it. Anomalous as the right may appear, was it a whit less intolerable than several of the manifold exactions which* free-born Britons quietly endured at home, and abroad in their colonies, where they imported their institutions? Take Massachusetts and the other New England states, for instance; what would a citizen of the model republic now say, were it attempted to resuscitate the ancient order of things? What would be the feelings of a Nova Scotian, were his legislators to revive the tenure under which were originally granted the broad acres on which he prides himself to-day? On the other hand, what a glorious field for law-suits, what green pasturage for Chancery lawyers the interpretation of these old land charters would open! Why! it would be a perfect California for the gentlemen of the long robe.

I shall now submit in a condensed form, an extract from an English royal charter; it is a most dainty tit-bit, which I can commend to the admirers of legal yore. Every one has heard of Nova Scotia knights; indeed, if I am well informed, we have one at present within the precincts of this city. Few are aware of the marvellous array of rights and privileges contained in the charter creating them, granted in 1621 by James I. of England, and confirmed and re-enacted by Charles

* I can scarcely forbear a smile when I hear the word mentioned, from its being connected with a very ludicrous recent incident: The enterprising proprietors of the Jacques Cartier Salmon River, desirous of improving their *fish preserve*, had determined to import from England an English game-keeper, to watch over it. John Crisp was the lucky individual: but John was a hard hitter, a pugnacious soul,—the type of the sturdy race which the Norman duke had mercilessly crushed under his iron heel at Hastings: he came in this country with the feelings not of an equal, but of a conqueror, and concluded that as such, he would be exposed to the ill will and vengeance of the discendants of Frenchmen; he depicted to himself the peaceful *habitant* as a blood-thirsty savage, the sworn enemy to his race. Mr. John Crisp was really a singular compound—he vowed everything in Canada was villainous—that the country was unbearable, that he was likely to die soon, as he had not tasted a mug of English porter, or drinkable ale since he left the Thames—the latter insinuation was highly censurable, in several points and more specially disrespectful towards one of his employers. The absence of "London stout" so depressed the spirit of John, that he had to resort to the *wine of the country*, 50. O.P. whisky to keep them up, but all in vain, he unstrung his nerves and, under incipient d...t..., he would rise in the middle of the night and discharge his fowling piece, at two gate posts near his dwelling, swearing horribly at them, and calling them "D.......d French Canadians." At last he became quite dangerous, and his loyalty to the Queen was one morning abruptly interrupted by one of his English masters, with the help of some *habitant* clapping handcuffs on him, and picketing him for an hour before his tent, with a rope, until he could be removed. His imprecations then became sublime. "To think," he would exclaim, "of a free-born Briton, picketed before a tent, with manacles on his arms, like a felon, in a Canadian wilderness." Colonial habits did not suit Mr. John Crisp, and after a short time, the Atlantic steamer re-conveyed him to the land of the free.

I., in 1625, in favor of Sir William Alexander de Menstrie, subsequently made Earl of Sterling. This precious document, written in Latin, covers twenty-four quarto pages. After enumerating the titles of the earl's lands in Nova Scotia, &c., it descends into the most minute particulars concerning the rights vested in him over his vassals and tenants in his extensive domain, which comprised Nova Scotia, New Brunswick, Cape Breton, St. John, Newfoundland, and even the Gaspé district. This royal grant divided Nova Scotia into one hundred and fifty fiefs or seigniories, and conferred on the mighty chieftain (who, by the bye, was also a poet) the power to knight any one who would become the purchaser of any of his lots, which he valued each at two hundred pounds sterling. How pleasant it must have been for the land speculator, on signing his deed of sale, to have the magic words tingling in his ears: "Rise, Sir N. Fortunatus," &c., or other words to the same effect. It has often been my lot to hear intelligent Britons commiserate most feelingly on the intolerable hardships which French charters imposed on the *benighted* French Canadians, but I have not yet had the good fortune to light on a French land patent embodying a greater number of exactions, restrictions and privileges in favor of the lord of the manor than the following charter, sanctioned by two English monarchs :—

"We also grant the possession of houses, buildings erected and to be erected, gardens, valleys, woods, swamps, roads, cross roads, ponds, streams, meadows, pasture lands, mills, the exclusive right to grind corn, the shooting of birds and wild animals, the right to fish, the right to turf and turf lands, coal and coal pits, rabbits and warrens, doves and dove cotes, workshops, forges, heaths, wheat fields, forests, merchantable timber, small trees, quarries, limestone, courts of justice and their dependencies, the right to remit sentences, the right of receiving gifts in marriages, the right to erect gallows and gibbets, the right of *cul de fosse*, the right of franche court, of sokman, of sak, of thole, of thane, of infangthief, of outhangthief, of outwark, of wavi, of week, of venysone, of pit and gallous," &c., &c., &c. The Lord have mercy on the poor vassal or tenant who had to comply with all these exactions! it must have been doubtful to him whether his *soul* as well as his body did not belong to the earl, his master.

So much for English charters. I shall now, in order to illustrate one of the peculiar institutions of the country, and for the benefit of non-legal readers, insert, as a sample, a *donation entre vifs*, in plain English, a Deed of Annuity, which I shall translate from a city paper, the *Courrier du Canada*. This form of donation was formerly and is still used by some country notaries. It is unnecessary to remark what a fruitful source of litigation its contradictory stipulations must have furnished.

Before giving this legal gem, I shall, as a preliminary, relate in a few words what occurred to an English millionaire who had acquired a large tract of land in the country parts of Canada, and who wanted more. Nothing was requisite to round off his estate but a small farm, owned by a very ancient Canadian lady: sell, she would not; but she agreed to dispossess herself if her rich neighbour would allow her an annuity of about £50; this amount was not to be paid in money; it was to be represented by the ordinary conditions of a *donation entre vifs* the preparing of which was left to the village notary,* as is usual in such cases. When the French document was read, John Bull could make neither head nor tail of it, and instructed the notary to have a literal and exact translation made; it was not quite Addisonian English, but it could be understood; the choleric Englishman restrained himself until the notary public arrived at that stipulation in the deed, whereby the donee (the Englishman) was required to "bind himself to harness the donor's (the old lady's) horse and drive her to the parish church," when, quietly rising from his chair, he collared the notary and kicked him out.

AN OLD FRENCH DONATION.

"Amongst other things the donor reserves for his use, an immortal horse, a cow which will never die, a ewe which renews herself forever, at the will of the donor; twenty minots of royal and merchantable wheat, good measure, made into flour, together with the bran, to be

* The village notary of former days was sometimes quite a character. One of those worthies had formerly "elected domicile" at St. Paul's Bay. His name was S——le. He belonged to the thirsty brotherhood, and was a bit of a wag. His notarial instruments did not always read intelligibly, owing to the fact that, when he was a little *tight*, his pen would wander beyond the paper, and he would continue to scribble on the wood of the high desk at which he sat with magisterial dignity; a portion of the text would remain there, and he would restore the missing words from memory, when he had to deliver copies. Some of his poor clients were addicted to the low habit—in the eyes of professional men—of *marchandeing* (bargaining) about the fees they intended to pay him. There being no help, the notary would quietly put in his pocket the coin of the realm, but slily insinuate that for such a miserable fee, nothing but a very indifferent deed could be expected—*it might hold good, it might not.* "Why don't you order a first class one,"—he would say. "You know my charges; one dollar for a first rate deed, *warranted*; half a dollar for a fair one, which may turn out well, and for a third-class deed a quarter, but a third-class I cannot recommend—you can only expect to have for your money. It is a mere chance if it is good for anything."

deposited in the garret of the donor and nowhere else; a reasonable* pig weighing 200 lbs. without legs or head, but with its fat, and if any should be wanting, it shall be taken from another reasonable pig of the donee, where the fat is the thickest and where there are no bones; also 15 lbs. of herbs salted, at proper season, and placed in a suitable cask; also each year the young of the cow and of the ewe, whether they have any young or not. The horse, cow and ewe will be renewed when it is necessary, according to the wish and will of the donor, expressed or not expressed. The donee will wait at all times on the donor, in sickness and in health, whether the donor asks him to do so or not; will go and fetch the priest and the physician *in extremis* — will drive them back, even should the donor die. The horse will be harnessed becomingly to a suitable vehicle with cushions and furs, in winter as well as in summer; the donee will be bound to drive the donor to church on Sundays; the donor shall also have a quarter of beef, or cow meat which the donee will kill himself, also a dead lamb, with its dependencies, just as if it were alive. The donor also reserves a bed; but when he dies, he leaves the enjoyment thereof to the donee who will be bound to keep it neat and clean."

As I do not wish the reader to be carried away with the errôneous idea that French Canadian notaries have the monopoly of bad grammar and barbarous phraseology, I shall close this hasty sketch with a curious but litteral quotation from a high English authority on the Law of Contracts; it will serve to illustrate what extraordinary gibberish the learned ancestors of Englishmen used to convey their ideas in, and exceeds in quaintness the clauses of a *Donation entre vifs*." †Si jeo vend chivall que ad null oculus la null action gist, auterment lou il ad un counterfeit, fau et bright eye!" This being interpreted, means: "If I sell a horse that has lost an eye, no action lies against me for so doing; but if I sell him with a false and counterfeit eye, then an action lieth."

---

* "Un cochon raisonnable." Very warm discussions used to ensue between donor and donee; one insisted on a fat pig; the other resolutely resisted the introduction of this clause, from the great expense and trouble to fatten the grunter; the notary would then propose, by way of compromise, to insert a "reasonable pig."

† Southerne *vs.* Howe, Addison on Contracts; American Edition, page 54, the note.

It would take me too long to show how, under these apparently incongruous terms, a great deal of sound meaning was conveyed.

Lord Monck's Residence.

CHAPTER IV.

(From the Morning Chronicle.)

THE reconstruction of the gubernatorial mansion at Spencer Wood, on the banks of the St. Lawrence, affords us an opportunity for saying something about a spot so celebrated for its natural beauty. We cannot do better than publish the following interesting sketch, for which we are indebted to J. M. LeMoine, Esq., of Spencer Grange, the author of the *Ornithology of Canada*:—

SPENCER WOOD.

"Along those banks full oft' has peal'd
The blow of tomahawk on shield,
As braves rushed on to fight,
And bow and blade and war-whoop fierce
Sent all their clamour dread to pierce
The stilly ear of night." K. K. K.

The tourist, descending the St. Lawrence, is struck with the number of beautiful villas, which ever and anon, nestling under groves of maple, oak and pine, line the river heights from Cape Rouge, the western extremity of the promontory, to Cape Diamond, the eastern end, which Champlain selected for his capital in 1608—Quebec.

These country seats, without possessing the extent of English noblemen's estates, are in many instances superior to them in point of scenery; they cover, frequently, about one hundred acres, although some (such as Holland Farm and Kilmarnock) have as many as two hundred acres attached to them. In former days a grand military road skirted the river heights, where they are located. Several remains of intrenchments and masonry testify to past strife and to the presence, in days of yore, of the white and the red man, the former sometimes armed with the cross, and bent on an errand of peace and good-fellowship; the latter hunting for skulls, and tracking relentlessly his fellow-man through forest wilds. It is on record that one of the first missionaries of Canada met with his death in this vicinity, in a most cruel manner, at the hands of the Indians he was christianizing. The Abbé Ferland is of opinion that the scalping scene took place on the very spot on which at present stands Clermont, the Honorable Mr. Justice Caron's residence. Certain it is that long ere the environs of Quebec had derived interest for having been the battle field of European armies, their soil had been frequently crimsoned with the blood of the aboriginal tribes, who used the St. Lawrence and its banks as their great highway. We shall now quote from a paper we previously prepared on this subject.

Among the many lovely sites which dot the banks of the broad St. Lawrence, one above all others has for years back been an unceasing object of admiration to strangers, and a legitimate boast to all Quebec—one might say, to all Canada.

A glorious old manor, comprising at one time a couple of hundred acres, with its luxuriant and primitive growth of forest trees; its unrivalled river scenery, its spacious, sloping, verdant lawn, fit for a ducal residence; its fairy garden plots; its curious artificial devices of tropical plants, clustering under glass, amongst the green foliage of the orange, the fig, and the pine-apple trees, bent down with golden fruit; its luscious sparkling grapes; its crystal fountains, whose sweet murmur blended with the rustling of shady oaks, under the influence of strong winds; its serpentine shady avenues: such was at one time Spencer Wood, for twenty-five years the elegant home of Henry Atkinson, Esq., and afterwards of the Earl of Elgin, whose exquisite entertainments many can yet recall to memory. Spencer Wood is enclosed between two small streams, the *ruisseau* St. Denis and the *ruisseau* Belle Borne, its natural boundaries; these streams have considerably diminished since the time when they were used, two hundred years ago, to propel two mills, then situated in the neighborhood and mentioned in old titles. It was formerly called Powel Place, after General Powel; it was subsequently named Spencer Wood, when the Spencer Percival family owned it: and had been, after the conquest of the country, the residence of the governors.*

* Sir James Craig resided in summer at a country house about four or five miles from Quebec, and went to town every morning to transact business. This residence is called Powel Place, and is delightfully situated in a neat plantation, on the border of the bank which overlooks the St. Lawrence, not far from the spot where General Wolfe

These extensive grounds are beautifully diversified by hills and clumps of old oak and maple, and although from the important *reserve* of Spencer Grange, comprising nearly the whole of the road front, when the rest was sold to government in 1854, they can have but little value for small building lots, still for the specific objects to which nature seems to have intended them, they seem to stand unequalled in Canada. It lies beautifully exposed to the morning sun, with a southerly aspect, in which direction it is bounded by perpendicular cliffs at whose feet the noble river sweeps past in majestic grandeur. A great deal remains to be said about the scenery of this spot: two of the most striking objects are two promontaries or points of land, one to the east, the other to the south-west of the property. A pavillion stands on the south-west point, from which many a tea-party was enjoyed in days of yore. Here a most glorious panorama presents itself. It would, however, be difficult to tell whether the view obtained from this point is not surpassed in magnificence by that which can be witnessed from the easterly point.

Spencer Wood is situate in the parish of St. Columba of Sillery, not very far from the ancient Jesuit mission at Sillery, close to Pointe-à-Puiseaux. It therefore possesses, in addition to beautiful scenery, historical recollections connected with some of the greatest events of the colony. Let us hear a grave historian and keen admirer of nature on this subject:—

" A chart of Quebec, by Champlain, exhibits, about a league above the youthful city, a point jutting out into the St. Lawrence, and which is covered with Indian wigwams. Later on, this point received the name of Puiseaux, from the first owner of the Fief St. Michel, bounded by it to the south-west. On this very point at present stands the handsome St. Columba church, surrounded by a village.*

" Opposite to it is the Lauzon shore, with its river *Bruyante*† (the Etchemin), its shipyards, its numerous shipping, the terminus of the Richmond Railway, the villages and churches of Notre Dame de Lévi

---

landed, and ascended to the heights of Abraham. Sir James gave a splendid public breakfast, *al fresco*, at this place, in 1807, to all the principal inhabitants of Quebec; and the following day he allowed his servants, and their acquaintances, to partake of a similar entertainment at his expense.—*J. Lambert's Travels*, 1808, *page* 310.

Contiguous to this property is the beautiful estate of the Hon. Mr. Percival, called Spencer Wood, formerly known as Powel Place, and which used to be the country residence of the Governor General.—*Bouchette's Typography of Canada*, 1815.

* Abbé Ferland's Notes on the Environs of Quebec, 1855.

† From the noise it makes before easterly gales.

St. Jean Chrysostôme, and Saint-Romuald. To your right and to the left, the St. Lawrence is visible for some twelve or fifteen miles covered with inward and outward bound ships. Towards the east, the landscape is closed by Cap Tourmente, twelve leagues distant, and by the cultivated heights of the *Petite Montagne*, and of St Féréol, exhibiting in succession the coast of Beaupré (Beauport, L'Ange Gardiens &c.), the green slopes of the Island of Orleans; Cape Diamond, crowned with its citadel and having at its feet a forest of masts; Abraham's Plains, the Coves and their humming, busy noises; St. Michael Cove-forming a graceful curve from Wolfe's Cove to Pointe-à-Puiseaux. Within this area thrilling events once took place, and round these divers objects, historical souvenirs cluster, recalling some of the most important occurrences in North America: the contest of two powerful nations for the sovereignty of the New World; an important episode of the revolution which gave birth to the adjoining republic. Such were some of the events of which these localities were the theatre. Each square inch of land, in fact, was measured by the footsteps of some of the most remarkable men in the history of America: Jacques Cartier, Champlain, Frontenac, Laval, Phipps, d'Iberville, Wolfe, Montcalm, Arnold, Montgomery, have each of them, at some time or other, trod over some part of this expanse

"Close by, in St. Michael's Cove, M. de Maisonneuve and Mademoiselle Mance passed their first Canadian winter with the colonists intended to found Montreal. Turn your eyes towards the west, and although the panorama is less extensive, still it awakens some glorious memories. At Cap Rouge, Jacques Cartier established his quarters, close to the river edge, the second winter he spent in Canada, and was succeeded in that spot by Roberval, at the head of his ephemeral colony. Near the entrance of the Chaudière river stood the tents of the Abnaquiois, the Etchemins, and the Souriquois Indians, when they came from the shores of New England to smoke the *calumet* of peace with their brethren, the French. The river Chaudière in those days was the highway which connected their country with Canada. Closer to Pointe-à-Puiseaux is Sillery Cove, where the Jesuit Fathers were wont to assemble and evangelize the Algonquin and Montagnais Indians, who were desirous of becoming Christians. It was from that spot that the neophytes used to carry the faith to the depths of the forest: it was here that those early apostles of Christianity congregated before starting with the gladsome tidings for the country of the Hurons, for the shores of the Mississippi, or for the frozen regions of Hudson's Bay. From thence went Father P. Druilletes, the bearer of the words of peace on behalf of the Christians of Sillery, to the Abnaquiois of Kennebcki, and to the Puritans of Boston. Near this same mission of Sillery, Frère Liegeois was massacred by the Iroquois, whilst Father Poncet was carried away a captive by these barbarous tribes.

"Monsieur de Sillery devoted large sums to erect the necessary edifices for the mission, such as a chapel, a missionary residence, an hospital, a fort, houses for new converts, together with the habitations for the French. The d'Auteuil family had their country seat on the hill back of Pointe-à-Puiseaux; and the venerable Madame de Monceau, mother-in-law of the Attorney General Ruette d'Auteuil, was in the habit of residing there, from time to time, in a house she had constructed near the chapel."

It would indeed be a pleasant task to recall all the remarkable events which occurred in this neighborhood. One thing is certain: the cool retreats studding the shores of the St. Lawrence were equally sought for by the wealthy in those days as they have been since by all those who wish to breathe pure air and enjoy the scenery.

If all Canada were ransacked over, it is doubtful whether a single spot could be selected, combining as a vice-regal residence in as high a degree, natural beauty and comfort: the exterior of the structure, however, argues in the designer's bad taste, or a very impoverished exchequer; it is built of common red brick, with pine window sills; the fences are exceeded in architectural design only by those about Governor Hincks, at Thornhill,* which is opposite.

May our worthy Governor General, forgetting for a time the sweet scenery of his own lordly mansion on the banks of the Dargle, of Charleville, enjoy the cool shades of Spencer Wood, the representative of British institutions amongst us, the honored ruler over two peoples who, however different they may be in race and language, have learned the secret of respecting each other's strength, and of uniting for the common good into bonds of indissoluble brotherhood.

* N.B.—The Thornhill fence is an ancient mosaic, in which spruce, cedar and tamarack are combined in curious proportions, or rather without proportion: figuratively it resembles an Act of Parliament having many flaws in it, some wide enough to admit—if not a carriage and four—at least adult pigs and dogs of large dimensions. (Since this was written, matters are mending.)

Le Chien d'Or---The Golden Dog.

CHAPTER V.

" Je suis un chien qui ronge l'os,
En le rongeant je prends mon repos,
Un jour viendra qui n'est pas venu,
Que je morderai qui m'aura mordu.
1736."

MY Quebec friend, when you take your daily " constitutional," on Durham Terrace, contemplating with undisguised pride the unrivalled surrounding scenery, and at your feet, the famous harbour, in which a whole fleet of Great Easterns could ride at ease, or else, when communing with your own thoughts, you stroll homewards from a brisk walk in the neighborhood of the city, after viewing the smiling country seats of successful citizens along the St. Louis road, until that imposing pile, the new Jail, the Ladies' Home, and the Military Asylum, successively break on your view, has it ever occurred to you, in the presence of these unmistakable and healthy signs of progress, to recall the past, the rude primitive times? and when passing by the magnificent corporation lots on the *Grande Allée*—a spot destined to become the Belgravia, the Fifth Avenue of the future metropolis of Confederated British America, have you ever, while stepping over this portion of the Plains of Abraham, reflected that from where you now stand, perchance the old Scotch pilot of the St. Lawrence, Abraham Martin, or *Maître Abraham*, as he was then styled—may also, two hundred years ago, while dreaming of Bruce and Wallace, have stood surveying with inward complacency his valuable " thirty-two acres "* after wending

* Can no heir of the old sea dog make good his title to this nice little family estate, on which the greatest portion of St. Louis and St. John's Suburbs are built, down to the Coteau Ste. Geneviève. To the late Rev. Mr. Maguire and to the Abbé Ferland is due the discovery of the origin of the name of the Plains of Abraham, a mystery which had puzzled many an antiquarian. Abraham Martin dit l'Ecossais, King's Pilot on the St. Lawrence, owned the whole land from St. Louis road to Cote d'Abraham, called after him, down to the Coteau Ste. Geneviève; the east boundary was the street in front of St. Mathew's cemetery, the west, Claire Fontaine-street, with that portion of the Plains called after him.—(*See Col. Beatson's Notes.*)

his way under secular oaks, and majestic pines to the brow of Cape Diamond, to ascertain if any of his royal master's argosies were rounding Point Levi? You are no doubt aware, that in those days it was rather a dangerous experiment to stray *unarmed* beyond the view of the Chateau St. Louis; that at times every bush, every rock concealed an implacable foe. Would you, think ye, have been swift enough of foot (although, no doubt, a great pedestrian) to follow through the underbrush and winding paths of the forest which then crowned the *Plateau*, the lithe and fierce Iroquois, stealthily dogging the footsteps of an unsuspecting colonist fresh from old France, until the grim warrior had added his scalp to the clanking belt of human bones and hair which girt his loins? Well, reader, let us float down the stream of time one whole century; let us view Champlain's city just a few years before the red cross of Albion streamed over its battlements. Let us look at Quebec when most gigantic plunder was going on in the colony. I do not mean in 185–, when British railway contractors were promising to the cormorants of the London and Manchester Exchange 11 per cent. dividends; I mean 175–, during the fast career of the French Intendant Bigot—a man to whom Roupell, Calvert, Sir Dean Paul could have taught nothing in the art of "raising the wind." Gentle reader, if you will accompany me towards the Quebec Post Office, I will briefly tell you a tale of those times.

When you get half way between Holiwell & Alexander's news depôt and the door of a jolly ex-Commissioner of Crown Lands—a door, by the by, immortalized by the pencil of our Canadian artist, Kreighoff,* just cast your eye above what formerly was the chief entrance to the City Post Office and notice a Golden Dog, in a crouching position, rudely carved in relievo, with the following inscription underneath:—

"Je Svis Vn Chien Qvi Ronge Lo,
en le rongeant je prends mon Repos,
Vn temps viendra qvi n'est pas venv,
Qve je morderay qvi m'avra mordv.
1736."

Are you aware that these identical words retrace a deed of blood, contain a record of vengeance long deferred but terrible: such, for

* "Pour l'amour de Dieu," and "Va au Diable," are the inscriptions to these two life-like pictures by Kreighoff, of the Indignant Beggar, which every one has seen.

instance, as a Corsican mother would glory in? If you have access to the Rev. Mr. Bourne's work, or to Col. Cockburn's *Quebec and its Environs*, published some thirty years since, you will obtain a meagre account of the tragedy enacted on this spot about one hundred and fourteen years ago. As you are likely to derive but little interest or amusement from the scanty details these writers furnish, I shall condense the elegant French sketch written by a brother advocate, now no more (the late Auguste Soulard), and shall incorporate in it the learned criticism which Mr. Soulard's narrative elicited from Monsieur le Commandeur Jacques Viger; he also, alas! is gone to his long home.

Nicolas Jacquin Philibert, a Quebec merchant, was, in 1748, the occupant, probably the proprietor, of the house on which the Golden Dog is now carved; the date, 1736, is supposed to commemorate the year in which the building was erected. Somehow or other he had incurred the displeasure of the Intendant (Bigot), perhaps for refusing to aid him in his peculations and extortions. The Intendant, in order to annoy Philibert, had billeted troops on him, and ordered a French lieutenant by the name of Pierre Legardeur, Sieur de Repentigny, to quarter on the Quebec merchant. This incensed Mr. Philibert very much, and, when the lieutenant attempted to enter the house with the order, Philibert objected, saying he would have the order recalled, to which De Repentigny replied, "You are a fool." A blow from a walking-stick was the answer. The officer then drew his sword and inflicted on his opponent a wound, of which he died on the 21st of January, 1748. The deadly thrust is supposed to have been given on the very steps of the Chien d'Or building; which steps were also, about a century later, the occasion for extensive litigation when the Chien d'Or belonged to a well-remembered millionaire, Jacob Pozer. De Repentigny, in order to elude a criminal prosecution, escaped from Quebec, and retired to Nova Scotia, then called Acadie, where he applied to Louis XV. for his pardon. Letters of reprieve and pardon were sent out from Paris, and De Repentigny returned to Quebec in 1749 with these letters, in order to meet any opposition which the Widow Philibert might urge, when he should apply to the Superior Council of the colony to have them registered. Madame Philibert having, as was customary in those days, been indemnified by pecuniary compensation for the loss of her husband, did not oppose the registration of De

Repentigny's letters of indemnity. The French lieutenant remained in the colony, and had been promoted to a captaincy in 1760; at that time, he was serving under the Chevalier de Lévis. Everything seemed to presage to De Repentigny forgetfulness of the past, and a promising future; every one seemed to have forgotten Philibert's untimely end, and how the family's respected chief had been cut off in the prime of manhood, and its prospects blighted forever, by the dastardly act of one of the Intendant's sycophants; all seemed to have forgotten these facts, all save one person, and this was a young man who had just seen twenty-three summers: his name was Pierre Nicolas Philibert.* Severe in his demeanor, studious and reserved in his habits, young Philibert had grown up to manhood, the chief support and consolation of his widowed mother. At times, several had remarked on his austere but beautiful face a sombre expression, which would immediately melt into a subdued sadness, the real cause of which few seemed to suspect. Beloved, as he certainly was, by all who knew him, it was a mournful day for the forlorn widow when, followed by some friends, she escorted her eldest son to the Lower Town wharf, on his way to old France to obtain a commission in the army.

Ten months after his departure, Madame Philibert one morning received a letter; it came from Europe. On breaking the seal, the first words which met her eye were as follows :—

"My Dearest Mother,—We are avenged; my father's murderer is no more."

The two had met at Pondicherry, in the East Indies. DeRepentigny had fallen under a sword wound which young Philibert had inflicted on him in a duel.

---

* An indefatigable searcher of old records furnishes the additional particulars about the Philibert family :—Marie Anne, born 1st September, 1734; Marie Magdeleine, born 2nd June, 1736; Pierre Nicholas, born 17th May, 1737; Pierre, born in 1738; Nicholas, born 10th Nov., 1740; Marguerite, born 30th October, 1742.—Sons and daughters of Mr. and Madame Philibert.—*Notes of le Commandeur Viger.*

Canadian Names and Surnames.

CHAPTER VI.

A CONTRIBUTOR to *Blackwood*, under the heading "The Scot in France," reviewing Mr. Francisque Michel's book, "Les Ecossais en France," graphically delineates the honorable part played some centuries back in the affairs of France, by Scotchmen. The learned critic, amongst other things, successfully traces to their origin several modern French names, and clearly demonstrates, after divesting them of the transmogrifications of time and language, that many of these names formerly belonged to brawny, six feet Scotchmen, whom little Johnny Crapaud, out of spite, had christened on account of their aldermanic appetites "wine bags"; in fact, the same distinguished class which we, moderns, on the undoubted authority of Judge Barrington, would designate "Twelve bottle men,"—select individuals scarcely ever heard of in these degenerate teetotal times, and of which class, Marshal de Saxe, Mdlle. Lecouvreur's friend, was in the last century a pretty fair representative. Might it not also be worth our while to examine into some of the ludicrous changes to which, in our own country, some old names have been subjected? Every one knew that Normandy and Brittany had furnished the chief portion of the earliest settlers of our soil; the exact proportion in which this emigration took place cannot at present be a subject of debate, now that we have in print the Abbé Ferland's laborious researches. We accordingly find, in the appendix to the first volume of his "Cours d'Histoire du Canada," a list and address of all the French who settled in Lower Canada, from the year 1615 to 1648. No one, perhaps, except a searching student of the Abbé's school, would have taken the trouble to trace the pedigree of all the families in Canada; on this subject, it is not too much to say, that the veteran historian is a living cyclopedia. It is true, he had ample sources of information at command, having had access to the "Register of Marriages, Births and Burials of the Roman Catholic Cathedral at Quebec," and these took him, uninterruptedly, as far back as 1640, in which year they were destroyed by fire, and restored from memory; he could also consult the ample details of the several census tables, compiled by order of the French government, yet in manuscript in our public libraries.

It is really singular to notice what a large portion of settlers came from Normandy to New France. Almost all the educated Frenchmen, such as Messrs. Rameau, Ampère, De Puibusque, Aubry, Fenouillet and others who have visited Canada, have been struck with the resemblance between the customs, manners and language of the French Canadian peasantry of this day, and those of the peasantry of Brittany and Normandy. All of them admitted that, as a general rule, our *habitants* spoke better French than the same class in the country parts of France. Of course, it is not pretended that even the educated in this country could compare for the purity of their idiom with Parisians, who alone claim the right to speak *pure* French. Parisian writers, on this point, have promulgated canons which seem rather exclusive. It is pretended, for instance, that the nicety of Parisian taste is such, that *even* a Parisian writer who removes for four years from his native city to the provinces, is liable to be detected when he writes. This is going far, and naturally reminds one of the fish-woman of Athens, who, by his accent, detected a new customer as belonging to the suburbs of the city.

When Mr. Rameau was in Quebec, I took occasion to ask him what he thought of our best writers. "Sir," said he, "I will relate to you what occurred to me in Paris last winter. I was acquainted with Canadian literature before I came here, and in order to test the correctness of my own opinion, I assembled some literary friends and told them that I intended reading them a chapter out of two new books which they had never seen before; they assented; this done, and replacing the books in my book-case, I requested them to tell me candidly where they could have been written. 'Why, in Paris, where else?' they replied; 'none but Parisians could write such French.' "Well, gentlemen," said I, "you are much mistaken, these books were written on the banks of the St. Lawrence, at Quebec. Etienne Parent, and the Abbé Ferland are the authors." My friends could scarcely credit the fact. I take pleasure in recording this incident, because such a circumstance does honor to the country. I also take particular pleasure in noticing this honorable fact, because it effectually bears on a stupid assertion not altogether uncommon, viz: That French Canadians speak nothing but *patois*—whereas, if the truth were known, it would appear that our peasantry talk* better French than does one half of the rural population of France; in fact, it is not rare to find the French peasantry of one department scarcely able to understand the idiom of the corresponding class in another department. Several causes might be adduced in explaining this singular feature; the first settlers in Canada had left France about the time when literature was at its zenith, and when the language was singularly beautiful. Whatever success may have been achieved in literature by modern France, no writer since the great revolution, has surpassed Corneille, Racine, Boileau, Voltaire or Sevigné, in each of their several departments; the language of the peasantry in New France has remained what it was two hundred years ago; it is not purer, but it is just as pure. If, on one hand the French element in Canada has escaped the disorganizing influence of the revolutionary era † of '89, on the other hand, it has received the infusion of no new blood; the race is essentially conservative, too much so, perhaps, according to men of the 19th century; still, as the component part of a great nationality, who can complain of its being too cohesive; who, on looking across the line, and viewing

---

* In connection with this fact, it appears that the French Canadians have alone retained in their original purity the simple old Norman songs which their ancestors brought into the country; that these same popular ballads have become so altered in France by time, that a request has been sent out to Canada to have them collected in their original purity. An eloquent young professor of the Laval University (Dr. Larue) has turned his attention to the subject.

† Our Canadian ancestors had long since realised the difference which the conquest had made in their situation, when their beloved and eloquent pastor, Bishop Plessis, in 1794, from the pulpit of the same French Cathedral which now faces the Upper Town Market place in Quebec, publicly, and in the name of his flock, thanked Almighty God that the colony was English, and therefore would be free from the horrors enacted in the French colonies of the day; that there were no human butchers in Canada, to slaughter any nobles, priests, women and children.—See the Funeral oration of Bishop Briand, pronounced on the 27th June, 1794, by Monseigneur Plessis.—(*Christie's History of Canada*, vol. I, pp. 356–7.) Could he have then foreseen what happened Louisiana later on, he might again have expressed his thankfullness that Canada did not belong to France—else it might have been included in the deed of sale and bargain executed between Napoleon the Great and the occupant of the White House in 1805. Verily, colonists are considered small fry by rulers of empires.

Our people were again in forcible terms reminded of the superiority of English over French institutions, when civil and religious liberty is at stake. Who has forgotten Dr. Cahill's eloquent appeal! "Three Bishops," said he, "cannot dine together in Paris without the permission of the police: no new place of worship can be opened without the consent of government. Why was the charitable society the *St. Vincent de Paul* broken up? Why were Protestant chapels summarily closed by the Police and the congregation dispersed?—Why is the press muzzled? Yes, why? Thank your stars," said the talented lecturer, "that you live here under the British flag!"

democracy in full rout, and possibly a renewal of the horrors of '89, in this land of the west, close at hand; who would not prefer at least one million of staunch conservative people, who, under proper treatment, would understand loyalty to their sovereign, as the Vendéens did, to a God-forsaken, atheistical, democratic* rabble, worshipping no other deity than the almighty dollar?

But this is wandering away from the subject which heads this sketch; *revenons a nos moutons*.

There is, in this country, a spice of drollery about some transformations of names worthy of notice. These queer changes do not necessarily imply abject ignorance in the class which adopts them. We may have in this country backwoodsmen† excessively stupid and ignorant, but where (except within the precincts of a lunatic asylum) would you find even a brat of a boy who would give the same reply which the free-born Briton gave to Lord Ashley, one of the commissioners appointed to enquire into the condition of the lower classes in England, "that all he knew about God was, that he had often heard the workmen say, God damn!" We say we thank Providence for this, for whatever other colonial drawbacks we may labor under, and they may be numerous, we are spared the spectacle of extreme social degradation side by side with fabulous wealth. Now to the point. Did you ever, my dear reader, know from whence the first Know-Nothing hailed? Perhaps you will meet me with

* It would be unmanly to abuse a great nation who has pledged itself to solve the grand Monroe problem, "America for the Americans," merely because the evil passions of social strife place it for a time under a cloud. The Americans have, doubtless, boundless resources, and in the energy of their people the elements of future greatness. Unfortunately, their lying journalists have succeeded in making them appear a very abject community. We who do not live amongst them, know them only by their scurrilous press.

† "Backwoodmen." A worthy but eccentric missionary, once enlivened a stirring appeal he was making to the sympathy and purse of a Quebec church meeting with the following anecdote, illustrative of the multitudinous hardships he had experienced in the course of his evangelizing duties in the backwoods of Canada. The holy man was very long and slender in the legs. "It was once my fate," said he, "to put up for the night in a log shanty, the dwelling of the headman in the mission; the bed did seem very short, but being a deal one, nailed to the floor, it had to remain where it was; I only became fully aware that either I was too long, or that it was too short for my humble self, when after extinguishing my candle, I tried to extend my weary limbs; my feet, I found, struck the window, which was nearly smashed by the operation. In despair I got up, and after cogitating a short time, I came to the conclusion that no other alternative existed but to remove the obstruction and open the window, through which, when lying down, my feet protruded some eighteen inches. I felt it was not a peculiarly dignified position for the pastor to be seen by the flock, but what could I do. I slept soundly from fatigue, but awoke early, feeling a great weight on my feet; on raising my head to see what it was, I found, that the patriarch of the farm yard—a very large turkey cock had made roosters of my nether extremities." He of course carried his point.

the common-place reply, *cui bono?* Is not Know-Nothingism dead and buried? True, I reply; so is the builder of the pyramids dead, (or at least, unless he can beat old Methusaleh, he ought to be,) and still the enquiry about the originator has been going on for some time, and is likely to continue, although for any practical purpose, the origin of the Pyramids or of Know-Nothingism is of the same moment. Well, I assert clearly and most emphatically, that the first Know-Nothing, nominally designated as such, lived at Cacouna, some seventy years ago. Now for the proof. About the end of the last century, an English vessel was stranded in the fall of the year, at Bic; the crew had lost everything, and as in those days the country below Quebec was thinly populated, they had to travel upwards on foot. Along the road they obtained their food by begging it from the French Canadian peasantry, and of course, various questions were put to them, as to who they were, where they came from, where they were going to? This constant questioning became troublesome to the honest tars, who knew naught of the language of Louis XIV. The first effort they made was to attempt to say that they could not understand the question put, and in a very few days, the stereotyped reply to all enquiries was "J'en sçais rien." "*I don't know.*" One of them was rather a good-looking fellow, and not being accustomed to snow-shoes, he got the *mal de raquette*, and had to stay behind; a wealthy Canadian peasant took pity on him, and admitted him under his hospitable roof. Jack was not long before falling a victim to the tender passion; and Mdlle. Josephte, the daughter of the house, having shewn him some kindness in his forlorn state, the gallant Briton could do nothing less than lay his heart at her feet.

"Amour, tu perdis, Troie!"

as old Lafontaine said in his fable of the cocks and hens; but for Jack the effect was diametrically opposite; it was his salvation, the dawn of a bright future. It was, however, love under difficulties in the beginning. To the fair one's enquiries, the interminable reply was returned-"J'en sçais rien." Mdlle. Josephte soon began to fancy that the words sounded musically in her ears;—she facetiously christened her Saxon friend *J'en sçais rien*, and soon the curé of the parish was called on to pronounce the magical "Conjungo vos" over madamoiselle and the English sailor. The union of the Norman and the Saxon, which seven hundred years before was a daily occurrence on the banks of Thames, was re-celebrated on the banks of the St. Lawrence, and with the same happy results. In the course of time, English Jack became the respected pater familias of a patriarchial circle of small "Sçaisriens," genuine Jean Baptistes in every thing, except that they were handsomer than the rest of the children of the parish. An addition to the family name soon took place, and to "J'en sçais rien," was affixed the words *dit l' Anglais*, (*alias the Englishman.*) It is a common practice amongst the French Canadians to have this addition, for instance, J. B. Portugais dit La Musique, Sansouci dit L'Eveillé, Picard des Trois Maisons. To this day there is a large progeny of "Scais rien, dit l'Anglais" in the parish of Cacouna. Now, reader, if I have made out my case, I pray for a verdict, for, verily this is the first mention of a Know-Nothing I find in history.

There is a very worthy N.P., on the Island of Orleans, a descendant of an Englishman or Scotchman, whose name was Richard somebody, but his heir has never been able to clear up the point; and still a family name he must have, by hook or by crook; so the Richard was made into Dick, and *Monsieur le Notaire Jean Dick* is now known all over the island, and executes deeds under that and no other name. I do not believe that he understands or speaks English.

A locality near this city, the village on the St. Lewis Road, which the Hon. Wm. Shepherd, formerly of Woodfield, laid out, has undergone several strange appellations.

It was, of course, intended to be named Shepherdville, and did at one time bear that name, under which several know it still;—a number of French Canadians having settled there, considered that as there was no saint in the calendar hailing under the name of Saint Shepherd, it was not right to give such a name to the Parish; however, on finding out that the parish was not canonically erected by the bishop, they consented to leave the original name, if it was only translated into French, and Shepherd meaning Berger, why they would put up,—until a saint was chosen,—with Bergerville: this was considered however, such a concession to anglification, that the knowing ones suspected that had not the Hon. William's ground rent agent interfered, holding over non-paying malcontents the fear of sundry writs of ejectment, the Saxon name would have been swept away and blotted out for ever. Matters were going on smoothly until a number of Irish having also elected domicile in

Bergerville, were much shocked at the liberty the French Canadian tenants had taken, in daring to re-christen the settlement; they were of opinion that as a considerable portion of the residents would not be out of place in St. Giles, in London, it might be more suitable to call the place Beggarville,* and not Bergerville; and just as party denominations have been in England in time of yore, by-words for strife between the houses of York and Lancaster, so it has been on the estate of the Hon. William on the St. Louis Road, near Quebec!

In October last, Tom Everell, an octogenarian Greenwich pilot died at Cap Rouge, near Quebec. Tom was well known all round; he had many years before married into a French Canadian family, and gradually lost his family name of Everell; he was called by the *habitants* Tom, le père Tom; he left a large number of children; they are all called Toms—there is Norbert Tom, George Tom, Henriette Tom, Jean Bte. Tom, but as a compensation to this loss of nationality in his offspring, a glorious distinction was made for his eldest son, in which primogeniture shines forth; of the whole family, he alone is allowed to bear the family patronomic as a christian name; he is not called Tom or Thomas Everell, but is recognised as EVERELL TOM.

In looking over English periodicals, I find that the transformation of names is not merely confined to Scotchmen in France, or to Englishmen in Canada, but also to Englishmen in their own country. Listen to this extract of *The Cornhill*, with which I shall close:—

"Surnames are by no means fully established in some parts of England In the colliery districts, particularly, hereditary designations seem to be the exception rather than the rule. A correspondent of *Knight's Quarterly Magazine* says, that clergymen in Staffordshire 'have been known to send home a wedding party in despair, after a vain essay to gain from the bride and bridegroom a sound by way of name.' Every man in these colliery fields, it seems, bears a personal sobriquet, descriptive of some peculiarity, but scarcely any person has a family name either known to himself or others. A story is told of an attorney's clerk who was professionally employed to serve a process on one of those

* Odd names seem fashionable in this village; there is one family composed of boys; several are very hard cases; one of them, aged about 17, combines all the vices of the rest; he is singularly vicious, just a shade better than a highwayman; he goes by the name of *Grand Père B......*; why? I never have been able to find out. I have come to the conclusion that it might be from his being supposed to unite the vices of three generations!

oddly-named persons, whose supposed real name was entered in the instrument with legal accuracy. The clerk, after a great deal of inquiry as to the whereabouts of the party, was about to abandon the search as hopeless, when a young woman, who had witnessed his labors, kindly volunteered to assist him. 'Oy say, *Bullyed*,' cried she to the first person they met, 'does thee know a mon named Adom Green? The bull-head was shaken in token of ignorance. They then came to another man. '*Loy-a-bed*, dost thee?' Loy-a-bed could not answer either. *Stumpy*, (a man with a wooden leg), *Cowskin*, *Spindleshanks*, *Cockeye*, and *Pigtail* were successively consulted, but to no purpose. At length, however, having had conversation with several friends, the damsel's eye suddenly brightened, and slapping one of her neighbors on the shoulder, she exclaimed—'Dash my wig! whoy he means moy feyther!' Then turning to the astonished clerk, she cried—'You shoul'n ax'd for *Ode Blackbird!*' So it appeared that the old miner's name, though he was a man of substance, and had legal battles to fight, was not known even to his own daughter."*

* A very slight investigation has already produced a list of patronymics which throw all Dickens' ideal ones, grotesque and clever as many are, into hopeless distance. In proof whereof, a correspondent of the London *Times* states that a friend of his made the following curious selection of surnames from the wills in the Prerogative Court in Doctors' Commons:—Asse, Bub, Belly, Boots, Cripple, Cheese, Cockles, Dunce, Dam, Drinkmilke, Def, Flashman, Fatt, Ginger, Goose, Beaste, Bearhead, Bungler, Bugg, Buggy, Bones, Cheeke, Clod, Codd, Demon, Fiend, Funcke, Frogge, Ghost, Gready, Hag, Humpe, Holdwater, Headache, Jugs, Jelly, Idle, Kneebone, Kidney, Licie, Lame, Lazy, Leakey, Maypole, Mule, Monkey, Milksop, Mudd, Mug, Phisike, Pighead, Pot, Poker, Poopy, Prigge, Pigge, Punch, Proverb, Quicklove, Quash, Radish, Rumpe, Rawbone, Rottengoose, Swette, Shish, Sprat, Squibb, Sponge, Stubborne, Swine, Shave, Shrimps, Shirt, Skim, Squalsh, Silly, Shoe, Smelt, Skull, Spattell, Shadow, Snaggs, Spittle, Teate, Taylecoate, Villian, Vittels, Vile, Whale.

All nature seems to have been ransacked for the purpose of producing even the above list, which is no doubt, only a small sample of that which some further investigation might have produced. Earth and water throw in their ridiculous contributions in the names of Asse, Goose, Beast and Codd; and the mysteries of the unknown world are represented by a Shadow and a Ghost. And Demon, Fiend, and Hagg, find also their nominal representatives on this upper earth. The ideal is, however, by no means alone drawn on, for we find, in a suspicious juxtaposition—Jugs, Punch, Headache.—This combination, it must be conceded, is rational enough.

The Holland Tree.

CHAPTER VII.

"Woodman spare that tree."

IT has often been stated that the chief glory of Quebec consisted in being surrounded on all sides by magnificent country seats, which in the summer season, as it were, encircle the brow of the old city like a chaplet of flowers: those who, on a sunny June morning, have wandered through the shady groves of Spencer Wood, Woodfield, Marchmont, Benmore, Kilmarnock, and fifty other old places, rendered vocal by the voices of myriads of winged choristers and with the sparkling waters of the great river at their feet, are not likely to gainsay this statement.

Amongst these beautiful rural retreats few are better known than Holland Farm, the family mansion of Surveyor General Holland, who purchased it about the year 1780. Four years previously it had been the head-quarters of General Montgomery, who choose it as his residence during the siege of Quebec. This fine property, running back as far as Mount Hermon Cemetery, and extending from the St. Louis or Grand Allée road, opposite Spencer Wood, down to the St. Foy road, which it crosses, is bounded to the north by the *Cime du cap*, or St. Foy heights. For those who may be curious to know its original extent to an eighth of an inch, I shall quote from Major Holland's title-deed wherein it is stated to comprise "in superficies, French measure, two hundred and six arpents one perch seven feet eight inches and *four eighths of an inch*," from which description one would infer the major had surveyed his domain with great minuteness, or that he must have been considerably of a stickler for territorial rights. What would his shades now think could they be made cognizant of the fact, that that very chateau garden, which he possessed and bequeathed to his sons in the year 1800, has been taken possession of for military purposes by the Imperial authorities, and held to this day by them, without any compensation, it is said, being tendered? Major Samuel Holland had distinguished himself as an officer, under General Wolfe, on the Plains of Abraham,—lived at Holland House * many years, as was customary in those days, in affluence, and at last paid the common debt to nature.

The major after having provided for his wife, Mary Josephte Rolet, bequeathed his property to *Frederick Brehm, John Frederick, Charlotte, Susan,* and *George Holland,*† his children. In 1817, Frederick Brehm Holland, who, at that time was an ordinance storekeeper at Prince Edward Island, sold his share of the farm to the late William Wilson, of the Customs department. Ten years later, John Frederick and Charlotte Holland also disposed of their interest in this land to Mr. Wilson, who subsequently having acquired the rights of another heir, viz., in 1835, remained proprietor of Holland Farm until 1843, when the property by purchase passed over to Geo. O. Stuart, Esq., of this city. Mr. Stuart built on it a handsome mansion, now known as Holland House, which he subsequently sold to R. Cassells, Esq., then of Quebec, and manager of the Bank of British North America: it is the house recently leased by Col. Lysons.

Holland Farm has been gradually dismembered. The pretty cottage opposite Spencer Wood, now owned by Major Campbell, is built on Holland Farm. A successful gold digger by the name of Sinjohn purchased last year a large tract of the farm fronting the St. Louis road, with Thornhill as its north-eastern, and Mr. Stuart's new road as its south-western boundary. His neat cottage, shaded by the Thornhill Grove, a nice garden and lawn now indicate that he does not intend to allow his Australian nuggets to rust in his coffers. A large portion of the gold hunter's land is a level pasturage entirely denuded of shrubs and forest trees. To a person looking from the vice-regal gate, at Spencer Wood, in the direction of the south gable of Holland House, exactly in a straight line, no object intervenes, except a fir tree, which detaches itself on the horizon, conspicuous from afar, over the plantation which fronts the St. Foy road. That tree is the Holland Tree. Well! what about the Holland Tree? What! you a Quebecer and not to

* The original Holland House stood a little behind the present mansion.

† The last will and codicil of S. Holland was executed before Chs. Voyer and colleague, N.P., at Quebec, and bear date 14th and 25th December, 1800. The Chateau St. Louis property is therein thus described :—" Un grand emplacement proche le Chateau St. Louis, donné et accordé au dit Sieur Testateur, cultivé actuellement en jardin."

know about the Holland Tree, its duel, and the slumberers who have reposed for so many years under its shade!!

"Oh! but I am not a Quebecer. So tell me about the Holland Tree." Well walk down from the St. Louis road along Mr. Stuart's new road and we shall see first how the rest of the "slumberers" has been respected. Hear the words which filial affection dictated to Frederick Brehm, John Frederick and Charlotte Holland, when on the 14th July, 1827, they executed a deed in favor of Wm. Wilson, conveying their interest in their father's estate:

"Provided always, and these presents as well as the foregoing deed of sale and conveyance are so made and executed by the said Robert Holland, acting as aforesaid (as attorney of the heirs Holland), upon and subject to the *express* charge and *condition*, that is to say, that the said William Wilson, his heirs and assigns shall for ever hold sacred and inviolable the small circular space of ground on the said tract or piece of land and premises, enclosed with a stone wall and wherein the remains of the late Samuel Holland, Esquire, father of the said vendors, and of his son the late Samuel Holland, jr., Esq., are interred, and shall and will allow free ingress and egress at all times to the relatives and friends of the family of the said Samuel Holland, for the purpose of viewing the state and condition of the said space of ground, and making or causing to be made such repairs to the wall enclosing the same or otherwise providing for the protection of the said remains as they shall see fit.*"

Not many years back, this "small circular space" which Mr. Wilson bound himself to hold sacred and inviolable, and which contained two neat marble slabs with the names of Messrs. Holland, senior and junior, and other members of the family engraved on them, was inclosed within a substantial stone wall, to which access was had through an iron gate: the walls were covered with inscriptions and with the initials of those who had visited a spot, to which the fatal issue of a deadly encounter lent all the interest of a romance. Nothing now is visible except the foundation, which is still distinct; the monument stones have disappeared;

* This deed was passed at Quebec before W. Fisher Scott, N. P. It purports to have been executed "in the Gaoler's Room," *entre les deux guichets*, in the Common Gaol of the District of Quebec. Some of those who signed it must have been in custody, why or wherefore does not appear.

the wall has been razed to the ground, some modern Vandal,* some descendant of the Ostrogoths (for amongst all civilized nations the repose of the dead is sacred) has laid violent hands on them ! ! When Mr. Wilson sold Holland farm in 1843, he made no stipulation about the graves of the Hollands : he took no care that what he had agreed to hold inviolable should continue to be so held. If his representatives are amongst those who now seek for reparation of the injury inflicted by this act, the loss of the "chateau" garden, will furnish to those who believe in Alison's doctrines of retributive justice in this world, a new exemplification of the principle.

The tragical occurrence connected with the Holland Tree is so much out of the ordinary run of events, that it seems where like the plot of a sensation novel—a dark tale redolent with love, jealousy and revenge. Two men stood, some sixty years ago, in mortal combat, not under the Holland Tree, as it has generally been believed, but somewhere on the mountain behind Montreal : one of them a Holland, the other was Major Ward of the 60th, the father of the Major Ward who, many years after, fought a memorable duel in Montreal with Mr. Sweeney. The cause of the bloody affray originated at a fancy ball in the St. Louis Chateau. It is said that when Major Holland saw the lifeless corpse of his son, and the fatal pistols, after first giving vent to parental grief, he uttered the following words :—"My beloved son, when General Wolfe presented me on the Plains of Abraham with those beautiful weapons, little did I think that they would be used to bring you to a dishonored grave." On that fatal day probably a dense wood hid the combatants from public gaze. I cannot say more without perhaps saying too much, and I must leave the young who are curious to question their grandfathers and their grandmothers about Holland Tree. I have said enough, I hope, to induce the reader to repeat with me,

"Woodman spare that tree !"

* A truculent gardener, it is said, who had been left in charge, some years back, converted the monumental slabs into grinding stones.

A Chapter on Canadian Nobility.

CHAPTER VIII.

"The names and memories of great men are the dowry of a nation. They are the salt of the earth, in death as well as in life. What they did once, their descendants have still and always a right to do after them."—*Blackwood.*

THESE are democratic times: men eminent for their intellect and world-wide fame,—Brights and Cobdens,—citizens of the most aristocratic country, members of a highly intelligent community, boldly and successfully set at defiance privilege, when propagating their favorite dogma of the sovereignty of the people, it may therefore be hazardous to readily expect from an enlightened and progressive Canadian public the gratuitous recognition of title and privilege, as implied in a Canadian nobility. Many considerations lead to this belief. The air we breathe, the tone of our people, the habits and customs of all classes here, although they may savour of monarchy, do not point out to this our native land as a soil in which titled nobility could, for many years to come, strike out deep roots or yield wholesome and palatable fruit.

Indeed, there are in our midst persons perverse enough to insinuate that a certain august visitor engrafted on the old trunk of our nationality sufficient titles to last us a whole century.

A young barrister, snatched too soon from fame and friends, thus embodied in verse Canada's motto:

> "Sur cette terre encor sauvage
> Les vieux titres sont inconnus;
> La noblesse est dans le courage,
> Dans les talents, dans les vertus."
>
> F. R. Angers.

True nobility must consist, for us, in courage, talent and virtue; such we consider the genuine guinea's stamp; the rest is all plated ware, which once tarnished by vile or unworthy sentiments, not all the blue blood of all the Howards could rescue from contempt. No not even the profound peace enjoyed under the protection of a mighty and free power, in these eventful times, when anarchy is inaugurating a reign of terror on our borders: not even the gratitude towards a strong protector could make us willingly kneel to a title unrecommended by merit or virtue.

We may feel differently on some points in both sections of the Province; we are not prepared to say whether the inhabitants of Western Canada (those whom one of our governors is said to have, facetiously, we presume, christened the *superior race*) are steadfast in their attachment to monarchical principles; we hope and trust they are, although several—their enemies, no doubt—depict them as thorough democrats: people dazzled by the glitter of Uncle Sam's dollars, whose chink they can hear from their own thresholds, inducing them to mingle with a nation identical with themselves in race, religion and language. One thing, however, we do know, and that is, that no community of feeling or interest can exist between our republican neighbors and the majority of the inhabitants of Lower Canada, alien in race, religion and language. Any alliance between the two must be founded on the abasement and ruin of the weaker of the contracting parties.

On one point the Latin and the Teuton of Lower Canada do seem to understand one another thoroughly, viz., in their estimate of monarchical ideas. They respect the sovereign and honor his chief men, the nobles—not the men of pleasure such as those with which Louis XV. surrounded his throne and oppressed his subjects, but honorable men such as Victoria and the English people are proud of; well represented by that aristocracy of merit "specially charged to perpetuate traditions of chivalry and honor;" whose door is open to the people, as the highest recognition of popular merit; whose worth is testified to by the English as well as the French; who is eulogized in high terms by men of commanding intellect, such as Montesquieu, Montalembert, Guizot, Chateaubriand.* Merit is then the touch-stone which wrung from these brilliant writers the unqualified praise they bestowed on the nobility of old England.

* "The nobility of Great Britain is the finest modern society since the Roman Patriciate," has said the illustrious Chateaubriand. His vast researches, his presence at the English court as French ambassador in 1822, had given him ample opportunity of judging. This estimate does not quite agree with that of the author of "Representative Men," Emerson: "Twenty thousand thieves landed at Hastings. These founders of the House of Lords were greedy and ferocious dragoons, sons of greedy and ferocious

Let us see whether we can apply this test to one of the oldest and most honored names in our own history—we mean that of the Baron de Longueil.

In former times, too, we had bloody wars to wage; merciless foes existed on our frontiers; the soil then found generous and brave soldiers to defend it: men who went forth each day with their lives in their hands, ready to shed the last drop of blood for all they held dear, their homes, their wives, their children. Has the stout race of other days degenerated, grown callous to what its God, its honor, its country may command in the hour of need? We should hope not. We said the Baron de Longueil.

Who was the Baron de Longueil? With your permission, kind reader, let us peruse together the royal patent erecting the seigniory of Longueil into a barony: it is to be found in the Register of the proceedings of the Superior Council of Quebec, letter B, page 131, and runs thus: "Louis, by the Grace of God, King of France and Navarre, to all present, Greeting: It being an attribute of our greatness and of our justice to reward those whose courage and merit led them to perform great deeds, and taking into consideration the services which have been rendered to us by the late Charles LeMoyne*; Esquire, Seigneur of Longueil, who left France in 1640 to reside in Canada, where his valour and fidelity were so often conspicuous in the wars against the Iroquois, that our governors and lieutenant governors in that country employed him constantly in every military expedition, and in every negotiation or treaty of peace, of all which duties he acquitted himself to their entire satisfaction;—that after him, Charles Le Moyne, Esquire, his eldest son, desirous of imitating the example of his father, bore arms from his youth, either in France, where he served as a lieutenant in the Régiment de St. Laurent, or else as captain of a naval detachment in Canada since 1687, where he had an arm shot off by the Iroquois when fighting near Lachine, in which combat seven of his brothers were also

pirates. They were all alike; they took everything they could carry. They burned, harried, violated, tortured, and killed, until everything English was brought to the verge of ruin. Such, however, is the illusion of antiquity and wealth, that decent and dignified men now existing boast their descent from these petty thieves, who showed a far juster conviction of their own merits, by assuming for their types the swine, goat, jackal, leopard, wolf, and snake, which they severally resembled.

"It took many generations to trim, and comb, and perfume the first boat-load of Norse pirates into royal highnesses and most noble knights of the garter; but every sparkle of ornament dates back to the Norse boat."—*English Traits.*

* He was nephew to the celebrated Surgeon Adrien Duchesne.

engaged ;—that Jacques Le Moyne de Ste. Hélène, his brother, for his gallantry, was made a captain of a naval detachment, and afterwards fell at the siege of Quebec, in 1690, leading on with his elder brother, Charles Le Moyne, the Canadians against Phipps, where his brother was also wounded; that another brother, Pierre Le Moyne d'Iberville, captain of a sloop of war, served on land and on sea, and captured Fort Corlard in Hudson's Bay, and still commands a frigate ; that Joseph Le Moyne de Bienville was commissioned an ensign in the said naval detachment, and was killed by the Iroquois in the attack on the place called Repentigny ; that Louis Le Moyne de Chateaugay, when acting as lieutenant to his brother, d'Iberville, also fell in the taking of Fort Bourbon, in the Hudson's Bay; that Paul Le Moyne de Maricourt is an ensign in the navy, and captain of a company in the naval detachment, acting in the capacity of ensign to his brother d'Iberville ; that, in carrying out our intentions for settling Canada, the said Charles Le Moyne, the eldest son, has spent large sums in establishing inhabitants on the domain and seigniory of Longueil, which comprises abou two leagues in breadth on the St. Lawrence, and three leagues and a half in depth, the whole held from us with *haute, moyenne et basse justice*, wherein he is now striving to establish three parishes, and whereat, in order to protect the residents in times of war, he has had erected at his own cost a fort supported by four strong towers of stone and masonry, with a guard house, several large dwellings, a fine church, bearing all the insignia of nobility; a spacious farm yard, in which there is a barn, a stable, a sheep pen, a dove cot, and other buildings, all of which are within the area of the said fort; next to which stands a *banal* mill, a fine brewery of masonry, together with a large retinue of servants, horses and equipages, the cost of which buildings amount to some 60,000 livres; so much so that this seigniory is one of the most valuable of the whole country, and the only one fortified and built up in this way; that this has powerfully contributed to protect the inhabitants of the neighboring seigniories; that this estate, on account of the extensive land clearings and work done and to be done on it, is of great value, on which thirty workmen are employed; that the said Charles Le Moyne is now in a position to hold a noble rank on account of his virtue and merit: For which consideration we have thought it due to our sense of justice to assign not only a title of honor to the estate and seigniory of Longueil, but also to confer on its owner a proof of an honorable distinction which will pass to posterity, and which may appear to the children of the said Charles Le Moyne a reason and inducement to follow in their father's footsteps: For these causes, of our special grace, full power and royal authority, We have created, erected, raised and decorated, and do create, erect, raise and decorate, by the present patent, signed by our own hand, the said estate and seigniory of Longueil, situate in our country of Canada, into the name, title and dignity of a barony; the same to be peacefully and fully enjoyed by the said Sieur Charles Le Moyne, his children and heirs, and the descendants of the same, born in legitimate wedlock, held under our crown, and subject to fealty (*foi et hommage avec dénombrement*) according to the laws of our kingdom and the custom of Paris in force in Canada, together with the name, title and dignity of a baron;—it is our pleasure he shall designate and qualify himself baron in all deeds, judgments, &c.; that he shall enjoy the right of arms, heraldry, honors, prerogatives, rank, precedence in time of war, in meetings of the nobility, &c., like the other barons of our kingdom—that the vassals, *arrière vassaux*, and others depending of the said seigniory of Longueil, *noblement et en roture*, shall acknowledge the said Charles Le Moyne, his heirs, assigns, as barons, and pay them the ordinary feudal homage, which said titles, &c., it is our pleasure, shall be inserted in proceedings and sentences, had or rendered by courts of justice, without, however, the said vassals being held to perform any greater homage than they are now liable to. .... This deed to be enregistered in Canada, and the said Charles Le Moyne, his children and assigns, to be maintained in full and peaceful enjoyment of the rights herein conferred.

"This done at Versailles, the 27th January, 1700, in the fiftieth year of our reign.

"(Signed) LOUIS."

We have here in unmistakable terms a royal patent, conveying on the Great Louis' loyal and brave Canadian subject and his heirs, rights, titles, prerogatives, vast enough to make even the mouth of a Spanish grandee water. It is a little less comprehensive than the text of the parchment creating Nova Scotia knights, but that is all.

The claims of the Longueil family to the peaceable enjoyment of their honor are set forth so lucidly in the following document, that we shall insert the manuscript in full;—it was written in Paris by an educated English gentleman, M. Falconer.

"When I was in Canada, in 1842, a newspaper in Montreal contained some weekly abuse of the Baron Grant de Longueil, on account of his assuming the title of Baron de Longueil. It appeared to me to be somewhat remarkable that a paper which very freely abused people for being republicans, and affected a wonderful reverence for monarchial institutions, should make the possession of monarchial honors, in a country professedly governed by monarchial institutions, the ground of frequent personal abuse, and was certainly a very inconsiderate line of conduct.

"But it was in fact the more blameable, as the possession of that honor by Baron de Longueil is connected with some historical events in which every Canadian ought to feel a pride, as being part of the history of his country.

"I can of course only give a short note of the family of Longueil.

"In the early settlement of Canada, one of the most distinguished men in the service of Government was Charles Le Moyne; he was in the war with the Iroquois, and contributed very materially to the pacification of the country and the defence of the frontier. He had eleven sons and two daughters; the names of the sons were—

"1st. Sieur Charles Le Moyne, Baron de Longueil. He was *Lieutenant du roi de la ville et gouverement de Montréal.* He was killed at Saratoga, in a severe action.

"2nd. Sieur Jacques Le Moyne de Sainte-Hélène, whose name was given to the island opposite Montreal, which was, until lately, part of the property of the family He fell at the siege of Quebec in 1690.

"3rd. Pierre Le Moyne d'Iberville, who was born at Montreal, in 1662, was the third son. He made his first voyage to sea at fourteen years of age. In 1686, he was in an expedition to Hudson's Bay, under Sieur de Troyes. In the same year the Marquis de Denonville made him commander of a fort, established in this expedition, and for his conduct in this post he received the thanks of the Governor of Canada. In 1690, with his brother, De Sainte-Hélène, he attacked some Iroquois villages, and prevented the attack of some Indians on Lachine and La Chenaye. He was made captain of a frigate in 1692—his instructions being dated 11th April of the same year. In 1694 he made an attack on Fort Bourbon, where his brother, De Chateaugay, was killed—but the fort was taken. On the 21st October, 1695, M. de Pontchartrain wrote to him a letter of commendation. In 1696 he carried troops to Acadia. He visited France in 1698. He left it with three vessels, in order to make a settlement in the Mississippi; he was the first person of European origin who entered the Mississippi from the sea; he ascended the river nearly one hundred leagues, established a garrison, and returned to France in 1699; in consequence of this success, he was decorated with the cross of the order of Saint Louis. In 1699 he was again sent to the Mississippi; his instructions were dated 22nd September of the same year, and directed him to make a survey of the country and endeavor to discover mines; this voyage was successful, and he returned to France in 1700, and was again sent to the Mississippi in 1701, his instructions being dated August 27th, of that year; he returned to France in 1702, and was made 'Capitaine de vesseau.' On July 5th, 1706, he again sailed for the Mississippi, charged with a most important command; but in 1706, on July 9th, this most distinguished discoverer and navigator died at Havannah. He was born at Montreal, and obtained an immortal reputation in the two worlds.

"4th. Paul Le Moyne de Maricourt, *capitaine d'une compagnie de la marine*. He died from exhaustion and fatigue in an expedition against the Iroquois.

"5th. Joseph Le Moyne de Serigny, who served with his brother, D'Iberville, in all his naval expeditions; we subsequently find him holding a lieutenant's commission in the navy at Rochefort.

"6th. François Le Moyne de Bienville, *officier de la marine*. The Iroquois surrounded a house in which he and forty others were located, and, setting fire to it, all except one perished in the flames.

"7th. Louis Le Moyne de Chateaugay, *officier de la marine*. He was killed by the English at Fort Bourbon—afterwards called Fort Nelson, by the English, in 1694.

"8th. Gabriel Le Moyne d'Assigny—died of yellow fever* in St. Domingo, where he had been left by his brother, D'Iberville, in 1701.

"9th. Antoine Le Moyne—died young.

"10th. Jean Baptiste Le Moyne de Bienville, 'Knight of the Order of St. Louis,' whose name is still remembered with honor among the people of New Orleans; he was, with his brother, a founder of that city, and *Lieutenant du Roy à la Louisianne*, in the Government of the Colony.

"11th. Antoine Le Moyne de Chateaugay, second of the name, *Capitaine d' une compagnie de la Marine à la Louisianne*. He married Dame Marie Jeanne Emilie des Fredailles.

"Such are the names of eleven sons; ten of whom honorably, and with distinction, served in the government of their country, receiving in the new colonies the honors and rewards of the King, who made no distinction between the born Canadian and the European.

"There were two daughters, sisters of the above; the eldest married Sieur de Noyan, a naval officer, and the second Sieur de la Chassagne.

"In a memorial of M. de Bienville, dated New Orleans, January 25th, 1723, after setting forth his services, he describes himself as Chevalier of the order of St. Louis, and Commander General of the Province of Louisianna; he states in it, that of *eleven* brothers, only four were then surviving: Baron de Longueil, himself, Bienville, Serigny, and Chateaugay, and that they had all received the cross of Knights of St. Louis.

"The patent creating the Seigniory of Longueil into a barony is dated 19th May, 1699. It relates that the late Charles Le Moyne, Seigneur of Longueil, emigrated from France to Canada in 1640, and had highly distinguished himself upon many occasions—that his son, Charles Le Moyne, had borne arms from an early age, and that Jacques Le Moyne de Sante Hélène, was killed by the English at the head of his company when Quebec was attacked, on which occasion, the said Charles Le Moyne, leading on the Canadians, was also wounded. It also names with honor D'Iberville, De Bienville, De Chateaugay, De Maricourt. The patent then states that on account of the services rendered by the family, Louis XIV. had determined to give to the Seigniory of Longueil, as well as to the said Charles Le Moyne himself, a title of honor, in order that an honorable distinction should pass to posterity, and be an object of emulation to his children to follow the example which had been set to them. It therefore creates and erects the Seigniory of Longueil into a barony, to be enjoyed by the said Charles Le Moyne, his

* Singularly enough, another Canadian William L. Le Moyne, Esq., of Quebec, my brother, expired also in St. Domingo, of yellow fever, some 138 years after—viz., in 1837.

children and successors, *et ayans cause*, and that they should enjoy the honors, rank and precedence in the assembly of nobles, as are enjoyed by other barons of the kingdom of France.

"This patent is remarkable therefore for creating a territorial barony—that is, whosoever possesses Longueil, whether male or female, is entitled to the title and distinction of a baron of the kingdom of France. I had some doubts if it was so, but submitted the case to a very eminent lawyer, at Paris, who assures me that there can be no dispute on the subject.

"There was another barony erected in Canada in 1671, in favor of M. Talon, the Intendant of the Province: it was called '† La terre des Islets,' which I believe is at this time owned by some religious community. However, I have pointed out above the title which, under a monarchy, this family has to distinction in Canada.

"The cession of Canada by France to England made no change in the legal right to hold honors, and a title to honors is as much a legal right as a title to an estate.

"No person by the accession was deprived of any legal right. At Malta, the old titles of honor are respected, and the Queen recognizes them in the commissions issued in her name in Malta. Whatever right French noblemen had in Canada under the French government continues at this time: in this instance the honor is greater than most titled European families can boast of.

"It is not, however, as a family matter I regard it. I wish you to remark that it was a Canadian who discovered the Mississippi from the sea, (La Salle having failed in this though he reached the sea sailing down the Mississippi), and also that the first and most celebrated Governor General of Louisianna was a French Canadian."

Here ends M. Falconer's ably written paper. We think we have made out a fair case for an old Norman house, who originally descended from the Count of Salagne, *en Biscaye*, and who enlisted on the side of Charles VII. in 1428. This count married Marguerite de la Tremouille, daughter of the Count des Guines, and Grand *Chambellan de France*, one of the oldest families of the Kingdom. We must now leave to our readers to decide, and we are willing also to accept for the house of Longueil * the motto—

"Sur cette terre encor sauvage
Les vieux titres sont inconnus;
La noblesse est dans le courage,
Dans les talents, dans les vertus."

† Chateau Bigot stands within its limits.—see page 9.

* The Baron de Longueil was succeeded by his son Charles, born 18th October, 1657. He served quite young in the army, when he distinguished himself, and died Governor of Montreal, 17th of January, 1755—he was the father of upwards of fifteen children. The third Baron of Longueil was Charles Jacques Le Moyne, born at the Castle of Longueil, 26th July, 1724—he commanded the troops at the battle of Monongahela, 9th July, 1755. He was also made Chevalier de St. Louis and Governor of Montreal, and died whilst serving under Baron Dieskau, as the Marquis of Vaudrueil states in one of his dispatches, the 8th September, 1755, at 31 years of age, the victim of Indian treachery ont he border of Lake George. His widow was re-married by special license, at

Montreal, on the 11th September, 1770, to the Hon. William Grant, Receiver-General of the Province of Canada—there was no issue from this second marriage, and on the death of the third baron the barony reverted to his only daughter, Marie Charles Josephte Le Moyne de Longueil, who assumed the title of baroness after the death of her mother, who expired on the 25th February, 1782, at the age of 85 years. She was married in Quebec, on the 7th May, 1781, to Captain David Alexander Grant, of the 94th, by the Rev. D. Francis de Monmoulin, chaplain to the forces. Capt. Grant was a nephew of the Honorable William Grant, his son, the Honorable Charles William Grant, was fourth baron and a member of the Legislative Council of Canada, and seigneur of the barony of Longueil. He assumed the title of Baron of Longueil on the death of his mother, which event occurred on the 17th February, 1841. He married Miss N. Coffin, a daughter of Admiral Coffin, and died at his residence, Alwing House, at Kingston, 5th July, 1848, aged 68. His remainswere transferred for burial in his barony. The fifth baron who assumed the title married in 1849, a southern lady, and now resides at Alwing House, at Kingston. The house of Longueil is connected by marriage with the Babys, De Beajeus, Le Moines, De Montenach, Delanaudieres, De Gaspés, Delagorgendieres, and several other old families in Canada.

On some very Peculiar Feudal Institutions.

"LE DROIT DE GRENOUILLAGE."

CHAPTER IX.

[*Ladies are invited to skip over this chapter, which treats of dry, legal technicalities.*]

"Et le dit Sieur, en sa qualité de gentilhomme, a déclaré ne savoir signer."

IN this eminently progressive age of railroads, telegraphs and balloons, when the subjugation of time and space so loudly proclaims the royalty of genius, the sovereignty of mind over matter, few will dare to revert, except for the sake of contrast, to those times which, with so much self-complacency, we style the dark ages; and still this is precisely what we intend to do, less however to show that this condemnatory expression is misapplied—in fact a misnomer,—less to disturb the verdict of posterity and demand a new trial, than in the spirit of the old judge who, during his leisure hours, reads over the notes of evidence on which he based his judgments on former trials. Like over him, an indistinct sense of doubt occasionally creeps over us, which in the secret of our hearts, now and again forces on our attention the following questions:—Have we thoroughly sifted, in all its bearings, the subject on which we have adjudicated? Have those same middle ages brought before our tribunal, had a fair trial? Have we not, perchance, given too much weight to the crown witnesses, and not enough to those summoned for the defence? Has the defendant had an opportunity of bringing into court all the documentary evidence available in such a momentous inquiry? In other words, when we lavish such wholesale abuse on our ancestors, are we sure we fully understand, truly appreciate the hidden motives which actuated their actions? Are we certain some designing men have not for a purpose traduced this eventful period of the world's history, purposely vilified its institutions, knowingly libelled its actors? Fortunately it is not our province to answer satisfactorily and fully these grave inquiries. We will be quite content for the present with merely raising a corner of the veil which stands between us and the past; and, reader, if perchance during the operation, your peering eye should detect the nakedness of some of our forefathers' queer conceits, we beseech you not to judge of them by the standard of to-day, but rather look on, like Shem and Japheth, *i. e.* with charity. Rest assured, little analogy can exist between the present time and the customs and manners of a period, in which it was not considered out of place to lavish stores of the most recondite learning in solving the unimportant problem "how many spirits can stand on the point of a needle without jostling one another?" and in which another subject of deep research then, but which will doubtless now appear of secondary moment to the general welfare of mankind, was "what was the colour of the Virgin Mary's hair?" Some profound thinkers, by elaborate arguments, showed that it must have been red; our taste would have inclined for auburn.

We are led to the present inquiry by the perusal of a cleverly written book, compiled by Louis Veuillot, ex-rédacteur of the *Univers*, a Paris newspaper recently suppressed by the elect of thirty-two millions of free men, either because his people were not sufficiently advanced to have a free press, or that a free press was a *malum per se*. We know of some of his subjects in Canada who, in their writings, deny both these doctrines.

But—says the utilitarian—practically, what have we in Canada to do with Louis Veuillot or his book? Nothing, certainly, more than this: it contains, over and above, a most interesting controversy waged by the champion of the ultramontane party in France and the late Attorney General and present President of the Cour de Cassation, Mr. Dupin, on this occasion the mouth-piece of the French Liberal party—a new confirmation of an opinion frequently set forth here, viz.: *that the Feudal tenure, in its mildest form only, was introduced into Canada*, although France, England and Germany for centuries groaned under its most obnoxious features.

According to Veuillot those feudal barons, whom we depict to ourselves so intent on oppressing and so ready for trivial offences to roast and quarter their unfortunate serfs, were in very many cases the very reverse of cruel; nay, some were humane and considerate to a degree. He tells of some being quiet satisfied with the gift of a pig, a goose, a sheep, for the right to pasture the whole flock on the domain of the landlord; sometimes their eccentric humors betrayed them into strange fancies. He shows us a seigneur in France to whose manor the peasantry drove each year, in a vehicle drawn by four horses, a lark; in another locality, an egg was substituted. We are also told that at Boulogne the Benedictine monks of Saint Proculus exacted from those who had leasehold property under them, the *steam* of a boiled capon; the operation was performed thus: on a fixed day in each year, the tenant drew near the table of the seigneur, bearing the boiled chicken between two dishes, when the upper dish was removed to allow the fumes to escape; this done he would remove the dish and the chicken.* He had acquitted

* We find several instances of tenures equally singular in England:—"A farm at Brookhouse, in Langsett, in the parish of Peniston, and county of York, pays yearly to Godfry Bosville, Esq., a snow ball in midsummer and a red rose at Christmas."

William de Albemarle holds the manor of Loston "by the service of finding for his lord the king, two arrows and a loaf of *oat* bread, when he should hunt in the forest of Dartmore."

Solomon Attefeld held land at Reperland and Atherton, in the county of Kent, upon condition "that as often as our lord the king would cross the sea, the said Solomon and heirs ought to go with him to hold his head on the sea if it was needful."

John Compes had the manor of Finchingfield given him by King Edward III., for the service of turning the spit at his coronation."

Geoffry Frumband held sixty acres of land in Wingfield, in the county of Suffolk, by the service of paying to our lord the king *two white doves* yearly.

John de Roches holds the manor of Winterslew, in Wiltshire, by the service that when the king should abide at Clarendon, he should go into the butlery of the king's palace there, and draw out of what vessel he chooses, as much wine as should be needful for making *a pitcher of claret*, which he should make at the king's expense; and that he should serve the king with a cup, and should have the vessel whence he took the wine, with all the wine then in it, together with the cup whence the king should drink the claret.

The town of Yarmouth is, by charter, bound to send the sheriffs of Norwich *a hundred herrings*, which are to be baked in *twenty-four pies or paties*, and delivered to the lord of the manor of East Carlton, who is to convey them to the king.

At the coronation of James II., the lord of the manor of Heydon, in Essex, claimed to hold the *basin and ewer* to the king by virtue of one moiety, and the *towel* by virtue of the other moiety of the same manner, whenever the king washed before dinner, but the claim was allowed only as to the towel.

Sir Walter Scott gives the following anecdote relative to James V. of Scotland:—"Another adventure, which had nearly cost James his life, is said to have taken place at the village of Cramond, near Edinburgh, where he had rendered his addresses acceptable to a pretty girl of the lower rank. Four or five persons, whether relations or lovers of his mistress is uncertain, beset the disguised monarch, as he returned from his rendezvous. Naturally gallant, and an admirable master of his weapon, the king took post on the high and narrow bridge over the Almond river, and defended himself bravely with his sword. A peasant, who was thrashing in a neighboring barn, came out upon the noise, and whether moved by compassion or by natural gallantry, took the weaker side, and laid about with his flail so effectually, as to disperse the assailants, well thrashed, even according to the letter. He then conducted the king into his barn, where his guest requested a basin and towel, to remove the stains of the broil. This being procured with difficulty, James employed himself in learning what was the summit of his deliverer's earthly wishes, and found that they were bounded by the desire of possessing, in property, the farm of Braehead, upon which he laboured as a bondsman. The lands chanced to belong to the crown, and James directed him to come to the Palace of Holly-Rood, and enquire for the gudeman (*i. e.* farmer) of Ballangeich, a name by which he was known in his excursions, and which answered to *Il Bondocani*

his feudal service. Now we do not wish to speak ill of Benedictine or any other monks, but we do state, without fear of contradiction, even by M. Veuillot, that at that remote period there existed many abbés, whose appetite was not satisfied merely from inhaling the steam of a boiled chicken. Some of these feudal land owners, however, were right good fellows. It is recorded that before the year 1450, the peasantry of Vaulx, in Normandy, residing within five miles of the Abbey of the Holy Trinity of Caën, were annually treated, on the *fête* of the Holy Trinity, to a substantial repast within the walls of the monastery. The *carte de cuisine* stood thus: "They were first to wash their hands (not altogether a superfluous preliminary for laboring men); then all sat down, a cloth was spread before them; to each was served out a small loaf of bread weighing from twenty to twenty-two ounces, a square piece of pork six inches long, after which came a slice of grilled ham (*lard routi sur le greil*), a panikin of bread and milk, and cider and cervoesie *ad libitum* during a four hour's sitting. With such royal cheer and such considerate masters, it is not at all surprising to hear a king of France—Louis X.—in 1315, after publishing edicts to liberate his subjects from the feudal servitude, complain that some of his people, being *ill advised*, preferred to remain as they were to becoming free. A learned writer, Delisle, from these and other instances, concludes that several of the customs which now appear to us as the most obnoxious, were the very ones which in the feudal times were considered the lightest, as their performance was attended with no trouble. And to this class belonged the famous *Droit de Grenouillage*, the subject of Messrs. Dupin and Michelet's irreverent mirth. These writers had perversly furbished up some old worm eaten charters on whose authority they accused the landed aristocracy of the middle ages with being in the habit of compelling their serfs to turn out on the wedding night of the lord of the manor, to beat the frog ponds, in order that his lordship's rest might not be disturbed by the noisy croakings of the frogs; and what was worse in the eyes of Veuillot,

of Haroun Alraschid. He presented himself accordingly, and found with due astonishment that he had saved his monarch's life, and that he was to be gratified with a crown-charter of the lands of Braehead, under the service of presenting an ewer, basin, and towl, for the king to wash his hands, when he shall happen to pass the Bridge of Cramond. In 1822, when George IV. came to Scotland, the descendant of this John Howison of Braehead, who still possesses the estate which was given to his ancestors, appeared at a solemn festival, and offered his Majesty water from a silver ewer." This gave rise to the old song "We'll gae nae mair a roving."

certain jolly friars, such as the Abbé de Luxeuil and the Abbé de Prüm, stood also charged with having required the performance of this sardanapalian service, not of course on their wedding night, (for none but bad Abbés married in those times), but whenever they resided in their domains, as the following lines showed :—

"Pâ! Pâ! rainotte, Pâ! (silence, frogs, silence!)

"Voici monsieur l'abbé que Dieu gâ. (Near you rests monsieur l'abbé, whom may heaven watch over)."

Not only were the peasants compelled to beat the frog ponds, but during the operation, in order to keep themselves awake, they were expected to croak out (in a subdued voice, we should imagine) this cabalistic formula. The performance of the croaking service was confined to those vassals whose land had on that condition been freed from *servitude*. A large portion of the volume before us is taken up in discussing this custom, of which few instances can be found; amongst others, the case of a drowsy German emperor is adduced, who having to sojourn over night in the village of Freinsenn, was threatened with being kept awake by the concerts of frogs; fortunately for his Highness, the peasantry mustered in time and compelled Aristophanes' noisy heroes to knock under, on which the mighty emperor freed his considerate vassals. Although it is said that at one time it was considered a special seigniorial priviledge for a baronial benedict to sleep soundly on his wedding night, nothing exists to show that this is the real cause why Mynheer Deutchman had so highly prized his uninterrupted nap; the probability is that he felt tired after travelling and wanted more than "forty winks."*

* Pity it is, the *Droit de Grenouillage* should be obsolete, especially in such a locality as Lake Beauport, where bull-frogs of fabulous size occasionally make the night hideous and sleepless with their *boomings*. The reader is reminded not to confound these plethoric individuals with the ordinary piping frog, *rana pipiens*, whose shrill squeak ceases about the 21st of June of each year, and who caused the cockney's mistake: "My dear parients," wrote young hopeful to his Bow-bells relatives, the day after his arrival in Canada, "Canada is a strange place: it is swarming with papists. The gentlemen leave, on their residence out of the city, a great deal of fine fir and furniture wood *uncut*. There is one peculiarity which struck me: the birds are not numerous, but some have a singularly loud song, and sing all night. Of this class is the Canadian nightingale, whose shrill note kept me from sleeping all last night. I hope, however, to get accustomed to it in time. I am spending a day or two at a place called Lake Beauport. Your dutiful son."

Speaking of the nightingale reminds me of another unjustifiable joke, a roguish bird fancier played on another cockney gentleman. This bird fancier's son had purchased on the market a common snow bird, for one penny; in transferring it from one cage to the other, he accidentally pulled out its tail; the bird was, however, exposed for sale in his window, and a verdant young Englishman, with more money than brains, was attracted by the comical figure it cut:—"What a very singular bird," he said, "was it born so?" "Why, yes," said the bird seller, "of course it was." "What

Mr. Veuillot thinks that this *Droit de Grenouillage* was not a whit more humiliating than the obligation the ordinary seignior was under to pour out drink for his superior, and his superior did not consider himself degraded for having to hold the shirt of his royal master when dressing. Counts and barons stood protracted law suits to enforce their rights to do homage to those above them, and these struggled as hard to get rid of an homage too expensive for them to keep up. When the Count of Cahors, who was also a bishop, approached his chief city, the Baron of Cessac was wont to precede him to a certain spot, indicated in old titles, where he was bound to meet him. Once arrived there, he would dismount, and having saluted the prelate with his hat off, his right leg bare and wearing a slipper, he would take the bishop's mule by the bridle and thus lead it towards the cathedral, from thence to the episcopal palace, where he would wait on the bishop during dinner time; this performed he would retire, taking with him the bishop's mule and *silver plate.* This ceremony took place as late as 1604, for the Bishop Etienne de Poppian; it resulted in a law suit, which was adjudicated on by the parliament of Toulouse. The complaint preferred by the Baron de Cessac was that the silver plate used on this occasion was not suitable to the *status* of the parties concerned, nor in accordance with the terms of his charter. The court condemned the count to provide the baron with a gilt set of silver plate, or else its legitimate value *à dire d'experts,* due regard being had to the quality of the individuals and to the grandeur of the occasion. The *experts* decided that the value of the plate was 3,123 livres. Etienne de Poppian's successor, Pierre de Habert tried to enter the city in 1627 without notifying the Baron de Cessac; the latter summoned him; the bishop pleaded that he was not

species do you call it, then?" "I never saw the like of it before," replied the bird fancier. "A stranger just told me it was a Jersey nightingale, a very rare bird." "What will you take for it?" "I could not think of parting with it." A few days passed, and the young man returned and begged as a favor to be allowed to purchase it. Finally, the bird fancier accepted seven and sixpence for it, *as a favor.* A month after, there was a *tall* row in the bird store, which nearly ended by a prosecution for assault and battery. This I know to be a fact.

Strange birds may, however, puzzle more learned men than a cokney youth. Every one remembers how a very learned professor of natural history was perplexed one day by the trick a waggish pupil played on him. A bird unclassified in the European, American, or any other fauna, was pompously brought forward and presented to the erudite doctor for examination. His brow got as dark as Erebus, and finally he made the humiliating confession, "*he was non plussed in toto.*" The mischevious pupil then gravely stated that he had only been trying to see "how a woodcock would look with a spruce partridge's head on it," when properly joined together by a good bird stuffer.

liable; that it was optional with the seignior to require the attendnace of his vassal at any ceremony whatever; that the attendance herein alluded to was particularly humbling for the vassal, for which reason he had dispensed him with it. The Baron de Cessac replied that it was a special prerogative of his to be allowed to attend on the count on his entry in his chief town, quoting various old Roman customs and Latin texts in support of his position. The bishop lost his suit in that court and in the Court of Appeals, and by decree (*arrêt*) of the 16th July, 1630, the baron was maintained in his cherished homage toward the count. Mr. Veuillot having shown pretty conclusively that all feudal rights and services were not necessarily oppressive and odious, discusses with his usual eloquence another feudal custom, which, if well authenticated, is undoubtedly one of the gravest charges against the morality of those times. This custom is known to old French writers as the *Droit de Jambage;* the apologist of the middle ages calls it simply *Droit du Seigneur;* he summons to his aid all his erudition, all his ingenuity, to explain off the *arrêts* and passages* invoked by Messrs. Dupin and Michelet, with what degree of success the reader of his book can judge for himself.

The want of space compells us, albeit reluctantly, to adjourn this inquiry into the institutions of times gone by. We may again revert to it hereafter, but before concluding, we must, on the authority of Mr. Veuillot, and we do so with pleasure, deny the correctness of a charge frequently made respecting the penmanship of our ancestors, as embodied in the words prefacing this sketch, and said to be found at the end of several old deeds and charters:—"Le dit Sieur, en sa qualité de gentilhomme, a déclaré ne savoir signer." A careful examination of many thousand deeds and charters enabled him to assert the contrary most positively. Here we are at the end of this communication without having scarcely redeemed our promise "to raise a small corner of the veil of the past," in order to lay before the reader the grounds for philisophical doubts as to the entire correctness of the verdict arrived at by posterity respecting the feudal times.

* The following is one of the chief quotations on which Mr. Dupin rests his theory: "J'ai vu. dit Boërius (décision 297), juger dans la Cour de Bourges, devant le métropolitain, un procès d'appel où le curé de la paroisse prétendait que de vieille date, il avait la *première connaissance charnelle* avec la fiancée; laquelle coutume avait été annullée et *changée en amende*.

Since writing the foregoing, a friend has placed in our hands the pungent and elaborate reply which Mr. Veuillot's book has elicited from a French *savant*, under the heading, "*Refutation du Livre de M. Veuillot sur le Droit du Seigneur.* Par Jules Delpit."

In such a fiery controversy as the one raging between the two writers, and on which we merely look as disinterested outsiders, it would be presumptuous for us to decide who is right. Veuillot, as a pamphlet writer, a publicist, and the organ of what is denominated the clerical party in France, is undoubtedly a great name—a tower of strength to his party. On the other hand, the confident tone, biting irony, and formidable array of erudition, law quations, old charters, arrèts, produced by his adversary, challenge enquiry and investigation. Jules Delpit asserts positively that the *Droit du Seigneur*, in its worst acceptation, existed in several European kingdoms, and quotes *seventy-two* instances. We are quite satisfied, in appreciating this subject, which to us is of no actual moment, to inscribe over both combatants—

"Adhuc sub judice lis et."

The Loss of the "Auguste."

FRENCH REFUGEES.

CHAPTER X.

IT was on the 22nd February, 1762; night's silent shades had long since closed round the grist mill of St. Jean Port Joly, County of L'Islet; the clock had just struck nine, when a tall man, in tattered garments, walked in and begged for a night's rest. Captain D'Haberville, as he was wont to do, when unoccupied, was seated in a corner of the room, his head depressed, evidently a prey to sombre thoughts. It requires considerable resolution to reconcile with poverty he, who was previously cradled in ease and luxury, especially when a numerous family depends on that man; still greater courage is needed to bear up with fate when misfortune cannot be traced to improvidence, expensive habits, prodigality, bad conduct, but is simply the result of uncontrolable events. The man whose folly causes his own downfall, whilst smarting under remorse, if he is reflective, soon discovers the expediency of speedily submitting to circumstances.

Captain D'Haberville felt no remorse; in the solitude of his heart, he would occasionally repeat to himself: "I cannot think I deserved such a heavy blow. O Heaven! grant me strength; give me courage, since it has pleased you to smite me down."

The voice of the stranger had caused the captain a thrilling emotion. Why? he did not know. Pausing a second, he said:

"My friend, you are welcome to stay here over night; you will also have your supper. My miller will provide you with a resting place in the mill."

"Thanks," replied the stranger, "but I am very exhausted; pray, give me a glass of spirits."

D'Haberville, feeling little inclined to divide with the unknown the scanty supply of brandy he kept on the premises, in case of sickness said he had none.

"If you only knew who I am, D'Haberville," listlessly rejoined the stranger, "you would give me the last drop of brandy you have in your house."

The captain felt indignant at being thus familiarly addressed by a mere vagrant; still there was something in the man's accent which convulsed him with emotion, and the indignant rebuke ready to escape, died on his lips.

At this moment Blanche, his daughter, entering the room, with a lighted candle, the whole family were struck with unutterable horror; motionless, there stood in their presence a veritable skeleton, in height a giant, a hideous giant, whose bones seemed ready to burst through the skin. An emaciated countenance; bloodless veins, from whence vampires seemed to have sucked the stream of life; leaden pale eyes, like those of Banquo's ghost, *without speculation,* such was what remained of the Chevalier Lacorne De Saint Luc, one of the richest and most distinguished men in the colony, under French rule. One moment more and Captain D'Haberville flew into his arms.

"What, you here, my dear De St. Luc; why, the sight of my bitterest foe would cause me less horror! Speak, speak, I beseech you. Tell us how our relatives, our dear friends have exchanged the deck of the *Auguste* for the insatiable deep, whilst you, the sole survivor, are now here to announce the harrowing tale."

The unbroken silence of De Saint Luc, his downcast, sorrowful countenance, revealed more than words could utter.

"Accursed, then, be the tyrant,"* roared out D'Haberville, "accursed

* Not the least interesting part of Mr. DeGaspé's work are the notes. "I have," says he, "attempted in this book to portray the misfortunes which the conquest brought on the greater portion of the Canadian *noblesse*, whose descendants, now forgotten, languish on the very soil which was once defended and soaked with the blood of their ancestors. Let those who say they were deficient in ability or energy, remember that their education and habits having been totally military, it was not easy to exchange them for new occupations.

"The old families who remained in Canada after the conquest, used to say that General James Murray, through hatred of the French, had insisted on their immediate expulsion; that he had them put on board of an old condemned vessel, and that before they sailed he was constantly repeating, with an oath, 'It is impossible to distinguish the victors from the vanquished when you see these damned Frenchmen pass, wearing their uniforms and swords.' Such was the tradition in my youth. Happily, these times are far away and forgotten."—[P. A. DeG.]

be the man who, through hatred of the French, has been the means of wilfully consigning to a watery grave so many brave hearts, by compelling them to depart in the most stormy season of the year, in an old, unseaworthy vessel."

"Instead of venting curses on your enemies," said De Saint Luc, in a harsh tone, "thank heaven that General Murray has granted you and yours a reprieve of two years to dispose of your property and return to France."

The chevalier then related all that had happened since the *Auguste* had sailed from Quebec, on the 15th October; how, after a succession of storms, shipwreck on the 15th November—finally consigned to the depths of the ocean, all the passengers and the crew, except six sailors; how the seven survivors had to dig graves for the unfortunate exiles—on the shores of Cape Briton, where the ship was stranded,—in all *one hundred and fourteen corpses;* how, in the depth of winter, half clad and starving, he had travelled some sixteen hundred miles on snow-shoes, after successively tiring out several Indian guides.

The reader will have recognized in this extract a translation from a passage of that charming volume *Les Anciens Canadiens,* recently published by our respected townsman, P. A. DeGaspé, Esq., Seigneur of St. Jean Port Joly: himself not a bad personification of the courteous, well-bred, feudal dignitary of former times. The loss of the ship which was conveying back to France the expatriated Canadians, and the melancholy death of so many distinguished inhabitants, whom Governor Murray, it is said, had compelled to sail in the *Auguste,* naturally created considerable excitement amongst the friends and relatives of the victims, and contributed powerfully to render the English governor odious to the colonists. Amongst the victims were Madame de Meziere,—a grand aunt of Mr. DeGaspé, and daughter of Baron de Longeuil,—who perished with her child. Mr. DeGaspé also furnishes a lively account of the interview of the Chevalier de Lacorne with the governor of the colony, in the Château St. Louis.† How Governor Murray was moved to pity by the

† The compilers of Hawkin's picture of Quebec, the late gifted Andrew Steuart and the late Dr. J. C. Fisher, thus graphically describe the Chateau St. Louis:—"Few circumstances of discussion and enquiry are more interesting than the history and fate of ancient buildings, especially if we direct our attention to the fortunes and vicissitudes of those who were connected with them. The temper, genius and pursuits of an historical era are frequently delineated in the features of remarkable edifices: nor can any one contemplate them without experiencing curiosity concerning those who first formed the plan, and afterwards created and tenanted the structure. These observations apply particularly to the subject of this chapter.

sight De Saint Luc's emaciated form presented. How he gradually softened towards the portion of the *old noblesse* which remained in the country, and eventually became the friend of the chevalier. This interview of De Saint Luc* and Captain D'Haberville is not an imaginary

The history of the ancient Castle of St. Lewis, or Fort of Quebec, for above two centuries the seat of government in the province, affords subjects of great and stirring interest during its several periods. The hall of the old fort, during the weakness of the colony, was often a scene of terror and despair at the inroad of the persevering and ferocious Iroquois; who, having passed or overthrown all the outposts, more than once threatened the fort itself, and massacred some friendly Indians within sight of its walls. There, too, in intervals of peace, were laid those benevolent plans for the religious instruction and conversion of the savages, which at one time distinguished the policy of the ancient governors. At a later era, when, under the protection of the French kings, the province had acquired the rudiments of military strength and power, the Castle of St. Lewis was remarkable as having been the sight whence the French governors exercised an immense sovereignty, extending from the Gulf of St. Lawrence, along the shores of that noble river, its magnificent lakes,—and down the course of the Mississippi, to its outlet at New Orleans. The banner which first streamed from the battlements of Quebec, was displayed from a chain of forts, which protected the settlements throughout this vast extent of country: keeping the English colonies in constant alarm, and securing the fidelity of the Indian nations. During this period, the council chamber of the castle was the scene of many a midnight vigil,—many a long deliberation and deep-laid project,—to free the continent from the intrusion of the ancient rival of France, and assert throughout the supremacy of the Gallic lily. At another era, subsequent to the surrender of Quebec to the British arms, and until the recognition of the independence of the United States, the extent of empire, of the government of which the Castle of Quebec was the principal seat, comprehended the whole American continent, north of Mexico! It is astonishing to reflect for a moment, to how small, and, as to size, comparatively insignificant an island in the Atlantic ocean, this gigantic territory was once subject!

Here also was rendered to the representative of the French king, with all its ancient forms, the fealty and homage of the noblesse, and military retainers, who held possessions in the province under the crown—a feudal ceremony, suited to early times, which imposed a real and substantial obligation on those who performed it, not to be violated without forfeiture and dishonor. The King of Great Britain having succeeded to the rights of the French crown, this ceremony is still (in 1835) maintained. [Fealty and homage is rendered at this day by the seigniors to the governor, as the representative of the sovereign in the following form: His Excellency being in full dress and seated in a state chair, surrounded by his staff, and attended by the attorney general, the seig nior, in an evening dress and wearing a sword, is introduced into his presence by the inspector general of the royal domain and clerk of the land roll, and having delivered up his sword, and kneeling upon one knee before the governor, places his right hand between his, and repeats the ancient oath of fidelity; after which a solemn act is drawn up in a register, kept for that purpose, which is signed by the governor and seignior, and countersigned by the proper officers.]

In England, it is also still performed by the peers at the coronation of our kings, in Westminster Abbey, although the ceremony is much curtailed of its former impressive observances.

The Castle of St. Lewis was in early times rather a strong hold of defence, than an embellished ornament of royalty. Seated on a tremendous precipice,—

On a rock whose haughty brow
Frown'd o'er St. Lawrence foaming tide—

and looking defiance to the utmost boldness of the assailant, nature lent her aid to the security of the position. The cliff on which it stood rises nearly two hundred feet in perpendicular height above the river. The castle thus commanded on every side a most extensive prospect, and until the occupation of the higher ground to the south-west, afterwards called Cape Diamond, must have been the principal object among the buildings of the city.

* We follow in history and in old memoirs the subsequent career of the Chevalier de

occurrence: it retraces what really did take place between Mr. De Gaspé's grandfather, Ignace Aubert DeGaspé, at one time a captain in the French navy, and the chevalier, as related to Mr. DeGaspé, some fifty years ago, by his aunt, Madame Bailly de Messein, who was about fifteen years of age when this occurred.

We are thus brought face to face with those fierce spirits of the *ancien régime*, who, like the Sewells, Smiths, Robinsons, and other United Empire Loyalists, later on, had preferred renouncing fortune, position, and friends, to accepting a foreign yoke. It would be curious to follow up the destinies of the Canadian exiles: some returned to the mother country to rot in the Bastile; others, such as the DeLerys, culled laurels and titles in the wars of the Republic and of the first Empire.* Possibly some of their grandchildren, now counts or barons under the new *regime*, may enjoy the distinguished honor of an entrée to the *cercle imperial*, together with the privilege of dancing "*La Salammbo*," under the approving eye and bewitching smile of the *Grandes Dames de la Cour*.

We are not, however, prepared to assert whether the departure of those proud aristocrats, tainted by the impure exhalations of the French court of the day, and to whom Magna Charta and the institutions of a free people were unknown—we are not, we repeat, ready to say whether their voluntary exile was not a blessing instead of a loss to the country. For the sake of the family honor, we hope and trust our ancestors were all they are cracked up.

Let us thank that old hand which has seen seventy-eight summers and which, its owner says, "must soon be colder even than Canada's winters," for having assisted in thus raising the veil on times little known, and graphically delineated the doings and sayings of the

---

Lacorne, and find him serving under General Burgogne. There is a spirited letter still extant of the Chevalier to the General, in which he tells him hard truths.

* He formed part of the distinguished Canadians who, on the 8th June, 1775, offered their services to Mayor Preston, at Montreal, to retake and hold Fort St. John from the Americans, and effectually did so on the 10th June, placing it into the hands of a detachment of the 7th Reg. or Royal Fusileers, under Capt. Kineer. They were the Chevalier de Belestre, De Longueil, De Lotbinière, De Rouville, De Boucherville, De Lacorne, De Labruère, De St. Ours, Perthuis, Hervieux, Gamelin, De Montigny, D'Eschambault and others. For this service General Carleton publicly thanked them. In September of the same year, this party, with the assistance of a number of Quebec and Three Rivers volunteers, viz: Messrs. De Montesson, Duchesnay, De Rigouville, De Salaberry, De Tonancour, Beaubien, Demusseau, Moquin, Lamraque, Faucher and others, started for St. Johns, near Montreal, to relieve the 7th and 26th regiments, then in charge of the fort, and who expected a siege, but after being beleaguered, the fort surrendered on 2nd November to General Montgomery. The Canadians and the two regiments were carried away prisoners of war—Congress refusing to exchange the Canadians, "*they being too much attached to the English government and too influential in*

Murrays,* the Carletons, the Haldimands, as well as those of the De Lanaudières, the Lacornes, the Babys, the Longueils, the Dunieres, &c.; may it be spared some time longer, and furnish us with more of those life-like sketches of "*Ancient Canadians.*"

---

their own country." Two, Messrs. Demontesson and De Rigouville, died prisoners of war; De Lacorne, Perthuis and Beaubien had been killed during the siege; De Lotbinière had an arm shot off; De Salaberry was twice wounded.

*Is there not some inaccuracy in the opinion conveyed of the conduct and character of General Murray? It is possible that, like many others, the general may, on his arrival in Canada, have been misled in judging of the French Canadians; but the state papers he addressed to the imperial authorities show what a favorable opinion he then entertained of the fidelity and honor of the Canadian *noblesse.*

These national antipathies, which fortunately are fast disappearing, formerly manifested themselves, sometimes very ludicrously. In the stormy days of the ninety-two resolutions, when the eloquent leader of the Commons of Canada, Louis Joseph Papineau, was nightly carried home in triumph to his hotel on the shoulders of an enthusiastic crowd, there were also in parliament Marchildons and L—wills, men of original views, but better acquainted with the plough or the anvil than with the amenities of social intercourse, and ever ready to fancy themselves slighted. It is related that an M.P.P. named Beaudoin, having received a card to a château ball, made it his business to attend; the evening was sultry, and ice-cream in corresponding demand. The rustic legislator, whose palate had never come in contact with the frigid delicacy, soon came to the conclusion that what every one asked for must be very desirable. "Waiter," said he, "*emportez moi, comment appelez-vous ca, ice-creme?*" "Yes sir," replied lacquey; and instanter, the Canadian Solon was provided with an ample plate of ice-cream, from which he transferred to his unsuspecting palate a large spoonful. But, O horror! his teeth immediately chattered from cold, as if he had a fit of ague—boiling over with patriotic rage, he roared to the frightened waiter, "Pendard! si c'eut été pour un Anglais, tu l'aurais fait chauffer!" "You abominable rascal! had you intended this for an Englishman, you would have taken the chill off!" The company, from His Excellency downwards, were convulsed with laughter.

Marie Josephte Corribeau,---A Canadian Lafarge.

CHAPTER XI.

THAT we have had in Canada very great rascals, some of imported stock, others of home growth, few who will take the trouble to scan this department of our history will be disposed to deny. Colonial crime has not yet, however, stalked forth in those fantastical forms, nor has it attained that luxurance of developement, which it occasionally assumes in the old world. Several types are still unrepresented. The religious scoundrel, notwithstanding several fair attempts, has never yet been becomingly typified in Canada, nor has the philosophical executioner: whereas, old England, in one of her knights, in the sanctimonious, sleek, white gloved Sir Dean Paul, presents to our gaze the life portrait of a full fledged villain, one whose pious donations were exceeded by his frauds only, and civilized France, in her world renowned Robespierre,* discoursing with the eloquence of Plato on the immortality of the soul, during those short intervals not taken up in signing death warrants, furnishes a finished picture of a monster of whose very existence we would fain doubt. The colonial historian, whose duty hereafter it may be to inscribe conspicuously on the role of infamy the names of such characters, must be content to do like those sensible Grand Trunk shareholders, who still expect eleven per cent. dividends: *he must wait until they come.* I hope he may have to wait as long.

Murders, more or less cold-blooded; robberies of every hue, our assize testify to. Bubbles, like the "South Sea Bubble" of yore, entailing ruin on myriads of victims, we also have had. An occasional case of poisoning amongst the peasantry, has now and again startled provincial ears, but a Brinvilliers we never yet had, such at least as history depicts the guilty friend of Sainte Croix. This fiend incarnate was beheaded

* Any one turning up Alison's History of Europe, will read with astonishment some of Robespierre's discourses; you notice the most lofty, the most enabling sentiments uttered by a man whose instincts were those of the hyena.

after poisoning her two brothers, her father and her sister; her husband escaped by good luck more than good management. Madame DeSevigné quaintly tells us how: "Comme elle voulait épouser Sainte Croix, elle empoisonnait fort souvent son mari; mais Sainte Croix qui ne voulait, point d'une femme aussi méchante qu'elle, donnait du contre-poison à ce pauvre mari, de sorte qu'ayant été ballotté cinq ou six fois de cette sorte, tantot empoisonné, tantot désempoisonné, il est demeuré en vie." Sainte Croix managed to save the life of the marquis each time in order himself to escape marriage with such a monster as the marchionness was.

I intend now to rescue from the oblivion of the past, a hideous figure, a being whose supposed fate stamped on the early times of British rule in Canada, a brand of ferocity which they scarcely deserve. An authentic document, discovered within a few years, throws a very desirable light on a question much debated at one time,—I allude to the mode of execution adopted by one of General Murray's court-martials in 1763, with respect to Marie Josephte Corriveau. These court-martials were quite odious enough to the people without it being necessary to impute to them acts of which they were not guilty.

There are few in Quebec who do not recollect having heard of, or seen, in 1850, when it was exhibited in this city, a rusty iron cage, very antique in appearance It somewhat resembled in shape a human form, having hollow iron arms, extended at right angles with the body, with legs attached to it, and a sperical iron structure, to receive the head. This cage came in the possession of the man who exhibited it after having been clandestinely abstracted from the Pointe Levy grave yard. The exhibitor realised a handsome amount, previous to disposing of his relic to the prince of modern humbugs, in whose museum the "Point Levy relic," as it was styled, remained on view for a long time, where, next to the woolly horse, the Aztecs, and other modern wonders, it attracted considerable attention. Nothing was visible in the rusty old coop but a piece of blanched bone. A mysterious tale of crime, however, invested this frail remnant of mortality, with vivid interest. Tradition has supplied several accessories to a fact, which recent historical researches have placed beyond the region of doubt. Until lately this cage was supposed to have been the instrument of torture and last abode before death, of a Canadian Lafarge, who had murdered her two husbands in an extraordinary way; in one instance adopting a process calculated to leave behind, no traces of violence.

Shortly after the cession of Canada to England, namely, in 1763—an awful murder occured in the parish of St. Vallier, district of Montmagny; although a hundred years have rolled by, the memory of the deed, disfigured by local and fantastical legends, is still vividly impressed on the minds of the peasantry.

In November, 1749, Marie Josephte Corriveau, (an ominous name by the by) was wedded to a farmer of St. Vallier. Eleven years after, on the 27th April, 1760, the man died. A vague rumor gradually became current that this woman had murdered her husband by pouring molten lead in his ear, when he was asleep. No action, however, seems to have been taken by the authorities, and three months after the death of her first husband, on the 20th July, 1760, she married Louis Dodier, another farmer of St. Vallier. It is said that after living with her second husband three years, Marie Josephte Corriveau seized on the opportunity, when he was sound asleep, to slip a noose round his neck; she then quietly passed the end of the rope through a pine knot-hole in the framework of her rude dwelling, and leisurely retiring outside, tried her best to produce strangulation on her liege lord. The agonizing man struggled hard, calling loudly for help, when the inhuman monster, having made fast the end of the rope outside the house, rushed in to feast her eyes on the inanimate form of the man whom, shortly before, she had sworn "to love, respect and obey," but instead of confronting a hideous corpse, with protruding eyes and stiffened limbs, her astonished gaze rested on the figure of a man quietly seated on a chair, close to her bed. It was her husband, who, having caught a glimpse of the rope under his bed, had suspected treachery: he had therefore feigned sleep, and even allowed the heartless wife to place the halter round his neck; when waiting, until she had passed one end of it through a flaw in the house gable, and retired outside, he inserted his pillow where his neck had been, gently shaking it occasionally, and uttering now and then a stifled groan. Madame Corriveau must have been wonderfully clever to have succeeded in obtaining forgiveness from her husband, after such henious conduct, or else the intended victim must have been next thing to an idiot to spare her; she, however, soon decided in ridding herself of a man whose revelations might bring her to the gallows, and shortly after, took occasion of his being in a sound sleep to batter in his brains with a pitch-fork; after which feat, she dragged the body to the stable, placed it behind a horse, to induce the belief that her husband had died from the effects of a kick from the animal. The treacherous wife was charged with the murder, jointly with her father and with a woman named Sylvain. The law was in those days administered by military tribunals—court-martials. It was established at the trial that the horse was a quiet animal, and proved that the wounds could never have been inflicted by a horse's kick: *she was convicted.* One fact yet remains unexplained, and that is, the extraordinary influence which the murdress exercised on her father, Joseph Corriveau, and which was such as to induce him to allow himself to be tried for a crime of which it does not appear he was guilty. The facts of the case are summarily related in a document recently discovered at Murray Bay, amongst the papers of the Nairn family. This document, no doubt, found its way at Murray Bay through some of the officers who sat on the court-martial, and who belonged to* Fraser's Highlanders, who settled in numbers at Murray Bay, in 1782, and were the immediate progenitors of genuine Jean Baptistes—such as the Warrens, the McLeans, the Harveys, the Blackburns, and several other families, who of their Scotch ancestry have retained nothing save the name. They are all Roman Catholics, and speak nothing but French The document in question runs thus:—

QUEBEC, 10*th April*, 1763.

[GENERAL ORDER.]

"The court-martial, whereof Lieutenant-Colonel Morris was president, having tried Joseph Corriveau and Marie Josephete Corriveau, Canadians, for the murder of Louis Dodier, as also Isabelle Sylvain, a Canadian, for perjury on the same trial, the governor doth ratify and confirm the following sentence:—That Joseph Corriveau having been found guilty of the charge brought against him, he is therefore adjudged to be hung for the same.

"The court is likewise of opinion that Marie Josephte Corriveau, his daughter, and widow of the late Dodier, is guilty of knowing the said

* Major John Nairn and Capt. Fraser of this corps were the ancestors of the late John Nairn, Esq., seigneur of Murray Bay, and of the late Hon. Malcolm Fraser, also seigneur of another portion of Murray Bay. They stood in high favor with General James Murray, who presented each with a seigneury.

murder, and doth therefore adjudge her to receive sixty lashes, with a cat-o'-nine tails on her bare back, at three different places, viz.: under the gallows, upon the market-place at Quebec, and in the parish of St. Vallier, twenty lashes at each place, and to be branded in the left hand with the letter M.

"The court doth also adjudge Isabelle Sylvain to receive sixty lashes with a cat-o'-nine tails on her bare back, in the same manner and at the same time and place as Marie Josephte Corriveau, and to be branded in the left hand with the letter P.

"The Court-martial, whereof Lieutenant-Colonel was president, is dissolved."

"The general court-martial having tried Marie Josephte Corriveau, for the murder of her husband, Dodier, the court finding her guilty, the Governor (Murray) doth ratify and confirm the following sentence:—That Marie Josephte Corriveau do suffer death for the same, and her body be hung in chains wherever the governor shall think fit.

(Signed,) "THOMAS MILLS,
"Town Major."

Until the discovery of the proceedings of the court-martial which tried the Corriveaus, popular superstition, ever prone to distort and magnify distant and mysterious events, had awarded to Marie Josephte Corriveau's crimes a punishment of which a parallel exists in that inflicted by Louis XI. on a cardinal and bishop named Baluc, who having been detected in a treasonable intrigue, was confined for many years in an iron cage, which, till lately, was shown in the castle of Loches, France.—(See Hallam's Middle Ages, page 516—the note.)—and fully as horrible as the Massachusetts law courts had inflicted on Margaret Jones,* and on Mrs. Ann Hibbens, the lady of a respectable Boston citizen who were both put to death as witches, the first in 1645, the second in 1656.

* Hutchinson's History of Massachusetts Bay.

It is bad enough to have to admit that the red hand of slavery* has branded the early times of Canada with its plague spot, without having to acknowledge that the tribunals of the country inflicted on a miserable woman, however guilty, a punishment which would place her judges mostly on a level with Iroquois savages. And it was generally thought until recently that Marie Josephte Corriveau, instead of being hanged, as it appears she was, on the "*buttes à Nepveu*" near Abraham's hill, had been starved to death in an iron cage, fastened to a gibbet erected close by the Temperance Monument at St. Joseph, Point Levy, where four roads intersect one another; that in this iron cage the victim was thrust, and that from the narrowness of this receptacle, she had to stand erect in it; that this instrument of torture hung by chains to the gallows; that the groans of the famishing prisoner were heart-rending, but that each successive day, they became less audible, until nothing was heard but the creaking of the chains to the night wind. There is enough of the horrible about her fate, without admitting, contrary to the text of the sentence rendered by the court-martial, that this fiendish woman was placed in an iron cage to starve to death; and still, if her execution and the hanging up after death of the body were merely intended to strike terror, why place it inside an iron cage, *well rivitted together?* † Certain it appears that the iron cage hung for several months high in the air close to the spot where the Temperance Monument now stands. Whether it once contained a living being, or merely a lifeless corpse, none perhaps will ever ascertain. The awful noises caused by the creaking of the cage gave rise amongst the uneducated peasantry to innumerable tales and ghost stories; at last, the terror became so universal that some intrepid young men, after consulting, doubtless, with the *curé* of the parish, as to where the loathsome object should be stowed away, determined to rid the place of the nuisance. One dark winter night, the posts were cut down, and next morning no vestige of *La Corriveau* could be seen; nor any vestige of her was seen until eighty-seven years after, when the grave-digger of the parish, in making a grave, struck on the rusty cage containing a thigh bone only, and

* The Quebec Gazette of 1764 contains an advertisement offering, on behalf of Mrs. Perault, an old resident, a slave for sale. There are also extant several royal declarations regulating the condition of slaves in the colony, bearing date respectively the years 1721, 1742 and 1745.—(See Sir H. Lafontaine's notes.)

† It was the custom for a long time in England to allow great criminals to hang in chains, *after death*, in public roads and public places.

which, after puzzling the brains of all the antiquarians of Quebec, was at last identified. The presence of the corpse of a "gallows bird" in consecrated ground was explained by the fact that in 1830, after the burning of the church, the cemetery had been enlarged by taking in an extensive piece of adjoining land. It is this popular tradition which our old friend, M. DeGaspé, has introduced with happy effect in his late work "Les Anciens Canadiens."

An Episode of the War of the Conquest.

CHAPTER XII.

"We burned and destroyed upwards of fourteen hundred fine farm houses."—*Journal quoted by Smith.*

"A priest with about four score of his parishioners have fortified themselves in a house, a few miles to the eastward of our camp, on the north side of the river, where they indiscreetly pretend to brave our troops....The priest who fortified himself on the north side of the river, sent a written invitation to an officer who commanded in a house in his neighborhood 'to honor him with his company to dinner, with an assurance that he, and any officer of his detachment who would be kind enough to accompany him, should return with the greatest safety;' he added, 'that as the English officer fought for his king and for glory, he hoped he himself would be excused for fighting for his poor parishioners and defending his country.' * * *

"The unfortunate priest is defeated; a detachment of light troops laid an ambuscade in the skirts of the wood near his fortified house, and as soon as the field-piece was brought up and began to play, he with his men sallied out, when, falling into the ambush, thirty of them with their leader were surrounded, *killed* and *scalped:* the reason of their being treated with such cruelty, proceeded from the wretched parishioners having disguised themselves like Indians. In this rencontre we had five men wounded. * * * *

"The parish of Richet, with the stately house lately occupied by the indiscreet priest, called Château Richer, are now in flames."—*Knox's Journal, Vol. II.*

THE heading of this paper indicate sufficiently that war, horrid war, will be my theme Close on two thousand years ago, a literary Roman branded the *ultima ratio regum* with the appropriate epithet "Bella, horrida, bella." The monster which heaven in its stern justice lets occasionally loose to chastise the earth, has not abated one jot of its ancient ferocity. Thirty-two millions of members of the human family, between whose country and ours an imaginary boundary exists, are within hail of our doors to attest that truth. See the charred walls of their once happy homes on devastated plantations—see the blanched bones of fathers, sons, brothers, and lovers, uncoffined and unshrouded promiscuonsly strewing the green sward in the Sunny South; whose balmy zephirs, full of the wail of anguish and death, laden with the miasma of putrifying corpses, are wafted towards our fertile fields: this, is war.

Did the grim phantom never stalk through our own land? How deep have we to dig before getting to the mouldering bones of those whom he formerly smote in our midst? Barely three generations: this, takes us down to the conquest.

Canada, like England, was conquered ; in one case an Anglo-Saxon kingdom was overrun by Norman invaders: in the other a Norman colony was wrested by the descendants of Anglo-Saxons from its French masters—both invasions left behind them a " Memory of sorrow." In both countries the conquest was a boon, the means of extending public liberty. In the first, the Saxon and Norman blended and formed a composite nationality, stranger that each of its separate elements would have constituted it: in the other, like causes may produce like results. I said that we too, Canadians, had our "Memory of sorrow." Let us hear a conscientious historian and an elegant writer :—" Are you," asks the learned Abbé Ferland, " desirous of studying antiquities, traditions and old Canadian customs? Go then and examine the ruins of Château Richer and the remains of the house of the Sieur Carré*: you will notice in the Church of Ste. Anne, the offerings of the Marquis of Tracy, of the Chevallier d'Iberville† ex votos suspended to the walls shortly after the

---

* Carré was that fighting *habitant*, who, at the head of a company of young Canadians, rushed up to Quebec, in 1690, to repel invasion. After the departure of Phips, the French commander was so pleased with Carré's bravery, that he made him a present of two small cannons used in the seige.

† We find an interesting editorial notice of a visit to the Ste. Anne's Church, in the Quebec *Mercury*, of 23rd July, 1863:—

"Steaming down the channel north of Orleans, the first object of interest that strikes the eye of the tourist after the beautiful and varied scenery of the parishes of L'Ange-Gardien and Chateau-Richer, presenting every diversity of hill and dale, wild, rocky promontory, and advancing and receding mountain and forest views, is the pretty little church of Ste. Anne, nestling under the brow of a steep hill, with its tall spire glistening in the rays of the morning sun. Standing on a gentle undulation sweeping up from the river, the church of Ste. Anne, or *La Bonne Ste. Anne*, as it is more frequently called, forms one of the most attractive features in the landscape. Hither annually repair the blind, the lame, the halt, the rheumatic, and those afflicted with every species of bodily ailment, who come to invoke the interposition of the saint to make them whole. Crowds of persons thus afflicted, with their friends or relatives, are then to be seen on the roads with the above object, to pray, or return thanks. That cures, either partial or whole, have been effected by these annual devout pilgrimages, there can be little doubt, as several have been attested by eye witnesses. A number of crutches left behind by persons cured, were formerly hung up in the church, but within late years they have been removed to the sacristy. On entering, the eye is struck with the neatness of the interior and the beauty of the decorations.

"The walls are adorned with strange paintings, of a primitive nature, with singular explanations which we could with difficulty understand.

"One is a wreck scene, with Ste. Anne represented as descending from heaven to the aid of a fleet during a storm, with the following curious inscription, which we copied *verbatim et literatim*:—

EX. VOTO. LE. NAVJRE. LE. ST. FRANCOIS. DE. CANADA. DEMATTE. DETROYS. LES. MATS. LE. 29BRE. 1732: COMMANDE. PAR. PIERRE. D'ASTARGIR. ARME. PAR. M. LAMDRILLE. LE. JEVNE.

"Another painting on the wall immediately opposite represents the landing of emigrants sometime before the year 1717; another not far distant a squadron of three war vessels, bearing a tri-colored flag of red, white and green. Out of this last one, we could extract no meaning, further than supposing it represented some notable instance of the saint's providential intervention.

middle of the 17th century; you will meet with families there who still own the lands conceded to their ancestors about the year 1640; in the *habitant* of the *Côte de Beaupré*, you will recognise the Norman peasant of the reign of Louis XIV., with his chronicles, his songs, his superstitions, his customs.

"But since I now have you on this soil of this *Côte de Beaupré*, I shall lay before you an episode of the war of 1759, of which the locality we now occupy was the theatre. This narrative will serve to disprove the English chronicler (Knox)—whose name heads this communication. A priest massacred by the English,—a convent of nuns burned by them, this is the only true portion of the English writer's record.

"Twenty years ago, at the foot of the cape on which the Château Richer Church is built, the blackened and crumbling walls of this convent could yet be seen: there they stood, a silent but eloquent monument of the horrors of a war in which buildings sacred to religion and to science, were ruthlessly destroyed by the hands of a civilised nation. Rebuilt through the exertions of the Rev. Mr. Baillargeon, when he had the spiritual charge of the Château Richer parish, this edifice was in part restored to its original destination: it is now the parish school.

"'T was on the evening of the 23rd June, 1759, a number of women and some old men were standing in groups in front of the church of Château Richer; close by a bonfire, in honor of the patron saint of Canada, St. Jean Baptiste, was slowly flickering out. Gaiety was the order of the day; several children, with live coals in their hands which they agitated high in the air, were trying to imitate an Indian

---

"The environs are also very pleasing; the neat white houses or cottages, ever and anon peering out from a dense covert of evergreens, maple or birch. Many places of no little interest to tourists and others also abound in the neighborhood, such as the Falls of Ste. Anne, the St. Fereol Fall, and the Seven Falls. From the top of the hill overhanging the village, the view is extensive, taking in the whole northern shore of the island, with Grosse Isle looming up in the distance.

"Yesterday morning being set apart by the Church for the annual celebration of the Festival, over three hundred passengers, bound to the shrine, left by the 'Voyageur.' A large number also went down overland, and arrived a considerable time before the steamer hove in sight. About half-past nine o'clock, all having disembarked, a solemn high mass was sung, and a relic of Ste. Anne, encased in a crystal globe, was exposed to the gaze of the devout during the ceremony. The interior of the church was densely crowded, and many were forced to remain outside during the service. The scene was very solemn and impressive, and the devotion of many of those who had congregated from all quarters, in the hope to being relieved of their bodily ills, was edifying in the extreme. The ceremony concluded towards noon, and the time between that and the hour fixed for the departure of the boat was employed by some in devotion, and by others in visiting the spots of interest in the vicinity."

war dance, such as they had seen performed by a band of Ottawas which had visited the place a few days previously, at the invitation of the governor of Canada, the great Onontio, as they called him. It was evident the elder folks entered little in the innocent fun and frolic which occupied the mind of the juveniles; surrounding the curé of the parish, the Rev. J. F. Duburon, who at this moment was standing on the point of the cape on which the parochial church is erected, some old people appeared in earnest conversation; the respected pastor had rested his telescope on the twig of one of the stunted cedar trees which grow in the crevices of the cape, and was scanning the horizon in the direction of the Traverse, just then lighted up by the last rays of the setting sun, whilst his parishoners were surveying the majestic expanse of water before them, the green beaches dotted over with kine, and the uplands clothed in verdure, showing fair promise of a luxuriant harvest. 'Watch well, my friends, along the north shore capes, if you do not see small white objects! They seem to be like sails. Oh, if it only were the relief for the colony, from France? what a rich joke we would play upon the English! Look now at the effect of the sun on the white sails!' At that moment a vessel, crossing from Cape Tourmente in the direction of the channel, which was then used between Pointe d'Argentenay and Madame Island, could be distinctly made out. 'Count them!' hurriedly exclaimed the reverend gentleman; 'one —two—three!'

"But the sun has gone down; the shade of the lofty capes reaches as low as the *traverse,* shutting out all objets from view.

"'My poor country!' exclaims the priest, closing the spy-glass; 'my poor country; what is to become of you, if these are English ships? What with Sir William Johnson, and the New England militia towards Lake Champlain, you stand a poor chance, now that an enemy shows himself in the very heart of Canada.'

"'Cheer up! reverend sir,' retorted the village notary; 'we have at Quebec, Montcalm and a fine army to defend us; and have we not also there one of our own people, a Canadian, the Marquis of Vaudreuil?'

"'My dear notary, let us place our hope in God; we have but little help to expect from men,' gloomily rejoined the minister of religion.

"'What?' said the warlike N. P.; 'do you forget how often French soldiers and Canadian militia have repulsed the New Englanders?'

"'I do not, I assure you, good friend; but, then we were united, and had no traitors amongst us;—to-day, dissentions and jealousy exists between the French regulars and the Canadian militia. We can trust our leaders; but, my dear notary, rest assured that those who have plundered our treasury will find means to effectually conceal their rascality. If there is not treachery, there will certainly be lukewarmness displayed, in the defence of the country. I *warn* you of the fact.'

"At that moment the arrival of a messenger from Quebec interrupted the conversation.

"'Here is a letter for you, reverend sir. I am also the bearer of two other letters for the priests of the neighboring parishes.'

"'Thank you, my friend,' replied M. Duburon—adding, 'Have you seen your brother since he has joined the regiment in Quebec?'

"'Oh yes, sir, and I can tell you that he is not afraid to meet an Englishman, even should he resemble Old Nick himself. The boys are in good spirits there, and they say that if they meet any more of the kilties, such as they met at Carillon, they will lead them a dance. My brother, pointing towards the earthworks near the Falls of Montmorency, said: Look there; if the English presume to attack us, with these works to protect us, we will give them the d—l to eat.'

"The *curé* having glanced over the letter, read out aloud the contents, thus:

"'Sir,—The English fleet is coming up the St. Lawrence. Agreeable to the plan decided on by the governor general, you and your parishioners will take to the woods, with whatever you can carry away of the church property. You will use your influence over your people to make them remain in their hiding-places so long as the English are in the vicinity of Quebec. May the Almighty soon deliver us from such unpleasant neighbors, &c.

"'†H. M., Bishop of Quebec.'

"'Just as I thought,' added M. Duburon; 'it is the English fleet we have just seen lower down than the Traverse. With a fair wind, to-morrow they will be in front of the city. To-morrow, we shall start for the woods; you,' addressing the village notary, 'please notify the inhabitants of this fact, whilst I dispatch these letters to the priests of Ste. Anne and St. Joachim.'

"The Reverend Mr. Duburon, my readers will remark, does not seem to be of such a warlike disposition as the historian Knox makes him out. Neither does the notary, Monsieur Crespin, appear to have been a more fighting character than his pastor. He held from his seigneur a kind of judicial office, and lived in state at the seigniorial manor, which was called the château.

"Monsieur Crespin was a man of peace: his motto was, *Cedat armis toga:* and having made a bundle of his 'minutes,' he placed his *greffe* under his arm, and, followed by Madame Crespin and Monsieur Crespin, junior, his son and lawful heir, he sorrowfully directed his steps towards the forest.

"During a short period, a great uproar existed in all the parishes of the *Côte de Beaupré*. Each parish had a place of concealment for its inhabitants at the foot of the mountain. It was a general stampede from the Falls of Montmorency as low down as Cape Tourmente. The valuables too heavy for removal to the woods, were deposited on the skirts of the woods; the farm cattle were driven back to out-of-the-way grazing-grounds; women, children, and old men, after bidding a sorrowful adieu to the homes of their youth, hurried to the interior with what they valued most. Some old men who were removed in their beds, were taken back in the fall in their coffins.

"Several births took place in the woods, and baptism administered. A few years back a venerable old man died at Ste. Anne, who was born on the banks of *Rivière aux Chiens*, under the shade of a walnut tree (*un noyer*), which he used to call his godfather; in commemoration of the fact, the word 'Noyer' was added to his family name, and his descendants bear it to this day.

"Two months had run over, Wolfe's army was kept in check by Montcalm, and could not advance on Quebec. Rendered impatient by this vigorous defence, which threatened to render abortive their expensive expedition, the English vented their spleen in the rural district by pillaging and burning the houses. It was easy to follow the march of the invaders in the lower parts of the district* of Quebec, by the blaze of the conflagrations they had lit up. Generally, the lives of prisoners were spared—they were even allowed to choose

* The dwellings at Rivière Ouelle, Ste. Anne, St. Roch, and St. Jean Port Joly, were burnt and pillaged,—even to the banal mill of Three Salmons, the only means for the inhabitants of grinding their corn for a distance of thirty miles, was consigned to the flames.

between the alternative to perish of cold or of hunger during the coming winter. Until then, the *Côte de Beaupré* had escaped the common fate; the scouts sent from the mountain were gratified to find their houses still uninjured. At last their turn came. The companies of the Louisbourg Grenadiers, under Captain Montgomery, were instructed to take possession of all the cattle, and to burn all the houses from Cape Tourmente until Ange Gardien.

"These troops followed the shore until they had got opposite the *Grande Ferme* at St. Joachim, where they landed and began their awful work. The Quebec Seminary owned at this spot a magnificent farm: close to it was the *presbytère* and church of St. Joachim. Philippe Réné de Portneuf, the priest of the parish of St. Joachim, was a member of the ancient family of Béeancour. Several of his ancestors, and three of his brothers, had served with distinction in the army; and he himself was not the man to fly from his parish at the sight of the English. Some forty of his parishioners, all handy with the gun, seeing the Scotch soldiers busy burning the church and *presbytère* of St. Joachim, and being led to believe that their own homes would soon share the same fate, determined to defend their property. Well armed, they ensconced themselves on the declevity of a thickly-wooded hill, which commanded the road the enemy had to follow. The brave *curé* considered it his duty to stand by them in this emergency; he therefore remained to encourage them by his counsel, and administer spiritual rites. The Canadians fought well, but a superior force threatening to surround them, they retired, leaving behind seven or eight of their comrades killed or wounded. The Highlanders had dearly bought their advantage, having lost several men by the bullets of the Canadian *chasseurs*. Many years after, Mr. Fraser, who had been present at this engagement, asked an old man named Gagnon, if he had not grieved for the death of a brother of his who had then fallen? 'No;' was his stern reply, 'for I avenged his death on the spot: I fired eight shots, and each time took down one of your men.' Though seriously wounded, Mr. de Portneuf followed his parishioners in their flight. But, weakened by loss of blood, he fell on a stone, which is yet pointed out, near the mill: the enemy soon came up, and hacked him to pieces with their sabres. This melancholy event took place on the 23rd of August. A few days after, the priest of the next parish, the Reverend Mr. Parent, his friend, gave Christian burial to Mr. de Portneuf's remain, and to those of seven of his flock. His body lies inside of the church, but outside of the railings and close to the seigniorial pew.

"The work of destruction having been completed at St. Joachim, the English detachment, with a similar errand on hand, marched upwards, towards the Montmorency, on whose banks the bulk of the forces were camped. After crossing the river Ste. Anne, the scouts noticed a group of men at the spot where the cross road begins, which leads through the woods to the back concession of St. Féréol. Some soldiers were sent in this direction, but fearing an ambush, they returned without striking a blow. It was merely a small band of *chasseurs* of Saint Féréol armed with fowling pieces, but impelled merely by curiosity to see what those English looked like whom they were told were the enemies of God and of France. The sight of his satanic majesty would not have been a greater curiosity for these simple-minded peasants than that of Englishman was in their exalted imaginations in these stormy days. During the few days of march of the Scotch companies, the *habitants* of Ste. Anne and Château Richer could, from their lofty hiding places, witness the conflagration which consumed their houses and farm buildings. At Ste. Anne's, the church and four houses only escaped the torch, and even then, if we credit a local tradition, the church, which was fired three times, only escaped through the especial protection of Sainte Anne! In the whole extent of Château Richer, a bakery alone was spared.

"When the British arrived at the village of this parish, they took their lodgings partly in the convent and partly in the houses situate near to the church, and busied themselves in carrying away the cattle and in destroying the harvests which were not yet cut.

"In the meantime, the Château Richer people became tired of living in the woods; the nights got cool; they were threatened with starvation, and many wished to find out how matters stood, on the shores of the St. Lawrence. At the request of the Rev. Mr. Duburon, two lads, Gravel and Drouin, undertook to go and explore for the rest. When they got on the heights behind the church of the parish, they saw large crowds of men ascending the Ange Gardien Hill. Red coats and glistening steel soon marked them as British troops. 'They are on the move, they are off for Quebec,' exclaimed Drouin, after a few moments of observation; 'a good riddance! Let us go back and tell our people.' 'Of course,' replied the other; 'but suppose we take a run to the convent and see what is going on there.' In a trice they got there: Drouin's hand has just seized the handle of the door, when it was violently thrown open, and twenty Highlanders point their guns towards them at the word 'Surrender.' As if struck by an electric shock, the young men bound off towards the hills, and a discharge of musketry follows: a bullet grazes Drouin's hair and skin, whilst the Highlanders seem particularly anxious to catch Gravel, a very tall youth. But fear adds wings, and soon they leave their pursuers in the rear; the noise of shot fired after them in the leaves gets fainter and fainter, and after a laborious race of three miles, they arrive quite exhausted and speechless amongst their comrades.

* * * * *

"Quebec had surrendered. About the end of September the *curé* of Château Richer had arrived from the mountain, leading his flock, and set to work to erect huts on the spot where their homes had previously stood. The young folks felt delighted at again seeing the banks of the St. Lawrence; the old men shed tears at having lived to see the day when the English were masters of the country; the fathers of families pondered sorrowfully over the waste and destruction which had befallen their lands. Monsieur Crespin, N.P., was cogitating on the legal difficulties which would surround him if he had to administer justice in the English language; it was doubly trying to a man of his years, after the trouble he had taken to master the French tongue. Behind the crowd, on stretchers, were conveyed the two youths, Drouin and Gravel; they had not yet rallied from the effects of their race.

* * * * *

"Sixteen years had passed over. Brought to the lowest ebb, by the pillage* and destruction perpetrated by the British soldiery, the inhabi-

---

* The canny Scots who played such a conspicuous part in the War of the Conquest, if they did suffer in their numbers, rather increased their "material guaranties."

"The following interesting anecdote is told of Fraser's Highlanders. It is related from the words of the venerable Mr. Thompson, who was present at the battle of Montmorenci:

"General Murray, being in want of funds to carry on his government during the winter, summoned all the officers and enquired if they had any money, and if their soldiers had any money that they could lend to the Governor until the supplies arrived from England in the spring. We were told of the wants of the governor, and the next day we were paraded, every man, and told that we should receive our money back, with interest, as soon as possible; and in order to prevent any mistake, every man received his receipt for his amount, and for fear he should lose it, the Adjutant went along the ranks, and entered in a book the name and sum opposite to every man; and *by the Lord Harry!* when they came to count it up, they found that our regiment alone, Fraser's Highlanders, had mustered *six thousand guineas!* It was not long after we had lent our money, that one morning a frigate was seen coming round Pointe Lévi with supplies. We were soon afterwards mustered, and every man received back his money, with *twelve months* interest, besides the thanks of the general."'—*Hawkin's Picture of Quebec.*

tants saw a brighter future in store for them; some had even retrieved their losses. Amongst the latter might be counted Gravel, who was now a *pater familias*, and whose loyalty had been rewarded by a lieutenancy in the militia. One day, an English officer of rank called at his house. He was the bearer of an order to the militia officers to furnish him with relays of horses to travel. As he spoke French fluently, the lieutenant thought he would drive him himself. 'What ruins are those?' enquired the Englishman when he passed close to the convent. 'Why, one could see them from St. Joachim, and even from Quebec.'

"'It was formerly a convent, sir; it was destroyed in '59 when the country was ceded. I have reason to know something about it. I can tell you I felt tolerably nervous on that day.' He then related his and Drouin's mission, their utter surprise, and how they were chased, also the serious illness which it caused them.

"'Well, my friend,' said the English officer, 'I see you and I are old acquaintances. We have met before. I was the lieutenant in charge of the company stationed in that convent, to prevent any attack on our rear. I saw you come down the hill, and it occurred to me we might get important information if we could catch one or the other of you two. Before I could utter a word of French to you, you were off. We fired, in hopes of frightening you and making you surrender. If you gave us no information, we had a hearty laugh at your expense. I have just arrived from England, and I felt curious to revisit this portion of the country, which I once visited in a very different way. I am glad to meet in you an acquaintance, at a time when I have to meet in the field an older acquaintance still, in the person of my old friend General Montgomery.'"*

---

* Montgomery, whose loyalty to the King had been so conspicuous in burning the dwellings of the French Canadians at St. Jean Port Joly and elsewhere, in 1759, fell at the head of American soldiers, at Pres de Ville, in the Lower Town of Quebec, 31st Dec., 1775.

A literary friend, to whom I was reading this chapter, and to whom I put the rather embarassing question, "What nationality will finally prevail in Canada?" answered, "It is hard to determine now what changes lie unrevealed in the womb of time. Judging from the march of events since the conquest, seeing the enormous and unparalleled strides taken by the French Canadians, who, without any emigration from France, and in spite of all obstacles, have attained 800,000 from 80,000 they then were, some of whom as merchants, &c., have realized fortunes of £350,000, like Hon. Mr. Masson, and others, farmers, some £300,000; who have founded most flourishing banks, such as the *Banque du Peuple*, the Jacques Cartier Bank, at Montreal, the *Banque Nationale*, at Quebec. Commercial companies, realizing *safely* their 40 per cent., like the Richelieu line of steamers, purchasing Saxon homesteads in Quebec and out of Quebec; in fact almost, to use Mr. Rameau's expression, elbowing the sturdy English race out of Lower Canada. I should," he observed, "fancy that these people, united as they are, can always hold their own, provided they are loyal to England; on the other hand, we know what British

De Breboeuf and Lalemant.

THE SHORES OF LAKE SIMCOE.

CHAPTER XIII.

" It may be in an earlier day
Some Indian strife disturb'd the scene,
And man's red blood, of man the prey,
Mix'd with thine azure waves serene.
It may be that with maddening yells
These wood-clad shores and isles have rung,
And chiefs, whose name no legend tells,
Dead in thy rocky depths were flung.

—*Bishop Mountain's " Songs of the Wilderness."*

THE Indian missions,* which formerly existed in the neighborhood of Lake Simcoe, will be ever memorable, as furnishing to the historian the materials for one of the most glorious pages of the early history of the colony: indeed, it may be safely asserted, that nowhere on this continent has human heroism shone with brighter lustre. The reader is doubtless aware that many of our early missionaries have sealed their faith with their blood. Foremost in this devoted band stand out two men, distinguished alike by birth and by the extraordinary amount of physical suffering which preceded their death.

Let us place before the reader a truthful sketch of these two Christian heroes, whose fate, as Canadians, as Christians, and as men, is equally creditable to Canada, to Christianity and to manhood. Let us watch them leaving behind the gaieties of Parisian life, the attributes of birth, the advantages of science and mental culture, in order to dive through the pathless forest in quest of the red man of the woods,—the bearers of a

energy, English capital, and perseverance can do. The English are a conquering, absorbing, powerful race. If, however, they want to hold their place on the continent of America, they will have to join their strength and destinies to the other chief element of the population—to British America, which is a little more extensive in area than the American Union, are reserved a bright future, if strongly knit together." I thought there was a good deal of truth in all this.

* According to recent researches, the St. Ignace mission would have been in the township of Medonte; the St. Louis Mission in the township of Tay. Until recently, there existed ruins of the St. Mary mission, on the banks of the River Wye. The present village of Coldwater must be in the vicinity of these ancient Huron missions. All these localities, according to Mr. Devine's map of 1859, must be included in the county of Simcoe.

joyous message,—with privation and suffering as a certainty before them, and generally a horrible death as the crowning reward: perchance the spectacle of self-sacrifice may still awaken an echo, even in an age in which selfishness and mammon seem to rule supreme.

Gabriel Lalemant was born in Paris; some of the members of his family had attained eminence at the French bar; he himself, had discharged for several years the duties of a professor of languages: of a delicate frame, he had attained his thirty-ninth year when he landed in Canada.

His colleague, Jean de Brebœuf, on the other hand was a person of most commanding mien, endowed with colossal strength and untiring endurance. Like the brave Dr. Kane in our own day, he was not long before discovering that no truer way existed to secure the respect of the savage hordes he had to deal with, than by impressing them with an idea of physical superiority. With this object in view, he would not hesitate when a *portage* occurred, to carry, unassisted, the travelling canoe heavily laden, accomplishing also, with ease, a variety of other feats indicative of extraordinary muscular strength: the Hurons would look with awe on the black robed giant. Himself a man of education and literary taste, he was the uncle of the poet De Brebœuf, who versified in French Lucian's poem of Pharsalia: it has also been stated that from his family sprung the English house of Arundel.

In 1648, these two men undertook the spiritual charge of the five missions or residencies in the Huron country, on Matchedache Bay, near Lake Simcoe: these five settlements were but a few miles apart from each other; a deadly hatred at that time existed between the Hurons and Iroquois. In the fall of 1648, a thousand Iroquois warriors, well provided with fire-arms, procured chiefly at the Dutch settlements, resolved to exterminate entirely the Hurons: they accordingly spent the winter hunting in the woods, stealthily drawing nearer and nearer to their foes; they thus advanced, unperceived, some three hundred miles. On the 16th March, 1649, they had arrived in the neighborhood of the St. Ignace settlement, which they reconnoitred during the night time. A deep ravine protected three sides of the residency, the fourth side being surrounded with a palisade fifteen or sixteen feet high. At one point alone the place was accessible, and there at the break of day the attack commenced. Operations had proceeded so noiselessly, that the place was in possession of the enemy before the garrison had time properly to provide for its defence: this was owing to the few warriors left in charge, the bulk having gone out on a distant hunt and war expedition. The assailants lost but ten men: mostly all the inmates were scalped, these were the best off—horrible tortures awaited those whose lives were spared. The attack having taken place at night, the only survivors who escaped were three Hurons, who made their way over the snow to the next residency in a state bordering on complete nudity. The tidings they brought created the utmost consternation: close on their heels the blood thirsty Iroquois followed, hurrying on before the enemy could prepare: they arrived at the next settlement—the St. Louis residency—about sunrise: the women and children had barely the time to quit, ere they surrounded it. Eighty stout Hurons rushed to the palisades to conquer or die. They actually succeeded in repelling two attacks and in killing thirty Iroquois, but overpowering numbers prevailed. With axes the besiegers cut down the stakes or palisades, rushed through the breach, when an indiscriminate slaughter took place inside. Fire was then set to the fort, and the smoke and flames soon warned the inhabitants of the third settlement,—the St. Mary's residency,—distant but three miles, that the Iroquois were butchering their comrades. Some few had fled from the St. Louis fort, in which Lalemant and De Brebœuf were located: they were not the men to fly from death. De Brebœuf's herculean form might be seen close to the breach, admonishing the fallen warriors how to die, and encouraging them in their last moments. Both were seized and marched prisoners to the St. Ignace settlement. Scouts were immediately sent out to ascertain whether the St. Mary's settlenent could stand an assault, and on their report a war council decided on attacking it the next day; amongst the inmates of this fort were some Europeans, who were determined to sell dearly their lives. The Iroquois, then numbering about two hundred, had to retreat for shelter into what remained of the St. Louis settlement. Several engagements followed, and finally the Iroquois remained in possession of the field of battle, having lost about one hundred of their bravest men.

The Indians, who had got possession of Fort St. Ignace, hurried to prepare the two missionaries to undergo the usual tortures reserved to prisoners. De Brebœuf had previously stated, on his arrival in the colony, that he expected to be soon put to death, nor was he long kept in suspense before seeing his prophecy verified.

A large fire was lit, and an iron caldron placed over it; the prisoners were then stripped and tied to a post erected near each fire; they were first beaten with sticks; then a necklace was made of the war-axes heated in the fire, and this was tied round their neck; bark sashes were also tied round them, on which rosin and pitch was smeared, and then set on fire. In derision of the holy rites of Christian baptism, the savages then poured boiling water on their heads. Amidst these horrible sufferings, Lalemant would raise his eyes towards heaven, asking strength and courage to endure them. De Brebœuf seemed like a rock, perfectly insensible to pain; occasionally he moved his lips in prayer;—this so incensed his executioners that they cut off his lips and nose, and thrust a red hot iron down his throat. Firm and resigned, the Christian giant, of a whole head taller than his torturers, would look down on them; even in his agony, he seemed to command his executioners. The implacable savages then untied Lalemant, much younger and more delicate than De Brebœuf; he threw himself or fell immediately at the feet of his intrepid colleague and prayed earnestly to the Almighty for help. He was then brought back and tied to his post—covered over with birch bark, and soon became a mass of living flames: the smell of blood awakening the ferocity of these cannibals, they, without waiting till his flesh was baked, cut out with their hunting knives large slices out of the fleshy part of his arms and legs, and then amidst horrible yells, devoured greedily the reeking repast; they then substituted burning coals for pupils in his eye sockets. De Brebœuf's sufferings lasted three hours; his heart was extracted after death and eaten. Lalemant was less fortunate; life was not extinct till next day; a savage more human than the rest put an end to his existence by cleaving open his skull with his tomahawk; at the departure of the Iroquois, the mutilated and charred remains of the two missionaries were found, and Christian burial given to them on the 21st March, 1649.

De Brebœuf's skull was taken to Quebec: his family sent out from France a silver case, in which it was placed, and remained in the Jesuits' College (now the Jesuits' Barrack, Upper Town Market place), until the last of the order, Father Casot, who died in 1800, presented it a short time before his death to the Religious Ladies of the Hotel Dieu Nunnery, where it can be seen to this day. Amongst the numerous witnesses of the Gospel put to death by the Indian tribes of Canada, none fell more heroically than De Brebœuf and Lalemant; the forests of new France had been selected at a very early period as a most appropriate field for apostolic labours, and when the Earl of Elgin, in one of his despatches to the home government called the early period of this colony, the "heroic times of Canada," he did nothing more than sum up in one happy expression a characteristic which recent researches are every day corroborating.*

* The friends of archeological enquiry will doubtless hail with joy the work which Dr. C. Taché promises the public shortly, on the wonderful discoveries and relics he has met with in the course of his explorations and searches in the territory formerly occupied by the Huron Indians. This gentleman has presented to the museum of the Laval University a great number of skeletons and Indian curiosities. He has had the good fortune to discover the exact spots on which, two hundred and twenty-four years ago, stood the Huron missions, near Lake Simcoe, in which the Iroquois massacres, herein alluded to, took place; he has penetrated into the very mounds and tombs wherein rested the bones of the redskins, after receiving the family and the national burial. But we must not anticipate.

Fin and Feather in Canada.

CHAPTER XIV.

" The shootings in Breadalbane and Athole are leased at the following rents : Blair —Athole, £3485 , Fortingall, £1,934 ; Legierait, £674 ; Moulin, £670 ; Little Dunkeld, £1,432 ; Dull, £984 ; Weem, £207 ; Kenmore, £300 ; Killin, £984 ; Balquhidder, £785. Maharajah Dholeep Singh has sublet the shootings of Auchlyne and Sine, for which he paid £750, and has taken the Moors of Grandtully, where he will shoot this season."—(Late English Papers.)

IN collecting together some facts relating to the finned and feathered game of Canada, we thought we could not do better than preface this short sketch with acurate *data* and figures, exhibiting what the killing of a few deer, hares, grouse and pheasants annually costs some of the sporting gentry of Britain ; indeed, we know of a recent instance, in which three rich young sportsmen of the " land o' cakes" purchased for £600, the right to shoot on some of the moors of Scotland, and actually brought home *two braces of grouse, each* ; expensive sport, was it not ?

What hecatombs of deer, what pyramids of wild turkey, what hampers of snipe, quail, ducks and grouse, we would now ask, the renting of a Scotch shooting range, such, for instance, as Blair Athole, viz., £3,485, would procure to a score of Canadian Nimrods ? Why, to use a metaphor, which some may consider as savouring of Federal war telegrams, a ship a trifle smaller than the *Great Eastern* would be freighted with the proceeds of such a gigantic *battue !*

When we read of Lord Dufferin's pic-nic to Iceland, in the yacht *Foam,* to witness, among other things, an eruption of Mount Hecla ; when we hear of an enterprising young Englishman having recently sailed for Greenland to practice rifle-shooting on walrusses, we naturally wonder why more of the venturesome spirits amongst our transatlantic friends do not tear themselves away, even for a few months, from London fogs, to our distant and more favored climes. How is it that so few, comparatively speaking, come to enjoy the bracing air and bright summer

* From the London " Canadian News."

skies of Canada? With what zest the enterprising and eccentric amongst them could undertake a ramble with rod and gun in hand, over the Laurentian chain of mountains from Niagara to Labrador, choosing as rallying points, whereat to compare notes and discuss politics, old port and sandwiches, the summit of Cape Eternity, in the Saguenay district, the peak of Cape Tourment and the Cave of the Winds under the Niagara Falls, after ransacking for fish and game the fifteen hundred intervening leagues of coast! We imagine that the atmosphere of those airy positions is as brisk as that of Ben-Mac-Dui or Cairn-gorum, and that the divers incidents of travel and sport therein combined, ought effectually to dispel *ennui* and restore their spirits for, as the author of Childe Harold truly says:

> "There is a pleasure in the pathless wood,
> There is a rapture on the lonely shore,
> There is society where none intrudes
> By the deep sea, and music in its roar."

If this were insufficient to rouse them, a smart trudge to the shores of the frozen ocean might be added; our distinguished travellers would shoot, on the route, ptarmigan, blue or sooty foxes, arctic hares, polar bears and the musk ox, after camping on the shores of the Copper Mine and the Great Slave Lake; the party on its return might now and again lunch at the Hudson Bay posts, in the absence of better fare, on pemmican, whale or walrus steaks—and who can say, whether combining with amusement, the cause of humanity, they might not be fortunate enough to elicit further tidings of the fate of Sir John Franklin's gallant band? This attractive programme, however, we merely display to tempt the most enterprising among the English sporting world; as for us *natives*, we find abundance of fish and game without venturing so far.

Volumes have been written to make known the inexhaustible mineral, agricultural, industrial and commercial wealth of this colony, but little efforts have yet been used to place on record the noble game, the inexhaustible treasures of wholesome food which a kind Providence has stored in the streams, in the rivers, in the forests of this magnificent country, for the benefit, for the daily use, of the million as well as of the millionnaire. Few—some, through interested motives, have suppressed the fact—have published to the world, that Canada, *without the stringent game laws of England*, without scarcely any expense, but with the mere consent of the people and the fostering care of the government, can be made what it was formerly—one of the most favored localities on the earth for game—yea, a veritable Canaan—a land of promise—abounding with the " milk and honey" of amusement for all those who rejoice in the manly and exhilarating pleasures of the chase.

It is true that for two centuries back the people have struggled hard to extirpate* its fish and game, and that, had the advice of the sportsmen not been heard in time, every estuary in the province would have been depopulated ; the forests, the sea shores, the whole country, instead of harboring quantities of luscious game, myriads of insect-devouring birds, would soon have become a kind of howling wilderness. Much harm has undoubtedly been done ; but the curing of the evil is fortunately still within our reach.† Intending to notice elsewhere the glorious results which have crowned the protective policy of successive administrations towards‡ fish and game, we shall now confine ourselves merely to mentioning, succinctly, the chief hunting grounds in the province.

Old writers, one and all, have spoken with astonishment, nay, with rapture, of the abundance and varieties of the sea fowl and birds frequenting the shores of the St. Lawrence, and we all know how thousands of the aboriginal races for centuries subsisted exclusively on the produce of the chase, throughout the boundless forests of Canada.||

* One of the greatest enormities perpetrated by the Indian, is the extinction in eastern, and in the greater portion of western Canada, of the wapite or Canadian stag, the noblest of the species, which roamed through our mountains—as large as a horse, with round, sharp antlers five feet high. It is now abundant in the western prairies and the eastern side of the Rocky Mountains, from the 56th or 57th parallel of north latitude to Texas. In the Hudson Bay territories, according to Sir John Richardson, its eastern limit is a line drawn from the south end of Lake Winnipeg to the Saskatchewan, in the 103rd degree of longitude, thence till it strikes the Elk river in the 111th degree.

† The increasing and successful efforts of the Quebec and Montreal Fish and Game Protection Clubs must necessarily be a source of pleasure to the many patriotic sportsmen interested in the cause of its preservation. Amongst many zealous members, one above others, in my opinion, deserves a passing word of encouragement, for his untiring efforts and energy—poachers, hucksters, pot-hunters, and every other species of obstructive, have in vain tried to put him down—I mean F. W. Austin, Esq., for several years Secretary to the Quebec Fish and Game Protection Club.

‡ With this object were written " *La Pêcheries du Canada.*"

|| To illustrate the enormous quantity of game in the north of Canada, and in the Hudson Bay territory, I cannot do better than subjoin the following extract from a valuable paper read before the Montreal Natural History Society, by Geo. Barnston, Esq., of the Hudson's Bay Company, in 1861. A long residence in that territory, and a patient investigation of the game it contains, renders Mr. Barnston's statement particularly valuable.

The Jesuits, generally accurate in their statements, in describing, in 1662, the Bird Rocks, at the entrance of the gulf, say that a boat might be easily loaded with eggs of the sea fowl, who build on these desolate islands, and that so numerous are they, that human beings ascending these rocks are in danger of being prostrated to the ground by the flapping of the wings of these feathered denizens.

We subjoin two extracts from the *Relations des Jesuites*, in their own quaint French.*

"It is very difficult," says he, "to form anything like an accurate idea of the various species of geese that have just been passed in review, viz: the Canada grey goose, the lesser grey goose, the Brant goose, the snow goose, and the white fronted goose. Of the quantity shot at particular points where they become an article of provisions, we may arrive at a wide but still a better estimate. Seventeen to twenty thousand geese are sometimes killed by the Albany Indians in the autumn or fall of the year, and ten thousand or more in the spring, making a total for these coast

Crees alone of at least	30,000
Not speaking so certainly of other natives, I would place the Moose Indians as killing at all seasons	10,000
Rupert's River natives	8,000
Eastmain and to the north, including Esquimaux	6,000
The Severn coast I cannot compute as yielding less than	10,000
The York Factory and Churchill Indians, with Esquimaux beyond, must dispose of	10,000
Making a total of geese killed on the coast, of	74,000

As many geese must die wounded, and others are got hold of by the foxes and wolverines, we may safely allow the total loss to the flocks while running the fiery gauntlet as equivalent to 80,000. I was at one time inclined to believe that two-thirds of this number was, or might be, the proportion for the autumn hunt, but it is probably nearer three-fourths, and we have thus 60,000 in round numbers brought down from the newly-fledged flocks, as they pass southward along the bay. I have lately been informed by an old and experienced hunter, that he believes that for every goose that is killed, above twenty must leave the bay without scaith, as although there is sometimes destruction dire among some lots that approach the gun, and that feed in quarters frequented by hunters, yet innumerable families of them alight on remote and quiet feeding ground, remain there unmolested, and take wing when the cold sets in, with their numbers intact. I must allow the correctness of this remark, and the deduction to be drawn from it is, that 1,200,000 geese leave their breeding grounds by the Hudson's Bay line of march for the genial south. Of the numbers to the westward along the arctic coast, that wend their way to their winter quarters straight across the continent, we can form but a very vague opinion, but computing it at two-thirds or more of the quantity supposed to leave the eastern part of the arctic coast, we cannot have less than two millions of geese, composing the numerous battalions which pass over the continent between the Atlantic and the Rocky Mountains, borne aloft generally like the scud, and as swiftly hastened on, by the force of the boreal blast.

"I ought to observe that the Brant geese, *Bernicla Brenta*, are not included in the above estimate. They are pretty numerous on the Atlantic coast, but are quite neglected by the Indians in general of Hudson's Bay."

* "A l'entrée de ce golfe (de St. Laurent) nous vîmes deux rochers, l'un rond, l'autre barré. Vous diriez que Dieu les a plantés au milieu des eaux comme deux colombiers pour servir de lieux de retraite aux oiseaux qui s'y retirent en si grande quantité, qu'on marche dessus; et si l'on ne se tient bien ferme ils s'élèvent en si grande quantité qu'ils renversent les personnes; on en rapporte des chaloupes ou des petits bateaux tous pleins quand le temps permet qu'on les aborde: les Français les ont nommés les Iles aux Oiseaux." (Relation des Jésuites. Le Père Paul Le jeune.)

"L'Isle-aux-Coudres et l'Isle-aux-Oies méritent d'être nommées en passant. La première est souvent remplie d'elans qui s'y recontrent; la second est peuplée en

Although egg-stealers* (a bad set, by the by, whose operations Audubon properly stigmatises) have considerably thinned their numbers, Dr. Bryant, who, in 1860, made an ornithological survey of these islands for the Smithsonian Institution, found them still tenanted by large numbers of gannets, puffins, gillemots, auks and kittiwakes. In the fall of the year the shores of the St. Lawrence literally swarm with ducks, teal and other sea fowl. We have ourselves counted thousands busy gobbling up the shell-fish, barnacles and sea weed which cling to the shelving rocks round Plateau and Bonaventure islands, at Gaspé. We have watched the gannet, the herring-gull, the cormorant, hovering in clouds over Percé Rock, on whose verdant summit they build and find an asylum secure from their great destroyer, man, whilst their discordant voices are heard above the roar of the surf, miles away. We have seen their young shot for food by hundreds in the month of August.

It is not an uncommon thing in the fall of the year for the Gaspé fishermen to kill as many as twenty ducks in one shot, in the air holes among the ice, down which the hungry birds crowd to feed. Where is the Canadian sportsman who would not give the world for a week on the Mille Vaches shoals in September? Where is the fowler who has not heard of the sport which Jupiter river, on Anticosti, affords, over and above the chance of putting an occasional bullet through a bear attracted to the sea shore for his morning meal of kelp and seaweed, in the absence of green oats and young mutton, his favorite provender? It would be unfair, however, to lead sportsmen to believe that one has to go as far as Anticosti to get a crack at "Bruin," when there are instances on record of snipe shooters killing bears on the beaches close to Quebec. We will mention one recent occurrence. A sporting member of the Quebec bar,† whom the summer vacation had seduced away from the Pandects and Blackstone, to the swampy Chateau Richer flats, was bagging as usual, a few dozen birds before breakfast. On firing his first shot, he heard a rustling in some tall rushes, and out stepped leisurely a —snipe? no, a bear. Sympathy for a fellow sportsman ought to have saved Bruin's life. Not so; his presence on the swamp was construed

---

son temps d'une multitude d'oies, de canards, d'outardes, dont *l'île que est plate et chargée d'herbe comme une prairie en parait toute converte. Les lieux circonvoisins retentissent incessamment des cris de ces oiseaux."*

* As recently as four years back Capt. Fortin, of the coasting service, pounced on four Yankee schooners in the very act of robbing the Bird Rocks of their eggs.

† Richard Pentland, Esquire.

by the disciple of St. Hubert into a clear case of trespass. Nothing could be more *inconvenient*, one will admit, than for a bear to take possession of the feeding grounds of teal and snipe. *Qu'a l'ait-il faire dans cette galère?* A heavy charge at close quarters, and Bruin's spirit was wafted to where all good bears go.

What clouds of sand-pipers, curlews and plover September brings forth from their breeding places, in the barren wilds of Labrador, the secluded lakes and islands of the north, up to the frozen ocean! Look, friend, look at that dense vapor that hovers over that long sand bar, *La Batture aux Alouettes* on the North Shore of the Saint Lawrence.—From afar, you might take it for a squall of hail or rain; but wait a minute until the sun's rays light up the picture. Now, see the snowy breast of myriads of chubby little northern strangers, the ring plovers; look out for them as they settle, by thousands, on the sand; now is your time. Enfilade their serried ranks, fire low; bang! One shot suffices, you have one hundred victims; to fire again would only cause unnecessary carnage. Father Point, lower down than Rimouski, during strong easterly winds, affords capital stock: Canada geese, Brent geese and ducks are perpetually hovering over the extreme end of the point: the fowler carefully concealed, pours a deadly volley into the flock, and his faithful Newfoundland dog springs in the surf and fetches out the dead birds.—You can either continue to *beat* the shore or cross over with us to Seal Rocks, in the Traverse, a delightful small game preserve, so bountifully stocked with ducks, teal and plover, that a club of *chasseurs* of St. Jean Port Joly have leased it from government; a rare thing in Canada for natives to pay for the privilege to shoot game; it is so plentiful everywhere. We are now at Crane Island; *Quantùm mutata ab illâ!* Night shooting has effectually scared the ducks from their resting places. Of swans, Lord Gosford seems to have got the last. As to cranes, two only have been seen of late years. This wary stilted stranger, *Gruem advenam*, as Horace calls it, can only be an accidental visitor, as its range is considerably more to the west. How often have we seen its solitary figure looming up at low tide, far beyond the range of a gun? Where is the time when a Crane Island *chasseur* thought he had had a poor season if he had bagged less than one hundred *outardes* (Canada geese), together with a few dozen snow-geese: wild in the extreme, yea, as hard to catch as southern generals, are those noisy swamp-feeders, who spend the summer months, winging every alternate day their wedgelike flight from the St. Joachim beaches, to the Crane Island flats, where they congregate at low water mark, some 3,000 feeding beyond a rifle's range. We know of a hunting ground not one hundred miles from Quebec, in which the protection of game is strikingly exemplified. None but the proprietors have access to this preserve, in which *outardes* and ducks assemble in astonishing multitudes. Recently two men shot fifty wild geese there in two days. The place is a source of revenue to its owners, and those birds, which are not sent to market, are salted and preserved for the farm servants' daily use.

It would be impossible for us, in this short sketch, to name all the localities where game is to be had in Canada. The two shores of the St. Lawrence, from Gaspé to the upper lakes, and the greater number of the tributaries of the great river, especially in the Ottawa district, are our chief shooting grounds—some seven or eight hundred leagues—plenty of elbow-room, as you may see. The Chateau Richer swamp, in spite of the indiscriminate slaughter of birds, still furnishes some 3,000 or 4,000 snipe per season. The Bijou marsh, formerly an excellent hunting ground, under the St. Foy heights, is pretty well destroyed at present for game purposes. What a splendid game preserve the Bijou would become in the hands of a sporting millionnaire! Woodcock are still numerous at Cote-à-Bonhomme, near Charlesbourg, at La Baie du Febvre, Les Salines, and in fifty other places. Wild pigeon shooting, especially in western Canada, yields an abundant harvest. The passenger pigeon still resorts to the Niagara district in such quantities that Audubon's graphic description of the flights of wild pigeons in Kentucky ceases to appear overdrawn. Until 1854, there existed in the woods back of Chateauguay, at a place called the Five Points, a pigeon roost; the devastation caused by this countless host in the wheat fields became very great, but in presence of the incessant attacks of man, a general pigeon stampede took place—the roost is now deserted.

Grouse shooting, which in Canada commences on the 20th August, affords also some amusement. *Grouse and partridge are shot and snared in Canada, the * Hon. Grantley F. Berkley to the contrary notwith-*

* We find in the London *Times* of the 18th September, 1863, in a letter subscribed Grantley F. Berkely, *valuable* (?) information respecting the Canadian partridge, and the mode of capturing it:—"The Americans," says this learned Nimrod, "are profoundly ignorant of the way to shoot winged game in any quantities, or to take them

standing—not poisoned with strychnine. A great falling off is certainly now observable in the number of birds, in consequence of the wanton slaying of the old ones in the breeding season; but dive into the interior about forty miles, at the time when the maple tree is decked with tints of unsurpassing loveliness, and then let us hear from you. We remember, one balmy September morning, beating for grouse in the wooded slopes of the Chateau Richer mountain, just at the hour when the rising sun was pouring forth floods of golden light. Never before had we seen our hardwood trees more gorgeously decorated. The bright red, deep green, and the orange-colored leaves sparkling with dew-drops, and bathed in autumnal sunshine, recalled to our mind Tasso's description of Armida's enchanted forest. We could compare it to nothing else but to a huge flower-garden in full bloom. Our rêverie was briskly interrupted by the *whirring* sound of the grouse, flushed from its cover by our dog.

Grouse is not the only game which you meet in the woods during a September ramble; perhaps you may be lucky enough to have a shot at the king of birds, the golden eagle, or his pilfering compeer the bald eagle, soaring high above your head amongst the crags. Do not be alarmed if, in crossing a mountain gorge, the hoarse croak of the raven should catch your ear. And if, perchance, camped for the night on the mountain brow in a deserted sugar-hut, you hear the horrible hooting of the great horned owl, fear nothing; *it is not the evil one:* wait until the nocturnal marauder lights on the large tree next to your resting place, and, by the light of the moon, your Manton will soon add to your museum, if you have such a fancy, one of the noblest and fiercest birds of the Canadian fauna.

If there should be anything of the Jules Gérard or the Gordon Cumming in your composition, and you have a hankering for larger game, without being able to go to the Rocky Mountains, go and ask that peasant in the market place the particulars of the raid which bears have recently made in his oat-field, after decimating his flock. Go in quest of the sheep-slayer; your guide will take you where bruin and her cubs

alive, and it is not unlikely they have adopted strychnine as a method of death." He, further on, explains why they poison the birds they intend for food, viz., for "the love of the almighty dollar, which makes men not over nice in the means they take to get it." Mr. Grantley F. B.'s peculiar insanity is becoming chronic.—In Canada we should try the cold water cure.

hold their nightly revels. Take care not to miss your intended victim; if you do, or only wound her, she won't miss you.

When you are tired of shooting bears, Canada geese, ducks, snipe, woodcock, pigeon and grouse, take the train for the western prairies and plains, and eight or ten days will bring you to where countless herds of buffalo browse; a subject upon which the Prince of Wales, our governor general, Lord Monck, Lord Mulgrave, and the other governors of British provinces, from their recent visit, are now in a position to speak *ex cathedrâ*. You can occasionally vary your sport by looking after wild turkeys and prairie hens, reserving deer and caribou hunting for the winter season, but when you get there, with Mr. Russell's fate before your eyes, do not desecrate the Sabbath. Before we part, let me give you a solemn piece of advice. By the mighty shades of Hawker, by the ramrod of the great Saint Hubert, I adjure you not to waste powder and shot in the neighborhood of large cities! Spring shooting and pot-hunters have for the most part extirpated the game in such localities. Go to Sorel, Deschambault, Mille Vaches, Lancaster, Long Point on Lake Erie, for ducks; to Chateau Richer, Grondines, St. Pierre les Becquets, for snipe; beat Côte à Bonhomme, the whole range of heights from Charlesbourg to the Jacques Cartier river, for woodcock; but if you wish for sport in earnest, go to western Canada, to the St. Clair marshes,*

* We read in the Toronto *Leader*, of November, 1860:—"Captain Strachan and Mr. Kennedy returned last evening from a fortnight's shooting in the St. Clair marshes, where they had excellent sport, bagging, to the two guns, two swans, three snipe, five wild geese, and 570 ducks,—black, mallard and grey ducks—weight 1,860 lbs."

"Cols. Rhodes and Bell, of this city, returned to town recently, from a hunting excursion in the woods north of Quebec. During their trip they met with a run of good sport, having killed ten caribous, four lynxes, a porcupine, and a large number of white partridges, hares, &c. Such an amount of game brought down by two guns must be considered a decidedly good *battue*. We understand that one of the large caribous has been obtained by several officers of the garrison for the purpose of being sent to England."—*Morning Chronicle*, 29th December, 1862.

"Ten tons of prairie chickens and quail were shipped from Chicago to New York by one of the Express companies recently."—*Ibid*, 6th January, 1863.

"SALMON FISHING.—Mr. Law's party returned from Godbout yesterday morning, three rods having killed 194 salmon, weighing 2196 lbs; the average weight of each being 11 lbs. and one-third."—*Mercury*, 7th August, 1863.

Messrs. Boswell and Kerr, the proprietors of the Jacques Cartier salmon stream, 27 miles from Quebec, have caught, with the fly, more than 200 fine salmon in July, 1863. The pools are fairly alive. [We now have before us a tabular statement showing the catch, each day, of three rods in the river Moisie, on the gulf coast, in 1862, viz: 318 salmon; average weight, 15 to 17 lbs.; and, also, a similar authentic statement for the river Godbout for June and July, showing 287 fish; weight, 3,116 lbs.]

The Essex *Record* says that "Bob Renardson" and two others have just returned from a shooting expedition at Baptiste Creek, where they have been for the last seven weeks. During that time they bagged sixteen hundred ducks, two bugle swans, one weighing 35 and the other 40 lbs., besides a quantity of smaller game. Most of the ducks have now left, owing to the freezing of the marshes.

where you will find swans, geese, ducks, teal, snipe, even eagles; in fact all the game of Canada congregated. Rely for success on good dogs, a good guide, a sure aim, and, our word for it, a plethoric game bag will be your reward.

The Montreal *Witness* says:—"We learn that the Hon. Col. Annesley, M.P., the Hon. Capt. Elphistone and Mr. Morland, returned to Montreal after a two days' shooting excursion, having bagged 232 head of duck and other game."

I could, *ad infinitum*, multiply quotations from the press, but I have said enough to induce English sportsmen to come and ascertain for themselves whether or not Canada contains game.

Acclimatization.

CHAPTER XV.

AMONGST the several subjects which of late years have seriously engaged the attention of statesmen and economists in other countries, few have had the privilege more so than the question of increasing the food for the sustenance of the people, by developing the natural resources of the country. Various means have been used to arrive at this very desirable result. The artificial propagation of fish, ever since the days of Remy and Gehin, has been and still continues to be in great favor; this, joined to the protection of deep sea fisheries and to a carefully organized system of public bounties, has produced in several of the more enlightened communities in the old world, an ample harvest for the rich man, as well as for perishing millions. Our own favored land has not been slow in following in the wake of the most illustrious nations, the English, the French, &c.; we, too, have our organized system of bounties for successful industry;* we have, at considerable cost, recently inaugurated a comprehensive protective policy over the hundreds of fruitful salmon rivers which intersect our thousand miles of sea coast. This branch of science has been eloquently descanted on, ably expounded by intelligent strangers, such as Dr. Henry, Chas. Lanman and others, who seemed perfectly amazed at our ignoring the inexhaustible resources which our lakes, our rivers, our majestic St. Lawrence contained in its limped waters. The writings of these gentlemen soon called forth an echo from our shores, and in a very short time we had "the Salmon Fisheries of the St. Lawrence," "Salmon Fishing in Canada," "Piscatorial Sketches," which would have gladdened the heart of "Old Isaac," and which place beyond contradiction the fact that Canada is a kind of terrestrial paradise for anglers. And if I abstain from placing before the public the names of these useful writers, it is merely because their known

* I hav shown elsewhere how the system worked: it rests with others to apply the remedy.

modesty dictates such a course to me; although I must confess, it does seem cruel to withhold the only recognition which the successful literary laborer can count on for his toil, in this new country, wherein no golden harvest is in store for him. Pisciculture is doubtless, at present, a recognized fact, a great, a wonderful science; and unquestionably those illiterate fishermen of the Vosges, Gehin and Remy, who restored its long forgotten secret, fancying it was quite a new discovery, are greater benefactors to the human race than he, who in Grecian story, is supposed to have stolen from heaven the divine fire. It were idle for me to attempt adding anything on a subject at present thoroughly known and appreciated. I wish merely to mention another matter closely connected with the propagation and increase of the animal kingdom by artificial means, quite as practicable, quite as valuable, to any country; I mean the acclimātization of foreign animals, the introduction in this country of valuable species hitherto considered indigenous to other climates. If I am asked why I urge the idea at present, I shall merely reply, that as the time draws near when the indefatigable members of the "Fish and Game Protection Club" will be called on to propose wholesome amendments to the Fish and Game Laws now in force, it may not be out of place for an humble advocate of the cause, to suggest to them that possibly they might enlarge their scope of usefulness, by enquiring whether Canada cannot respond to the appeal England and France are making to us through the press and through their scientific periodicals. Every one knows the immense undertakings of the Imperial Acclimatization Society of Paris. It was presided over, until his death, by a leading French naturalist, Isidore Geoffroy Saint Hilaire. It is patronized by several of the most eminent French *savants* and by the Emperor himself. Every month the proceedings are printed in a Scientific Bulletin, sent to its corresponding members all over the globe.

A similar institution also exists in London. It is comparatively recent, but its object is warmly advocated by the *Times*, and by several eminent men. I shall now make known its programme.

The purposes of the society are:—

1st. The introduction, acclimatization and domestication of mammalia, birds, fishes, insects and vegetables, whether useful or ornamental.

2nd. The perfection, propagation, and hybridisation of races already domesticated.

3rd. The spread of indigenous and naturalized animals, &c., from parts of the United Kingdom where they are already known, to other localities where they are not known.

4th. The procuration, whether by purchase, gift, or exchange, of animals, &c., from British Colonies and foreign countries.

5th. The transmission of animals, &c., from England to her colonies and foreign parts, in exchange for others sent from thence to the society.

6th. The holding of periodical meetings, and the publication of reports and transactions for the purpose of spreading knowledge of acclimatization, and of enquiry into the causes of failure.

As the *Times* correctly remarks, the doctrine of acclimatization, or domestication of animals, is not new ; nor was it considered a chimæra by our forefathers ; for, whence comes the horse, the sheep, the domestic pig, the turkey, the potato, the pheasant ? Almost all our domestic animals, and most of our useful vegetables, have been notoriously acclimatized. Look at the efforts to introduce into England the Chinese sheep, which multiplied very rapidly; look at the endeavors to acclimatize the guan, the curassow, and other valuable tropical poultry, in English farm-yards ? Who has not been agreeably surprised to hear of the striking success with which the Marquis of Breadalbane has restored to Scotland those noble birds, the black game, which had nearly become extinct ? It would appear that they are now breeding so fast that fears are entertained that they may dwarf. The *Bulletins* of the French society describe a beautiful species of duck, recently introduced from Canada, in France; it is called the Labrador duck. Mention is also made of an endless variety of animals and birds successfully domesticated. The Angora goat, acclimatized in Sicily, another species of goat imported into France from Thibet,—dromedaries, sent by the society to the Brazilian government,—merino sheep, reared in France,—Cuban animals and birds, which might be with advantage introduced in other countries,—the breeding of turtles, as objects of food, and fifty other experiments, many of which, if of no practical bearing for us in Canada, still evince the lively interest which European communities take in this practical pursuit.

Why, therefore, should not our "Fish and Game Protection Club" devote some moments to enquire what animals or birds the inhabitants of the banks of the St. Lawrence could exchange with those who reside on the shores of the Thames or the Seine? Does not every mail bring out enquiries and orders for the finest specimens of our fauna? Suppose our friends of the county of Essex, or of Chatham, send us down some of their magnificent wild turkeys, some of their red deer, or occasionally a gigantic whapite or Canadian stag; we might add, a few beavers, ruffed and spruce grouse, with a few couple of live ptarmigan; such gifts would grace any English or French park. Although the naturalizing and making barn fowls of the Australian black swan may not fill our pockets, there are several animals now introduced into France, England, and Australia, the acquisition of which might be very desirable. Cannot we, too, profit by the experience of other countries?

A Parting Word.

CHAPTER XVI.

MANY have already visited—many intend to visit—the Hermitage. It is as well for the latter to know that no time of the year can be selected with more advantage than the second week in September, when the foliage of the hard wood trees assumes its autumnal brilliancy—not even Kreikoff's forest scenery, dazzling though it be, can equal in brightness the leaves of a Canadian forest in September, during about a fortnight.

Should this first instalment of *Maple Leaves* be acceptable to my readers, they can count on a second at no distant period. Amongst the notes and sketches still remaining in my portfolio, I notice many which merely require some long winter evenings to be expanded into readable form. The history of the mysterious French officer, who, after assuming holy orders, spent the remainder of his days on the Island St. Barnabé, opposite Rimouski, and of which we find mention in *Emily Montague's letters, written from Sillery in 1767, will doubtless be much relished by romantic readers; and as my agents, Messrs. Holiwell & Alexander, tell me that my book is obtaining many romantic readers, it may be as well to inform them that a literary friend has just become possessed of a manuscript memoir of the old hermit of the Island St. Barnabé. I think I am safe in promising them the first reliable intelligence in English of this saintly individual. The pirate of Anticosti, Gamache, also claims attention; and I think I can furnish a sketch of the parliamentary career of the Honorable Louis Jos. Papineau; a chapter on Indian customs, the war-whoop, burials, &c. One of the most attractive historical legends will be the melancholy fate of Françoise Brunon, the converted daughter of an Iroquois chief; an abridged account of Indian ferocity at Detroit, as depicted by the Abbé Casgrain; the story about Mdlle. Granville's brother, the Gosse Island captive; the historical legend of Massacre Island, at Bic; and a variety of stirring events, founded on history, in connection with local traditions, together with sporting intelligence.

---

* Vol. i., page 161.

MAPLE LEAVES:

A BUDGET OF

LEGENDARY, HISTORICAL, CRITICAL,

AND SPORTING INTELLIGENCE.

(Second Series.)

By J. M. LeMoine, Esq.

(Copyright Secured.)

QUEBEC:

1864.

TO THE READER.

This series contains, properly speaking, the historical portion of the "Maple Leaves," viz. :—Sketches of the origin, ancestry and military prowess of our forefathers in Eastern and Western Canada, from the earliest days down to the close of the last American invasion of Canada. That we have had plenty of fighting in this country, few who choose to investigate the subject will be inclined to deny; and as there are yet amongst us some who profess to consider as skirmishes, engagements in which several thousands of corpses strewed the ground, I thought it would not be out of place to undeceive them by bringing into Court the record of history. Not wishing to be charged with putting my own construction on past events, I have produced the very text of Bancroft, Christie, Garneau, and others, allowing the reader to form his opinion; in such cases, scarcely ever obtruding any comments of my own. Two documents I shall specially commend to the attention of the student of Canadian history—one, the narrative of the Fort George Massacre, by an eye witness; the other, a sketch furnished by George Coventry, Esq., of Cobourg, of the United Empire Loyalists.

I have also devoted considerable space to the Fish and Game of the country, and to setting forth amendments in the laws advocated by the Quebec and Montreal Fish and Game Protection Clubs, and by others. In a third series, I hope yet to redeem a promise I made in the first, and to furnish to the patrons of "Maple Leaves" a deal of new and interesting intelligence on literary and other subjects connected with Canada.

Spencer Grange, near Quebec,
20th May, 1864.

MAPLE LEAVES.

HISTORY AND SPORT.

Augustus Sala on Canada.

"I AM bold enough to think that about nine-tenths even of my educated countrymen have about as definite an idea of Montreal, Toronto, and of Quebec, as they have of Owyhee or of Antannarivo. Is it impertinent in me to assume that my friends at home are as ignorant as I was the day before yesterday? It seems to me that, abating a few merchants, a few engineers, and a few military men, it has hitherto been nobody's business in England to know what the Canadians are like. It is not the thing to go to Canada. One can "do" Niagara without penetrating into the British Province. English artists don't make sketching excursions thither. The Alpine Club ignore it. Why does not some one start a Cataract Club? We let these magnificent provinces, with their inexhaustible productiveness—for asperity of climate is no sterility—their noble cities, their hardy and loyal population, go by. We pass them in silence and neglect. We listen approvingly while some college pedant, as bigoted as a Dominican, but without his shrewdness, as conceited as a Benedictine, but without his learning, prates of the expediency of abandoning our colonies. If we meanly and tamely surrender these, into whose hands would they fall? What hatred and ill-will would spring up among those now steady and affectionate people in their attachment to our rule, but from whom we had withdrawn our countenance and protection! But Canada has been voted a 'bore,' and to be 'only a colonial' would ap-

2

ply, it would seem, to a province as well as to a bishop. I have not the slightest desire to talk guidebook, or even to institute odious comparisons, by dwelling on the strength and solidity, the cleanliness and comeliness, the regard for authority, the cheery but self-respecting and self-exacting tone which prevails in society; the hearty, pleasant, obliging manners of the people one sees at every moment in this far-off city (Montreal) of a hundred thousand souls, with its cathedrals, its palaces, its schools, its convents, its hospitals, its wharves, its warehouses, its marvelous tubular bridge, its constantly growing commerce, its hourly-increasing prosperity, its population of vivacious and chivalrous Frenchmen, who, somehow, do not hate their English and Scottish fellow-subjects, but live in peace and amity with them, and who are assuredly not in love with the Yankees. But it really does make a travelling Englishman 'kinder mad,' as they would say south of the forty-fifth parallel, when he has just quitted a city which, in industry, in energy, and in public spirit, is certainly second to none on the European continent, and which, in the cleanliness of its streets, the beauty of its public buildings, and the tone of its society, surpasses many of them—to know that a majority of his countrymen are under the impression that the Canadian towns are mere assemblages of log-huts, inhabited by half-savage backwoodsmen in blanket coats and moccassins, and that a few mischievous or demented persons are advocating the policy of giving up the Canadas altogether. Happily there is a gentleman in Pall-Mall who has been to Canada—who has seen Quebec, and Toronto, and Montreal. The name of that gentleman—the first in our realm—is Albert-Edward, Prince of Wales; and he knows what Canada is like, and of what great things it is capable."—So says the late editor of the *Cornhill Magazine*.

Champlain

NO name in Canadian history is surrounded with more lustre and deeper veneration than that of the founder of Quebec. As a statesman,—a discoverer,—a brave and successful commander, Samuel de Champlain's fame will be handed down from generation to generation. The late Dr. J. C. Fisher thus describes* his career:—

"On the 13th April, 1608, Pontgravé having been already despatched in a vessel to Tadoussac, Champlain, who had obtained the commission of Lieutenant, under De Monts, in New France, set sail from Honfleur, with the express intention of establishing a settlement on the St. Lawrence, above Tadoussac, at which post he arrived on the 3rd June. After a short stay, he ascended the river, carefully examining the shores; and on the 3rd July, reached the spot called Stadacona, now Quebec, rendered so remarkable by the first visit of Jacques Cartier in 1535. Champlain, whose ambition was not limited to mere commercial speculations—actuated by the patriotism and pride of a French gentleman, a faithful servant to his king, and warmly attached to the glory of his country,—thought more of founding a future empire than of a trading post for peltry. After examining the position, he selected the elevated promontory which commands the narrowest part of the great river of Canada, the extensive basin between it and the Isle of Orleans, together with the mouth of the little River St. Charles, as a fit and proper seat for the future metropolis of New France, and there laid the foundation of Quebec, on the 3rd July, 1608. His judgment has never been called in question, or his taste disputed in this selection. Its commanding position, natural strength, and aptitude both for purposes of offence and defence, are evident on the first view—while the unequalled beauty, grandeur, and sublimity of the scene mark it as worthy of extended empire:—

* In *Hawkins's Picture of Quebec.*

——— hoc regnum gentibus esse,
Si quà fata sinant, jam tum tenditque fovetque.

This noble site, prove fate hereafter kind,
The seat of lasting empire he designed.

"Here, on the point immediately overlooking the basin and on the site reaching from the grand battery to the Castle of St. Lewis, he commenced his labors by felling the walnut trees, and rooting up the wild vines with which the virgin soil was covered, in order to make room for the projected settlement. Huts were erected, some lands were cleared, and a few gardens made, for the purpose of proving the soil, which was found to be excellent. The first permanent building which the French erected was a store-house, or magazine for the security of their provisions. Champlain thus describes his first proceedings, which will be read with interest by the inhabitant at the present day :—'I reached Quebec on the 3rd July, where I sought out a proper place for our dwelling; but I could not find one better adapted for it than the promontory, or Point of Quebec, which was covered with walnuts and vines. As soon as possible, I set to work some of our laborers to level them, in order to build our habitation. ...... The first thing which we did was to build a store-house to secure our provisions under shelter, which was quickly done. ...... Near this spot is an agreeable river, where formerly wintered Jacques Cartier.' A temporary barrack for the men and officers was subsequently erected on the higher part of the position, near where the Castle of St. Lewis now stands. It must be remembered that at the time of the landing of Champlain, the tide usually rose nearly to the base of the rock, or *côte* ;* and that the first buildings were of necessity on the high grounds. Afterwards, and during the time of Champlain, a space was redeemed from the water, and elevated above the inundation of the tide, on which store-houses, and also a battery level with the water were erected, having a passage of steps between it and the fort, on the site of the present Mountain street, which was first used in 1623.

---

* Old residents still remember a red bridge which formerly existed at the end of St. Peter Street, opposite the Montreal Bank; and vessels were moored, some sixty years ago, to the buildings which stood on the site on which the Quebec Bank was erected last year.—(J. M. L.)

"Champlain had now, humble as they were, successfully laid the foundations of the first French Colony in North America. One hundred and sixteen years had elapsed since the discovery of the New World; and it was only in the year previous that, on the whole continent, north of Mexico, a European nation had at length succeeded in establishing any settlement. This was effected by the English under Captain Christopher Newport, who laid the foundation of a settlement at Jamestown, Virginia, on the 13th May, 1607, two hundred and fifty-seven years ago. The chivalrous character and adventures of Captain John Smith, and the interesting story of Pocahontas, have conferred a peculiar interest on the early history of this colony. It may be noted, as a singular contrast with the growth of the English colonies afterwards, that at the death of Queen Elizabeth, in 1603, there was not a European family in all the northern continent: at present the great State of Virginia alone, —of which the germ was a colony of one hundred souls, of whom fifty died during the first year; and which, as described by Chalmers in his political annals, 'feeble in numbers and enterprise, was planted in discord, and grew up in misery,'—numbers upon its soil no less than twelve hundred thousand inhabitants! The disappearance and eradication of the Indians has been still more extraordinary. Of the countless tribes who filled up the back country of Virginia at the time of the first settlement by the English, it appears by the census of 1830 that there existed only *forty-seven* Indians in the whole state!

"The summer was passed in finishing the necessary buildings; when clearances were made around them, and the ground prepared for sowing wheat and rye, which was accomplished by the 15th October. Hoar frosts commenced about the 3rd October, and on the 15th the trees shed their leafy honors. The first snow fell on the 18th November, but disappeared after two days. Champlain describes the snow as lying on the ground from December until near the end of April, so that the favorite theory of those who maintain the progressive improvement of the climate, as lands are cleared in new countries, is not borne out by the evidence of Canada. From several facts it might be shown that the wintry climate was not more inhospitable in the early days of Jacques Cartier and Champlain than in the present. The winter of 1611 and 1612 was extremely mild, and the river was not frozen before Quebec.

"From the silence of Champlain respecting the hamlet or town of Stadacona, which had been visited by Cartier so often in 1535, it would seem probable that it had dwindled, owing to the migratory predilections of the Indians, to a place of no moment. He certainly mentions a number of Indians who were "*cabannés*," or hutted near his settlement; but the ancient name of Stadacona never once occurs. It will be recollected that Cartier spoke of the houses of the natives as being amply provided with food against the winter. From the evidence of Champlain, the Indians of the vicinity appear to have degenerated in this particular. They are represented as having experienced the greatest extremities for want of food during the winter of 1608; and some who came over from the Pointe Lévi side of the river were in such a state of wretchedness as hardly to be able to drag their limbs to the upper part of the settlement. They were relieved and treated with the greatest kindness by the French.

"The ice having disappeared in the spring of 1609, so early as the 8th April, Champlain was enabled to leave the infant settlement of Quebec and to ascend the river on the 18th, for the purpose of further exploring the country. He resolved to penetrate into the interior; and his mingled emotions of delight and astonishment may easily be conceived, as he proceeded to examine the magnificent country of which he had taken possession. During this summer, he discovered the beautiful lake which now bears his name; and having returned to Quebec in the autumn, he sailed for France in September, 1609, leaving the settlement under the command of Captain Pierre Chauvin, an officer of great experience.

"Champlain was well received on his arrival by Henry IV., who invited him to an interview at Fontainebleau, and received from him an exact account of all that had been done in New France, with a statement of the advantages to be expected from the new establishment on the St. Lawrence,—at which recital the king expressed great satisfaction. De Monts, however, by whose means the settlement of Quebec had been formed, could not obtain a renewal of his privilege, which had now expired: notwithstanding which, he was once more enabled by the assistance of the company of merchants, to fit out two vessels in the spring of 1610, under the command of Champlain and Pontgravé. The latter was instructed to continue the fur trade with the Indians at Tadoussac, while Champlain, having with him a reinforcement of artisans and laborers, was to proceed to Quebec. He sailed from Honfleur on the 8th April, and arrived at Tadoussac in the singularly short passage of eighteen days. Thence ascending the river to Quebec, he had the gratification of finding the colonists in good health, and content with their situation. The crops of the previous year had been abundant, and everything was in as good order and condition as could be expected.

"To pursue further the proceedings of Champlain, and his discoveries in the interior, does not properly fall within the scope of this work, but belongs to the History of Canada. It may be well, however, to observe in this place, that owing to the political error committed by this otherwise sagacious chief, when he taught the natives the use of fire-arms, and joined them in an offensive league against the Iroquois, who were at first supported by the Dutch, and afterwards by the English colonists of New York, Champlain not only laid the foundation of that predatory and cruel warfare which subsisted with little intermission between his countrymen and the five nations, notwithstanding the conciliatory efforts of the Jesuits; but he may with reason be considered as the remote, although innocent, cause of the animosity afterwards engendered between the Provincialists and the French, owing to the excesses of the Indians in the interest of the latter, and of a war which terminated only with the subjugation of Canada by the British arms in 1760.

"Champlain, who made frequent voyages to France in order to promote the interests of the rising colony, and who identified himself with its prospects by bringing out his family to reside with him, was wisely continued, with occasional intermission, in the chief command until his death. In 1620, he erected a temporary fort on the site of the Castle of St. Lewis, which he rebuilt of stone, and fortified in 1624. At that time, however, the colony numbered only fifty souls. It appears from the Parish Register then commenced to be regularly kept, that the first child born* in Quebec of French parents was christened Eustache on the 24th October, 1621, being the son of Abraham Martin† and Margaret

* The first marriage in the colony took place between Guillaume Couillard and Guillemette Hebert. Two months previously the first marriage in the New England States was celebrated on the 12th May, 1621, at Plymouth, between Ed. Winslow and Susannah White. Couillard's house, the first built in the city, appears to have stood on the Battery, close to the old small-pox cemetery.—(J. M. L.)

† Abraham Martin dit L'Ecossais, *alias*, *Maitre Abraham*, King's pilot, after whom the Plains were called.

L'Anglois. In 1629, Champlain had to undergo the mortification of surrendering Quebec to an armament from England under Louis Kertk, who, on the 22nd July, planted the English standard on the walls, just one hundred and thirty years before the battle of the Plains of Abraham. Champlain was taken as a prisoner of war to England, whence he returned to France, and subsequently to Canada in 1633. The inhabitants were well treated by Kertk, who was himself a French Huguenot refugee, and none of the settlers left the country; which was restored to France by the treaty of St. Germain-en-Laye, on the 29th March, 1632.

"Champlain, who combined with superior talents and singular prudence a temperament of high courage and resolution, after a residence in New France of nearly thirty years, died full of honors, and rich in public respect and esteem, in the bosom of the settlement of which he was the founder, about the end of December, 1635. His memoirs are written in a pleasing and unaffected style, and show that he was deficient in none of the qualities which are so essential in the leader of difficult enterprises, and the discoverer of new countries. His obsequies were performed with all the pomp which the colony could command; and his remains were followed to the grave with real sorrow by the clergy, officers, and the civil and military inhabitants, Father Le Jeune pronouncing an appropriate funeral oration.

"At the death of Champlain, the French possessions in Canada consisted of the fort of Quebec, surrounded by some inconsiderable houses, and barracks for the soldiers, a few huts on the Island of Montreal, as many at Tadoussac, and at other places on the St. Lawrence, used as trading and fishing posts. A settlement had just been commenced at Three Rivers; and in these trifling acquisitions were comprised all that resulted from the discoveries of Verazzano, Jacques Cartier, Roberval, Champlain, and the vast outlay of De la Roche, De Monts, and other French adventurers. At the time we are writing, (1834,) the Colony or Province of Lower Canada contains nearly six hundred thousand inhabitants—Quebec posseses over three thousand houses, and a population of near thirty thousand souls (now some sixty-five thousand souls). That of Montreal is as numerous; and Three Rivers is progressively improving in wealth and resources. The social and commercial intercourse between these flourishing towns is maintained by means of magnificent steamboats of unrivalled safety and expedition — those floating palaces in which a thousand human beings are often transported from city to city. The trade of the province, instead of being limited to a few small craft engaged in the fisheries or the fur trade, employs more than a thousand vessels of burthen, enriching the province with an annual immigration of from twenty-five to fifty thousand souls, the aggregate of whose capital is immense; and conveying in return the native produce of the Canadas to almost every part of the empire. Pitt must have been prophetically inspired when he gave to the great seal of Canada its beautiful legend, for nothing could be more applicable to the double advantages of one extensive branch of its commerce—the Timber trade—

—— AB IPSO
DUCIT OPES ANIMUMQUE FERRO—
Gains power and riches by the self-same steel.

Instead of a few huts on the river's side, the country on each bank of the St. Lawrence has been long divided into rich seigniories, and the fertile soil cultivated by an industrious, a virtuous and contented population—by a people to whom foreign dominion, instead of deteriorating their former condition, has been the herald of all that can render life precious. It has given to them the unrestricted enjoyment of their rights, language and religion—protection against external foes, together with the full security of their domestic usages, customs, laws and property—perfect exemption from the burthens of taxation, and a state of rational happiness and political freedom unequalled on the face of the globe. The following beautiful lines from Virgil will strike every one, as singularly applicable to the condition of the Canadian farmer, or *habitant:*

"O fortunatos nimium, sua si bona nôrint,
Agricolas! quibus ipsa, procul discordibus armis,
Fundit humo facilem victum justissima tellus."

Let us now see the same subject treated by one of our most

eloquent statesmen. The speech* is in reply to the following sentiment:—

"*The memory of Sieur de Champlain*, the fearless navigator and accomplished statesman; the first to explore and designate these shores; whose plans of empire, more vast and sagacious than any of his time, failed of success, only through the short-sightedness of his sovereign, in allowing the Atlantic shores of New England to fall into the hands of his rivals, thereby changing the history of the New World."

The Hon. Thos. D'Arcy McGee, President of the Executive Council of Canada, addressed the assemblage in response to this sentiment. He said: I beg to assure you, Mr. President, and the gentlemen of the Maine Historical Society, who have done me the honor to invite me here, that I feel it a very great privilege to be a spectator and a participant in the instructive, retributive ceremonial of this day. This peninsula of Sabino must become, if it is not already, classic ground, and this 29th of August, the true era of the establishment of our language and race on this continent, one of the chief *fasti* of the English speaking people of North America. It is, on general grounds, an occasion hardly less interesting to the colonies still English, than to the citizens of Maine, and, therefore I beg to repeat in your presence, the gratification I feel in being allowed to join in the first of what I trust will prove but the first, of an interminable series of such celebrations. I would be very insensible, sir, to the character in which I have been so cordially presented to this assembly, if I did not personally acknowledge it; and I should be, I conceive, unworthy of the position I happen to occupy as a member of the Canadian Government, if I did not feel more the honor you have paid to Canada, in the remembrance you have made of her first Governor and Captain General, the Sieur de Champlain. That celebrated person was in truth, not only in point of time, but in the comprehension of his views, the audacity of his projects, and the celebrity of his individual career, the first statesman of Canada; and no one pretending to the character of a Canadian statesman could feel otherwise than honored and gratified when Champlain's name is invoked, publicly or

* This report of the Hon. Mr. McGee's speech at the Fort Popham (State of Maine) celebration, in 1862, we copy from the Portland *Advertiser*.

privately in his presence. We have no fear that the reputation of our great founder will not stand the severest test of historical research; we have no fear that his true greatness will dwindle by comparison with the rest of the Atlantic leaders—the chiefs of the renowned sea—chivalry, of whom we have already heard such eloquent mention. We Canadians ardently desire that he should be better known—be well known—and, perhaps, you, Mr. President, will permit me to indicate some of the events in the career, to point out some of the traits in the character, which hallow for us, forever, the name and memory of the Sieur de Champlain.

"What we esteem most of all other features in the life of our founder, is that chief virtue of all eminent men—his indomitable fortitude; and next to that we revere the amazing versatility and resources of the man. Originally a naval officer, he had voyaged to the West Indies and to Mexico, and had written a memoir, lately discovered at Dieppe, and edited both in France and England, advocating among other things the artificial connexion of the Atlantic and Pacific oceans. From the quarter-deck we trace him to the counting rooms of the merchants of Rouen and Saint Malo, who first entrusted him, in 1603, with the command of a commercial enterprise of which Canada was the field. From the service of the merchants of Rouen, Dieppe and Saint Malo, we trace him to the service of his sovereign—Henry IV. For several successive years we find his flag glancing at all points along this rock-bound coast on which we are now assembled, from Port Royal to Massachusetts Bay. Whenever we do not find it here, we may be certain it has advanced into the interior, that it is unfurled at Quebec, at Montreal, or towards the sources of the Hudson and the Mohawk. We will find that this versatile sailor has become in time a founder of cities, a negotiator of treaties with barbarous tribes, an author, a discoverer. As a discoverer, he was the first European to ascend the Richelieu, which he named after the patron of his latter years—the all-powerful Cardinal. He was the first to traverse that beautiful lake, now altogether your own, which makes his name so familiar to Americans; he was the first to ascend our great central river, the Ottawa, as far north as Nippissing, and he was the first to discover what he very justly calls "the fresh water sea" of lake Ontario. His place as an American discoverer is, therefore, amongst the first;

while his claims as a colonizer rest on the firm foundation of Montreal and Quebec, and his project—extraordinary for the age—of uniting the Atlantic with the Pacific by artificial channels of communication. As a legislator, we have not yet recovered, if we ever shall, the ordinances he is known to have promulgated; but as an author we have his narrative of transactions in New France, his voyage to Mexico, his treatise on navigation, and some other papers. As a diplomatist, we have the Franco-Indian alliances, which he founded, and which lasted a hundred and fifty years on this continent, and which exercised so powerful an influence, not only on American but on European affairs. To him also it was mainly owing that Canada, Acadia, and Cape Breton were reclaimed by, and restored to France, under the treaty of Saint German-en-Laye, in 1632. As to the moral qualities, our founder was brave almost to rashness. He would cast himself with a single European follower in the midst of savage enemies, and more than once his life was endangered by the excesses of his confidence and his courage. He was eminently social in his habits—as witness his order of *le bon temps*—in which every man of his associates was for one day host to his comrades, and commanded in turn in those agreeable encounters of which we have just had a slight skirmish here. He was sanguine as became an adventurer, and self-denying as became a hero. He served under De Monts, who for a time succeeded to his honors and office, as cheerfully as he had ever acted for himself, and in the end he made a friend of his rival. He encountered, as Columbus and many others had done, mutiny and assassination in his own disaffected followers, but he triumphed over the bad passions of men as completely as he triumphed over the ocean and the wilderness.

"He touched the extremes of human experience among diverse characters and nations. At one time he sketched plans of civilized aggrandisement for Henry IV, and Richelieu; at another he planned schemes of wild warfare with Huron chiefs and Algonquin braves. He united, in a most rare degree, the faculties of action and reflection, and like all highly reflective minds, his thoughts, long cherished in secret, ran often into the mould of maxims, and some of them would now form the fittest possible inscription to engrave upon his monument.

"When the merchants of Quebec grumbled at the cost of fortifying that place, he said :—'It is best not to obey the passions of men; they are but for a season; it is our duty to regard the future.' With all his love of good fellowship and society, he was, what seems to some inconsistent with it, sincerely and enthusiastically religious; among his maxims are these two—that 'the salvation of one soul is of more value than the conquest of an empire,' and, that 'kings ought not to think of extending their authority over idolatrous nations, except for the purpose of subjecting them to Jesus Christ.'

"Such, Mr. President, are, in brief, the attributes of the man you have chosen to honor, and I leave it for this company to say, whether in all that constitutes true greatness the first Governor and Captain General of Canada need fear comparison with any of the illustrious brotherhood who projected and founded our North American States. Count over all their honored names; enumerate their chief actions; let each community assign to its own his meed of eloquent and reverent remembrance; but among them from the south to the north, there will be no secondary place assigned to the Sieur de Champlain.

"Mr. President, your Excellency has added to the sentiment in honor of Champlain, an allusion and an inference as to the different results of the French and Enghish Colonial policy, on which you wil probably expect me to offer an observation or two before resuming my seat. Champlain's project originally was, no doubt, to make this Atlantic coast the basis of French power in the New World. His government claimed the continent down to the 40th parallel, which as you know intersects Pennsylvania, Ohio and Illinois, while the English claimed up to the 45th, which intersects Nova Scotia and Canada.

"Within these five degrees of latitude the pretentions of France were long zealously maintained in diplomacy, but were never practically as serted, except in the 44th and 45th, by colonization. I am not prepared to dispute the inference that the practical abandonment, by France, of the coast discoveries of her early navigators, south of 45, may have changed, as you say, 'the destiny of the New World.' It may be so; it may be, also, that we have not reached the point of time in which to speak positively as to the permanent result; for Divine Providence moves in His orbit by long and insensible curves, of which even the clearest-sighted men can discern, in their time, but a very limited section. But we know, as of the past, that the French power, in the reign of Louis XIII. and XIV., was practically based on the St. Lawrence, with a southern aspect, rather than on the Atlantic with a western aspect. All the consequences of that great change of plan and policy, I am not prepared here so much as to allude to, for that would carry me where I have no wish to go—into international issues, not yet exhausted.

"I may be permitted, however, to question that French influence, as developed in its Roman Catholic religion, its Roman law and its historical fascinations, was ever really circumscribed to Canada, or was really extinguished, as has been usually assumed, by the fall of Quebec. It is amazing to find in the colonial records of the period between the death of Champlain and the death of Montcalm, a century and a quarter, how important a part that handful of secluded French colonists played in North American affairs. In 1629, Champlain could have carried off all his colonists in 'a single ship;' more than a hundred years later, they were estimated at some 65,000 souls; in the Seven Years' War they were, according to Mr. Bancroft, but as 'one to fourteen' of the English colonists. The part played by the Canadians in war, under the French kings, was out of all proportion to their numbers; it was a glorious but prodigal part; it left their country exposed to periodical scarcity, without wealth, without commerce, without political liberty. They were ruled by a policy strictly martial to the very last, and though Richelieu, Colbert, de la Gallissionere, and other supreme minds, saw in their 'New France' great commercial capabilities, the prevailing policy, especially under Louis XIV. and XV., was to make and keep Canada a mere military colony. It is instructive to find a man of such high intelligence as Montcalm justifying that policy in his despatches to the President de Mole on the very eve of the surrender of Quebec. The Canadians, in his opinion, ought not to be allowed to manufacture, lest they should become unmanageable, like the English colonists, but, on the contrary, they should be kept to martial exercises, that they might subserve the interests of France in her transatlantic wars with England. Such was the policy which fell at Quebec with its last French Governor and Captain General, and it is a policy, I need hardly say, which no intelligent Canadian now looks back to with any other feelings than those of regret and disapprobation. A hundred years have elapsed since the international contest to which you refer was consummated at Quebec, and Canada to-day, under the mild and equitable sway of her fourth English sovereign, has to point to trophies of peaceful progress, not less glorious, and far more serviceable, than any achieved by our predecessors who were subject to the French kings. The French speaking population, which, from 1608 till 1760, had not reached 100,000, from 1760 to 1860 has multiplied to 880,000. Upper Canada, a wilderness as Champlain found it and Montcalm left it, has a population exceeding Massachusetts, of as fine a yeomanry as ever stirred the soil of the earth. If French Canada points with justifiable pride to its ancient battle-fields, English Canada points with no less pleasure to its newly reclaimed harvest-fields; if the old *regime* is typified by the strong walls of Quebec, the monument of the new era may be seen in the great bridge which spans the St. Lawrence within view of the city I represent, and whose four and twenty piers may each stand for one hour sacred to every traveller who steams through its sounding tube on his way from the Atlantic to the Far West.

"In conclusion, Mr. President, allow me again to assure you that I have listened with great pleasure to the speeches of this day—especially to the address of my old and long-esteemed friend (Hon. Mr. Poor). I trust the sentiments uttered here, at the mouth of the Kennebec, in Maine, will go home to England, and show our English relatives that the American people, unmoved by any selfish motive, are capable of doing full and entire justice to the best qualities of the English character. I am sure nothing was further from your minds than to turn this historical commemoration to any political account—and certainly I could not have done myself the pleasure of being here, if I had imagined any such intention —but after all the angry taunts which have been lately exchanged between England and America, I cannot but think this solemn acknowledgment of national affiliation, made on so memorable a spot as Fort Popham, and made in so cordial a spirit, must have a healing and a happy effect. We have been sitting under your authority, Mr. President, in the High Court of Posterity—we have summoned our ancestors from their ancient graves—we have dealt out praise and blame among them—I trust without violence to truth or injustice to the dead: for the dead have their rights as the living have: injustice to them is one of the worst forms of all injustice—and undue praise to the underserving is the worst injustice to the virtuous and meritorious actors in the great events of former ages.

" When we leave this place, we shall descend from the meditative world of the Past to mingle in the active world of the Present, where each man must bear his part and defend his post. Let me say for myself, Mr. President, and I think I may add I speak in this respect the general settled sentiment of my countrymen of Canada, when I say that in the extraordinary circumstances which have arisen for you, and for us also, in North America, there is no other feeling in Canada than a feeling of deep and sincere sympathy and friendliness towards the United States. As men loyal to our own institutions, we honor loyalty, everywhere; as freemen we are interested in all free States; as neighbors we are especially interested in your peace, prosperity and welfare. We are all anxious to exchange everything with you except injustice and misrepresentation; that is a species of commerce which—even when followed by the fourth estate (pointing to the reporters at his right)—I trust we will alike discourage, even to the verge of prohibition. Not only as a Canadian, but as one who was originally an emigrant to these shores as an Irishman, with so many of my original countrymen resident among you, I shall never cease to pray that this kindered people may always find in the future, as they always have found in the past, brave men to lead them in battle, wise men to guide them in council, and eloquent men like my honorable friend yonder (Hon. John A. Poor) to celebrate their exploits and their wisdom from generation to generation."

A "Green-back" of the last Century.

"A LITERARY gentleman of this city, well known for his antiquarian researches in connection with the early history of Canada, showed us,* yesterday, a slip of once negotiable 'paper,' which may not inaptly be termed a 'shinplaster' of the last century. It was one of the Intendant Bigot's famous bills on Paris, which he drew so liberally when the fate of the colony of New France was imminent, and the approaching fall of French power in America gave to the avaricious a capital chance of making money while a state of war and confusion lasted—an opportunity which, if history speaks true, they did not neglect. The bill is in an excellent state of preservation, and is printed on a quarter-sheet of rough foolscap." On next page appears a *fac simile* of it.

This was a Treasury note when a Bourbon reigned in France, and the North American colonies were still faithful to King George. It was worth fully as much in 1764 as Mr. Chase's "kites" are worth in 1864.

The following words appear on the back of the note:—

Payé à l'ordre de Mons. Perrault valeur reçûe comptant à Québec, le 7e septembre 1763.

LOFFICIALE.

Payé à l'ordre de Monsieur D. Vialars valeur accompte à Québec, le 20e septembre 1763.

PERRAULT.

---

* *Quebec Morning Chronicle.*

A COMPTE DES DÉPENSES GÉNÉRALLES.

Troisième. *A Québec, le 7e Octobre* 1758.

POUR 774 lvs.

EXERCICE 1758.

No. 17.

MONSIEUR, au quatre juillet mil sept cent soixante-un, il vous plaira payer par cette troisième de Change, ma première ou seconde ne l'étant, à l'ordre de M. Lofficiale, le somme de sept cent soixante-quatorze livres valeur reçûe en acquits. De laquelle somme je vous rendrai compte sur les dépenses de la Marine de cette Colonie. Je suis,

Monsieur,

Vu par nous Intendant de la nouvelle France.

BIGOT.

Votre très-humble & très-obeissant serviteur,

IMBERT.

A MONSIEUR
Monsieur PERICHON,
Trésorier général des Colonies,
Rue Neuve St. Eustache,
A PARIS.

"KITE-FLYING" ONE HUNDRED YEARS AGO.

Under the above caption "L" adds the following interesting note (says the same paper), *apropos* of the Intendant Bigot's "shinplater":—

"In order to complete, for the benefit of the curious, the particulars respecting Bigot's bill of exchange, mentioned in your last issue, it may be as well to state that this bill and several others were negotiated at fifty per cent. discount by London brokers, about the year 1764. 'Daniel Vialars,' to whom the present bill was endorsed, appears to have been an extensive London merchant. With the bill there was a long and ably-written letter, in which he proposes a kind of business partnership to Mons. Perrault, of Quebec. Mr. Perrault was in those days a very extensive Lower Town merchant; his business store seems to have occupied the spot on which now stands, in St. Peter-street, Mr. Daniel McGie's and the Express office. Amongst other strange pieces of information contained in the letter referred to, is a request to Mr. Perrault to call on Mr. Zachary Thompson, 'Capitaine du Port à Québec,' to procure a certificate of the tonnage of the ship *La Marie*, Capt. Cornillard—'qui fut fretté par le Général Amherst pour transporter en France le Chevalier de Levis et sa suite, après la capitulation de Montréal.' This is the hero of the battle of St. Foy. Daniel Vialars' letter covers eight pages. It is written in elegant French. He begins by expressing the hope that the fact of his being a Protestant won't interfere in the mercantile connection likely to ensue between him and Mr. Perrault, as 'la probité se trouve dans toutes sortes de religions.' On the 12th February, 1763, Mr. Vialars writes to say that he trusts peace will soon be proclaimed between England and France, and that the final treaty respecting Canada was deferred merely to afford the English time to withdraw their funds from Martinique, Guadeloupe, and Havana. 'According to private advices,' says he, 'from Holland, the preliminaries between the Queen of Hungary, the King of Prussia and the Elector of Saxe, are signed; if so, we shall soon have a general peace.'

"This odd document was found many years ago, with several others, in the garret of the Lower Town house which Mr. Perrault had occupied A number were used by a merciless old cook to singe chickens. This fact reminds one of some manuscripts of priceless value for the history of Canada, discovered at Quebec in the wood-box of Mr. Ryland's office, some years back. Unfortunately a portion had already been consigned to the flames."

Ex-Councillor Estebe on Colonial Matters,

24TH FEBRUARY, 1760.

THE reader has just seen a *fac simile* of a Canadian "greenback" of the last century. The kindness of a friend—David A. Ross, Esquire—enables me to submit another document of this period. It is a letter from Estebe, a leading man in the last days of French rule in the colony.

Monsieur Estebe was a member of the Superior Council, at Quebec, one of the advisers of the notorious Bigot, as such condemned, justly or unjustly, three years after the date of this letter, to restore to the King of France some 300,000 livres. This communication, recently discovered, and which has never yet been published, is also addressed to Monsieur Perrault, l'ainé, an eminent Lower Town merchant of that day. It is important as throwing additional light on an eventful period of the history of Canada; having been written four months after the battle of the Plains of Abraham, two months before that of Ste. Foy, and at a time when war was still raging in the colony. The English held the territory enclosed in the walls of Quebec and some forts, but Montreal and the rest of Canada, defended by a celebrated commander and by a numerous army, still belonged to France; and after the brilliant victory of Ste. Foy in April following, as Captain John Knox says, "the fate of Quebec depended on whether it were English or French frigates which entered the harbor first"—defeat, famine and disease (scurvy) had so thinned the ranks of General Murray's brave legions. This old document, indited by an educated gentleman, will also be read with interest, as furnishing a vivid picture of the extreme misery at that time existing in France; still this state of things was doomed to endure some twenty-nine years longer before culminating in the horrors of the French Revolution of '89. Canada had ceased to be prized by France as far back as 1735; disappointment at not finding gold mines being one of the chief causes: the auriferous Chaudière region and its fabulous wealth were not talked of in those days. The eyes of the French were then turned towards Louisiana, whose fate was decided a few years after the surrender of Quebec. Louisiana was, in 1768, handed over to the tender mercies of the Spaniards, who, under General O'Reilly, inaugurated their rule with exploits which throw in the shade those of General Butler in the Crescent City, at the head of Federal soldiers. Twelve of the principal men in the colony, including the Attorney-General, Lafrenière, a French Canadian, were, without trial, seized and loaded with chains: six of them were shot. Compared with the rule of Spain in Louisiana, even the arbitrary measures of a Haldimand and a Craig, and the civil and religious persecutions of the old Family Compact in Canada, ought to have appeared to the old French colonists mildness itself.

[TRANSLATION.]

BORDEAUX, 24*th February*, 1760.

To Monsieur PERRAULT, Quebec:

SIR,—It was with heartfelt pleasure I received your favor of 7th Nov. last, since, in spite of your misfortunes, it apprized me of the fact that both you and your lady were well.

I feel grateful for the sympathy you express in our troubles, during our passage from Quebec to Bordeaux. I wish I could as easily forget the misfortunes of Canada as I do the annoyances we suffered on the voyage.

We learned, *viâ* England, by the end of Oct. last, the unfortunate fate of Quebec. You can imagine how we felt on hearing such dreadful news I could contain neither my tears nor my regrets, on learning the loss of a city and a country, to which I owe everything, and to which I am as sincerely attached as any of the natives. We flattered ourselves that the silence the English had kept during all last summer on their operations, was of good omen for us, and that they would be ignominiously compelled to raise the siege; we had even an indistinct knowledge of the repulse they had met with at Montmorency; we knew that our troops followed them closely wherever they attempted to land. We have erred like you in the hopes we cherished. What fatality, what calamities, and how many events unknown to us, have led to your downfall?

You do not yet know, my dear sir, of the extent of your misfortunes; you imagine that the loss of the remainder of the colony is close at hand; you are right. This cannot be otherwise, since the relief which is sent to you from France cannot prevent that. The small help which Canadians expected from the payment of some Treasury notes is taken away from them; none are paid since the 15th of October last. This, this is the overwhelming blow to all our hopes! The Treasury notes of the other colonies are generally in the same predicament: the King pays none, and the nation groans under taxation. No credit, no confidence anywhere. No commerce, nor shipments—a general bankruptcy in all the cities of France. The kingdom is in the greatest desolation possible—our armies have been beaten everywhere—our navy, no more exists—our ships have been either captured or burnt on the coasts, where the enemy has driven them ashore, Admiral de Conflans having been defeated on getting out of the harbor of Brest. In one word, we are in a state of misery and humiliation without precedent. The finances of the King are in fearful disorder. He has had to send his plate to the mint. The *seigneurs* have followed his example, and private individuals are compelled to sell their valuables, in order to live and to pay the onerous taxes which weigh on them. At the present moment, by royal order, an inventory is being taken of the silver in all the churches of the kingdom. No doubt, it will have to be sent to the mint, and payment will be made when that of the Treasury notes takes place, that is, *when it pleases God.* Such is a summary of what now occurs here. How I regret, my dear sir, the merry days I spent in Canada! I would like to be there still, if matters were as formerly. I could own a turn-out there, whereas I go on foot, like a dog, through the mud of Bordeaux, where I certainly do not live in the style I did in Quebec. Please God this iron age may soon end! We flattered ourselves this winter that peace would soon be proclaimed. It is much talked of, but I see no signs of it. It will, it is said, require another campaign to complete the ruin, and to postpone more and more the payment, of the Treasury notes.

What will be the ultimate fate of these bills, is very hard to say. It is unlikely any settlement of them will be made before peace is concluded. My opinion is, that nothing will be lost on the bills which are registered, but I cannot say the same of the exchange which is not registered, since payment has been stopped. The Government has refused to register any bills, even some which had been sent to me, and which were payable in 1758. I negotiated some registered ones, here and in Paris at 50 per cent. discount—non-registered ones are valueless—and you get few purchasers even for registered bills. Four richly laden vessels belonging to the West India Company (*Compagnie des Indes*) have arrived lately. This was very opportune, as the company was rather shaky. However, it never failed to pay the "Beaver" bills, and has even accepted those which had not yet fallen due. Our affairs on the coast of Coromandel are like the rest—in a bad way. Fears are entertained for Pondicherry. The English are arming a large expedition for Martinique. That island will have the same fate as Guadeloupe.

The succor sent out to you, if ever it reaches, of which I doubt, consists in six merchant ships, laden with 1,600 tons of provisions, some munitions of war, and 400 soldiers from Isle Royal. I believe this relief is sent to you, more through a sense of honor than from any desire (as none exists) to help you. Many flatter themselves you will retake Quebec this winter. I wish you may, but I do not believe you will. This would require to be undertaken by experienced and determined men, and even then such attempts fail. Remember me to your dear wife. Kiss my little friend (your boy) for me; I reserve him, when he comes to France, a gilt horse and a silver carriage. My wife and family beg to be remembered.

Yours, &c.,

(Signed) ESTEBE.

P.S.—Your brother is always at La Rochelle. Since I am at Bordeaux, out of 80 vessels which left South America, one only has arrived here. You can fancy how trade stagnates. A singular distrust exists everywhere. The Exchange of ——— and other good houses is refused. Those who want to remit to Paris have to get their specie carried.

6th March.

The hospital of Toulouse is just short of nine millions. Bankrupts everywhere, merchants and others.

Why Louis the Fourteenth

BOASTED THAT CANADA CONTAINED MORE OF HIS OLD NOBILITY THAN THE REST OF THE FRENCH COLONIES PUT TOGETHER.

OF the numerous colonial possessions of France and England, few have had the privilege in the same degree as Canada, of associating with the fortunes of the colony, the names of several of the leading spirits in both kingdoms. Amongst those who, under French dominion, were connected with New France, by titles, honors, civil or military, were several noble dukes, a Montmorency, a Cardinal Duke of Richelieu, a Vendome, a Prince of Condé, a Ventadour, a Lévis, a Daimville; proud Marquises such as DeFeuquières, De Menneville, De Tracy, DeVaudreuil, De Beauharnois, DuQuesne, DeMontcalm, DeVillerai, DeRepentigny; great sea captains such as the Count D'Estrée, DeBougainville, Vice-Admiral Bedout, De Voquelin, Count de la Galissonnière, the victor of Admiral Byng in the Mediterranean, Count de Tilly; engineer officers of great merit, such as the Delérys, one of whom fortified Quebec, whilst another was created Baron de l'Empire, under the first Napoleon, for his services in the Imperial armies, and Viscount by Louis XVIII. Several of these and others were born in the colony and *annoblis* in the mother country. When we find these historical names heading the galaxy of young noblemen, who alone, in the days of *privilege*, could claim as a right, commissions in the French regiments serving in Canada, we can understand why, as Charlevoix relates, the great monarch Louis XIV. boasted that Canada contained more of his old nobility than the rest of the French colonies put together.

This is not at all to be wondered at, considering the kind of colonists sent to Canada from France as soon as it became a Crown colony, that is, in 1663. "Measures were adopted," we are told, "to infuse a more liberal spirit into the colony, to raise the quality and character of the settlers, and to give a higher tone to society. The King took a most judicious method to accomplish this. He resolved to confer upon the Government a degree of comparative splendor, worthy of the great nation of which it was a dependency. In 1664, he sent out to Quebec the most brilliant emigration that had ever sailed from France for the New World. It consisted of a Viceroy, a Governor General, an Intendant, and other necessary officers of the civil government—the regiment of Carignan, comanded by Colonel de Salières, and officered by sixty or seventy French gentlemen, most of whom were connected with the *noblesse*. Many of these gentlemen settled in the province, and having obtained concessions of the waste lands, became the *noblesse* of the colony, and were the ancestors of the best French families of the present day. The beneficial manner in which this infusion of superior blood, education and accomplishments must have operated, as regards the social and domestic manners of the colonists, previously devoted to the humblest occupations of trade, may be easily imagined. Liberal tastes were encouraged—sentiments of honor and generosity pervaded the highest rank in society, the influence of which was speedily felt through every class of the inhabitants. The Marquis de Tracy, who had the commission of Viceroy, staid little more than a year in the province. He made a successful expedition against the Irequois, and returning to France, carried with him the affections of all the inhabitants. He maintained a state which had never before been seen in Canada, rightly judging that in a colony at so great a distance from the mother country, the royal authority should be maintained before the public eye in all its external dignity and observances. Besides the regiment of Carignan, he was allowed to maintain a body guard, wearing the same uniform as the *Garde Royale* of France. He always appeared on state occasions with these guards, twenty-four in number, who preceded him. Four pages immediately accompanied him, followed by six valets,—the whole surrounded by the officers of the Carignan regiment, and of the civil departments. M. De Courcelles, the Governor General, and M. De Talon, the Intendant, had each a splendid equipage. It is mentioned in an interesting French manuscript, from which we have taken much valuable information never before published, that as both these gentlemen were men of birth, education, handsome figure and accomplished manners, they gave a most favorable impression of the royal authority, then first personally represented in New France."* Nor do titled men seem to have been scarce in the colony since it has become a British dependency—the brightest jewel in Victoria's Crown. Without dwelling on the several instances in which British noblemen have been identified with the colony, either by marriage, residence, real estate, or otherwise; without describing the visits paid to Canada by members of the Royal family, peers of the realm and others—as early as the 14th August, 1787, the royal banner of England streamed from the quarter-deck of the *Pegasus* frigate, snugly moored in the port of Quebec, when the future sovereign of England (William IV.) was on a friendly visit to his august father's new subjects. The 10,000 U. E. Loyalists, who had crowded into Canada, insisted on this occasion on his leaving his name to Sorel, one of their strongholds.

The subject of the following notice—which we find in the Montreal *Gazette*—was known in the upper circles of society in this city. One would fancy that the Norman and the Saxon have become one on the banks of the St. Lawrence, as well as on those of the Thames. The Duke of Richmond was one of our best governors; the Chevalier de LaCorne, one of our greatest warriors:

"The parish church bells tolled yesterday in commemoration of the death of Miss Mary Ann Margaret Lennox, daughter of Major the Earl of Lennox, who died last Monday morning. Miss Lennox, by her father, was a granddaughter of the Duke of Lennox and Richmond, in the peerage of Great Britain, Duke of Aubigny in that of France, and Earl of March in that of the United Kingdom. By her mother she was a descendant of the LaCorne family, a race which is eminent in the early history of Canada for its services to the State, and as such was related to the DeBouchervilles, DeLanaudières, Duchesnays, and other ancient Canadian families. Her sister, Miss Charlotte Lennox, died about two months ago. The funeral services were held yesterday, when her remains were placed in the vaults of the church of Notre-Dame-de-Toutes-Grâces, at Coteau-St.-Luc."

CAPTAIN BEDOUT.

A correspondent, over the signature of "Query," writes us (*Quebec Morning Chronicle*) as follows:

"We read in McGee's History of Ireland, volume 2, page 691, that on

* *New Historical Picture of Quebec*

the 16th December, 1796, a French fleet, carrying a formidable army, under Hoche and Grouchy, sailed from Brest to invade Ireland. It was composed of 17 sail of the line, 13 frigates and 13 smaller ships, one of the largest, the *Indomptable*, carrying 80 guns, was commanded by a *Canadian* named Bedout. Who was this Capt. Bedout, whose merit and nautical science could procure him from the French Government (never too prone to recognize talent in colonists) such an exalted post as commander of a line-of-battle ship? Can no one tell?"

A correspondent, over the signature of "E. G.," sends the following reply to the query published in yesterday's issue:

"The Rear-Admiral Bedout mentioned in McGee's History of Ireland was born in Quebec, in 1751. His father was a seignior and a member of the *Conseil Supérieur*. The whole family removed to France at the time of the cession, in 1763, and Jacques, the subject of this notice, entered the French navy, where he distinguished himself on several occasions, and was promoted by Napoleon to the rank of Rear-Admiral, and afterwards decorated with the *Croix de la Légion d'Honneur*. He died in 1816. Our historians, Bibaud and Garneau, have recorded Bedout's name as well as those of other French celebrities whose early years had been passed on the borders of the St. Lawrence." He was one of the ancestors of the Panet family.

OBITUARY.

The parish of St. François de la Beauce, says the *Journal de Quebec*, was, on the 11th inst., the scene of a solemn and touching ceremony. Almost 3,500 persons, congregated from the different parishes of the county, and even from this city, thronged the choir, nave and galleries of the spacious and magnificent local church. This multitude had gathered together to pay the last tribute of respect to a man regretted by all who had the pleasure of his acquaintance, by all who had an opportunity of appreciating the generosity and benevolence of his heart.

Charles Joseph Chaussegros de Léry, Esq., one of the seigneurs of Rigaud-Vaudreuil and other places, eldest son of the Honorable Charles Etienne Chaussegros de Léry, member of the Executive Council, and of the late Marie Josephte Fraser, and nephew of the late Viscount de Léry, Lieutenant-General in the service of France, was born at Quebec on the 2nd September, 1800. Descended from one of the oldest families of the province, whose members, both under French rule and the present government, filled, with approbation, the most important offices of trust in the colony; allied to the best Canadian families, and by the mother's side, to one of the most illustrious houses of Scotland, Mr. de Léry nobly bore his honorable name. After having, with honor and success, devoted the first and greatest portion of his life to the service of his country, in the career followed by his father before him, he abandoned —now some fifteen years since—public life to devote himself exclusively to the advancement and colonization of his seigniory, Under his management, and that of an able and worthy friend, the respected curé of the parish, St. François, now noted for its gold mines, progressed rapidly and soon became the most important parish in the county. Mr. de Léry was frequently solicited to re-enter the arena of politics, but always persistently refused; he preferred to devote his leisure hours to the interests of his *censitaires*, who all respected him as a father, and often submitted their mutual petty disagreements to his arbitration. His wealth, social rank, knowledge, and above all, his urbanity, rendered the task to him an easy and an agreeable one, and all who came to consult him and lay before him their little differences, invariably returned home satisfied with his decisions.

COMTE DE DOUGLAS,

Born at Montreal in 1747; died at Paris in 1842. Louis Archambault, Comte de Douglas, it appears, had obtained rank in the peerage of France with that title. He had succeeded, in 1770, his uncle, Charles Joseph de Douglas, Comte et Seignieur de Montréal, in France, who, with one of his brothers, had accompanied Charles Edward in his chivalrous attempt to recover the throne of his ancestors, and was taken prisoner at the battle of Culloden. Thus the French Canadian Comte de Douglas, is said to have sprung from one of the most illustrious families in Europe; and it is stated that his maternal grandfather was governor of Montreal, when Canada was a French colony.†

---

† An Earl of Douglas was made *Duc de Touraine*, and a Duke of Hamilton became *Duc de Chatelherault* in France, about 1425. (*Les Ecossais en France*, par Francesque Michel.

U. E. Loyalists.

"OUTLINE OF A FEW CONSPICUOUS U. E. LOYALISTS, WHO FLED TO NOVA SCOTIA AND UPPER CANADA AFTER THE AMERICAN REVOLUTION (1783), WITH PERSONAL REMINISCENCES OF EARLY SETTLERS."—*Parliamentary Manuscripts collected by G. Coventry, Esq.*—(REVIEWED BY J. M. L.)

THE foregoing is a subject about which, in our opinion, the bulk of Lower Canadians, notwithstanding their knowledge of Canadian history, know very little; in fact, those who have the courage to be candid, will promptly admit that in their minds a haze of uncertainty has hovered for a long time as to the exact meaning of the word "U. E. Loyalists," and that they do not clearly understand what is meant by "Nova Scotia Knights." They can readily tell you how many trips Jacques Cartier or Champlain made to New France; of the thrashing General Levis gave General Murray on the Ste. Foy heights in 1760; of the harrowing tale of the shipwrecked French refugees on Cape Breton in 1761; of the arbitrary banishment of the Acadians: but be cautious how you parade before their eyes the mystic combination "U. E. Loyalists," else many will fancy you are attempting to enlist their sympathy in favor of some new Masonic order, mayhap an Orange lodge, or perchance some secret political organization possibly like the Knights of the Golden Circle, or the D. M. D.† With all due deference to their historical lore, I see no cogent reason why the 10,000 English refugees who, Mr. Coventry tells us, "were the founders of the present prosperity of Upper Canada," should be more ignored in the annals of this, our common country, than were the French refugees who returned to the parent state a century back. At their removal, honors were lavished on both classes by their respective sovereigns, and several of them have left their mark in history.

† Defenders of the Monroe Doctrine.

Before proceeding further in this inquiry, let us award our meed of praise to the enlightened statesmen who have been instrumental in rescuing from oblivion the memories of the brave and honorable men who, at the close of the American revolutionary struggle, made the western portion of Canada their home. To the late Hon. William Hamilton Merritt and to the Hon. James Morris, the descendants of these worthies owe a debt of gratitude for having procured the support and sanction of the legislature to the measures they devised in order to compile the important parliamentary papers and manuscripts now styled "The Simcoe Papers and Manuscripts relating to the U. E. Loyalists;" and if I should venture to say that what has been collected can only be considered as a first instalment, it is not with the view of disparaging the labours of Mr. Coventry, the gentleman employed by Parliament to transcribe these documents. I merely wish to record my opinion, that compared to the rich mines of historical facts and data procured at government expense in France, in the United States and elsewhere, relating chiefly to Lower Canada, the Coventry Manuscripts appear but the forerunners of a comprehensive compilation necessary for a full history of that progressive western portion of the Canadas. Any one viewing what material the *Archives de la Guerre*, the *Archives de la Marine*, the *Albany State Documents*, and the old census tables of France have furnished to Mr. Faribault, Mr. Garneau, Mr. Bibaud and others, for the history of Lower Canada, will confess that our portion of the country has been dealt with most liberally. It is not every day, be it remembered, that a Lower Canadian is warranted in stating that Lower Canada has in one respect had a larger portion of the loaves and fishes than its sister province!

To prevent disappointment, let us, at the onset state, for the benefit of the 20,000 descendants of the famous 10,000 "founders of western prosperity," that it is not in this short sketch, penned by a French Canadian in a leisure hour, that they are to look for the whole pedigree and domestic history of their worthy grandfathers.

Should the nephews of U. E. Loyalists be as kindly treated by the government of the day, *when Canada will be received as a Sovereign State, in the great Republic, some time about the year* 1964, as their fathers were by the house of Hanover in the last century, they will, indeed, be accounted a fortunate race.

Let us now hear Mr. Coventry, without adopting all his conclusions:

"Upper Canada may be said to have been founded by American Loyalists, who were driven from their country at the Revolutionary War. The whole country was a wilderness, as the French, who were the previous occupiers, had taken no pains to clear or colonize it.* 'Tis true that at Detroit, where they had a fort, they induced a few individuals to settle around, and also on the Canadian shore, the descendants of whom remain there to the present day. After the British flag triumphed, they remained unmolested, as well as those who chose to remain in the Lower Province.

"The great work, therefore, of subduing the forests and of bringing the rich tracts of land under cultivation, was left to the indomitable courage, energy, and perseverance of the settlers, protected and encouraged by the mother country.

"The principal object of the line of division of Canada, as established by Mr. Pitt's Act, was to place them, as a body, by themselves, and to allow them to be governed by laws more congenial than those which were deemed requisite for the French, on the St. Lawrence.

"This decision arose from the tenor of the Treaty of Capitulation at Montreal, which was on so liberal a scale that when finally ratified at Fontainebleau, the French [the Canadians, Mr. Coventry means] were to enjoy, unmolested, their own religion, their own laws, their civil rights, to retire when they pleased, and to dispose of their estates to British subjects.

"Of course they came under the general rules laid down by the British Government and Governor; nor were they entitled to grants of land, which were so freely given to Loyalists and soldiers who had so bravely fought under the British flag. They continued to pursue their old-fashioned way of living, and for many years gave no political trouble.

"Previous to Mr. Pitt's Act coming into operation in 1791, many large grants of land were made, but the names of the parties were not registered in the Crown Land Department, nor were the locations known, as it frequently happened that such grants were sold and not taken up until many

* It is only necessary to refer to the chronicles of the past to ascertain whether or not the French took pains to colonize New France.—*J. M. L.*

years afterwards. Consequently our information is very meagre relative to the progress of the colony whilst under military rule.

"There were no official surveys of lands until 1792, when about 20,000 acres were surveyed in York, Scarboro' and Cramahe. Old settlers, from the taking of Fort Niagara in 1759 to the above period, located where they pleased, with the grant of "Land Warrants," which held good in after years by proof of possession and clearance.

"Some of the old settlers in the Niagara district have told me that the property they now hold has not been registered to this day;—they hold possession by prescriptive right, having been on their farms for upwards of eighty years.

"As our enquiry is confined to Upper Canada, we need not enter upon the surveys of the Lower Province; suffice it to say, that after the Treaty of Fontainebleau, in 1763, the Crown was desirous to establish the boundary of the Roman Catholic grants. Consequently 5,000 acres were awarded to the Seminary Domain, and the outskirts of the City of Quebec parcelled out to the British settlers who remained with the government. Up to the year 1780, about 80,000 acres were surveyed by order of the British governors, part of which the government retained, and the remainder was given to the military. The rise and progress of a newly-settled country is at all times an interesting topic. Nothing affords so much entertaing information to young people as the adventures of Robinson Crusoe, the result of De Foe's fruitful imagination; and the pleasing picture of Paul and Virginia, by Bernardin de St. Pierre, in the Mauritius, will be handed down to succeeding generations; the result, however, of such utopean lives is of no practical use to families in the present organized state of society.

"Settlers in a Canadian wilderness had to bear the burthen and heat of the day; had to exist by the sweat of their brow; to undergo wonderful privations and to pass through realities which would scarcely be credited in a work of fiction. Still a century has passed and proved the truth of the assertions of Macaulay, that the British Colonies have become far mightier and wealthier than the realms which Cortez and Pizarro had added to the dominions of Charles the Fifth.

"The history of the country, therefore, during the last century, is eminently the history of physical, of moral and intellectual improvement.

"The history of the settlers; the progress of agriculture, of horticulture, of the useful and ornamental; the change in the habits and manners of the people; the exchange of the spinning wheel for imported finery; the daily luxury and comforts of the inhabitants, contrasted with the privations of their ancestors, will all form subjects of interesting moment in the results of our inquiries.

"The people having their daily duties to perform, with a constant succession of work from sunrise to sunset, were cut off from all intercourse with the world, and for months together never saw a white man's footstep around their dwellings. A solitary Indian occasionally crossed their grounds with whom they traded for skins and deer. They might almost literally be said to have existed in a state of nature—old associations were their thoughts and the reflection that they were laying the foundation of prosperity for their children. The Bible they carried with them formed their principal solace and consolation—and their endeavors were blessed. The superstition so characteristic of the aboriginies seemed to form no part of their existence. Their minds were constantly occupied with some useful work, and as the shades of evening drew around them they retired, and in such sound sleep that a monarch would have envied. At that period there was but one road through the country, a sort of military highway leading from Toronto to Montreal, and an Indian path leading to Penetanguishine, where a fort was erected and garrisoned by a few soldiers. Between these two points messages were sent backwards and forwards with unerring certainty by Indian guides, similar to David and Solomon's running footmen.

"There was no money except that which Government distributed for the pay of the troops

"Those who were fortunate enough to have located in the vicinity of an encampment, or a fort, were liberally paid for their produce, and the cash was speedily put away in an old stocking, or locked up for posterity to gloat the eye upon.

"Thieves were unknown, and crime of any description was a rare occurrence.

"The Government was as liberal as the most fastidious could desire. It gave them land, tools, materials for building, and the means of subsisting for two or three years, and to each of their children, as they be-

6

came of age, two hundred acres of land. Families at the present day speak with pride, pleasure and thankfulness of the liberality of the British Government in affording them assistance in the wilderness—they continued staunch and loyal to their sovereign, ever ready in any emergency to preserve untarnished the honor of the country. 'THANK GOD I AM A TRUE BRITON' was instilled into the mind from infancy. Intimately connected with the rise and progress of Upper Canada, there is an important class of settlers who demands our especial attention. I allude to the U. E. Loyalists.

"Those extraordinary men underwent the severest trials and privations for their determined loyalty to the House of Hanover.

"No one can have the slightest conception of the misery that civil war entails until after the perusal of Mr. Sabine's History; every refined cruelty of which the human mind is susceptible was practised on those upholders of the cause of a limited monarchy.

"Doubtless, retaliation was, in a measure, the order of the day; so that scenes were daily witnessed as harrowing to a philanthropist as during the reign of terror in France under Robespierre and Danton.

"The lives that were sacrificed during the seven years' struggle for independence can never be ascertained; so that, rather than prolong the war, and to spare the further effusion of blood, the Minister adopted the humane principle of completing a treaty that was by no means satisfactory to the greater portion of enlightened politicians.

"Those who are interested in the history of nations should, by all means, obtain Mr. Sabine's useful and interesting work; but as it is now scarce, I shall subjoin a few notices of extraordinary characters who figured in the revolutionary struggle, who afterwards took refuge in Canada and Nova Scotia, and who acted as pioneers in clearing the wilderness, and by perseverance and industry reared families whose descendants have since shone conspicuous in the annals of the country. As Upper Canada had few actual settlers previous to the termination of American hostilities, nor any accommodation for the reception of refugees, we have to trace the stream of loyalists who made their escape to the shores of New Brunswick and Nova Scotia, where they arrived in British ships by thousands, and afterwards branched out in various directions as they obtained grants of land in various sections of the colony.

"Some few came over by way of Niagara, under the auspices of Sir William Johnson, and afterwards under the administration of General Simcoe. Their history is extremely interesting, shewing the wonderful vicissitudes of human life, and may be held up as beacons to those grumblers of the present day, who have not the same manliness, fortitude and presence of mind to meet the casualities incidental to the changes that at times take place under every form of government.

"The loyalist officers at the close of the war retired on half-pay.

"This stipend they received during life, and they also received grants of land according to their rank.

"Many were appointed to responsible and lucrative civil offices, and some even administered the Government of the colony in which they resided: General Simcoe, for instance, who commanded the Queen's Rangers in the Revolutionary war. Nothing in the history of those extraordinary men is so remarkable as their longevity. Several lived to enjoy their pay for upwards of half a century, and so common among them were the ages of eighty and eighty-five, ninety and even ninety-five, that the saying became proverbial—'Loyalist half-pay officers never die.' So courteous and liberal was the British Government, that even after the death of those old officers, many widows and orphans were recipients of various sums, amounting to between £20,000 and £30,000 per annum, (aye and as much as £50,000.)

"We have previously remarked that those who are curious to know the fate of from 7,000 to 10,000 loyalists should consult Mr. Sabine's valuable work.

"In our selection we shall notice a few conspicuous families who fled from the States at a very early period of Upper Canadian history."

It is with those prefatory remarks that Mr. Coventry ushers in the bright galaxy of loyal men whose allegiance to the House of Hanover was so substantially rewarded, whose orphans and widows received as much as £50,000 per annum from the British Exchequer. Good olden time, Mr. Coventry! Happy age this was! Let us not, however, dwell on the sunny picture too long, lest it should call forth an invidious comparison between the treatment experienced by Governor Simcoe's and Sir William Johnston's friends, and that meted out to the successful reformers of abuses in 1838-9, in Eastern and Western Canada. They, too, were the sons of men who had stood up for Britain's flag in 1775 and 1812; but "let the past bury its dead." The U. E. Loyalists were brave, let us honor them; they sacrificed their comforts, their worldly means, to the shrine of consistency, and consistency is a jewel; let us cherish their memory!

But how shall we becomingly recount the odyssey of their sufferings in the wilds of Western Canada? How shall we depict their valor in war? Let Chrysler's Farm, let Lundy's Lane, let Queenston Heights, let the battle fields of 1812-13-14 unfold their honored records.

The Coventry manuscripts contain sketches of the following U. E Loyalists and early settlers of Upper Canada:

The Smiths, Gambles, Andersons, Jones, Lymans, Robinsons, Baldwins, Sir James McCaulay, Hon. John Wilson, John Strachan, Capt. James Dittrick, Roger Bates, Mrs. White, Joseph Brant, Thomas Horner, Hon. M. DeBoucherville,* Hon. John Stewart, Hon. W. Morris, Mohawk Chief Martin, Hon. Samuel Crane, Nicholas Browse, Jacob De Witt, Hon. George Crookshank, Sir Joseph Brook, Hon. James Crooks, George Brouse, M.P.P.; Dr. Schoefield, Hon. John Molson, Hon. John McDonald, Thomas Merritt, Jacob Bowman, Hon. Henry Ruttan, Hon. John Elmsley, Chief Justice; Hon. Peter Russell, Administrator; Hon. Henry Allcock, Chief Justice; W. Weeks, M.P.P.; John White, Attorney-General; Mrs. Secord, of Chippewa; Col Clark, Port Dalhousie; Hon. W. Hamilton Merritt, Philemon Wright, the first settler on the Ottawa; Rev. John Stuart, Frontenac; Tecumseh; Mrs. Clench, of Niagara; Mrs. John Gibson, of Grantham; John Kilburn; James Richardson, of Glover Hill; also a statement of the sufferings of the clergy at the American revolution. This paper is particularly interesting.

Out of such a rich casket of historical gems, who will dare to select? Here is a lively sketch of an Indian warrior, Tecumseh—a genuine product of an American forest: as such I shall add it to the *Maple Leaves* and insert it possibly in a subsequent paper. And here are traits of devotion and disinterestedness, scraps of family history, feats of personal prowess, inci-

*Hon. Mr. DeBoucherville is a lineal descendant of the old Governor of Three Rivers, and founder of the village of DeBoucherville.

dents of the battlefield; how shall I crowd them all in the narrow limits of this record of Canadian worth and Canadian gallantry? Yes, how? I acknowledge the idea distresses me much; enough at any rate for to-day. But before closing listen to the quaint gossip of a very worthy and ancient dame of some 79 summers, Mrs. White.† "The Bay of Quinté was covered with ducks, of which we could obtain any quantity from the Indians. As to fish, they could be had by fishing with a scoup. I have often speared large salmon with a pitch fork." Only fancy, spearing salmon with a pitch fork! "Now and then provisions ran very scanty, but there being plenty of bull frogs, we fared sumptuously." Good gracious! to think that the U. E. Loyalists were veritable frog-eaters. "Eating bull frogs a sumptuous fare!" Oh, Mrs. White! Mrs. White! However, there was just as excellent a reason for eating bull frogs in Upper Canada in 1788, as there was for eating horse flesh‡ in Lower Canada some thirty years previously: *there was nothing else to eat.* Let us continue. "This," says Mrs. White, "was the time of the famine, I think, in 1788; we were obliged to dig up our potatoes, after planting them, to eat. We never thought of these privations, but were always happy and cheerful. No unsettled minds; no political strife about church government, or squabbling municipal councils. We left everything to our faithful Governor.§ I have often heard my father and my mother say

---

† Reminiscences of Mrs. White, of White's Mills, near Cobourg.

‡ Montcalm had had 1500 horses slaughtered for the inhabitants of Canada in 1758.

§ "Let us do justice to the memory of a really great man; that first Governor (Simcoe) was no mere soldier. While his military designs entitled him to rank with Wolfe and Brock, as the preserver of Canada to the Crown of Great Britain, his large views of civil policy went far beyond all the men—civilians by profession—who have been entrusted with the supreme direction of affairs in this country. I was glad to see that at the great pioneer festival held at London a few weeks ago, the name of General Simcoe was not forgotten, for it is a name that must always remain inscribed on the corner stone of the history of Western Canada. I do not know a more interesting or instructive picture of any Canadian Governor, not even that which Peter Kalm gave, in 1745, of the renowned Marquis de la Gallissonière, than is given by the Duke de la Rochefoucault Liencourt, of Lieut.-Governor Simcoe, in his travels in North America in the year 1795. The French Duke found Upper Canada 'a new country, or rather,' he says, 'a country about to be formed;' and its Governor, 'a man of independent fortune,' whose only incitement to accept the office was the hope of thereby rendering a great service to his native land. 'Governor Simcoe,' he says, 'was of opinion that not only would Upper Canada be found quite able to sustain all her own inhabitants, but that she might become a granary to England'—a statesman's hope which has been fully realized! De la Rochefoucault describes an incident of his rule, which came under his own notice. 'We met,' he says (speaking of an excursion he made with the

that they had no cause of complaint in any shape, and were always thankful to the Government for its kind assistance in the hour of need. Of an evening, my father would make shoes of deerskin for the children, and my mother, make home-spun dresses. We had no doctors, no lawyers, no stated clergy. We had prayers at home, and put our trust in Providence. An old woman in the next clearance was chief physician to the surrounding country as it gradually settled. A tree fell one day and hurt mother's back very much; we sent for the old woman, who came, steeped some wheat, made lye and applied it very hot in a flannel; in a very short time she was as well as ever. Flax was cultivated in those halcyon days. One year we grew 700 cwt.; we spun and wove it into wearing apparel and table linen. It lasted a long time. A handy fellow came along and made us our chamber looms, so that we might work away. We had no occasion for imported finery, nor, if we had, we could not have procured any. As the girls grew up and settlers came round, a wedding occasionally took place. There was but one minister, a Presbyterian, named Robert McDonald, a kind, warm-hearted man, who came on horseback through the woods from Kingston, and when he saw smoke from a house he straight made up to the residence, where he was always welcome. He had a most powerful voice, when he became excited; he could be heard a mile off. All who were inclined to marry he spliced, with many a kind word to the young folks—'that they were sure to prosper by industry and perseverance.' He married Mr. White and myself.

"When the other girls would smirk and look pleasant at him, and think him a great benefactor, he would chuck them under the chin and say—''t will soon be your turn.'"

Governor beyond Niagara), 'an American family, who, with some oxen, cows and sheep, were coming to Canada. 'We come, said they to the Governor—whom they did not know—'to see whether he will give us land.' 'Aye, aye,' the Governor replied, 'you have tired of the Federal government; you like no longer to have so many kings, you wish again for your old father;' (it is thus the Governor calls the British monarch when he speaks with Americans); 'you are perfectly right; come along, we love such good royalists as you are; we will give you land.' Such, sir, was the spirit of the founder of Upper Canada—such was the beneficient policy which breathed into that soulless wilderness the breath of life: and lo! your country became a living spirit. 'Come along! we like such good royalists as you are; we will give you land!' This was the policy of Governor Simcoe, three-quarters of a century ago—a policy which rebukes and puts to shame the narrow, illusory and vexatious quackery which obstructs the settlement of our remaining lands at this moment, and stands sentry for barbarism in the North-West."—*McGee's Letter to Dr. Parker in* 1863.

Further on Mrs. White speaks of steamboats and railroads, with much greater respect, however, than the late Mr. Marchildon, M.P.P., and winds up this picture of a Canadian arcadia, by saying—"Give me the spinning wheel days, when girls were proud to wear a home-spun dress of their own spinning and weaving, not dreaming of high-heeled boots, thin shoes, hoops and crinoline, and salt-cellar bonnets."

So mote it be.

THE "U. E." LOYALISTS.

"A Volunteer" writes us† as follows, viz:—

"Among the many communications which have graced your journal, and for which we are indebted to the facile pen of our respected townsman, J. M. LeMoine, there are few who possess so great an interest for us Anglo-Saxons, born on the soil, as the subject matter of Mr. LeMoine's letter of yesterday. Our fathers, through good and through evil report, stood firm in their allegiance to the British flag, and shed their blood in many a well-fought field. Is there no history of the Provincial corps, raised in the different revolted states, which fought by the side of the British regulars? Are there no returns on file in the War Office, showing when and where these different corps were raised; how they were commanded and officered, and what battles they fought? What officers survived the war, and chose Lower Canada as their home? Have we no Napier to write in full the history of the U. E. Loyalists?

† *Quebec Morning Chronicle.*

The Battle Fields of Canada.

AN attempt is here made to supply a gap which no guide-book as yet has filled. That a brief narrative of the chief encounters which have taken place on Canadian soil and on its borders, between rival armies, will prove acceptable, many firmly believe. These accounts will be collated from reliable sources: Charlevoix, Bancroft, Garneau, Christie, Bibaud, John Gilmary Shea, the New York *Historical Magazine*, the *New Historical Picture of Quebec*, compiled by the late Dr. John C. Fisher and the late Andrew Stuart, men distinguished alike for their vast erudition and high authority as writers. In these fighting days, when our American neighbours have on foot larger armies than the old world can boast of, a glance at battle fields is not out of place. Although the narratives of our battles, in many cases, have been made up from letters and reports written by the leaders of regulars, and are calculated to exhibit in bright colors their superiority over volunteers or militia, enough occasionally transpires to show that the regulars met with hearty co-operation from the militia, and that in some hard fights, east and west, the militia can justly lay claim to the greater portion of the success. It may be neither an unpleasant nor an unprofitable task to enquire how the bone and sinew of the country repelled aggression: the enquiry will give us no occasion to be ashamed of our fathers. If, when the time comes, we can meet the invader as stoutly as they did during the seven years' war, and during the two American invasions; if we are then fortunate enough to entwine our banner with wreaths as redolent of heroism as that of Carillon, Ste. Foy, Chateauguay, Queenston, Lundy's Lane, we need not fear the verdict—either of posterity or of new masters, should "manifest destiny" ever hand us over to republican rule. We may then have a right to expect to be treated as men, having acted as such, in fulfilling one of the most sacred laws of nature fighting for our hearths—our homes—our country.

The Sieges of Quebec, 1629.*

ONE who is conversant only with the petty and broken lines of European geography, cannot form any adequate conception of the political importance of our impregnable fortress. Placed, as if by the most consummate art, at the very lowest point that effectually commands the navigation of the largest body of fresh water in the world, Cape Diamond holds, and must forever hold, the keys not only of all the vast and fertile regions drained by our magnificent river, but of the almost untrodden world between Lake Superior and the Rocky Mountains. On one side the icy barriers of the north, on the other, the dangers, delays and distempers of the Mississippi will for ever secure an almost exclusive preference to the great highway of the St. Lawrence. In Quebec and Montreal, respectively, must centre the dominion and the wealth of half a continent.

Quebec has been styled the Gibraltar of America—a comparison that conveys a more correct idea of its military strength than of its commercial and political importance. Let the European reader complete the comparison by closing the Baltic, the Elbe, and the Rhine—turning the Danube westward into the English channel, and placing Gibraltar so as to command that noble stream's navigation of two thousand miles.

Quebec, moreover, derives a vast degree of relative importance from its being almost the only fortified spot in North America. Over the whole continent nature has not planted a single rival; while art, in the more level districts of the south, was in a great measure suspended by swamps and forests.

The spirit of the French system of American colonization appreciated fully the unrivalled advantages of Quebec, and made Cape Diamond the fulcrum of a lever that was to shake the English colonies from their foundations. Every page of the earlier history of these regions forces on the reflecting mind a fundamental distinction between the English and the French colonies in North America. The former were planted by an intelligent people; the latter were founded by an ambitious government.

* From *Hawkins's Picture of Quebec.*

The English settlements, forming, as it were, so many neutrally independent States, directed their unfettered energies into the natural channels of agriculture and commerce. The French ones, entangled in the meshes of a net of unparallelled extent, were but the inert parts of a political machine, powerful indeed, but unwieldy, expensive and unproductive. The French sought dominion in military power—the English cherished the spirit and enjoyed the blessings of freedom. Their fundamental destruction, while it gave France a temporary preponderance, could not fail to secure the ultimate triumph of her more enlightened, though less crafty, rival.

From the struggles between the hereditary rivals sprung most of the eventful scenes which form the subject of this chapter ; and one cannot but wonder that Quebec, the source of all the evils that afflicted the English settlement, was not more frequently the main object of attack.

Sieges are from various causes, such as the vicissitudes of fortune, the concentration of interest, the pre-eminent display of valor and generosity, and other popular virtues, the most spirit-stirring occurences in warfare ; but one of the sieges of Quebec is peculiarly interesting and important, from its cutting off the contending commanders in the decisive hour of victory, changing the civil and political condition of vast and fertile regions, and bringing to a close the European warfare which had rendered the basins of the St. Lawrence and the Mississippi one vast field of blood and battle.

Many years, however, before the political jealousies of France and England rendered Quebec the object of unremitting and vigorous contention, several Indian tribes, influenced partly by a natural dislike of foreign intruders, and partly by hereditary hostility towards the native allies of the strangers, had attempted to sweep away the scarcely-formed germs of our ripe and rich metropolis. In the year 1621, when the whole population of Quebec fell short of three score souls, the Five Nations, or, as they are often termed, the Iroquois, surrounded a fortified post on the shore of the River St. Charles, but fearing the consequences of an actual assault, turned their murderous wrath on the chief objects of their vengeance, the Indian allies of the colony. It is but just here to offer the tribute of applause to the superiority of the French over the English in conciliating the aboriginal savages of the North American continent.

While the English fought their way by inches in almost every settlement, the French generally lived on fraternal terms with their immediate neighbors, and engaged in hostilities with distant tribes rather as allies than principals. The Indian wars of the English were generally civil ones; those of the French were almost universally foreign. In the incursions, of which we have instanced one, the aim of the Iroquois was not so much the French as the Hurons and the Algonquins. After a lapse of eight years of dubious security, Quebec, as if in anticipation of its final and permanent destiny, fell into the hands of the hereditary enemies of France.

In the preceding year, that is in 1628, Sir David Kertk, accompanied by William de Caen, a traitor to his country, penetrated as far as Tadousac with a powerful squadron, and thence summoned the Governor of Quebec to an immediate surrender. Champlain, who had founded the colony, and whose name will live forever in a lake rich in historic recollections, had at that time the command of Quebec. The gallant commander, relying perhaps as much on a bold front as on the strength of the defences or the prowess of the garrison, saved the settlement from Kertk's irresistible force by the spirited reply of himself and his companions.

In July following, an English fleet under two brothers of Sir David Kertk, who remained himself at Tadousac, anchored unexpectedly before the town. Those who know the difficulty, even in the present day, of conveying intelligence between Quebec and the lower parts of the river, will not be surprised that the fleet should have almost literally brought the first intelligence of its own approach.

The brothers immediately sent, under the protection of a white flag, the following summons, which breathes at once a consciousness of strength and a feeling of generosity:—

"*July* 19*th*, 1629.

"SIR,—Our brother having last year informed you that sooner or later he would take Quebec, he desires us to offer you his friendship and respects, as we also do on our part; and, knowing the wretched state of your garrison, we order you to surrender the fort and settlement of Quebec into our hands, offering you terms that you will consider reasonable, and which shall be granted on your surrender.

CHAMPLAIN'S ANSWER.

"GENTLEMEN,—It is true that, owing to the want of succour and assistance from France, our distress is very great, and that we are incapable of resistance: I therefore desire that you will not fire on the town, nor land your troops until the articles of capitulation can be drawn up."

Articles of Capitulation proposed by Champlain.

"That Messieurs Kertk shall produce the King of England's commission, by virtue of which they summon the place to surrender, as an evidence that war had been declared between France and England. That they should also produce authority by which they were empowered by their brother, David Kertk, admiral of the fleet. That a vessel should be furnished for transporting to France all the French, without excepting two Indian women. That the soldiers should march out with their arms and baggage.

"That the vessel to be provided to carry the garrison to France shall be well victualled, to be paid for in peltries. That no violence or insult shall be offered to any person. That the vessel to be procured shall be ready for departure three days after their arrival at Tadoussac, and that they shall be transported."

ANSWER OF THE KERTKS.

"That they had not the commission from the King of England, but that their brother had it at Tadoussac; that they were empowered by their brother to treat with Mr. Champlain.

"That a vessel would be provided, and if not sufficiently large, they would be put on board the ships of the fleet of England, and from thence sent to France.

"That the Indian women could not be given up, for reasons to be explained when they met.

"That the officers and soldiers should march out with their arms, baggage and other effects."

Champlain's own proposals of capitulation satisfactorily demonstrate that, down to 1629, France had hardly any permanent footing in the country. By stipulating for the removal of "all the French" in Quebec, Champlain seems to have considered that the province was virtually lost to France; and the single vessel which was to furnish the means of a removal, reduces "all the French" in Quebec to a very paltry number. The humanity of the victors, however, had the effect of inducing most of the colonists to remain under the English government.

With Quebec fell, of course, the whole of Canada into the power of England.

Champlain, with the partiality of a father for his child, strove by the most pressing entreaties, and by the most natural exaggerations, to make his country wrest Quebec from England by negotiation or by arms. His countrymen, however, did not unanimously second the unsuccessful commander's blended aspirations of patriotism and ambition. With the exception of a few placemen, and of a few zealots for commercial intercourse and maritime enterprise, most of the leading men of France considered Canada merely as an expensive toy. The Government, therefore, permitted three years to elapse without employing any active means of recovering the lost colony, and at last adopted the alternative of negotiation, its cheapest and most powerful weapon against the generous prowess of England.

In 1632, France recovered, by treaty of St. Germain-en-Laye, Canada, along with the Acadian Peninsula and the Island of Cape Breton.

Connected with this point of our interesting subject, a few observations on the colonial supremacy of Britain may not be deemed impertinent by the intelligent reader.

Before the decay of the feudal system, and the establishment of standing armies had consolidated the gigantic kingdoms of Spain and France, England was more than a match, in a fair field, for either of her more populous and more extensive rivals. Subsequently, however, to the introduction of those political and military innovations, England was induced, as well by necessity as by inclination, to cherish her navy as the safest and most efficient means of maintaining her high position among the powers of Europe. Not only has her navy secured to her uninterrupted blessings of national independence, and the proud rank of arbitress of Europe, but it has enabled her to reap the rich fruits of the colonial enterprize of France, Portugal and Holland. *Sic vos non vobis!* would have been the appropriate, though a haughty inscription of her omnipresent and omnipotent banner. As if by the unerring hand of destiny, colony after colony, from Gange's banks to Erin's side, has been made to submit, notwithstanding repeated restitutions, to the permanent dominion of the British name; and a nation separated from all other nations, owes chiefly to that very separation the mastery of a world far more extensive than the "whole world"* of the Roman bard. But, however humiliating to rivals may have been the colonial conquests of England, the conquered colonies have found, in the blessings of political liberty and comparatively unrestricted commerce, an ample recompense for their share of national humiliation, and have generally acquiesced, with a feeling of peaceful gratitude, in the milder and happier order of things.

Champlain was reinstated in the government of the recovered colony, and during the remaining years of his honorable life was exempted from the troubles, at least, of foreign invasion. Quebec seems to have enjoyed a kind of dubious tranquility until, about twenty years after Champlain's death, the Five Nations, to the unusually large number of seven hundred warriors, after having massacred the natives and the colonists in the open country, and committed the most cruel devastations, blockaded Quebec for several successive months. Such a siege may occupy a very small share of our consideration, but the recollections of the tomahawk and the knife† of the yelling children of the forest are still vivid enough in Canada to rouse our definite sympathies for the dangers and the distresses of the unhappy citizens. The scene must have teemed with picturesque horrors, and many bold and thrilling achievements, doubtless, deepened its terrible interest. This siege, although ultimately baffled, was very prejudicial to the welfare of Quebec: its dangers and terrors drove many of the settlers to France in despair, and almost led to the ruin of the colony.

---

* How singularly these words, penned in 1835 by one of the most gifted Canadians, now sound in 1864, when the debates in the Imperial Parliament anent the rejection of the Lyson's militia bill are still fresh in the memory of all: "Ships, colonies and commerce," was a grand idea then, not now.—*J. M. L.*

† That the Indians were dangerous allies, the following incident, related in Moore's *Indian Wars of the United States*, clearly shows:—"Mr Jones, an officer of the British army, had gained the affections of Miss Macrea, a lovely young lady of amiable character and spotless reputation, daughter of a gentleman attached to the Royal cause, residing near Fort Edward, and they had agreed to be married. In the course of service, the officer was removed to some distance from his bride, and became anxious for her safety and desirous of her company. He engaged some Indians, of two different tribes, to bring her to camp, and promised a keg of rum to the person who should deliver her safe to him. She dressed to meet her bridegroom, and accompanied her Indian conductors; but, by the way, the two chiefs, each being desirous of receiving the promised reward, disputed which of them should deliver her to her lover. The dispute arose to a quarrel, and according to their usual method of disposing of a disputed prisoner, one of them instantly cleft the head of the lady with a tomahawk."

Phipps before Quebec in 1690.†

AFTER a lapse of about thirty years, Quebec, under the command of the gallant Count de Frontenac, made a vigorous and honorable defence in 1690, against the forces of Sir William Phipps, Governor of Massachusetts.

As this seige, in addition to its intrinsic interest, was the fruit of the colonial system of France previously noticed, it demands a fuller and more circumstantial detail in any historical sketch of Quebec.

For some years before the date of this seige, the French had vigorously availed themselves of their geographical position not merely to harass, but to circumscribe the colonies in New England and New York. The possession of Acadia, which had been restored by England, in defiance of the remonstrance of the neighboring provinces, enabled France to command and cripple the commerce and the fisheries of the eastern colonies; while the discovery of the Mississippi, in the year 1673, and the subsequent attempts of France to colonize its banks, excited serious alarms for the security of the more westerly settlements.

The English colonies, roused to a sense of the impending dangers, made unparalleled exertions, both by land and sea, to deliver themselves from their crafty and restless neighbors.

In 1690, they took Port Royal, in Acadia, with a small force of seven hundred men; and, in the same year, made a judiciously planned attempt on Quebec, the true centre of the French power in America. The immediate cause of this attempt was the cruel invasion of the State of New York by the French in the beginning of the year. The French had concerted an attack on the City of New York, to be made simultaneously by sea and land; but, though their main design was disappointed by unforeseen circumstances, they sent forth marauding parties to the south, that laid waste the country with fire and sword, and murdered in cold blood the unresisting inhabitants of Schenectady with more than barbarian ferocity.

The English colonists, provoked by an attack so cowardly, so atrocious and so uncommon even in the annals of American warfare, and haunted

† From *Hawkins's Picture of Quebec.*

by undefined terrors of future encroachments and cruelty, determined, by means of their commissioners assembled at New York, to carry the war into Canada with all possible diligence. Having in vain requested from the mother country a supply of ships and ammunition, the colonists gallantly resolved to bear the whole burden of the invasion, and to extricate themselves, at all hazards, from the rapidly closing net of the French. It is more than probable that had their invasion of Canada been successful, they would have resisted, by something more than remonstrances, the restitution of the province to their inveterate and implacable enemies, and have anticipated by a permanent conquest the triumphs of the immortal Wolfe.

The invading forces consisted of an army, that was to cross the country under General Winthrop, and a naval squadron under the command of Governor Phipps. Of the army nothing more needs be said, than that like every other army on a similar errand, it was completely unsuccessful; to the squadron, which conducted the siege of Quebec, our last attention must be given.

As soon as the Count de Frontenac, who had turned his earlist attention to the operations of the land army, was apprised of its retreat, he led back his troops with all possible diligence to reinforce the garrison of Quebec, having ordered the governors of Montreal and Three Rivers to follow him with all their disposable forces of militia and regulars.

By extraordinary exertions, the gallant count put the city in a state at least of temporary defence before the arrival of the hostile squadron, and seems to have infused into his soldiers his own heroic confidence of success.

Sir William Phipps appeared before the town on the 5th October, old style. Charlevoix, who uses the new style adopted by the French as early as 1582, calls it the 16th. Although he was certainly neither a traitor nor a coward, the delay and irresolution of the general were afterwards complained of, probably owing to the great disappointment of the English colonists, at the failure of the expedition and the fruitless expense which had been incurred. On the 6th October "it was concluded," says Major Walley in his narrative, "that a summons should be sent ashore, of which the following is a copy:

"To Count Frontenac, Lieutenant General, and Governor for the French King, at Canada, or in his absence, to his deputy, or him or them in chief command.

"The war between the two crowns of England and France does not only sufficiently warrant, but the destruction made by the French and Indians under your command and encouragement, upon the persons and estates of their Majesties' subjects of New England, without provocation on their part, hath put them under the necessity of this expedition, for their security and satisfaction, and although the cruelties and barbarities used against them by the French and the Indians, might upon the present occasions prompt to a severe revenge; yet being desirous to avoid all inhumanity and unchristian-like actions, and to prevent the shedding of blood as much as may be, I, William Phipps, Knight, do hereby and in the name and on behalf of their most excellent Majesties, William and Mary, King and Queen of England, Scotland, France and Ireland, defenders of the faith, and by order of their Majesties said government of the Massachusetts colony in New England, demand a surrender of your forts and castles and the things and other stores, unembezzled, with a seasonable delivery of all captives, together with a surrender of all your persons and estates to my disposal.

"Upon the doing whereof you may expect mercy from me, as a christian, according to what shall be found for their Majesties' service and the subjects' security, which if you refuse forthwith to do, I come provided, and am resolved, by the help of God, on whom I trust, by force of arms, to revenge all wrongs and injuries offered, and bring you under subjection to the Crown of England; and, when too late, make you wish you had accepted the favor tendered.

"Your answer positive in an hour—returned with your own trumpet, with the return of mine, is required, upon the peril that will ensue."

* * * * * * * * * * *

Finding the place prepared for defence, Sir William, after a fruitless attempt to capture it on the land side, by an attack on the River St. Charles, contented himself with a bombardment of the city, and retired after staying a week in the harbor. All the English naratives of the siege plausibly enough ascribed the defeat to Sir William's procrastinating disposition, but he seems on this occasion, at least, to have had sufficient justification in the obvious impropriety of attacking a city almost impregnable by nature, and swarming with zealous defenders.

Charlevoix mentions that he was delayed by head winds and by bad pilots. But Sir William's delay, from whatever circumstances it sprung, was indubitably the sole cause of the subsequent disgrace and disaster. Had the English forces arrived but three days sooner, they could not have failed to achieve an easy and almost bloodless conquest; but during that period, time for defence was afforded, and M. de Callieres, Governor of Montreal, had reinforced the garrison with the troops of the upper country, and rendered the beseiged numerically superior to the besiegers. But even in this apparently untoward circumstance Phipps might have discerned the gleams of certain victory, for the increased consumption of supplies, originally scanty, would soon have enlisted on his side the powerful aid of famine.

Our French manuscript clearly shows that even before Sir William's hasty departure, the garrison had deeply tasted the horrors of famine. The nuns restricted themselves to a daily morsel of bread; and the loaves which they furnished to the soldiers were impatiently devoured in the shape of dough—terror and distress reigned in the city, "for," in the simple but affecting language of the writer, "every thing diminished excepting hunger." To add to the general confusion, the English squadron kept up a tremendous cannonade more to the alarm than to the injury of the inhabitants. Major Walley's Journal, besides being too prolix for our limits, is less likely to interest the sympaties of the reader than the narrative of one of the beseiged. We therefore take the following extracts from our French manuscript:

"It is easy to imagine how our alarms redoubled, when we heard the noise of the cannon we were more dead than alive, every time that the combat was renewed. The bullets fell on our premises in such numbers, that in one day we sent twenty-six of them to our artillerymen to be sent back to the English. Several of us thought that we were killed by them; the danger was so evident that the bravest officers regarded the capture of Quebec as inevitable. In spite of all our fears we prepared different places for the reception of the wounded, because the combat had commenced with an air to make us believe our hospital would not be capable of containing those who might have need of our assistance: but

God spared the blood of the French; there were few wounded and fewer killed. Quebec was very badly fortified for a siege; it contained very few arms and no provisions; and the troops that had come from Montreal had consumed the little food that there was in the city." "The fruits and vegetables of our garden were pillaged by the soldiers; they warmed themselves at our expense and burned our wood." "Every thing appeared sweet to us, provided we could be preserved from falling into the hands of those whom we considered as the enemies of God, as well as of ourselves. We had not any professed artillerymen. Two captains M. De Maricourt* and De Lorimier, took charge of the batteries and pointed the cannon so accurately as hardly ever to miss. M. De Maricourt shot down the flag of the admiral, and, as soon as it fell, our Canadians boldly ventured out in a canoe to pick it up, and brought it ashore under the very beard of the English."

Abortive Expedition in 1711.†

THE defeat of Sir William Phipps was sensibly felt by the people of New England, who indeed were called upon to defray the expense, amounting to one hundred and fifty thousand pounds. They frequently represented to the British Ministry the commercial advantages, which would result from the total expulsion of the French from North America. At last, in 1707, during the military glories of the reign of Queen Anne, distinguished by a Marlborough, as this age has been by a Wellington—the Earl of Sunderland, Secretary of State, determind to make another attempt to dislodge the French from their almost impregnable position at Quebec. The armament intended for this object, under the command of General Macartney, was, however, diverted from its destination, and ordered to Portugal, in consequence of the disastrous condition to which

* One of the Baron de Longueil's heroic brothers.—See chapter on "Canadien Noblesse," in first series of *Maple Leaves*.

† From *Hawkins's Picture of Quebec*.

the affairs of the Queen's ally, Charles III., King of Spain, had been reduced by the defeat of the allied forces at Almanza.

In 1711, the project was resumed, only to result in a signal and mortifying failure. The plan of this expedition was suggested by a provincial officer, General Nicholson, who had just taken possession of Nova Scotia, on which occasion he had given the name of Annapolis to Port Royal. This officer had brought to London four Indian Chiefs, and had the address to persuade the ministry to enter into the views of the New England States. The expedition consisted of five thousand troops from England, and two thousand provincials, under Brigadier General Hill, brother to the Queen's favorite, Mrs. Masham. The naval force was very strong, and was placed under the command of Sir Hovenden Walker. The fleet met with constant fogs in the Gulf of St. Lawrence, and was nearly destroyed on the Egg Islands, on the 22nd August. Despairing of success, the admiral called a council of war, and it was determined to return to England without making any further attempt. Eight transports* were lost on this disastrous day, with eight hundred and eighty-four officers, soldiers and seamen. The provincial land forces under General Nicholson, which had advanced as far as Albany, and had been joined by six hundred Iroquois, returned to their respective quarters on hearing of the failure of the naval expedition. It is remarkable that during the heat of the factions of that day, the Whigs affected to consider this attempt on Quebec so perfectly desperate an undertaking, that it was made one of the articles of impeachment against Harley, Earl of Oxford, that he had suffered it to go on.

The Marquis De Vaudreuil, then Governor General of Canada, omitted no duty of a brave and prudent officer on this occasion. The rejoicings at Quebec were naturally great at so signal a deliverance; and the Church of *Notre Dame de la Victoire*† spoke the pious gratitude of the religious inhabitants, by assuming the title of *Notre Dame des Victoires.*

---

* It is supposed that the old hull of a wreck, still extant, on Cape Despair, Gaspé, belonged to this ill-fated expedition.—(*J. M. L.*)

† It is the same church standing, to this day, opposite Blanchard's Hotel in the Lower Town Market.—(*J. M. L.*)

Defeat of Washington at Fort Necessity.*

JULY, 1754.

AMIDST these preparations, M. de Contrecœur received intelligence that a large corps of British was advancing against him, led by Colonel Washington. He forthwith charged M. de Jumonville to meet the latter, and admonish him to retire from what was French territory. Jumonville set out with an escort of thirty men; his orders were to be on his guard against a surprise, the country being in a state of commotion, and the aborigines looking forward for war; accordingly his night campaigns were attended by great precaution. May 17, at evening-tide, he had retired into a deep and obscure valley, when some savages, prowling about, discovered his little troop, and informed Washington of its being near to his line of route. The latter marched all night, in order to come unawares upon the French. At day-break, he attacked them suddenly; Jumonville was killed along with nine of his men. French reporters of what passed on the occasion declared that a trumpeter made a sign to the British that he bore a letter addressed to them by his commandant; that the firing ceased, and it was only after he began to read the missive which he bore that the firing recommenced. Washington affirmed, on the contrary, that he was at the head of his column; that at sight of him the French ran to take up arms, and that it was false to say Jumonville announced himself to be a messenger. It is probable there may be truth in both versions of the story; for the collision being precipitate, great confusion ensued. Washington resumed his march, but tremblingly, from a besetting fear of falling into an ambuscade. The death of Jumonville did not cause the war which ensued, for that was already resolved on, but only hastened it. Washington proceeded on his march; but staid by the way to erect a palisaded fastness, which he called *Fort Necessity*, on a bank of the Monongahela, a river tributary to the Ohio, and there waited for the arrival of more troops to enable him to attack Fort Duquesne (Pittsburg), when he was himself assailed.

* Garneau's *History of Canada*, Bell's translation.

Contrecœur, upon learning the tragic end of Jumonville, resolved to avenge his death at once. He put six hundred Canadians and one hundred Savages under the orders of the victim's brother, M. de Villiers, who set out directly. Villiers found, on his arrival at the scene of the late skirmish, the corpses of several Frenchmen; and near by, in a plain, the British drawn up in battle order, and ready to receive the shock. At Villiers' first movement to attack them they fell back upon some intrenchments which they had formed, and, armed with nine pieces of artillery, Villiers had to combat forces under shelter, while his own were uncovered. The issue of the battle was doubtful for some time; but the Canadians fought with so much ardor that they silenced the British cannon with their musketry alone; and, after a struggle of ten hours' duration, they obliged the enemy to capitulate, to be spared an assault. The discomfited British engaged to return the way they came; but they did not return in like order, for their retrograde march was so precipitate that they abandoned all, even their flag. Such were the unglorions exploits of the early military career of the conqueror of American Independence. The victors having razed the fort and broken up its guns, withdrew. War now appeared to be more imminent than ever, although words of peace were still spoken. Villiers' victory was the first act in a great drama of twenty-nine years' duration, in which Great Britain and France were destined to suffer terrible checks in America.

JUMONVILLE AND WASHINGTON.*

It is somewhat curious to have, at this day, an examination of Washington's culpabilities in the Jumonville affair from a member of the French officer's family. In the recently published work, *Les Anciens Canadiens*, of Philippe Aubert de Gaspé, p. 396, is the following:

Colonel Malcolm Fraser, during Wolfe's invasion of Canada, was in a detachment which burnt the houses of the Canadians from Rivière Ouelle to the Rivière des trois Saumons. Having become, after the conquest, the intimate friend of my family, he replied to my grandfather's complaints about this act of vandalism: "How could we help it, my dear friend: *à la guerre comme à la guerre.* Your Frenchmen, in ambush in the woods, killed two of our men when we landed at Rivière

* From the *New York Historical Magazine.*

Ouelle." "You should, at least," said my grandfather, "have spared my flour-mill; my poor tenants would not then have been reduced so low as to eat their corn in sagamity like Indians." "In war as in war," added my grandmother; "I admit your maxim, but was it fair war to kill my brother, Villiers de Jumonville, as Washington, your countryman, did at Fort Necessity?" "Ah, madam!" replied Col. Fraser, "for mercy's sake do not, for the honor of the English, ever again mention that atrocious murder."

I once slightly reproached our celebrated historian, Mr. Garneau, with passing lightly over that horrible assassination. He replied that it was a delicate subject, that the great shade of Washington hovered over the writer, or something of the kind.

This may be, but it is incumbent on me to clear the memory of my great uncle, whom Washington in his works sought to blacken in order to justify his assassination.

The tradition in my family is that Jumonville presented himself as bearer of a summons requiring Major Washington, Commandant of Fort Necessity, to evacuate that post erected on French territory, that he raised a flag of truce, showed his despatches, and that, nevertheless, the English commander ordered his men to fire on him and his small escort, and that Jumonville fell dead with a part of those who accompanied him.

There is a discrepancy, easily explained, between the tradition of my family and the truth of history. Moreover, this discrepancy has no bearing on the murder of the bearer of the flag of truce, whose mission was to summon the English to evacuate the French possession and not Fort Necessity, which was not thrown up till after the event. (After citing Contrecœur's instructions to Coulon de Villiers, and the capitulation signed by Washington, he proceeds): Now no one is more disposed than myself to render justice to the great qualities of the American hero; when in my family the conversation turned on the cruel and premature death of our noble kinsman, assassinated in the onset of what promised to be a brilliant career, I used to seek to excuse Washington on account of youth, as he was then but twenty. I expatiated on his virtues, his humanity, when twenty-two years afterwards he directed the cause of his countrymen and created a great and independent nation.

I never, indeed, should have thought of drawing from oblivion this deplorable event, had not Washington himself made it necessary by seeking, in order to clear himself, to blacken the reputation of my great uncle Jumonville in the memoir which he published several years after the catastrophe.

"We were informed," said he, "that Jumonville, disguised as an Indian, was prowling for several days around our posts, and I had to consider him as a spy."

This excuse has no probability, because Washington could not but know that not only the soldiers, but also the officers of the French army, when fighting in the woods, adopted the Indian dress, a short coat, leggings, breech-cloth, and moccasins. This light and easy dress gave them a great advantage over enemies always dressed in European style. Nor could Jumonville, without culpable temerity, proceed directly to the English posts without taking great precautions, the wood being infested with hostile Indians, who, acting on a first impulse, would show no great respect to a flag of truce.

After disposing of this accusation of his being a spy, of which Washington did not think till years after the murder when writing his memoir, let us see what he says in justification in his despatches to his government immediately after the affair. It is necessary to observe here that the crowns of France and England were then at peace; that war was declared by Louis XV. only after that event; that the only hostilities committed were the invasion of French territory by the English, and that it was against this very act that Jumonville was sent to protest.

But let us return to Washington's justification in his despatches. He says that "he regarded the frontier of New England as invaded by the French; that war seemed to him to exist, &c.; that the French in his sight ran to arms, and then he ordered his men to fire; that the action lasted a quarter of an hour, in which the French had ten men killed, and one wounded, and twenty-one prisoners; and the English one killed and three wounded; that it was false that Jumonville read a summons, &c.; that there had been no ambush, but surprise and skirmish, which is lawful war."

Lawful war indeed for a strong detachment to attack suddenly a handful of men in full peace. It was not getting badly out of it for a Major of twenty; some generals of the Northern American army, who pique themselves on address, would not do better to-day. The phrases "that war seemed to him to exist," "that the French in his sight ran to arms," are of admirable simplicity. These French dogs forgot, apparently, that it was more christian to allow themselves to be killed like sheep.

If we accept Washington's assertion, how can we explain the cry of horror and indignation that resounded through all Canada and even Europe? Yet the French have never been reproached with bewailing like women the loss of even their best generals or a signal defeat; why then their indignation, their fury at the tidings of the death of that young man, who was, so to speak, making his first apprenticeship in arms, if he perished in an action fought according to the rules of civilized nations? All the French prisoners, and even Manceau, who alone escaped the massacre, the very Indian allies of the English declare that Jumonville waved his handkerchief over his head, invited the English, by an interpreter, to stop, having something to read them, that the firing ceased, and that while an interpreter was reading it, he was shot through the head, and that but for the interposition of the Indians the whole party would have been massacred. * * * Washington should never have signed a capitulation where the words assassin and assassination are thrown in his face.

The reader must judge whether I have rescued my grand uncle's memory from the accusation of being a spy. Had Jumonville acted the vile part his enemy attributes to him, to justify a shameful assassination, the French would never have shed so many tears on the victim's grave. So writes the author of "Les Anciens Canadiens," M. De Gaspé.

Beaujeu, the Victor of Washington and Braddock.*

9TH JULY, 1755.

THE battle of the Monongahela, as the French more properly style the action fought between the English and French near Fort Duquesne on the 9th July, 1755, has always been, and probably always will stand in our annals as Braddock's defeat. The victory to which that general

* From the *New York Historical Magazine.*

went so confidently, the extent and equipment of his army, the finest ever sent by England to America; the haughty superiority of the regulars over the provincials, all made the terrible and sudden disaster a thing to link forever with the name of the hapless general rather than a battle; and national pride was flattered by an epithet that perpetually punished the guilty commander, paraded on the scaffold of public opinion as Byng had been on a real one.

The battle-field still goes by the name of Braddock's field, and with Germantown and Gettysburg, makes the three great battle-fields of the Keystone State.

It is somewhat remarkable that, though Braddock's expedition has within a few years been made the subject of a monograph constituting a stately octavo, so little has been done to investigate the French accounts, or the life and career of the petty officer who, with a handful of Canadian militia and Indians, routed the finest English army ever seen beyond the Atlantic to astonish the provincials and annihilate the French.

A little volume in Mr. Shea's cramoisy series contains all the French accounts of the battle, with a brief memoir of the French commander, whose family still exist in Canada, holding prominent positions in the government of a province divided from Pennsylvania by an imaginary line.

The general events are well known. As part of the scheme for the conquest of Canada, Braddock was to advance with a considerable army from Virginia on Fort Duquesne, which, dilapidated, almost ungarrisoned, seemed a certain prize, and every preparation was made to celebrate with due exuberance of joy the triumph of Britannic power.

M. de Contrecœur, a Canadian officer, had for some time commanded the fort, but had been relieved by Daniel Hyacinthe Marie Lienard de Beaujeu, a captain in the marines, all the land troops in Canada being of this arm, as Canada and other transatlantic possessions of France depended on the naval department, causing incongruities not without their parallel in our day and country.

As Captain Beaujeu fell in the action, no official report was apparently made, and the accounts which reached Quebec, and which, forwarded to France, formed the basis of the account printed at the Louvre, speak incorrectly of Contrecœur as commander of Fort Duquesne ; but the register kept by the chaplain of the fort, Friar Denis Baron, a Franciscan, who was one of the first to chant the service of Rome in the "Chapel of Our Lady's Assumption on the Beautiful River," and a journal of Mr. Godefroy, an officer in the fort, and an account of the War Department, concur in calling Mr. de Beaujeu commandant of the fort and of the forces there.

Beaujeu belongs to the family of the naval officer whose disagreement with La Salle contributed to the unhappy result of that explorer's attempt to reach the mouth of the Mississippi, and was born at Montreal, August 9, 1711 : his father, also a captain, having been for a time King's Lieutenant at Three Rivers.

His son Daniel had won the cross of a Knight of St. Louis, and for a time commanded at Niagara. When placed temporarily in Fort Duquesne, he saw that it could not stand the siege. Extravagance and corruption, such as we know too well, had made the fort a costly affair to the French king, without rendering it a formidable work to an English force.

To await Braddock's approach was therefore madness ; but Beaujeu, full of the pride of a French officer, resolved to attack the English general on the way, and if possible ambuscade the line of his march. From the influence which, during a long service on the frontiers, he had acquired over the Indian tribes, he had little doubt of his ability to gather a considerable number around him for the attempt. On the fifth of June they had learned of Braddock's departure from Will's Creek, and as the month advanced, small parties brought tidings of his approach. On the eighth of July the two brothers de Normanville came in with tidings that the enemy were only eighteen miles off.

While Braddock thus, almost at the end of his march, meeting no opposition, was doubtless congratulating himself on a bloodless victory and a successful campaign, Beaujeu was forming his last plan for an attack on the invader, resolved to die on the field rather than surrender the fort. He now called the war chiefs to a council. Despite the influence which he had acquired by long years spent in service with them, he found them reluctant. The notes of English preparation, the reports of scouts and runners, the experience of a party sent out under La

Pérade, all had impressed the savage mind. "What, Father," they cried, "would you kill and sacrifice us? The English are over four thousand strong and we only eight hundred, and you talk of attacking them. You see well that you are mad. We must have till to-morrow to decide."

Thus deserted by his dusky allies, Beaujeu doubtless passed a gloomy night, prepared to die as became a Chevalier of St. Louis and a French officer commanding an advanced post. At an early hour in the morning he, with probably all his command, assembled in the little chapel of the fort, where the grey-robed friar said mass for the warriors, and in the funeral entry in his register he noted the fact that Beaujeu then approached the tribunal of penance and received the Holy Eucharist, preparing for the death which seemed so certain to be his portion before the close of the day. After lingering a short time before the altar, Beaujeu formed his command, and the small squad of one hundred and forty-six Canadians and seventy-two regulars filed from the fort, Beaujeu at their head, arrayed in his hunting shirt, the silver gorget suspended from his neck alone showing his rank. As he passed the Indian camp he asked the result of their council. "We cannot march," was the reply. "I am determined to meet the enemy," retorted Beaujeu; "will you let your father go alone?" His cool, almost contemptuous manner, seems to have decided the matter. The Indians encamped under the Bourbon lilies by the waters of the Alleghany, were Hurons, Iroquois, Shawnees. Pontiac, Anastase, Cornplanter, were among them; men insensible to fear, warriors who had achieved renown in many a foray. To sit by and see two hundred Frenchmen go to meet the English host of twice as many thousands would be a perpetual disgrace. They silently took up their arms and followed the French line.

Beaujeu had selected as the point at which to assail the Enlish line a ravine beyond the Monogahela where the army would certainly cross. The delay had however been so great that the van had crossed the stream before he could reach the spot. As he came to the crest of a hill over which the trail passed, he came full in view of the English line coming proudly on, the summer sun glittering from the bayonets and muskets of the men, and the brilliant scarlet uniforms contrasting with the green foliage of the woods. They, too, marked with astonishment the sudden apparition of the French. Beaujeu was in the front bounding on, brandishing his carbine and cheering his men to a mad attack on the very front of the well appointed army before him, with artillery enough to sweep his whole command from the earth.

As the rattling fire of the French and Indians told on the ranks of Braddock's men, they formed and opened with their cannon, pouring grape into the French party, which soon, in backwoods fashion, took to the trees, and stealing towards the English flank, kept up a steady and deadly fire. At the third discharge of cannon Beaujeu fell dead, and Captain Dumas, his second in command, succeeded, and inspired equal energy.

As we all know, the great error of Braddock was that he kept his men in solid column, and supposing that the French, who were attacking him along his whole van, were as numerous as his own men, kept pushing columns forward to drive back an imaginary corps in front, at every step exposing his flank to a small but concealed body of sharpshooters, who cut them down without mercy. The Indians, who were at first startled by the cannon, at last, tired of musketry, seized their tomahawks and rushed out on the English, who, already deprived of many of their officers, and demoralized by the unwonted system of war, gave way in utter route.

Washington had in vain endeavored to induce Braddock to adopt the backwoods style of fighting, and to him was due the safety of the remnant of the army, his Virginia troops alone remaining cool and meeting the enemy as they had done in former struggles.

The route was a massacre. The Indians cut down all, many perishing in the river; over a thousand dead were strewn over the bloody field amid cannon, caissons, mortars, small-arms, tents, wagons, cattle. The plunder tempted the Indians from the pursuit, or the English could scarcely have borne from the field their dying general.

The French lost three officers killed in the action, Captain Beaujeu, Lieutenant de Carqueville, and Ensign de la Perade, and had several wounded. Their whole killed amounted to thirty, three-quarters of whom were Indians, the savages avenging their death by burning the few prisoners that fell into their hands.

The victors took up the body of their fallen commander and bore it back to the fort which he commanded, and by his daring had so effectually preserved. It apparently lay in state, for it was not interred till the twelfth. The following is the entry of Father Baron in his register:

"Burial of Mr. de Beaujeux, Commandant of Fort Duquesne.

"In the year one thousand seven hundred and fifty-five, the ninth of July, was killed in the battle fought with the English, the same day as above, Mr. Lienard Daniel, Esquire, Sieur de Beaujeu, Captain in the Infantry, Commandant of Fort Duquesne and of the army, who had been to confession and made his devotions the same day, his body was interred on the 12th of the same month in the cemetry of Fort Duquesne, under the title of the Assumption of the Blessed Virgin by the Beautiful River, and that with the ordinary ceremonies by us the undersigned Recollet priest, King's Chaplain in said fort, in testimony whereof we have signed,

"FRIAR DENYS BARON, P. R,
Chaplain."

Some have attempted to make Beaujeu merely wounded in battle, but the word is *tué*, killed, in this entry, and in every account of the fight, and the word would never be used to mean wounded. The burial notices of those who died of wounds are given with precision, and all note the administration of the sacrement of extreme unction which would not have been omitted in the case of Beaujeu, had he survived the battle.

The entries bearing on the battle are, 1st, Pierre Simar, scalped near the fort on the fifth of July, of whom F. Baron notes that he had satisfied his Easter duty (*i.e.* been to confession and received communion). 2, Limoges, killed in the battle and buried on the field. 3. Jean B. Tallion, wounded in the battle on the 9th, and buried at the fort on the 10th, after confessing and receiving extreme unction. 4. Mr. Dericherville, Esquire, Sieur de Carqueville, killed on the 9th, after having been to confession the same day, buried on the 10th in the fort. 5. Jean B. de la Perade, Esquire, Sieur de Parieux, wounded on the 9th, died on the 10th after receiving the sacrements of penance and extreme unction, buried in the fort. 6. Beaujeu. 7. J. B. Dupuis, wounded the 9th, died the 29th, after receiving sacrements of penance, the holy eucharist, and extreme unction. 8. Joseph, Sieur de Ste. Therèse (wounded on the 9th), died, July 30, after receiving the sacrements of penance, the eucharist, and extreme unction.

There can, therefore, be no doubt on the point. Before starting from the fort, Carqueville went to confession; Beaujeu not only did this, but received communion, and both were killed on the 9th, Carqueville being interred on the 10th and Beaujeu on the 12th.

Captain Beaujeu, who thus died achieving one of the greatest victories in French annals, left, it is said, by his wife, Michelle Elizabeth de Foucault, a son who went to France at the conquest of Canada, and a daughter who married Carles de Noyan, Governor of Guiana; but further nothing has yet reached me concerning them.

Collateral branches remained in Canada and have since been distinguished.

Defeat of Washington at Monongahela,

9TH JULY, 1755.

DEATH OF BRADDOCK.

"We have been beaten, shamefully beaten, by a handful of French."—*Washington's letter after the battle.*

The historian, Garneau, thus describes the same engagement:—

"M. DE CONTRECŒUR commanded at Duquesne (Pittsburg). One of his scouts informed him (July 8) that the British were but six leagues off. He resolved to attack them on the way, and proceeded himself to mark a place of ambuscade. Next day, two hundred and fifty-three Canadians and six hundred savages, led by M. de Beaujeu, left the fort, about 8 A.M., to take post in the ravines and thickets bordering the road along which the British were about to pass. This troop was in the act of descending the slope bordering the plain above noted, just as Colonel Gage began to ascend it. The two masses soon met in mid-career, and before the French were able to reach the ground they had been directed to take up. There was now nothing for it but for each party to try its strength in driving its adversary off the line of road. The British, taken by surprise, had to sustain a hot fire, galled by which their ranks gave way somewhat, and Gage was fain to fall back upon the main body of Braddock's force. The path being thus cleared, the French were enabled to complete the operation planned beforehand, and mostly ensconced themselves in every covert of brushwood and behind each rock which could be turned to sheltering account, while the mounted Canadians took post on the river, as if it were only they who meant to dispute the passage, whereas the foot soldiers and savages, posted at intervals, right and left, formed a half circle, the horns of which curved outwards so as to enclose the approaching enemy.

"The British van, its ranks reformed and closely supported by the main body, were advancing confidently, when a semi-concentric fire, from unseen gun-muzzles, was opened upon them, seemingly from every side, under which they first staggered, were then brought to a halt, and finally threw their ranks into confusion. Braddock, however, by great exertion restoring order, they opened fire on as many of their foes as they could see, and the artillery coming up, began to play upon the French central corps. One of the first cannon balls shot killed M. de Beaujeu. M. Dumas, second in command, placed himself at the head of the French not under cover, and, well sustained by M. de Ligneris and other officers, dashed forward on the British: a desperate struggle ensued. The savages, who had been scared by the cannonade, observing that the Canadians did not flinch under it, with yells resumed the sheltering-places they had left. The British long put a good face on the matter, and even made a forward movement, the men being impelled onward by their officers, sword in hand; but fairly confounded by the murderous fire kept up, and which ever thinned their ranks the more they further advanced, the whole body of regulars fell into hopeless disorder; so perplexed were some fusileers, that, firing at random, they killed several of their officers and some of their own comrades. The colonial militia alone seemed to preserve their presence of mind on this occasion, but even they were in the end borne backward by the panic-stricken regulars. Meanwhile Braddock did his best to reform his men, and lead them back to the charge, but all in vain. The balls flew round him like hail, two horses he rode were killed; he mounted a third, but only to receive a mortal wound, for the most of the French and savages from under shelter were able to single out at their leisure all those whom they chose to hit. After three hours' struggle the British column gave way entirely, abandoning their cannon. The Canadians now advanced, hatchet in hand, and the savages quitting their lurking places simultaneously, both fel upon the rear of the retreating British and Americans, and made frightful havoc; those whose swiftness of foot did not exceed that of their pursuers were cut down or drowned in the Monongahela, in a fruitless attempt to gain the opposite bank.* M. Dumas, knowing that Colonel Dunbar's corps was still intact and would serve as a rallying body for such fugitives as had gained the advance, pursued them no longer; and called a halt the rather, as the savages had betaken themselves to pillaging, and it would have been a hard matter to get them off their prey.

"The carnage thus concluded had scarcely an example in the annals of modern war.† Nearly 800 out of the 1200 men led to battle by Braddock were killed or wounded; out of 86 officers, 26 were slain and 32 hurt; for they made heroic attempts to rally and inspirit their baffled men; several officers killed themselves in despair. Washington excepted, all the mounted officers received wounds, mortal or other. The luckless general was carried to Fort Necessity, where he died July 13, and was buried at the roadside near that paltry post. He was a brave and experienced officer, but an arrogant man; contemning his enemy, despising alike militia and savages; yet had he the mortification to see his regulars madly flee, while the Virginians stood firmly and fought bravely to the last.

"The beaten soldiers, when they reached those of Durham, infested them also with their own panic, and in an instant the corps broke up. The cannon were spiked, the ammunition destroyed, and most of the baggage burnt; by whose direction no one knew. There was no semblance of order had till the fugitive rout attained Fort Cumberland, in the Alleghanies.‡ Washington wrote thence: "We have been beaten, shamefully beaten by a handful of French, who only expected to obstruct our advance. Shortly before the action we thought our forces were equal to all the enemies in Canada; we have been most unexpectedly defeated, and now all is lost."

"The French gained a great booty. The baggage of the vanquished, their provisions, fifteen cannon, many small arms, and much munitions of war, the chest, Braddock's papers—in fine, all became fair spoil for the

* Mr. Pouchot, "Memoirs on the late War in America."

† Mr. Jared Spark's "Life of Washington."

‡ Life, Correspondence, &c., of Washington.

victors. These documents revealed the projects of the British Ministry, and served to justify the indignant sentiments expressed against its polity in a memorial addressed by the Duke de Choiseul to the different European courts. There were taken, after the battle, from amidst the dismounted and broken vehicles left on the field, from 400 to 500 horses, including those which had been killed or hurt. The victory cost the French about forty men. M. deBeaujeu was much regretted by the Canadians, his compatriots, and by the Indian tribes, who held him in great respect. This ended the combat of Monongahela, one of the most memorable battles known to American history. The news of this discomfiture spread universal consternation throughout the whole of British America."

The Fort George Massacre,

AUGUST 9TH, 1757.

"Kill me," cried Montcalm, using prayers and menaces and promises, "but spare the English who are under my protection."—*Bancroft's United States, Vol. IV.*

OF the many stirring incidents which marked the "seven years war" culminating in the conquest of Canada, few have been more loudly denounced than the deed of blood perpetrated by the aborigines on the garrison and inmates of Fort George, called by the British Fort William Henry, subsequent to its capitulation; few occurrences of that day have left, between the militias of New France and New England, more bitter memories. Neither "2,000" nor 1,000, nor 500, not even 200 individuals were slaughtered on this occasion; there were enough, however, to exhibit in its true features Indian warfare in former times. The barbarities to which British soldiers and New England colonists were subjected, in direct violation of the articles signed by General Montcalm and accepted by the thirty-six Indian tribes present, have furnished those inclined to make capital out of national wrongs a welcome pretext to charge the French commander with being, in some degree, accessory to the commission of these horrors. Cooper's attractive novel "*The Last of the Mohicans*," and other works,* have also helped to render current a belief to which the whole of Montcalm's career, as well as history, gives the lie. True, the American novelist does not go so far as to accuse the Marquis with counselling the deed, but he asserts that, during its execution, the French showed "an apathy which has never been explained." Here is a grave accusation levelled at the fair name of the chivalrous rival of Wolfe; fortunately for his posthumous fame, there is such a thing as historical truth; there are also honorable men, whose nature spurns the cheap popularity acquired by circulating a lie calculated to ruin or vilify a national enemy. To this class belongs George Bancroft, the gifted historiographer of the United States. Let us now quote from his beautiful writings:

"How peacefully rest the waters of Lake George between their ramparts of highlands! In their pellucid depths, the cliffs and the hills, and the trees trace their image, and the beautiful region speaks to the heart, teaching affection for Nature. As yet (1757), not a hamlet rose on its margin; not a straggler had thatched a log-hut in its neighborhood; only at its head, near the centre of a wider opening between its mountains, Fort William Henry stood on its banks, almost on a level with the lake. Lofty hills overhung and commanded the wild scene; but heavy artillery had not, as yet, accompanied war-parties into the wilderness.

"Some of the Six Nations preserved their neutrality, but the Oneidas danced the war-dance with Vaudreuil. 'We will try the hatchet of our father on the English, to see if it cuts well,' said the Senecas of Niagara; and, when Johnson complained of depredations on his cattle, 'You begin crying quite early,' they answered, 'you will soon see other things.'†

"'The English have built a fort on the lands of Onontio,' spoke Vaudreuil, governor of New France, to a congress, at Montreal, of the warriors of three-and-thirty nations, who had come together, some from the

---

* "This treaty of capitulation was violated by Montcalm in a manner which fixes eternal disgrace on his memory."—*Moore's Indian Wars in the United States*, p. 194.

† Vaudreuil to the Minister, 13th July, 1757.

rivers of Maine and Acadia, some from the wilderness of Lake Huron and Lake Superior. 'I am ordered,' he continued, 'to destroy it. Go, witness what I shall do, that, when you return to your mats, you may recount what you have seen.' They took his belt of wampum, and answered—'Father, we are come to do your will.' Day after day, at Montreal, Montcalm nursed their enthusiasm by singing the war-song with the several tribes. They clung to him with affection, and would march to battle only with him. They rallied at Fort St. John, on the Sorel, their missionaries with them, and hymns were sung in almost as many dialects as there were nations. On the sixth day, as they discerned the battlements of Ticonderoga, the fleet arrayed itself in order, and two hundred canoes, filled with braves, each nation with its own pennon, in imposing regularity, swept over the smooth waters of Champlain, to the landing place of the fortress. Ticonderoga rung with the voices of thousands; and the martial airs of France, and shouts in the many tongues of the red men, resounded among the rocks and forests and mountains. The Christian mass, too, was chaunted solemnly; and to the Abenaki converts, seated reverently, in decorous silence, on the ground, the priest urged the duty of honoring Christianity by their example, in the presence of so many infidel braves.

"It was a season of scarcity in Canada. None had been left unmolested to plough and plant. The miserable inhabitants had no bread. But small stores were collected for the army. They must conquor speedily, or disband. 'On such an expedition,' said Montcalm to his officers, 'a blanket and a bearskin are the warrior's couch. Do like me, with cheerful good-will. The soldier's allowance is enough for us.'(‡)

"During the short period of preparation, the partisans were active. Marin brought back his two hundred men from the skirts of Fort Edward, with the pomp of a triumphant warrior. 'He did not amuse himself with making prisoners,' said Montcalm, on seing but one captive (§); and the red men yelled with joy as they counted in the canoes two-and-forty scalps of Englishmen.

"The Ottawas resolved to humble the arrogance of the American boatmen; and they lay hid in ambuscades all the twenty-third of July,

‡ Montcalm's Circular to his officers, 25th July, 1757.
§ Montcalm to Vaudreuil, 27th July, 1757.

and all the following night. At day-break of the twenty-fourth, Palmer was seen on the lake, in command of two-and-twenty barges. The Indians rushed on his party suddenly, terrified them by their yells, and after killing many, took one hundred and sixty prisoners. 'To-morrow, or next day,' said the captives, 'General Webb will be at the fort with fresh troops.' 'No matter,' said Montcalm; 'in less than twelve days, I will have a good story to tell about them.'(*) From the timid Webb there was nothing to fear.' He went, it is true, to Fort William Henry, but took care to leave again with a large escort, just in season to avoid its siege.

It is the custom of the red men, after success, to avoid the further chances of war, and hurry home.

"'To remain now,' said the Ottowas, 'would be to tempt the Master of life.' But Montcalm, after the boats and canoes had, without oxen and horses, by main strength, been borne up to Lake George, held on the plain above the portage one general council of union. All the tribes, from the banks of Michigan and Superior to the borders of Acadia, were present, seated on the ground according to their rank; and, in the name of Louis the Fifteenth, Montcalm produced the mighty belt of six thousand shells, which, being solemnly accepted, bound all, by the holiest ties, to remain together till the end of the expedition. The belt was given to the Iroquois, as the most numerous; but they courteously transferred it to the upper nations, who came, though strangers, to their aid. In the scarcity of boats, the Iroquois agreed to guide De Levi, with twenty-five hundred men, by land, through the rugged country which they called their own.

"The Christian savages employed their short leisure at the confessional; the tribes from above, restlessly weary, dreamed dreams, consulted the great medicine men, and, hanging up the complete equipment of a war-chief as an offering to their Manitou, embarked on the last day of July.

"The next day, two hours after noon, Montcalm followed with the main body of the army, in two hundred and fifty boats. The Indians whom he overtook, preceded him in their decorated canoes. Rain fell in torrents; yet they rowed nearly all night, till they came in sight of

* DeBougainville to the Minister, 19th August, 1757.

the three triangular fires that, from a mountain ridge, pointed to the encampment of De Levi. There, in Ganousky, or, as some call it, Northwest Bay, they held a council of war, and then, with the artillery, they moved slowly to a bay, of which the point could not be turned without exposure to the enemy. An hour before midnight, two English boats were descried on the lake, when some of the upper Indians paddled two canoes to attack them, and with such celerity that one of the boats was seized and overpowered, two prisoners being reserved; the rest were massacred. The Indians lost but one warrior, a great chieftain of the nation of the Nepissings.

"On the morning of the second day of August, the savages dashed openly upon the water, and forming across the lake a chain of their bark canoes, they made the bay resound with their war-cry. The English were taken almost by surprise. Their tents covered the plains. Montcalm disembarked without interruption, about a mile and a half below the fort, and advanced in three columns. The Indians hurried to burn the barracks of the English, to chase their cattle and horses, and to scalp their stragglers. During the day, they occupied, with the Canadians under La Corne, the road leading to the Hudson, and cut off the communication. At the north was the encampment of De Levi, with regulars and Canadians, while Montcalm, with the main body of the army, occupied the skirt of the wood on the west side of the lake. His whole force consisted of six thousand French and Canadians, and about seventeen hundred Indians. Fort William Henry was defended by Lieutenant-Colonel William Munro,* of the 35th regiment, a brave officer and a man of strict honor, with less than 500 men, while 1700 men lay entrenched near his side, on an eminence to the south-east, now marked by the ruins of Fort George.

"Meantime, the braves of the Nepissings, faithful to the rites of their fathers, celebrated the funeral honors of their departed brother. The lifeless frame, dressed as became a war-chief, glittered with belts and ear-rings, and the brilliant vermilion; a riband, fiery red, supported a gorget on his breast; the tomahawk was in his girdle, the pipe at his lips, the lance in his hand, at his side the well-filled bowl. And thus the departed warrior sat upright on the green turf, which was his death-

---

* Captain Christie to Governor Pownall, 10th August, 1757.

couch. The speech for the dead was pronounced; the death-dances and chants began; the murmurs of human voices mingled with the sound of drums and the tinkling of little bells. And thus arrayed, in a sitting posture, he was consigned to the earth, well provided with food, and surrounded by the splendors which delighted him when alive.

"On the fourth of August, the French summoned Munro to surrender, but the gallant old soldier sent an answer of defiance. Montcalm hastened his works; the troops dragged the artillery over rocks and through forests, and with alacrity brought fascines and gabions. The red men, unused to a siege, were eager to hear the big guns. Soon the first battery of nine cannon and two mortars was finished; and amidst the loud scream of the savages, it began to play, while a thousand echoes were returned by the mountains. In two days more a second was established, and by means of the zig-zags, the Indians could stand within gun-shot of the fortress. Just then arrived letters from France, conferring on Montcalm the red riband, with rank as Knight Commander of the Order of St. Louis.'

"'We are glad,' said the red men, 'of the favor done you by the great Onontbio, but we neither love you, nor esteem you the more for it; we love the man, and not what hangs on his outside.' Webb, at Fort Edward, had an army of four thousand, and might have summoned the militia from all the near villages to the rescue. He sent nothing but a letter, with an exaggerated account of the French force, and his advice to capitulate. Montcalm intercepted the letter, which he immediately forwarded to Munro. Yet, not till the eve of the festival of St. Lawrence, when half his guns were burst, and his ammunition was almost exhausted, did the dauntless veteran hang out a flag of truce.

"With a view to make the capitulation unviolably binding on the Indians, Montcalm summoned their war chiefs to council. The English were to depart with the honors of war, on a pledge not to serve against the French for eighteen months; they were to abendon all but their private effects; an escort was to attend them on their departure; every Canadian or French Indian made captive during the war was to be liberated. The Indians applauded; the capitulation was signed. Late on the ninth of August the French entered the fort, and the English retired to their entrenched camp.

"Montcalm had kept from the savages all intoxicating drinks, but they solicited and obtained them of the English, and all night long they were wild with dances and songs and revelry. The Abenakis of Acadia excited the angry passions of other tribes, by recalling the sorrows they had suffered from English perfidy and English power. At day-break they gathered round the entrenchment, and, as the English soldiers filed off, began to plunder them, and incited one another to swing the tomahawk recklessly. Twenty, perhaps even thirty, persons were massacred, while very many were made prisoners. Officers and soldiers, stripped of everything, fled to the woods, to the fort, and to the tents of the French. To arrest the disorder, De Levi plunged into the tumult, daring death a thousand times. French officers received wounds in rescuing the captives, and stood at their tents as sentries over those they recovered. 'Kill me,' cried Montcalm, using prayers, and menaces and promises; 'but spare the English, who are under my protection;'* and he urged the troops to defend themselves. The march to Fort Edward was a flight; not more than six hundred reached there in a body. From the French camp Montcalm collected together more than four hundred, who were dismissed with a great escort, and he sent De Vaudreuil to ransom those whom the Indians had carried away.

"After the surrender of Fort William Henry, the savages retired. Twelve hundred men were employed to demolish the fort, and nearly a thousand to lade the vast stores that had been given up. As Montcalm withdrew, he praised his happy fortune that his victory was, on his own side, almost bloodless, his loss in killed and wounded being but fifty-three. The Canadian peasants returned to gather their harvests, and the lake resumed its solitude. Nothing told that civilised man had reposed upon its margin but the charred rafters of ruins, and, here and there, on the side-hill, a crucifix among the pines to mark a grave."

In perusing Bancroft's narrative, we find nothing to support the allegation of British and of some American writers, "that the French at Fort William Henry acted as fiends." We cannot, either, detect any circumstance calculated to warrant Cooper's charge against Montcalm, of "extraordinary apathy" during the massacre. The reverse in fact is

* Montcalm to the Minister, 8th September, 1757.

apparent in every line. I am indebted to the kindness of our old historian, the Abbé Ferland, for a most interesting letter, from an eye-witness of the whole proceedings. It not only corroborates entirely Bancroft's and Garneau's version of the Fort William surrender, but discloses circumstances which I have not yet read in any English work. This letter was written in French by the Abenakis missionary of the St. François village, near Montreal, and bears date 21st October, 1757; it is to be found in the *Recueil de Lettres Edifiantes et Curieuses*, reprinted at Toulouse in 1810, vol. 6. It is referred to by Bancroft and other historians, but its text in English is not given.

(*Translation.*) " ST. FRANCOIS, near Montreal,
21*st October*, 1757.

On the 12th July, I left St. François, chief village of the Abenakis mission, for Montreal, to present to M. De Vaudreuil a deputation of twenty Abenakis who accompany Father Virot in his undertaking to found a new mission amongst the Wolfe Indians of the River Oyo, or *Belle Rivière*.

We soon received orders to join the French army, which was camped one league higher up, towards the *portage*, close to a spot where a waterfall compelled us to convey overland to Lake St. Sacrement (George) the implements necessary for the siege. Preparations were being made for a start, when an occurrence took place which rivetted the general attention. A small fleet of canoes was seen in the distance, coming up an arm of the river, decked out with trophies, heralding a victory. It was M. Marin, a Canadian officer of much merit, returning triumphantly from the expedition confided to his charge. About 200 savages had been placed under his orders to go towards Fort Lydis; he had, with a small flying camp, the courage to attack and the good fortune to take possession of—a large portion of the outer works of the fort. His savages had just sufficient time to remove the scalps from the two hundred dead warriors left on the spot, without losing a single one of their own party. The enemy, three thousand strong, in vain sought to wreak vengeance in the pursuit they made of the savages. It was whilst we were engaged in counting the number of English scalps displayed about the canoes, that we observed a French boat bearing towards us five Englishmen, tied and escorted by Outaouacks, whose prisoners they were.

The sight of these unfortunate captives caused great rejoicings amongst the savages present: these barbarous feelings they gave vent to, by horrible yells and by conduct distressing to humanity. More than one thousand savages, taken from thirty-six different tribes, under the banner of France, were at that moment lining the shores of the lake. At one instant, and seemingly without any preconcerted plan, they all ran in hot haste towards the adjoining woods. I knew not at first how to explain this unexpected movement. I was not long in suspense. The barbarians in a minute returned with clubs ready to inflict on the unfortunate English the most dreadful treatment. At sight of these cruel preparations, my heart sank in me; I felt my eyes bathed with tears; my sorrow did not however render me inactive. Without a moment for thought, I flew towards those wild beasts, in hopes of restraining them; alas! of what avail was my feeble voice, but to articulate a few sounds, which the tumult, the diversity of languages, the surrounding ferocity rendered inaudible. At least I made bitter reproaches to some Abenaquis who were near me; my determination awoke humane sentiments in their breasts. Ashamed, they slank off from the murderous crowd, throwing away their clubs. But what was a few less in a mass of 2,000, bent on giving no quarter? Seeing the futility of my interference, I was in the act of withdrawing in order not to witness the bloody tragedy which would soon commence. I had scarcely gone a few steps when a feeling of compassion brought me back to the bank, from which I cast my eyes on the victims doomed to certain death. Their present state caused me a new pang. Terror had so overpowered them that their strength failed them completely—they could barely stand up; death was written on their downcast and convulsed features. They were doomed; they seemed certain of being battered to death, when, lo and behold! their salvation sprung from the very acts of their murderers. The French officer who had charge of the boat had noticed what had taken place on the shore. Moved by that feeling of commiseration which misfortune rings from a brave man, he undertook to create a similar sentiment in the heart of the Outaouacks, masters of the prisoners. He played his part so well that he succeeded to inspire in them compassion for the captives. They immediately adopted a plan which succeeded to its fullest extent. As soon as the boat was within hailing distance from the shore, one of its inmates, an Outaouack, proudly uttered the following threat: *"These prisoners are mine; my property shall be respected; touch them, any of you, and you touch me!"* One hundred French officers might have spoken thus; they would only have been laughed at, and have brought on the captives an increase of cruelty; but a savage fears his fellow, and him only; the most trifling insult may have to be atoned for by death only: this makes them cautious. The will of the Outaouack was respected, as soon as made known; the prisoners were disembarked without any tumult, and lodged in the fort, free from insult. They were then separated and closely questioned, and soon revealed all we wanted to know. Terror made them communicative to a degree. I visited one who was placed in a room in which one of my friends was. I tried to inspire him with hope, and procured him refreshments, for which he seemed grateful.

Having given pent to my feelings of compassion, and having solaced an unfortunate, I hastened to get my own little party on board of the boats, which was done instantly. The distance was short: two hours were sufficient to get to the end of our journey. The tent of the Chevalier de Lévi stood at the entrance to the camp. I took the liberty to pay my respects to this personnage, whose name is synonymous with merit, and who is still better than his name. The conversation turned on the circumstance which had saved the life of the five English prisoners, whose perillous adventure I have just related. I was far from knowing the details, which are indeed startling, viz.: M. De Corbesse, a French colonial officer, had been ordered the night previous to cruize on Lake St. Sacrement. His detachment consisted of about fifty French and a little over three hundred savages. At dawn of day, he discovered in boats a detachment of three hundred English. These boats being more lofty and stronger in build than birch canoes, more than compensated the superiority we had over them in numbers. Our men did not hesitate to attack them, and the enemy at first seemed ready to fight, but this resolve did not last. The French and savages, whose only chance of victory rested in their boarding the boats, and who fought at a disadvantage, being at a distance, closed in, in spite of the heavy fire poured on them. The British no sooner saw them drawing near, than terror disarmed them. It was not a fight: 'twas a rout. Of all alternatives, the most dangerous, though the less honorable, was for the English to seek to land: they choose it. They made their way towards the shore accordingly. Some jumped in the water to swim ashore, in hopes of hiding in the woods: a bad plan, the folly of which brought sorrow on them. However swift their boats might be, could they expect to beat the birch canoes which fly through the liquid element with the swiftness of an arrow? Soon did the French and savages catch up to them. In the first heat of the fight all were massacred without quarter—torn to pieces. Those who took to the woods did not fare better. An Indian in the woods is in his own element; he can run through them as nimbly as a deer. The enemy was hacked to pieces. At last the Outaouacks, seeing that they had to deal, not with fighting men, but with beings who allowed themselves to be slaughtered without resisting, set to making prisoners. There were 157 prisoners taken and 131 killed; twelve only escaped captivity and death. The boats, equipments, provisions, all was taken and plundered. No doubt you fancy that such a victory cost us dear. The fight took place on water, that is in an open place, where no ambush could be laid. The enemy had time to prepare; he had the advantage of attacking from boats with lofty sides, frail bark canoes which a little skill or coolness would have sunk with their crews. Well, this is all true, and still this success only cost us one Indian, disabled by a shot in the wrist.

Such was the fate of the British under the unfortunate Mr. Copperel, who, it was thought, was drowned. The English speak of this engagement in terms denoting as much sorrow as surprise at its results. They frankly admit the extent of their losses; it would, indeed, be difficult to deny the slightest detail: the corpses of their men floating on the waters of the lake or strewing its beaches, tell the fearful tale. As to those made prisoners, the greater portion are still in the dungeons of M. Le Chevalier de Lévi. I saw them fyling off in detachments escorted by the victors, who, barbarously occupied with their triumph, thought little of softening the pangs of a defeat. In the space of a league which I had to walk before joining my Abenaquis Indians, I met several small squads of these prisoners. More than one Indian stopped to exhibit to me, with pride, his capture, expecting I would applaud his success.

The love of country certainly did not make me insensible to a triumph favorable to our nation. But misfortune commands respect, not only on behalf of religion, but even from nature. Moreover, these prisoners seemed in such a plight; their eyes swimming in tears, their faces covered with prespiration and blood, and a halter round their necks: in presence of such a spectacle, compassion and humanity asserted their rights. The rum, which the savages had freely imbibed, had gone to their heads and increased their natural ferocity. I feared to witness every minute, some of the prisoners slaughtered and falling at my feet, victims of cruelty and drunkenness; I scarcely dared to look up for fear of meeting the sorrowful glance of some captive. A spectacle more horrible than what I had yet seen was soon to take place.

My tent had been pitched in the centre of the Outaouack camp. The first thing I noticed on arriving there was a large fire: wooden stakes, stuck in the earth, announced a feast. It was one, but, good heavens! what a feast: the remains of an Englishman's corpse cut up and half eaten. I saw these fiends a short time after greedily devouring a human creature: they were helping themselves from the pot with large ladles to the reeking flesh as if they could never swallow enough. I heard that they had prepared themselves to this feed, by drinking brimful, out of the skulls, human blood; their smeared faces and gory lips confirmed the statement. What was still more awful, they had placed, close by, ten English prisoners to witness the abominable repast! The Outaouack's nation resembles that of the Abenaquis; I thought that by gently rebuking them for this act, I might make some impression on their mind. I erred: a young warrior said, "You speak and act like a Frenchman, but I am an Indian, human flesh is good for me." He then handed me a baked fragment cut from the English corpse. To his words I made no reply, but his offer I rejected with visible horror. Convinced, by what I had just witnessed, that I could do nothing to alter the state of things in respect to the dead, I thought I would see what I could do for those still living, whose fate was much more to be pitied. I walked up to the English, one of whom attracted my notice; by his uniform I saw he was an officer; I resolved to purchase him, and thereby save his life and liberty. I made up, with this object in view, to an old Outaouack, thinking that the ice of age would have tempered his ferocity, and that he would be more manageable; I extended my hand to him, bowing civilly at the same moment. It was not a man I had to deal with; it was a being even more ferocious than a wild beast, as wild animals often yield to kindness. "*No*," he thundered out, in accents which might have awed me, had my heart, in that moment, been susceptible to harbour any other feeling but that of compassion and horror, "*No! I do not want your friendship; avaunt!*" I did not wait for a repetition of the threat. I withdrew to my tent, to brood over the thoughts which religion and humanity can inspire on such an occasion. It did not occur to me as necessary to dissuade my Abenaquis Indians from committing such horrible excesses. However powerful example may be with all men in matters of customs and habits, they were incapable of perpetrating such acts; even before they were christianized, they never were cannibals. Their humane and tractable disposition, at that period, distinguished them from the greatest portion of the Indians of this continent. These thoughts kept me awake a considerable portion of the night.

Next morning, on rising, I had hoped no vestige would remain round my tent of the repast of the preceding day. I flattered myself that the fumes of rum and the fierce feelings they engender, having been dissipated, calmness and humanity would again return. I knew not the Outaouack's character and disposition. It was as a luxury, a *bonne bouche*, that they had banquetted on human flesh. At the dawn of day, their execrable repast had been resumed; they were only waiting for the moment to set to and devour the last remains of the English corpse. I have already said that we were three missionaries attached to this mission. During the entire campaign, we lodged, thought, and acted together on all points; this community of feelings rendered our duties more bearable during the fatigues of warfare. We came to the conclusion that it would not be proper to celebrate our holy mysteries in the head-quarters of barbarism, inasmuch as these superstitious tribes might use the holy vases to assist them in, and to decorate their, juggleries. For this reason we left a spot polluted by so many abominations, and dived into the depths of the forest. This could not be effected, however, without separating myself a little from my Abenaquis. It had, however, to be done. This step was in the end productive of regret, as you will see by the sequel. I had not been long in my new abode before I witnessed with what new fervor my neophytes drew towards the tribunal of repentence. * * * * * Whilst many of my Abnaquis sought the succour of religion, others strived to irritate Heaven, and by their acts to call down punishment from above. Ardent spirits are the favorite drink, the universal passion of the savage tribes, and unfortunately, despite of laws human and divine, too many furnish them with this curse. Unquestionably however the missionary, by his character, by the influence he exerts, prevents much disorderly conduct. I lived close to my flock, a small wood alone intervening. I could not, however, after night-fall visit the encampment, without running the risk of hostile attacks not only on the part of the allies of the English, the Iroquois, who had, a few days previously, scalped one of our grenadiers, but also at the hands of the idolatrous portion of our own savages, to whom experience had taught me not to trust. Some young Abnaquis, together with Indians of several tribes, took advantage of my absence and of darkness, to go and steal some ardent spirits from the French tents, whilst the inmates were asleep. Once in possession of the liquor, they used it freely and soon felt its influence. Drunkenness amongst Indians makes itself known seldom by silence, generally by noise. They commenced to sing, to dance, to cry out, and then set to fighting. At the dawn of day, disorder was at its height; I then learned of it and hastened to where trouble existed; alarm and confusion everywhere—caused by intoxication. My Indians soon were calmed. I took each of them by the hand in succession and conducted them to their tents, bidding them to lie down. This scandalous scene seemed ended, when a Moraigan Indian, naturalized amongst the Abnaquis and adopted by the tribe, re-enacted it in a still more serious manner. After having had words with a drunken comrade, an Iroquois, they came to blows. The first, a more powerful man, having thrown his opponent, was belaboring him unmercifully, and what was worse, lacerating his shoulder with his teeth. The combat was at its height when I drew near them. I could only use my own strength to separate them. Indians fear one another too much to interfere, no matter for what reason, into one another's quarrels. I was unable to cope with them, and the victor was too infuriated to quit his victim so readily. I was tempted to leave these demons chastise one another for their own excesses, but I feared the death of one of them would be the *finale.* I increased my efforts; by dint of pulling at the Abnaquis, he felt some one shaking him; turning his head round: he had trouble in recognizing me; he was still excited, but gradually became calm, when he allowed the Iroquois liberty to escape, of which the latter was not slow to avail himself. * * * *

[Further on the good missionary relates the trouble he experienced in preventing his Indians from blowing up the boats containing the powder, a feat they had undertaken for mere amusement sake.]

The forced inactivity of our Christian Indians, together with the presence of so many idolatrous nations, made me tremble, not for the sake of religion itself, but on account of their future conduct. I longed for the day when the preparations for the expedition would allow us to start. When the mind is engaged the heart is less liable to err. That day at last came, and on the 29th of July the Chevalier de Lévis, with 3,000 men, marched overland to protect the arrival of the army which was to proceed by water conveyance. His march was not accompanied with any of those facilities which high roads in Europe, built with princely magnificence, offer. Impenetrable forests, rugged mountains, slimy bogs, such was the route composed of. Three leagues a day was a good performance; we took five days to travel twelve leagues. These obstacles had been foreseen, and hence why this detachment had, in marching, started a few days before the other. On the Sunday we embarked with the Indians, only about 1,200 at that time, the rest having gone by land.

We had scarcely made four or five leagues on the lake before we noticed evident traces of our last victory in the shape of abandoned English boats which, after being buffetted a long while with the winds and tide, had floated ashore on the beach. The most striking spectacle was a tolerable large quantity of English corpses strewing the shore or scattered here and there in the woods. Some were hacked to pieces, and mostly all were mutilated in a most horrible way. What an awful visitation war then seemed to me! It would have been highly agreeable to me to have the remains of our enemies buried, but we had only landed by accident in this cove. Duty and necessity compelled us to journey on, in conformity with orders; we had to lose no time. It was night when we reached the spot marked out as a camping ground—a locality overrun with wild thorns and alive with rattlesnakes; our Indians brought us several they had caught. This venomous reptile, if ever there was one, has a head much too small in proportion to its body; the skin is sometimes regularly spotted with a dark black and a pale yellow colour. He has no sting, but very sharp teeth, a bright sparkling eye; he carries under his tail several small scales which he can inflate prodigiously, and which he rattles violently one against the other when irritated: hence his name. His virus after being exposed to smoke is a specific against toothache; his flesh when smoked and pulverised is also a good cure for fever. Salt is applied as a cure on the part affected by his bite, which otherwise proves fatal in less than an hour.

The next day about 4 P.M., M. de Montcalm arrived with the remainder of the forces; we had to start in spite of the rain which fell in torrents; we marched on the greater portion of the night until we discovered M. de Lévis' camp, by three fires lighted in a triangle on the crest of the mountain. We halted there; a general council was held; and then started for Lake George, distant twelve miles. At twelve o'clock, noon, we took to the canoes to ascend, paddling slowly in order to allow the boats bearing our artillery to come up, but they could not do it, and at night they were more than three miles astern. Having arrived at an indenture, the point of which we could not pass without revealing ourselves to the enemy, we resolved, until we received fresh orders, to pass the night there. It was marked by a small incident which was the prelude to the siege.

About eleven, two boats from the fort appeared on the lake; they soon had reason to alter their calm and measured movements. A neighbor of mine, who kept watch for the benefit of all, noticed them at a fair distance. All the Indians were apprised of the fact, and preparations made to receive them, in haste but in silence. I was ordered to seek safety by going ashore and concealing myself in the woods. It was not through mistaken bravery, unsuited to a minister of religion, that I disregarded the mandate. I thought the order was not serious, having reason to doubt the statement about the boats. It was not likely that our lynx-eyed enemies had failed to notice the presence, since two days, on the waters of the lake, of our four hundred boats; on this hypothesis I could scarcely persuade myself that two boats would have the foolhardiness to appear in our presence, much less to engage in combat forces so much superior. A friend of mine who had seen all, reprimanded me in strong terms for not being where I ought to be: he was right; a boat tolerably large held all the missionaries; a tent was spread over it to protect them against the inclemency of the weather during the cool nights. This white pavillion, under which we took shelter, was visible at a distance by moonlight, and the English were curious to find out what it was. To come towards us or to run straight to destruction was one and the same thing. Few could have escaped, if, fortunately for them, a small incident had not warned them a few minutes too soon for the success of our plans. One of the sheep forming part of the army supplies began to bleet; this sound, which presaged an ambuscade, caused the enemy to stop short, face about, and urge on their boats double quick, in order to escape, favored by darkness and the woods.

What then remained to be done? Twelve hundred savages pursued the fugitives, with yells as loud as they were incessant. Both parties seemed to hesitate; not a shot was fired. The assailants not having had time to form regularly, were afraid to fire lest they should hit one another; moreover they wished to make prisoners. The fugitives struggled hard to get away, and were in the act of doing so, when the Indians fired. The British, being too close to the first canoes, returned the fire, and soon an ominous silence succeeded to all this noise. We were hoping for victory, when a pseudo-brave, who was not in the *mêlée*, shouted that the Abnaquis Indians had met with severe loss Immediately, seizing hold of the religious vases wherewith to administer the last rites, I hurriedly jumped into a canoe to get to where the fight had taken place. I was however not wanted, as I learned from another Indian who had been in the thick of it; none of our forces had been struck except a Nipissingue who was killed, and another Indian warrior wounded, whilst boarding the enemy. I did not wait for the end of his narrative, but hastened back to our people, leaving the matter in the hands of the Nipissingue missionary, Mr. Mathaveh. I arrived by water and met M. de Montcalm, who, on hearing the firing, had landed lower down and made his way through the woods; an Abnaquis Indian, at my request, related to him what had taken place in a very few words. The darkness of the night prevented the number of dead being known; the enemies' boats had been captured and also three prisoners; the remainder strayed through the forest. M. de Montcalm, pleased with the success, then withdrew to ponder over, with his usual sagacity, the operations of the morrow.

Day had scarcely dawned, when the warriors of the Nipissingue nation present, proceeded with the funeral of their dead warrior (a pagan,) killed in the engagement of the previous night.

The funeral was accompanied with all the pomp and show customary with savages. The body was decked out, or rather completely covered, with all the grotesque ornaments which vanity could devise for such a melancholy occasion; porcelain necklace, silver bracelets, rings in the ears and nose, sumptuous dresses, all was brought into requisition; paint and vermilion was resorted to in order to replace, by freshness and an appearance of life, the palor of death. The wearing apparel of an Indian warrior was also used;—a fiery red ribbon tied upon his breast; a gorget; his gun rested on his arm; a tomahawk in his girdle; his pipe in his mouth; his lance in his hand; a well-filled can at his side. Thus gaudily attired as a warrior, he was seated on a grassy mound as on a couch. Ranged in a circle round this corpse, the Indians observed a solemn silence, as if oppressed with grief. The orator interrupted it by pronouncing the funeral oration on the dead; to this succeeded war songs and dances, with the noise of tambourines and bells for music: a death-like solemnity, in keeping with the occasion, reigned throughout. The pageant ended by the burial of the Indian warrior with a large quantity of eatables deposited in the grave, no doubt to prevent the possibility of his dying a second time for want of food. I cannot, as to this ceremony, speak as an eye witness; the presence of a missionary would indeed be out of place at a pageant dictated by superstition and adopted by stupid credulity. I had these facts from spectators. * * * *

Fort George was a square, flanked by four bastions, with outer works and ditches eighteen to twenty feet deep; the scarp and counter scarp were sloped with moving sand; the walls consisted of large pine trunks supported by massive stakes, about fifteen to eighteen feet high, the interstices filled up solidly with sand. Four or five hundred men, with nineteen cannon, defended it. Two or three of these were thirty-six pounders, the others were of smaller caliber; there were also four or five mortars. The place was protected by no other external works than a fortified rock, surrounded by a palisade and piles of stone, the garrison of which consisted of 1700 men which constantly sent reinforcements to the fort itself. The chief strength of this entrenchment consisted in its peculiar position, which commanded all surrounding objects, and which, on account of the mountains and swamps in its neighborhood, could only be attacked with artillery from the fort. Such was Fort George from what I saw and heard of it after its capitulation. It was impossible to invest and attack it on all sides. 6,000 French or Canadians and 1700 savages, our whole strength, were not enough to compass its surrender with any degree of success. 20,000 men would scarcely have sufficed. The enemy had always a kind of back door, whereby they could retreat to the forest —a good plan—had they to evade enemies which were not Indians; but from such escape under cover of the woods is more than hazardous. The Indian warriors were encamped on the Lydis road, so close to the woods and in such numbers that this plan of evasion could scarcely avail them. On the heights of the land close by and within hail, were located the Canadians. Lastly, the French regulars—to whom, properly speaking, were confided the siege operations—were disposed on the edge of the wood, close to where the trench would open; then came the reserve camp, sufficiently strong to ward off assault.

These preliminaries settled, M. de Montcalm sent proposals to the enemy, which, had they been accepted, would have saved a great deal of blood and sorrow. The following are very nearly the terms of the letter sent to M. Moreau (Col. Munro), the British officer in charge:

"Sir,—I come at the head of forces large enough to take possession of the place under your command, and to intercept any succour which might come to you from elsewhere. Among my followers is a crowd of savage tribes, whom any blood spilt might render deaf to any sentiments of mercy and moderation. My love of humanity induces me to ask from you a surrender, now that I may yet obtain from them terms of capitulation honorable to yourselves, and useful to all.—I remain, &c.

(Signed) "Montcalm."

M. de Lévis' aide-de-camp, M. Fontbrane, was the bearer of this letter. The English officers, several of whom he knew, received M. Fontbrane with that courtesy customary between honorable men in times of war. But no surrender was granted. The reply ran thus:

"Monsieur le Général, I feel obliged to you in particular for the gracious offers you make. I fear not barbarous treatment. My men, like myself, are determined to conquer or die.—I am, &c.

(Signed) "MOREAU (Munro.)"

This proud reply was accompanied with a salvo of guns. We were far from being able to answer. Before establishing a battery, we had to carry our guns through woods and over rocks, fully a mile and a half. Thanks to the voracity of our Indian allies, we were deprived of the use of our horses for this duty. Tired of salt meat, they had not hesitated to seize hold of them some days previously, killing and eating them, without taking counsel of any one except their stomachs. In the absence of beasts of burthen, so many strong arms and loyal men set to work that the task was soon completed. During all this, I was lodged close to the hospital, a spot from whence I could easily afford to lend the help of my ministry to the dying and wounded. I remained there some time without having any news about my Indians. This silence caused me uneasiness. I was very desirous of assembling them once more, to inspire them with sentiments becoming religion, in the perilous position in which they were. I determined on going to seek them. The trip, over and above its length, was beset with perils. I had to pass by the trench where a soldier, close by me, had met his death, whilst examining the curious indenture a bullet had made on a tree. On my road, I must confess I was struck with the way the French and the Canadians performed the dangerous duties devolving on them. On seeing the joy with which they carried to the scene of danger felled trees and other siege implements, one would have imagined they considered themselves invulnerable against the incessant fire of the enemy. Such acts denote pluck and love of country, and this is the true character of the nation. I went all round without finding any one except a few stray squads of Abnaquis, so that my journey resulted in nothing except in shewing my good will. At that distance from my people I could be of but very little use to them; still I rendered some service to a prisoner, a Moraigan, whose tribe is favorable to, and mostly entirely under, the dominion of Britain. This man's face was quite repulsive; an enormous head with small eyes, a heavy body and diminutive stature, thick and short legs: these traits and many others classified him amongst deformed men; nevertheless he was a human being, and as such entitled to the offices of christian charity, being still more the victim of his looks than of misfortune. He was bound to the trunk of a tree, where his grotesque face attracted the curiosity of passers-by; jeers and taunts were his lot at first, then came blows: he was struck so violently as nearly to cause him the loss of an eye. Such conduct revolted me; I ran to the relief of this unfortunate, and pained by his misfortune, I authoritatively expelled from the spot idle spectators. I mounted guard near him a portion of the day, and played my part so well that I enlisted in his behalf his masters' (the savages) sympathies, so that the persecutions ceased without my remaining there. I do not know whether he felt grateful; he gave me only a wild glance; but independently of religion, I was more than compensated by the pleasure I had experienced in saving an unhappy being. There were plenty of other unfortunates. Every day Indian skill and bravery added to their numbers, in the shape of prisoners. The enemy could not stir out of the fort without meeting captivity or death. The following will show: an English woman took into her head to go in quest of vegetables, in a cultivated patch close to the ditch of the fortress; her daring cost her dear. A savage, secreted in a cabbage bed, saw her and shot her dead. The enemy tried in vain to remove her body; the victor stood sentry all day long, and finally scalped her.

In the meantime, the savages got very desponding at not hearing any shots fired from the *big guns*, as they called our cannon. They grew impatient at not being allowed to carry on the war alone. To satisfy them, we had to hasten to begin the siege and to mount our first battery. When it opened for the first time, the whole mountains resounded with their yells and joyous cries. We were dispensed during the operations from taking much trouble to ascertain the effect of our firing; the wild yells of the Indians soon carried this information in every direction. I seriously thought of changing my quarters; the distance which intervened between them and where my neophytes were, left me no duties to perform, but before this change took place an alarming incident occurred. The frequent trips which the enemy made during the day towards their boats made us suspect some grand move was in contemplation. A rumor got abroad that they intended to burn our war and commissariat supplies. M. de Launay, captain of a French regiment of grenadiers was instructed to watch over the boats which contained them. The skilful measures he had devised rendered it almost a subject of regret to us that the enemy did not show himself. I, subsequently to this, joined my Abnaquis and remained with them during the remainder of the campaign. Nothing of note took place for some days, except the promptitude with which the siege operations progressed. Our second battery was erected in two days. This was for the Indians the occasion for a new holiday, which they celebrated in a style befitting warriors. They were constantly hovering around our gunners, whose skill they admired. Nor was their admiration barren in results. They were resolved to make themselves useful in every way; undertaking to act as gunners, and one in particular got very expert. A savage having himself pointed a gun, struck exactly a retreating angle, on which he had been told to take aim. He however declined trying a second shot, alleging that as he had at the onset attained to perfection, he ought not to risk his reputation on a second attempt. But what seemed to astonish the savages most in our siege operations was the several zigzags of a trench which, like subterranean passages, are so useful in protecting the besiegers from the fire of the besieged. They witnessed with unbounded curiosity the finish and perfection which the French grenadiers bestowed on their works. The force of example soon induced them to set to, with pick and hoe, to open a trench towards the fortified rock, a task confided to them. They soon had extended the trench so far that they got within gun shot. M. de Villiers, brother to M. de Jumonville, an officer whose name alone indicated merit, took advantage of this trench to march up with a detachment of Canadians in order to open fire on the outer defences of the enemy. The action was sharp, long and bloody for the enemy, who abandoned these outer works;—the chief entrenchments would also have been carried that day if their capture could have ensured the fall of the place. Each day was signalised by some brilliant feat of arms, either by the French, the Canadians or the savages. In the meantime the enemy held out resolutely, buoyed up with the hopes of a prompt relief. A trivial occurrence which happened then ought to have greatly decreased these hopes. Our scouts met in the woods three messengers, who had left Fort Lydis (Edward): they killed the first, captured the second, and the third escaped by swiftness of foot. A letter was discovered in a hollow bullet concealed on the body of the dead messenger with so much art, that none save a soldier experienced in these matters could have detected it. This letter was signed by the commander of Fort Lydis, and addressed to the commander of Fort George. It contained the summary of the confession extorted from a Canadian, made prisoner on the first night of our arrival. He had stated that our army consisted of 11,000 men, and our Indian allies of 2,000, with most formidable artillery. This was erroneous, and our forces were considerably over-estimated. But the error did not proceed from fraud, which, however useful it can be to any country, cannot be pardoned by an honorable man, be he ever so patriotic. Until this campaign, the largest armies from Canada had rarely exceeded 800 men; surprise and wonder magnified ours to those unaccustomed to see considerable ones. I have often, during the campaign, witnessed greater illusions in this way. The commander of Fort Lydis concluded his letter by informing his colleague that the interest of the king, his master, did not permit him to send any soldiers from the fort: that it was his duty to capitulate and make the best of terms.

The best use Montcalm fancied this letter could be applied, was to have it delivered to its address by the surviving despatch-bearer, who had been captured. The English officer (Munro) thanked him, and hoped he would continue to act with the same courtesy. This act either indicated that he was joking, or else a prolonged resistance. The actual state of the place did not presage the latter: one-half of its batteries dismounted and rendered useless by our guns; terror amongst the besieged, whose courage was only kept up by rum; finally, frequent desertions—all combined to show that surrender was close at hand. Such was the opinion of deserters, who would have come in crowds had not our Indian allies increased the perils attending such a feat.

Amongst those who sought refuge in our ranks, there was an individual belonging to a neighboring republic, our faithful ally, who enabled me to claim him soon, as a returned son of the church. I visited him soon at the hospital, where he lay wounded. On my return, I noticed a general movement in all quarters of the camp—French, Canadians and Indians, all ran to arms. The rumor of the arrival of succor to the enemy had caused this commotion. Amidst alarm, M. de Montcalm, with that coolness which marks a master mind, made arrangements for the safety of our trenches, of our batteries and boats, and then left to head the army. I was quietly seated at the door of my tent, from which I could see our troops go by, when an Abnaquis put an end to my contemplative mood, by unceremoniously saying to me: "*Father, you pledged yourself that no danger would deter you from coming to administer to us the rites of your religion; do you think our wounded men could come to you from the battle-field, across these mountains? We now start to fight, and look to you to fulfil your promise.*" This strong appeal made me forget my fatigues. I took my position with alacrity in front of our regulars. After a forced march, I arrived at a spot where my people, in front of all the troops, were waiting for the battle to begin. I deputed, on the spot, messengers to bring them all together, and gave them a general absolution before meeting the enemy; but no enemy came. M. de Montcalm, in order not to lose the advantage of his preparations, sought to bring them out by the following stratagem. He proposed that the French and Canadians should simulate a fight, whilst the Indians, secreted in the woods, should lie in wait for the enemy, who would assuredly make a sortie. Our Iroquois approved of the plan, but alleged that the day was too far gone. The other savages were in favor of the *ruse de guerre*, but the excuse of the Iroquois prevailed; so that all had to withdraw without seeing anything more than the preparations for a fight. At last, the next day being the eve of the *fête* of Saint Lawrence and the seventh after our arrival, the trenches having been pushed as far as the gardens, we were just going to mount our third and last battery. The closeness of the fort led us to hope that in three or four days it might be assaulted by all our forces, and breached; but the enemy saved us the trouble and danger: they hung out the white flag, and asked to surrender.

We are now drawing near to the capitulation of the fort, and to the bloody catastrophe which ensued. No doubt that every corner of Europe has echoed with the news of this melancholy event, whose odious character (unexplained) is calculated to cast a stigma on France. Your equity will soon be in a position to decide whether this horrible charge rests, or not, on malignity or on ignorance of the facts. I shall merely adduce circumstances so public and so incontrovertible, that I can even, without fear of contradiction, appeal to the testimony of the English officers who saw them and suffered from them. The Marquis of Montcalm, before granting any capitulation, had thought proper, in order to have the capitulation respected, to consult all the Indian tribes present. He assembled all their chiefs, and laid before them the terms of the surrender; it granted to the garrison the right to march out of the fort with all the honors of war, imposing on them the obligation not to serve for eighteen months against the King of France, and to release all the Canadians made prisoners during this war. These terms received general assent and approbation, and were signed by the generals of both armies. Consequently, the French army, drawn up in line of battle, advanced towards the fort, to take possession of it in the name of His Most Christian Majesty, whilst the English troops, in good order, left it to go and post themselves, until the next day, in the retrenchments. Their march was not interrupted by a violation of the rights of nations. But soon the savages gave good cause of complaint. Whilst the French were entering the fort, the savages had crowded in numbers, in its interior, by the port-holes, in order to plunder, as plunder had been promised to them, but plunder did not suffice. Several sick, being too ill to follow their friends in their honorable capitulation, had remained in the casemates; these fell victims to the unmerciful cruelty of the savages: they were butchered in my presence. I saw one of those fiends issue from one of those pestiferous casemates, which thirst of blood alone could have induced him to enter, bearing triumphantly in his hand a human head all bloody; he would not have been more proud of the richest trophy imaginable.

This was but the prelude to the tragedy to be enacted on the morrow. At daybreak, the Indians crowded round the defences. They began by asking the English for all the effects, provisions and valuables which their covetous eyes could detect; but their demand was made in terms indicating that a refusal would be attended with a thrust from a lance. Everything was given up instantly, even to the wearing apparel in actual use. This condescension was calculated to soften the mind, but an Indian's heart is not like the heart of ordinary men; you would fancy that Nature itself has intended it as the seat of inhumanity. The savages were disposed to commit the greatest excesses. A detachment of 400 French regulars arrived to protect the retreat of the British. The English filed off. Alas for those who could not follow, or lagged behind from the main body! Their corpses strewed the soil and the interior of the works. This butchery, which at first had been attempted by a few Indians only, was the signal on which all the rest became like so many infuriated wild beasts. They struck right and left with their war-axes at those within their reach. The massacre, however, was not so great, nor did it last as long, as their fury would make one fancy; it attained to some forty or fifty cases. The patience of the British, who contented themselves with bowing their heads under the hatchets of their executioners, appeased it all at once, without bringing back reason and justice amongst them. Amidst incessant yells, the savages continued to make prisoners.

I arrived at that moment. It is more than man can do to possess insensibility in such heartrending scenes. The son wrested from a father's arms, the daughter violently separated from a mother's embrace, the husband dragged from his wife's bosom, officers despoiled of every garment except their shirt, without regard to their rank or to common decency: crowds of unfortunate beings rushing wildly, some towards the French tents, some towards the fort,—in fact filling up any place likely to afford shelter; such was the doleful spectacle which broke on my sight. In the meantime the French were neither idle nor indifferent spectators of the catastrophe. The Chevalier de Lévis hurried wherever the tumult was the greatest, with a courage dictated by clemency and natural to so illustrious a name. A thousand times he braved certain death, from which he would not have escaped, notwithstanding his rank and merit, without the interposition of a special Providence, which withheld the arm ready to strike. The French officers and the Canadians followed his example, with a zeal worthy of the humane treatment which has always characterized this nation, but the bulk of our forces, employed in guarding our batteries and the fort, was prevented by the distance from helping in this work. Of what avail could 400 men be against 1,500 infuriated savages who confounded us with the enemy? One of our sergeants who had actively resisted their cruelty, received a lance thrust which prostrated him. One of our French officers, in recompense of similar devotion, received a large wound which brought him to death's door: moreover, in those moments of alarm, no one knew which way to run. The measures seemingly the most judicious ended in a miserable failure. M. de Montcalm, who heard of these doings late, on account of the distance between his tent and the spot, as soon as informed of them, used such speed in coming there as proved the goodness and generosity of his heart. He seemed to be everywhere at once: prayers, threats, promises,—he tried everything; at last he resorted to force. The position and merit of Colonel Youn (Young) induced him to exert his authority and use violence to tear from the hands of a savage, (Colonel) Young's nephew. But, alas! the deliverance of this young man cost the life to some prisoners, who were butchered on the spot, lest they too should be rescued alive. The tumult still continued, when some one thought of telling the British to march off "to the double quick." This plan succeeded. The savages, finding pursuit useless and having made some prisoners, desisted. The British continued unmolested their retreat on Fort Lydis, where they arrived, at first only three or four hundred strong. I cannot state the number of those who, having taken to the woods, succeeded in getting to the fort, guided by the report of the guns, which were, during several days, fired for their guidance.

The rest of the garrison had not, however, met with death, nor was it detained in captivity; several had saved themselves by retreating to the fort or to the French tents. It was at the latter place I went as soon as the tumult was over. A crowd of forlorn women bemoaning their fate, surrounded me; they threw themselves at my feet, kissed the skirt of my garment, uttering lamentations which were heartrending. Nor had I the power to remove the cause of their grief. They called aloud for their sons, their daughters and husbands, torn from them forever, as if I could restore them. An opportunity presented of lessening at least the number of these unfortunates. I eagerly availed myself of it. A French officer informed me that in his camp there was a Huron who had in his possession a child, six months' old, whom the savage would certainly put to death, unless I hastened to rescue it. I hurried to the savage's tent, and found him holding in his arms the innocent victim, who was covering with kisses the hands of its executioner, and playing with some porcelain ornaments which hung about his person. This spectacle inflamed me with a new ardor. I commenced by awarding to the savage all the praise which was due to the bravery of his tribe. He saw through me at once.

"*Here,*" said he, civilly, to me; "*do you see this child? I have not stolen him; I found him stowed away in a hedge. You want him, but you shall not get him.*"

In vain I tried to convince him how useless it would be for him to attempt to retain the infant as his prisoner, as, from the want of proper nourishment, it was sure to die.

He produced some tallow to feed it with, adding: "That even if the child did die, he could always find a corner to bury it in; and that then, I might, if I choose, give it my blessing."

I replied by offering him for his little captive a tolerably large sum of money. He declined; but consented in the end, if I would give him in exchange another British prisoner. I had made up my mind to seeing the negotiation end by the death of the child, when I noticed the Huron converse in the Indian dialect with another savage. Our dialogue had heretofore been carried on in French. This gave me fresh hope: nor was I disappointed. The result was that the child would be mine, if I gave in exchange the scalp of an enemy.

"*You shall have it very shortly,*" said I, "*if you will keep to your bargain.*" I ran to the Abnaquis camp and asked the first savage I met, if he owned any scalps, and if so, that I would consider it a favor to be presented with one. He immediately, with much kindness, untied his wallet and allowed me the pick of scalps. Possessed with one of these barbarous trophies, I carried it triumphantly, followed by a crowd of French and Canadians, who were curious to see the end of this singular adventure.

Joy lent me wings: I ran in an instant to my Huron friend: "*Here,*" said I; "*here is your pay.*"

"*You are right,*" said he; "*it is really a British scalp; the hair is red!*"* (Red hair often distinguished the British colonists.) "*Take the boy; he is yours.*"

I did not allow him time for a second thought, and seized hold of the child, who was mostly naked, wrapping him up in the folds of my robe. The little fellow was not accustomed to be so roughly handled, and uttered cries, which indicated as much awkwardness in me as pain with him.

* Probably it belonged to a Scotchman, as a large number of Scotch served in the British armies in America before and at the time of the conquest of Canada.

I consoled myself with the hope that he would soon be confided to more experienced hands. I arrived at the fort. The infant's wailings caused all the women to rush towards me; all hoped to find a lost child. They examined him eagerly, but neither their hearts nor their eyes could discover a son. They withdrew to vent again their grief in loud lamentations. My embarrassment was great to find myself with my charge, some forty or fifty leagues from any French settlement. How could I provide for so young an infant?

I was overwhelmed with my thoughts, when I happened to see passing by a British officer who spoke French fluently. "Sir," said I, "I have just rescued this child from captivity, but he is certainly doomed to die, unless you order some of these women to nurse it, until I find means to provide for it. The French officers present backed my prayer.

The British officer then spoke to the women. One offered to nurse the child if I would guarantee her life and that of her husband, and have them conducted safe to Boston *viâ* Montreal. I accepted these terms, and asked Mr. de Bourlamarque to allow me three grenadiers to escort the English to the camp of the Canadians, where I hoped to find means to fulfil my engagements. This worthy officer acceded to my proposal.

I was just in the act of leaving the fort, when the child's father turned up: he had been struck by a shell, and lay quite helpless; he entirely concurred in what had been planned to save the life of his child. I started with my English friends,* escorted by the three grenadiers. After a fatigueing but successful march of two hours, we arrived at the quarters of the Canadians. I shall not pretend to pourtray the crowning feat of my undertaking: there are some things which are beyond the power of words. We had scarcely arrived in the neighborhood of the camp, when a loud exclamation caught my ears. Was it from grief? was it from joy? It proceeded from all this, and from more. It was the voice of a mother. From afar, the piercing eye of the parent had recognized her darling boy; who can deceive a mother? She rushed wildly towards the English lady who held the child, tearing it from her arms frantically, as if she feared to lose it a second time. One can imagine her transports

* The English woman who had consented to take charge of the infant, and her husband.

on finding again her child, and on being told that her husband—to whom she thought she had said adieu for the last time—was still alive. One thing was still wanting to my entire happiness, that is, re-uniting the father and the mother of the child.

I again retraced my steps towards the fort. I felt very weak; it was later than one o'clock P.M., and I had had yet nothing to eat. On my arrival I mostly fainted. The kind offices of the French officers soon allowed me to finish my good work. I had the fort searched for the Englishman I was looking for, but the search for a long time was unavailing. The pain caused by his wound had made him seek for rest in the most solitary part of the fort. He was found at last; and I was just going to conduct him back to his wife, when the mother and her son made their appearance. Orders had been issued to assemble together all the English dispersed in different directions, numbering about 500, and to conduct them to the fort, where their subsistence might be provided for more easily, until they could be sent to Orange; this was happily done a few days after. I was cordially thanked,—not only by those I had saved, but also by the English officers,—and that repeatedly. As to the offers to serve me, they merely flattered me, as springing from a sense of gratitude. A missionary like me has no recompense to look for except from the Almighty.

I cannot help noticing the recompense which the English woman met with, who had consented to nurse the child in the absence of its real mother. Providence, through the instrumentality of my colleague, M. Picquet, restored to her her missing child. I remained a few days longer in the neighborhood of the fort, and my ministry was crowned with more success, in rescuing more prisoners, and in saving the lives of some French officers, jeopardized by the acts of some drunken savages

Such are the circumstances of the unfortunate expedition which has thrown dishonor on the bravery evinced by the Indians during all the siege operations, and which has rendered burthensome to ourselves even their good offices. They pretend to justify their conduct. The Abnaquis in particular allege their right to wreak vengeance for the treatment experienced by their warriors no later than last winter, when, during peace or pending a truce, they were betrayed and slaughtered by the British of the Acadian forts. For my part, I do not pretend to place on its trial a nation, who, although it may be our enemy, has not the less many titles to our respect. I have not sufficient knowledge of facts to do so. I am not aware that I have mixed up with this narrative a single circumstance which could be gainsaid, nor do I see that malignity can discover any fact calculated to affix on the French the odiousness of this event. We had got the Indians to agree to the conditions of surrender; what could be more calculated to prevent any infraction of its terms?

A guard of four hundred men had been assigned to the enemy, as an escort, to protect their retreat: some of the escort fell, in their zeal to prevent the tumult: could any stronger means have been devised to ensure the observance of the treaty? Finally, large sums were expended to repurchase the English prisoners from the savages, so that nearly four hundred are at Quebec, ready to embark for Boston. Could the violation of the treaty be more efficaciously repaired? These queries seem to me unanswerable. The savages are then alone responsible for this violation of the rights of nations; with their unquenchable ferocity, with their utter disregard of all control, lies the cause. The news of this carnage, spread in the English colonies, has struck such universal terror, that a single Indian dared to go and make prisoners at the very doors of Orange (Albany), without being opposed or molested in his retreat.

The enemy did nothing to oppose us in the interval which followed the capture of the fort, and still the situation of the French army was most critical. The savages, except the Abnaquis and Nipistingues, had disappeared on the day of the massacre. Twelve hundred men were occupied in destroying the fort; about one thousand were busy conveying away the immense military stores and provisions which had fallen into our hands. There was a mere handful of soldiers remaining to meet the enemy, had he shown himself. This inactivity gave us the means of completing our work. Fort George has been completely destroyed, and the remains consumed by fire. It was only when it was burnt, that we understood the extent of the enemy's losses. There were casemates and subterranean recesses filled with corpses, which, during some days, furnished material to the flames. Our loss was merely 21 killed (of which three were Indians) and 25 wounded. I then returned to Montreal on Assumption Day.

Battle of Carillon,*

8TH JULY, 1758.

JULY 1.—Montcalm made a movement in advance, *echeloning*† his troops from Fort Carillon to the foot of Lake George, to curb the enemy, and obstruct their landing.

July 5.—The British embarked, at the lake head, in 900 barges and 130 bateaux, while on numerous rafts cannon were mounted, constituting so many floating batteries. "The sky was serene," says Mr. Dwight, "and the weather superb: our flotilla sped its way in measured time, in accord with inspiriting martial music. The standards' folds floated gaily in the sunshine; and joyous anticipations of a coming triumph beamed in every eye. The firmament above, the earth below, and all things around us, formed together a glorious spectacle. The sun, since his course in the heavens began, rarely ever lighted up a scene of greater beauty or grandeur."

The British van, 6000 strong, led by Lord Howe, reached the lake foot early on the 6th, and landed at Camp Brûlé. As it approached Bourlamaque fell back on La Chute, where Montcalm was posted, after waiting, but in vain, the return of M. de Trépézée, whom he had sent on a reconnaissance to Mont Pelée, with 300 men. The latter, at sight of the enemy, meant to rejoin Bourlamaque, but lost his way in the woods; thereby, through the delay ensuing, just as he reached the spot whence he had set out, his corps was surrounded by the enemy, and two-thirds of the men were killed, or drowned in attempted flight. The rest, who formed his rear-guard and had taken another route, arrived safely at La Chute, whither Trépézée and another officer were borne mortally wounded. It was also in this fortuitous skirmish that Lord Howe lost his life. He was a young man, but an officer of much promise, whose death was greatly mourned over by his compatriots.

The amount of the enemy's force, and his intents, were now alike dis-

* Garneau's *History of Canada*, Bell's translation.

† *Echelon*, Fr., is a stepping-bar or round in a ladder; hence the military term *échelonner*, dispose parties of soldiers *en échelon* (ladder-fashion); *i. e.* range them in detachments on a line, with interspaces at determinate intervals.—*B.*

cernible. Montcalm broke up his camp at La Chute; while, supported by the colonial regulars and 400 to 500 Canadians, just come up, he defiled towards the heights of Carillon, where he proposed to do battle; for it had been determined that, whatever might be the disparity in the numbers of the two armies, the entry to Canada should not be given up without a struggle. Montcalm at first elected to make his stand at Fort St. Frederic (Crown-Point); but M. de Lotbinière, who knew the country well, counselled him to prefer the heights of Carillon: the enemy, he said, could not pass that way, if it were (judiciously) occupied; and it would be easy to strengthen the pass by entrenching, under the cannon of the fort; whereas, he observed, the works needful to cover St. Frederic would take two months to execute: not to mention that Carillon, once cleared, the enemy could safely descend Lake Champlain, leaving the former stronghold unassailed, in his rear. Montcalm, feeling the cogency of this reasoning, halted the troops as soon as they reached Carillon in their retrograde march; then he gave them orders to take up a position in advance of the fort, and there entrench themselves, as proposed.

The heights of Carillon are situated within a triangle formed by the discharge of the superflux waters of Lake George, named La Chute River, and Lake Champlain, into which they here flow. Some bluffs (*buttes*), which are not lofty, and rise highest at the summit of the triangle, terminate, by an easy slope, towards the lake, but present a steep frontage (*escarpement*) to the river, the latter having a strand alongside it about 50 yards broad. At the extremity of the triangle, on the edge of the frontage aforesaid, was a small redoubt, the fire from which radiated on the river and lake; enfilading, too, the sloping ground along the course of the stream. This redoubt was connected by a parapet with Fort Carillon (the ruins of which may still be seen). The fort, which could contain 300 to 400 men, lay in the lap of the triangle, and commanded the centre and right side of the plateau, as well as the plain below, in the direction of Lake Champlain and the River St. Frederic. The enemy in our front bivouacked during the night of July 6–7. The glare of their numerous fires indicated that they were in great numbers near the portage. The French entrenchments, of zigzag outline, were begun in the evening of the 6th, and carried on most actively on the

7th. They began at the fort, followed for some length the crest of the heights, in the direction of La Chute River, and then turned to the right, in order to traverse the triangle at its base, following the sinuosities of a gorge of little depth, running across the plateau, and finally descended to the hollow (*bas-fond*) which extends to the lake. The lines of entrenchment might have about 600 yards of development, and a height of five feet: they were formed of felled trees, placed each on others, and all disposed in such sort, that the larger branches, stripped of their leaves and pointed, turned outwards and formed a rude kind of chevaux-de-frise. Each battalion as it arrived, first taking the place it was to occupy in action, constructed its part of the defences intended to cover all. Every man worked with ardour at his separate task. The Canadians, who did not obtain hatchets till noon on the 6th, began their assigned portion of the abattis, in the hollow towards Lake Champlain, and finished it just as the advancing British came into view. As the intermediate country between the troops and the enemy was thickly wooded, Montcalm had caused the nearest parts of it to be cleared, so that the latter should be the sooner seen, and have no covert when within gun-range.

Meanwhile, Abercromby was completing the disembarkation of his army. Some prisoners he took misinformed him that the French had entrenched themselves merely to gain time, expecting the arrival of 3000 additional men, under De Lévis, said to be on the way. The *wily* Abercromby determined to fall on at once, before the (imaginary) succour could come up. An engineer, sent by Abercromby to reconnoitre, returned and reported that the French works were incomplete; upon which he (boldly) put his army in motion. The vanguard, led by Colonel Bradstreet, did not halt till it came within a short mile of the French entrenchments, late on 7th July. Here the enemy's advanced corps passed the night; the line of adversaries on each side of the narrow interspace making ready for next day's action.

The British army, deducting a few hundred men left at La Chute (probably for guarding the boats at the foot of the lake), consisted of 15,000 prime soldiers, under experienced officers—all full of confidence in their superior numbers proving irresistible; while the French forces were only 3600 strong, including 450 Canadians and marines; there being no armed savages present. Montcalm put Fort Carillon in charge of 300 men; the rest lined the entrenchments, three men deep. Order was given to each battalion to keep in reserve a grenadier company and a piquet of soldiers, to take post behind, and repair, on accasion, to any overpressed part of the line. De Lévis, who arrived just that morning (the 8th), commanded the right wing; under him were the Canadians and their chief, M. De Raymond; Bourlamaque commanded the left wing, Montcalm the centre. Such was the French order of battle.

About half-past 12, noon, the outposts re-entered the abattis, after skirmishing with those of the British. A cannon-shot, fired from the fort, gave the signal to the men within to stand to their arms, and be ready to open fire.

Abercromby divided his army into four columns, the heads of which were ordered to attack simultaneously. The grenadier companies, posted in front of all, had directions to force the entrenchments at the bayonet's point, but not to fire till they had fairly cleared the barricade. At the same time, an alloted number of gun-barges were to fall down La Chute River, and menace the French right flank. By one o'clock P.M. the British columns were moving onward; they were intermingled with light troops and savages. The latter, as they advanced under tree-covert, kept up a galling fire on the French. The enemy's four columns, leaving the uncleared woods behind, descended into the gorge in front of our entrenchments, advancing upon them with great boldness and in admirable order; two of the four columns being directed against the French left wing, one against the centre, and the fourth against the right, following the sinuosities in the slope of the hollow where the Canadians were posted. The firing was commenced by the marksmen (*tirailleurs*) of the column opposed to the French right wing, and extended gradually from that point to the French left, the column facing which, composed of Highlanders and grenadiers, tried to penetrate the barrier on M. De Lévis' side. That officer, discerning the danger, ordered the Canadians to make a sortie and assail the flank of this column. The manœuvre succeeded; for the Canadians' fire, and that of the two battalions on the sloping ground or hillock (*coteau*), forced this column to incline towards the next, in order to avoid a cross flanking-fire.

The four columns, obliged to converge a little in advancing, either to protect their flanks or the better to attain select points of attack, became massed in debouching near the heights. At that instant, 30 barges appeared on La Chute, sent to inquiet the French flank. A few shots from the fort, which sank two of them, and an assault upon the others, from the banks, by a few men, caused their crews to retreat.

Montcalm had given an order that the enemy should be allowed to come unresisted within twenty paces of the entrenchments, and it was punctually obeyed. Arrived at the marked line, the musketry which assailed their compact masses told so promptly and terribly, that they were first staggered, and then fell into disorder. Forced to fall back an instant, the broken forward ranks were re-formed, and returned to the attack; but forgetting their consign (not to fire, themselves, till they had surmounted the barricade with fixed bayonets), they began to exchange shots, at a great disadvantage, with the ensconced French. The firing on both sides, along the whole line, became very hot, and was long continued; but, after the greatest efforts, the surviving assailants were obliged to give way a second time, leaving the ground behind them strewed with dead. Once again, however, they rallied at a little distance, re-formed their columns, and, after a few moments' halt, threw themselves anew upon the entrenchments, despite the hottest opposing fire imaginable.

Our generalissimo (Montcalm) exposed himself as much as the meanest of his soldiers. From his station in the centre, he hastened towards every point where there was most danger, giving orders and bringing up succour. Finally, the British, after unexampled efforts, were again repulsed.

Astonished more than ever at so obstinate a resistance, Abercromby, who thought nothing would withstand his forces, could not yet believe that they would ultimately fail before enemies so much inferior in numbers; he thought, that let his adversaries' courage be ever so great, they would at last renounce a contest which, the more violent and prolonged it were, would end all the more fatally for them. He resolved, therefore, to continue his assaults with added energy till he should achieve a triumph. Accordingly, between 1 and 5 o'clock P.M. (four hours), he ordered up his troops six times, to be as often driven back, each succeeding time with increasing loss. The fire kept up against them by the French was so hot and close, that part of the fragile ramparts which protected the assailed ignited more than once.

The enemies' columns, not succeeding in their first attacks made simultaneously but independently against the whole French line, now conjoined their strengths, and in a solid body tried to force, sometimes the centre of the French, at other times their right, and again their left wing—all in vain. But it was the right of the French works that was longest and most obstinately assailed; in that quarter, the combat was most sanguinary. The British grenadiers and Highlanders there persevered in the attack for three hours, without flinching or breaking rank. The Highlanders above all, under Lord John Murray, covered themselves with glory. They formed the head of the troops confronting the Canadians, their light and picturesque costume distinguishing them from all other soldiers amid the flames and smoke. This corps lost the half of its men, and 25 of its officers were killed or severely wounded.* At length this mode of attack failed, as the preceding had done, owing to the cool intrepidity of our troops; who, as they fought, shouted *Vive le roi!* and cried "Our general for ever!" During the different charges of the enemy, the Canadians made several sorties, turned their flanks, and took a number of them prisoners.†

At half-past five, Abercromby, losing hopes of success for a moment, withdrew his columns into the woods beyond, to allow the men to recover their breath; yet he resolved to make one last attempt before quite giving up his enterprise. An hour having elapsed, his army returned to the charge, and with its massed strength, once again assaulted the whole French line. This final attack failed even as the others. Thus fairly baffled, the British had perforce to retreat, leaving the French masters of the field; the rear of the former being protected by a swarm of

---

* Scarcely any of the wounded Highlanders ever recovered, even those sent home as invalids; their sores cankered, owing to the broken glass, ragged bits of metal, &c., used by the Canadians, instead of *honest* shot.—*Bell.*

† Some Highlanders taken prisoners by the French and Canadians, huddled together on the battle-field, and expecting to be cruelly treated, looked on in mournful silence. Presently a gigantic French officer walked up to them, and whilst exchanging in a severe tone some remarks in French with some of his men, suddenly addressed them in Gælic. Surprise in the Highlanders soon turned to positive horror. Firmly believing no Frenchman could ever speak Gælic, they concluded that his Satanic majesty in person was before them—it was a Jacobite serving in the French army.

riflemen, who skirmished with the Canadians sent in pursuit till nightfall.

By this time, the French were exhausted with fatigue, but intoxicated with joy. General Montcalm, accompanied by Chevalier de Lévis, and the staff-officers, passed along the ranks and thanked the victors, in the king's name, for their good conduct during this glorious day, one of the most memorable in the annals of French valour. Scarcely believing, however, that the present retreat of the British army would be definitive, and fully expecting that they would renew the combat next day, he issued orders to prepare for their reception as before. The troops therefore had to pass the night in their position; they cleaned their arms, and when daylight dawned next morning, set to work to complete and add to the entrenchments; constructing two batteries, one to the right with four cannon mounted, and another on the left, with six. After a pause of some hours and no enemy appearing, Montcalm sent out some detachments to reconnoitre, one of which, pushing on beyond La Chute, destroyed an intrenchment which the British had formed there, but abandoned. Next day (July 10), De Lévis advanced to the foot of Lake George with his grenadiers, volunteers, and Canadians, and there found many evidences of the precipitation of Abercromby's retreat. During the night following the battle, he continued his retreat, without stopping, to the lake; and this retrograde movement must have become a veritable flight. His soldiers left by the way their field implements (*outils*), portions of the baggage, and many wounded men (who were all picked up by De Lévis); their general having re-embarked his remaining troops by the first morning light, after throwing all his provisions, etc., into the lake.

Such was the battle of Carillon, wherein 3,600 men struggled successfully, for six hours, against 15,000 picked soldiers. The victory gained on this memorable day (July 8, 1757) greatly raised the reputation of Montcalm, whom good fortune attended ever since he came to America, making him the idol of the soldiers. In his army but 377 men were killed or wounded, including 38 officers. Amongst those hurt was M. de Bourlamaque, who was severely wounded in the shoulder; M. de Bougainville, who had just been promoted to the grade of assistant-quarter-master (*aide maréchal de logis*), was wounded likewise. De

Lévis' clothes and hat were ball-pierced in several places. The British owned to a loss of 2,000 killed or wounded, including 126 officers; but the contemporary French accounts estimated the British loss at from four to five thousand.

"Montcalm," said M. Dussieux, "stopped invasion by his brilliant victory of Carillon; *certes*, that was a deed to be proud of. But Montcalm spoke modestly of what he had done: 'The only credit I can lay claim to,' wrote he next day to M. de Vaudreuil, 'is the glory accruing to me of commanding troops so valorous......The success of the affair is due to the incredible bravery manifested both by officers and soldiers.'

"During the evening of the battle-day, the fortunate and illustrious general wrote, upon the battle-field itself, this simple and touching letter to his friend M. de Doreil: 'The army, the too small army of the king, has just beaten his enemies. What a day for (the honour of) France! Had I had two hundred savages to serve for the van of a detachment of a thousand chosen troops, led by De Lévis, not many of the fleeing enemies would have escaped. Ah! such troops as ours, my dear Doreil —I never saw their match.'"

Engagement at Beauport Flats,*

31st July, 1759.

As the left bank of the Montmorency, just beyond its embouchure is higher than the right, Wolfe strengthened the batteries he already had there, the gun-range of which enfiladed, above that river, the French entrenchments. The number of his cannon and pieces for shelling was raised to sixty. He caused to sink, on the rocks level with the flood below, two transports, placing on each when in position fourteen guns. One vessel lay to the right, the other to the left, of a small redoubt which the French had erected on the strand, at the foot of the Courville road, in order to defend, not only the entry of that road, which led to heights occupied by the French reserve, but also the ford

* Garneau's *History of Canada*, Bell's translation.

of the Montmorency below the falls. Cannon-shots from the transports crossed each other in the direction of the redoubt. It became needful, therefore, to silence the fire of the latter, and cover the march of the assailants, on this accessible point of our line; therefore the *Centurion*, a 60-gun ship, was sent afterwards to anchor opposite the falls, and as near as might be to the shore, to protect the ford which the British forlorn-hope was to cross, as soon as the attacking force should descend from their camp of l'Ange-Gardien. Thus 118 pieces of ordnance were about to play upon Montcalm's left wing.

Towards noon, July 31, all this artillery began to play; and, at the same time, Wolfe formed his columns of attack. More than 1,500 barges were in motion in the basin of Quebec. A part of Monkton's brigade, and 1,200 grenadiers, embarked at Pointe-Lévi, with intent to re-land between the site of the *Centurion* and the sunken transports. The second column, composed of Townshend's and Murray's brigades, descended the heights of l'Ange-Gardien, in order to take the ford and join their forces to the first column at the foot of the Courville road, which was ordered to be ready posted, and only waiting for the signal to advance against the adjoining French entrenchments. These two columns numbered 6,000 men. A third corps of 2,000 soldiers, charged to ascend the left bank of the Montmorency, was to pass that river at a ford about a league above the falls, but which was guarded (as already intimated) by a detachment, under M. de Repentigny. At 1 P.M. the three British columns were on foot to execute the concerted plan of attack, which would have been far too complicated for troops less disciplined than Wolfe's.

Montcalm, for some time doubtful about the point the enemy would assail, had sent orders along his whole line for the men to be ready everywhere to oppose the British wherever they came forward. As soon as the latter neared their destination, De Lévis sent 500 men to succour Repentigny (at the upper ford), also a small detachment to espy the manœuvres of the British when about to cross the lower ford; while he sent to Montcalm for some battalions of regulars, to sustain himself in case of need. The general came up, at 2 P.M., to examine the posture of matters at the left. He proceeded along the lines, approved of the dispositions of De Lévis, gave fresh orders, and returned to the centre,

15

in order to be in a position to observe all that should pass. Three battalions and some Canadians, from Trois-Rivières, came in opportunely to reinforce the French left. The greatest part of these troops took post, as a reserve, on the highway, and the rest were directed on the ford defended by M. de Repentigny. The latter had been already hotly attacked by a British column, but he forced it to give way, after some loss of men. The retreat of this corps permitted that sent to succour Repentigny to hasten back to the arena of the chief attack.

Meanwhile, the barges bearing the Pointe-Lévi column, led by Wolfe in person, after making several evolutions, meant to deceive the French as to the real place for landing, were directed towards the sunken transports. The tide was now ebbing; thus part of the barges were grounded on a ridge of rock and gravelly matter, which stopped their progress and caused some disorder; but at last all obstacles were surmounted, and 1,200 grenadiers, supported by other soldiers, landed on the St. Lawrence strand. They were to advance in four divisions; and Monkton's brigade, which was to embark later, had orders to follow, and, as soon as landed, to sustain them.. From some misunderstanding these orders were not punctually executed. The enemy formed in columns, indeed; but Monkton's men did not arrive to time. Still the van moved, music playing, up to the Courville road redoubt, which the French at once evacuated. The enemy's grenadiers took possession of it, and prepared to assail the entrenchments beyond, which were within musket-shot distance. Wolfe's batteries had been pouring, ever since mid-day, on the Canadians who defended this part of the line, a shower of bombs and bullets, which they sustained without flinching. Having re-formed, the British advanced, with fixed bayonets, to attack the entrenchments; their showy costume contrasting strangely with that of their adversaries, wrapped as these were in light capotes and girt round the loins. The Canadians, who compensated their deficient discipline only by their native courage and the great accuracy of their aim, waited patiently till the enemies were a few yards distant from their line, meaning to fire at them point-blank. The proper time come, they discharged their pieces so rapidly and with such destructive effect,* that the two British columns,

* "Their (men of) small-arms, in the trenches, lay cool till they were sure of their mark; they then poured their shot like showers of hail, which caused our brave grenadiers to fall very fast."—*Journal of a British officer.*

despite all their officers' endeavours, were broken and took flight. They sought shelter at first against their foes' fire behind the redoubt; but not being allowed to re-form ranks, they continued to retreat to the main body of the army, which had deployed a little further back. At this critical time, a violent thunderstorm supervened, which hid the view of the combatants on both sides from each other, while the reverberations of successive peals rose far above the din of battle. When the rain-mist cleared off, the Canadians beheld the British re-embarking with their wounded,* after setting fire to the sunken transports. Their army finally drew off, as it had advanced, some corps in the barges; others marched landward, after re-crossing the Montmorency ford. The fire of their numerous cannon, however, continued till night set in; and it was estimated that the British discharged 3,000 cannon-balls during

---

* "As our company of grenadiers approached, I distinctly saw Montcalm on horseback riding backwards and forwards. He seemed very busy giving directions to his men, and I heard him give the word to fire. Immediately they opened upon us, and killed a good many of our men, I don't recollect how many. We did not fire, for it would have been of no use, as they were completely entrenched, and we could only see the crown of their heads."............"We were now ordered to retreat to our boats, that had been left afloat to receive us; and by this time it was low water, so that we had a long way to wade though the mud. A Serjeant Allan Cameron, of our company, seeing a small battery on our left with two guns mounted, and apparently no person near it, thought he would prevent it doing us any mischief on our retreat, so he picked up a couple of bayonets that lay on the beach, and went alone to the battery, when he drove the points of them into the vents as hard as he could, and then snapped them off short.

"When the French saw us far enough on our retreat, they sent their savages to scalp and tomahawk our poor fellows that lay wounded on the beach. Among the number was Lieutenant Peyton, of the Royal American Battalion, who was severely wounded, and had crawled away as far as the pains he endured would allow. After the savages had done their business with the poor fellows that lay nearest to the French batteries, they went back, except two, who spied Lieutenant Peyton, and thought to make a good prize of him. He happened to have a double-barrelled fusil, ready loaded, and as he had seen how the savages had treated all the others that came into their clutches, he was sure that if they got the better of him they would butcher him also. Fortunately, his presence of mind did not forsake him, and he waited until the first savage came near enough, when he levelled his fusil, and brought him to the ground; the other savage, thinking that the Lieutenant would not have time to reload, rushed in upon him boldly, with his tomahawk ready to strike, when Lieutenant Peyton discharged his fusil right into his chest, and he fell dead at his feet. We saw no more of the savages after that, at least on that occasion; but we saw enough of them afterwards.

"While poor Lieutenant Peyton lay upon the ground, almost exhausted from his exertions and loss of blood, he was accosted by Serjeant Cameron, who had no other means of helping him than carrying him away; and he was well able to do it, for he was a stout, strong, tall fellow. He slung the Lieutenant's fusil over his shoulder along with his own, and took him on his back, telling him to hold fast round his neck. As he had a long way to carry him, he was obliged every now and then to lay him down in order to take breath, and give the lieutenant some ease, as his wound was exceedingly painful. In this way he got him at last to one of the boats, and laying him down, said, 'Now, sir, I have done as much for you as lay in my power, and I wish you may recover.'"—*Hawkins's Picture of Quebec.*

the day and evening; while the French had only a dozen pieces of cannon in action, but these were very serviceable in harassing the disembarking British. The loss of the French, which was due almost entirely to artillery fire, was inconsiderable, if we remember that they were for more than six hours exposed to it. The enemy lost about 500 men, killed and wounded, including many officers.

The victory gained at Montmorency was due chiefly to the judicious dispositions made by De Lévis, who, with fewer troops in hand than Wolfe, contrived to unite a greater number than he did at every point of attack. Supposing the British grenadiers had surmounted the entrenchments, it is very doubtful whether they would have prevailed, even had they been sustained by the rest of their army. The ground from the strand to the Beauport road rises into slopes, broken by ravines, amongst which meanders the Courville road; the locality, therefore, was favorable to our marksmen. Besides, the regulars in reserve were close behind, ever ready to succour the militiamen.

General Wolfe returned to his camp, in great chagrin at the check he had just received. Imagination depicted to his apprehensive mind's eye the unfavorable impression this defeat would make in Britain; and he figured to himself the malevolent jibes which would be cast at him for undertaking a task which he had proved himself to be incompetent to perform! He saw vanish, in a moment, all his proud illusions of glory; and Fortune, in whom he had trusted so much, as we have seen, seemed about to abandon him at the very outset of his career as a commander-in-chief. It seemed as if his military perceptions had lost somewhat of their usual lucidity, when, after losing all hope of forcing the camp of his adversary, he afterwards sent Murray, with 1,200 men, to destroy the French flotilla at Trois-Rivières, and to open a communication with General Amherst at Lake Champlain. Murray set out with 300 barges, but did not go far up the country. Repulsed twice at Pointe-aux-Trembles by De Bougainville, who, with 1,000 men, followed his movements, he landed at Sainte-Croix, which place he burnt, as has been already noticed. Thence departing, he fell upon Deschambault, where he pillaged the French officers' baggage. [!] He then retired precipitately, without fulfilling his mission. His incursion, nevertheless, much disquieted Montcalm at first; for he set out *incognito* for the

Jacques Cartier, as fearing lest the British might take possession of its lower course, gain a firm foothold there, and cut off his communications with western Canada; but learning that the latter were in full retreat when he arrived at Pointe-aux-Trembles, Montcalm retraced his steps.

After this new repulse, a malady, the germ of which was present in the bodily frame of Wolfe long before, now suddenly developed itself and brought him almost to death's-door. As soon as he convalesced, he addressed a long despatch to Secretary Pitt, recounting the obstacles against which he had to struggle, and expressing the bitterness of his regret at the failure of all his past endeavours. This letter (if it did little else) expressed the noble devotedness to his country's weal which inspired the soul of the illustrious warrior; and thus the British people were more affected at the sorrow of the youthful captain than at the checks his soldiers had received.

The spirit of Wolfe, no less than his bodily powers, sank before a situation which left him "only a choice of difficulties;" thus he expressed himself. Calling those lieutenants in aid, whose character and talents we have spoken of, he invited them to declare what might be their opinions as to the best plan to follow for attacking Montcalm with any chance of success; intimating his own belief, also, which was, that another attack should be made on the left wing of the Beauport camp. He was also clear for devastating the country as much as it was possible to do, without prejudicing the principal operation of the campaign.

The Battle of the Plains of Abraham,*

13TH SEPTEMBER, 1759.

ANY one who visits the celebrated Plains of Abraham, the scene of this glorious fight—equally rich in natural beauty and historic recollections—will admit that no site could be found better adapted for displaying the evolutions of military skill and discipline, or the exertion of physical force and determined valor. The battle-ground presents

* From *Hawkins's Picture of Quebec.*

almost a level surface from the brink of the St. Lawrence to the Ste. Foy road. The *Grande-Allée,* or road to Cape Rouge, running parallel to that of Ste. Foy, passed through its centre,—and was commanded by a field redoubt, in all probability the four-gun battery on the English left, which was captured by the light infantry, as mentioned in General Townshend's letter. The remains of this battery are distinctly seen near to the present race-stand. There were also two other redoubts, one upon the rising ground, in the rear of Mr. C. Campbell's house*—the death scene of Wolfe—and the other towards the Ste. Foy road which it was intended to command. On the site of the country seat called Marchmont, the property of the Honorable J. Stewart, and at present residence of Mr. Daly, Secretary of the Province,† there was also a small redoubt, commanding the intrenched path leading to the Cove. This was taken possession of by the advanced guard of the light infantry, immediately on ascending the heights. At the period of the battle, the Plains were without fences or enclosures, and extended to the walls to the St. Lewis side. The surface was dotted over with bushes, and the woods on either flank were more dense than at present, affording shelter to the French and Indian marksmen.

In order to understand the relative position of the two armies, if a line be drawn to the St. Lawrence from the General Hospital, it will give nearly the front of the French army at ten o'clock, after Montcalm had deployed into line. His right reached beyond the Ste. Foy road, where he made dispositions to turn the left of the English. Another parallel line somewhat in advance of Mr. C. Grey Stewart's house on the Ste. Foy road, will give the front of the British army, before Wolfe charged at the head of the grenadiers of 22nd, 40th, and 45th regiments, who had acquired the honorable title of the Louisbourg Grenadiers, from having been distinguished at the capture of that place, under his own command, in 1758. To meet the attempt of Montcalm to turn the British left, General Townshend formed the 15th regiment *en potence,* or presenting a double front. The light infantry were in rear of the left, and the reserve was placed in rear of the right, formed in eight sub-divisions, a good distance apart.

* Occupied this year by Col. Alex. Bell.

† At present the family mansion of John Gilmour, Esq.

The English had been about four hours in possession of the Plains, and were completely prepared to receive them, when the French advanced with great resolution. They approached obliquely by the left, having marched from Beauport that morning. On being formed, they commenced the attack with great vivacity and animation, firing by platoons. It was observed, however, that their fire was irregular and ineffective, whereas that of the English was so well directed and maintained, as to throw the French into immediate confusion. It must be stated, that although the French army was more numerous, it was principally composed of colonial troops, who did not support the regular forces as firmly as was expected of them—(some of them had not even bayonets.) Montcalm, on his death bed, expressed himself bitterly in this respect. The English troops, on the contrary, were nearly all regulars, of approved courage, well officered and under perfect discipline. The grenadiers burned to revenge their defeat at Montmorency; and it was at their head that Wolfe, with great military tact, placed himself at the commencement of the action.

About eight o'clock, some sailors had succeeded in dragging up the precipice a light six-pounder, which, although the only gun used by the English in the action, being remarkably well served, played with great success on the centre column as it advanced, and more than once compelled the enemy to change the disposition of his forces. The French had two field pieces in the action. The despatches mention a remarkable proof of coolness and presence of mind, on the part of troops who had no hopes but in victory, no chance of safety but in beating the enemy—for had they been defeated, re-embarkation would have been impracticable. The English were ordered to reserve their fire until the French were within forty yards. They observed these orders most strictly, bearing with patience the incessant fire of the Canadians and Indians. It is also stated that Wolfe ordered the men to load with an additional bullet, which did great execution.

The two generals, animated with equal spirit, met each other at the head of their respective troops, where the battle was most severe. Montcalm was on the left of the French, at the head of the regiments of *Languedoc*, *Bearne* and *Guienne*—Wolfe on the right of the English, at the head of the 28th, and the Louisbourg Grenadiers. Here the greatest exertions were made under the eyes of the leaders—the action in the centre and left was comparatively a skirmish. The severest fighting took place between the right of the race-stand and the Martello towers. The rapidity and effect of the English fire having thrown the French into confusion, orders were given, even before the smoke cleared away, to charge with the bayonet. Wolfe exposing himself at the head of the battalions, was singled out by some Canadian marksmen, on the enemy's left, and had already received a slight wound in the wrist. Regardless of this, and unwilling to dispirit his troops, he folded a handkerchief round his arm, and putting himself at the head of the grenadiers, led them on to the charge, which was completely successful. It was bought, however, with the life of their heroic leader. He was struck with a second ball in the groin; but still pressed on, and just as the enemy were about to give way, he received a third ball in the breast, and fell mortally wounded. Dear, indeed, was the price of a victory purchased by the death of Wolfe—of a hero whose uncommon merit was scarcely known and appreciated by his country, before a premature fate removed him for ever from her service. It might have been said of him, as of Marcellus,

> Ostendent terris hunc tantùm fata, neque ultrà
> Esse sinent. Nimium vobis Romana propago
> Visa potens, superi, propria hæc si dona fuissent.

He met, however, a glorious death in the moment of victory—a victory which, in deciding the fate of Canada, commanded the applause of the world, and classed Wolfe among the most celebrated generals of ancient and modern times. Happily, he survived his wound long enough to learn the success of the day. When the fatal ball took effect, his principal care was, that he should not be seen to fall.—"Support me,"—said he to an officer near him,—"let not my brave soldiers see me drop The day is ours, keep it!" He was then carried a little way to the rear, where he requested water to be brought from a neighboring well to quench his thirst. The charge still continued, when the officer—on whose shoulder,* as he sat down for the purpose, the dying hero leaned—exclaimed, "They run! they run!"—"Who runs?" asked the gallant

* The position of the dying hero is faithfully given in West's celebrated picture.

Wolfe, with some emotion. The officer replied,—"The enemy, sir: they give way every where!"—"What?" said he, "do they run already? Pray, one of you go to Colonel Burton, and tell him to march Webb's regiment, with all speed, down to St. Charles River, to cut off the retreat of the fugitives from the bridge.—Now, God be praised, I DIE HAPPY!" So saying, the youthful hero breathed his last. He reflected that he had done his duty, aud he knew that he should live for ever in the memory of a greatful country. His expiring moments were cheered with the British shout of victory,

——pulchrumque mori succurrit in armis.

Such was the death of Wolfe upon the Plains of Abraham, at the early age of thirty-two years! It has been well observed, that "a death more glorious attended with circumstances more picturesque and interesting, is no where to be found in the annals of history." His extraordinary qualities, and singular fate, have afforded a fruitful theme of panegyric to the historian and the poet, to the present day. How they were appreciated by his gallant companions in arms, may be learned by the subjoined extract from a letter written after the battle by General, afterwards Marquis Townshend, to one of his friends in England:—"I am not ashamed to own to you, that my heart does not exult in the midst of this success. I have lost but a friend in General Wolfe. Our country has lost a sure support, and a perpetual honor. If the world were sensible at how dear a price we have purchased Quebec in his death, it would damp the public joy. Our best consolatian is, that Providence seemed not to promise that he should remain long among us. He was himself sensible of the weakness of his constitution, and determined to crowd into a few years actions that would have adorned a lengthy life." The feeling and affecting manner in which Wolfe is spoken of in this letter, and its elegance of expression, confer equal honor upon the head and heart of the accomplished writer. The classical reader will agree with us in thinking, that he had in his mind at the time the eulogy of Marcellus which we have quoted above.

The spot consecrated by the fall of General Wolfe, in the charge made by the grenadiers upon the left of the French line, will to the latest day be visited with deep interest and emotion. On the highest ground considerably in advance of the Martello towers, commanding a complete view of the field of battle—not far from the fence which divides the race-ground from the enclosures on the east, and opposite to the right of the English—are the remains of a redoubt against which the attack was directed which Wolfe so gallantly urged on by his personal example. A few years ago a rock was pointed out, as marking the spot where he actually breathed his last; and in one of the enclosures nearer to the road is the well whence they brought him water. It is mentioned in the statistical work of Colonel Bouchette, that one of the four meridian stones, [placed in 1790 by Major Holland, then Surveyor General of Canada, "stood in the angle of a field redoubt where General Wolfe is said to have breathed his last." As he had been conveyed a short distance to the rear after being struck with the fatal ball, it must be presumed that this redoubt had been captured; and that the grenadiers were pressing on, when he received his mortal wound. This is corroborated by a letter which we have met with, written after the battle by an officer of the 28th Regiment, serving at the time as a volunteer with the Louisbourg Grenadiers under Colonel Murray. He speaks of the redoubt in question as "a rising ground," and shows that Wolfe was in possession of it previously to his last wound: "Upon the general viewing the position of the two armies, he took notice of a small rising ground between our right and the enemy's left, which concealed their motions from us in that quarter, upon which the general did me the honor to detach me with a few grenadiers to take possession of that ground, and maintain it to the last extremity, which I did until both armies were engaged, and then the general came to me; but that great, that ever memorable man, whose loss can never be enough regretted, was scarce a moment with me till he received his fatal wound."

The place is now, however, about to be marked to posterity by the erection of a permanent memorial. Permission has been given to the writer of this account, to announce the intention of His Excellency the Lord Aylmer to erect a small column on the spot where Wolfe expired. This act of soldier-like generosity will be duly appreciated: and posterity will have at last amply redeemed their long neglect, and wiped away a reproach of more than seventy years' duration. The Monument in Quebec, common to Wolfe and Montcalm—the stone placed in the Ursuline Convent in honor of the latter—and the smaller column on the

Plains, dyed with the blood of Wolfe, will form a complete series of testimonials—honorable to the spirit of the age, and worthy of the distinguished individuals under whose auspices they have been executed

The memorial on the Plains now bears the following inscription :

HERE DIED
WOLFE:
VICTORIOUS.

Death of Montcalm.*

A DEATH no less glorious closed the career of the brave Marquis de Montcalm, who commanded the French army. He was several years older than Wolfe, and had served his king with honor and success in Italy, Germany and Bohemia. In the earlier campaigns of this war he had given signal proofs of zeal, consummate prudence and undaunted valor. At the capture of Oswego, he had with his own hand wrested a color from the hand of an English officer, and sent it to be hung up in the Cathedral of Quebec. He had deprived the English of fort William Henry; and had defeated General Abercromby at Ticonderoga (Carillon). He had even foiled Wolfe himself at Montmorency; and had erected lines which it was impossible to force. When, therefore, he entered the Plains of Abraham at the head of a victorious army, he was in all respects an antagonist worthy of the British general.

The intelligence of the unexpected landing of Wolfe above the town was first conveyed to the Marquis de Vaudreuil, the Governor General, about day-break. By him it was communicated without delay to Montcalm. Nothing could exceed the astonishment of the latter at the intelligence; he refused at first to give credence to it, observing: "It is only Mr. Wolfe with a small party, come to burn a few houses, look

* From *Hawkins's Picture of Quebec.*

about him and return." On being informed, however, that Wolfe was at that moment in possession of the Plains of Abraham,—"Then," said he, "they have at last got to the weak side of this miserable garrison. Therefore we must endeavor to crush them by our numbers, and scalp them all before twelve o'clock." He issued immediate orders to break up the camp, and led a considerable portion of the army across the River St. Charles, in order to place them between the city and the English. Vaudreuil, on quitting the lines at Beauport, gave orders to the rest of the troops to follow him. On his arrival at the Plains, however, he met the French army in full flight towards the bridge of boats; and learned that Montcalm had been dangerously wounded. In vain he attempted to rally them—the route was general—and all hopes of retrieving the day and of saving the honor of France were abandoned.

Montcalm was first wounded by a musket shot, fighting in the front rank of the French left,—and afterwards by a discharge from the only gun in the possession of the English. He was then on horseback, directing the retreat—nor did he dismount until he had taken every measure for the safety of the remains of his army. Such was the impetuosity with which the Highlanders, supported by the 58th Regiment, pressed the rear of the fugitives—having thrown away their muskets and taken to their broad swords—that had the distance been greater from the field of battle to the walls, the whole French army would inevitably have been destroyed. As it was, the troops of the line had been almost cut to pieces, when their pursuers were forced to retire by the fire from the ramparts. Great numbers were killed in the retreat, which was made obliquely from the River St. Lawrence to the St. Charles. Some severe fighting took place in the field in front of the Martello Tower, No. 2. We are informed by an officer of the garrison, that, on digging there some years ago, a number of skeletons were found with parts of soldiers' dress, military buttons, buckles, and other remains.

It is reported of Montcalm, when his wounds were dressed, that he requested the surgeons in attendance to declare at once whether they were mortal. On being told that they were so—"I am glad of it," said he. He then enquired how long he might survive? He was answered, "Ten or twelve hours, perhaps less." "So much the better," replied he; "then I shall not live to see the surrender of Quebec." On being afterwards visited by M. de Ramesay, who commanded the garrison, with the title of Lieutenant du Roi, and by the Commandant de Roussillon, he said to them: "Gentlemen, I commend to your keeping the honor of France. Endeavor to secure the retreat of my army to-night beyond Cape Rouge: for myself, I shall pass the night with God, and prepare myself for death." On M. de Ramesay pressing to receive his commands respecting the defence of Quebec, Montcalm exclaimed with emotion: "I will neither give orders, nor interfere any further; I have much business that must be attended to, of greater moment than your ruined garrison, and this wretched country. My time is very short—so pray leave me. I wish you all comfort, and to be happily extricated from your present perplexities." He then addressed himself to his religious duties, and passed the night with the bishop and his own confessor. Before he died, he paid the victorious army this magnanimous compliment: "Since it was my misfortune to be discomfited and mortally wounded, it is a great consolation to me to be vanquished by so brave and generous an enemy. If I could survive this wound, I would engage to beat three times the number of such forces* as I commanded this morning, with a third of British troops."

Almost his last act was to write a letter, recommending the French prisoners to the generosity of the victors. He died at five o'clock in the morning of the 14th September; and was buried in an excavation made by the bursting of a shell within the precincts of the Ursuline Convent—a fit resting place for the remains of a man who died fighting for the honor and defence of his country.

* Great jealousy existed in those days between the regulars and the militia—the militia was badly armed, not having even bayonets.

The Battle of Ste. Foy,

27TH AND 28TH APRIL, 1760.

"Militiamen were seen to crouch on the ground to load their pieces; rise up after the cannon shot passed over them, and dash forward to shoot the British gunners."

THE events of the 27th and 28th of April, 1760, in this country, afford us, if nothing else, a subject of reflection, concerning the manner in which the militia of Canada deported itself on the occasion. In the endless and bloody warfare which raged for so many years between the colonists of New England and those of New France, our militia had previously established its efficiency as an auxiliary to regulars. In the defeat of Abercromby, at Carillon; of Wolfe, on the Beauport Flats; of Murray, at Ste. Foy, it had left its mark. Its onset was less fierce than that of the other auxiliaries in those days, the Redskins. It was less handy than them at scalping, but more manageable, more docile. The New Englanders and British troops left this bloody work to the Iroquois, who, it must be confessed, grew very expert at it. The French enlisted, for the nonce, the services of the Hurons, Abenaquis, Algonquins, &c. Occasionally the European soldiers tried their hand at it. Capt. John Knox, Wolfe's companion, and one who has never been charged with underrating British successes, relates in his journal that the British did a trifle in the scalping line on the 23rd of August, 1759, at St. Joachim, whose parish priest, with thirty followers, were "scalped and killed," as Knox ingeniously states, "for having disguised themselves like Indians." Knox does not say they were taken for Indians. The grave charges of atrocities freely bandied round by English and French historians, against the rival commanders might be, in nine cases out of ten, traced to the savages they employed as auxiliaries. An Indian under the influence of intoxicating liquor is more like a wild beast than a human being—ready, at the first impulse of the demon lurking in his veins, to slaughter friend or foe. Scalping, although a dangerous experiment, was not always followed by loss of life: a well-authenticated instance is on record of a scalped Montrealer who lived fourteen years afterwards. He appears to have been mostly as hardy as the celebrated St. Denis, who has the credit of having walked about Paris with his head in his hands after decapitation.

There are so many accounts of the Ste. Foy battle, that it seems superfluous to dwell at length on the subject. We have the story of eye-witnesses, such as Mante, Knox, Fraser; also of Chevalier Johnstone, a Scotchman, fighting in Canada for the cause of France. We also have Smith's account, not over-correct; and Garneau's narrative, probably the most complete, and collated from documents, many of which had never seen the light before.

He computes the English force at 7,714, exclusive of officers. The French force were more numerous: there were amongst them 3,000 Montreal and Three Rivers militia, and 400 savages; the Quebec district militia having been compelled by General Murray to swear allegiance to the English monarch during the preceding winter. As a set-off, the English general had twenty to twenty-two field pieces, and De Lévis had been able to bring through the slush of the Suede Swamp at Ste. Foy only three small pieces. The battle of the 28th lasted, according to General Murray, one hour and three-quarters. He acknowledges, in his despatch of the 25th May, 1760, to Pitt, having lost one-third of his men, and the French 2,500; this would make some 4,000 corpses strewing the environs of the spot where the monument now stands. This ought to be a sufficient answer to those who fancy it was merely a skirmish. We read in Garneau's history of Canada:

"The savages, who were nearly all in the wood behind during the fight, spread over the battle-field, when the French were pursuing the enemy, and felled many of the wounded British, whose scalps were afterwards found upon the neighbouring bushes. As soon as De Lévis was apprised of this massacre, he took vigorous measures for putting a stop to it. Within a comparatively narrow space, nearly 2,500 men had been struck by bullets; the patches of snow and icy puddles on the ground were so reddened with the blood shed that the frozen ground refused to absorb; and the wounded suivivors of the battle, and of the savages, were immersed in pools of gore and filth ankle deep."—(J. M. L.)

STE. FOY MONUMENT FESTIVAL.*

THE INAUGURATION CEREMONY, 19TH OCTOBER, 1863.

"Our ancient city witnessed, on Monday, the rare spectacle of a public festival.

"Before entering upon our report of the proceedings, it is right that we should place in concise form before our readers some details of the battle in memory of which the Ste. Foy Monument was raised. The battle of Ste. Foy, sanguinary and fiercely contested, when we consider the number of men engaged, was fought upon the plains bordering the Ste. Foy road, on the 28th April, 1760, and the fiercest struggle took place on the very spot now occupied by the pillar. The circumstances under which it was fought were of a peculiar nature. It was the first and only action which was fought in the course of the De Lévis' bold attempt to take the Fortress City from the British. It was also the last victory won by French arms on Canadian soil. It must be admitted that the occasion was most auspicious for the French, and the consummation of their brightest hopes seemed at hand. Quebec was held in the winter of 1759-60 by a handful of British troops. The daring young soldier who had led them to victory was no more. They were three thousand miles from the mother country, and completely cut off from all prospect of aid or succour throughout the winter months. Reinforcements from England were out of the question until the spring of 1760 burst the icy bonds of the St. Lawrence. Reinforcements from the then friendly Provinces of Boston and New York were equally impossible,

---

* Abridged from *Quebec Morning Chronicle*.

because of the dense forests, and the other impassable natural barriers which extended south of the St. Lawrence from the Gulf to the great lakes. On the other hand the French were still in considerable strength throughout Canada. The hearts of the people were with King Louis and French connexion, whatever oppression they might have suffered from tyrannical governors and speculating intendants. Montreal, Three Rivers, and all other posts throughout Canada—except Quebec—were held by French garrisons and the Canadian militia and Indian auxiliaries."

[Here the editor has inserted extracts from *Smith's History of Canada*, and, in order that the other side may be heard, an account of the battle, which, strange to say, was written in English by Chevalier Johnstone, a Scottish Jacobite, who served in the French army in Canada. We substitute for these narratives M. Garneau's account in his *History of Canada*, which was written from both French and English records. We copy from Mr. Bell's translation]:

"The wood whence the French were issuing was 400 yards distant from the enemy's front: now, as the forest soil was marshy, the French could debouch only upon the highway. The space between the wood and the British was not wide enough to allow De Lévis to form his men and lead them on without disadvantage. His situation thus became difficult, for the hill of Sainte-Geneviève and the River St. Charles alike barred his way, if he elected to march on Quebec either by the road of St. Ambroise or that of Charlesbourg; and the enemy might reach the above eminence before the French, having only the cord of the arc to pass along; he therefore resolved to attain the Ste. Foy road by a flanking march. Nightfall come, he ordered his troops to defile, on the right, along the skirts of the wood, till they would have got beyond the British front, and turn round their left flank. This manœuvre, if successful, gave him both a good position and a chance for cutting off the corps of observation posted at the Red River outlet on the St. Lawrence; but the stormy weather, and the dfficulty of countermarching at that season with wearied men, prevented the operation being essayed with due celerity. Next day Murray, who hastened to the imperilled spot, had leisure to extricate his troops with the loss only of their baggage, &c. Becoming pressed in his own retreat, he took shelter in the church of

Ste. Foy, which he fired as he left it; and he was finally able to resume his march to Quebec, leaving De Lévis master of a field of battle which he would otherwise have had much difficulty to conquer.

"The French horsemen dogged Murray's retrograde steps, and skirmished with his rear-guard as far as Dumont's mill. Murray posted a strong guard within the mill, with orders to hold it (if attacked) till night. The French troops took lodging in the houses between the church and the mill. The rain fell, meanwhile, in torrents, and the weather was frightful.

"During the night the British left the mill, fell back on the Buttes-à-Neveu, and began to entrench themselves there. When the day broke, De Lévis took possession of the mill and the whole plain of Abraham as far as the flood, in order to cover the Anse-du-Foulon (Wolfe'e Cove), whither the French vessels, laden with provis ions, artillery and baggage, which had not effected their discharge at St. Augustin, had received orders to repair. While this was effecting on the 28th, our army was to take repose, so as to be ready next day to assail the British at the Buttes, and drive them into the city.

"No sooner, however, was Murray within the walls, than he determined to make a sortie with all his troops; intending either to give bat tle if anoccasion presented, or else to fortify himself at the Buttes-à-Neveu, should De Lévis' force appear to be too considerable to resist in open field; for the report of a French cannoneer (who fell in while disembarking, was floated down the flood, and rescued by some British soldiers on guard) left no further doubt in his mind that the force so long spoken of had now arrived. He left the city in the morning of April 28, at the head of his whole garrison, the regulars in which, not including officers, alone numbered 7714 combatants. Excepting some hundred sick in hospital, Murray left in the place only soldiers enough to mount guard, and, with a force from 6,000 to 7,000 strong, advanced in two columns, with 22 cannon.

"De Lévis, who rode out, with his staff officers, far in advance of his men to reconnoitre the position of the British on the Buttes-à-Neveu, no sooner perceived this forward movement than he sent orders to his main army to quicken its march towards the Plains of Abraham. Murray, seeing only the French van as yet, resolved to attack it before the soldiers could take breath after their march; but he had to deal with an adversary of mark, and cool temperament withal. The former ranged his troops in advance of the Buttes, his right resting on the hill (*coteau*) of Sainte-Geneviève, and his left touching the cliff (*falaise*) bordering the St. Lawrence; his entire line extended about six furlongs. Four regiments, under Colonel Burton, formed his right, placed astraddle (*à cheval*) on the road of Ste. Foy. Four regiments, and the Scotch Highlanders, under Colonel Fraser, forming the left, were similarly ranged on the road of St. Louis. Two battalions were kept as a reserve: and besides these last, the right flank of the British army was covered by a corps of light infantry under Major Dalling; the left flank by Captain Huzzen's company of Rangers and 100 volunteers, led by Capt. Macdonald. All being arranged in the form described, General Murray gave orders to advance.

"The French van, composed of six companies of grenadiers, set in battle order, part on the right, in a redoubt erected by the British, the year preceding, to the eastward of the Anse-du-Foulon; part on the left, in Dumont's mill, the miller's house, the tannery, and other buildings close by, on the road to Ste. Foy. The rest of the army, on learning what was toward, hastened its march, the men closing ranks as they came near; but the three brigades were hardly formed, when the British began the attack vigorously.

"Murray felt the importance of getting hold of Dumont's mill, which covered the passage (*issue*) by which the French were debouching, and he assailed it with superior numbers. He hoped that, by overpowering the grenadiers who defended it, he should be able to fall afterwards upon the centre of the force still on its way, push them far off the line of operation, and cut off the French right wing, hemmed in, as it were, on the road of St. Louis.

"Lévis, to prevent this design, withdrew his right to the entry of the wood which was in its rear, and caused the grenadiers to evacuate the mill, and fall back, in order to lessen the distance for the arriving brigades. At this turn, Bourlamaque was severally wounded by a cannon-shot, which also killed his horse. His soldiers, left without orders, seeing the grenadiers hotly engaged and overmatched, simultaneously flew to their support, and formed in line just as the enemies bore down on this point in mass with all their artillery; their field-pieces and howitzers, loaded with ball and grape, plying upon the space occupied by this wing, which staggered under so deadly a fire. The French grenadiers advanced quick step, re-took the mill after an obstinate struggle, and kept it.* These brave soldiers, commanded by Captain Aiguebelles, almost all perished this day. While those events were passing on the left, De Lévis caused the soldiers to re-capture the redoubt they had evacuated in order to fall back. The Canadians of the Queen's brigade, who occupied that petty redoubt and the pine wood on the margin of the cape, regained their ground and soon charged in turn, supported by M. La Corne de St. Luc and some savages. The combat was not less hot on this line than at the left. All the troops were now in action, and the fire was heavy on both parts. Militiamen were seen to crouch on the ground to load their pieces, rise up after the cannon-shot passed over them, and dash forward to shoot the British gunners. Those of Montreal fought with great courage, especially the battalion led by the brave Colonel Rhéaume, who was killed. This brigade posted in the centre, and commanded by M. de Repentigny, itself arrested on open ground (*rase campagne*) the British centre, when advancing at quick step, and with the advantage of high ground. It also repulsed several charges, and slackened, by its firmness and rapid firing, the enemy when pressing the grenadiers of the left; thereby facilitating their after-march onward: in fine, this was the only brigade that maintained its ground during the whole time the obstinate struggle lasted.

"By this time, the attack which gave the British the mastery, for a moment, over the positions occupied by the French van when the fight began, was everywhere repulsed, and our people in re-possession of all the ground they temporarily lost; thus Murray's offensive movement by the road of Sainte-Foy had failed, and that check enabled the French to attack him in their turn.

"De Lévis, observing that the British General had over-weakened his left to strengthen his right, resolved to profit by it. He ordered his

* With this old windmill is associated one of the most thrilling episodes of the conflict. Some of the French Grenadiers and some of Fraser's Highlanders took, lost, and re-took the mill five times, their respective officers looking on in mute astonishment and admiration; while a *Scotch piper, who had been confined for bad conduct ever since 13th Sept.*, 1759, *was piping away within hearing*,—so says an old chronicle.—*J.M.L.*

troops to charge the enemy's left wing with the bayonet, and to thrust the British off the St. Louis road on to the Ste. Foy. By this manœuvre he took in flank the whole of Murry's army, drove the corps off the height of Sainte-Geneviève, and cut off the enemy from the line of retreat to the city. Colonel Poulardier dashed forward at the head of the Royal Roussillon brigade, attacked the British impetuously, transpierced their whole mass and put them to flight. At the same time their light troops gave way, and the fugitives, throwing themselves in front and in rear of the enemy's centre, caused his fire to be suspended. De Lévis profited by this disorder to cause his own left to charge the British right wing, which the former completely routed.

"Then the whole French army advanced in pursuit of the beaten foe; but as his flight was rapid, the short distance they had to run did not allow of throwing them towards the river St. Charles. De Lévis, nevertheless, might have been able to effect this object, but for an order ill-delivered by an officer whom he charged to call upon the Queen's brigade to sustain the charge of the Royal Roussillon brigade at the right; and who, instead of causing it to execute the prescribed movement, thus made it take place behind the left wing.

"The enemy left in their victors' hands their whole artillery, ammunition, and the intrenching tools they brought with them, besides a portion of the wounded. Their loss was considerable; nearly a fourth of their soldiers being killed or wounded. Had the French been less fatigued than they were, and assailed the city without allowing the enemy time to recover themselves, it would probably have fallen again under the domination of its former masters, says Knox; for such was the confusion that the British neglected to re-man the ramparts; the sentinels were absent from their posts when the fugitives sought shelter in the lower-town; even the city gates stood open for some time. But it was impossible to exact further service from the conquerors. They had to oppose to the fire of the enemy's 22 cannon, that of three small pieces, which they painfully dragged across the marsh of La Suède. They, too, experienced great loss, having been obliged to form rank and remain long immoveable under the enemy's fire. A brigadier, six colonels or majors (*chefs de battaillon*) and 97 other officers, with a savage chief, were killed or wounded.

"The numbers of the two contending armies were nearly co-equal, for De Lévis left several detachments to protect his artillery, barges, and the bridge of Jacques Cartier river, in order to assure himself a way of retreat, in case he were worsted. The cavalry took no part in the action.

"The savages, who were nearly all in the wood behind during the fight, spread over the vacated battle-field, when the French were pursuing the enemy, and felled many of the wounded British, whose scalps were afterwards found upon the neighboring bushes. As soon as De Lévis was apprised of this massacre, he took vigorous measures for putting a stop to it. Within a comparatively narrow space, nearly 2,500 men had been struck by bullets: the patches of snow and icy puddles on the ground were reddened with the bloodshed that the frozen ground refused to absorb; and the wounded survivors of the battle and of the butchery of the savages were immersed in pools of gore and filth, ankle-deep.

"The transport of the wounded, which took up much time, formed the concluding act of the sanguinary drama performed this day. The wounded were borne to the General Hospital, the distance to which was much increased by the deviations from the straight way to it that had to be made. 'It wants another kind of pen than mine,' wrote a *religieuse* from the house of suffering, 'to depict the horrors we have had to see and hear, during the twenty-four hours that the transit hither lasted, the cries of the dying and the lamentations of those interested in their fate. A strength more than human is needful at such a time, to save those engaged in tending such sufferers from sinking under their task.

"'After having dressed more than 500 patients, placed on beds obtained from the king's magazines, there still remained others unprovided with resting-places. Our granges and cattle-sheds were full of them. * * * We had in our infirmaries 72 officers, of whom 33 died. Amputations of legs and arms were going on everywhere. To add to our affliction, linen for dressing ran out, and we were fain to have recourse to our sheets and chemises. * * * * * * *

"'It was not with us now as after the first battle, when we could have recourse, for aid, to the *hospitalières* of Quebec * * * the British having taken possession of their house, as well as those of the Ursulines and private dwellings, for the reception of their wounded, who were even in greater number than ours. There were brought to us twenty British officers, whom their own people had not time to carry away, and whom we had to take charge of." * * * * * * *

"After the action, which lasted three hours, the French took post on the Buttes-à-Neveu, and established their camp on the same plains where they had just so gloriously avenged their defeat thereupon in the preceding year."

De Lévis' triumph did not last long. On the evening of the battle he broke ground within 600 or 700 yards of the walls, and next day commenced to bombard the town, but without producing much effect. On the night of the 15th May, news was received of the approach of the English squadron from Halifax, and De Lévis abandoned the siege with great precipitation, leaving his whole battering train, camp and camp furniture, entrenching tools, &c., behind him. He was pursued and several prisoners taken, and thus ended the French attempt to retake Quebec. The brave garrison pent up amid a hostile population, and worn down by service and sickness, welcomed the succor with that grateful joy which might be expected from men in their position.

THE MONUMENT—ITS HISTORY.

"The idea of erecting a monument to the slain of 1760 was conceived many years ago. For a long time the plough of the farmer and the shovel and pick-axe of the workman, as he labored at the foundation of new buildings along the Ste. Foy road, turned up human remains—evidently the relics of those who were slain. Rusty, half decayed arms, accoutrements and buttons, bearing the arms or regimental numbers of French and British regiments, found in close proximity to those remains, told to whom they belonged. In 1853–54, an unusual number of these bleached fragments of humanity—sad memorials of a by-gone struggle—were found, and the St. Jean Baptiste Society conceived the idea of having them all interred in one spot. They were accordingly collected, so far as possible, and the Christian intention of the society was carried out on the 5th June, 1854. The ceremony is doubtless fresh in the minds of the great majority of our citizens. A splendid procession was organized, and the national socities, public bodies, troops, volunteers, &c.,

followed a magnificent funeral car, containing the bones of the slain French and English soldiers, to the French Cathedral, where a solemn *Requiem* was sung. The remains were then conveyed in the same state to the field on the Ste. Foy road, adjoining the mansion of the late Mr. Julien Chouinard, where the death-struggle had taken place between the 78th Highlanders, (Fraser's) and the French "Grenadiers de la Reine," where they were deposited in a common grave. An eloquent funeral oration was delivered by Col. Sir Etienne Pascal Taché. The project of an appropriate monument was started about the same time, and appeared to meet with general approval. It was, however, the French Canadian national society which took the lead, as it had done on the previous occasion, and as it has done since. Arrangements had progressed to such an extent that it was intended to lay the corner-stone of the monument on the 24th June, 1855, but it was thought desirable to postpone it until the 19th June following, when the presence of His Imperial Majesty's corvette *La Capricieuse* in the harbor of Quebec added new solemnity to the occasion. A procession, exceeding in magnitude that of the previous year, was organized; and the presence in its ranks of the British garrison of Quebec, and the crew of a French war vessel, was indicative of the cordial alliance then as now existing between these two great powers, and formed an auspicious spectacle for their decendants in the new world. On that occasion, the Hon. P. J. O. Chauveau was the orator of the day. His speech was a most brilliant effort, worthy of his reputation as a public speaker, replete with brilliant imagery, couched in the most eloquent language, governed throughout by sound judgment and good taste. During the following year, the St. Jean Baptiste Society labored earnestly and unceasingly for the purpose of collecting subscriptions to complete the monument. Theirs was, indeed, no easy task, as may be well supposed, for the excitement of the thing had all passed away with the public display, and those who would have willingly contributed before the laying of the corner-stone, took but little interest in it afterwards. Success was, however, attained, and in four or five years, the base was crowned by the noble pillar which now rears its fine proportions on the historic heights of Ste. Foy. Without being invidious in the least, we may say that to Dr. P. M. Bardy belongs in a great degree the credit of this success; indeed, his fellow members of the St. Jean

Baptiste Society are the first to concede to him the merit of his exertions. Baron Gauldrée Boilleau, the Consul General of France in Canada, obtained from His Highness Prince Napoleon the beautiful statue of Bellona, which forms such an appropriate ornament on the summit of the monument. The memorial to the slain of 1760 having been thus completed, the plan of an inauguration ceremony was projected, and was consummated yesterday in presence of His Excellency the Governor General, Lord Monck, the garrison, the public bodies, the national societies, and at least twenty-five thousand persons, citizens of Quebec and residents of the adjacent villages. The Ste. Foy monument is decidedly the handsomest public monument we have in this city or its vicinity. Of bronzed metal, standing on a stone base, and surmounted by a bronze statue, it is a most prominent object in the landscape. The face of the pedestal fronting Ste. Foy road has the simple inscription, surrounded by a laurel wreath, 'AUX BRAVES DE 1760, ERIGÉ PAR LA SOCIÉTÉ ST. JEAN BAPTISTE DE QUÉBEC, 1860.'* On the face looking towards the city is the name 'MURRAY,' on an oval shield surmounted by the arms of Great Britain and Ireland, and supported by British insignia. On the other side is a shield bearing the name 'LEVIS,' surmounted by the arms of France under the Bourbons, the crown and lilies, with appropriate supporters at each side. In rear looking towards the valley, there is a representation of a wind-mill in bas-relief—in allusion, we suppose, to the wind-mill which was an object of alternate attack and defence to both armies on the occasion of the battle. This portion of the column also bears the national arms of Canada. The site of the monument is beautiful in the extreme. You reach it from the Ste. Foy toll-gate after five or six minutes' walk through an avenue bordered on either side by handsome villas, and fine gardens, and half shaded by over-arching trees. It stands on an open field on the brow of the cliff over-hanging the valley of the St. Charles. As you turn towards the monumental pillar, you have before you the valley of the St. Charles, along which the populous suburbs of St. Roch and St. Sauveur are gradually making their way. Beyond the limit of

* It has occurred to many that the incription "Erigé par les citoyens de Québec" would have been more appropriate, considering that many citizens, certainly not "Jean Baptistes," subscribed liberally to the Monument fund, amongst others the Hon. Francis Hincks, Geo. B. Symes, Esq., Col. Rhodes, and a host of others.—J. M. L.

the level ground, the hills rise up terrace-like, bright, even in the late autumn with the verdure of gardens, and rendered still more attractive by the endless succession of villas, farm-houses and villages which dot the rising ground at intervals until they are lost in the distance, far away in the rear, behind Lorette, Charlesbourg and Beauport, where the blue summits of the Laurentian range rise to the skies. On the left, at one end of the valley, the prospect is rendered still more grand by the mountain heights and thickly-wooded skirts of the valley, bright with the orange, crimson, and russet hues of autumn. Along the whole landscape you can trace the winding of the St. Charles, from the foot of the mountains on the one side until it mingles with the broad St. Lawrence on the other. In fact it is impossible, within the narrow limits of our report, to describe the scene. It contains every variety of physical feature which can add to beauty of landscape; and viewed as it was yesterday, under the warm sun of the Indian summer, it was indeed rarely beautiful. It is needless to say that the attraction was heightened by the moving crowd, the bright uniforms, the glistening arms, and waving banners of the thousands who thronged the field of Ste. Foy during the sunny afternoon."

A NOBLE SENTIMENT.

The Montreal *Transcript* terminates an article about the Ste. Foy Monument celebration with the following sentiment:—

"Thus terminated a ceremony which fitly opens the second century of British rule in La Nouvelle France; in the first, French, British and Indians meet as deadly enemies to shed each other's blood, and contend for domination over Canada; in the second, the descendants and representatives of the same races assemble to bury their hostility with the bones of the victims of that century's old contest beneath a monument in their common valour, which is a memorial also that the three races are blending into one people. Let us hope that before a third century dawns the fusion will be complete, and as Briton, Roman, Saxon, Dane, and Norman blended to form the English people, so all the races that find in Canada a home may by forbearance, mutual respect, strict justice, and an enlarged view of their nationality, bury in a common grave the dead bones of their militant prejudices, whether of faith or origin, and look smiling down on them as a united Canadian nation, not ignoring, but recognizing and drawing wisdom from past struggles and contentions, making past war the mother of present and future peace."

Arnold's Expedition in 1775.*

The invasion of Canada by the troops of the American Congress, rendered the year 1775 remarkable in the annals of the Province. The principal points which will demand our attention are the expedition of Arnold, the storming of Quebec, and the death of Montgomery.

Canada, supposed to be perfectly secure, had been left almost destitute of regular troops, nearly all of which had been removed to Boston. The whole force of this description consisted of only two regiments of infantry, the 7th Fusileers, and the 26th, amounting to no more than eight hundred men. Of these the greater part were in garrison at St. John's, the rest dispersed through the various posts. The province was, however, extremely fortunate in the character, talents and resources of the governor, General Carleton.

On the 17th September, 1775, Brigadier General Richard Montgomery, who had formerly been in the British service, appeared at the head of an army, before the fort of St. John's; which, after a gallant defence, surrendered on the 3rd November, the garrison marching out with the honors of war. Montreal, which was entirely defenceless, capitulated on the 12th November; and General Carleton, conceiving it of the utmost importance to reach Quebec, the only place capable of defence, passed through the American force stationed at Sorel, during the night, in a canoe with muffled paddles;† and arrived in Quebec on the 19th, to the great joy of the garrison and loyal inhabitants, who placed every confidence in his well known courage and ability.

While the province was thus threatened with subjugation on the side of Montreal, a new danger presented itself from a quarter so entirely

* From *Hawkins's Picture of Quebec.*

† Piloted by Captain Bouchette, the ancestor of our respected townsmen, R. S. M. Bouchette, Joseph Bouchette, Esqrs., Captain Jean Bouchette, &c.

unexpected, that, until the particulars were ascertained, the fears and superstitions of the inhabitants of the country parishes had ample subject for employment and exaggeration. An expedition of a singular and daring character had been successfully prosecuted against Quebec from the New England States, by a route which was little known and generally considered impracticable. This expedition was headed by Colonel Arnold, an officer in the service of the Congress, who with two regiments, amounting to about eleven hundred men, left Boston about the middle of September, and undertook to penetrate through the wilderness to Point Levi, by the means of the rivers Kennebec and Chaudière.

The spirit of enterprise evinced in this bold design, and the patience, hardihood and perseverance of the new raised forces employed in the execution, will forever distinguish this expedition in the history of offensive operations. A handful of men ascending the course of a rapid river, and conveying arms, ammunition, baggage, and provisions through an almost trackless wild—bent upon a most uncertain purpose—can scarcely be considered, however, a regular operation of war. It was rather a desperate attempt, suited to the temper of the fearless men engaged in it, the character of the times, and of the scenes which were about to be acted on the American continent. The project, however, of Arnold was by no means an original thought. It had been suggested by Governor Pownall, in his "Idea of the service of America," as early as the year 1758. He says,—"The people of Massachusetts, in the counties of Hampshire, Worcester and York are the best wood-hunters in America. * * * I should think if about a hundred thorough wood-hunters, properly officered, could be obtained in the County of York, a scout of such might make an attempt upon the settlements by way of Chaudière river."

On the 22nd September, Arnold embarked on the Kennebec river in two hundred batteaux; and notwithstanding all natural impediments—the ascent of a rapid stream—interrupted by frequent *portages* through thick woods and swamps—in spite of frequent accidents—the desertion of one-third of their number—they at length arrived at the head of the river Chaudière, having crossed the ridge of land which separates the waters falling into the St. Lawrence from those which run into the sea.

They now reached Lake Megantic, and following the course of the Chaudière river, their difficulties and privations, which had been so great as on one occasion to compel them to kill their dogs for sustenance, were speedily at an end. After passing thirty-two days in the wilderness, they arrived on the 4th November at the first settlement, called Sertigan, twenty-five leagues from Quebec, where they obtained all kinds of provisions. On the 9th, Colonel Arnold arrived at Point Levi, where he remained twenty-four hours before it was known at Quebec; and whence it was extremely fortunate that all the small craft and canoes had been removed by order of the officer commanding the garrison. On the 13th, late in the evening, they embarked in thirty-four canoes, and very early in the morning of the 14th, he succeeded in landing five hundred men at Wolfe's Cove, without being discovered, from the *Lizard* and *Hunter*, ships of war. The first operation was to take possession of what had been General Murray's house, on the Ste. Foy road, and of the General Hospital. They also placed guards upon all the roads, in order to prevent the garrison from obtaining supplies from the country.

The small force of Arnold prevented any attempt being made towards the reduction of the fortress, until after the arrival of Montgomery from Montreal, who took the command on the 1st December, and established his head-quarters at Holland House.* Arnold is said to have occupied the house near Scott's Bridge, lately inhabited by the Honorable Mr. Justice Kerr, (and since owned by Mr. Langlois.)

The arrival of the governor on the 19th November, had infused the best spirit among the inhabitants of Quebec. On the 1st December, the motley garrison amounted to eighteen hundred men, all, however, full of zeal in the cause of their king and country, and well supplied with provisions for eight months. They were under the immediate command of Colonel Allan Maclean, of the 84th Regiment or Royal Emigrants, composed principally of those of the gallant Fraser's Highlanders, who had settled in Canada.

STATEMENT OF THE GARRISON, 1ST DECEMBER, 1775.

70 Royal Fusileers, or 7th Regiment.
230 Royal Emigrants, or 84th Regiment.
22 Royal Artillery.

* Now occupied by Fred. Woods, Esq., manager Bank of B. N. America.

330 British Malitia, under Lt. Col. Caldwell.
543 Canadians, under Colonel Dupré.
400 Seamen under Captains Hamilton and Mackenzie.
50 Masters and Mates.
35 Marines.
120 Artificers.

1800 Total bearing arms.

The siege, or rather the blockade, was maintained during the whole month of December, although the incidents were few and of little interest. The Americans were established in every house near the walls, more particularly in the suburbs of St. Roch, near the Intendant's palace. Their riflemen, secure in their excellent cover, kept up an unremitting fire upon the British sentries, wherever they could obtain a glimpse of them. As the Intendant's palace was found to afford them a convenient shelter, from the cupola of which they constantly annoyed the sentries, a nine-pounder was brought to bear upon the building; and this once splendid and distinguished edifice was reduced to ruin, and has never been rebuilt. The enemy also threw from thirty to forty shells every night into the city, which fortunately did little or no injury either to the lives or the property of the inhabitants. So accustomed did the latter become to the occurrences of a siege, that at last they ceased to regard the bombardment with alarm. In the meantime, the fire from the garrison was maintained in a very effective manner upon every point where the enemy were seen. On one occasion, as Montgomery was reconnoitering near the town, the horse which drew his cariole was killed by a cannon shot.

During this anxious period the gentry and inhabitants of the city bore arms, and cheerfully performed the duties of soldiers. The British militia were conspicuous for zeal and loyalty, under the command of Major Henry Caldwell, who had the provincial rank of Lieutenant Colonel. He had served as Deputy Quartermaster General with the army, under General Wolfe, and had settled in the province after the conquest. The Canadian militia, within the town, was commanded by Colonel Le Comte Dupré, an officer of great zeal and ability, who rendered great services during the whole siege.

General Montgomery, despairing to reduce the place by a regular siege, resolved on a night attack, in the hope of either taking it by storm, or of finding the garrison unprepared at some point. In this design he was encouraged by Arnold, whose local knowledge of Quebec was accurate, having been acquired in his frequent visits for the purpose of buying up Canadian horses. The intention of Montgomery soon became known to the garrison, and General Carleton made every preparation to prevent surprise, and to defeat the assault of the enemy. For several days, the governor, with the officers and gentlemen off duty, had taken up their quarters in the Récollet Convent, where they slept in their clothes. At last, early in the morning of the 31st December, and during a violent snow storm, Montgomery, at the head of the New York troops, advanced to the attack of the Lower Town, from its western extremity, along a road between the base of Cape Diamond and the river. Arnold, at the same time, advanced from the General Hospital by way of St. Charles street. The two parties were to meet at the lower end of Mountain street, and when united were to force Prescott Gate. Two feint attacks in the meantime on the side towards the west, were to distract the attention of the garrison. Such is the outline of this daring plan, the obstacles to the accomplishment of which do not seem to have entered into the contemplation of the American officers, who reckoned too much upon their own fortune and the weakness of the garrison.

When, at the head of seven hundred men, Montgomery had advanced a short distance beyond the spot where the inclined plane has since been constructed, he came to a narrow defile, with a precipice towards the river on the one side, and the scarped rock above him on the other. This place is known by the name of Près-de-Ville. Here, all further approach to the Lower Town was intercepted, and commanded by a battery of three-pounders placed in a *hangard* to the south of the pass. The post was entrusted to a captain of Canadian militia, whose force consisted of thirty Canadian and eight British militiamen, with nine British seamen to work the guns, as artillerymen, under Captain Barnsfare, master of a transport, laid up in harbor during the winter. At day-break, some of the guard being on the look out, discovered, through the imperfect light, a body of troops in full march from Wolfe's Cove upon the post. The men had been under arms waiting with the utmost steadiness for the attack, which they had reason to expect, from the reports of deserters; and in pursuance of judicious arrangements which had been previously concerted, the enemy was allowed to approach unmolested within a small distance. They halted at about fifty yards from the barrier; and as the guard remained perfectly still, it was probably concluded that they were not on the alert. To ascertain this, an officer was seen to approach quite near to the barrier. After listening a moment or two, he returned to the body; and they instantly dashed forward at double quick time to the attack of the post. This was what the guard expected: the artillerymen stood by with lighted matches, and Captain Barnsfare at the critical moment giving the word, the fire of the guns and musketry was directed with deadly precision against the head of the advancing column. The consequence was a precipitate retreat—the enemy was scattered in every direction—the groans of the wounded and of the dying were heard, but nothing certain being known, the pass continued to be swept by the cannon and musketry for the space of ten minutes.

The enemy having retired, thirteen bodies were found in the snow, and Montgomery's orderly sergeant desperately wounded, but yet alive, was brought into the guard room. On being asked if the general himself had been killed, the sergeant evaded the question by replying that he had not seen him for some time, although he could not but have known the fact. This faithful sergeant died in about an hour afterwards. It was not ascertained that the American general had been killed, until some hours afterwards, when General Carleton, being anxious to ascertain the truth, sent an aide-de-camp to the Seminary, to inquire if any of the American officers, then prisoners, would identify the body. A field officer of Arnold's division, who had been made prisoner near *Sault-au-Matelot barrier, consenting, accompanied the aide-de-camp to the Pres-de-Ville guard, and pointed it out among the other bodies, at the same time pronouncing, in accents of grief, a glowing eulogium of Montgomery's bravery and worth. Besides that of the general, the bodies of his two aides-de-camp were recognized among the slain. The defeat of Montgomery's force was complete. Colonel Campbell, the second in command, immediately relinquished the undertaking, and led back his men with the utmost precipitation.

* Sault-au-Matelot street, until 1830, was the fashionable quarter of the city. The *élite* resided there. It was *bad taste* to live in the Upper Town.

The exact spot where the barrier was erected before which Montgomery fell, may be described as crossing the narrow road under the mountain, immediately opposite to the west end of a building which stands on the south, and was formerly occupied by Mr. Racey as a brewery. It is now numbered 58. At the time of the seige this was called the Potash. The battery extended to the south, and nearly to the river. An inscription commemorating the event might properly be placed upon the opposite rock.

Soon after the repulse of the enemy before the post at Près-de-Ville, information was given to the officer in command there, that Arnold's party, from the General Hospital, advancing along the St. Charles, had captured the barrier at the Sault-au-Matelot, and that he intended an attack upon that of Près-de-Ville, by taking it in the rear. Immediate preparations were made for the defence of the post against such an attack, by turning some of the guns of an inner barrier, not far from the old Custom House, towards the town; and although the intelligence proved false,—Arnold having been wounded and his division captured,—yet the incident deserves to be commemorated as affording a satisfactory contradiction to some accounts which have appeared in print, representing the guard at Près-de-Ville as having been paralysed by fear,—the post and barrier "deserted,"—and the fire which killed Montgomery merely "accidental." On the contrary, the circumstances which we have related, being authentic, proved that the conduct of the Près-de-Ville guard was firm and collected in the hour of danger; and that by their coolness and steadiness they mainly contributed to the safety of the city. Both Colonel Maclean and General Carleton rendered every justice to their meritorious behaviour on the occasion.

In the meantime the attack by Arnold, on the north-eastern side of the Lower Town, was made with desperate resolution. It was, fortunately, equally unsuccessful, although the contest was more protracted; and at one time the city was in no small danger. Arnold led his men by files along the river St. Charles, until he came to the Sault-au-Matelot, where there was a barrier with two guns mounted. It must be understood that St. Paul street did not then exist, the tide coming up nearly to the base of the rock, and the only path between the rock and the beach was the narrow alley which now exists in rear of St. Paul street under the precipice itself. Here the curious visitor will find a jutting rock, where was the first barrier. The whole of the street went by the name of the Sault-au-Matelot from the most ancient times. Arnold took the command of the "forlorn hope," and was leading the attack upon this barrier, when he received a musket wound in the knee which disabled him, and he was carried back to the General Hospital. His troops, however, persevered, and having soon made themselves masters of the barrier, pressed on through the narrow street to the attack of the second, near the eastern extremity of Sault-au-Matelot street. This was a battery which protected the ends of the two streets called St. Peter street and Sault-au-Matelot, extending, by means of *hangards* mounted with cannon, from the rock to the river. The Montreal Bank,* then a private house, had cannon projecting from the end windows, as had a house at the end of Sault-au Matelot street. The enemy took shelter in the houses on each side, and in the narrow pass leading round the base of the cliff towards Hope-Gate, where they were secured by the angle of the rock from the fire of the guns at the barrier. Here the enemy met with a determined resistance, which it was impossible to overcome; and General Carleton having ordered a sortie from Palace Gate under Captain Laws, in order to take them in the rear—and their rear-guard, under Captain Dearborn, having already surrendered—the division of Arnold demanded quarter, and were brought prisoners to the Upper Town. The officers were confined in the Seminary. The contest continued for upwards of two hours, and the bravery of the assailants was indisputable. Through the freezing cold, and the pelting of the storm, they maintained the attack until all hope of success was lost, when they surrendered to a generous enemy, who treated the wounded and prisoners with humanity.

The Americans lost in the attack about one hundred killed and wounded, and six officers of Arnold's party, exclusive of the loss at Près-de-Ville. The British lost one officer, Lieutenant Anderson of the Royal Navy, and seventeen killed and wounded. The following is a statement of the force which surrendered:

1 Lieutenant Colonel,	Not wounded.
2 Majors,	
8 Captains,	
15 Lieutenants,	

* This bank formerly occupied the building which stood last year, where the new Quebec Bank has since been built.

1	Adjutant,	Not wounded.
1	Quarter-Master,	
4	Volunteers,	
350	Rank and file,	
44	Officers and soldiers, wounded.	
426	Total surrendered.	

By the death of Montgomery the command devolved upon Arnold, who had received the rank of Brigadier General. In a letter, dated 14th January, 1776, he complains of the great difficulty he had in keeping his remaining troops together, so disheartened were they by their disasters on the 31st December. The siege now resumed its former character of a blockade, without any event of importance, until the month of March, when the enemy received reinforcements that increased their numbers to near two thousand men. In the beginning of April, Arnold took the command at Montreal, and was relieved before Quebec by Brigadier General Wooster. The blockading army, which had all the winter remained at three miles distance from the city, now approached nearer the ramparts, and re-opened their fire upon the fortifications, with no better success than before. In the night of the 3rd May, they made an unsuccessful attempt to destroy the ships of war and vessels laid up in the Cul-de-Sac, by sending in a fire ship, with the intention of profiting by the confusion, and of making another attack upon the works by escalade. At this time they had reason to except that considerable reinforcements, which they had no means of preventing from reaching the garrison, would shortly arrive from England; and giving up all hope of success, they became impatient to return to their own country. A council of war was called on the 5th, by General Thomas, who had succeeded Wooster; and it was determined to raise the siege at once, and to retire to Montreal. They immediately began their preparation, and in the course of the next forenoon broke up their camp, and commenced a precipitate retreat.

In the means time the gallant Carleton and his intrepid garrison were rejoiced by the arrival, early in the morning of the 6th May, of the *Surprise* frigate, Captain Linzee, followed soon after by the *Isis*, of fifty guns, and *Martin* sloop of war, with a reinforcement of troops and supplies. Nothing could exceed the delight of the British at this seasonable relief. After the toil and privation of a six months' seige, it may be imagined with what feelings the inhabitants beheld the frigate rounding Pointe Lévi, and how sincerely they welcomed her arrival in the basin. The *Isis* was commanded by Captain, afterwards Admiral, Sir Charles Douglas, Baronet, father of Major General Sir Howard Douglas, the late popular Lieutenant Governor of New Brunswick. Captain Douglas had made uncommon exertions to force his ship through fields of ice,—having by skilful management and a press of sail carried her, for the space of fifty leagues, through obstacles which would have deterred an officer less animated by the zeal which the critical service on which he was employed required. The troops on board the vessels, consisting of two companies of the 29th Regiment, with a party of marines, amounting in all to two hundred men, were immediately landed, under the command of Captain Viscount Petersham, afterwards General the Earl of Harrington. No soon had they arrived in the Upper Town, than General Carleton, who had learned the retreat of the enemy, determined to make s sortie and to harass their rear. He accordingly marched out at the head of eight hundred men; but so rapid was the flight of the enemy, that a few shots only were exchanged, when they abandoned their stores, artillery, scaling ladders, leaving also their sick, of whom they had a great many, to the care of the British. The humanity with which they were treated was afterwards commemorated by Chief Justice Marshall in his life of Washington.

The conduct of Generaly Carleton throughout the siege was beyond all praise. He always wore the same countenance, and as his looks were watched, his conduct infused courage into those of the inhabitants, who unused to a siege, sometimes gave way to despondency. He was, indeed, a man of true bravery, guided by discrimination, conduct and experience. During the attack of the 31st December, he had taken post at Prescott Gate, where he knew would be made the combined attack of Montgomery and Arnold, had they succeeded in passing the barrier at Près-de-Ville and the Sault-au-Matelot. Here he took his stand, and there is every reason to believe that he would have defended the post even to death. He had been heard to say, that he would never grace the triumph of the enemy, or survive the loss of the town.

The despatches announcing the retreat of the American forces from before Quebec were taken home by Colonel Caldwell, who received the usual present on the occasion. His Majesty immediately bestowed the Knighthood of the Bath upon General Carleton. The following extract from his despatches to Lord George Germaine, Secretary of State, shows his own sense of the general conduct of the officers and men under his command. Among the Canadian officers who particularly distinguished themselves, were Colonel Dupré, Major Ecuyer, and Captains Bouchette, Laforce and Chabot, of the marine.

"Thus," says General Carleton, "ended our siege and blockade, during which the mixed garrison of soldiers, sailors, British and Canadian militia, with the artificers, from Halifax and Newfoundland, showed great zeal and patience, under very severe duty, and uncommon vigilance, indispensable in a place liable to be stormed, besides great labor necessary to render such attempts less practicable.

"I cannot conclude this letter without doing justice to Lieutenant Colonel Maclean, who has been indefatigably zealous in the king's service, and to his regiment, wherein he has collected a number of experienced good officers, who have been very useful. Colonel Hamilton captain of His Majesty's ship *Lizard*, who commanded the battalion of seamen, his officers and men, discharged their duty with great alacrity and spirit. The same thing must be acknowledged of the masters, inferior officers and seamen, belonging to His Majesty's transports, and merchantmen, detained here last fall: only one seaman deserted the whole time. The malitia, British and Canadian, behaved with a steadiness and resolution that could hardly have been expected from men unused to arms. Judges, and other officers of government, as well as merchants, cheerfully submitted to every inconvenience to preserve the town: the whole, indeed, upon the occasion, showed a spirit and perseverance that do them great honor.

"Major Caldwell, who commanded the British militia all winter, as Lieutenant Colonel Commandant, and is bearer of these despatches to your Lordship, has proved himself a faithful subject to His Majesty, and an active and diligent officer. He, and, indeed, almost every loyal subject are very considerable sufferers by the present hostile invasion."

Battle of Queenston,

13TH OCTOBER, 1812.

"ON the morning of the 11th October, 1812," says *Christie*,* "the American forces were concentrated at Lewistown opposite that place, with a view of making an attack upon the latter; but through the neglect or cowardice of the officer entrusted with preparing and conducting the boats to the place of embarkation, the attack miscarried. Early in the morning of the 13th, their forces were again concentrated at Lewiston, and the troops embarked under cover of a battery of two eighteen and two six pounders. This movement being soon discovered, a brisk fire was opened upon them from the British shore by the troops, and from three batteries. The Americans commenced a cannonade to sweep the shore, but with little effect. The first division, under Colonel Van Ransalaer, effected their landing unobserved under the heights a little above Queenston, and, mounting the ascent, attacked and carried an eighteen pounder battery, and dislodged the light company of the 49th Regiment. The enemy were in the meantime pushing over in boats, and notwithstanding the current and eddies, here rapid and numerous, and a tremendous discharge of artillery which shattered many of their boats, persevered with dauntless resolution, and effected a landing close upon Queenston, where they were opposed by the grenadiers of the 49th Regiment and the York volunteer militia, with a determination verging upon desperation. The carnage became terrible. The British being overwhelmed with numbers, were compelled to retire some distance into a hollow. General Brock, who was at Niagara, a short distance below, having heard the cannonade, arriving at that moment, the grey of the morning, with his provincial aid-de-camp, Lt.-Col. M'Donnell, from that place, and having rallied the grenadiers of his favorite 49th, was leading them on to the charge, when he received a musket ball in his breast, which almost imme-

* *History of Canada.*

diately terminated his existence. In the interim, the light company, supported by a party of the Yorkers, rallied, and reascended to dislodge the enemy from the heights. They formed and advanced to the charge, exposed to a smart fire, but finding the enemy posted behind trees, so that a charge could have little effect, they desisted, and separating, posted themselves in like manner, and kept up a sharp fire for some time. Lieut.-Col. M'Donnell, who had joined them while forming for the charge, and was encouraging the men, received a ball in his back, as his horse, which had been wounded, was in the act of wheeling. He survived his wound but twenty-four hours, in the most excruciating pain. The Americans having effected their landing with an overwhelming force, the British were obliged to give way, and suspend the fight until the arrival of reinforcements, leaving the Americans in possession of the heights. General Sheaffe soon after came up with a reinforcement of three hundred men of the 41st Regiment, two companies of militia, and two hundred and fifty Indians. Reinforcements having also arrived from Chippawa, the general collected his whole force, amounting to upwards of eight hundred men, and leaving two field pieces, with about thirty men under Lieutenant Holcroft of the Royal Artillery, in front of Queenston, as a check to prevent the enemy from occupying the village, proceeded by a circuitous route to gain the rear of the heights upon which the enemy were posted. The Indians, being more alert than the troops, first surmounted the hill, and commenced the attack, but were repulsed and fell back upon the main body, who formed with celerity, and upon the word, advanced to the charge under a heavy shower of musketry. The British set up a shout, accompanied with the war-whoop of the Indians, and advanced at the double quick pace, when the Americans, struck with terror, gave way and fled in all directions, some concealing themselves in the bushes, others precipitating themselves down the precipice and being either killed by the fall or drowned in the attempt to swim the river. A terrible slaughter ensued by the Indians,* whose vengeance it was impossible to restrain, until a white flag was observed ascending the hill with offers of an unconditional surrender, which were accepted. An armistice of three days was proposed by the

* Shall we also say, "Oh! the English and their savages, they were fiends!"

American and granted by the British general, in order to take care of their wounded and bury their dead, on condition of destroying their batteaux, which was immediately complied with. One general officer (Wadsworth), two lieutenant-colonels, five majors, a multitude of captains and subalterns, with nine hundred men, one field piece, and a stand of colors, were the fruits of this important victory; the enemy having lost in killed, wounded, missing, and prisoners, upwards of fifteen hundred men. General Van Ransalaer, before the arrival of the reinforcements from Niagara, under General Sheaffe, finding the fate of the day still undetermined, his troops almost exhausted with fatigue, and falling short of ammunition, had returned to the American shore, to urge across reinforcements from the embodied militia; but they, notwithstanding every menace and entreaty on his part, unanimously refused. In this dilemma, he wrote a note to General Wadsworth, who remained with the Americans on the Queenston heights, informing him of the situation of things, and leaving the course to be pursued much to his own judgment, assuring him that if he thought best to retreat, he would send as many boats as he could command, and cover his retreat by every fire he could make. But before the latter had time to resolve upon any mode of security or retreat, the spirited advance of the British had decided the fate of the day.

"Thus ended, in their total discomfiture, the second attempt of the Americans to invade Upper Canada. The loss of the British is said to have been about twenty killed, including Indians, and between fifty and sixty wounded. The fall of General Brock, the idol of the army, and of the people of Upper Canada, was an irreparable loss, and cast a shade over the glory of this dear-bought victory. He was a native of Guernsey, of an ancient reputable family, distinguished in the profession of arms. He had served for some years in Canada, and in some of the principal campaigns in Europe. He commanded a detachment of his favorite 49th Regiment, on the expedition to Copenhagen with Lord Nelson. He was one of those men who seem born to influence mankind, and mark the age in which they live. As a soldier he was brave to a fault, and not less judicious than decisive in his measures. The energy of his character was expressed in his robust and manly person. As a civil governor, he was firm, prudent and equitable. In fine, whether viewed as a man, a statesman, or a soldier, he equally deserves the esteem and respect of his contemporaries and of posterity. The Indians, who flocked to his standard, were enthusiastically attached to him. He fell at the early age of forty-two years. The remains of this gallant officer were, during the funeral service, honored with a discharge of minute guns from the American, as well as British, batteries, and with those of his aid-de-camp, Lieutenant-Colonel M'Donnell, interred in the same grave at Fort George, on the 16th of October; amidst the tears of an affectionate soldiery and a grateful people, who will revere his memory, and hold up to their posterity the imperishable name of Brock."

Battle of Beech Woods, 1813.*

THOROLD, *July 5th*, 1813.

AFTER the brilliant affair of Stoney Creek, the force under the command of Gen. Vincent, at Burlington Heights—regular militia and Indians—quietly advanced to Grimsby (40 Mile Creek), and took up their position on the west bank of that creek, their left extending to the lake side; the Crook's House being their head-quarters. When in this position a reinforcement of 100 warriors of the Caughnawagians arrived from Lower Canada, with their officers and chiefs.

Those people and the Six Nation warriors were, in appearance, more civilized than our western allies, but in no instance better warriors.

Those, our vigilant aids, were permitted to perambulate the country between our position and that of the enemy on the Niagara river, and were thereby instrumental in being useful by keeping the enemy in close quarters.

The gallant and indefatigable Captain Fitzgerald (recently one of the Knights of Windsor, England), was permitted to organize a scouting party of 100 men from the 49th Regiment of Foot, the Glengaries and the militia, which were on all occasions a corps in advance to watch the movements of the enemy.

* Coventry Manuscripts.

It was on one fine morning in July, 1813, that Colonel Boestler, of the United States army, sailed forth from Fort George, Niagara, with a force of 500 picked men in quest of Fitzgibbon's scouting party, and to lay them low. No doubt led by some of the tame ones unfortunately among us at that time, he pursued his course directly to the rendezvous of Fitzgibbon, and his allies in the Beech Woods, on arriving in an open field near the woods, commenced to prepare for action without the enemy in view; when after some straggling shots were fired from the woods, whereby the enemy felt and discovered its deadly effect without a possibility of making a defence against the foe.

The brave and honorable Fitzgibbon, deprecating such a warfare, issued orders for the firing to cease, which was partially done; still a desultory fire was kept up on the enemy,

When Fitzgibbon, with a flag in hand, rushed from the ambuscade, and said to Colonel Boestler that he would not be accountable for his command if they did not surrender; which, after some consultation, was agreed upon.

Major Dehein, coming up at this time with a reinforcement of Glengary men, dismissed the prisoners and escorted them to head-quarters, Grimsby, where they were disposed of as prisoners of war—being sent to Toronto.

(Signed) COL. JOHN CLARK,
Port Dalhousie.

The Battle of Chateauguay,

26TH OCTOBER, 1813.

THIS celebrated battle field furnishes us an opportunity for introducing to the reader's notice a Canadian, who has deserved well from the British crown and from his fellow countrymen. We quote from Mr. Morgan's *Biographical Dictionary*, p. 197 to end:

"The family of De Salaberry is descended from a noble family of the

Pays des Basques (Navarre). The father of the subject of this notice was a legislative councillor, and devotedly attached to his sovereign, so much so indeed, that he placed his four sons in the army. The one here noticed rose to great distinction, as will be seen; one of the others was killed at Badajos, and the other two died in the East Indies, employed in active warfare.

"The Honorable Charles Michel d'Irumberry de Salaberry, C. B., Seigneur de Chambly et de Beaulac, member of the Legislative Council, surnamed the Canadian Léonidas, was born at the Manor House of Beauport, November 19, 1778. He married Demoiselle Hertel de Rouville, and continued, as is before stated, to serve in the army, as well as his brothers. He served also, during the space of eleven years, in the West Indies, under General Prescott. At the seige of fort Matilda, under Prescott, and at the evacuation thereof, he commanded the grenadier company of the 4th battalion, 60th Regiment, which covered the retreat with credit to themselves. In 1795, he served at the conquest of Martinique; became aid-de-camp to Major-General de Rottenburg and accompanied him in the Walcheren expedition. Circumstances recalled him to this country, where he, in a very short time, formed the Voltigeurs, the organization of which reflected great honor upon him; lieutenant-colonel commanding and superintendent of this fine corps, he was also selected as one of the chiefs of the staff of the militia. Attacked at Lacolle, at the end of 1812, together with M. D'Eschambault's advance guard, by one thousand four hundred Americans of General Dearborn's army, he fought them until night; in attempting to surround him, they fired against each other, which soon terminated in their retreat; thus resulted the first victory of De Salaberry and the Voltigeurs. Part of this corps participated in the defeat, no less humiliating to the American army, at Chrysler's Farm. Dearborn and Wilkinson thus baffled in their project of invasion, there only remained General Hampton to contend with. De Salaberry, in proceeding to discover his whereabouts, obstructed the road from Odeltown to L'Acadia, by cutting down a great many trees. After several skirmishes, the Americans, not daring to hazard a general action in the woods, retired to a place called Four Corners. His adversary made an incursion into his camp, at the head of 200 Voltigeurs and 150 Indian warriors of the tribes of Lower Canada, and threw the enemy into disorder, without any loss on his own side. Hampton being repulsed on the Odeltown route, resolved wisely to effect a junction with his chief general, in taking the route leading to Chateauguay, which he was approaching, believing the road to be open; but access thereto was everywhere prevented by being blockaded by field works. De Salaberry was too sagacious not to discover that this strategic point was the road which Hampton would be sure to take in order to join Dearborn. The former, in the meantime, swept away the English pickets; and Major Henry with difficulty resisted them; when De Salaberry ably shifted his position, and threw himself on the route to face that general. The Canadian hero, who had the advantage of being acquainted with the whole of the country above Chateauguay, during an excursion on the American frontier some weeks before, then ascended to the left of the bank of the river Chateauguay, to reach the other extremity of a wood, where he knew there was an excellent position in a swamp, intercepted by deep rivulets. On four of these he established lines of defence in succession. The fourth was about half a mile in the rear, and commanded a ford on the right shore, which was a very important point of defence, with a view to the protection of the left bank. He caused to be erected on each of these lines a sort of breastwork, which was extended to some distance in the woods, to protect his right. The breastwork on his first line formed an obtuse angle on the right of the road. The whole of the day was taken up with fortifying this position, so as to force the enemy, in case he should feel disposed to make an attack, to cross a large space of settled country, and removing himself to a great distance from his supplies; whereas, on the contrary, the Voltigeurs had everything at hand, and were well supplied; more especially, as on the second line after the Voltigeurs and Indians, came the Watteville regiment. Sir George Prevost was on the third line, at Caughnawaga, with some troops and militia, from the Montreal district, having brought them down with him from Kingston, to oppose the junction of the American army. De Salaberry did not confine himself to the foregoing arrangements. He ordered a party of thirty axemen of the division of Beauharnois to proceed in front of the first line of defence, for the purpose of destroying the bridges and obstructing the roads. All the bridges within a league and a half were destroyed; and a formidable obstruction was formed on the road to the extent of a mile in advance of the first line of defence, which extended to the edge of the river, and continued to a distance of three or four acres through the woods, joined by a swamp on the right, almost impassible. The four lines of defence were thus completely sheltered, even from the fire of artillery. To this fortified position so well selected, and to the heroism displayed, is mainly due the victory which succeeded. The talents and abilities of a commander are distinguished, no doubt, as well in the selection of a position, as in leading an army into and out of the field of battle. Major-General de Watteville, who visited De Salaberry's camp, approved of all his arrangements. There was some skirmishing, which led to the retreat of the workmen and their escort to the camp, at about two leagues above the confluence of the waters, between a little river belonging to the British, and that of Chateauguay, supported on the left by the river Chateauguay, and in front and on the right, by *abattis* and a species of *chevaux de frise*. On the 24th October, having made a large opening on the road through the woods and swamps, within a distance of five miles of the Canadian encampment, in which De Salaberry was at the head of three hundred Voltigeurs, Fencibles and Indian warriors, who had just received reinforcements in a few companies of sedentary militia; the American general advanced at the head of seven thousand infantry and four hundred horse, with twelve pieces of artillery, sending, during the night, Colonel Purdy to take possession of the ford, but this officer lost his way in the woods. The next day, Hampton made an advance in person towards the *abattis*, with three thousand five hundred men, and placed Purdy at the head of one thousand five hundred men, to attempt again to turn the Canadians, leaving in reserve the remainder of his troops. De Salaberry, warned of this movement by the fire directed on his advanced pickets, now seeing before him an enemy whom he had on two former occasions brought to the charge, advanced in front; and giving the signal, placed himself in the centre of the first line of defence, leaving the second in charge of Lieutenant-Colonel McDonnell, the same who had taken Ogdensburg. The firing commenced smartly on both sides, but badly directed by the Americans. They fired better afterwards; meanwhile, the circumstance of hearing incessantly the report from the corps at different intervals, led them to believe that the Canadians were advancing in great numbers, and their ardor began to weaken. Purdy's column arrived at the ford during the engagement, but was repulsed and thrown into disorder by De Salaberry, who had directed his attention to that particular spot. Seeing his plan disconcerted by the defeat of that division, the American commander ordered a retreat, which he effected with considerable loss. De Salaberry slept on the field of battle, and on the following day at daybreak, he was joined by Captain de Rouville, his brother-in-law, with his company of Voltigeurs, the Watteville grenadiers, together with a few of the native warriors. On the 28th, he sent Captain Ducharme, the hero of Beaver Dam, together with one hundred and fifty warriors, to reconnoitre, and they assured him that the American army had abandoned their camp on Piper's road, and had returned to Plattsburg. Wilkinson, who was at Cornwall, hearing of the defeat of his colleague, retired to Salmon river, and fortified himself. The victory at Chateauguay permitted the Baron de Rottenburg, and afterwards Sir Gordon Drummond, his successor in command, to resume the offensive in Upper Canada. Great Britain commemorated the victory by causing a gold medal to be struck; the Voltigeurs were presented with colors, ornamented with devices; and De Salaberry, besides the gold medal, had the order of the Bath conferred upon him, transmitted with an autograph letter from his Royal Highness the Prince Regent. The two houses of the provincial legislature passed a vote of thanks to him. The Voltigeurs took part in the second victory, obtained at Lacolle, in March, 1814. De Salaberry laid down the sword for the pen. He became a senator; being called to the Legislative Council in 1818, at the same time as Monseigneur Plessis. He died at Chambly, on the 26th February, 1829, aged 51 years; and was buried in the new church of that place, which was erected in the room of the one destroyed by fire in 1806. The late commander, Viger, possessed his likeness, painted by Dickinson, and engraved by Durand. De Salaberry is represented attired in the uniform worn by the Voltigeurs, decorated with the Chateauguay medal, and the cross of the Bath, with his sword under his arm. His family crest is also seen. The escutcheon of our compatriot bears the motto becoming to the *parfait chevalier:* "*Force à superbe; mercy à faible.*" A medallion representing a battle in the woods. On the trunk of a tree, reversed is written: "Chateauguay, 26th October, 1813." A serpent biting his tail, symbol of immortality, encircles the medal. With respect to the English medal of Chateauguay, Britannia is seen bearing a palm in hand, crowning a lion lying at her feet. On the reverse is engraved Chateauguay. De Salaberry would have become a great officer of light troops, and even in the armies of Bonaparte would certainly have attained the first rank."

The Montreal *Gazette* of 3rd November, 1813, contains an interesting account of this battle, furnished by an eye-witness (Adjutant Michael Sullivan, afterwards Judge Sullivan). The want of space permits us merely to clip the following extract:—

"It is highly gratifying to add, that the 300 men engaged, together with their brave commander, were all Canadians, with the exception of the gallant Captain Ferguson, three of his company and three officers belonging to other corps. Let this be told wherever mention is made of the battle of Chateauguay, and prejudice must hide its head, and the murmurs of malevolence will be hushed into confusion.

"To the officers and troops engaged on this memorable day the the highest credit is certainly due. Captain Ferguson, of the Canadian Light Infantry, and the two Captains Duchesnay, of the Voltigeurs, highly distinguished themselves in the command of their respective companies, and by their skill and coolness in executing several difficult movements with as much precision as at a field day. Nothing could exceed the gallantry of Captain Daly, of the militia flank brigade, who literally led his company into the midst of the enemy. Equally conspicuous for the spirit and bravery throughout this arduous contest were Captains Lamothe, of the Indian department, Lieut. Pinguet, of the Canadian Light Infantry, Lieut. and Adjutant Hebden, of the Voltigeurs, and Lieut. Schiller, of Captain Daly's company, Lieut. Guy and Lieut. Wm. Johnson, of the Voltigeurs, who formed their retiring picquest in the line of defence, and behaved with great spirit during the engagement. Captain Ecuyer, of the Voltigeurs, and Lieut. Powell, of Captain Levesque's company, deserve great credit for their exertions in securing the prisoners in the wood at an imminent risk. Captains Langtin and Hunan of the Beauharnois militia behaved remarkably well. The former knelt down with his men at the beginning of the action, said a short prayer in his own good way, and told them that *now they had done their duty to their God, he expected they would also do their duty to their king.*

"Louis Langlade, Noel Annance and Bartlet Lyons of the Indian Department were in the action of the 26th and the affair of the 28th. Their conduct throughout was highly meritorious. Nor shall I omit the names of privates Vincent, Pelletier, Vervais, Dubois and Carron of the Voltigeurs, some of whom actually swam across the river and made prisoners those who refused to surrender.

"With respect to Lieut.-Col. De Salaberry, the most selfish must admit that his important services entitle him to the thanks and gratitude of his country.

"It is difficult which to admire the more, his personal courage as an individual, or his skill and talents as a commander. We find him long before the battle displaying the greatest judgment in the choice of his position, and strengthening it when chosen, with every means within the reach of his ingenuity. We see him in the heat of action embracing every object with a comprehensive view, defending every point, and providing for every contingency; but his merit and that of his little army become more conspicuous when we reflect upon the critical nature of the times at the eve of this splendid victory. Affairs in our sister province had assumed a gloomy aspect; despondency had already begun to spread its baneful effects. We had been even told from high authority, that 'the period was in all probability fast approaching when it was to be *finally* determined whether the arrogant expectations of the enemy were to be realized, by his successful invasion of this province, or whether he was to meet with defeat and disgrace in the attempt.' That period is now past; the friends of their country will look back to it with grateful recollection; the face of things is changed. The enemy, to use a favorite phrase, did indeed 'pollute our soil;' but he was repulsed by Canadians not the one-twentieth part of his force, led on by a Canadian commander."*

---

* For this interesting extract, and other valuable documents, I am indebted to Lieut.-Col. the Hon. Juchereau Duchesnay, L.C., whose father and uncle played such an honorable part in this engagement.—(*J. M. L.*)

Reminiscences of 1812 and 1813—Close of the War.*

THE great disturber of Europe, Napoleon the 1st, having been sent a prisoner to the Island of Elba, European nations enjoyed a brief period of tranquility, which enabled Great Britain to send a portion of her veteran army, under the illustrious Wellington, to prosecute the war with America—the brunt of which had, for two years, been nobly sustained by the militia of Canada, assisted by the mere handful of regulars which had been left in the country.

The Americans soon perceived that they had nothing to gain, but everything to lose, by prolonging the struggle, and held out the olive branch, the very name of Wellington having filled their hearts with terror.

Peace was accordingly concluded, which we fervently hope may never again be interrupted by the unhallowed ambition and thirst of territory of our "American Cousins."

My purpose being now gained, that of sustaining the character of our militia in the day of trial, I will therefore dismiss them to their homes, though they were found present for duty at Chippawa, at Lundy's Lane, and at Fort Erie, which actions I may have an opportunity of detailing to you hereafter. In corroboration of the account I have written of the character of our militia in 1812, I would beg leave to offer the words of General Brock to the magistrates of the Niagara district, after the capture of Detroit, and also the resolutions of the Hon. W. H. Merritt, which passed the Legislature unanimously for awarding the medals to the militia of 1812.

When General Brock returned to the Niagara frontier, after the capture of Detroit, the magistrates of this district presented him with a complimentary address.

The gallant general replied most emphatically, "That had not Western

* Coventry Manuscripts.

Canada rose as one man in defence of their rights, and in support of the Constitution of Britain, his hands would have been as if tied, being without the aid of British troops, who were nearly all engaged at this time in the European war."

The following resolutions were proposed by the Hon. Mr. Merritt in the House of Assembly, on Wednesday, September 8th, 1852:—

"That an humble Address be presented to Her Majesty, representing the disappointment of many of the inhabitants of this province, when they discovered that the hardest fought battles in Canada were not included in the General Order of the first of June, 1847, which awarded medals for certain actions.

"That the said General Order confined the distribution of medals to those actions only where the general or superior officers of the several armies or corps engaged had already received that distinction; consequently, many of the battles of this country do not come under the rule thus laid down; and this House has reason to believe it will not be departed from in behalf of the Canadian Militia, without a strong representation from this House.

"That Her Majesty's attention be accordingly called to the distinguished services of the Canadian Militia during the late war with the United States, with the view of removing the inviduous distinctions caused by the distribution of these medals—the Canadian Militia having acquired, in common with the British troops, a reputation for loyalty and gallantry of which their posterity may feel justly proud.

"That Her Majesty be therefore prayed to confer a similar medal to that awarded for the battles of Detroit, of Chrysler's Farm and Chateauguay, on the now few survivors who successfully defended their country in the various other battles fought during the war.

"That His Majesty King George the Third ordered that the word 'NIAGARA' should be inscribed on the colors of the Glengary Light Infantry and the incorporated militia of Canada, for their gallant conduct on that frontier; and if they deserved such marked distinction, they surely deserve a medal to commemorate it."

An Address, embodying the foregoing resolutions, was accordingly presented and read, when the Hon. Mr. Mathieson said he had much pleasure in seconding this Address, and he sincerely hoped that the Imperial Government, at this late period, would acknowledge the services rendered by the Militia, by granting some allowance to the very few remaining officers of the war of 1812.

These men shared the dangers and privations of that period.

He had no pecuniary interest in this Address, as he then belonged to the regular army, and still enjoyed half-pay; but when he remembered that these men left their farms and profession to defend the country against foreign agression, and risk their lives to continue the connection with the mother country, he did hope they would merit consideration and have some remuneration made to them.

When he remembered that the population of Upper Canada in 1812 was only between 70,000 and 75,000 souls, of which there were about 15,000 men for actual service, and these, in addition to two or three weak regiments, to defend a frontier of nearly a thousand miles!

Such an extent of country to be defended, and successfully defended, against the whole force of the United States, he should say such defenders should be amply rewarded.

In those days he had seen women ploughing the fields, and their daughters harrowing after them, when their husbands and brothers were on the frontier defending the country.

The men of those days were not annexationists; they opposed it to the death; nor had they any desire to quote what was done in the State of New York, or any other State of the American Union.

They had the privilege of making their own laws, and were contented.

(Signed) A LINCOLN MILITIA FLANKER OF 1812.

Battle of Chippawa,*

JULY, 1814.

"THE campaign of 1814 was opened on the Niagara frontier by Gen. Brown of the American army, who crossed from Black Rock to Fort Erie, July 3rd, with two divisions of his army, computed at not less than 5000 men.

After driving in a picket of the garrison of Fort Erie, and that fort being in a defenceless state, both from the nature of the fortification and smallness of its garrison, under Major Buck of the King's, it was at once surrendered.

General Ryall's despatch to General Drummond, of July, 1814, states: "I was made acquainted with the landing of the American army at Fort Erie, on the morning of the 3rd instant, at 8 o'clock, and orders were given for the immediate advance on Chippawa of five companies of the Royal Scots, under General Gordon, to reinforce the garrison of that place.

"Colonel Pearson had moved forward from thence with the light company of the 100th Regiment, some militia and Indians.

"The following morning, a body of the enemy's troops were reported to be advancing by the river.

"I moved to reconnoitre, and found them in a considerable force, with cavalry, artillery and riflemen.

"Having been joined by the King's on the morning of the 5th, I made my dispositions for an attack at 4 o'clock in the afternoon.

"The light companies of the Royal Scots and 100th Regiment, with the 2nd Lincoln Militia, under Colonel Thomas Dickson, formed the advance, under Colonel Pearson.

"The Indian warriors were posted on our right flank, in the woods; the troops moved in three columns, the King's regiment being in advance.

"The enemy had taken up a position with his right resting on some buildings and orchards, close on the Niagara river, and strongly sup-

* Coventry Manuscripts.

ported by his artillery; his left towards the woods, having a considerable number of riflemen and Indians in front of it.

"Our militia and Indians were shortly engaged with them.

"The enemy's riflemen and Indians at first checked their advance, but the light troops being brought to their support, they succeeded, after a short contest, in destroying them in handsome style.

"I immediately moved up the King's Regiment to the right, when the Royal Scots and 100th were directed to charge the enemy, and they advanced in the most gallant manner under a destructive fire.

"I am sorry to say, however, that in this attempt they suffered so severely, I was obliged to withdraw them, finding their further efforts against the superior numbers of the enemy would be unavailing.

"Colonel Gordon of the Royal Scots, and most of the officers of the 100th, were wounded.

"I directed a retreat to be made upon Chippawa, which was conducted with great order and regularity, covered by the King's under Maj. Evans, and the light troop under Colonel Pearson, and I have the pleasure of saying not a single prisoner fell into the hands of our enemy, excepting those disabled from wounds.

"Some of the prisoners taken report the enemy's force to have been 6,000, with a numerous train of artillery; our force, in regular troops, not more than 1,500, exclusive of the militia and Indians, of which last description there was not above 300.

"Our forces retired to Fort George, and General Brown crossed the Chippawa and advanced to Queenston, where he remained without striking a blow, from the 8th to the 23rd July, unless an occasional demonstration before Fort George and the unprovoked conflagration of the village of St. David's.

"The gallant General Ryall, on learning that General Brown had retreated across the Chippawa, immediately pushed forward his forces to Lundy's Lane, being reinforced by the 103rd Regiment, under Colonel Scott, within two and a half miles of the enemy's position, and there await to be reinforced by General Drummond.

"In the battle of Chippawa, Captains John Rowe and George Turney, and Privates Stephen Perr and Timothy Skinner, of the 2nd Lincoln Militia, were killed; and Colonel Dickson, commanding the 2nd Lincoln, Captain Lewis Clement, and several others, were wounded."

Battle of Lundy's Lane,*

25TH JULY, 1814.

No sooner had General Drummond heard the result of the battle of Chippawa, than he hastened from Kingston to Toronto, which place he left on the evening of the 25th July, and arrived at Niagara the next morning.

The greatest energy seems to have characterized General Drummond's movements, and we immediately find him advancing with about 800 men to the support of General Ryall.

As soon as he arrived at Lundy's Lane, he found the whole in position, and was soon after attacked by the enemy.

In the commencement of the action, the intrepid Ryall was severely wounded, and was intercepted in passing to the rear by a party of the enemy's cavalry, and taken prisoner.

Thus General Drummond was deprived of an officer whose bravery, zeal and activity had always been conspicuous.

In the centre, repeated and determined attacks were made by the 49th, and detachments of the King's Royals and light companies of the 41st with the most perfect steadiness and bravery: and thereby the enemy was constantly repulsed with very heavy loss.

In so determined a manner was their attacks directed against our guns, that our artillerymen were bayonetted by the enemy in the act of wadding, and the muzzles of the enemy's guns were sometimes within a few yards of ours.

Our troops having been pushed back for a few moments, in the darkness of the night, some of our guns remained a few minutes in the enemy's hand; they were, however, not only quickly recovered, but two pieces—a six-pounder and a 5½-inch Howitzer, which the enemy had had brought up, were captured, together with several tumbrels.

About nine o'clock—the action having commenced at six o'clock—there was a short intermission of firing, during which it appears the enemy

* Coventry Manuscripts.

were employed in bringing up their whole force, and shortly after renewed the attack with fresh troops, but were repulsed with equal gallantry and success.

The enemy's efforts to carry the hill were determined, and continued till about midnight, when, finding that he had suffered severely from the superior discipline and steadiness of His Majesty's troops, he gave up the contest, and retired with great precipitation to his camp beyond the Chippawa.

On the following day the Americans burnt the bridge, water mill, and also the bridge at the mouth of the Chippawa, abandoning their camp, throwing the greater part of their baggage, camp equipage and provisions into the rapids of the Niagara, and retreated in great disorder by the river road towards Fort Erie.

Our light troops, cavalry and Indian allies, were sent in pursuit to harrass the retreat, which was continued until the enemy reached their own shores.

The loss sustained by the enemy in this severe action was about 1500 men, including several hundred prisoners. Their two principal commanders, Scott and Brown, were wounded.

The number of troops under General Drummond, for the first three hours, did not exceed 1600, and the addition during the action of the 103rd regiment did not increase it beyond 2800 men of every descriptions, including militia and Indians.

Of the battles that were fought during the war, none can compare with that of Lundy's Lane for the obstinacy and courage exhibited on both sides.

At Chippawa, the contest was decided principally by musketry, but it was at Lundy's Lane the Americans first crossed bayonets with British troops, and the issue of that contest taught them, whatever their moral courage, their physical inferiority to British disciplined troops.

If any army was ever fairly beaten by another, the battle of Lundy's Lane furnishes such an instance, if remaining in possession of the field of battle, whilst the enemy retreats precipitately, is to be considered a proof of victory.

The writer was made a prisoner during the night of the engagement, but regained the British lines by finding his way through the enemy's masses before they retreated.

Siege of Fort Erie, 1814.

General Drummond's despatch to His Excellency the Governor General, Sir Geo. Prevost, dated Camp before Fort Erie, August 15th, 1814, contains the following:—

Having reason to believe that a sufficient impression had been produced on the works before Fort Erie, by the firing of the battery I opened on the morning of the 14th inst., and by which the stone buildings were much injured and the outside of the parapets and embrasures much shattered, I determined on assaulting the place, and accordingly made the necessary arrangements for attacking by a heavy column, directed to the entrenchments on the side of Snake Hill, and by two columns to advance from the battery to assault the fort and intrenchments on this side.

The troops destined to attack by Snake Hill marched at five o'clock yesterday afternoon, in order to gain the vicinity of that place of attack in sufficient time.

It is with the deepest regret I have to report the failure of both attacks, which were made two hours before daylight this morning.

A copy of Col. Fischer's report is herewith enclosed, which will enable Your Excellency to form a pretty correct judgment of the cause of the failure of his attack. Had the head of the column, which entered the place without difficulty, been supported, the enemy must have fled from their works, which were all taken, as contemplated in the instructions, or have surrendered.

The attack on the fort and entrenchments leading from it to the lake, was made at the same moment by two columns, one under Col. Drummond of the 104th Regiment, consisting of the flank companies of the 41st and 104th, and a body of seamen under Capt. Dobbs, of the Royal Navy; the other under Col. Scott of the 103rd Regiment, and two companies of the Royals.

These columns advanced to the attack as soon as the fire from Colonel Fischer's column was heard, and succeeded, after a desperate resistance, in making a lodgement in the fort through the embrasures of the bastion, and captured the guns, which they had actually turned against the enemy, who still maintained the stone building, when, most unfortunately, some ammunition which had been placed under the platform caught fire from the firing of the guns in the rear, and a most tremenduous explosion followed, by which almost all the troops that had entered the place were dreadfully mangled.

Panic instantly communicated to the troops, who could not be persuaded that the explosion was accidental, and the enemy at the same time pushing forward and commencing a heavy fire of musketry, the fort was abandoned, and our forces retreated towards the battery.

I immediately pushed forward the first battalion of Royals to support and cover the retreat, a service which that valuable corps executed with perfect steadiness. Our loss has been severe in killed and wounded; and, I regret to say, all those returned "missing" may be considered wounded or killed by the explosion, and left in the hands of the enemy.

The failure of these most important attacks had been occasioned by circumstances which may be considered as almost justifying the momentary panic they produced, and which introduced a degree of confusion in the extreme darkness of the night that the utmost efforts of the officers were inefficient in removing.

The officers appear to have behaved with the most perfect coolness and bravery, nor could anything exceed the steadiness and good order when the advance of Col. Fischer's brigade was made, until emerging from a thick cover, it found itself stopped suddenly by an abattis and within a heavy fire of musketry and guns behind a formidable entrenchment.

With regard to the centre and left columns under Colonels Scott and Drummond, the determined gallantry of both officers and men, until the unfortunate explosion took place, could not be surpassed.

Col. Scott and Colonel Drummond were unfortunately killed; every officer of those two columns were either killed or wounded by the enemy's fire or the explosion.

The result of the attack on Fort Erie was even more disastrous in its consequences to the British, than had been the attack on Toronto to the Americans.

In this affair 900 men were killed and wounded on the British side;

and so severe was the blow that had a less energetic commander than Drummond been in Upper Canada, or had a more able than General Brown commanded the Americans, the issue might have been of a most disastrous character.

As it was, whether from Brown's wounds or incapacity, the blow was not followed up, and sufficient time was afforded to Gen. Drummond to recover from the loss he had sustained.

(Signed) A LINCOLN FLANKER OF 1812.

The Capture of Fort Niagara

BY ONE WHO SERVED IN 1814.

THIS fort was one of much importance to the Americans in the war of 1812; as, standing on the right bank of the river where it falls into Lake Ontario, it commanded the entrance to the river, and served as a depôt to supply the army.

It was very strong for a fort in that part of the country; for, its *enceinte*, besides being of regular construction, and mounting many guns, including three stone towers at the west, south-west, and south angles of the fort, in addition to a long and strong stone barrack on the north face,—the whole having flat roofs, mounted with cannon.

It was accordingly, in December, 1814, determined to attempt its capture, and the attempt was made on the night of the 19th of that month.

The force destined for that purpose was composed of the 100th regt., the Grenadier company of the 1st, the flank companies of the 41st, and some artillerymen; the whole under command of Colonel Murray, of the 100th,—a better man than whom could not have been chosen.

Bateaux having been secretely conveyed overland from Burlington to a point about four miles up the British side of the river, the troops silently left their cantonments about 10 o'clock at night, concealed their march under cover of the adjacent wood, embarked without noise, and landed undiscovered on the opposite side, whence they descended cautiously towards the fort.

There lay, between them and their destination, a small hamlet, called (if I recollect aright) Youngston, about two miles, or somewhat less, from the fort, to which it served as an outpost, where it was known lay a detachment from the garrison.

It was necessary to surprise it, without alarming the fort.

A chosen body was therefore sent in advance, while the main body followed at a convenient distance.

When arrived near it, some of the former crept up stealthily to a window and peeped in.

They saw a party of officers at cards. "What are trumps?" asked one of them. "Bayonets are trumps!" answered one of the peepers, breaking in the window and entering with his companions, while the remainder of the detachment rapidly surrounded the house, rushed into it, and bayonetted the whole of its inmates, that none might escape to alarm the fort.

Not a shot was fired on either side; American sentries having retired from their posts into the building, to shelter themselves from the cold there was no time for resistance.

The assailants performed their work of human destruction in grim silence,—a lamentable but necessary act.

Resuming their march, they drew near the fort; not a word is spoken; the muskets are carried squarely, that the bayonets may not clash; the ice crackles audibly under their tread, but the sound is borne to their ear on the continuous gusts of a north-east wind—when lo! the charger of Colonel Hamilton (which, having lost a leg in Holland, could not march and would not stay behind) neighs loudly, and is answered by a horse in a stable not far from the front gate.

What a moment! The force instantly halts, expecting to hear the alarm suddenly given—the sound of drums and bugle, and of the garrison rushing to their posts. But all remains quiet. The sentries, crouching in their boxes, take the neigh of the charger for that of some horse strayed from its farm-house or from the neighboring hamlet; they feel no inclination—leaving their shelter—to explore, shiveringly, the thick darkness of a moonless wintry night.

It can be nothing. The approaching force, drawing freer breath, puts itself in motion, shuffles hastily and silently forward, and the crisis is near!

The "forlorn hope" is commanded by Lieut. Dawson, and led by Sergeant Andrew Spearman.

It halts at about the distance of twenty-five yards from the gate over which the sergeant (a tall, stalwart man) strides, and, strange to say, finds the wicket open!

The sentry, hearing some one approach, issues from his box, protrudes the upper part of his body through the doorway, and asks: "Who comes there?"

Spearman, imitating the nasal twang of the Americans, answers: "I guess, Mr., I come from Youngstown," quietly introducing, at the same time, his left shoulder through the half-opened wicket.

The sentry stares at him—perceives, by his accoutrements and by his action, that he is an enemy—turns round and runs inwards, exclaiming: "The Brit—!" He says no more: Spearman's bayonet is in his side!

The sergeant returns and calls, in a subdued tone, the "forlorn hope," which swiftly enters, followed by the column. The light company of the 100th makes a rapid circuit and escalades. The whole attacking force has entered.

Had the assailants been discreetly silent, they might have effected the capture without loss to themselves or to the enemy; but their blood being up, they uttered a terrific yell, which roused the sleeping garrison and occasioned some resistance.

A cannon, turned inwards, was fired from the roof of the south-western tower, followed by a slight pattering of musketry. To prevent repetition of the former, Lieut. Nolan, of the 100th, a man of great personal strength and ardent courage, rushed into the lower part of the tower, regardless of what foes he might find there, and by what friends he might be followed.

Next morning his body was found, the breast pierced by a deep bayonet wound, at the bottom of which were a musket ball and three buckshot.

But he had not died unavenged.

One American lay at his feet, whom he killed by a pistol shot; while the cloven skulls of two others attested his tremendous strength of arm and desperate valor.

Some of his men, however, had seen him plunge into the darkness, followed him, and although too late to save him, had taken the tower, slaying the defenders to a man.

This resistance exasperated our men, who rushed wildly about into every building, bayonetting every American they met.

The carnage, indeed, would have amounted to extermination, if the British officers had not zealously exerted themselves in the cause of mercy.

Lieut. Murray, of the 100th, particularly distinguished himself by his humane endeavors; for finding that the tide of fugitives set towards the southern angle, where a sally-port had been burst in, he made them lie down, protected them, and thus saved many. In half an hour the fort was fully captured: all was quiet, and the panting victors sought to drown their excitement in sleep.

Thus fell Fort Niagara, with such unexpected facility as gave rise to a report that treason had contributed to its capture.

Indeed, it was said that its commander, Capt. Leonard, had betrayed it by giving to the British general on that part of the frontier the necessary information and instructions and the countersign, by means of which countersign, and not in the manner above stated, Spearman, it was said, had obtained admission.

Certain it is, that Leonard, on the night of the assault, had left the fort and slept at his farm about four miles distant, and that next morning, he rode into the fort in apparent ignorance of its capture,—an ignorance not easily reconcileable with the firing, especially of the cannon, on the preceding night. The short contest cost the British the gallant Nolan and five men killed, and two officers and three men wounded.

The Americans lost 65 men and two officers killed and twelve men wounded.

In the fort were found several pieces of ordnance, of which twenty-seven were mounted on the works, besides small arms, ammunition, clothing and commissariat stores in abundance.

It was known that a large sum in specie was in the fort at the time of the assault; but, when matters had somewhat calmed down, and examination of the captured stores was formally made, no specie was to be found!

It was said in a whisper, which indignation afterwards swelled into bold and loud assertion, that after the resistance had been subdued, three officers of the 100th had made their way into the magazine, where the specie lay in kegs, got it rolled out of the building and of the fort down to the water's edge, had it put on board a bateau and conveyed to the opposite shore, where it was conveyed inland and secreted in a friend's house, saying to the men employed that it was ammunition.

The men, however, were not so credulous as to believe that, at such a moment, officers, detaching themselves from the force to which they belonged, would secure ammunition that would not fit the British musket.

It was ever afterwards confidently believed that those officers had embezzled the specie: an imputation that their increased expenditure seemed in some degree to justify.

No inquiry, however, was made (which led to further suspicions), and the prize money, which had been expected to be large, was disappointingly small.

The next morning, the ground within the fort was strewed with arms and clothing, and with pieces of harness that had been stored for the American artillery.

A rifle was to be had for a trifle, and a greatcoat for little or nothing. As to the pieces of leather, two utilitarian officers of the 100th had it carried into their rooms, where they set some saddlers to work, and made them manufacture sets of harness, which they sold to Canadian farmers at a very handsome profit.

On the departure of the snow, the fort assumed a new appearance, our bricklayers facing the ramparts, within and without, with sods of the size of bricks, giving them a very neat and regular aspect, which brightened when the ensuing spring covered with verdure.

Lieutenant Dawson was deservedly promoted to a company, while Spearman remained a serjeant, and never, as far as we know, received any reward for his gallantry but the esteem of his officers and comrades.

If he be still alive, he lives in Richmond, U.C., where the 100th, after its disbandment in 1818, received lands and settled.

Last summer, being upwards of seventy years of age, he walked fort miles to where he supposed me to be, to obtain my certificate as to his services, to support his petition to the Commander-in-Chief for a small pension which might enable him to exist, now that he is past labour.

I was not there, but my son was, who gave him a cordial reception, rest and refreshment, and promised to procure from me the certificate.

I have given it, conscientiously declaring that Andrew Spearman, then serjeant in the 100th Regiment and leading the forlorn-hope, was the person to whose tact and daring was principally due the success of the British force in "the capture of Fort Niagara."

(Signed) JOHN CLARK.*

* The accounts of these late battles are taken from the Parliamentary Manuscripts collected by Mr. G. Coventry. Colonel John Clark, who lately died, was well and favorably known all over Canada, for his staunch support of British institutions.

List of Salmon and Trout Rivers.*

THE following is a list of the principal salmon and trout rivers of Canada and New Brunswick, with the distances of the former from Quebec, and such information as could be obtained concerning their character and condition. Those marked in *italics* have been leased to private individuals, but the others are open to all comers.

The *Jacques Cartier* is the only† river near Quebec which, at the present time, affords any salmon.

From Quebec to Murray Bay is.................... 78 miles.

Here there is a river that furnishes a few salmon and many fine trout.

From Murray Bay to the Saguenay is.......... 44—120

There is excellent sea trout fishing in the Saguenay, and its tributary, the *St. Marguerite*, is a superior salmon river.

River Escoumain 23

Between it and the Saguenay are the two *Bergeronnes*, and both furnish a few salmon and many trout.

Portneuf.. 26

Plenty of trout and salmon.

Sault au Cochon.. 9

Impassable for salmon, but affording excellent trout fishing at its mouth.

La Val.. 2

Superior salmon and trout river.

Bersemis.. miles 24—84

Affording in its tributaries many fine salmon; between it and the La Val are the Colombia, Plover and Blanche, all poor salmon streams.

---

* From "*The Game Fish of the North,*" by Barnwell.

† There is also the Ste. Anne, a few miles from Quebec, a good salmon stream. The Jacques Cartier is owned by J. K. Boswell, Esq., of Quebec, and Wm. H. Kerr, Barrister, of Montreal, two keen sportsmen. Upwards of 200 salmon were caught last year in the Jacques Cartier. Since the above list was prepared, the rush of sportsmen to Canada has much increased; and persons now wishing to lease salmon rivers have to apply early in the season to the Commissioner of Crown Lands for Canada.—[*J. M. L.*]

Outardes.. 11
Manicouagan 16
Mistassini 12
Betscie 3

Of these rivers I can obtain no satisfactory information.

Godbout.. 15—57—261

A celebrated salmon river, one of the best in the province.

Trinity.. 15

Good salmon and trout fishing.

Little Trinity 10
Calumet.. 3
Pentecost 14

Not a salmon river.

St. Margaret.. 36

One of the best salmon and trout rivers.

Moisie .... 23—103—364

Fine large salmon are taken in this river, and it is widely celebrated.

Trout.. 7
Manitou 35

Good trout fishing; the salmon are obstructed by falls.

Sheldrake 16
Magpie.. 22

Furnishes a few salmon.

St. John 5

An admirable salmon stream.

Mingan .... 16—101—465

Probably the best river in the province for salmon, and excellent for trout.

Romaine.. 9

An excellent stream for both salmon and trout.

Wascheeshoo 53
Pashasheboo 18

A few salmon.

Nabesippi 7
Agwanus.. 5

A fair supply of salmon.

Natashquan .... 14—106—571

Salmon fine and abundant.

Kegashka 23

Salmon impeded by falls.

Musquarro 15

Affords good salmon fishing.

Washeecootai 12

Olomanosheebo 11

Coacoacho 18

Contains some salmon.

Etamamu 21

Fine salmon fishery.

Netagamu 16

A fine trout stream.

Mecattina 4

Good salmon fishing.

Ha! Ha! 9

St. Augustine 6

Affords many salmon.

Esquimaux .... 14—149—720

An excellent salmon river, somewhat run down.

In New Brunswick there are salmon in the St. John and its tributaries, but the best of the latter, the Nashwaak, has been closed with an impassable dam. From St. John it is easy to take the cars to Shediac, and cross to Prince Edward's Island, where there is magnificent trout fishing, especially near Charlotte, and tolerable accommodation ; or one can take the Quebec steamer to Bathurst and fish the Nipisiquit, which is admitted to be the best river in the province, or the Restigouche and its tributaries, an excellent stream, but much injured by spearing; or the Cascapediacs, which furnish some salmon and innumerable grilse. The Miramichi, between Shediac and Bathurst, is a fine large stream.

The streams in Canada emptying into the St. Lawrence from the south shore, are hardly worth mentioning as salmon rivers, having been ruined by mill-dams, with the exception of those that empty into Gaspé Basin, but they all afford superior trout fishing. I would here remark, that where the name trout is mentioned in connection with the British Provinces, the *Salmo Trutta Marina*, or sea trout, is always intended; and the salmon fishing spoken of is fly fishing. The rivers that empty into Gaspé Basin, such as the Dartmouth, York and St. John, are leased, as also the Bonaventure, that flows into the Bay of Chaleurs.

As explicit directions for travelling through the benighted regions called the British Provinces, the following are given from a somewhat unwillingly extended experience:

Take the night train or any route that will bring you to Boston before half-past seven A.M., for at that hour the boat leaves for St. John, not St. Johns, which is in Newfoundland. If you are too late, you may still, by means of the cars, intercept the same vessel at Portland. This boat does not leave daily, but generally advertises in the New York and always in the Boston papers. It touches at Portland, where you may take a steamboat on its arrival to Calais, and proceed thence by railroad to the Scoodic River, where there is fine white, not sea, trout fishing, or stop at St. Andrews, whence there is a railroad in progress to Woodstock, on the St. John River. The Boston boat reaches St. John in about thirty-two hours, or at three o'clock; the fare is six dollars; the meals extra, and, consequently, extra good.

Salmon Fishing in Canada.*

WE have much pleasure in laying before our readers the following account of the fishing this season (1863), in some of the rivers the property of the province, which incontestibly proves two things. First, that there is better sport to be obtained, by amateur fishermen, in Canada than in any of the far-famed rivers in Europe; and secondly, that the system of protection adopted by the Commissioner of Crown Lands is not only increasing the number of the salmon, but enabling them to attain to a larger size. Never were our markets so abundantly and so cheaply furnished with this noble fish as during the past summer:

RIVER ST. JOHN.

Salmon taken in the river St. John, with the fly, during July, 1863, by two rods—July 1st, eleven fish were caught at Trent Rapid and Camp Pool; 2nd, sixteen at Trent and Camp; 3rd, twenty-three, at Seal and Trent; 4th, sixteen at Seal, Trent, and Fall; 5th, Sunday; 6th, twenty-two, at Seal, Trent, and Camp; 7th, thirteen, at Seal and Fall; 8th, sixteen, at Trent, Seal, and Fall; 9th, no fishing; 10th nineteen, at Seal, Trent, and Camp; 11th, eight, at Trent and Seal; 12th, Sunday; 13th, fifteen, at Trent and Seal; 14th, six at Trent; 15th, four, at Trent and Seal; 16th, river very small; 17th, (one rod) two fish, at Trent; 18th, little fishing; 19th, Sunday; 20th, three at Seal, one rod, river rising; 21st, three, at Seal, one rod, river rising; 22nd and 23rd, no fishing; 24th, ten, at Falls and Trent; 25th, seven at Falls and Seal; 26th, Sunday; 25th, five, at Seal and Camp. Total number of fish, 199; total weight, 1960 lbs.; average weight, 10 lb.

RIVER GODBOUT.

Salmon taken with the fly by three rods, in the river Godbout, during June and July, 1863:—June 8th, one fish was caught at Cayley's Stone;

* From the *Quebec Mercury* (Government organ.)

9th, one at Sandbank; 10th, two, at Bear and Camp; 11th, one, at Camp; 15th, three, at Bear and Glassy; 16th, two, at Fall, Bear; 17th, four, at Eddy, Belle, Cayley; 18th, eight, at Glassy, Belle; 19th, two, at Camp, Glassy; 20th, three, at Camp, Cayley; 21st, Sunday; 22nd six, at Kate, Belle, Upper, Bear; 23rd, five, at Belle, Glassy, Kate, Upper, Cayley; 24th, six, at Fall, Belle, Upper; 25th, seven, at Cayley, Shea, Upper; 26th, eleven, at Doctor, Indian, Kate, Bear, Cayley, Upper; 27th, seventeen, at Kate, Belle, four in Haworth, Upper; 28th, Sunday; 29th, twelve, at Upper, Shea, Haworth; 30th, eight, at Belle, Upper, Indian, Haworth; July 1st, nine, at Shea, Upper; 2nd, eight, at Indian, Upper; 3rd, seven, at Fall, Upper, Haworth; 4th, twelve, at Upper, Belle, Shea; 5th, Sunday; 6th, five, at Upper; 7th, two, at Haworth, Upper; 8th, thunder and rain, fish down; 9th, five, at Upper, Shea; 10th, three at Indian, Upper; 11th, nine, at Upper; 12th, Sunday; 13th, seven, at Upper, Haworth; 14th, four, at Upper, Haworth, Indian, Shea; 15th, four, at Haworth, Indian, Upper; 16th, three, at Upper, Belle; 17th, one, at Upper; 18th, two, at Indian, Upper; 19th, Sunday; 20th, three, at Upper; 21st, two, at Upper; 22nd, two, at Upper; 23rd, one, at Shea; 24th, five, at Fall, Eddy, Haworth, Upper; 25th, none; 26th, Sunday; 27th, one, at Shea; 28th, one, at Upper. Total number of fish, 194; total weight, 2158 lbs; average weight, 11¼ lbs.

RIVER MOISIE.

Messrs. C. & G. Bacon, and Mr. B. Williams, of Boston, lessees of the fly-fishing division of the river Moisie, returned from their expedition last Saturday, and left the same night for their homes. They started from Quebec on the 6th June, in the steamer *Napoleon III.*, with the other parties for Godbout, Mingan, &c. Their fishing began on the 21st June, and the last fish was killed on the 5th of July, when a sudden fall of the river, occasioned by the continued dry weather, brought their sport to a close. Taking into consideration the shortness of time—a fortnight—the fishing was good. They caught 139 salmon, of which thirty weighed 30 lb., and ten over 30 lb. The largest fish caught weighs 30 lb. They caught in the same river last year 318 fish, the largest weighing 42 lb.

RIVER NIPISSIGUIT.

The following record of eleven days' salmon-fishing on the river Nipissiguit, Bay of Chaleurs, New Brunswick, by Messrs. Adshead & Rintoul, shows what excellent sport these gentlemen obtained during their trip:—Killed by Mr. J. E. Adshead, July 6, one salmon; 8th, seven; 9th, six; 10th, seven and one grilse; 11th, two; 13th, four; 14th, two; 16th, two; 17th, one; 18th, two; 20th, four and two grilse—total, thirty-eight salmon and three grilse; weight, 384½ lb. Killed by Mr. Rintoul, July 6, one salmon; 7th, two; 8th, four; 9th, eight; 10th, five; 11th, one; 13th, one; 14th, one; 15th, three; 16th, two; 17th, three; 18th, five; 20th, two—total, 38 fish; weight, 341 lb.

RIVERS MINGAN AND MANITOU.

Salmon killed in the rivers Mingan and Manitou by three rods during the season of 1863: June 15th, four fish; 16th, 17th, and 18th, flood; 19th, two; 20th, six; 22nd, eight; 23rd, four; 24th, two; 25th, eleven; 26th, two; 27th, two; 29th, fifteen; 30th, nine; July 1st, one; 2nd, four; 3rd, seven; 4th, seven; 6th, twelve; 7th, fourteen; 8th, nine; 9th, two; 10th, five; 11th, two; 13th, fifteen; 14th, four; 15th, thirteen; 16th, five; 17th, two; 18th, six; 20th, nineteen; 21st, eleven; 22nd, two; 23rd, ten; 24th, three. Total number of fish, 218; total weight, 2,226 lb.; average weight, 10 1-5 lb.

To this we may add that we are credibly informed that four gentlemen from New Brunswick, who leased the river Natashquhan, killed over 500 fine fish, and that one of the party took *forty-six* of them in one day, with his own rod, a feat which we believe to be unparalleled in any river in Great Britain or Norway.

We have much pleasure in stating that there is every probability that a fine seaworthy steamer will make a fortnightly trip during the months of June and July, 1864, to the principal streams belonging to the Government, affording an opportunity to the tourist, the invalid, and the fisherman to visit the most interesting localities, to invigorate their health, and to enjoy their sport, thus tending to increase the revenue already derived from these rivers, and enabling their valuable fisheries to be more fully appreciated.

Professor Hind on the Fisheries of the St. Lawrence.*

THE Labrador Peninsula, with the coast and islands of the Gulf of St. Lawrence, possess a colonial and imperial interest which can scarcely be over-estimated in contemplating the possible future of British North America.

The annual value of the fisheries in British American waters exceeds four millions sterling, besides being the best nursery for seamen "the world ever saw."

The fisheries on the Atlantic coast of Labrador alone yield a yearly return of at least one million sterling; and yet, since the destruction of the town of Brest, at the gulf entrance of the Straits of Belle Isle, more than two hundred years ago, no attempts have been made to form settlements on an extensive scale on or near the coast.

In the great interior valleys, some ten or fifteen miles from the coast, timber, fit for building purposes and fuel, exists in abundance, and the climate and soil admit of the successful cultivation of all common culinary vegetables.

West of the Mingan Islands large areas exist suitable for settlement. Limestones and sandstones occupy the coast, and extend about ten miles back over a space of eighty miles on the Straits of Belle Isle, and great facilities exist in many other places for the establishments, by which an annual saving of more than a quarter of a million sterling would be secured at the outset, with the prospect of an indefinite increase. Local establishments for the supply of salt, food, and all the requirements of a vast fishing trade, are particularly demanded on the Gulf and Atlantic coast.

* Explorations in Labrador.

The British American fisheries will eventually acquire a wholly unlooked for importance by direct trade with the Southern States for cured fish, upon the return of the peace, and with the great valley of the Mississippi for fresh salt-water fish, conveyed in ice. The connection of the present terminus of the Grand Trunk Railway of Canada at Rivière du Loup with the Bay of Chaleurs would bring the rich living treasures of the Gulf within easy reach of the cities of the Western States.

As a nursery for seamen, the great North American fisheries have no equal, and the day will yet arrive when the hitherto desolate shores of Labrador, north, east and west, will possess a resident population capable of contributing largely to the comfort and prosperity of more favored countries.

Deep-Sea Fisheries of Canada.

"Judicious laws have been passed and will be enforced by the Canadian Government, and the American fisherman may find in neighboring waters, what he will never again in his own, these noble fish (the salmon) dwelling in abundance, and protected from worthless, wanton and unreasonable destruction. . . .

"In Canada the people have discovered, fortunately for them, not too late, the importance of stringent protective laws."—*The Game Fish of the North*, by BARNWELL.

IF, on one hand, it is a proud boast for Canada to be in advance of the rest of the continent by her wise legislation touching the natural resources in her rivers,—if even an enlightened American is compelled to admit that it would be well for the Great Republic to borrow a leaf from our book, it is also singularly strange that through the recent lengthy newspaper discussion anent this same subject, scarcely a word has been written, or even mention made of the most valuable portion of our fisheries, I mean the deep-sea fisheries. Whatever praise the British Provinces may be entitled to for what they have done to protect and foster this prolific source of wealth, let us not, however, run away with the idea that our legislation is perfect, especially the portion relating to the deep-sea fisheries. Much has undoubtedly been performed; something yet remains to be done. The Abbe Sieyès boastingly asserted of the legal reforms he had introduced, that he had perfected the French Constitution; pray, how many new constitutions have been since his day adopted and discarded in France? In assuming that our legislation respecting deep-sea fisheries requires amendment, as well as that relating to the salmon fisheries, I am merely repeating a trite observation, which doubtless has been often made by those conversant with the subject.

Let us look, for the present, into the bounty question, as connected with the pecuniary outlay of the fishery organization. Several questions will naturally arise in the course of this inquiry. Receipt and expenditure are cardinal points either in government or in private undertakings; it may be reasonably asked whether, with the present outlay differently apportioned, greater efficiency in enforcing the law, results of more magnitude for the public weal might not follow? The law places $14,000 annually at the disposal of the government to pay bounties; by many it is questioned whether this amount might not be more advantageously bestowed. Protection to the fisheries has only become an established fact in Canada since 1858; it is, therefore, still in its infancy, and requires an artificial stimulus before it can be expected to bring forth the matured fruits of age. To afford this artificial impulse, the bounty system in this country, as elsewhere, has received its legal existence. It cannot be considered a *permanency;* it is merely intended to arouse the energy of those engaged in the prosecution of the fisheries: no industry which could not prosper unless such a stimulus were made *permanent* would be worth having for any people. This principle is well understood by the nations who have granted the largest bounties. *What is wanted on the Gaspé and Labrador coasts is, less bounties to fishermen, than complete and effectual protection and security to persons and property.* In the opinion of many, the operation of the clause of the Act awarding bounties might be, for a time, suspended, and the granting of bounties made contingent on the sufficiency of revenue derived from the fisheries. Another point about the bounty system which invites consideration is, the principle on which the bounty is given. In my opinion, the whole, or nearly the whole, ought to be awarded, not to the lazy drone called the outfitter, but to the successful and intelligent fisherman himself; the outfitter, without prohibiting the bounty, might be just as much benefitted, only it would be in an indirect way; instead of calculating on a catch of 100 cwts. for profit, he would have 150 or 200 cwts. for exportation, and the fisherman's skill or industry would receive its fitting reward. Another important feature would be, punctuality in the payment of bounties. How can a poor Gaspé fisherman be expected to leave his home and wait in Quebec six months, as was the case formerly, until it suits the government, or the collector of the port, to pay him his bounty? On reference to Moses H. Perley's Report—a masterpiece of practical information, we find, that in 1851, one of the sister provinces voted also $2000 to form societies on the principle of the agricultural societies, destined to award prizes, not only to those who caught the most fish, but also to the fishermen who prepared the finest, the most marketable article. In many European marts, none but fish of first quality find a purchaser. Doubtless, the bounty question will be thoroughly sifted by the Parliamentary Committee appointed to report on the fisheries; it may be questioned, however, whether adequate sources of information can be open to it. The European governments send intelligent men abroad to rifle, as it were, the brains of other nations; in our country, we patch up and tinker up, *ad infinitum*, our home ideas and indigenous systems.

J. M. L.

Habits of Spawning Fish.

THE following interesting letter appeared in the *Field* newspaper of the 23rd February, 1863, published in London:—

" During three seasons past I have observed salmon whilst breeding in one of the tributaries of the Saguenay. The *locus in quo* is a shoal and rapid spot, with sheltering boulders, and long spits of pebbly bottom. The current is lively, but not heavy or strong. Autumn leaves cannot lodge in it, and branches or small drift-wood sticks hurry past upon its rippling surface, as if conscious that their presence might inconvenience the family parties already in possession of the shallow homestead. Many preconceived and some favorite notions about the habits of this fish were rudely shaken. Books had taught me peculiarities such as at no time could I then actually observe. The most prominent of contradictions were, that the fish did not root with snouts amongst the gravel to make troughs for the ova; nor did the pairs work by turns; neither was the male accustomed to perform alone his milting in the furrow where her ladyship had just left those delicately-colored eggs, of the 'pale pearly pink of sea shells.' I saw nothing of such ascribed habits. The female alone was industrious; the male fierce and pugnacious. She, filled with the cares of her maternity, seemed diligently absorbed in the success of her feminine instincts; he, sexual, masculine, selfish, and bullying—a very 'fancy man:' ever and anon jostling her; now running his beak into little ridges of sand or gravel in some furious rush after rival salmon or maraudering trout, and kicking up a most unbecoming dust: then, again, rudely overturning her in the awkward conflict, and tumbling into the nest a new pile of gravel, to her intense disgust. The way this active and tidy fishwife does her busy duty is curious. She wriggles herself among the small stones, and with rapid motions of the caudal and anal fins, and a winnowing action of the tail and body (turning over alternately upon one side and another), she keeps quantities of gravel in suspense, almost afloat in the edding hollow. Sand and lighter particles trail down the current behind her. It seemed to me as if the power exercised by her motions in the water had almost, if not quite, as much to do with the displacing of gravel and sand as the bodily movement against them. The same thing may be seen where the screw of a steamer stirs and draws up mud and dirt from the bottom of water several feet beneath the keel. The bed once made to her satisfaction, she settles down into it, as if resting from her labors; and should her attendant lord be not near and ready, she turns over upon her side as if to signal and invite him. The bully of the throng then settles alongside her; and, as nearly as I could perceive, their milt and ova are thus expressed in actual contact, both lying almost upon their sides during a strong quivering pressure. This function performed, she slinks lazily away. She remains for a few moments quiet, as if to let things settle; and soon recommences her previous winnowing along either side of the furrow, but this time advancing a little, and stirring down some gravel from above. I was much interested, and not a little surprised, with what I saw. You may depend upon it, sir, although the salmon is a fine, genteel and noble fish, he is not half so platonic a breeder as some amateur and theoretic naturalists have reported him to be. He is a creature of like passions with all others—cold-blooded, if you please, but not therefore insensate. A trout can be tickled; why should not the higher and richer-fed member of that respectable family—*Salmonidæ*—feel occasionally a trifle ticklish? Oh, no! Mr. Salar is not a sentimental and ultra-domestic Chinaman. He does not lie a-bed and sympathise, pain for pain, with his laboring mate. He has more of the Indian nature, and if he had 'portages' to make, would leave his squaw to bear the heaviest burdens. My native gallantry forbids me to think so highly as before of this king of fresh-water fish. Bold, agile, powerful, sagacious (though sometimes suicidally bent on poking his head into meshes, and darting into apertures that he *won't* again come out through), often, too, wide-awake for anxious anglers, and too fertile in combative resources for the hand and tackle of nervous fly-fishers,—withal I put down this lord of salmondom as a selfish water-type of that terrestrial lord of creation sung about in the old song.

"There is one point upon which my experience differs from that of Walsh. He says the cartilaginous appendage disappears after the breeding season. I have seen it of great prominence in several specimens taken during May and June. In one male salmon of 63lb. weight, the gristly substances, hard as bone, measured 5¼ inches long. The fish had caught himself by this hook at the outside net meshes, and twisting and struggling around to get free had drowned in the slack of the net. That this extra jaw is not much used, and is most probably a natural weapon, appears likeliest from the fact of its being longer while the fish is foul than when fresh. The nasty condition of the fish at breeding time may account somewhat for its being then uglier and more conspicuous. Consider how much larger appears the head, and how coarse is every point of the fish, during and after spawning season."

W. F. WHITCHER.

Quebec, Canada East, 1863.

The Fisheries of Canada.*

SIR,—Those who are desirous to see the riches of the country opened up will have felt gratified by the assurances contained in your issue of the 19th April inst., of the earnest manner in which the legislative wisdom of Canada are prosecuting the enquiry into one of its most inexhaustible resources. I mean the fisheries. Lest any desirable amendment in the law should escape attention, permit me again to place before the public a summary of the reforms I advocated last year in the work I published in French, LES PECHERIES DU CANADA; which reforms I had occasion to urge in the *Mercury* of the 10th July last, in the course of a lively newspaper discussion respecting the abuses and frauds of our Bounty system.

A careful investigation of the river and deep sea fisheries of Canada, in my opinion, embraces the consideration of the following, among other points:

1.—The present mode of catching codfish, mackerel, herring, salmon: what improvements could take place therein?

2.—When ought these fishes to be caught? Is it a fact that herring is caught out of season, when it is unwholesome and consequently of little value?

3.—The method of salting, curing and barrelling fish intended for foreign markets—what improvements can be here introduced?

4.—Ought we to have, as they have in England and in some of the United States, a compulsory law for the inspection of fish and oil? Has the free port of Gaspé fulfilled its object?

5.—The evil of seining herring on its spawning ground, merely as manure for the land?

* Letter to the Editor of the *Quebec Mercury*.

6.—What is the quantity of fish exported annually? Is it a fact that foreign crafts trespass within the limits assigned by the Reciprocity Treaty for fishing purposes?

7.—Is there any other fish or muscle, which in times of dearth, could be substituted to herring, caplin and squid for bait?

8.—What new legislation is required on the bounty question? Are bounties of any use to us?

9.—Would it not inure to our ultimate advantage and to that of the lessee to grant long leases of the Salmon Rivers, as short leases induce the lessee to derive the largest possible return in fish in a comparatively short period—that is, to ruin the river by over-fishing it?

10.—The wholesome system of control exercised in other departments of the public service, viz:—The appointment of a visiting inspector, an outsider, unconnected in any way with this branch, to report to the government, on the internal management of it. There are inspectors of railroads, inspectors of registry offices, inspectors of ports, inspectors of customs, inspectors of prisons, of warehouses, &c.—Why should there not be an inspector of the fishery revenue? Let us have a cheap but an efficient supervision.

11.—The existing necessity of renewing correspondence with New Brunswick in order to secure her joint co-operation in new legislation to regulate the fisheries on the boundaries of both provinces, the Ristigouche river, for instance, and also other places.

12.—That a more efficient law should be passed to prevent the peasantry in the rural parts from indulging any longer in the wholesale destruction of young fish who are caught each tide by the thousand in the stake fisheries and other engines of destruction, without being able to make their escape, and are left to rot and decay in the fishery, such as young white fish, sturgeon, shad, herring, salmon smoult, &c.

13.—That it would be highly useful to have a map of each salmon estuary and river, to furnish reliable information to persons who are prepared to pay high rents, if they can ascertain beforehand full particulars about the fishing location; that this can now be done at a trifling expense.

14.—Expediency of republishing and circulating amongst the fishermen of Gaspé those admirable and eminently practical directions to be found in Mr. Perley's Reports, page 264, prepared by the Imperial Board of Commissioners of the Fisheries of the United Kingdom.

15.—That the time to catch trout should be altered, so as to make it legal to do so from 1st January to 20th of September, but no later, as in some places trout is known to spawn early in September.

16.—The capture of salmon fry ought also to be strictly prohibited: all such taken to be returned instanter, alive, to their native element.

17.—The necessity of substituting a small screw steamer and fast-sailing revenue cutters, drawing but little water, to the present coasting service? Would English gunboats answer or not? Query.

18.—Reorganization of the judiciary system of the Magdalen Islands.

19.—Declaratory clause to explain some of the obscure provisions of the Fisheries Act; and certain discretion left with the Judge to temper, in some cases of fine or imprisonment, the severity of the law.

Such are some of the amendments I set forth in the French press of this city last winter, and which were inquired into by a Parliamentary Committee.

Yours, &c.,

J. M. LeMoine.

Quebec, 6th April, 1864.

The Birds of Canada.

ARRANGED BY J. M. LEMOINE,

According to classification and nomenclature of the Smithsonian Institution.

(The figures refer to those of the catalogue of North American birds published by the Institution in 1858.)

ORDER I.—BIRDS OF PREY.

Duck Hawk,	5.	Golden Eagle; Ring-tailed Eagle,	39.
Pigeon Hawk,	7.	Northern Sea Eagle,	40.
Jer Falcon,	11.	Gray Sea Eagle,	42.
Sparrow Hawk,	13.	Bald Eagle,	43.
Goshawk,	14.	Fish Hawk,	44.
Cooper's Hawk,	15.	Great Horned Owl,	48.
Sharp-shinned Hawk,	17.	Mottled Owl,	49.
Swainson's Hawk,	18.	Long-eared Owl,	51.
Brown, or Canada Hawk,	21.	Short-eared Owl,	52.
Red-tailed Hawk,	23.	Great Gray Owl,	53.
Western Red-tail,	24.	Barred Owl,	54.
Red-shouldered Hawk,	25.	Sparrow Owl,	55.
Broad-winged Hawk,	27.	*Kirtland's Owl,	56.
Sharp-winged Hawk,	28.	Saw-whet Owl,	57.
Rough-legged Hawk,	30.	Snowy Owl,	61.
Black Hawk,	31.	Hawk Owl,	62.
Marsh Hawk,	38.		

ORDER II.—CLIMBERS.

Yellow-billed Cuckoo,	69.	Yellow-bellied Woodpecker,	85.
Black-billed Cuckoo,	70.	Black Woodpecker,	90.
Hairy Woodpecker,	74.	Red-bellied Woodpecker,	91.
Downy Woodpecker,	76.	Red-headed Woodpecker,	94.
Three-toed Woodpecker,	82.	Yellow-shafted Flicker,	97.
Banded three-toed Woodpecker,	83.		

* This rare owl, lost sight of for fifty years in the fauna of the United States, is mentioned by Professor Arch. Hall, of Montreal—there is one specimen in the Museum of Natural History, of Montreal; Thomas McIlwraith, Esq., of Hamilton, owns one, and I have had the good fortune to capture one alive, which is still in my possession.

ORDER III.—PERCHERS.

Humming Bird, 101.
Chimney Swallow, 109.
Whip-poor-will, 112.
Night Hawk, 114.
Belted King-fisher, 117.
King Bird; Bee Bird, 124.
Pewee, 135.
Wood Pewee, 139.
Green-crested Flycatcher, 143.
Yellow-bellied Flycatcher (?), 144.
Wood Thrush, 148.
Hermit Thrush, 149.
Wilson's Thrush, 151.
Olive-backed Thrush (?), 153.
Robin, 155.
Varied Thrush, 156.
*Stone Chat, 157.
Blue Bird, 158.
Ruby-crowned Wren, 161.
Golden-crested Wren, 162.
Tit-lark, 165.
Long-billed Creeper, 167*a*.
Prothonotary Warbler, 169.
Maryland Yellow-throat, 170.
Mourning Warbler, 172.
Connecticut Warbler, 174.
Kentucky Warbler, 175.
Golden-winged Warbler, 181.
Nashville Warbler, 183.
Golden-crowned Thrush, 186.
Black-throated Blue Warbler, 193.
Yellow-rump Warbler, 194.
Blackburnian Warbler, 196.
Bay-breasted Warbler, 197.
Pine-creeping Warbler, 198.
Chestnut-sided Warbler, 200.
Blue Warbler, 201.
Black Poll Warbler, 202.
Yellow Warbler, 203.
Black and Yellow Warbler, 204.
Cape May Warbler, 206.
Hooded Warbler, 211.
Small-headed Flycatcher, 212.
Canada Flycatcher, 214.
Redstart, 217.
Scarlet Tanager, 220.
Summer Red Bird, 221.
Barn Swallow, 225.
Cliff Swallow, 226.
White-bellied Swallow, 227.
Bank Swallow, 229.
Purple Martin, 231.
†Wax Wing, 232.
Cedar Bird, 233.
Great Northern Shrike, 236.
White-rumped Shrike, 238.
Red-eyed Flycatcher, 240.
Yellow-green Vireo, 241.
Cat Bird, 254.
Brown Thrush, 261.
Long-billed Marsh Wren, 268.
House Wren, 270.
Wood Wren, 272.
Winter Wren, 273.
American Creeper, 275.
Red-bellied Nuthatch, 279.
Black-cap Titmouse, 290.
Hudsonian Titmouse, 296.
Sky Lark, 302.
Evening Grosbeak, 303.
Pine Grosbeak, 304.
Purple Finch, 305.
Yellow Bird, 313.
Pine Finch, 317.
Red Crossbill, 318.
White-winged Crossbill, 319.
Lesser Red Poll, 320.
Mealy Red Poll (?), 321.
Snow Bunting, 325.
Lapland Longspur, 326.

* I insert the stonechat and the evening grosbeak on the authority of Mr. William Couper, of this city,—who was presented with a specimen of each, shot in Canada—I am also indebted to him for several suggestions in preparing this list.

† Care ought to be taken not to confound this bird with its small summer congener—the cherry or cedar bud—the wax-wing is altogether a winter visitor.

White-crowned Sparrow, 345.
White-throated Sparrow, 349.
Black Snow Bird, 354.
Tree Sparrow, 357.
Field Sparrow, 358.
Chipping Sparrow, 359.
Song Sparrow, 363.
Fox-colored Sparrow, 374.
Black-throated Bunting, 378.
Rose-breasted Grosbeak, 380.
Indigo Bird, 387.
Boblink ; Reed Bird, 399.
Cow Bird, 400.
Red-winged Blackbird, 401.
Meadow Lark, 406.
Orchard Oriole, 414.
Baltimore Oriole, 415.
Rusty Blackbird, 417.
Crow Blackbird, 421.
American Raven, 423.
Common Crow, 426.
Magpie, 432.
Blue Jay, 434.
Canada Jay, 443.

ORDER IV.—GALLINACEOUS.

Wild Pigeon, 448.
Common Dove, 451.
Wild Turkey, 457.
Spruce Partridge, 460.
Ruffed Grouse, 465.
Rock Grouse, 468.
American Ptarmigan, 470.
Partridge; Quail, 471
Sand-hill Crane (?), 479.

ORDER V.—WADERS.

Great Blue Heron, 487.
Least Bittern, 491.
Bittern ; Stake Driver, 492.
Night Heron, 495.
*Glossy Ibis, 500.
Golden Plover, 503.
Killdeer, 504.
Wilson's Plover, 506.
Semipalmated Plover ; Ring Plover, 507.
Black-bellied Plover, 510.
Turnstone, 515.
†American Avoset, 517.
Northern Phalarope, 520.
American Woodcock, 522.
English Snipe, 523.
Red-breasted Snipe, 524.
Gray-back ; Knot, 526.

ORDER VI.—PALMATED.

Jack Snipe, 531.
Least Sandpiper, 532.
Sanderling, 534.
Semipalmated Sandpiper, 535.
Tell-tale ; Stone Snipe, 539.
Yellow Legs, 540.
Solitary Sandpiper, 541.
Spotted Sandpiper, 543.
Field Plover, 545.
Buff-breasted Sandpiper, 546.
Marbled Godwit, 547.
Hudson Godwit, 548.
Long-billed Curlew, 549.
Hudsonian Curlew, 550.
Esquimaux Curlew, 551.
Clapper Rail, 553.

* A beautiful specimen of this rare bird was shot at Grondines, on the 28th of April, 1864, and contributed to my collection by P. J. Charlton, Esq., of Quebec, to whom I am also indebted for a wood duck and a large blue heron.

† Three avosets were shot in the bay opposite Toronto, in October, 1863.

§ Temminck calls this Crane *Canadensis*. Charlevoix also mentions cranes in Canada, and still many assert the crane does not stop here in its migrations westward.

Virginia Rail,	554.	Ring-necked Duck,	590.
Yellow Rail,	557.	Red-head,	591.
Coot,	559.	Canvas-back,	592.
American Swan,	561*a*.	Golden Eye,	593.
Snow Goose,	563.	Barrow's Golden Eye,	594.
White-fronted Goose (?),	565.	Butter Ball,	595.
Canada Goose,	567.	Harlequin Duck,	596.
Hutchin's Goose,	569.	South Southerly,	597.
Brant,	570.	Labrador Duck,	600.
Mallard,	576.	Velvet Duck.	601.
Black Duck,	577.	Surf Duck,	602.
Sprig-tail; Pin-tail,	578.	Scoter,	604.
Green-winged Teal,	579.	Eider Duck,	606.
Blue-winged Teal,	581.	King Eider,	608.
Shoveller,	583.	Ruddy Duck,	609.
Gadwall,	584.	Sheldrake,	611.
Baldpate,	585.	Red-breasted Merganser,	612.
Summer Duck,	587.	Hooded Merganser,	613.
Greater Black-head,	588.	Smew.	614.
Little Black-head,	589.	*American Pelican,	615.

* Mr. McIlwraith, the well known naturalist of Hamilton, in a letter to me under date 6th May, 1864, thus describes the recent appearance of a flock of pelicans:—

HAMILTON, *May 6th*, 1864.

J. M. LeMoine, Esq., Quebec, C. E.

DEAR SIR,—On the evening of Friday, the 15th April last, a flock of eight pelicans was observed to alight on Burlington Bay, where they soon attracted attention by their unusual shape and motion. They sit much lighter on the water than swan or geese, and, on rising to fly, can do so with less exertion, while the bill and pouch form distinguishing marks not to be mistaken. By daylight on Saturday morning the gunners were early astir, and finding the pelicans still there, started in pursuit, the birds seemed unwilling to rise from the water, but not at all disposed to admit of a close inspection, and so vigorously did they ply their large and powerful paddles that though the wind was *high* and *fair*, it was only after a chase of about two miles that the skiffs got sufficiently near to risk a long shot, which crippled two of the number; one was wing-broken and could not rise, another, though evidently hit, kept sailing round still rising, till on making a sudden turn against the wind to join his companions, the fractured pinion gave way, and he fell from a great height into the water, where he was soon secured. The remainder of the flock returned in the evening, and were seen for two or three days afterwards evidently seeking their companions, but were extremely wary and could not again be approached within gunshot. About fifteen years ago a small flock spent a day or two about the bay, and one was shot, which is all I have heard of being observed here, though there is no doubt that like other migratory birds which breed in the far countries, they must pass this way every spring and fall, the probable reason why we do not see them oftener is that when migrating they fly at an immense height, and may perform the whole journey without stoppage. The individuals procured were both males in adult plumage; one is now stuffed and in my possession, the skin of the other has been sent to England.

On the 25th of April while paddling along the bay shore, I observed some strange looking birds sitting on a submerged stump about 100 yards from shore opposite a point of woods which runs out into the bay; creeping on under shadow of the trees, I found the group consisted of five cormorants, three large and brownish in color, and two

Gannet,	617.	Fork-tailed Gull,	680.
Common Cormorant,	620.	Marsh Tern,	681.
†Leach's Petrel(?),	642.	Wilson's Tern,	689.
Mother Cary's Chicken,	645.	Loon,	698.
Sooty Shearwater,	648.	Red-throated Diver,	701.
Pomarine Skua,	653.	Red-necked Grebe,	702.
Arctic Skua,	654.	Horned Grebe,	706.
White-winged Gull,	658.	Razor-billed Auk,	711.
Great Black-backed Gull,	660.	Arctic Puffin,	715.
Herring Gull,	661.	Least Auk,	723.
Ring-billed Gull,	664.	Black Guillemot,	726.
Bonaparte's Gull,	670.	Murre,	730.
Kittiwake Gull,	672.	Sea Dove,	738.
Ivory Gull,	676.		

The *Canadian Journal* for January, 1861, contains an excellent paper on "The Birds of Canada West," by Thomas McIlwraith, Esquire, of Hamilton, an accurate observer and keen admirer of the feathered tribe. The fauna of Lower Canada is greatly similar to that of Western Canada; birds, indigenous to warm climates, are not, however, so numerous down here. We have neither the wild turkey, quail, meadow lark, nor pelican; but our severe winters bring us, occasionally, several feathered denizens of the extreme north.

"Following," says he, "the arrangement referred to (Audubon's), we find highest on the list the family *falconidæ*, which includes all our diurnal birds of prey, such as eagles, hawks, buzzards, &c. These are distinguished by their short and powerful beaks, strong hooked talons, and

---

smaller and darker. I watched them for some time, their motions were graceful in the extreme, as they sat pruning their plumage, their long slender necks curving in every conceivable direction, while every now and then one of the number would dart off into the water and presently return with a fish, which was swallowed with no ceremony save turning the head downwards. At length they seemed aware of my proximity, and that the distance between us was diminishing. I was anxious to secure one of each kind, and just as they got up made use of the means in my power to accomplish that object, but was only partially successful, as the larger of the two, though evidently struck by the shot, managed to get away, the other was a fine specimen, and agrees in every particular with Professor Baird's description of the Florida cormorant, though I would scarcely have expected to find that bird so far north. It may be that being in company with the larger species which breeds in the north, they have been led away from their usual haunts.

Regarding the glossy Ibis, I may mention that a pair of these birds were shot here in 1857, and are now in my possession. I have a specimen of Kirtland's owl, and have also obtained recently a fine specimen of the great cinereous owl.

† These birds have been mostly all described in my *Ornithologie du Canada*.

the great length and breadth of their wings; this class is well represented in our woods, and along the (Burlington) bay shore; the most conspicuous member of it being the *bald eagle,* whose grand circling flight makes him an object of interest wherever he appears. With us this species is seldom seen during summer; but at the approach of winter, when the fish-hawk has gone south, and game gets scarce in the woods, a few pairs are usually observed about Land's Bush, and along the beach, where they prey on musk-rats, and feed on such animal matter as may be thrown up by the waters of the lake. During the two past winters, the fishermen residing on the beach have been offered a liberal price for a mature specimen of this bird; but so difficult are they of approach, that although individuals have been seen nearly every day during two months in each season, yet all the exertions of the hunters have been quite unsuccessful. Occasionally, after the report of some heavily-laden pieces a single broken feather has been seen winnowing its way downward, but as yet no mature specimen of the eagle has been procured. Latterly, the hunters being foiled in the chase, have resorted to stratagem, and have tried to poison the birds by putting strychnine into the body of a small animal, and leaving it near their usual haunts. By this means two or three individuals were obtained, but all of them have been young birds, which are of a brownish color, more or less blotched with white. The only instance I have heard of the capture of the mature bald eagle, in this vicinity occurred some years ago, but may be worth repeating, as tending to illustrate the habits of the bird. A laboring man, residing in the outskirts of the city, found that some depredator was levying black mail upon his chickens, and resolved to put a stop to it. At midnight he visited the roosts with his musket, but all was quiet, and no trace of mink or fox visible; about day-break, however, there was a disturbance among the fowls, when, jumping up, he was just in time to take a hurried aim at a large eagle, which was gliding off with a plump chicken clutched firmly in his talons. The shot took effect in the outer joint of the wing, which brought the spoil-encumbered marauder to the ground; pursuit and struggle then ensued, the eagle, according to custom, throwing himself on his back, and fighting fiercely with his feet. In this curious engagement the gunner, for a time, had the worst of it, as, owing to the hurried way in which he had been called into the field, he was ill-prepared to contend with the sharp claws of his powerful adversary. On further assistance arriving from the house, the eagle was secured alive and brought into the city (Hamilton) by his captor, who happened to be at work at the gaol and court-house, then in course of erection. Here he was put for convenience into one of the cells, where he was visited by many of our citizens, some of whom gave expression to their wit over the circumstance of the first prisoner confined in the gaol being the rapacious symbol of American freedom.*

" The young of this species differs from the adult so much in appearance that, till within the last few years, they were considered as distinct species, the former being described as the *grey sea-eagle;* Wilson, who closely observed their habits, had suspicions that they were identical, but the fact was not proved till after his time.

" The same mistake was made with the *golden eagle* of Britain, the young of which was described as the *ring-tailed eagle,* till they have now been proved beyond doubt to be the same. This species is also American, several specimens having during the past winter been found near Toronto. Besides the foregoing, there are various other species of eagle said to be found on this part of the continent, one of which was discovered by Audubon, and named by him after Washington; but from the real scarcity of the species, and the difference which exists among birds of different ages, we cannot at present speak of them with any degree of certainty.

" The most interesting genus of the falconidæ is that which includes the true falcons: these are distinguished from the other members of the family by their comparatively short and hooked beak, long and pointed wings, by a tooth-like process near the tip of the upper mandible, and by the dash and courage they exhibit when striking their prey on the wing; there is probably no other bird so admired by the sportsman, or feared by the water-fowl, as the *peregrine falcon.* We have often heard those who periodically visit Long Point or Baptiste Creek, to practise duck shooting, speak with enthusiasm of the exploits of the bullet hawk, as he is termed by the gunners; he is described as flying at considerable height above the marshes, which are dotted with flocks of geese, ducks, teal and

* While the above was in type the writer procured a fine specimen of the adult animal, measuring three feet by six feet six inches.—January, 1861.

widgeon, his quick eye marking every movement that is made below. While these keep the water, they are comparatively safe, as they can elude their pursuer by diving; but if, in the excitement caused by the presence of so dreaded an enemy, they should attempt to escape by flight, then is the time to witness the swoop of the falcon, who, singling from the affrighted flying flock the victim he has destined for his prey, descends with a rush, which the eye can scarcely follow, and strikes it to the earth in an instant. So suddenly does the bird fall on being struck, that it was long supposed the blow was given by the breast-bone of the hawk. This opinion has, by close observation, been proved incorrect,—and specimens so prostrated, when picked up, are found to be so lacerated on the back as to leave no doubt that the stroke is given by the feet. This noble bird is well known to the residents on Burlington beach, where he has frequently been observed coursing along in quest of his favorite prey; but from the uncertain nature of his visits, and the rapidity of his flight, no specimen has yet been procured. A recent writer professes to have found specific distinctions between this and the British bird of the same name, but these do not seem to be clearly made out, and the general opinion is that it is identical with the peregrine falcon, so much in favor when hawking was a princely amusement in Europe; with us he follows the full bent of his own wild nature, and unencumbered by hood or bell, roams the whole Atlantic coast, from Greenland to Cuba, and inland to the Rocky Mountains, and is known in the different districts he visits by the various names of peregrine falcon, bullet hawk, duck hawk, and wandering falcon.

"Following falcons in order come the *owls*. Birds of this family are easily distinguished by the largeness of the head and eyes, and the forward direction of the vision; of this class I have noticed eight different species near the city, none of which are plentiful, yet, from their strictly nocturnal habits, they may be more so than we are aware of. They are all migratory, and, from sometimes meeting with two or three individuals in a single excursion, and again not seeing any during that season, we infer that they pass along in bands, keeping up the communication by their loud hooting, which is frequently heard at night during spring and fall. The *snowy owl*, styled by Wilson the 'great northern hunter,' is during some winters quite common around the shores of the bay, though in others only a very few are seen; during the winter of 1858–59, I am aware of seventeen specimens having been brought to the market by fishermen and others, while during the last winter, only two individuals have been killed. All the birds of this class have the plumage remarkably full and soft, which enables them to skim noiselessly on their prey, and clutch it ere it is aware of the danger.*

"Passing the *goatsuckers*, of which we have two species, the whip-poor-will and the night hawk, we come to the *swallows*, of which we have five; in this group we have an instance of the way in which birds sometimes adapt their habits to suit particular circumstances. The republican or cliff swallow, which is but a recent addition to the *fauna* of the continent, in its original character, builds its nest in caves, and under the overhanging ledges of perpendicular rocks; when lured to this district probably by the abundance of their favorite insect food, which is found along our marshy lands, and not finding rocks suitable for their purpose in the breeding season, they frequently choose, as a substitute, the end of a barn or other outhouse. I have seen such a republic in the country, where the upper part of the end of a barn was literally covered with clay, and perforated with numerous circular holes, out of which the full dark eyes and gaping bills of the callow inmates were frequently seen protruding; there must have been from two to three tons of clay used in the work, and the constant visits of the parent birds at this interesting season give the building, at a short distance, much the appearance of a great bee-hive.

"In the habits of the *swift* or *chimney swallow* is another deviation from the established custom. When we see these birds circling round in the air and dropping perpendicularly into our chimneys to roost and rear their young, the question very naturally arises, where did they build before the invention of chimneys? Naturalists tell us that their nesting place then was in hollow trees, broken off midway and open at the top, but that now, even where these can be had, the chimney is preferred. We can easily understand that in settled parts of the country, when their favorite trees are all cleared away, they must either leave the district or

* It is worth noting, as an instance of adaptation to circumstances, that the eyes of the snowy owl and the hawk owl, which migrate to the arctic regions, are so constructed, as to enable them to procure their prey by day as well as by night—an evident necessity where there is no night for six weeks.

change their abode, but why they should, in places where they have their choice, leave the open tree for the open chimney, is still, I believe, an unanswered question.

"Next in order come the *flycatchers*, birds of small size, but in their habits much resembling the birds of prey. These have the upper mandible overhanging and notched at the tip, and the voice, in most cases, harsh and discordant. The mode of taking their prey varies in different species, some, taking up a station on a post or limb of a tree, dart after the passing insect, making the snapping of the bill distinctly heard; others, more expert of wing, keep skipping about among the bushes, and take by surprise anything suitable which comes in the way. A prominent member of this group is the *king bird*, or tyrant flycatcher, well known on account of his depredations among hive bees; he is also remarkable for the courage he displays when guarding his nest and young, being known to drive even the bald eagle from his vicinity.

"Nearly allied to the flycatchers, but differing from them in form and habits, are the *wood-warblers*. There is no class of small birds so much sought after by collectors as these; they are a numerous family, generally graceful in form, sprightly in manner, and brilliant in color; they arrive here about the beginning of May, a month which, above all others, is enjoyed by those who are fond of rambling in the woods. Their food seems to consist chiefly of insects, which they find lurking among the opening buds and blossoms of the trees. A few species remain with us during summer and rear their young, but the great body pass on farther north to breed, returning again in September, though from the trees being more full in leaf at that season, and the birds silent, they are not much observed. I have noticed twenty-two species belonging to this family, in our woods, some of them of rather rare occurrence, among which I may mention *sylvia maritima* or *Cape May wood-warbler*. Wilson met with this species only once, and Audubon mentions it as being exceedingly rare. I found it in the spring of 1857 along with others of the same family, while on their annual journey northward.

"The family of *creepers* includes, besides the tree creeper (the type of the class), the genus *wren*, of which we have three species, viz.: the *marsh wren*, which builds in all the marshes round the bay; the *winter wren*, which is identical with the common wren of Britain; and the *house wren*, which seems to have discovered Hamilton only within the last two or three years. This little bird is strongly attached to the dwellings of man, and in the United States is frequently accomodated with a house fixed to a post or tree in the orchard, which is taken possession of as soon as the birds arrive from their winter quarters. During the past two summers several pairs of house wrens have raised their brood in our city gardens, though previous to that date I have nct heard of their being observed.

"Of *thrushes* we have five species, among which is an instance of the difference of habit which is frequently noticed even among birds which in many respects are closely allied to each other. The red-breasted thrush or *robin* is well known for his familiarity, frequently rearing his young close to our dwellings, yet his near relation, the *wood-thrush*, is one of our most retiring songsters, and is seen only in the most secluded parts of the woods; perched on the highest twig of a tall tree, his full sweet notes are frequently heard, but the moment he is aware of being observed he drops under the tree tops and glides off in silence.

"This group includes our best songsters, some of which make the very woods ring with their thrilling notes. I have frequently heard the remark that our Canadian birds, though gaudy in plumage, are quite deficient in song. My opinion of this matter is, that comparing the birds of North Britain with those of Canada, we have only to strike from the former list the British skylark, to be able to compete successfully, either as regards the number of performers or the variety and sweetness of their notes. I have often imagined (but it may be only a fancy) that their is a strange harmony existing between the voices of birds and their particular places of resort; I have noticed this in winter in the short, sharp note of the nuthatch, which as he hurries about seems ever to say that he must bestir himself as the days are short. The lively twittering of the warbler seems to blend with the first fluttering of the young leaves; the shrill piping of the plover is quite in unison with the whistling of the sea-breeze, which comes up over the treeless barren which they usually frequent, and surely if we had sought through the whole feathered race for a tenant to our gloomy cedar swamps, we could not have found one more suitable than the great horned owl, the solemn aspect and singular voice of which makes the solitude of such places still more intense.

The family of *finches* is one of our most comprehensive groups; it has been divided by Audubon into 18 different genera, and contains, according to that author, 55 species. Of these a fair proportion are found in our fields and gardens, where they render considerable service by ridding the ground of the seeds of such troublesome plants as the dandelion and the thistle. The greater number are summer residents only; a few remain all the year round, and one or two species visit us from the north only in severe winters; of the latter class a rare species has during the past winter been observed in considerable numbers round the city. I refer to the pine grosbeak, which was first observed about the 5th or 6th of January, in a garden in Merrick street, feeding on the berries of the mountain ash. They attracted attention by the unsuspicious way in which they followed their occupation, almost within reach of the people who were passing on the side-walk, shewing clearly that they were little accustomed to the society of man. In small flocks, they continued to frequent the gardens where their favorite berries were to be obtained, till about the 23rd February, when a strong west wind, accompanied by warm rain prevailed for a day and night, after which they were no more seen. In the winters of 1856–1857 they paid a similar visit, but have not been observed in any other year. Nearly all those which visited this part of the country were either young males or females. The adult male was much sought after on account of his showy crimson plumage, but only a few of them were procured. It is worthy of remark, that the grosbeaks are frequently, if not always, accompanied by true Bohemian chatterers; which latter feed on the stem and pulp of the berries of the mountain ash, rejected and thrown down by their hard-billed fellow travellers.

"The small family of *marsh blackbirds* is next in order, two species of which are well-known on account of their gaudy colours. One is the red-winged blackbird so common in our marshes during summer, and the other is the *Baltimore oriole*, whose pensile nest we sometimes see suspended from the drooping twigs of our willow shade trees. The former of these enjoys the unenviable reputation of being a notorious corn thief, and though several writers have endeavored to clear his character from this imputation, yet if brought to the bar on such a charge, we might expect to hear very strong condemnatory evidence given against him by the farmer, and unless he could succeed in getting upon the jury a majority of his friends, the *crow blackbirds*, which had themselves tasted the corn, the chances are that the case would go against him. Admitting, however, that he does occasionally take what was intended for others, he amply compensates for it by the destruction of innumerable grubs and caterpillars, whose ravages among the corn would have far exceeded his own. A more remarkable species than either of these is the *cow-bunting*, which, like the British cuckoo, builds no nest, but dropping its egg into that of another bird, leaves the care of its offspring to those not related to it even by family ties. With us, the cow-birds are summer residents only, usually making their appearance about the beginning of April, and retiring to the south about the end of October. It is possible that a few individuals may spend the winter with us, in sheltered situations; as when visiting a farm house near Dundas, early in March (1857), I was surprised to see half a dozen of these birds nestling close together on a beam just above the cattle in the cow-house. On enquiry, I found they had been there all winter, coming out for a few hours about mid-day, and gleaning seeds from among the fodder of the cattle. They were all males, and seemed in excellent condition.

"It was long a subject of remark among those who were fond of observing the habits of birds, that the nest of the cow-bunting was seldom, if ever, found, and suspicions were entertained that some irregularity existed in their mode of perpetuating their race, but Wilson was the first to establish the fact that they not only shirk the duties of incubation, but that the whole tribe live in a state of the most unrestrained polygamy. Their conduct, in this respect, forms a striking contrast to that of all our other summer birds: these, as soon as they arrive from their winter quarters, lay aside the instinct which has kept them in flocks during their migratory course, and scattering about in pairs, each pair makes choice of a particular tree or bush, which is to be their home for the season. To this spot they are devotedly attached, and near it the male may be constantly seen, either cheering his mate with a song, or fighting bitter battles of disputed boundary with his troublesome neighbours. Even the woodpeckers, which, some writers say, have the smallest share of enjoyment of all the feathered tribes, may at this season be seen chattering and chasing each other round the favorite decayed tree, whose hollow recess is to be the cradle for their young. During all this excitement, the cowbirds remain in a state of callous indifference, and in small flocks, keep roaming about the clearings like bands of vagrants, with no song save a few spluttering notes, holding no intercourse with other birds, and with no attachment to any locality, save that where food is most abundant.

" As the season of incubation advances, the female cow-bird leaves the flock, and having made choice of a nest to suit her purpose, deposits therein one egg, and leaves it, not only without hesitation, but, judging from her manner, with evident satisfaction. The nest so selected is usually that of a fly-catcher or warbler, in which the owner has made a similar deposit. Wilson, who spent much time in investigating this matter, tells us, that the egg of the cow-bird is hatched in less time than the others, and that the female being obliged to leave the nest to provide for the wants of the youngster, the unhatched eggs are exposed to the weather, and do not come to maturity, but, in a few days, disappear altogether, leaving the intruder in undisputed possession of the nest. It has ever been a puzzle to naturalists to account for this singular habit, and as it may be interesting to hear what has been said on the subject, I will here make one or two short extracts.

" Wilson, after devoting more space to the description of this than any other bird he met with, says, 'what reason nature may have for this extraordinary deviation from the general practice, is, I confess, altogether beyond my comprehension. Many conjectures, indeed, may be formed as to the probable cause, but all of them, which have occurred to me, are unsatisfactory and inconsistent. Future and more numerous observations may throw some light on the matter, till then, we can only rest satisfied with the fact.' Mr. Selby, the eminent English naturalist, suggests, regarding this habit in the cuckoo, that the old birds retire to the south before the young are able to accompany them, and *therefore* they have to be confided to the care of others. The writer of an article on this subject, in the *British Cyclopædia of Natural History*, says regarding Mr. Selby's theory, 'this is perhaps about as good an explanation of the cuckoo's peculiarities as has yet been offered, but it fails, like all the others, in being quite inapplicable to the North

American cow-bunting. The true cause, whatever that may be, of this extraordinary deviation, must, we are persuaded, be the same in both, nor can we at present accept of any explanation as satisfactory, which will not alike apply to either.'

"I have been particular in making these extracts, because it occurs to me that an important consideration connected with the subject has been overlooked, it is one which applies alike to the cuckoo and the cowbird, and will, I think, if carefully followed up, go far to explain the seemingly unnatural conduct of both species. We recognize in it, as in accordance with the all-wise laws which regulate animated nature, that over each class there is imposed a salutary check, to prevent excess in production; this is specially observable among the feathered tribes, some of which have their eggs carried away by the ship-load from the breeding places; others, such as the grouse and waterfowl, are greatly reduced in number by sportsmen, or those who make a business of sending them to market, while the finches and blackbirds contribute largely to the support of the birds of prey, and in the southern part of the continent, are, during the winter, taken in numbers with the net and sold for the table. None of these causes, however, in any way affect the class which embraces the fly-catchers and warblers, as from their small size and the nature of their food, they are not sought after for these purposes. The check which applies to this class must therefore be of a different description from those referred to, and finding no way in which their numbers are reduced to any extent, *except* by the sacrifice made of their own young while rearing that of the cowbird, leads me to conclude, that the habit has been given for the special purpose of keeping within proper bounds a class of birds which might otherwise have exceeded their due proportion in the economy of nature. If we suppose the habit to be the result of any physical defect in the cowbird, we might naturally expect that it would confide the care of its young to a bird nearly allied to its own species, but in nine cases out of ten, the foster parents belong to a group which are different both in size, habit and the nature of their food; it is evident, therefore, that the *result* of the peculiarity is intended by nature to bear specially on the class to which the foster parents belong, and any one who has noticed the flocks of cowbirds which pass along on their migratory course in spring and fall, and estimated that for each bird in these flocks, from three to five of a different class have been prevented from coming to maturity, must admit that it is no small influence which the cowbird exercises in maintaining the balance of power which so admirably prevails among the feathered tribes.

"If we could imagine such a thing in nature, whose movements are all so well ordered as that the cow-buntings should at any time get in excess of the other class referred to, it would be curious to estimate the results; the flycatchers would then be fully occupied in rearing foster children, and not being permitted to perpetuate their own species, must soon die out, when the cowbirds, finding themselves without a substitute in the rearing of their young, would either be driven by necessity to make the attempt themselves, or they too would soon be added to the list of extinct species.

"Passing the *jays* and the *crows* (both of which are well deserving of notice did our limits permit), we come to a species which, in our vicinity, is the sole representative of his family.* This is the *American shrike*, or *butcher bird*, so called from his habit of impaling his prey on thorns. With us this species appears about the end of September, and a few adults remain over the winter. The male frequently makes choice of a particular district as his hunting ground during his stay, and, I am inclined to think, returns to it, year after year. His aspect bespeaks both strength and courage; the short neck, broad head, and notched beak, giving him much the appearance of a bird of prey. His favorite food consists of grasshoppers and other insects, but in winter when these cannot be procured, he does not hesitate to hunt down the smaller finches, killing them with a blow of his powerful beak. In October last, when passing through an open field west of the race course, I noticed one of these birds, whose motions led me to suspect he was engaged in the occupation which has gained his name; he was too shy to allow a close inspection of his operations, but on examining the thorn bush I found too of his victims still in life on the spikes. I did not observe anything which could lead to an explanation of this singular habit, except that it seemed to take great delight in the pastime, skip-

* Since writing the above, I have found a second species near the city, which appears to be the *Lanius Exeubitoroides* of Baird.

ping about between the ground and the bush, and warbling a few rather musical notes in evident token of satisfaction.

"To those who have occasion to be in the woods in winter, there is no bird so familiar as the *white breasted nuthatch;* it is one of the few which remain with us all the year round, and is remarkable for its restless, inquisitive habits; as a climber it has no equal, and may often be seen running downward on the smooth bark of a perpendicular tree, a feat which no other Canadian bird ever attempts. An examination of its feet shows a remarkable adaptation for this peculiar habit. It is furnished with a long and strongly-hooked hind claw which enables it to hang firmly in that position. It is said to roost head downward, and I have often seen it when shot, hanging in this position after death. The red-breasted nuthatch is another species of the same genus; it resembles the other, but is more migratory in its habits, less in size, and slightly different in colour.

"The family of *woodpeckers* is well represented in our woods, seven different species being observed. Of these the most common are the two spotted varieties, which resemble each other in colour, but differ considerably in size; they are partially migratory, only a few remaining during the winter. In the fall, when passing along to the south, they are frequently seen on the shade trees of the city, jerking themselves round to the off side of the branch when observed, or again startling the inmates of our frame dwellings, by rattling loudly on the decaying boards.

"A very beautiful species of this family is the *red-headed woodpecker*, which has been remarked by those who are observant of our native birds, to be less common in this district than formerly. This can only be accounted for by the removal of the heavy decaying timber which forms the nursery of its favorite insect food, and as the country gets more under cultivation, we may look forward to the time when it will only pay us a passing visit on its way to and from the woody regions to the north of us.

The least common species of this class which I have observed is the Arctic three-toed woodpecker. Wilson does not appear to have met with it at all, and Audubon mentions the northern part of the state of New York, as the southern limit of its migration; it resembles the spotted woodpeckers in size and manners, but differs from them in color, and in wanting the hind toe. Why one class of these birds should have four toes, and another, similar to it in habits, should have only three, we are at a loss to determine. I may remark, however, that the three-toed species belongs exclusively to the north, being seldom found among deciduous trees, and I have no doubt that a careful examination of the feet of this bird, and their mode of application to the bark of the pine, would give a satisfactory explanation of the seeming defect.

Passing the pidgeons and the grouse, which are equally interesting to the sportsman and the naturalist, we come to the waders and swimmers. Here my remarks will be general, as the haunts of these birds being beyond the reach of morning excursions I cannot say much from personal observation.

Of the first division of this group, which includes the plovers, sand-pipers, curlew, &c., little can be said, except that they visit the sandy shores of Burlington beach in considerable numbers every spring and fall, when on their migratory course to and from their summer residence in the north. In spring these visits are usually made during the month of May, occasionally the flocks remain for a day or two, but more frequently they move off after a rest of only a few hours, and are succeeded by others bound on the same journey. By the first of June they have all disappeared except the little spotted sand-piper, which stays with us during the summer, rearing its young on the shores of the bay.

Of the heron family, we have four species: viz., the great blue heron, the black crowned night heron, and the greater and lesser bitterns. Much information has yet to be gained regarding the birds of this class. Being all more or less night feeders, the study of their habits is attended with peculiar difficulty. On the breast of the great blue heron, covered by the long plumage of the neck, is a tuft of soft tumid feathers, which, when exposed in the dark, emit a pale phosphorescent light. The use of this does not appear to be fully understood, though the fishermen aver that when the heron retires at night to his feeding ground, he wades knee deep in the water, and shewing this light attracts the fish within his reach, much in the same way as the Indian does when fixing the torch of pitch-pine on the bow of his canoe.

"Of the flocks of the larger water-fowl which periodically pass along on their migratory course, only a very few now visit us; occasionally, in thick or stormy weather a few stragglers alight on the bay to rest and recruit themselves, though they generally forfeit their lives by so doing. Last fall three specimens of the American swan were thus procured, and a single individual of what has hitherto been considered the young of the snow goose was also obtained; doubts still exist as to the identity of the latter bird, some writers maintaining that it is a separate and distinct species, while others declare it to be the young of the snow goose in immature plumage. There are good arguments on both sides, but conclusive information on the subject can only be obtained from their breeding grounds in the far north.

"Of ducks I have noticed, in the market and elsewhere, twenty different species, the gayest of which is the *wood-duck*, so called from its habit of building its nest in the hollow of a decayed tree. A few pairs of this species annually raise their broods near the shores of the Dundas marsh; the *teal* and *mallard* have also been observed leading out their young from the ready inlets of the bay, but there are exceptional cases, as the great body pass farther to the north, paying us a short visit going and returning.*

"Nearly allied to the ducks is the small family of *mergansers*, which contains only three species† peculiar to the American continent, all of which are, at certain seasons of the year, found round the shores of the bay. The birds of this class subsist chiefly by fishing, and have the bill compressed and deeply serrated, to enable them to hold their slippery prey. They are also furnished with a crest, the use of which has been a matter of conjecture among naturalists, one of whom suggests that the elongated feathers of the head being acted on by the water, serve to give precision to the blow when striking the fish, much in the same way as a feather acts on the shaft of an arrow. The most beautiful of this

---

* It has been remarked by fishermen and others, who have had occasion to be on the waters of the bay during the summer months, that there are usually about a dozen ducks which keep together in a small flock, and do not seem to take any share in the duties of the breeding season. The flock is composed of both sexes, and frequently of different species. Various conjectures have been formed as to the cause of this singular conduct, but the probability is, that they are birds which, from being wounded or otherwise in ill health, have been unable to perform the journey northwards, and prefer spending the summer in retirement, joining their comrades on their return in the fall.

† The smew, or white nun, is mentioned in some works as an American bird, but its occurrence is very rare and considered accidental.

class is the hooded merganser, whose fine erectile crest extends from the bill right over to the hind head. With us this species is never abundant, but a few pairs are seen every spring as soon as the ice begins to shove from the sides of the bay. Their stay at this season is short, as they soon pass on to the north to breed; in the fall they again pay us a visit accompanied by their young, and follow their avocation round the bay till they are frozen out, when they move off to the south to spend the winter.

"Two species of tern visit the bay in spring, and during winter three species of gull have been observed at the beach. Of the latter class the most conspicuous is the great black-backed gull, which arrives from the north at the approach of winter, and leaves again on the first appearance of spring. The woid *gull*, as applied to the human species, is often used to denote dullness or stupidity, but such a meaning could not be suggested by the character of the birds to which it belongs, as there is not, among all other water-fowl, a more vigilant species than that which we have just referred to; it never comes within gun-shot, and the only specimen ever procured at the beach, met his death by following the example of an eagle in tasting a poisoned carcase, a few minutes after which, both were stretched dead upon the ice.

"Lowest on the list as being least perfect in their organization, are the grebes, a class of birds which frequent the borders of our smaller lakes and ponds, finding their sustenance chiefly in the shallow waters, which abound with water-plants. Three different species of this genus are found in the bay, all of which are known to the gunners by the somewhat suggestive name of 'helldiver.' An examination of these birds shows the most wonderful adaptation to their peculiar mode of life. Their food being obtained entirely under water, and their nest being only a few inches above its level, they have little occasion to be on land. When surprised in that situation, they seem most helpless, their legs being placed so far aft, they are unable to keep the body in anything like a horizontal position, and so make poor progress in walking, but the moment they reach the water they disappear under the surface, and are not again seen while the cause of alarm remains. The plumage of this species is of the most compact and silky texture, and is never penetrated by water while the bird is in life. The legs are placed far behind the centre of gravity, to give it greater power in swimming, and are much compressed so as to offer the least possible resistance to water, while the toes, in place of being connected with a web as in the duck, are each furnished with a separate membrane, which enables the bird to pass with ease and celerity through the tangled masses of water-plants, among which its favorite food is found. In some part of the European continent the skin of the grebe is much prized as trimming for ladies' dresses; and in olden time, when the fowling-piece was a less perfect instrument than at present, considerable difficulty was found in supplying the demand, as the grebe being a most expert diver, disappeared at the first flash of the gun, and was under water ere the shot could reach it. Since the invention of the percussion cap, however, they are more readily killed, and were any of our Hamilton ladies desirous of having a dozen or two of grebe's skins for trimmings, I have no doubt the birds would be forthcoming. At present, there being no demand for the skins and the flesh being unsuitable for the table, they are not much disturbed.

"Of the three species alluded to, one is a winter visitor, the other two remain during the summer, and rear their young in Dundas marsh and the reedy inlets of the bay. They are well protected with feathers, yet seem very sensitive to the cold, moving off to the south at the first touch of frost; returning again about the latter end of April.

"I have thus alluded to only a few of our more remarkable birds. The total number of species observed in the near vicinity of the city, from May, 1856, to the present time, amounts to 206, each of which has a separate and distinct history of its own, though in many cases it is very imperfectly known to us. If sportsmen and others, who have opportunity of observing the birds in their native haunts, could be induced to make notes of their observations, and communicate them to public bodies having the means of making them known, much new information would no doubt be gained, and we could with tolerable certainty ascertain the the geographical distribution of many species, a point at present undetermined."

Fauna and Flora of the extreme North-East.

AT a recent meeting of the Chicago Academy of Sciences, Dr. Kennicott gave some interesting particulars of a large tract of land called the Barren Ground, in the occupation of the Hudson's Bay Company, being the extreme north-east portion of North America, east of Hudson's Bay, whither he had been under the auspices of the Audubon and other learned societies, to make collections and observations in natural history. The speaker described the Barren Land as of vast extent, covering thousands of square miles which had never yet been trodden by the foot of white man, and probably was unknown to the Indian. Nothing but lichens and mosses grow on this vast territory, and the animal and *flora* which are found on it are very marked and peculiar. He said that the immense tract of land bore about the same relation to the prairie as the prairie bears to the wooded country. With very few exceptions, there was nothing to be seen but the lowest kind of *flora*. His visit there was in the winter, and he had felt the weather quite warm. The speaker spoke of the migration of birds northward, across the tract during spring. In high winds, when they flew low, he had shot several of them; and found, upon examination of the seeds they had eaten, that they were such as could have come only from the State of California or the neighbourhood of Oregon. He stated that he had observed several specimens of granite and very fine copper, the latter so pure that the Indians had had no difficulty in making it into spear-heads; and he had lit his pipe at a fire caused by the spontaneous combustion of a peculiar kind of coal which had been burning for thousands of years. The artificial heat produced by these fires was very considerable, and where the heat existed, quite a peculiar odour of plants was produced. The country abounded with lakes, but the geographical description of them, which had been generally furnished by Indians, could not be relied upon. The lecturer spoke of the aquatic habits of the Esquimaux to be found on Copper river, and made some interesting allusions to the magnetic pole and the discoveries of Sir John

Ross and his nephew in connection therewith. In reply to Professor Andrews, the lecturer said that he had not observed any description of *fungi* growing on the Barren Ground. The color of the lichens and mosses was from a grayish white to a dull brown. He had seen trees thirty feet high growing on the rock with not more than a peck of earth for their roots. They offered very little resistance to the wind, and were frequently blown down. The Indians made their bows from the roots. He spoke at length upon the indigenous animals to be found on the Barren Ground, and their peculiarities, mentioning the musk ox, the barren ground reindeer, the barren ground bear, and the polar bear.

APPENDIX.

The Quebec Fish and Game Protection Club Report.

At the annual general meeting of the Fish and Game Protection Club, the undermentioned gentlemen were elected to form a Committee for the ensuing year:—

Col. Rhodes, *President.*	J. B. Forsyth, Esq.
J. Gilmour, Esq., *Vice-President.*	W. Marsden, Esq., M.D.
F. W. G. Austin, Esq., *Sec'y.-Treas.*	P. V. Robin, Esq.

The following report of the retiring Committee, for the past year, was then read, and unanimously adopted:

GAME.

The wasteful practice of the Indians in slaying the moose, for the purpose of obtaining skins alone, is still perseveringly carried on during the close season in many of the districts frequented by this game, which is, in consequence, rapidly diminishing from year to year; other results cannot possibly be anticipated, as no steps are taken by the government of the country, by the municipal or other local authorities in the new and distant settlements, to arrest these wanton proceedings. In the existing state of the law, it is the conscientious sportsman alone who is precluded from enjoying a brief excursion during winter, in pursuit of these monarchs of the Canadian forest.

The caribou have increased in numbers; their habits differ from the habits of the moose; they are more erratic and difficult of approach, their spreading hoofs and light action assist their flight over the deep snows when followed by the huntsman; their hides, as objects of traffic, are not of such value to the Indians as the skins of the moose.

An experienced craftsman, a member of this Club, killed recently, in a single foray, no less than ten caribou, together with a great quantity of other game, of which ptarmigan formed the largest proportion. These birds, met with in numbers, were generally found in glades and open spaces in the coverts, where their food—wild fruits and buds of particular trees and shrubs—was plentiful.

Hares and Canada grouse were also met with in unusually large quantities.

Col. Rhodes, as well as other sportsmen, observed that the herds of caribou were large, and contained a promising number of young animals.

The chase of this wary and swift-footed game is highly appreciated by the true Canadian sportsman, who, to hunt it successfully, must possess the staunch qualifications of the deer stalker and chamois hunter combined, as these animals are usually found in herds roaming over the bleak mountain-sides and frozen lakes of our northernmost districts. When the surface of the snow is soft and yielding, and a suitable wind prevails, the caribou may be approached by careful stalking; but during calm weather, or when the snow is crusted, the only chance of obtaining a shot is for the sportsman to hide himself to the leeward of his game, an attendant is then ordered to make a distant circuit and give the caribou his wind. When these keen-scented animals discover the presence of an enemy, they become alarmed, and move away in the direction opposed to that from which they imagine the danger to proceed, and thus encounter a real foe in the person of the concealed hunter. An unusual number of caribou have been disposed of in the markets of this city.

Red deer (locally so called,) were also last season abundant, and were disposed of at reasonable prices.

A sportsman, who, during a short excursion in the Ottawa District killed some of these fine animals, on his return reported that about thirty head of this game were last autumn shot by two gentlemen in that neighborhood.

Great numbers of red deer are annually killed during the fence time by the operatives engaged in the manufacture of timber, in the same locality.

The mode usually adopted by sportsmen of hunting these animals is to drive the woods with hounds, when the startled deer fly at once to the water, where the hunter, in a light skiff or birch canoe, awaits the approach of his game, which plunges in, and tries to escape by swimming; at this crisis, an exciting aquatic contest sometimes ensues. Later in the season, when the rivers and lakes are ice-bound, the deer are shot in the "runs;" they are also sometimes "still-hunted"—a good many, too, are shot at night with the aid of a torch.

A good number of bears were killed during the past summer and autumn in the neighborhood of this city—these animals made some bold attacks upon a few of the sheep-folds in this district.

Feathered game generally was abundant, tracts deserted for may years were again resorted to, and grounds usually tenanted were frequented by increased numbers of the different species. The country around Chicago, also, where efficient game laws exist, swarmed with prairie fowl and quail; one Express company alone, at that place, forwarded to New York no less than ten tons of these birds.

Wild ducks of various kinds were also plentiful in different sections, and the markets were well supplied with them. It is, however, much to be deplored that the Act does not entirely prohibit the killing of water-fowl of different species in the coupling season, and that no provision of law is yet made to prevent the shooting of woodcock while congregated on their feeding grounds between sunset and sunrise; by suffering this wholesale method of destruction, which is extensively followed in this district, many coverts become entirely denuded of this excellent game.

Rumors prevailed last spring that the shooting of snipe was a good deal indulged in during the breeding time, and it was not only to the lower orders that illegal practices in this respect were imputed.

Information of infringements of the Game Act was sent to your Committee in three instances during the past year, and prosecutions were brought accordingly, which resulted in two convictions. Owing, however, to the paradoxical opinions expressed in relation to the protection of fish and game by the magistrate who happened to preside, the third case was withdrawn by the Club.

Your Committee regret that no legislation has yet been adopted towards arresting the practice of shooting the singing and small birds of the country. It is generally on a Sunday that the dissolute emerge with their guns and other engines to carry on a warfare against the pretty songsters, whose bodies, when dead, are useless, but whose cheerful notes, while living, awaken pleasure and delight. From the fact that the existence of the small birds confers great benefits upon agriculture, by destroying insects hurtful to vegetation, it is surprising that no philanthropic legislator has yet introduced a law to save them from destruction. The Humane Society, recently organized in this city, within whose province the repression of heedless acts of cruelty naturally lies, will no doubt consider whether it would not become that body to arrest this wanton destruction of life.

This Club is deeply indebted to J. M. LeMoine, Esq., for several excellent communications published by that gentleman, connected with the objects of this association.

Your Committee cannot close this part of their report without congratulating their fellow members upon the marked increase apparent last season in some of those objects of human food, which their Society desires to promote, and they also believe that the humble efforts of this Club, aided by similar associations now established in different parts of the province, as well as in Nova Scotia, have not been altogether uninteresting to those who really appreciate an increase in the game of Canada as a desirable object.

SALMON AND SALMON FISHERIES.

The restoration of our salmon and trout fisheries, which has been attempted by the government, is a subject which interests the public as deeply as it does every member of this association.

The coasts, rivers and lakes of Canada, which nature and nature alone had stocked with a rich provision of wholesome food, requiring neither expense to maintain nor labor to cultivate, in numerous instances from the improvidence of the Indian, the greed of the white man, and the long-continued indifference of the government, had become entirely barren—and in other cases the supply had so diminished as to render every exertion towards the preservation and increase of these fisheries an object of paramount importance. This Club, therefore, has never failed to regard with great interest the late efforts of the Executive to rescue these fisheries from the state of depression to which years of recklessness and inattention had reduced them. These struggles have been attended with much benefit in promoting the increase of salmon in some of the rivers* of the Lower St. Lawrence—other rivers would, no doubt, have equally profitted had the well-intended efforts of the government been fully seconded by an efficient and laborious staff.

The system of leasing salmon fishing stations and fishing rights, although at one time regarded as a somewhat speculative measure, has successfully contributed towards promoting an increase of these valuable fish.

The Moisie, which sent so large a supply of excellent salmon to this market during the past summer, and which river has been managed for the past two or three years by an experienced tacksman, affords an apt illustration of the results to be obtained by careful and prudent fishing; the boon conferred by placing so large a quantity of wholesome food within reach of all classes of the community was fully appreciated.

The incredible rapidity with which the young salmon increase in development and gain flesh has been recently ascertained with great accuracy, twenty months sufficing from the deposition of the ova to produce marketable fish; each fortnight of their stay in the salt water, after their first descent of their native river, adds over a pound to their weight.

From the rapid increase in size and weight of these fish, in the sea, it is interesting to know what composes their natural food while there. Professor Queckett thinks they live upon the ova of the sea-urchin; Professor Huxley considers that their food consists of small crustaciæ. This question admits of no difficulty with regard to the fish frequenting the Gulf of St. Lawrence and its coasts, as the operatives engaged in splitting and curing salmon invariably find their stomachs gorged with caplin and young herrings.

The advantages resulting from the artificial propagation of salmon over the natural way, are also remarkable; it is estimated that not more than one ovum in a thousand naturally deposited in a river becomes a marketable fish, while one in each hundred placed in a hatching-box be-

* Since the Jacques Cartier has fallen into the hands of private individuals, the catch of salmon, in 1863, attained the unprecedented figure of two hundred fish. The pools of the Ste. Anne were swarming with fish last year, and fresh salmon on the Quebec market was, from its abundance, as low as two pence half-penny per pound, one season. --(*J. M. L.*)

comes a perfect salmon. The superiority, therefore, of artificial breeding, in re-stocking rivers which have become barren, is obvious, and it is not by any means an expensive operation; the original cost of the ponds at Stormontfield, which annually send to sea 200,000 salmon, was only £600, and the yearly expense does not exceed £50.

Recent discoveries in the natural history of the *Salmo Salar* have also served to elucidate many points which were subjects of controversy among naturalists, as well as practical fishermen. It is now ascertained that the ova of salmon are only fecundated after leaving the fish, and the fecundation may be effected not only by the milt of the full-grown male, but also by that of the grilse and the parr.*

About one-half the ova hatched become smoults, which descends to the sea during the first year of their hatching, the remainder continuing in their native river till the following season, and in a few instances some of the latter remain in their nursery until the third year, before they are ready to migrate. Salmon ova are never hatched in the sea, nor can parr live in the salt water before assuming the smoult scales. All the smoults that have migrated to the sea do not the same year return to their native river as grilse, one-half returning the next year as small salmon. It appears to be a law of these fish, to descend to and return from the sea by double or divided migrations.†

A few breeding salmon do not suffice to re-stock an exhausted river, or to augment the supply in a productive one, as the waste which occurs in the ova is enormous; much is lost from not coming in contact with the vitalizing milt of the male—from not having been properly covered with gravel by the fish. The ova also are devoured by the larvæ of aquatic insects and water fowl; the young fry, too, are destroyed in great numbers by other fish.

None of our exhausted rivers have yet been re-stocked, nor has any determined effort been made by the government staff to restore any of them; twenty months sufficing to produce marketable salmon from the ova, several of these barren rivers, had they been subjected to active management, would now teem with fish.

No marked increase of trout affecting the smaller rivers and inland lakes has yet been observed, as the law affords no protection to these fish during the spawning time nature assigned to them. The proper close season for trout ought to commence on the first of September and terminate on the first of January.

In August, 1858, it was by law enacted that a fish-way should be attached and maintained to every dam or slide where fish might ascend. The present Act enjoins the same thing, and directs the Superintendent of Fisheries to see that such fish-way is maintained.

Your Committee regret to add that, notwithstanding that more than four years have now elapsed since the passing of the first law, there are yet salmon rivers in Lower Canada barred by mill-dams and slides, which

---

* *Brown's Natural History of the Salmon.* † *Ibid.*

have no fish-ways attached to them. There are also mill-dams having suitable fish-stairs, which, during the run of the salmon, are suffered to remain so encumbered by drift and mill rubbish as to be perfectly useless.

Mr. Fennell, the Irish Fisheries Commissioner, in his evidence given before the committee of the House of Lords in 1860, states that salmon can ascend any height by means of these stairs. A fish-way has been recently constructed in Ireland two miles long.

Authentic information from different sources reached your Committee last season, that the spearing of breeding salmon was indulged in as usual by the Indians. This practice, so long as it is persevered in, must neutralize all the efforts of the government to increase these fish. If it be deemed a hardship to deprive the Indians of this privilege, it would be an act of wisdom to substitute, in the autumn, such a moderate supply of other food as would aid in their support, while engaged during the winter at their hunting-grounds, as spearing the salmon destroys the seed, and devastates the seed-ground of these fisheries.

No provision is yet made for communicating by steam with the fisheries of the Lower St. Lawrence; until this be effected, the revenue from them must ever remain inconsiderable.

The Act now in force does not protect the fry of the salmon during their stay in their native rivers. The young fish are destroyed in great numbers in waters flowing through populous districts. To capture or have in possession at any time young salmon, under a certain weight, should be prohibited. The young of trout ought also to be protected. The practice of setting fixed or stationery lines in the inland lakes ought also to be forbidden.

F. W. G. AUSTIN,
Secretary-Treasurer.

Quebec, *2nd February*, 1863.

Annual Report of the Montreal Fish and Game Protection Club, for 1864.

THE Annual Meeting was held at "Dolly's," on the 5th March, 1864.

HENRY MCKAY, *President.*
JOHN OGILVY, *Vice-President.*
A. MURRAY, *Secretary* and *Treasurer.*

COMMITTEE.

A. HOWARD,	FREDERICK RAY,
GEORGE HORNE,	ALFRED RIMMER,
L. M. DUVERNAY,	L. BETOURNAY.

Mr. Henry McKay, the President, in the chair.

The Secretary read the following Annual Report:—

The Committee of the Montreal Fish and Game Protection Club have to report that during the past year every effort has been made to secure the enforcement of the law, in so far as it provides against the improper destruction of fish and game.

A reward of ten dollars offered to any one securing a conviction, was extensively advertised throughout the city and in country places, and the markets here have been so carefully watched that it has become a matter of more danger than profit to buy or sell at the prohibited seasons.

As large quantities of black bass and doré were openly exposed for sale as late in the season as April last, the Secretary prosecuted one of the dealers, but failed to secure a conviction, as evidence was brought to show that the fish in question had been taken before the 15th of March. The prosecution had a good effect, however, as the sale was at once put a stop to. Your Committee would recommend, that on the 15th instant, notice be given to all dealers that ten days will be allowed them to dispose of the stock on hand, but that after that time an information will be laid against any one having them in his possession.

A well-known trader from Verchères, who has been in the habit of supplying the markets and hotels with game, both in and out of season, was detected on one of the market boats in May last. His bag of game was confiscated, and himself convicted in ten dollars and costs. In this case, the Club reward was divided between the informer and the police constable who effected the capture.

On the 10th of June last, the reward was claimed for the conviction of one Ives, of the Township of Bolton, for having shot three partridges on the 25th April. A certified copy of the conviction before H. S. Foster, Esq., J. P. for Bedford, having been received, as also a letter from that gentleman, stating that the penalty awarded (sixteen dollars) had been enforced, the sum of ten dollars was remitted to the party who prosecuted.

It having come to the knowledge of the Committee, that fish and game, out of season, had been served at the St. James Club House, this was at once brought before the managers, and a letter was received from the secretary stating that the matter had been one of inadvertence, and that instructions had been issued that any fish or game which may be out of season should not again enter the Club.

The attention of the principal hotel and restaurant keepers has been, from time to time, called to these laws, and their observance of them, and co-operation with the Club generally, asked and promised.

The Committee are sanguine that by a steady perseverance in the course followed during the past year, one great object of the Club will be attained in the closing of all markets, here at all events, for the prohibited articles. It is really in the markets of large cities that the battle has to be fought, for it is almost impossible, for many reasons, to reach the first offender in country places. Stop the sale of his illicit wares, however, and you will do much to cure the evil.

For this reason, the Committee would express an earnest hope that organizations similar to this and the Quebec Club, will soon be found in every town in Canada. The object appeals not alone to the interests of sportsmen. In a country like ours, so recently wrested from the hands of nature, and blessed by Providence with such magnificent preserves for the finest of fish and game—preserves that, by proper management, could be made almost inexhaustible, and from which might be drawn a large and valuable portion of the food of the people,—it is surely lamentable to see a war of utter extermination so ignorantly and recklessly carried on,—to see that while other countries are, at great expense, carefully fostering both foreign and home fisheries—that while the people of Australia, for instance, are bringing the ova of salmon and trout twelve thousand miles to stock their barren streams, we, whose every inland creek once abounded with these fish up to the very foot of Niagara, have nearly succeeded in destroying all within our reach.

Mill dams and mill offal, stake nets, and the villanous spear upon the spawning ground, have all but done their work; and unless the efforts now being made are successful, and both government and people give themselves to the simple work of seeing that the *feræ naturæ* get common fair play, a few years more and we shall indeed have killed our goose for the sake of its golden eggs.

As the Club are aware, Mr. Price, M.P.P., has had before Parliament for several sessions bills to amend the Fishery and Game Acts. Your Committee have been in communication with that gentleman on the subject, and have pleasure in acknowledging the prompt attention which these suggestions received at his hands.

The Committee have recommended the following amendments to the present laws:—

GAME ACT.

Sect. 3.—This clause declares it unlawful to kill certain game by snaring, but it is defective in not providing against the buying, selling or having in possession game that has manifestly been killed by snaring. It is only by the enforcement of such a clause as this that the evil can practically be reached.

Sect. 4.—Referring to the killing of wild geese, ducks, &c., should be amended so as to prohibit their destruction between the 1st April and the 20th August, in every year. It would be better still to prohibit spring shooting altogether.

Sect. 11.—That it is highly desirable to prohibit altogether, and at all seasons, the destruction, carrying away, &c., of the eggs of wild fowl in all parts of Canada, or at least west of the River Saguenay—incalculable injury being done in this way every spring, especially on the Lakes St. Francis and St. Peter, and the marshes adjacent.

Sect. 13.—That in the opinion of the Club it has become of importance to consider how far it is right or necessary any longer to draw the marked distinction now existing between the Indians and all other of Her Majesty's subjects, especially in parts of Canada where the former have to a great extent adopted the habits and pursuits of civilized life, and where the practices complained of are carried on, not for sustenance, but pecuniary gain. There can be no doubt, for instance, that the great destruction of the eggs of game fowl perpetrated every year in the neighborhood of Lake St. Francis, is principally the work of the St. Regis Indians, and that there, and in other parts of Canada, the injurious consequences of the peculiar privileges granted to this class are becoming every day the more manifest.

FISHERY ACT.

One effect of the amended Act now before Parliament will be, if it passes, to shorten the present fence time for trout and lunge, substituting the 20th of September and 10th of December for the present dates. This the Committee regret, and have represented their desire that these fish should be kept out of market till at least the 1st January, and later if possible.

Your Committee also recommended that clauses similar to sections 10 and 15 of the Game Act should be inserted in the Fishery Act, providing that it shall be the duty of clerks of markets, &c., to seize and confiscate all fish exposed for sale, or otherwise, in contravention of the Act; and, also, that Custom-house officers should be invested with similar authority, as much of the fish killed at improper seasons, or in an improper manner, is carried for sale into the United States.

Your Committee have also recommended that a clause be introduced into the Act prohibiting mill offal, saw-dust, or tan bark, from being thrown into the rivers and streams. It is true the Agricultural Act provides for this to a certain extent, but saw-dust is not specified in the clause; and, in any case, it would be well to have this matter, which so particularly affects the fisheries, provided for in the Fishery Act.

The above suggestions have, with but few exceptions and alterations, been adopted by Mr. Price, and either have, or will be introduced into the bills which he has before Parliament. Whether they will become law or not, or if so, when, it is of course impossible to say. They have already been before the house for two sessions; perhaps during the present one a little time may be spared for the business of the country.

Among other suggestions which your Committee felt it their duty to press on the Legislature of the country, was one urging for the protection of the smaller insectivorous birds.

It is now well understood that the wanton destruction of these birds, which too commonly prevails, especially in the neighborhood of large cities, does much injury to the agricultural and horticultural interests of the country; and your Committee obtained from a gentleman of this city, who has devoted much attention to these subjects, a very complete list of the ornithology of Canada, discriminating between the birds injurious and those useful to the most important interests. This list was sent through the Hon. Mr. Rose to Mr. Joly, M.P.P., and the latter gentleman has introduced a bill which embraces the suggestions of your Committee, and which they trust may become law. This bill prohibits the destruction of the birds protected, except at *certain seasons.* It would be better to prohibit it altogether. There is no use in shooting them at any season; on the contrary, much evil.

Your Committee had in view the publishing in both languages of a full synopsis of the Fishery and Game Acts, accompanied by an appeal to the community in general for countenance and aid. This they intended to circulate widely throughout country places especially, and they hoped thus to be able to interest the influential and enlightened in their favor. They have delayed doing so, however, until it be known if any amendments to these acts are to be made. This will probably be ascertained in a few months, when the Committee would recommend to their successors to carry out the proposed publication.

Notwithstanding all the penalties that can be attached to the improper destruction of game, the practice will be carried on so long as the evil consequences are not evident to the people, and while, therefore, no general opprobrium attaches to the offence. Interest the multitude, however, in the matter,—create an enlightened public opinion as to the propriety and necessity of these laws for the general good,—and their infringement to an injurious degree, in any settled part of the country, would soon be an impossibility.

The Committee have been in communication, during the year, with a gentleman residing in Chateauguay county, who had taken a warm interest in the removal of the numerous obstructions to the ascent of salmon which exist in the river Chateauguay. The required orders for the erection of fishways on the dams have been given by the proper authorities, and if these orders are complied with—if edging slabs, saw dust and other injurious rubbish be kept out of the stream, and especially if the inhabitants on the banks of the of the river can only be induced to give the fish fair play, your Committee would strongly recommend that the attempt be made to stock it again with salmon.

This will not cost a large sum, as even under all the present disadvantages several were killed there last season. Doubtless a number of the public-spirited among the inhabitants of the county will contribute to pay the expense, and if successful, and there is no reason why it should not be so, salmon may in a few years be nearly as numerous in that river as was the case thirty or forty years ago.

Salmon River too, which flows into Lake St. Francis, and which derived its name from the abundance of that noble fish once found in its waters, might, were proper care observed, be re-stocked without much difficulty.

Your Committee would recommend this matter to the attention of the Club during the ensuing season. The re-establishment of several good salmon streams in the neighborhood of Montreal would be an object worthy of their efforts.

While on this subject they regret to have to say, that it is within their knowledge that over two hundred salmon were killed of the scoop-net last season at Brompton Falls, St. Francis River, near Sherbrooke. It seems that the fishway there is insufficient, and that the fish are captured with ease while attempting to ascend the dam. This is known to almost every man, woman and child in the neighborhood, and such things happening in one of the few streams that the salmon yet frequent, augurs ill for the success of such experiments as have been recommended.

They have also to report that Lake Memphremagog was given over in toto to the torch and spear last fall. During the preceeding year, some good was done by the presence and exertions of Mr. Nettle, the Superintendent of Fisheries; but during last October every lunge found on the spawning grounds, became sport and profit to the barbarians of the the spear. Many of the respectable among the inhabitants on its shores deeply regret this, and would do all in their power to prevent it, short of running the risk of having their houses and barns burned by the vagabonds who follow this nefarious trade, and who do not hesitate to threaten this as the result of taking any steps against them. It would be well did the law provide for the taking of the most notorious of such depredators to some distance, say to Sherbrooke, for trial; and your Committee would strongly recommend to their successors to urge upon the Crown Lands Department the necessity of sending to that locality a force of three or four special constables during the next spawning season. The laws are openly defied there, the local authorities quite inadequate; and the preservation of the black trout or lunge, in that noble lake, is well worth the small expense it would entail on the government.

With regard to general sporting interests during the past year, your Committee would observe that game of nearly all kinds has been somewhat more plentiful. Ducks of the different varieties were numerous. The partridge, or Canada grouse, appear to be increasing in number, the destruction by snaring seems to have been somewhat lessened of late years, and if the amendment to the bill asked for were passed, and snared game could be seized in the market, there is no doubt that this practice would soon cease, and this fine bird become exceedingly abundant.

Snipe have visited us in great numbers during the past year, and woodcock were very abundant during the breeding season; about the beginning of August, however, and earlier than usual, they took their accustomed flight to parts unknown, and did not return in September in numbers, by any means, as large as usual.

Deer appear to have been abundant, especially in Canada West, but the Committee is credibly informed that great numbers were wantonly slaughtered last spring, in the vicinity of Ottawa, at a time when neither carcase nor hide is of any value. The angler has had less reason to congratulate himself. There can be no doubt but that the black bass, the game fish *par excellence* of the waters in our immediate vicinity, are year by year diminishing in numbers. A few years ago they could be taken in plenty with the rod very near Lachine, now they are getting scarce even at St. Anns and the Cascades. Whatever the reason of this,—deficient protection at the spawning season, netting in the St. Lawrence and Ottawa, or the constantly increasing disturbance of the waters by our constantly increasing trade, all but the last reason is to be regretted; for whether as sport to the disciples of Isaac Walton, or food to the hungry, there are few finer fish in our waters than the bold and agile bass.

Your Committee have, in conclusion, to congratulate the Club on the large accession to its number since the beginning of the last year and the interest which has been taken in its objects.

Success, say we, to a cause so ably advocated and in whose favor we see enlisted many of the leading men of the great commercial metropolis of the Canadas.

MEMBERS OF THE MONTREAL FISH AND GAME PROTECTION CLUB.

Henry McKay,
Geo. Horne,
Alex. Ramsay,
Danl. Wylie,
Walter Macfarlane,
J. Thomson,
Wm. M. Freer,
Andrew Law,
Don. Ross,
Alex. Murray,
E. Atwater,
Jas. Baillie,
R. A. Brooke,
J. D. Crawford,
R. D. Collis,
Wm. Edmonstone,
Jas. Gordon,
Benj. Hutchins,
John Hope,
Jas. Hutton,
J. H. Joseph,
B. Lyman,
Wm. Mocdie,
David Mair,
Chas. Geddes,
Jessie Joseph,
J. M. Miller,
H. L. Macdougall,
M. McCulloch,
Thos. Ogilvy,
John Ogilvy,
Alfred Rimmer,
W. W. Ramsay,
F. H. Simms,
S. H. Thompson,
D. A. P. Watt,
Thos. Wilson,
C. J. Coursol,
Gordon McKenzie,
J. J. Brady,
J. E. Malhiott,
L. W. Marchand,
G. F. Prowse,
Duncan Robertson,
M. McCulloch,
Lewis S. Black,
L. A. Duvernay,
H. H. Merrill,

D. L. Macdougall,
Ed. Mackay,
W. S. Macfarlane,
W. Phillips,
E. A. Prentice,
Jackson Rae,
Gilbert Scott,
G. W. Warner,
Augustus Heward,
Jas. Walker,
Henry Budden,
Jas. Esdaile,
John Scott,
J. E. Caillet,
Thos. McDuff,
K. Nicolson,
Hy. Chapman,
A. McK. Forbes,
J. Kershaw,
W. C. Willis,
P. Leslie,
Capt. McFarlane, M T.,
Louis Betournay,
And. Robertson,
Alex. Cross,
Fredk. W. Kay,
Henry Starnes,
R. H. Buller, 60th Rifles,
Alphonse Boyer,
Major Gordon, 60th Rifles,
Hy. Thomas,
Adolphe Roy,
Thos. O. Rogers,
Alex. Molson,
Capt. Miller, 60th Rifles.

ERRATA.

Page 18, line 8—Read "la" instead of "le."

" 118, line 19—Leave out "the."

" 133, note at foot of page—Read "Wood" instead of "Woods."

" 136, " " " —Read "the *elite* in the commercial world" instead of "the *elite*."

" 138, " " " —Read "until last year" instead of "last year."

" 181, line 2—Read "eddying" instead of "edding."

" 188—The Sand-hill Crane is erroneously inserted amongst the Gallinacious, instead of amongst the Waders.

" 190—The note at foot of page applies to all the birds.

" 214—The Montreal Game Club Report is for 1863—not 1864.

MAPLE LEAVES.

CONTENTS OF FIRST SERIES.

CONTENTS OF SECOND SERIES.

MAPLE LEAVES.

CANADIAN HISTORY

AND

QUEBEC SCENERY.

(Third Series.)

By J. M. LeMoine, Esq.,

(COPYRIGHT.)

Quebec

1865.

INTRODUCTION.

THE present budget of *detached papers* on Canadian History and Canadian Scenery comprises two subjects, viz.: *Jottings of History, chiefly illustrative of the era of the Conquest*, and *Brief descriptions of several spots in the vicinity of Quebec*. The first is intended for the general reader; the second, of a more intimate and local nature, are not likely to possess for the public generally the same amount of interest as they may awaken in those immediately concerned, unless it be those seats so closely linked with historical events, that, as it were, they may be considered as forming portion of the history of the country. This volume, intended for tourists and persons of leisure, although strictly historical in all its parts, is written in a light, familiar style, the writer trusting that no offence will be taken where none was meant.

The Illustrations, by Livernois, speak for themselves. Had we had to deal with an artist less self-sacrificing, less public-spirited, probably none would grace our pages. Should an indulgent public continue to this *series* the favor extended to the two that preceded, the writer will feel that to Mr. Livernois' portraying of localities is due a fair portion of that success.

To the many kind friends who, in this arduous, though pleasant task, have staunchly stood by us, we return our grateful thanks. To some of the proprietors of country seats described, we owe an apology for having failed to set forth, in becoming language, the charms of their rustic homes.

SPENCER GRANGE,
(NEAR QUEBEC),
1st June, 1865.

CONTENTS.

MAPLE LEAVES.

CANADIAN HISTORY AND QUEBEC SCENERY.

The Campaign of 1759 in Canada.

"The campaign in which Wolfe met his death is interesting on his own account, and also because of the possibility, however remote, that the scene of it may one day witness a fresh contest for empire in Canada."—(*London Saturday Review*, 1864.)

THE seige operations of Quebec, and military incidents which took place in its environs during the summer of 1759, from the important results they ultimately led to, with regard to the rest of the continent, no less than from the change of rule they inaugurated in Canada, will ever be a theme of engrossing interest for every dweller in the Western hemisphere. The surrender of Canada, probably forever dissolved the gigantic *idea* of a French transatlantic empire, planned by Richelieu, extending from the shores of the north Atlantic through New France (with Quebec for its northern outlet), the Ohio Valley to Louisiana, (with New Orleans for its southern outlet), the whole to be connected by a chain of forts, etc.—an event brought round, as much through the neglect of the parent state and the successful propagation of the Goldwin Smith doctrines of that period, as it can be ascribed to British valour, this be it said without the slightest desire to lessen the glory of British arms during that memorable campaign. History has recorded the departure from Quebec, during the last year of French rule in Canada, of the delegates De Bougainville and Doreil, and their conference with the imperial authorities (on 8th April, 1759) on the other side of the Atlantic, assuring them that unless the mother country was prepared to do more to protect Canadian soil against foreign aggression, *the colony* *was lost to France.* History has also transmitted the brutal* reply of the oblivious mother to her colonial offspring, through the mouth of the Colonial Minister Berryer, La Pompadour's protegé; also, the spirited answer of the Canadian delegates who hurried home. The Canadians, though deserted, fought determinedly but ineffectually to defend their altars, their hearths their homes.

More than one century later history (in April, 1865) is again called on to chronicle the departure of delegates from Quebec to confer with the imperial authorities, and tell them that unless the mother country does more to protect her offspring, in this her dependency, the conquest of which has cost her so much blood and treasure, *the colony is lost to England*: history has yet to furnish the remaining links in the chain of future events. Now for the fighting times of 1759 and their results. As soon as the New England British provinces, ceased to be menaced on their northern frontier by their old and powerful foes, the French, a sense of security and growing strength kindled with increased ardor the spirit of independence fostered there for many long years; the civil and religious tyranny which had driven from their English homes the Pilgrim Fathers to the shores of the New World, had not been forgotten amongst their descendants, smarting under the oppressive policy of an obstinate monarch in opposition to Pitt and other liberal statesmen of England; sympathy and encouragement at the onset from the French, galled at the reverse their arms had met with in Canada—these and several other causes operated to hasten the great struggle for independence in '75. The traditions, causes, and results of successful revolution in the New World, brought back to the Old, by Lafayette and his victorious legions fresh from the battle-field, served to fan the flame of discontent and roused oppressed classes in France,—the whole culminating in the appalling horrors of 1789.

Thus British success in Canada, as predicted by Montcalm in his famous prophetic letter of the 24th August, 1759, written from the camp at Beauport, meant for England the loss of her American Provinces: *sic vos, non vobis!*

---

* Le ministre de la marine (colonies) l'inepte Berryer, reçut fort mal M. de Bougainville, et lui dit: "Eh! Monsieur, quand le feu est à la maison, on ne s'occupe pas des écuries."—"On ne dira pas du moins, Monsieur, que vous parlez comme un cheval," répliqua Bougainville. (Dussieux, p. 172.)

Cordons et Croix de St. Louis were however liberally sent from Versailles to soothe the victims.

Thus, as has been remarked by many eminent writers, the American rebellion was the forerunner and herald of the French revolution.

It would be presumptious for us to attempt to sum up the preparations of the Quebec military authorities for the coming campaign, in a more lucid and concise manner than has been done by one of our historians, Mr. Garneau :—

"While M. de Vaudreuil and the generals were at Montreal, they received despatches from France, which determined Montcalm to leave for Quebec, where he arrived May 22; followed soon afterwards by the Governor General and M. de Lévis. The ships had brought a confirmation of the report that a British fleet was on its way to the capital, which therefore became the first point to be defended. May 22, an express brought word of some enemy's ships having reached Bic. 'Coming events' thus 'casting their shadows before,' there was no time to lose, and all was now activity to realize means for a stout defence of the capital. In order to obstruct the enemy's approach, river-buoys and all other indicators for safely navigating the flood were removed; while fire-boats were prepared for igniting the enemy's ships as soon as they should reach the port. The garrison stores and government archives were removed to Three-Rivers, and the army magazines fixed at Montreal: only necessaries for one month were reserved at Quebec, to supply the daily wants of the troops and inhabitants. A portion of the little grain remaining in the upper country was purchased with money advanced by army officers. Finally, goods were bought to give as presents to those savage tribes about Niagara and Detroit, which either remained true to the French, or whose people disowned their alliances with the British. The gifts thus awarded would at least, it was hoped, secure their neutrality.

"These preliminaries arranged, the chiefs turned their attention to organizing the army, and to strengthening Quebec; the loss of the latter, it was likely, would eventuate in that of all Canada. But as for the city defences, they were judged to be anything but impregnable, and especially weak on the landward side; where the rampart, which was unprovided with parapet, embrasures, and cannon, was but six or seven feet in height, and protected outwardly neither by fossé, nor glacis: it was therefore decided unanimously, that the city should be put under cover of an entrenched camp, to be occupied by the bulk of the army.

"Quebec is built, as has been said before, at the extremity of a promontory. To the east and the south the St. Lawrence, here about a mile wide, rolls its deep waters; to the north is the fine valley of the St. Charles river, which, at its embouchure, along with the greater stream forms a basin three or four miles in extent. The St. Charles' lower bed is entirely covered at high tide; but at full ebb, it is fordable. The promontory on which Quebec stands, being very steep towards the St. Lawrence, with an elevation ranging between 160 and 300 feet, was considered inaccessible, especially on the city side.* The weakest points towards the port were protected by pallisades and walls; and the communications between lower-town and upper-town were cut, and defended by artillery. It was thought that batteries erected on the quays of the lower-town and on the scarp of the upper, would together bar all passage against an enemy, whether ascending from the lower, or descending by the upper flood. If this were so, all that was further wanted, in regard of the city's safety, was to close up the entry of the St. Charles river, and thence fortify its left strand, &c., (*la Canardière*), along with the northern shore of the St. Lawrence, from Beauport to the embouchure of the Montmorenci; said fortifying line to be continued inland for some distance along the right bank of the latter stream, which, descending from the Laurentian highlands, crosses the highway along the left side of the flood it falls into just below.

"The entry of the St. Charles, at a point facing the Porte du Palais, was boomed with masts chained together, kept in place by anchors, and protected in front by five barges, each mounted with a cannon. Behind the first barricade three merchant-vessels were sunk, having a platform laid across them, and a battery superimposed, armed with heavy ordnance, the gun-range of which radiated over the whole expanse of the bay. There was besides, at the near end of the Beauport and Charlesbourg roads, a bridge of boats, traversing the St. Charles, defended at each extremity by a hornwork. The right bank of the same river, from the pontoons over it to the Porte du Palais, was bordered with entrenchments, having artillery mounted to defend the entry of the suburb of St. Roch, and prevent the enemy from gaining by surprise the heights of Quebec.—The army now

* "There is no reason to believe"—thus was the order of battle worded (June 10)—"that the enemy will think of passing in front of the city and landing at the Anse des Mères; and, so long as the frigates remain to us, we have nothing to apprehend on that side."

changed position; it passed from the right bank (of the lower St. Charles), whereon it was first entrenched (on the city side), to the left bank of the St. Lawrence; following a line beginning at the bridge of boats just mentioned, and continued to the embouchure of the Montmorenci, with a short prolongation inland, as aforesaid. This line was covered by entrenchments, which followed the sinuosities of the ground, and were flanked by redoubts, with cannon mounted at every point where an enemy could land easily. In the centre of the line, at the issue of the Beauport stream, was moored a floating battery of 12 guns.

"The flotilla still remaining, consisting of two frigates, the barges, and fire-ships, were put in charge of Captain Vauquelin. Sentinels were posted at intervals, on the margin of the flood, from Quebec to as far above it as the Anse du Foulon ('Wolfe's Cove'), where a steep path (*rampe*) was formed to communicate with the Plains of Abraham, on the plateau above. A small redoubt, with cannon mounted, guarded that passage.—Such were the preparations made for defending Quebec and its environs.

"According to the plan adopted (always supposing the St. Lawrence were barred in front of Quebec, and the Beauport army too solidly entrenched to have its lines forced), there was no chance for the invaders but to land on the right of the flood, proceed a certain distance upward, cross to the opposite (left) shore, make a short detour inland and re-descend. By these means, the French army might have been assailed in its rear, if either the Charlesbourg or Bourg-Royal road were followed. But this operation would have been difficult, and doubtless was so considered (by the British), because an enemy's retreat would have been impossible in case of a repulse.

"The French army was strengthening daily, by the arrival of militia-men from all parts of the country. In rural homesteads, there remained behind only aged men, women and children. Every male fit to bear arms presented himself at Quebec, at Carillon, at lake Ontario, at Niagara, or at a post on lake Erie, or, in fine, at some point or other, even if as distant as that portion of the Ohio valley still possessed by the French.

"In the arrangement of the field forces, Montcalm's right wing, composed of the militias of Quebec and Trois-Rivières districts, 4,380 strong, under Messrs. de St.-Ours and de Bonne, occupied La Canardière (facing the city); the centre, composed of 2,000 regulars, under brigadier Sennezergues, guarded the space between the lower St. Charles and Beauport church; the left, composed of the militia of Montreal district, numbering 3,450 men, under Messrs. Prud'homme and d'Herbin, extended from said church to the river Montmorenci. General de Lévis commanded the whole left, Colonel de Bougainville the entire right, of the general position; while M. de Montcalm, taking charge of the centre, there established his head-quarters.* A corps in reserve, composed of 1,400 colonial soldiers, 350 horsemen and 450 savages, under M. de Boishébert (an officer just returned from Acadia), took up a position behind the centre of the army, on the heights of Beauport. If to these forces we add the sailors and 650 others in Quebec garrison (the latter being armed citizens), under M. de Ramesay, there is a resulting total of 13,000 combatants. 'We had not reckoned,' said an ocular witness, 'on realizing so large a force, because so great a number of Canadians was not expected to be present: those only being called on who were most able to bear the fatigues of war; but there was so great an emulation among the people, that we saw arrive in camp even octogenarians and lads of 12 to 13 years of age. Never were subjects of any king more worthy of his favour, whether regard be had to their constancy in toil, or to their patience in sufferings, which have really been extreme in this country. In the army itself, every heavy burden was laid upon them.'

"In the position we have described, then, the approaching enemy was to be confronted. The Governor General and the civil administrators quitted the city meantime, and repaired to Beauport; the chief families left for country places, taking with them their most precious effects.

"Meanwhile the first arrived British ships anchored at Bic (the inaction of which caused surprise) formed only the van squadron, under Admiral Durell, despatched from Louisbourg, to intercept and take vessels that might be sent from France. A powerful armament, under Admiral Saunders, sailed from England in February, to take on board, at Louisbourg, Wolfe's corps and transport the men to Quebec. But Saunders, finding the shores of Cape Breton clogged with ice, repaired to Halifax till the obstruction should clear itself. When Louisbourg *har-*

* The house stood on the spot where a dwelling has since been built on the *Jesuit's* Farm at Beauport, close to the Temperance Monument.

bour became accessible, Wolfe* there embarked with eight regiments of the line, two battalions of Royal American fusileers, three companies of Louisbourg grenadiers, three companies of rangers, an engineer corps, 1,000 royal marines; in all nearly 11,000 men."

We shall now lay before the reader a version of the Canadian events of 1759, which, from the high position of the writer as a historian, the care taken by him in 1837 to investigate the *local*, when on a visit to Quebec, and the no less important fact that his nationality is neither French nor English, ought to be impartial—we allude to that contained in George Bancroft's *History of the United States*:—

"As soon as the floating masses of ice permitted, the forces for the expedition against Quebec had repaired to Louisbourg; and already Wolfe, by his activity and zeal, his good judgment, and the clearness of his orders, inspired unbounded confidence. His army consisted of eight regiments, two battalions of Royal Americans, three companies of rangers, artillery, and a brigade of engineers,—in all, about eight thousand men; the fleet under Saunders had two-and-twenty ships of the line, and as many frigates and armed vessels. On board of one of the ships was Jervis, afterwards Earl St. Vincent; another, which followed, bore, as master, James Cook, the navigator, who was destined to explore and reveal the unknown paths and thousand isles of the Pacific. The brigades had for their commanders the brave, open-hearted, and liberal Robert Monckton, afterwards governor of New York, and conqueror of Martinico; George Townshend, elder brother of Charles Townshend, soon to succeed his father in the peerage, and become known as a legislator for America, a man of quick perception, but unsafe judgment; and the rash and inconsiderate James Murray. For his adjutant-general, Wolfe selected Isaac Barre, an old associate at Louisbourg; an Irishman of humble birth, eloquent, ambitious, and fearless. The grenadiers of the army were formed into a corps, commanded by Colonel Guy Carleton; a detachment of light infantry were to receive orders from Lieutenant-Colonel, afterwards Sir William Howe.

"On the 26th of June, the whole armament arrived, without the least accident, off the isle of Orleans, on which, the next day, they disembarked. A little south of west the cliff of Quebec was seen distinctly, seemingly

* Wolfe did not take ship at Louisburg, but at Portsmouth; having returned to England immediately after the capture of the former place.—*B.*

impregnable, rising precipitously in the midst of one of the grandest scenes in nature. To protect this guardian citadel of New France, Montcalm had of regular troops no more than six wasted battalions; of Indian warriors few appeared, the wary savages preferring the security of neutrals; the Canadian militia gave him the superiority in numbers; but he put his chief confidence in the natural strength of the country. Above Quebec, the high promontory on which the upper town is built expands into an elevated plain, having towards the river the steepest acclivities. For nine miles or more above the city, as far as Cape Rouge, every landing-place was entrenched and protected. The river St. Charles, after meandering through a vertile valley, sweeps the rocky base of the town, which it covers by expanding into sedgy marshes. Nine miles below Quebec, the impetuous Montmorenci, after fretting itself a whirlpool route, and leaping for miles down the steps of a rocky bed, rushes with velocity towards the ledge, over which, falling two hundred and fifty feet, it pours its fleecy cataract into the chasm.

"As Wolfe disembarked on the isle of Orleans, what scene could be more imposing? On his left lay at anchor the fleet, with the numerous transports; the tents of his army stretched across the island; the entrenched troops of France, having their centre as the village of Beauport, extended from the Montmorenci to the St. Charles; the city of Quebec, garrisoned by five battalions, bounded the horizon. At midnight on the 28th, the short darkness was lighted up by a fleet of fire-ships, that, after a furious storm of wind, came down with the tide in the proper direction. But the British sailors grappled with them, and towed them free of the shipping.

"The river was Wolfe's; the men-of-war made it so; and, being master of the deep water, he also had the superiority on the south shore of the St. Lawrence. In the night of the 29th, Monckton, with four battalions, having crossed the south channel, occupied Point Levi; and where the mighty current, which, below the town, expands as a bay, narrows to a deep stream of but a mile width, batteries of mortar and cannon were constructed. The citizens of Quebec, foreseeing the ruin of their houses, volunteered to pass over the river and destroy the works; but, at the trial, their courage failed them, and they retreated. The English, by the discharge, of red-shot balls and shells, set on fire fifty houses in a night, demolished the lower town, and injured the upper. But the citadel was beyond their reach, and every avenue from the river to the cliff was too strongly entrenched for an assault.

"As yet no real progress had been made. Wolfe was eager for battle; being willing to risk all his hopes on the issue. He saw that the eastern bank of the Montmorenci was higher than the ground occupied by Montcalm, and, on the 9th of July, he crossed the north channel and encamped there; but the armies and their chiefs were still divided by the river precipitating itself down its rocky way in impassable eddies and rapids. Three miles in the interior, a ford was found; but the opposite bank was steep, woody, and well entrenched. Not a spot on the line of the Montmorenci, for miles into the interior, nor on the St. Lawrence to Quebec, was left unprotected by the vigilance of the inaccessible Montcalm.

"The General proceeded to reconnoitre the shore above the town. In concert with Saunders, on the 18th of July, he sailed along the well-defended bank from Montmorenci to the St. Charles; he passed the deep and spacious harbour, which, at four hundred miles from the sea, can shelter a hundred ships of the line; he neared the high cliff of Cape Diamond, towering like a bastion over the waters, and surmounted by the banner of the Bourbons; he coasted along the craggy wall of rock that extends beyond the citadel; he marked the outline of the precipitous hill that forms the north bank of the river,—and everywhere he beheld a natural fastness, vigilantly defended, entrenchments, cannon, boats, and floating batteries guarding every access. Had a detachment landed between the city and Cape Rouge, it would have encountered the danger of being cut off before it could receive support. He would have risked a landing at St. Michael's Cove, three miles above the city, but the enemy prevented him by planting artillery and a mortar to play upon the shipping.

"Meantime, at midnight, on the 28th of the July, the French sent down a raft of fire-stages, consisting of nearly a hundred pieces; but these, like the fire-ships a month before, did but light up the river, without injuring the British fleet. Scarcely a day passed but there were skirmishes of the English with the Indians and Canadians, who were sure to tread stealthily in the footsteps of every exploring party.

"Wolfe returned to Montmorenci. July was almost gone, and he had made no effective advances. He resolved on an engagement. The Montmorenci, after falling over a perpendicular rock, flows for three hundred yards, amidst clouds of spray and rainbow glories, in a gentle stream to the St. Lawrence. Near the junction, the river may, for a few hours of the tide, be passed on foot. It was planned that two brigades should ford the Montmorenci at the proper time of the tide, while Monckton's regiments should cross the St. Lawrence in boats from Point Levi. The signal was made, but some of the boats grounded an a ledge of rocks that runs out into the river. While the seamen were getting them off, and the enemy were firing a vast number of shot and shell, Wolfe, with some of the navy officers as companions, selected a landing-place; and his desperate courage thought it not yet too late to begin the attack. Thirteen companies of grenadiers, and two hundred of the second battalion of the Royal Americans, who got first on shore, not waiting for support, ran hastily towards the entrenchments, and were repulsed in such disorder, that they could not again come into line, though Monckton's regiments had arrived, and had formed with the coolness of invincible valour. But hours hurried by; night was near; the clouds of midsummer gathered heavily, as if for a storm; the tide rose; and Wolfe, wiser than Frederic at Colin, ordered a timely retreat. A strand of deep mud, a hill-side, steep, and in many places impracticable, the heavy fire of a brave, numerous, and well-protected enemy, were obstacles which intrepidity and discipline could not overcome. In general orders, Wolfe censured the impetuosity of the grenadiers, he praised the coolness of Monckton's regiments, as able alone to beat back the whole Canadian army.

"This severe check, in which four hundred lives were lost, happened on the last day of July. Murray was next sent, with twelve hundred men, above the town, to destroy the French ships and open a communication with Amherst. Twice he attempted a landing on the north shore without success; at Deschambault, a place of refuge for women and children, he won advantages over a guard of invalid soldiers, and learned that Niagara had surrendered; that the French had abandoned Ticonderoga and Crown Point. The eyes of Wolfe were strained to see Amherst approach. Vain hope! The Commander-in-Chief, though opposed by no more than three thousand men, was loitering at Crown Point; nor did even a messenger from him arrive. Wolfe was alone to struggle with difficulties which every hour made more appalling. The numerous body of armed men under Montcalm 'could not,' he said, 'be called an army;' but the French had the strongest country, perhaps, in the world, on which to rest the defence of the town. Their boats were numerous, and weak points were guarded by floating batteries. The keen eye of the Indian prevented surprise. The vigilance and hardihood of the Canadians made entrenchments everywhere necessary. The peasantry were zealous to defend their homes, language and religion. Old men of seventy and boys of fifteen fired at the English detachments from the edges of the wood. Every one able to bear arms was in the field. Little quarter was given on either side. Thus for two months the British fleet had ridden idly at anchor; the army had lain in their tents. The feeble frame of Wolfe sunk under the energy of his restless spirit, and the pain of anxious inactivity.

"Yet, while disabled by fever, he laid before the brigadiers three several and equally desperate methods of attacking Montcalm in his entrenchments at Beauport. Meeting at Monckton's quarters, they wisely and unanimously gave their opinions against them all, and advised to convey four or five thousand men above the town, and thus draw Montcalm from his impregnable situation to an open action. Wolfe acquiesced in their proposal, and, with despair in his heart, yet as one conscious that he lived under the eye of Pitt and of his country, he prepared to carry it into effect. Attended by the Admiral, he examined once more the citadel, with a view to a general assault. Although every one of the five passages from the lower to the upper town was carefully entrenched, Saunders was willing to join in any hazard for the public service; 'but I could not propose to him,' said Wolfe, 'an undertaking of so dangerous a nature and promising so little success.' He had the whole force of Canada to oppose, and, by the nature of the river, the fleet could render no assistance. 'In this situation,' wrote Wolfe to Pitt, on the 2nd of September, 'there is such a choice of difficulties, that I am myself at a loss how to determine. The affairs of Great Britain require most vigorous measures; but then the courage of a handful of brave men should be exerted only where there is some hope.' England read the despatch with dismay, and feared to hear further tidings.

"Securing the posts on the Isle of Orleans and opposite Quebec, he marched, with the army, on the 5th and 6th of September, from Point Levi, to which place he had transferred all the troops from Montmorenci, and embarked them in transports that had passed the town for the purpose. On the three following days, Admiral Holmes, with the ships, ascended the river to amuse Bougainville, who had been sent up the north shore to watch the movements of the British army, and prevent a landing. New France began to feel a sentiment of joy, believing the worst dangers of the campaign over. De Levi, the second officer in command, was sent to protect Montreal with a detachment, it was said, of three thousand men. Summer, which in that climate hurries through the sky, was over; and the British fleet must soon withdraw from the river. 'My constitution,' wrote the general to Holdernesse on the 9th, just four days before his death, 'is entirely ruined, without the consolation of having done any considerable service to the state, and without any prospect of it.'

"But, in the mean time, Wolfe applied himself intently to reconnoitring the north shore above Quebec. Nature had given him good eyes, as well as a warmth of temper to follow first impressions.* He himself discovered the cove which now bears his name, where the bending promontories almost form a basin with a very narrow margin, over which the hill rises precipitously. He saw the path that wound up the steep, though so narrow that two men could hardly march in it abreast; † and he knew, by the number of tents which he counted on the summit, that the Canadian post (De Vergor's) which guarded it could not exceed a hundred. Here he resolved to land his army by surprise. To mislead the enemy, his troops were kept far above the town, while Saunders, as if an attack was intended at Beauport, set Cook, the great mariner, with others, to sound the water and plant buoys along that shore.

"The day and night of the 12th were employed in preparations. The autumn evening was bright; and the General, under the clear starlight, visited his stations, to make his final inspection, and utter his last words of encouragement. As he passed from ship to ship, he spoke to those in the boat with him of the poet Gray, and the elegy in a country churchyard. 'I,' said he, 'would prefer being the author of that poem to the glory of beating the French to-morrow;'‡ and while the oars struck the

* Wolfe to Wm. Rickson, 1st Dec., 1758.

† Vice Admiral Saunders to Secretary Pitt, 20th Sept., 1759.

‡ I owe my knowledge of this incident to Dr. J. C. Fisher of Quebec, to whose personal kindness I am indebted for explanations given me on the battle-ground itself. The *Picture of Quebec*, published by Hawkins, in 1834, is indebted to him for its historical value. (Bancroft.)

river as it rippled in the silence of the night air under the flowing tide, he repeated :

> 'The boast of heraldry, the pomp of power,
> And all that beauty, all that wealth e'er gave,
> Await alike the inexorable hour;
> The paths of glory lead but to the grave.'

"Every officer knew his appointed duty, when, at one o'clock in the morning of the 13th of September, Wolfe, with Monckton and Murray, and about half the forces, set off in boats, and, without sail or oars, glided down with the tide. In three quarters of an hour the ships followed, and, though the night had become dark, aided by the rapid current, they reached the cove just in time to cover the landing. Wolfe and the troops with him leaped on shore; the light infantry, who found themselves borne by the current a little below the entrenched path, clambered up the steep hill, staying themselves by the roots and boughs of the maple, and spruce, and ash trees that covered the precipitous declivity, and, after a little firing, dispersed the picket which guarded the height. The rest ascended safely by the pathway. A battery of four guns on the left was abandoned to Colonel Howe. When Townshend's division disembarked, the English had already gained one of the roads to Quebec, and, advancing in front of the forest, Wolfe stood at daybreak with his invincible battalions on the Plains of Abraham, the battle-field of empire.

"'It can be but a small party, come to burn a few houses and retire,' said Montcalm, in amazement, as the news reached him in his entrenchments the other side of the St. Charles; but, obtaining better information.—'Then,' he cried, 'they have at last got to the weak side of this miserable garrison : we must give battle, and crush them before mid-day.' And before ten the two armies, equal in numbers, each being composed of less than five thousand men, were ranged in presence of one another for battle. The English, not easily accessible from intervening shallow ravines and rail fences, were all regulars, perfect in discipline, terrible in their fearless enthusiasm, thrilling with pride at their morning's success, commanded by a man whom they obeyed with confidence and love. The doomed and devoted Montcalm had what Wolfe had called but 'five weak French battalions,' of less than two thousand men, 'mingled with disorderly peasantry,'* formed on ground which commanded the position of the English. The French had three little pieces of artillery; the English one or two. The two armies cannonaded each other for nearly an hour; when Montcalm, having summoned Bougainville to his aid, and despatched messenger after messenger for De Vaudreuil, who had fifteen hundred men at the camp, to come up, before he should be driven from the ground, endeavored to flank the British, and crowd them down the high bank of the river. Wolfe counteracted the movement by detaching Townshend with Amherst's regiment, and afterwards a part of the Royal Americans, who formed on the left with a double front.

"Waiting no longer for more troops, Montcalm led the French army impetuously to the attack. The ill-disciplined companies broke by their precipitation and the unevenness of the ground, and fired by platoons, without unity. The English, especially the forty-third and forty-seventh, where Monckton stood, received the shock with calmness; and after having, at Wolfe's command, reserved their fire till their enemy was within forty yards, their line began a regular, rapid, and exact discharge of musketry. Montcalm was present everywhere, braving danger, wounded, but cheering by his example. The second in command, De Sennezergues, an associate in glory at Ticonderoga, was killed. The brave but untried Canadians, flinching from a hot fire in the open field, began to waver; and so soon as Wolfe, placing himself at the head of the twenty-eighth and the Louisbourg grenadiers, charged with bayonets, they everywhere gave way. Of the English officers, Carleton was wounded; Barre, who fought near Wolfe, received in the head a ball, which destroyed the power of vision of one eye, and ultimately made him blind. Wolfe, also, as he led the charge, was wounded in the wrist, but still pressing forward, he received a second ball; and, having decided the day, was struck a third time, and mortally, in the breast. 'Support me,' he cried to an officer near him; 'let not

* Three several French accounts represent Montcalm's forces in the battle as only equal, or even inferior, to the British. Jugement Impartial sur les Opérations Militaires de la Campagne en Canada en 1759, 5, printed at Quebec in 1840. Compare, also, in the New York Paris Papers, Extrait d'un Journal, tenu à l'Armée, &c., and the letter of Bigot to the Minister, of October 25, 1759. Knox, in Journal, i. 74, which seems to be followed in the *New Picture of Quebec*, 345, makes the number of Canadian militia in the battle 5,000. But Bougainville had 2,000 up the river; 1,500 remained at the camp with Vaudreuil; De Levi had also been sent with a detachment to assist in opposing Amherst. There were not Indians enough with the French to be of moment. In the summer of 1837, I examined the country round Quebec. (Bancroft.)

my brave fellows see me drop.' He was carried to the rear, and they brought him water to quench his thirst. 'They run, they run,' spoke the officer on whom he leaned. 'Who run?' asked Wolfe, as his life was fast ebbing. 'The French,' replied the officer, 'give way everywhere.' 'What,' cried the expiring hero, 'do they run already? Go, one of you, to Colonel Burton; bid him march Webb's regiment with all speed to Charles River to cut off the fugitives.' Four days before, he had looked forward to early death with dismay. 'Now, God be praised, I die happy.' These were his words as his spirit escaped in the blaze of his glory. Night, silence, the rushing tide, veteran discipline, the sure inspiration of genius, had been his allies; his battle-field, high over the ocean-river, was the grandest theatre on earth for illustrious deeds; his victory, one of the most momentous in the annals of mankind, gave to the English tongue, and the institutions of the Germanic race, the unexplored and seemingly infinite West and North. He crowded into a few hours actions that would have given lustre to length of life; and filling his day with greatness, completed it before its noon.

"Monckton, the first brigadier, after greatly distinguishing himself, was shot through the lungs. The next in command, Townshend, brave, but deficient in sagacity and attractive power, and the delicate perception of right, recalled the troops from the pursuit; and when De Bougainville appeared in view, declined a contest with a fresh enemy. But already the hope of New France was gone.* Born and educated in camps, Montcalm

* The incidents of the battle are thus related by a Scotch Jacobite, aide-de-camp to general Levi, Chevalier Johnstone, whose chequered career in Canada, is thus alluded to in Francisque Michel's work: "*Les Ecossais en France*", Par un des articles de la paix, Louis XV s'obligeait à éloigner les Stuarts de ses états; le difficile était de décider Charles Edouard à quitter la France. Il fallut le faire arrêter, et ses gentilshommes, comme Sir John Graeme, Oxburgh, George Kelly, furent mis à la Bastille. Un seul eut la permission de lui tenir compagnie à Vincennes: c'était Macdonald MacEachen, ce fidèle compagnon qui lui donné autrefois le Laird de Clonronald et qui avait depuis renoncé à l'Ecosse pour la France. Le chevalier de Johnstone, qui en avait fait autant, ayant demandé à être replacé sur la liste des officiers de la suite de Charles Edouard qui recevaient des secours du roi de France s'était vu forcé d'accepter une commission d'enseigne dans un détachement d'infanterie de marine destiné pour le Cap-Breton. Il s'embarqua à Rochefort avec le chevalier de Montalembert et le chevalier de Trion, son cousin, officiers à demi-solde qui avaient aussi obtenu de l'emploi à Québec, et là il mena une vie semée de vicissitudes jusqu'à son retour définitif en France, au commencement de décembre 1760." "*Les Ecossais en France*"—Francisque Michel—Vol. II p. 442.

A singular ccincidence and one we have not seen noticed by any of our historians, is the fact of several Scotchmen after the battle of Culloden, joining the French regiments intended for Louisbourg and Canada; we find in the regiment of Languedoc an other Scotchman, "Monsieur Duglas" in charge of one of the Sillery outposts: this is evi-

had been carefully instructed, and was skilled in the language of Homer as well as in the art of war. Greatly laborious, just, disinterested, hopeful, even to rashness, sagacious in council, swift in action, his mind was a well-spring of bold designs; his career in Canada a wonderful struggle against inexorable destiny. Sustaining hunger and cold, vigils and incessant toil, anxious for his soldiers, unmindful of himself, he set, even to the forest-trained red men, an example of self-denial and endurance; and in the midst of corruption made the public good his aim. Struck by a musket-ball, as he fought opposite Monckton, he continued in the engagement, till, in attempting to rally a body of fugitive Canadian in a copse near St. John's gate, † he was mortally wounded.

"On hearing from the surgeon that death was certain, 'I am glad of it,' he cried; 'how long shall I survive?' 'Ten or twelve hours, perhaps less.' 'So much the better; I shall not live to see the surrender of Quebec.' To the council of war he showed that in twelve hours all the troops near at hand might be concentrated, and renew the attack before the English were entrenched. When De Ramsay, who commanded the garrison, asked his advice about defending the city, 'To your keeping,' he replied, 'I commend the honor of France. As for me, I shall pass the night with

---

dently an abbreviation for Douglas. Chevalier Johnstone's statement is curious and does not reflect much credit on the conduct of the French regulars, though he speaks highly of the Canadian militia and volunteers :—

"Our onset was neither brisk nor long. We went on in confusion, were repulsed in an instant, and it could not naturally be otherwise from the absence of our volunteers and grenadiers, and Bougainville at Cap Rouge with the best of our Canadians, the Montreal regiments with Poularies at Beauport, a league and a half from the battle-field. The example of the bravest soldiers in a regiment—the grenadiers and volunteers—suffice to infuse courage in the most timid, who can follow the road shown to them, but cannot lead the way. The brave Canadian militia, saw us with heavy hearts, grief and despair from the other side of the St. Charles river, cut to pieces upon the heights, stopped as they were in the hornwork and prevented by superior orders from rushing to our assistance. About two hundred brave and resolute Canadians rallied in the hollow at the bakehouse and returned upon the heights like lions. They fell instantly upon your left wing with incredible rage, stopped your army for some minutes from pursuing our soldiers in their flight, by attracting your attention to them, resisted undaunted the shock of your left, and when repulsed they disputed the ground mile by mile from the top to the bottom of the height pursued by your troops down the valley at the bakehouse opposite the hornwork. These unfortunate heroes who were most of them cut to pieces, saved your army the loss of a great many men, by not being hotly pursued, and if your left, who followed these two hundred Canadians down to the plain, had crossed it from the bakehouse to the river St. Charles, only three or four hundred paces, they would have cut off the retreat of our army, invested the three-fourths of them in Quebec without provisions, and M. Vaudreuil next day must have surrendered the town and asked to capitulate for the colony. But your conduct cannot be blamed, as it is always wise and prudent in giving, as Pyrrhus advises—a golden bridge to one's enemy in flight."

† Bigot to the Minister, 25th October, 1759. N. Y. Paris Documents, vi. 39.

God, and prepare myself for death.' Having written a letter recommending the French prisoners to the generosity of the English, his last hours were given to the hope of endless life, and at five the next morning he expired.

"The day of the battle had not passed, when De Vaudreuil, who had no capacity for war, wrote to De Ramsay at Quebec not to wait for an assault, but as soon as his provisions were exhausted, to raise the white flag of surrender.* 'We have cheerfully sacrificed our fortunes and our houses,' said the citizens; 'but we cannot expose our wives and children to a massacre.'† At a council of war, Fiedmont, a captain of artillery, was the only one who wished to hold out‡ to the last extremity; and on the 17th of September, before the English had constructed batteries, De Ramsay capitulated.

"America rung with exultation; the towns were bright with illuminations, the hills with bonfires; legislatures, the pulpit, the press, echoed the general joy; provinces and families gave thanks to God. England, too, which had shared the despondency of Wolfe, triumphed at his victory, and wept for his death. Joy, grief, curiosity, amazement, were on every countenance.|| When the parliament assembled, Pitt modestly and gracefully put aside the praises that were showered on him. 'The more a man is versed in business,' said he, 'the more he finds the hand of Providence everywhere.' 'I will own I have a zeal to serve my country beyond what the weakness of my frail body admits of;'§ and he foretold new successes at sea. November fulfilled his predictions. In that month, Sir Edward Hawke attacked the fleet of Conflans off the northern coast of France, and, though it retired to the shelter of shoals and rocks, he gained the battle during a storm at nightfall."

---

* Vaudreuil to De Ramsay, 13th Sept., 1759. N. Y. Paris Documents, xvi. 27.

† Relation du Siège de Québec.

‡ Procès Verbal du Conseil de Guerre, 15th September, 1759. N.Y. Paris Documents, xvi. 28, and other papers on the subject in the same volume.

|| Walpole's Memoirs of the Reign of Geo. II.

§ Report of the speech by Jared Ingersoll of Connecticut, in a letter dated 22nd December, 1759.

Frontispiece.

PLAN OF SIEGE OPERATIONS AND RIVER ST. LAWRENCE, DRAWN IN 1759 BY AN ENGLISH NAVAL OFFICER.

THIS plan shows distinctly the extensive entrenchments, redouts and earth-works at Beauport, from the bridge of boats on the St. Charles to the Montmorenci Falls. The bridge of boats was in a line with the earth-work at Ringfield on the Charlesbourg road. This earth-work is well exhibited on the plan, and from the Chevalier Johnstone's Diary, and an examination of the *local*, it is easy to understand all about it. Over what in those days was called the " Ravine at Beauport," a solid bridge, supported by masonry, at Brown's Mills, has since been built. The Rivière Larrey or Lairet is also well designated, likewise the vast front of the French army, extending from the heights in the neighborhood of the New Jail, down to the General Hospital. General Wolfe's camp at Ange Gardien is clearly depicted; the two hulls mounted with cannon in the St. Charles, which stopped the pursuit of the French, the boom of masts thrown over that river, where an old stone jettee had been constructed in 1720, to protect ships, in a line with the present Gas Works, all these objects can be taken in at one glance in this excellent drawing.

The small plan of the Battle of the Plains in the corner of the large one discloses the position of the two armies: near the brow of the hill the Colonial troops; then the famous Royal Roussillon regiment, commanded by Col. Poularies; next the regiments of Bearn, Languedoc, La Sarre; then came Colonials; then the Burghers of Quebec to the north-west; the Indians last; the thickets of course occupied by Canadian sharp-shooters—the whole formed *en potence*. The English regiments face towards them on a much less extended and stronger line: Otway's regiment first; the Louisbourg Grenadiers, Bragg's, Lascelles', Highlanders and Ansthruther's regiment, under Murray; Royal Americans and Light Infantry, under Amherst and Townshend. The old Sillery Chapel is visible to the west, leaving one to infer that the plan was taken somewhere from the ships at Sillery.

A Representative Man.—1758.

M. Luc de LaCorne Saint Luc.

IF there be an era in the primitive times of Canada, in which the martial spirit of its inhabitants shone forth more brightly than at others, of a verity it is that war-like period which immediately preceded the cession of the country by the French Crown, known to our historians as the "seven years' war." Nowhere in the annals or records of the past, did the Canadian militia and volunteers exhibit greater endurance,—more perseverance,—more stout and successful resistance on many a hard-fought battle field; though after all, it must have mattered little what the French commanders did achieve, having at their disposal merely a handful of regulars, aided by the militia of the country and their Indian allies. France also had in those days its Goldwin Smiths: the colony was voted a bore; and niggardly reinforcements sent out when the whim of the moment prompted—perhaps not at all. Pitt had vowed to plant the flag of England on the summit of Cape Diamond. A gigantic army for those times, 50,000 men—including regulars, New England militia and savages—were to invade Canada at three points: the St. Lawrence,—the lakes,—the interior, under the guidance of Wolfe, Amherst, Haviland, Johnston. Ardent admirers of General Levi, the victor of Murray, have ventured to assert that had this general, who had never suffered defeat, been present at the first battle of the Plains of Abraham, the fate of the colony would have been different; however great the military genius of the hero of St. Foy may have been, at best, he could in the face of the overwhelming forces sent merely have retarded the fall. At the time we allude to (1758), with much larger armies in the field, a new system of warfare had, to a certain extent, superseded the old desultory mode of attack; the midnight raid and murderous assault of former times—with Indian allies as guides and sharp-shooters—still continued for both combatants to be a military necessity in bush fighting; but the large armies of Europeans, to whom the savages acted as pioneers and auxiliaries, in a measure served as a check on the atrocious and peculiar system of fighting of the latter, although a memorable exception to the rule occurred in the Fort George tragedy; this outrage however was chiefly traceable to the effects of the ardent spirits purloined by the redskins from the English camp. Could we reasonably hold European commanders—English as well as French—responsible for the nameless horrors perpetrated on our soil by their Indian allies, one would be apt to believe our European forefathers had left their humanity at home to act the savage on our shores. Take for instance the great Lachine massacre. On the 25th April, 1689, during a profound peace, 1500 savages stealthily surround, before day-break, the habitations at Lachine, nine miles from Montreal; the unsuspecting inmates are soon secured, slaughtered in a few minutes; a lurid conflagration alone marks the spot where once stood a smiling, happy village—men, women and children are sacrificed indiscriminately. Some are burnt, others, disembowelled; mothers made to hold their live infants over the fire and turn the spit; everywhere groans, tortures, despair. Two hundred victims butchered in cold blood, and all this accomplished in less than an hour. "Ils poussèrent, dit Charlevoix, la fureur même à des excès dont on ne les avait pas cru capables. Ils ouvraient le sein des femmes enceintes, pour arracher le fruit qu'elles portaient; ils mirent des enfants tous vivans à la broche et contraignirent les mères de les tourner pour les faire rôtir. Ils inventèrent quantités d'autres supplices inouïs et deux cents personnes de tout âge et de tout sexe périrent ainsi en moins d'une heure dans les plus affreux tourments."

These scenes, Charlevoix relates, were repeated within one league of the city, and only when these infuriated demons were satiated with human gore, did they retire with two hundred prisoners whom they afterwards burnt. The island of Montreal remained in their possession until the fall following. In October, an Indian ally of the French, whom they had tortured and hacked, escaped and apprised the French that the Indians intended returning in the winter to have a repetition of these sickening horrors at the town of Three Rivers, after which Quebec was to be visited on the same errand; that when they would have extirpated the French settlers to the last man, they would meet in the following spring an English fleet at Quebec (no doubt Phipps' ships which did appear before

Quebec in October, 1690). Providence frustrated their dire designs. Of course, such doings were not confined to the allies of the New-Englanders. The savages in league with the French carried fire and the sword amidst the peaceful dwellers of the adjoining English provinces; Schenectady as well as Lachine has its bloody records. Our early history teems with such incidents. Happily the extension of the colony in 1758, and the rapidly-increasing power of the whites was calculated to render these scenes less frequent.

Apart from the several European commanders who acquired fame during the seven years' war, some of the settlers or *habitants** of Canada became famous in battle. It is one of the most remarkable soldiers of that day we purpose sketching here—Mons. Luc De LaCorne Saint Luc, previously introduced to our notice in Mr. De Gaspé's book, *The Canadians of Old*, and in the *Maple Leaves*, as one of the few survivors in the shipwreck of the *Auguste*, in 1761, on its voyage to France with the French refugees. The career of De LaCorne also commends itself to our attention from its analogy to that of other Canadians of later days: he fought as bravely under the flag of St. George, when it became that of his country, as he had done previously when the lily-spangled banner of the French monarch waived over the home of his youth. Being no utopian, LaCorne cheerfully accepted the new *regime* under which his hitherto distracted country was destined to enjoy peace, liberty and prosperity. Being a man of mark, talent and courage, high civil and military honors were soon within his reach. We purpose in this paper viewing the Chevalier De LaCorne as the type of the *Canadians of Old*, the representative man of that thrilling era of 1758—Carillon and its glories—when every Canadian peasant was a soldier, and when the parishes were so drained of their able-bodied men that the duties of husbandry devolved *entirely on the women and children.* History makes mention of two LaCornes. De LaCorne La Colombière, who commanded in Acadia, and fought with success against the English in 1756—he returned to France at the time of the conquest and became the friend and companion of the famous naval commander, De Suffren, in his sea voyages. The other, the subject of this notice, LaCorne de Saint Luc, a "Chevalier de Saint Louis," was a most influ-

**Habitants*: here is a word whose meaning has been singularly perverted. *Habitant* meant formerly the permanent settler, who came to *habiter le pays*, in contradistinction to the military and civil functionaries who were transient. The richest merchant might be a *habitant*: that is a permanent resident.

ential personage both amongst the Canadians and amongst the Indian tribes, under French and under English rule; one of his first feats was the capture of Fort Clinton in 1747. He also, at the head of the Canadians and Indians, distinguished himself at the battle of Carillon (Ticonderoga), in 1758, where Abercrombie was defeated by Montcalm and Lévis; LaCorne captured from the English general one hundred and fifty waggons of war stores. After serving through the hard-fought engagements of the campaign, we find him subsequently at the Battle of the Plains of Abraham; we thence follow him to Montreal, and see him under General Lévis at the head of his old friends, the Canadians and the Indians; in April following he was wounded at Murray's defeat on the St. Foy heights, and took a prominent part in the last victory of the French in Canada—a battle which permitted them, on leaving the country, to shake hands with their brave antagonists, the English.* In 1761 he decided to return with his brother, his children and nephews to France, and, having *plenty* of ready money (some £6,000), he was on the eve of purchasing a vessel at Quebec in September of that year for that purpose, when the generosity of General Murray made this unnecessary, and the *Auguste* was fitted up at Government expense. In this ill-starred ship, LaCorne and one hundred and twenty of the chief persons in the colony, including several ladies, officers and soldiers, sailed on the 17th October, 1761. The chevalier has left a Journal or Diary, kept by himself, of the appalling disaster which befel the *Auguste* on the coast of Cape Breton, where the ship was stranded on the 15th November, 1761. This narrative,† which has recently been published, is affecting from its truthfulness and simplicity; no boasting, no flourishes of rhetoric in this short record of death and human suffering. On reading of the seven survivors,—out of one hundred and twenty-one souls,—slowly wending their way over the foggy and snow-clad sea shore of *Isle Royale*, occasionally one dropping down benumbed, fatigued and exhausted, to sleep the long sleep of death, one is reminded of another gallant band who nearly a century

* How singular are the fortunes of war! Wolfe, Amherst, and several other English officers, who, under the "butcher" Cumberland and under Ligonier had been disastrously defeated by Marshal Saxe, at Fontenoy and Laufeldt, met on the Plains of Abraham their old rivals, with Scotch Jacobites fighting on both sides. A few months later and the second battle of the Plains—a brilliant though bootless victory—again asserted the martial qualities of the French legions.—(J. M. L.)

† Journal du Naufrage de l'*Auguste* par M. Luc De LaCorne Saint Luc en 1761—Coté et Cie, Québec.

later on, a few degrees closer to the pole, could be seen equally forlorn; they too dropped down and died as they walked along the ice-clad strand; "some were buried and some were not," as the old Esquimaux woman stated to McClintock's party—the latter was Sir John Franklin's devoted but despairing followers. We shall condense LaCorne's narrative of the shipwreck. The ship struck on the 15th November; LaCorne and his six surviving companions, including the captain, were washed ashore in a boat, more dead than alive; the 16th was employed in digging graves; none of his children, none of the ladies had been saved; the young, the fair, the high-born strewing in hideous confusion a rock-bound coast amidst fragments of the wreck,—in all one hundred and fourteen corpses. Such were the dismal objects which met the gaze of LaCorne and of his fellow-sufferers on the morning of the 16th November. Amidst the roar of the sea and of the tempest the last rites were performed by the sorrowing parent; and on the 17th, with a common feeling, all hurried from a spot in which everything reminded them of death, "*plurima mortis imago,*" and took to the woods, not knowing where they were; on the 17th a snow storm added to their misery; three of the party here gave out through fatigue, but LaCorne, who all along appears as the leading spirit, urged them on, and with success; on the 25th the Journal mentions, as a godsend, the discovery of some deserted huts;—in them they found two dead men; on the 26th two more of the party gave out, and were reluctantly left behind with some provisions. Twelve inches of snow had fallen that day.

On the 3rd December, after a tedious tramp through the forest, not knowing where they were, they struck on the sea coast and discovered an old boat, unseaworthy; the captain of the *Auguste* set to work to caulk her, and matters seemed likely to assume a more hopeful aspect, when a fresh snow-storm nearly caused the destruction of the whole party. "Our provisions running short," adds LaCorne, "we had to live on wild berries and sea-weed. On the 4th the storm having abated, we found our boat imbeded in the snow, but when we came to launch her, our captain, who until then had held out, declared he could go no further on account of the pains and ulcers he labored under; the three others mostly as bad, sided with him, and being alone, I was compelled, although suffering much less, to remain with them. I did not like to desert them, and we trusted to Providence, when two Indians made their appearance. Our men hailed them with loud cries and lamentations; in which I could catch the words 'have mercy on us.' I was then smoking, a quiet spectator of this sorrowful scene. Our men mentioned my name, and the Indians greeted me warmly. I had on several occasions rendered service to these tribes. I learned that we were ninety miles from Louisbourg (Cape Breton). They told me they were ready to conduct me to St. Pierre. I had our men crossed over a river which was there, and left with the Indians, for their wig-wam about three leagues distant. They gave me dried meat, and on the 5th I returned to my friends."

Thence we follow the hardy adventurer to St. Pierre, to Labrador Bay, and finally we find him, in spite of all remonstrance, starting in a birch canoe, in that inclement season, with two young men whom he had tempted to this fool-hardy enterprise, by offering them twenty-five louis d'or: they afterwards landed at Cheda-Bouctou, and after encountering great privation, fatigue, and divers perilous adventures, he arrived at Fort Cumberland, when after a short rest he continued his journey on foot, having worn out his strength and his snow shoes. The Temiscouata portage brought him subsequently to the lower parishes, then to Kamouraska; and the night he spent at the Manor of St. Jean Port Joli is graphically described in the *Canadians of Old.* He arrived at Quebec on the 23rd February, laid an account of his shipwreck before General Murray, and left for Montreal to see General Gage. This man of iron winds up his Journal by stating that the fatigues, dangers and starvation he was exposed to were very great—that the circuitous road he followed led him to believe he must have walked at least 1650 miles in the severest season in the year, and unprovided with any succour. "I used to see my guides and companions, the Indians and Acadians, giving out after eight days' marching, and often less. During all this time, I enjoyed excellent health, had no dread of the consequences, and fortunately withstood so much fatigue; had I had guides as vigorous as myself, I would have saved one hundred and thirty pounds which it cost me, and I would have arrived earlier." General Jeff. Amherst, then at New York, wrote to the chevalier a feeling letter, dated 28th March, 1762, condoling with him on this melancholy shipwreck.

We have no hesitation in saying that this feat of human endurance, this journeying during a Canadian winter through forests,—over bays in a frail bark canoe and frozen snow on snow shoes, some seventeen hundred miles, is almost without a parallel in modern times, and that we would be very unwilling to accept it as the truth, were it less authentically recorded.

The loss of family and friends, as previously stated, seems to have changed entirely the future plans of the chevalier; he bid adieu to La Belle France, and made up his mind to live in Canada—a British subject. We fail for a few years to trace clearly what occupations were followed by this singularly hardy man; probably, with his compeers, the Rocheblaves, DeRouvilles, St. Ours, Deschambault, DeBellestre, De Lotbinière, he took part in politics. At the arrival of General Burgoyne, LaCorne again, although close on seventy years of age, headed the militia and the Indian tribes which Sir Guy Carleton sent to assist the newly-arrived general. LaCorne was present at several engagements during the war of independence, and probably would have rendered important services to the English general, but Burgoyne neither understood nor took any pains to understand the character of his Indian allies. Matters went on tolerably well so long as the English commander met with success, but with reverse, discontent got to such a pitch in a short time that the Indian tribes and the small number of Canadians soon absolutely refused to be led on by a general about as fit to handle this arm of the service as the Baron Dieskau had shown himself twenty years before. The disgraceful capitulation of the English army at Saratoga to General Gates was the crowning feat. In vain Burgoyne,* on his return to England, and from his seat in Parliament, supported by a host of powerful friends, tried to explain off the shame he had brought on his brave army by accusing others; his violent, artful charges called forth a spirited letter from the Chevalier LaCorne, which appeared at the time

*John Burgoyne, an English general officer and dramatist, connected with this country in the former capacity, was the natural son of Lord Bingley, and entered early in the army. In 1762 he commanded a force sent into Portugal for the defence of that kingdom against the Spaniards. He also distinguished himself in the first American war by the taking of Ticonderoga, but was at last obliged to surrender with his army to General Gates at Saratoga. For this act he was much censured and condemned by all the English people. He was elected into the English Parliament for Preston, in Lancashire, but refusing to return to America pursuant to his convention, was ignominiously dismissed the service. He endeavored to exonerate himself, but without avail, in some pamphlets he published in defence of his conduct. As an author, he is more distinguished for his three dramas of the *Maid of the Oaks*, *Bon Ton*, and *The Heiress*, all in the line of what is usually called genteel comedy, they forming light and pleasing specimens.—M. B. L.

in the English papers; it being, doubtless, new to many English readers, a translation of this letter from old memoirs may prove acceptable:—

LE CHEVALIER DE ST. LUC TO GENERAL BURGOYNE.

"QUEBEC, 23rd October, 1778.

"SIR—I cannot say whether this letter will reach you; if it should, it is written to express my surprise at your lack of memory concerning myself and also concerning my companions-in-arms, the Canadians and Indians.

"I am at a loss to guess your motive, unless it be to bury my name, with your own, in obscurity—an achievement beyond your power. I was known long before you had attained the position which furnished you the opportunity of ruining one of the finest armies which my country ever saw.

"You say, sir, that I was unable to afford you any information; I am glad you should be the means of informing the public that you never sought advice from me. Allow me, however, to tell you that I have served under general officers who honored me with their confidence; men worthy of the position,—able to maintain their dignity,—distinguished by their abilities.

"You also charge me with having withdrawn from the army. You will permit me to inform you, sir, that those who, like myself, left it, did not, more than you, dread the perils of war. Fifty years' service will dispose of this charge. You, sir, better than any, know who made me leave the army—it was yourself.

"The 16th August, 1777, the day of the Bennington affair, you sent me, through Major Campbell, an order to hold myself in readiness to start on the morning of the 17th with the Canadians and Indians, ahead of General Fraser's brigade, to post ourselves at Stillwater. But that same day M. de Lanaudière informed you of the defeat of Lieut.-Col. Baum's detachment, and of that of Lieut.-Col. Breyman, who had advanced to support the latter. He apprised you that these two detachments had lost at least seven hundred men. You appeared to put little faith in his statement, and you told me the loss did not amount to one hundred and fifty men, although the real figure showed that the first report was exact. Counter orders were then issued to the whole army which had intended to march on that day, and the next day we were made to cross North River, and, with General Fraser's brigade, to camp at

Battenkill. The Indians, startled by your grand manœuvres, to which they were not accustomed, had noticed that you had sent no force either to collect the remnants of the corps dispersed at Bennington (some of whom, to my knowledge, returned to your camp five days after), or to succour the wounded, of which a portion were dying. This conduct of yours, sir, did not convey a very high idea of the care you would take of those who might fight under you. The indifference you exhibited to the fate of the Indians concerned in the Bennington encounter, to the portion of one hundred and fifty, had disgusted them very much; a good number of them had fallen there together with their great chief, and out of the sixty-one Canadians forty-one only had escaped.

"Bear in mind, sir, so that you may not form an erroneous opinion of this matter, what passed in council, when you represented our loss as trifling. I told you, on behalf of the Indians, whose interpreter you had made me, that they were very deserving. They said many things which it would have been useless to repeat; amongst others, that they wished to speak their sentiments to you in plain terms. I warned you of what would be the final result. Finally, sir, their discontent became such that they left on the spot, although you refused to allow them provisions, shoes and an interpreter.

"Two days subsequently, you had seen your error; Brigadier Fraser had anticipated what would be the consequences of your acts towards the Indians. You then sent for me, and I had the honor to meet you in the tent of the brigadier, when you asked me to return to Canada, the bearer of despatches to General Carleton, to induce His Excellency to treat the Indians kindly and send them back to you. I did so, and I would have rejoined the army, if the communication had not been cut off. After that, of what use could I have been, I, whom you had represented as good for nothing, and as one of the Indians who had left the army. Ah! sir, having ceased to be a general, do not at least cease to be a gentleman! On the latter point I am your equal. You bear the rank of a general and I may not be your equal in talent, but I am your equal in birth, and claim to be treated as a gentleman.

"Be that as it may, sir, notwithstanding my advanced age (67 years), I am ready to cross the sea to justify myself before the King, my master, and before my country, of the unfounded charges you have heaped on me, but I am quite indifferent as to what you personally may think of me."

A Legislative Councillor of Canada, in 1784, we find this sturdy old soldier at the ripe age of 74, equally ready in camp and in council,—manfully battling for the right of his countrymen to enjoy all the privileges of British subjects, and siding against the old family compact,—remonstrating loudly but respectfully, and holding forth in the resolutions he proposed, in favor of the constitution of 1774. When the stern old Roman died does not appear; he seems to have attained a very great age.

In a measure, are we not justified of saying of him what Clarendon wrote of Hampden, "that he was of an industry and a vigilance not to be tired out or wearied by the most laborious, and of parts not to be imposed on by the most subtle and sharp,—of a personal courage equal to his best parts"?

Canadian Homes.---Canadian History.

Introduction.

> "Oh give me a home where the maple and pine
> Around the wild heights so majestically twine;
> Oh give me a home where the blue wave rolls free
> From thy bosom, Superior, down to the sea."

"COULD you not write the history of 'Our Parish,' and also sketch briefly our country seats, marking out the spots connected with historical events?" Thus discoursed one day to us, in her blandest tones, a fair denizen of Sillery. There, was a poser for a *galant homme*; a crusher, for the first *litterateur* of......the parish. That innate civility of a Frenchman, quicker than thought, elicited from us an unreflective affirmative reply. Thus, compassionate reader, was entrapped, caught and committed the first *litterateur* of Sillery—irrevocably handed over to the tender mercies of all the critics, present and future, in and out of the parish. Oh, my friends, what a crunching up of literary bones in store! what an ample repast was thus prepared for all the reviewers—the Jeffreys and LaHarpes—in and out of the parish, should the luckless *litterateur* fail to assign fairy scenery—important historical events—great battles, not only to each renowned spot, but even to the merest potatoe-patch, turnip-ground or cabbage-garden within our corporate limits? Yes, tremble for him.

Joking apart, is there not a formidable difficulty besetting our path—the insipidity and monotony inseparable from the necessity which will devolve on us of having constantly to discover new beauties in spots identical in their main features; and should we, in order to vary the theme, mix up the humorous with the rural, the historical, or the antiquarian style, may not fun and humor be mistaken for satyre—a complimentary notice for flattery, above all others, a thing abhorrent from our nature? But 'tis vain to argue. That fatal "yes" has been uttered, and no true knight goes back from his plighted word. There being no help, we devoutly commend our case to St. Columba, and the archangel St. Michael, the patrons of our parish, and set to our task, determined to assume a wide margin, draw heavily on history,—season the whole with short anecdotes,—glimpses of domestic life, calculated to light up the past and present; and should you, dear reader, be dissatisfied in the end with the contents of the *third*, perhaps the last, series of *Maple Leaves*, on you alone rests the blame; had you not patronized the first and second, *no third series would have been inflicted.*

O critic, who would fain seek in our homes great architectural excellence, pause! for the majority of them, no such pretension is set up. Nowhere either on our soil are to be found ivied ruins, dating back to doomsday book, moated castle, or mediæval tower. We have no Blenheims, nor Chatsworths, nor Woburn abbeys, nor Arundel castles, to illustrate every style of architectural beauty, rural embellishment and landscape. Canadian cottages, the best of them, are not the stately country homes of

> "Old pheasant-lords,
> ....Partridge-breeders of a thousand years."

typifying the accumulated wealth of centuries, or patrician pride; nor are they the gay *chateaux* of *La Belle France*. In Canada we could—in many instances we had to—do without the architect's skill; nature having been lavish to us in her decorations, art could be dispensed with. Our country dwellings possess attractions of a higher class, yea, of a nobler order, than brick and mortar moulded by the genius of man, can impart. A kind Providence has surrounded them in spring, summer and autumn with scenery often denied to the turreted castle of the proudest nobleman in Old England. Those around Quebec are more particularly hallowed by associations destined to remain ever memorable amongst the inhabitants of the soil.

Some of our larger estates, like Belmont (comprising 450 acres), date back more than two centuries, whilst others, though less ancient, retrace vividly events glorious in the same degree to the two races, who, after having fought stoutly for the mastery, at last hung out the olive branch and united long since, willing partners, in the bonds of a common nationality, neither English nor French, though participating largely of either, and linked their destinies together as Canadians. Every traveller in

Canada, from Baron La Hontan, who "preferred the forests of Canada to the Pyranèes of France," to the Hon. Amilia Murray of "muffin memory," Charlevoix, LaGalissonnière, Peter Kalm, Isaac Weld, John Lambert, Heriot, Silliman, Ampère, Marmier, Rameau, Augustus Sala, have united in pronouncing our Quebec landscape so wild, so majestic, withal, so captivating, as to vie in beauty with the most picturesque portions of the old or the new world. So much for scenery, as to the historical associations which Quebec and its environs suggests to the mind of the visitor, they have been thus summed up by a well-known writer :—*

"History is everywhere around us, beneath us; from the depths of yonder valleys, from the top of that mountain, history rises up and presents itself to our notice, exclaiming 'behold me!' Beneath us, among the capricious meanders of the River St. Charles, the Cabire-Coubat of Jacques Cartier is the very place where he first planted the cross and held his first conference with the Seigneur Donacona. Here, very near to us, beneath a venerable elm tree (under the walls of the English Cathedral), which, with much regret, we saw cut down, tradition states that Champlain first raised his tent. From the very spot on which we now stand, Count de Frontenac returned to Admiral Phipps that proud answer, as he said, *from the mouth of his cannon*, which will always remain recorded by history. Under this rampart are spread the plains on which fell Wolfe and Montcalm, and where, in the following year, the Chevalier de Lévis and General Murray fought that other battle, in memory of which the citizens of Quebec have erected a monument. Before us, on the heights of Beauport, the souvenirs of battles not less heroic, recall to our remembrance the names of Longueuil, St. Helene and Juchereau Duchesnay. Below us, at the foot of that tower on which floats the British flag, Montgomery and his soldiers all fell, swept by the grape shot of a single gun pointed by a Canadian artilleryman. On the other hand, under that projecting rock, (in Sault-au-Matelot st.) now crowned with the guns of old England, the intrepid Dambourgès, sword in hand, drove Arnold and his men from the houses in which they had established themselves. History is then every where around us. She rises as well from these ramparts, replete with daring deeds, as from those illustrious plains equally celebrated for feats of arms, and she again exclaims, 'here I am!'

*Honorable P. O. Chauveau, the auther of *Charles Guerin*.

The History of Sillery.

CHAPTER I.

Henry IV. of France had for his chancellor Nicholas Brulart de Sillery, a worthy and distinguished magistrate, who, as State councillor, enjoyed the confidence of his sovereign until death closed his useful career in 1640, at the ripe age of 80. To this eminent lawyer and statesman was born a patriarchal family of sons and daughters. The youngest of his sons, Noël Brulart de Sillery,* having brilliantly completed his studies at Paris in the classics, entered, at the age of eighteen, the military order of the Knights of Malta, and resided twelve years in that island as a knight; his martial bearing and ability, modesty and uniform good conduct soon paved the way for him to the highest dignities in this celebrated Order. Soon the Grand Master appointed him "Commandeur de Troyes;" this preferment yielded him 40,000 livres per annum.

On his return to Paris in 1607, the favor of the court and the protection of Marie de Medicis was the means of having him nominated Knight of Honor. His talents and position soon procured him the appointment of French Ambassador to the Court of Spain in 1614, which high position he left for that of Ambassador at Rome in 1622, where he replaced the Marquis of Coeuvres. He spent two years in the Eternal City, and subsequently acknowledged that it was there that he conceived the first idea of embracing Holy Orders; Cardinal de La Valette replacing him at the Roman Court as French *Chargé d'Affaires*. From what can be gleaned in history, this distinguished personage led a princely life, his enormous rent-roll furnishing the means for a most lordly establishment of retainers, liveries and domains. His fancy for pomp and show, great though it was, never, however, made him lose sight of the poor, nor turn a deaf ear to the voice of the needy.

In 1626, the Pope (Barberini), Urbain VIII., having proclaimed a jubilee, the ex-ambassador, as if a new light had dawned on him, and under the guidance of a man famous for his pious and ascetic life, Vincent de Paul, determined to reform his house and whole life. Thus, a few years after, viz., in 1632, the Commandeur de Sillery sold to Cardinal

* A. Brulart de Sillery, Marquis de Puisieux, was Minister of Foreign Affairs in France from 1747 to 1751.—O'Callaghan's *Paris Document Table*, vol. x.

Richelieu his sumptuous and princely hotel in Paris, entered Holy Orders in 1634, and devoted all the energy of his mind and his immense wealth to the propagation of the faith amongst the aborigines of Canada, having been induced to do so by the Commandeur de Razili who previously had solicited him to join the company des "Cents Associés," or Hundred Partners, of which Razili was a member.

The Commandeur de Sillery inaugurated his benevolent purpose by placing 12,000 livres in the hands of Father Charles Lalemant, a zealous Jesuit; this was the beginning of the mission which, through gratitude to its founder, was called Sillery—it was distant about four miles and a half from Quebec, on the north shore of the St. Lawrence; date of the foundation, July, 1637.* History has preserved a letter addressed from Paris by the Commandeur de Sillery to the Chevalier de Montmagny, governor of the colony, in which the benevolent man asked the governor to ratify a grant of "twelve arpents" made to him in the city itself by the company of the Hundred Partners, and also to ratify a promised grant of other lands to open a seminary or school to educate Algonquin and Montagnais children, although, at the request of the Indians, the settlement became more extensive and comprised also the residence of the christianized Indians. Father Le Jeune, a learned Jesuit, had charge and control over the workmen who were sent out from France at the expense of the Commandeur de Sillery; and on the 22nd February, 1639, a permanent bequest was authentically recorded in favor of the mission by the commandeur placing at interest, secured on the Hôtel-de-Ville at Paris, a sum of 20,000 livres tournois. Palisades had been used originally to protect the settlement; in 1651 the governor of Quebec, Jean de Lauzon, strengthened the palisades and added redoubts.† In 1647 the church of the mission had been placed under the invocation of St. Michael the Archangel; hence why

* An authentic record still remains of the foundation of the mission; it is written in the language of Virgil, by Father Deguen, its first missionary, and heads the register of baptisms, marriages and burials of the mission. It runs thus: "Dominus de Sillery, eques militenses et sacerdos non adpridem factus, vir imprimis pius, reductionem Sancti Josephi, una et amplius leaca, suprâ Kebicum ad ripas magni fluminis." Jacta sunt fundimenta domûs, Julii, 1637, et 14 Aprilis anni, 1638.—*Bressani, Appendix*, p. 300.

† Il y avait (des petits forts) à Sillery, sur les fiefs Saint Michel, Saint François, Saint Sauveur, à Beauport, à l'Ile d'Orleans. "Les *Hiroquois*," dit la mère de l'Incarnation, "craignent extre mement les cannons; ce qui fait qu'ils n'osent s'approcher des forts." Les habitants, afin de leur donner la chasse et de la terreur, ont des redoutes en leurs maisons pour se defendre avec de petites pièces.—*Abbé Ferland's Notes, p.* 92.

Sillery Cove, once called St. Joseph's, was, in 1647, named St. Michael's Cove.

The Commandeur de Sillery extended his munificence to several other missionary establishments in Canada and other places. What with the building of churches, monasteries and hospitals in Champagne, France; at Anneey, Savoy; at Paris, and elsewhere, he must, indeed, have been for those days a veritable Rothschild in worldly wealth.

This worthy ecclesiastic died in Paris on the 26th September, 1640, at the age of 63 years, bequeathing his immense wealth to the Hôtel Dieu of that city. Such was, in a few words, the noble career of one of the large-minded pioneers of civilization in primitive Canada, Le Chevalier Noël Brulart de Sillery—such the origin of the name of "Our parish."

One of the first incidents, two years after the opening of the mission, was the visit paid to it by Madame de la Peltrie, the noble founder of the Ursuline Convent at Quebec. This took place on the 2nd August, 1639, the day after her arrival from Dieppe and stately reception by the governor, M. de Montmagny, who had asked her to dinner the day previous. This same year the nuns called *Hospitalierès* (Hôtel Dieu) opened a temporary hospital at Sillery, but the inmates and resident Indians suffered fearfully from the ravages of the small-pox. In attempting a sketch of the Sillery of ancient days, we cannot follow a truer nor pleasanter guide than the old historian of Canada in the interesting notes he published on this locality in 1855, after having minutely examined every inch of ground. "A year after their arrival at Quebec," says Abbé Ferland, "in August, 1640, the *Hospitalières* nuns, desirous of being closer to the Sillery mission, where they were having their convent built according to the wishes of the Duchess D'Aiguillon, left Quebec and located themselves in the house of M. de Puiseaux. They removed from this house at the beginning of the year 1641 to take possession of their convent, a mile distant. During that winter no other French inhabitants resided near them except the missionaries, and they suffered much from cold and want. But the following year they had the happiness to have in the neighborhood a good number of their countrymen. M. de Maisonneuve, Mlle. Mance, the soldiers and farmers recently arrived from France, took up their abode at M. de Puiseaux's. * * * They spent the winter there and paid us frequent visits, to our mutual satisfaction."*

* *History of the Hôtel Dieu.*

Sillery being constantly threatened by the Five Nations, the *Hospitalières* ladies were compelled to leave their establishment and seek refuge in Quebec on the 29th May, 1644, having thus spent about three years and a half amongst the savages. The locality where they then resided still goes under the name of "Convent Cove."

"Monsieur Pierre Puiseaux, Sieur de l'habition de Sainte Foy," after whom was called *Pointe à Pizeau*, at Sillery, seems to have been a personage of no mean importance in his day. Having realised a large fortune in the West Indies, he had followed Champlain to Canada, bent on devoting his wealth to the conversion of the aboriginal tribes. His manor stood, according to the Abbé Ferland, on that spot in St. Michael's Cove on which the St. Michael's Hotel*—long kept by Mr. W. Scott—was subsequently built, to judge from the heavy foundation walls there. Such was the magnificence of the structure that it was reckonned a perfect gem of a house,—"*Une maison regardée dans le temps comme le bijou du Canada*," says the old chronicler. Paul de Chomedey de Maisonneuve having arrived in 1641, with colonists for Montreal, the laird of St. Michel generously tendered him the use of his manor and seigniory of St. Foy. Under the hospitable roof of this venerable old gentleman, M. de Maisonneuve, Mlle. Mance, the founder of the Hôtel Dieu hospital at Montreal, and Mdme. de la Peltrie spent the winter of 1641-2, whilst the intended *colonists* for Villemarie were located close by in the Sillery settlement. During the winter a considerable rumpus took place between the future Governor of Montreal, M. de Maisonneuve, and the then present Governor of Quebec, Chevalier de Montmagny. It appears that on a certain festival a small cannon and also fifteen musket shots had been fired without authority; His Excellency Governor Montmagny, in high dudgeon at such a breach of military discipline, ordered Jean Gorry, the person who had fired the shots, to be put in irons; Mlle. Mance, had furnished the powder for this military display. The future Governor of Montreal, Monsieur de Maisonneuve, is said to have, on this occasion, publicly exclaimed: "Jehan Gorry, you have been put in irons for my sake and I affronted! I raise your wages of ten half crowns (dix écus), let us on only reach Montreal; no one there will prevent us from firing."† Bravo! M. de Maisonneuve!

* The hotel is that one now kept by one Pierre Letarte.

† Manuscript owned by G. B. Faribault, Esquire.

Peace, however, was restored, and His Excellency Governor Montmagny, headed, in person, the expedition which, on the 8th May following, sailed from St. Michael's Cove, Sillery, to found at Montreal the new colony. *Baron* Puiseaux accompanied M. de Maisonneuve, to take part also in the auspicious event, but his age and infirmities compelled him, soon after, to return to France, where he died a few years subsequently, and by his last will executed at La Rochelle, on the 21st June, 1647, he beqeathed his St. Foy property to the support of the future bishops of Quebec. "The walls of the Sillery Chapel," says the historian of Canada previously quoted, "were still standing about thirty years ago, and the foundations of this edifice, of the hospital and of the missionary residency are still perceptible to the eye on the spot now occupied by the offices and stores of Hy. LeMesurier, Esq., at the foot of the hill and opposite the residence of the Honorable Mr. Justice Caron."

"Amongst the French gentlemen of note who then owned lands at Sillery, may be mentioned *François de Chavigny, sieur de Berchêreau qui,*" adds, Abbé Ferland, "*occupait un rang elevè dans le colonie. En quelques occasions, il fut chargé de remplacer le Gouverneur, lors que celui-ci s'absentait de Québec.*" Now, dear reader, let it be known to you that you are to look, with every species of respect on this worthy old denizen of Sillery, he being, as the Abbé has elsewhere established beyond the shadow of a doubt, not only the ancestor of several old families such as the Lagorgendierès, the Rigaud de Vaudreuils and Tachereaus, but also the ancestor of your humble servant the writer of these lines.

"The Sillery settlement contained during the winter of 1646–7, of Indians only, about two hundred souls. Two roads led from Quebec to the settlement, one the Grande Alleé or St. Louis road, the other the Cove road, skirting the beach. Two grist mills stood in the neighborhood; one on the St. Denis streamlet which crosses the Grande Allée road (from Sinjohn's to Lord Monck's residence)—the dam seems to have been on the Spencer Wood property. 'This mill, and the *fief* on which it was built, belonged to M. Juchereau,' one of the ancestors of the Duchesnays. 'Another mill existed on the Belle Borne brook,' which crosses the main road, the boundary between Spencer Grange and Woodfield. Any one visiting these two streams during the August droughts, will be struck with their diminutiveness, compared to the time when they turned the two grist mills two hundred years back: the clearing of the adjoining forests, whence they take their source may account for the metamorphosis."

The perusal of the Rev. Mr. Ferland's work brings us to another occurrence, which, although foreign to the object of this sketch, deserves notice:—

"The first horse seen in Canada was landed from a French vessel about the 20th June, 1648, and presented as a gift to His Excellency, Governor Montmagny." Another incident deserving of mention, occurs under date 20th August, 1653. The Iroquois* surprised at Cap Rouge Rev. Father J. Antoine Poncet and a peasant named Mathurin Tranchelot, and carried them off to their country. The rev. missionary for three days was subjected to every kind of indignity from the Indian children and every one else. A child cut off one of the captive's fingers. He was afterwards, with his companion, tied up during two nights, half suspended in the air; this made both suffer horribly; burning coals were applied to their flesh. Finally, the missionary was handed over to an old squaw; he shortly after became free and returned to Quebec, on the 5th November, 1653, to the joy of everybody.

His comrade, Tranchelot, after having had his fingers burnt, was finally consumed by fire on the 8th September, 1653. Such were some of the thrilling incidents of daily occurrence at Sillery two centuries ago.

What with breaches of military etiquette by M. de Maisonneuve's colonists—the ferocity of skulking Iroquois—and the scrapes their own neophytes occasionally got into, the reverend fathers in charge of the Sillery mission must now and again have had lively times, and needed, we would imagine, the patience of Job, with the devotion of martyrs, to carry out their benevolent views.

We read in history how, on one Sunday morning in 1652, the Sillery Indians being all at mass, a beaver skin was stolen from one of the wig-

---

* The insecurity produced in the colony at this period by the incessant inroads of the Five Nations was such that several colonists were on the eve of, and some did—return to France.

"Les familles françaises éparses sur les bords du St. Laurent, se trouvaient exposées à des dangers continuels. Pendant le jour, les hommes étaient attaqués au coin des champs, à l'oreé d'un bois, sur les eaux du grand fleuve. Pour tomber tout-à-coup sur leurs victimes, les maraudeurs iroquois se tenaient cachés tantôt derrière un arbre renversé, tantôt dans un marais, ou au milieu des joncs du rivage; pendant la nuit, ils rôdaient autour des maisons, cherchant à surprendre quelques familles sans défense."—*Ferland, Histoire du Canada.* Vol. 1, p. 398.

Hence why the French houses in each settlement were generally close to one another for mutual protection; the church in the centre to sound the tocsin of alarm.

wams, on which, a council of the chiefs being called, it was decided that the robbery had been committed by a Frenchman,* enough to justify the young men to rush out and seize two Frenchmen then accidentally passing by, and in no wise connected—as the Indians even admitted—with the theft. The Indian youths were for instantly stripping the prisoners, in order to compel the governor of the colony to repair the injury suffered by the loss of the peltric. One of them, more thoughtful than the rest, suggested to refer the matter to the missionary father, informing him at the same time that in cases of robbery it was the Indian custom to lay hold of the first individual they met belonging to the family or nation of the suspected robber, strip him of his property, and retain it until the family or nation repaired the wrong. The father succeeded, by appealing to them as Christians, to release the prisoners. Fortunately, the real thief, who was not a Frenchman, became alarmed, and had the beaver skin restored.

Old writers of that day occasionally let us into queer glimpses of a churchman's tribulations in those primitive times. Champlain relates how a pugnacious parson was dealt with by a pugnacious clergyman of a different persuasion respecting some knotty controversial points. The arguments, however irresistible they may have been, Champlain observes, were not edifying either to the savages or to the French :—" J ay veu le ministre et nostre curé s'entre battre à coup de poing sur le differend de la religion. Je ne scay pas qui estait le plus vaillant et qui donnait le meilleur coup; mais je scay tres bien que le ministre se plaignoit quelque fois au Sieur de Mons (Calviniste, directeur de la compagnie) d'avoir ésté battu et vuidoient en ceste faccon les poincts de controverse. Je vois laisse à penser si cela éstait beau à voir; les sauvages éstoient tantôt d'un côté, tantôt de l'autre, et les François meslez selon leur diverse croyance, disaient pis que pendre de l'une et de l'autre religion." The fighting parson (no Plymouth brethren in those days) had evidently caught a tartar. However, this controversial sparring did *not* take place at Sillery.

The winter of 1666 was marked by a novel incident in the annals of

* *Histoire du Canada.*—Ferland. Vol. 1, page 109.

the settlement. On the 9th of January,* 1666, the governor of the colony, M. de Courcelles, with M. du Gas as second in command, and M. de Salampar, a volunteer, together with two hundred colonists who had volunteered, and three hundred soldiers of the dashing regiment of Carignan, which the viceroy, the proud Marquis de Tracy, had brought over from Europe, after their return from their campaign in Hungary, sallied forth from the capital on snow shoes. A century and a half later one might have met on that same road another viceroy—this time an English one, as proud, as fond of display, as the Marquis de Tracy—with the Queen's Household Troops, the British Grenadiers and Coldstream Guards—the Earl of Durham, one of our ablest, if not one of the most popular of our administrators. Let us now follow the French Governor of 1666, heading his light-hearted soldiers along the St. Louis road, all on snow shoes, each man, His Excellency included, carrying on his back from twenty-five to thirty lbs. of biscuit, &c. The little army is bound towards the frontiers of New Holland (the State of New York) on a nine hundred miles' tramp (no railroads in those days), in the severest season of the year, to chastise some hostile Indian tribes, after incorporating in its ranks, during its march, the Three Rivers and Montreal reinforcements. History tells of the intense suffering experienced during the expedition by these brave men, some of them more accustomed to Paris *salons* than to Canadian forest warfare on snow shoes, with spruce boughs and snow drifts for beds. But let us not anticipate. We must be content to accompany them on that day to

* "Monsieur de Courcelles, qui en fut le chef (de l'expedition), y apporta toute la diligence possible, de sorte qu'il se trouva prêt à partir le 9 Janvier, 1666, accompagné de M. du Gas, qu'il prit pour son lieutenant, de M. de Salampar, gentilhomme volontaire, du Père Pierre Raffeix, Jèsuite, de 300 hommes du Régiment Carignan Salières et de 200 volontaires, habitants des colonies françaises, chacun ayant aux pieds des raquettes, dont ils n'étaient pas accoutumés de se servir et tous sans en excepter les chefs et M. de Courcelles même étant chargés chacun de 25 ou 30 livres de biscuit etc. A peine pourrait on trouver dans toutes les histoires une marche plus difficile et plus longue, que le fut celle de cette petite armée, et il fallut un courage français et la constance de M. de Courcelles pour l'entrependre * * * il fallait faire trois cent lieues sur les neiges, traverser continuellement sur la glace des lacs et des rivières en danger de faire autant de chûtes que de pas, ne coucher que sur la neige au milieu des forêts, et souffrir un froid qui passe de beaucoup la rigueur des plus rudes hivers de l'Europe.

"Cependnant nos troupes estant allées le premier jour à Sillery, pour recommander le succès de leur entreprise à l'Archange Saint Michel, Patron de ce lieu là, plusieurs eurent des le troisième jour, le nez, les oreilles, les genoux et les doigts, ou d'autres parties du corps gelées et le reste du corps couvert de cicatrices."—*Relations des Jesuites*, 1666 Page 6.

the Sillery settlement,—a march quite sufficient for us degenerate Canadians of the nineteenth century.

Just picture to yourself, our worthy friend, the hurry and scurry at the Missionary residency on that day—with what zest the chilled warriors crowded round the fires of the Indian wigwams, the number of pipes of peace they smoked with the chiefs, the fierce love the gallant Frenchmen swore to the blackeyed Montagnais and Algonquin houris of Sillery, whilst probably His Excellency and staff were seated in the residency close by, resorting to cordials and all those creature comforts to be found in monasteries, including *Grande Chartreuse*, to restore circulation through their benumbed frame!—How the reverend fathers showered down the blessings of St. Michael, the patron saint of the parish, on the youth and chivalry of France!—How the Sillery duennas, the *Capitainesses*, closely watched the gallant sons of Mars, lest some of them* should attempt to induce their guileless neophytes to seek again the forest wilds, and roam at large—the willing wives of white men!

We shall clip a page from Father Barthelemy Vimont's *Journal of the Sillery Mission*, an authentic record, illustrative of the mode of living there; it will, we are sure gladden the heart even of an anchorite:—

"In 1643, the St. Joseph or Sillery settlement was composed of between thirty-five and forty Indian families, who lived there the whole year round except during the hunting season; other nomadic savages occasionlly tarried at the settlement to procure food, or to receive religious instruction. That year there were yet but four houses built in the European fashion; the Algonquins were located in that part of the village close to the French residences; the Montagnais, on the opposite side; the houses accommodate the chiefs only, their followers reside in bark huts, until we can furnish proper dwellings for them all. In

* Baron Vincent Saint Castin, was from Oleron, in Bearn. Originally a Colonel in the King's Guards, he came to Canada in 1665, a Captain in the Carignan Regiment. He was, in 1680-1, in command of Fort Penobscot in Maine. He married the daughter of Madockawando, Sachem of the Penobscots, by which tribe he was adopted and elevated to the rank of Chief. He played a conspicuous part in the wars of that day, signed treaties with the Governors of New England. Having amassed a property of 300,000 crowns, he retired eventually to France, where he had an estate. He was succeeded by his son in the Government of Penobscot. His daughters married advantageously in the colony. We find one of them, Mademoiselle Brigitte de Saint Castin, amongst the pupils of the Ursuline Nuns at Quebec, about the beginning of the last century.—"*Les Gouverneurs Generaux du Canada le menagent et ceux de la Nouvelle Angleterre le craignent*," says *La Hontan*.

this manner was spent the winter season of 1642-3, the French ships left the St. Lawrence for France on the 7th October, 1642; a period of profound quiet followed. Our Indians continued to catch eels, (this catch begins in September)—a providential means of subsistence during winter. The French settlers salt their eels, the Indians smoke theirs to preserve them. The fishing having ended about the beginning of November, they removed their provisions to their houses, when thirteen canoes of Atichamegues Indians arrived, the crews requesting permission to winter there and be instructed in the Christian religion. They camped in the neighborhood of the Montagnais, near to Jean Baptiste, the chief or captain of these savages, and placed themselves under the charge of Father Buteux, who undertook to christianize both, whilst Father Dequen superintended the religious welfare of the Algonquins. Each day all the Indians attend regularly to mass, prayers, and religious instruction. Catechism is taught to the children, and the smartest amongst them receive slight presents to encourage them, such as knives, bread, beads, hats, sometimes a hatchet for the biggest boys. Every evening Father Dequen calls at every hut and summons the inmates to evening prayers at the chapel. The *Hospitalières* nuns also perform their part in the pious work; Father Buteux discharged similar duties amongst the Montagnais and Atichamegues neophytes. The Atichamegues have located themselves on a small height back of Sillery. 'When the Reverend Father visits them each evening, during the prevalence of snow storms, he picks his way in the forest, lantern in hand, but sometimes loosing his footing, he rolls down the hill.' Thus passed for the Sillery Indians, the early portion of the winter. In the middle of January they all broke ground and located themselves about a quarter of a league from Quebec, to make tobogins and began the first hunt, which lasted about three weeks. Each day they travelled a quarter of a league to Quebec to attend mass, generally at the chapel of the Ursuline Convent, where Father Buteux and also the nuns instructed them. In February they sought the deep woods to hunt the moose." "On my return to Sillery," adds Father Vimont, "twelve or thirteen infirm old Indians, women and children, who had been left behind, followed me to the Hospital, where we had to provide for them until the return, at Easter, of the hunting party."

Whilst the savage hords were being thus reclaimed from barbarism at

Sillery, a civilized community a few hundred miles to the east of it were descending to the level of savages. We read in Hutchinson's *History of Massachusetts Bay*, of our Puritan brethren of Boston, occasionally roasting defenceless women for witchcraft; thus perished, in 1645, Margaret Jones; and a few years after, in 1656, Mrs. Ann Hibbens, the lady of a respectable Boston merchant. Christians cutting one another's throat for the love of God. O, civilization where is thy boast!

During the winter of 1646-7, Sillery contained, of Indians alone, about two hundred souls.

Let us now sum up the characteristics of the Sillery of ancient days in a few happy words, borrowed from the *Notes** published in 1855 on that locality by the venerable Abbé Ferland, whose loss Quebec just now deplores:—

"A map of Quebec by Champlain exhibits, about a league above the youthful city, a point jutting out into the St. Lawrence, and which is covered with Indian wigwams. Later on this point received the name of Puiseaux, from the first owner of the Fief St. Michel, bounded by it to the southwest.† On this very point at present stands the handsome St. Colomba church, surrounded by a village."‡

"Opposite to it is the Lauzon shore, with its river *Bruyante*|| (the 'Etchemin') its shipyards, its numerous shipping, the terminus of the Grand Trunk Railway; the villages and churches of Notre Dame de Lévis, St. Jean Chrysostôme and Saint Romuald. To your right and to your left the St. Lawrence is visible for some twelve or fifteen miles, covered with inward and outward bound ships. Towards the east the landscape is closed by Cap Tourment, twelve leagues distant, and by the cultivated heights of the *Petite Montagne* of St. Fereol, exhibiting in succession the *Côte de Beaupre*, (Beauport, L'Ange Gardien, &c.) the green slopes of the Island of Orleans, Cape Diamond, crowned with its citadel, and having at its feet aforest of masts, Abraham's Plains, the Coves and their humming, busy noises, St. Michael's Coves forming a graceful curve from Wolfe's Cove to Pointe

**Notes on the Environs of Quebec*, 1855.

†Occupied by Michael Stevenson, Esq.

‡The temple for Catholic worship erected at Pointe à Puizeau about 1854, is very picturesquely located; its stained glass windows add much to its beauty; the Rev. Father Harkin has been in charge ever since the late Abbé Ferland was appointed secretary to the Archbishop of Quebec and Military Chaplain to the Forces.

§||From the noise it makes before easterly gales.

à Puiseaux. Within this area thrilling events once took place, and round these diverse objects historical souvenirs cluster, recalling some of the most important occurrences in North America; the contest of two powerful nations for the sovereignty of the New World; an important episode of the revolution which gave birth to the adjoining Republic. Such were some of the events of which these localities were the theatre. Each square inch of land, in fact, was measured by the footsteps of some of the most remarkable men in the history of America: Jacques Cartier, Champlain, Frontenac, Laval, Phipps, d'Iberville, Wolfe, Montcalm, Arnold, Montgomery, have each of them, at some time or other, trod over this expanse

"Close by, in St. Michael's Cove, Mr. De Maisonneuve and Mademoiselle Mance passed their first Canadian winter, with the colonists intended to found Montreal. Turn your eyes towards the west, and although the panorama is less extensive, still it awakens some glorious memories. At Cap Rouge, Jacques Cartier established his quarters, close to the river's edge, the second winter he spent in Canada, and was succeeded in that spot by Roberval, at the head of his ephemeral colony. Near the entrance of the Chaudière river stood the tents of the Abnoquiois, the Etchemins and the Souriquois Indians, when they came from the shores of New England to smoke the calumet of peace with their brethren the French; the river Chaudière in those days was the highway which connected their country with Canada. Closer to Pointe à Puiseaux is Sillery Cove where the Jesuit Fathers were wont to assemble and establish the Algonquin and Montagnais Indians, who were desirous of becoming Christians. It was from that spot that the neophytes used to carry the faith to the depths of the forest; it was here that those early apostles of Christianity congregated before starting with the joyous message for the country of the Hurons, for the shores of the Mississippi, or for the frozen regions of Hudson's Bay. From thence went Father P. Druilletes, the bearer of words of peace on behalf of the Christians of Sillery, to the Abnoquiois of Kennebeki, and to the puritans of Boston. Near this same mission of Sillery, Friar Liegeois was massacred by the Iroquois, whilst Father Poncet was carried away a captive by these barbarous tribes.

"Monsieur de Sillery devoted large sums to erect the necessary edifices for the mission, such as a chapel, a missionary residence, an hospital, a fort, houses for the new converts, together with the habitations for the French. The D'Auteuil family had their country seat on the hill back of Pointe à Puiseaux; and the venerable Madame de Monceau, the mother-in-law of the Attorney General Ruette D'Auteuil, was in the habit of residing there from time to time, in a house she had constructed near the chapel."

It would be indeed a pleasant and easy task to recall all the remarkable events which occurred in this neighborhood. One thing is certain, the cool retreats studding the shores of the St. Lawrence were equally sought for by the wealthy in those days as they have been since by all those who wish to breathe pure air and enjoy the scenery.

The Sillery settlement commenced to be deserted about the beginning of the last century. After the conquest of the country the care of the buildings was neglected, and they soon fell to ruins; but the residence of the missionary fathers was preserved, and the ruins of the other structures remained standing long enough to be susceptible of identification with certainty. Several of the old inhabitants recollect having seen the church walls* demolished, and they were of great solidity. Abbé Ferland himself, twenty years ago, saw a portion of those walls standing above ground. The ruins of the hospital and the convent were razed about thirty years ago, and in demolishing them several objects were discovered, some of which must have belonged to the good ladies, the *Hospitalières* nuns.

For the benefit of those who might feel inclined to explore the remaing vestiges of M. Sillery's foundation, I shall furnish some details on the locality. About the centre of Sillery Cove can be seen a cape, not very high, but with its sides perpendicular. The position of surrounding objects point it out as the spot on which stood the fort intended to protect the village; there also, in a dry soil, stood the cemetery, from which several bodies were exhumed in the course of last summer (1854). At the foot of the cape, on your left, is the missionaries' house, now converted into a residence for the clerks of Hy. Lemesurier, Esq., to whom belongs that portion of Sillery. This building† has been kept in repair, and is still in a good state of preservation. In a

*This church is well shown in the Plan of the Seige Operations published in this volume.

† The hill which led down to it in primitive times was not Graddon's hill, but an old hill not used at present, on the property of Henry LeMesurier, Esq.

line with it, and nearest the St. Lawrence, can be discovered the foundation of the church. This edifice stood north-east and south-west.

Near the wall closest to the river ran a spring of water, perfectly clear, and, no doubt used for the wants of the church and of the presbytery or manse. Several other streams of excellent water run down the hill and intersect the grounds in all directions. No misconception can exist as to where the chapel stood, as there are still (in 1855) living several persons who saw the walls standing, and can point out the foundation. To the right of the small cape, and on a line with the chapel, stood the hospital, now deserted for more than two centuries. Over its foundation an elm has grown,—'tis now a handsome and large tree; six feet from the ground its circumference measures two fathoms (12 feet), which makes its diameter about three and a half. Heriot thus describes the locality in 1806:—

"From hence to Cap Rouge the scenery, on account of its beauty and variety, attracts the attention of the passenger. At Sillery, a league from Quebec, on the north shore, are the ruins of an establishment which was begun in 1637, intended as a religious institution for the conversion and instruction of natives of the country; it was at one time inhabited by twelve French families. The buildings are placed upon level ground, sheltered by steep banks, and close by the borders of the river; they now only consist of two old stone houses, fallen to decay, and of the remains of a small chapel (the chapel has of late been repaired and fitted up for a malt house, and some of the other buildings have been converted into a brewery).* In this vicinity the Algonquins once had a village; several of their tumuli, or burying places, are still discoverable in the woods, and

* Breweries, however, and other manufactories had been in operation in the colony, as early as 1668, as we glean from the following entry in the *Jesuits' Journal*. Of the brewery alluded to here, some remains still exist, we believe, in St. Charles street, where Lepper & Lloyd's brewery once stood:—

"Et parce qu un pais ne peut pas se former entièrement sans l'assistance des manufactures, nous voyons déjà celle des souliers et des chapeaux commencée, celle des toiles et des cuirs projetée, et on attend que la multiplication qui se fait des moutons, produise suffisemment des laines pour introduire celle des draps, et c'est ce que nous espérons dans peu puisque les bestiaux se peuplent assez abondamment, entr'autres les chevaux qui commencent à se distribuer dans tout le pais. La brasserie que Monsieur Talon fait construire, ne servira pas peu aussi pour la commodité publique, soit pour l'épargne des boissons enivrantes, qui causent ici de grands desordres, auxquels on pourra obvier par cette autre boisson qui est très saine et non malfaisante, soit pour conserver l'argent dans le pais qui s'en divertit par l'achat qu'on fait en France de tant de boissons, soit enfin pour consumer le surabondant des bleds qui si sont trouves quelquefois en telle quantité que les laboureurs n'en pouvaient avoir le débit."—*Relations des Jesuites*, 1668, p. 3.

hieroglyphics cut on the trees remain, in some situations, yet uneffaced."*

On the 6th June, 1865, we determined to afford ourselves a long-promised treat, and go and survey, with Abbé Ferland's *Notes on Sillery* open before us, and also the help of that eminently respected authority in every parish, the "oldest inhabitant," the traces of the Sillery settlement of 1637. Nor had we long to wait before obtaining ocular demonstration of the minute exactitude with which our old friend, the Abbé, had investigated aud measured every stone, every crumbling remain of brick and mortar. The first and most noticeable relic pointed out was the veritable house of the missionaries, facing the St. Lawrence, on the north side of the road, on Sillery Cove; it is still the property of Henry Le Mesurier, Esquire, of Beauvoir. Were it in the range of possible events that the good fathers could revisit the scene of their past apostolical labors and view their former earthly tenement, hard would be their task to identify it. The heavy three-feet-thick wall is there yet, as perfect, as massive, as defiant as ever; the pointed gable and steep roof, in spite of alterations, still stands—the true index of an old French structure in Canada. Our forefathers seemed as if they never could make the roof of a dwelling steep enough, to prevent the accumulation of snow. But here ends all analogy with the past; so jaunty, so cosy, so modern does the front and interior of the Sillery "Mansion House" look—so named for many years past. Paint, paper and furniture have made it quite a snug abode since it has been occupied by Thomas Beckett, Esq., the representative of the English house of R. R. Dobell, Esq., with Henry LeMesurier, Esq., joint occupant of Sillery Cove. Nor was it without a certain peculiar feeling of reverence we, for the first time, crossed that threshold, and entered beneath those fortress-like walls, where for years had resounded the orisons of the Jesuit Fathers, the men from whose ranks were largely recruited our heroic band of early martyrs—some of whose dust, unburied, but not unhonored, has mingled for two centuries with its parent earth on the green banks of Lake Simcoe, on the borders of the Ohio, in the environs of Kingston, Montreal, Three Rivers, Quebec—a fruitful seed of christianity scattered bountifully through the length and breadth of our land; —others, whose lifeless clay still rests in yon sunny hillock in rear, to the west of the "Mansion House"—the little cemetery described by Mr. Ferland. Between Mr. Beckett's residence and the river, about forty feet from

Heriot's Travels, 1806, p. 98.

the house, inclining towards the south, are the remains of the foundation walls of the Jesuits' church or chapel, dating back to 1640; they stand north-east and south-west, and are at present flush with the greensward; a large portion of them were still visible about thirty-five years ago, as attested by many living witnesses; they were converted into ballast for ships built at this spot, and into materials for repairing the main road by some vandal who will remain nameless. From Mr. Beckett's steps you notice the little cape to the south-west mentioned in Mr. Ferland's *Notes,* though growing smaller and smaller every year from the quantities of soil and stone taken from it, also to repair the road. The large elm pointed out by the Abbé as having grown over the spot where the hospital stood is there yet, a majestic tree. The selection of a site for the little cemetery is most judicious; several little streams from the heights in the rear filter through the ground, producing a moisture calculated to prevent decomposition, and explanatory of the singular appearance of the bodies disinterred there in 1855. Every visitor will be struck with the beauty, healthiness and shelter which this sequestered nook at Sillery presents for a settlement, and with its adaptability for the purposes for which it was chosen, being quite protected against our two prevailing winds, the north-east and south-west, with a splendid southern exposure.

Many years after the opening of the Algonquin and Montagnais school at Sillery, the Huron Indians, after being relentlessly tracked by their inveterate foes, the Five Nations, divided into five detachments; one of these hid on the Great Manitoulin Island, others elsewhere; a portion came down to Quebec on the 28th or 29th July, 1650, under the direction of Father Ragueneau, and, on the 28th July, 1650, settled first on the Jesuits' land at Beauport; in March, 1651, they went to *Ance du Fort,* on the lands of Mademoiselle de Grandmaison, on the Island of Orleans. But the Iroquois having scented their prey in their new abode, made a raid on the island, butchered seventy-one of them, and carried away some prisoners. The unfortunate redskins soon left the island in dismay, and, for protection, encamped in the city of Quebec itself, under the cannons of the fort, near the Jesuits' College (at present the Jesuits' Barracks); in 1667, they settled on the northerly frontier of Sillery, in Notre Dame de Foy (now St. Foy); restless and scared, they again shifted their quarters on the 29th December, 1693, and pitched their erratic tents at Ancienne Lorette, which place they also abandoned many years afterwards to go and settle at *Jeune* or Indian Lorette, where the remnants of this once warlike race, the *nobles* amongst Indian tribes, exist. A few mongrels, crossed with their Caucasian brethren, vegetate in obscurity: exotic trees transplanted far from their native wilds, and whose blossoms show the sear and yellow leaf long before they are full blown.

CHAPTER II.

"Along this road was the favorite drive of the Canadian belle."—*Hawkins' Picture of Quebec.*

Shall we venture to assert that Sillery equals in size some of the German principalities, and that, important though it be, like European dynasties, it has had its periods of splendor succeeded by eras of medieval obscurity. From 1700 down to the time of the conquest, we appeal in vain to the records of the past for any historical event connected with it; everywhere reigns supreme a cimmerian darkness. But if the page of history is silent, the chronicles of the *ton* furnish some tit-bits of drawing-room chit-chat. Thus, as stated in Hawkins' celebrated *Historical Picture of Quebec*, the northern portion of the parish skirting the St. Foy road "was the favorite drive of the Canadian belle." In these few words of Hawkins is involved an intricate question for history, a problem to solve, more abstruse than the one which agitated the Grecian cities respecting the birth of Homer. Who then was the Canadian belle of former days? The Nestors of the present generation still speak with admiration of a fascinating stranger who, close to the end of the last century, used to drive on the St. Foy road, when a royal duke lived in the city, in what is now styled "The Kent House," owned by Mr. Bourassa, in St. Louis street. The name of this distinguished traveller, a lady of European birth, was Madame St. Laurent; but, kind reader, have patience. The Canadian belle who thus enjoyed her drives in the environs of Quebec was not Madame St. Laurent, as it is distinctly stated at page 170 of Hawkins that this occurred before the conquest, viz., 1759. Might it have been that vision of female loveliness, that spotless and beautiful Mrs. De Léry, whose presentation at court, with her handsome husband, shortly after the conquest, elicited from His Majesty George III. the expression which history has preserved, "If such are all my new Canadian subjects, I have indeed made a conquest;" or must we picture to ourselves as the Canadian belle that peerless beauty, that witty and benevolent Mrs. Hughes Pean, Intendant Bigot's fair charmer, mysteriously hinted at, in all the old Quebec guide books, as "Mrs. P——." Madame Hughes Pean,* whose husband was Town Major of Quebec, owned a seigniory in the vicinity of the city—some say at St. Vallier, where Mons. Pean used to load with corn the vessels he dispatched elsewhere; she also was one of the gay revellers at the romantic Hermitage, Bigot's shooting lodge at Charlesbourg. Old memoirs seem to favor this version. Be this as it may, the St. Foy road was a favorite drive even a century before the present day; so says Hawkins' historical work on Quebec—no mean authority, considering that the materials thereof were furnished by that accomplished scholar and eminent barrister, the late Andrew Stuart, father of the present Judge Stuart, and compiled by the late Dr. John Charlton Fisher, one of the able joint editors of the New York *Albion*, and father of Mrs. Ed. Burstall, of Sillery. Who was the reigning belle in 1759, we confess that all our antiquarian lore has failed to satisfactorily unravel. The battles of 1759 and 1760 have rendered Sillery, St. Foy, and the Plains of Abraham classic ground. The details of these events, having appeared elsewhere, the reader is referred to them.

Those of the present day desirous to ascertain the exact spot in the environs of Quebec where past events have taken place, ought to be careful not to be misled by subsequent territorial divisions for municipal or canonical purposes. Many may not be aware that our forefathers included under the denomination of Abraham's Heights that plateau of comparatively level ground extending in a south-easterly direction from the *Coteau Ste. Geneviève* towards the lofty banks which line the river St. Lawrence, covering the greatest part of the land on which subsequently have been built the St. Lewis and St. John's suburbs, the hilly portion towards the city and river, where stands the *asile Champêtre*,† thence south-east, being then called *Buttes à Nepveu;* the land close by, between the Plains and Pointe à Puiseaux, as Côte St. Michel; the ascent from the valley of the St. Charles towards this plateau was through the hill known as Côte d'Abraham. The locality where Woodfield and Spencer Wood now stand, in the fief of St. Michael, was designated as the wood of Samos, thus called after a celebrated French ecclesiastic of Quebec, Bishop Dosquet, whose country seat

* Madame Pean's house in St. Louis street stood where the Officers' Barracks have been since built. We take her to have been that pretty Ang. De Meloises, a pupil of the Ursuline Nuns, mentioned in the *Histoire des Ursulines de Québec*.

† This old Canadian homestead, now owned by J. G. Irvine, Esquire, Barrister, is occupied by the Provincial Aide-de-Camp, Colonel Irvine.

Samos was in 1732—now Woodfield. The Gomin Wood was to the west. As strangers who read the account of what has been styled the two battles of the Plains get frequently confused, it would, in our opinion, render matters less complex by always calling the battle of the 13th September, 1759, "The first battle of the Plains of Abraham," and that of the 28th April, 1760, "The second battle of the Plains." There can be no doubt that recent territorial subdivisions are conducive to confusion so far as the student of history is concerned. The old Sillery settlement, which lay within the limits of the parish of St. Foy, was, in 1855, placed under the dististinguished tutelage of a saint dear to those who hail from the Emerald Isle, and called St. Columba of Sillery. In this manner the realms heretofore sacred to the archangel St. Michael have peacefully passed under the gentle sway of St. Columba, notwithstanding the law of prescription. The English residents of Sillery—and this ought to console sticklers for British precedents and the sacredness of vested rights—did not thus permit the glory of the archangel to depart, and soon after the erection of St. Columba into a parish, the handsome temple called St. Michael's Chapel* was built by some spirited parishioners in front of Mount

* This neat Gothic structure was erected in 1854, at a cost of $12,400, the proceeds of the munificent donations of several members of its congregation and others. The ground on which it stands was presented, as a gift, by Mrs. Jas. Morrin. Several handsome stained-glass windows, representing scriptural scenes, have been recently added. We read, amongst others, the following names on the list of subscribers to the foundation of the chapel, parsonage and school-house :—

Sir Edmund Head.
Colonel Rhodes.
Ed. Burstall.
Captain Retallack.
J. Walker.
Miss Mountain.
Miss Cochran.
F. Burroughs.
Wm. Petry.
W. Price.
T. K. Ramsay.
Lieut.-Colonel Mountain.
Miss Guerout.
J. F. Taylor.
G. Alford.
N. H. Bowen.
Charles Hamilton.
Rich. Tremain.
Miss Taylor.
Dr. Boswell.
Charles Wilson.
Preston Copeman.
Thomas Beckett.
Lord Monck.
Henry Lemesurier.
Charles E. Levey.
Captain Pemberton.
E. Jackson.
D. D. Young.
Rev. A. Mountain.
W. F. Wood.
Honorable W. Walker.
Michael Stevenson.
Mrs. Helmuth.
Honorable Henry Black.
Mrs. Montizambert.
Mrs. Forsyth.
G. Hall.
J. K. Boswell.
T. G. Penny.
W. Drum.
W. Herring.
John Giles.
Thomas Nelson.
Barthy W. Goff.
John Jordan.
The Lord Bishop Mountain.
Denis Godley.
Jos. B. Forsyth.
Colonel Boomer.
F. H. Andrews.
C. N. Montizambert.
Mrs. Carroll.
Robert Hamilton.
Mrs. J. Gibb.
Major H. W. Campbell.
Okill Stuart.
G. B. Symes & Co.
C. Coker.
H. S. Scott.
Mrs. G. R. Mountain.
James Gibb.
J. H. Oakes.
Mrs. Woodbury.
Miss George.
Charles O'Neill.
Society for the Promotion of Christian Knowledge.

We understand that, through the aid and efforts of Charles E. Levey, Esq., of

Hermon cemetery; a not unappropriate monument on their part to the memory of the ancient and worthy patron of the parish. St. Michael's chapel is weekly honored by the attendance of the Sovereign's representative, and *suite*; and on fine summer days by the rank and fashion of the neighboring metropolis—old Quebec.

In this neighbourhood is situated Mount Hermon Cemetery. It is about three miles from Quebec, on the south side of the St. Lewis road, and slopes irregularly, but beautifully, down the cliff which overhangs the St. Lawrence. It is thirty-two acres in extent, and the grounds were tastefully laid out by the late Major Douglas, U. S. Engineers, whose taste and skill had been previously shewn in the design of Greenwood Cemetery, near New York. A carriage drive, upwards of two miles in extent, affords access to all parts of the grounds, and has been so arranged as to afford the most perfect view of the scenery. The visitor, after driving over the smooth lawn-like open surface, finds himself suddenly transferred by a turn of the road into a dark avenue of stately forest trees, from which he emerges to see the broad St. Lawrence almost beneath him, with the city of Quebec and the beautiful slopes of Point Levi in the distance.

Many beautiful monuments now adorn the grounds, some of which are from Montreal and some from Scotland, but the great majority are the productions of Mr. Félix Morgan, of Quebec, and do great credit to his taste and skill. Many of them are beautiful and costly structures of Italian marble.*

A neat Gothic Lodge at the entrance of the grounds contains the office and residence of the superintendent. In the former a complete plan of the grounds is kept; every separate grave being marked upon it with its appropriate number, so that at any future time, on consulting it, the exact spot of interment can be ascertained, and the Register which is also kept affords information respecting the places of birth, age, and date of

Cataracoui, a handsome organ has been subscribed for in England, and that it will shortly grace St. Michael's Chapel.

* Who can visit this sylvan abode, sacred to the repose of the departed, without noticing one tomb in particular, in the enclosure of Wm. Price, Esq.—we allude to that of Sir Edmund Head's gifted son? "The troubled waters of the St. Maurice and the quiet grave at Sillery recall, as in a vision, not only the generous, open-hearted boy, who perished in one and sleeps in the other, but they tell also of the direct line of a good old family cut off—a good name passing away, or, if preserved at all, preserved only on a tomb stone."—*Notman's British Americans.*

death. A large vault, perfectly secured with iron doors, has been constructed for the purpose of receiving bodies during the winter, when immediate interment is not desired; and a suitable stone chapel, in the Gothic style, has been erected adjacent to the grounds, where Divine service, according to the rites of the Church of England, is performed.

On leaving this lovely spot, the ride continues through the woods on the edge of the banks rising from the shore. On the south side are distinguished the embouchures of the Etchemin and Chaudière pouring in their tribute of waters. At Pointe à Puiseaux the road leads down to Sillery Cove. The view from this point would afford an excellent composition for the brush of the landscape-painter. Before reaching the ascent to the villa of the late Mr. Macnider is an old stone house, formerly inhabited by the heroine of *Emily Montague*, near which are the ruins of what was once a large stone chapel. Such visitants as are unacquainted with this novel will find in it a faithful picture of the manners and condition of the colonist when Canada first became a British colony. A mile beyond is the villa of Kilgraston. Hence the tourist, instead of returning by a road conducting through a wood into St. Lewis road for Quebec, will do better by continuing his ride to the church of St. Foy, from which is seen below the St. Charles, gliding smoothly through a lovely valley, whose sides rise gradually to the mountains and are literally covered with habitations. The villages of Lorette and Charlesbourg are conspicuous objects.

The Wild Flowers of Sillery.

"Everywhere about us are they glowing,
Some like stars, to tell us spring is born;
Others, their blue eyes with tears o'erflowing,
Stand like Ruth amid the golden corn."

Are you an admirer of nature, and sweet flowers? Would you, most worthy friend, like to see some of the bright gems which spring, whilst dallying over the sequestered, airy heights and swampy marshes of our woods, drops along her path? Follow, then, sketch book and pencil in hand, the fairy footsteps of one of the most amiable women which old

England ever sent to our climes; accompany the Countess of Dalhousie on a botanizeing tour through Sillery woods; you have her note book, if not herself, to go by. For May, see what an ample store of bright flowers scattered around you; fear not to lose yourself in thickets and underbrush; far from the beaten track a noble lady has ransacked the environs over and over again, sometimes alone, sometimes with an equally enthusiastic and intelligent friend, who hailed from Woodfield; sweet flowers and beautiful ferns attract other noble ladies to this day in that wood. Are you anxious to possess the first-born of spring? Whilst virgin snow still whitens the fields, send a young friend to pluck for you, from the willow, its golden catkins:—

> "The first gilt thing
> Decked with the earliest pearls of spring."

The Gomin Wood will, with the dawn of May, afford you materials for a wreath, rich in perfume and wild beauty. The quantity of wild flowers, to be found in the environs of Quebec has called forth the following remarks from one of Flora's most fervid votaries, a gentleman well known in this locality:—"A stranger," says he, "landing in this country, is much surprised to find the flowers which he has carefully cultivated in his garden at home, growing wild at his feet. Such as dog-tooth violets, trilliums and columbines. I was much excited when I discovered them for the first time; the *trillium*, for which I had paid three shillings and six-pence when in England, positively growing wild. I could scarcely believe that I had a right to gather them; having paid so much for one, I felt that it was property, valuable property running wild, and no one caring to gather it. No one? Yes! some did, for *we* gathered all that we could find, and if the reader will stroll along the hedges on St. Lewis road he will find them in abundance: dark purple flowers, growing on a stalk naked to near the summit, where there is a whirl of three leaves, its sepals are three, petals three, stamens twice three, and its stigmas three, hence its name of *trillium*. We have a few of the white varieties. After the purple *trillium* has done flowering, we have the painted trillium in the woods; the *trillium grandiflorum* is abundant at Grosse Isle. The dog-tooth violet early arrested my attention; the spotted leaves and the bright yellow flowers, fully recurved in the bright sunshine, contrast beautifully with the fresh green grass of the banks on which they are usually found; the bulbs are deep-seated, and the plant will at once, from the general appearance of the flower, be recognized as belonging to the lily family.

"The marsh marigolds, with the bright yellow buttercup-looking flowers, are now in the full luxuriance of bloom in wet places near running water; they may not be esteemed beautiful by all, and yet all God's works, and all his flowers, are good and beautiful. Let any one see them as I have seen them, a large flower-bed of an acre and more, one mass of the brightest yellow, a crystal stream meandering through their midst, the beautiful Falls of Montmorenci across the river rolling their deep strains of Nature's music, the rising tide of the St. Lawrence beating with refreshing waves at his feet, and a cloudless azure sky over head, from which the rosy tints of early morn had hardly disappeared, and if his soul be not ready to overflow with gratitude to the Supreme Being who has made everything so beautiful and good, I do not know what to think of him. I would not be such a man, 'I'd rather be a dog and bay the moon.'"

The whole Gomin bog is studded with Smilacina *Bifolia*, sometimes erroneously called *the white lily of the valley*, also the Smilacina *Trifolia*, the *Dentaria*, the *Streptopus roseus* or twisted stem, a rose-colored flower, bearing red berries in the fall. There are also in this wood, trillium, the May flower, *Hepatica* and *Symplocarpus*, thickets crowned with *Rhodoras* in full bloom—a bush a few feet high with superb rose-colored flowers—the general appearance of a cluster of bushes is most magnificent. In the same locality, further in the swamp, may be found the *kalmia angustifolia* bearing very pretty compact rose-colored flowers like small cups divided into five lobes, also the beautiful Ladies' Slipper Orchis (*Cypripedum humile*) in thousands on the borders of the swamp,—such is Sillery wood in May. The crowded flora of June is the very carnival of nature, in our climes. "Our Parish" is no exception. The Ladies' Slippers, *Kalmia Smilacina*, etc., may still be gathered in the greatest abundance throughout most of this month. Here is also the Bunch or Pigeon berry, in full bloom, the Brooklime Spedwell, the Blue-eyed-grass, the Herb Bennet, the Labrador Tea, the *Oxalis Stricta* and *Oxalis acetosella*, one with yellow, the other with white and purple flowers: the first grows in ploughed fields, the second in the woods. "Our sensitive plant; they shut up their leaves and go to sleep at night, and on the approach of rain. These plants are used in Europe to give an acid flavor to soup." Here also flourishes the Linnea Borealis, roseate bells, hanging like twins from one stalk, downy and aromatic all round. In the middle of June, the Ragwort, a composite flower with yellow heads, and about one half to two feet high, abounds in wet places by the side of running streams. Also, the Anemone, so famous, in English song, principally represented by the Anemone Pensylvanica, growing on wet banks, bearing large white flowers; add the Corydalis, *Smilacina, racemosa* resembling Solomon's Seal. Here we light on a lovely Tulip bed; no,—'tis that strangely beautiful flower, the pitcher plant (*Sarracenia Purpurea*). Next we hit on a flower, not to be forgotten, the *Myosotis palustris* or Forget-me-not. Cast a glance as you hurry onwards on the *Œnothera pumila*, a kind of evening primrose, on the false Helebore—the the one-sided Pyrola, the Bladder Campion—*silene inflata*, the sweet-scented yellow Mellilot, the white Yarran, the Prunella with blue labrate flowers the Yellow Rattle, so called from the rattling of the seeds. The perforated St. John's Wort is now coming into flower everywhere, and will continue until late in August; it is an upright plant, from one to two feet high, with clusters of yellow flowers. The Germans have a custom for maidens to gather this herb on the eve of St. John, and from its withering or retaining its freshness, to draw an augury of death or marriage in the coming year. This is well told in the following lines:—

"The young maid stole through the cottage door,
And blushed as she sought the plant of power;
Thou silver glow-worm, O lend me thy light,
I must gather the mystic St. John's Wort to-night,
The wonderful herb whose leaf must decide
If the coming year shall make me a bride.
And the glow-worm came
With its silvery flame,
And sparkled and shone
Through the night of St. John;
While it shone on the plant as it bloomed in its pride,
And soon has the young maid her love-knot tied.
With noiseless tread
To her chamber she sped,
Where the spectral moon her white beams shed.

"Bloom here, bloom here, thou plant of power,
To deck the young bride in her bridal hour;

But it drooped its head, that plant of power,
And died the mute death of the voiceless flower,
And a withered wreath on the ground it lay.
And when a year had passed away,
All pale on her bier the young maid lay;
And the glow-worm came,
With its silvery flame,
And sparkled and shone
Through the night of St. John;
And they closed the cold grave o'er the maid's cold clay,
On the day that was meant for her bridal day."

Let us see what flowers sultry July has in store for us in her bountiful cornucopia. "In July," says a fervent lover of nature, "bogs and swamps are glorious indeed," so look out for Calopogons, Pogonias, rose-colored and white and purple-fringed Orchises, Ferns, some thirty varities, of exquisite texture,

" In the cool and quiet nooks,
By the side of running brooks;
In the forest's green retreat,
With the branches overhead,
Nestling at the old trees' feet,
Choose we there our mossy bed.

On tall cliffs that woo the breeze,
Where no human footstep presses,
And no eye our beauty sees,
There we wave our maiden tresses."

the Willow-herb, the true Partridge-berry, the Chimaphila, Yellow Lily, Mullein, Ghost Flower, Indian Pipe, Lysimacha Stricta, Wild Chamomile. August will bring forth a variety of other plants, amongst others the Spirantes, or Ladies' Tresses, a very sweet-scented Orchis, with white flowers placed as a spiral round the flower stalk, the purple Eupatorium, the Snake's head, and crowds of most beautiful wild flowers, too numerous to be named here.*

* For anything good in this short sketch of our Wild Flowers, the reader is indebted to Mr. S. S. Sturton, whose paper on the *Wild Flowers of Quebec* was our guide.—J. M. L.

The Woods of Sillery.

Rest now in the leafiest and coolest glen of Sillery, until July and August heats are over, or else steam down and take a briny dip at Murray Bay, Cacouna, or Tadousac; which do you prefer? Do you fancy the Canadian highlands? seek, then, the pleasant shades of Cap à l'Aigle or Pointe à Pic. Are you inclined for French gaiety, killing toilets, and perpetual motion, in the way of dancing? steer for Cacouna. Do you like the *grand monde*, the fashionable place *par excellence?* then try Tadousac. You will find at Burslam Terrace, Sand Cliff Terrace, Bethune Cottage, Knotty Lodge, or Elgin street many old acquaintances from Sillery, and at the Tadousac Hotel visitors from every part of the known world.

You, doubtless, imagine you have now seen Sillery under every aspect; there never was a greater mistake, dear reader. Have you ever viewed its woods in all their autumnal glory, when September arrays them in tints of unsurpassing loveliness? We hear you say, no. Let us then, our pensive philosopher, our romantic, blushing rose-bud of sweet sixteen, our *blase*-traveller, let us all have a canter over that sandy Cap Rouge road, out by St. Lewis gate, and returning through the St. Foy road, nine miles and more; let us select a quiet afternoon, not far distant from the Indian summer, when

> "The gentle wind, a sweet and passionate wooer,
> Kisses the blushing leaf, and stirs up life
> Within the solemn woods of ash, deep crimsoned,
> And silver beech, and maple yellow—leaved,"

and then you can tell us whether the glowing description below is overdrawn:—

"There is something indescribably beautiful in the appearance of Canadian woods at this season of the year, especially when the light of the rising or setting sun falls upon them. Almost every imaginable shade of green, brown, red and yellow, may be found in the foliage of our forest trees, shrubs, and creeping vines, as the autum advances; and it may truly be said that every backwoods home in Canada is surrounded by more gorgeous colorings and richer beauties than the finest mansions of the nobility of England.

"Have our readers ever remarked the peculiarly beautiful appearance of the pines at this season of the year? When other trees manifest symptoms of withering, they appear to put forth a richer and fresher foliage. The interior of the tree, when shaded from the sun, is a deep invisible-green, approaching to black, whilst the outer boughs, basking in the sunlight, show the richest dark-green that can be imagined. A few pine and spruce trees scattered among the more brightly-colored oaks, maples, elms and beeches, which are the chief denizens of our forests, give the whole an exceedingly rich appearance. Among the latter, every here and there, strange sports of nature attract attention. A tree that is still green will have a single branch, covered with red or orange leaves, like a gigantic bouquet of flowers. Another will have one side of a rich maroon, whilst the other side remains green. A third will present a flounce or ruffle of bright buff, or orange leaves round the middle, whilst the branches above and below continue green. Then again some trees which have turned to a rich brown, will be seen intertwined and festooned by the wild vine or red root, still beautifully green; or a tree that is still green will be mantled over by the Canadian ivy, whose leaves have turned to a deep redish-brown. In fact, every hue that painters love, or could almost imagine, is found standing out boldly or hid away in some recess, in one part or another of a forest scene at this season, and all so delicately mingled and blended that human art must despair of making even a tolerable imitation. And these are beauties which not even the sun can portray; the photographer's art has not yet enabled him to seize and fix them on the mirror which he holds up to nature. He can give the limbs and outward flourishes, but not the soul of such a scene. His representation bears the same relation to the reality that a beautiful corpse does to the flashing eye and glowing cheek of living beauty."

Literary Gossip in Olden Times.

Now for a little literary gossip. Are you aware of the early literary claims of Sillery on the world at large? On the 22nd March, 1769, a novelist of some standing, Mrs. Frances Brooke, an officer's lady, author of *Lady Julia Mandeville*, published in London a work in four volumes, which she dedicated to His Excellency the Governor of Canada, Guy Carleton, afterwards Lord Dorchester, under the title the *History of Emily Montague*, being a series of letters addressed from Sillery by Emily Montague, the heroine of the tale, to her lively and witty friend, Bella Fermor—to some military admirers in Quebec, Montreal, and New York—and to some British noblemen, friends of her father.

It is stated in all the old Quebec Guide Books, that the house in which the "divine" Emily then dwelled stood on the brow of the Sillery Hill, close to Mrs. Graddon's property at Kilmarnock.

This novel, whether it was through the writer's *entourage* in the world or her *entrée* to fashionable circles, or whether on account of its own intrinsic literary worth, had an immense success in its day. The racy descriptions it contains of Canadian scenery, and colonial life, mixed with fashionable gossip of our Belgravians of 1766, seven years after the conquest, caused several English families to emigrate to Canada. Some settled in the neighborhood of Quebec, at Sillery, it is said. Whether they found all things *couleur-de-rose*, as the clever Mrs. Brooke had described them,—whether they enjoyed as much Arcadian bliss as the author of *Emily Montague* had promised—it would be very ungallant for us to gainsay, seeing that Mrs. Brooke is not present to vindicate herself. As to the literary merit of the novel, this much we will venture to assert, that setting aside the charm of association, we doubt that *Emily Montague*, if re-published at present, would make the fortune of her publisher. Novel writing, like other things, has considerably changed since 1766, and however much the florid Richardson style may have pleased the great grandfathers of the present generation, it would scarcely chime in with the taste of readers in our sensational times. In Mrs. Brooke's day Quebecers appear to have amused themselves pretty much as they do now, a century later. In summer, riding, driving, boating, pic-nics at Lake St. Charles, the Falls of Montmorenci, &c. In winter tandems, sleigh drives, pic-nics at the ice cone, tomycod fishing on the St. Charles, Chateau balls, the formation of a *pont* or ice-bridge, and its breaking up in the spring—two events of paramount importance. The military, as now the promoters of conviviality, fun and social amusement, and in return obtaining the *entrée* to the houses of the chief citizens; toying with every English rosebud or Gallic lily, which might strew their path in spite of paternal and maternal admonitions from the other side of the Atlantic, occasionally leading to the hymeneal altar a Canadian bride, and next introducing her to their horror-stricken London relatives, astounded to find out that our Canadian belles, were neither the color of copper, nor of ebony; in education and accomplishments, their equals—sometimes their superiors when class is compared to class. Would you like a few extracts from this curious old Sillery novel, of which one copy only seems now extant at Quebec. Bella Fermor, one of Emily Montague's familiars, and a most ingrained *coquette*, thus writes from Sillery in favor of a military protégé, on the 16th September, 1766, to the "divine" Emily, who had just been packed off to Montreal to recover from the effects of a love fit. "Sir George is handsome as an Adonis * * * you allow him to be of an amiable character; he is rich, young, well-born, and he loves you * * *."

All in vain thus to plead Sir George's cause, a dashing Col. Rivers (meant, we are told, by the Hon. W. Sheppard, to personify Col Henry Caldwell, of Belmont) had won the heart of Emily, who preferred true love to a coronet. Let us treasure up a few more sentences fallen from Emily's light-hearted confidante. A postscript to a letter runs thus—"Adieu, Emily, I am going to ramble in the woods, and pick berries with a little smiling civil captain [we can just fancy we see some of our fair acquaintances' mouths water at such a prospect], who is enamoured of me. A pretty rural amusement for lovers." Decidedly; all this in the romantic woodlands of Sillery, a sad place it must be confessed, where even boarding school misses, were they to ramble thus, could scarcely escape contracting the *scarlet* fever. Here goes another extract :—

(Bella Fermor to Miss Rivers, London.)

"Sillery, Sept. 20th—10 o'clock.

"Ah! we are vastly to be pitied; no beaux at all at the general's, only about six to one; a very pretty proportion, and what I hope always to see. We—the ladies I mean—drink chocolate with the general to-morrow, and he gives us a ball on Thursday; you would not know Quebec again. Nothing but smiling faces now; all gay as never was—the sweetest country in the world. Never expect to see me in England again; one is really somebody here. I have been asked to dance by only twenty-seven. * * * * * *"

Ah! who would not forgive the frolicsome Bella all her flirtations? But before we dismiss this pleasant record of other days, yet another extract, and we have done:—

(Bella Fermor to Lucy Rivers.)

"Sillery—Eight in the evening.

"Absolutely, Lucy, I will marry a savage and turn squaw (a pretty soft name for an Indian Princess!) Never was anything delightful as their lives. They talk of French husbands, but commend me to an Indian one, who lets his wife ramble five hundred miles without asking where she is going.

"I was sitting after dinner, with a book, in a thicket of hawthorn near the beach, when aloud laugh called my attention to the river, when I saw a canoe of savages making to the shore. There were six women and two or three children, without one man amongst them. They landed, tied the canoe to the root of a tree, and finding out the most agreeable shady spot amongst the bushes with which the beach was covered, (which happened to be very near me) made a fire, on which they laid some fish to broil, and fetching water from the river, sat down on the grass to their frugal repast. I stole softly to the house, and ordering a servant to bring some wine and cold provisions, returned to my squaws. I asked them in French if they were of Lorette; they shook their heads—I repeated the question in English, when the eldest of the women told me they were not; that their country was on the borders of New England; that their husbands being on a hunting party in the woods, curiosity and the desire of seeing their brethren, the English, who had conquered Quebec, had brought them up the great river, down which they should return as soon as they had seen Montreal. She courteously asked me to sit down and eat with them, which I complied with, and produced my part of the feast. We soon became good company, and brightened the chain of friendship with two bottles of wine, which put them in such spirits that they danced, sung, shook me by the hand, and grew so fond of me that I began to be afraid I should not easily get rid of them.

"Adieu! my father is just come in, and has brought some company with him from Quebec to supper.

"Yours ever,

"A. Fermor."

Conclusion.

It behoves us now—albeit reluctantly—to say adieu to the flowery realms of romance in which *Emily Montague* has enshrined "Our Parish," and to view the settlement in our present day, such as Anglo-Saxon intelligence and Anglo-Saxon energy have chiefly made it: the permanent abode of many merchant princes—as they rejoice in being styled—engaged in the exportation of the great staple of Canada, the riches of its forests. Sillery, with a population of about 4,000, is skirted in its southern aspect with innumerable and valuable timber coves or berths, in which the wooded wealth of Western and Eastern Canada awaits European purchasers. Gilmour's or Wolfe's cove, Spencer cove, Woodfield harbor, St. Michael's cove, Pointe à Pizeau or Bogue's cove, Pemberton's cove, Sharples' cove, Union cove, New London cove, Ring's End cove, Safety cove, Bridgewater cove, Victoria cove, Crescent cove, Cap Rouge coves,—furnishing an export trade of $5,000,000. These coves are crammed with elm, oak, spruce, pine, tamarac, etc., from Pres-de-Ville to Cape Rouge river, some eight miles. What a theme for a disciple of Malthus to discuss! And how long and carefully, how minutely, did Prince Napoleon in his visit to Quebec in 1861, examine and note down, the boundless wealth of Canada for ship-building purposes, accumulated in the coves of Sillery.

Our Country Seats.

IN the preceding paper a general sketch has been attempted of that portion of the St. Lawrence highlands adjoining Quebec to the west—a locality remarkable for the numerous residences it contains of "the nobility of commerce," as a contemporary facetiously styles our merchants. We shall, in the following sketches, go over a great portion of the same ground, and detail, specifically, the most attractive of these residences, enlarging our canvass, however, so as to comprise also descriptions of rural homes beyond the limits of Sillery. Many other abodes we would also desire to take in these pages, but space precludes it. It is to be hoped we won't be misunderstood in our literary project: far is it from our intention to write a panegyric of individuals or a pæan to success, although sketches of men or domestic recollections may frequently find their place in the description of their abodes. No other desire prompted us but that of attempting to place prominently before the public the spots with which history or nature has more specially enriched Quebec. Quebecers ought to be proud of their scenery and of the historical ivy which clings to the old walls of Stadacona. Neighboring cities may grow vast with brick and mortar; their commerce may advance with the stride of a young giant; their citizens may sit in high places among the sons of men, but can they ever compare with our own fortress for historical memories or beautiful scenery? Such being the case, let us then stand up for and appreciate nature's gifts; let us use our best endeavors to make them known. A fitting preface to this paper will be found in a historical sketch of the mansion which still crowns the Montmorenci Falls, once the abode of the father of our Sovereign; we shall then view the residences on the St. Lewis road in succession, then those along the St. Foy road, and finally close this paper with the description of other remarkable spots in the neighborhood of Quebec.

The Duke of Kent's Lodge,—Montmorenci.

"Oh! give me a home where the cataract's foam
Is admired by the poor and the rich, as they roam
By thy banks, *Montmorenci*, so placid and fair,
Oh! what would I give, could I find a home there."

The Montmorenci heights and beaches have become famous on account of the successful defence made there during the whole summer of 1759, by Montcalm, against the attacks of Wolfe's veterans. Finally, the French lines having been deemed impregnable on the Beauport side, a fort and barracks* were repeatedly talked of at *Isle aux Coudres*, to winter the troops. Wolfe was, however, overruled in his councils, and a spot near Sillery pointed out for a descent, probably by a French renegade, Denis de Vitré,—possibly by Major Stobo, who, being allowed a good deal of freedom during his captivity, knew the locality well. Stobo had been all winter a prisoner of war in the city, having been sent down from Fort Necessity to Quebec, by the French, from whom he escaped in the beginning of May, 1759, and joined Durell and Saunders' fleet long before it reached Pointe Levi. These same heights, celebrated for their scenery, were destined, later on, to acquire additional interest from the sojourn thereat of a personage of no mean rank—the future father of our august Sovereign.

Facing the roaring cataract of Montmorenci stands the "Mansion House," built by Sir Frederic Haldimand, C.B.,† Governor of the Province from 1778 to 1791, a plain-looking lodge, still existing, to which, some years back, wings have been added, making it considerably larger. This was the favorite summer abode of an English Prince. His Royal Highness Edward Augustus, Colonel of the Royal Fusileers, subsequently Field Marshal the Duke of Kent, "had landed here," says the *Quebec Gazette* of 18th August, 1791, "from H. M. ships *Ulysses* and *Resistance*, in seven weeks from Gibraltar, with the 7th or

* *Knox's Journal*, Vol. ii., pp. 14, 21, 24, 28. Aug. 21. "The project of erecting a fortress on the Island of Coudres, for a garrison of three thousand men, is laid aside for want of proper materials, and the season being too far advanced for such an undertaking. The enterprise for storming Quebec is also given up as too desperate to hope for success." P. 28.

† "For sale, the elegant villa of the late Sir Frederic Haldimand, K.B., delightfully situated near the Falls of Montmorency, with the farm-house.—Quebec, 1st Dec., 1791."—*Supplement to Quebec Gazette*, 22nd *Dec.*, 1792.

Royal Regiment of Fusileers." The Prince had evidently a strong fancy for country life, as may be inferred by the fact that, during his prolonged stay in Halifax, as Commander-in-Chief of the Forces, he owned also, seven miles out of the city, a similar rustic lodge, of which Haliburton has given a charming description. 'Twas on the 11th of August the youthful colonel, with his fine regiment, landed in the Lower Town; on the 12th was held, in his honor, at the Château St. Louis, a levée, whereat attended the authorities, civil, military, and clerical, together with the gentry. In the afternoon "the ladies were presented to the Prince in the Château." Who, then, attended this levée? Did he dance? If so, who were his partners? No register of names; no list of Edward's partners, such as we have of the Prince of Wales.* No *Court Journal!* Merely an entry of the names of the signers of the address in the *Quebec Gazette* of 18th August, 1791. Can we not, then, re-people the little world of Quebec of 1791?—bring back some of the principal actors of those stormy, political but froliosome times? Let us walk in with the "nobility and gentry," and make our best bow to the scion of royalty. There, in full uniform, you will recognize His Excellency Milord Dorchester, the Governor General, one of our most popular administrators; next to him, that tall, athletic military man, is the Deputy Governor General, Sir Alured Clark. He looks eager to grasp the reins of office from his superior, who will set sail for *home* in a few days. See how thoughtful the Deputy Governor appears; in order to stand higher with his royal English master he chuckles before-hand over the policy which gives to many old French territorial divisions, right English names—Durham, Suffolk, Prince Edward, York, Granville, Buckinghamshire, Herdfordshire, Kent. The western section of Canada will rejoice in the

---

* The list of the partners of Prince Edward's grand son H. R. H. the Prince of Wales, at the ball, etc., given in his honor in Quebec, by the Mayor and citizens, at the Music Hall, on the 21st August, 1860, comprises: 1. Mrs. Langevin (wife of H. L. Langevin, Esq., M.P.P., and Mayor of Quebec); 2. Mrs. Cartier (wife of the Hon. George Etienne Cartier, Attorney General); 3. Miss Irvine (daughter of Colonel Irvine, Provincial Aide-de-Camp); 4. Miss Price; 5. Miss LeMesurier, 6. Miss Derbyshire; 7. Miss Sewell; 8. Miss Caron (daughter of the Hon. Justice Caron, and now wife of Mr. Justice Taschereau); 9. Lady Milne; 10. Miss Napier, of Montreal; 11. Mrs. Sericold (wife of Captain Serocold and daughter of the Hon. Chief Justice Duval); 12. Miss Dunscomb (daughter of the Collector of Customs at Quebec); 13. Miss Fischer (daughter of the Attorney General of New Bruuswick); 14. Miss Mountain (daughter of the late Bishop of Quebec); 15. Miss Anderson; 16. Mrs. Ross; 17. Mrs. Alex. Bell; 18. Miss Tilley (daughter of the ex-Provincial Secretary of New Brunswick); 19. Mrs. R. H. Smith.

9

new names of Hesse, Lunenbourg, Nassau, Mecklenbourg. That Deputy Governor will yet live to win a *baton** of Field Marshal under a Hanoverian sovereign. He is now in close conversation with Chief Justice William Smith, senior. Round them are a bevy of Judges, Legislative Councillors, Members of Parliament, all done up to kill, *à l'ancienne mode*, by Monsieur Jean Laforme,† court hair-dresser, with powdered periwigs, ruffles and formidable pigtails. Here is Judge Mabane, Secretary Pownall, Honorable Messrs. Finlay,‡ Dunn, Harrison, Collins, Caldwell, Fraser, Lymburner; Messrs. Lester, Young, Smith, junior. Mingled with them you also recognize the bearers of old historical names—Messrs. Baby, De Bonne, Duchesnay, Dunière, Gueroult, De Lotbinèire, Roc de St Ours, Dambourgès, De Rocheblave, De Rouville, Saint George Dupré, the terror of the Yankees, Taschereau, De Tonnancour, Panet, De Salaberry, and a host of others. Dear reader, you want to know also what Royal Edward did—said—was thought of—amongst the Belgravians of old Stadacona, during the three summers he spent in Quebec,

> "How he looked when he danced, when he sat at his ease,
> When his Highness had sneezed, or was going to sneeze."

Bear in mind then, that we have to deal with a dashing Colonel of Fusileers—age twenty-three—status, a prince of the blood; add that he was ardent, generous, impulsive, gallant; a tall, athletic fellow; in fact,

---

* He was created Field Marshal in 1827.

† Monsieur Jean Laforme was, indeed, a high authority on hair dressing. Our youthful grandmothers of 1791 would have no other than Monsieur Laforme to dress their hair for the *Chateau* balls. A memorable instance has been handed down to posterity of the awful dilemma in which, either a press of engagements or an oversight, placed the Court *peruquier*, from which his genius alone extricated him. The beautiful Mrs. P——t, the consort of the Speaker of the Legislative Assembly in 179–, had to attend at a ball at the Castle St. Louis. Unfortunately she had omitted engaging in time Laforme to arrange her hair for the evening in question; and every hour of the day on which the ball was to take place, being bespoken, the hair-dresser in despair said that he would guarantee she would yet go to the ball, but that she must place herself entirely in his hands. "Well," said the *Grande Dame*, "what, then, am I to do?" "Bah!" said the *peruquier*, "'tis easily settled; I shall *do* up your hair the day *previous*."—"But then how am I to sleep with my hair done up?" "Oh! that is again easily arranged—you will sleep in a *fauteuil*. I will have your hair and head padded and strapped down." And so she did.

‡ The Hon. Hugh Finlay was Deputy Postmaster General for Canada from 1774 to 1800, when he was succeeded by George Heriot, who wrote a folio of travels on Canada. Hugh Finlay had served under Benjamin Franklin, the first English Deputy Postmaster General for the *then* British American Provinces, from 1750 to 1774, when he resigned. When he took the appointment the postage on letters was insufficient to cover his salary, £300 per annum.

one of George III.'s big, burly boys—dignified in manner—a bit of a statesman; witness his happy and successful speech* at the hustings of the Charlesbourg election, and the biting rebuke it contained in anticipation—for Sir Edmund Head's unlucky post-prandial joke about the *superior* race. Would you prefer to know him after he had left our shores and become Field Marshal the Duke of Kent? Take up his biography by the Rev. Erskine Neale, and read therein that Royal Edward was a truthful Christian gentleman—a chivalrous soldier, though a stern disciplinarian—an excellent husband—a persecuted and injured brother—a neglected son—the munificent patron of literary, educational and charitable institutions—a patriotic Prince—in short, a model of a man and a paragon of every virtue. But was he all that? we hear you say. No doubt of it. Have you not a clergyman's word for it—his biographer's? The Rev. Erskine Neale will tell you what His Royal Highness did at Kensington Palace, or Castlebar Hill. Such his task; ours, merely to show you the gallant young colonel, emerging bright and early from his Montmorenci Lodge, thundering with his spirited pair of horses over the Beauport and *Canardière* road; one day, "sitting down to whist and partridges for supper," at the hospitable board of a fine old scholar and gentleman, M. de Salaberry, then M.P.P. for the county of Quebec, the father of the hero of Chateaugay, and who resided near the Beauport church. Another day you may see him dash past Belmont or Holland House or Powell Place, occasionally dropping in with all the *bonhommie* of a good, kind Prince, as he was—especially when the ladies were young and pretty. You surely did not expect to find an anchorite in a slashing Colonel of Fusileers—in perfect health—age, twenty-three. Not a grain of ascetism ever entered, you know, in the composition of "Farmer George's" big sons; York and Clarence, they were no saints; neither were they suspected of ascetism; not they, they knew better. And should Royal Edward, within your sight, ever kiss his hand to any fair daughter of Eve, inside or outside of the city, do not, my Christian friend, upturn to heaven the whites of your eyes in pious horror; princes are men, nay, they require at times to be more than men to escape the snares, smiles, seductions,

* "Away," exclaimed the Prince to the excited voters, "with those hated distinctions of English and Canadians; you are all my august father's beloved subjects!"

which beset them at every step in this wicked, wicked world. How was Montmorenci Lodge furnished? Is it true that the Prince's remittances, from Carleton House never exceeded £5,000 per annum during his stay here?—Had he really as many bells to summon his attendants in his Beauport Lodge as his Halifax residence contained—as he had at Kensington or Castlebar Hill? Is it a fact that he was such a punctual and early riser, that to ensure punctuality on this point, one of his servants was commanded to sleep in the day time in order to be awake at day-break to ring the bell?—Did he really threaten to court-martial the 7th Fusileers, majors, captains, subs and privates, who might refuse to sport their pig-tails in the streets of Quebec, as well as at Gibraltar?

Really, dear reader, your inquisitiveness has got beyond all bounds; and were Prince Edward to revisit these shores, we venture to say, that you would even in a frenzy of curiosity or loyalty do what was charged by De Cordova, when Edward's grandson, Albert of Wales, visited, in 1860, Canada and the American Union:—

> "They have stolen his gloves and purloined his cravat—
> Even scraped a souvenir from the nap of his hat."

Be thankful if we satisfy even one or two of your queries. He had indeed to live here on the niggardly allowance of £5000 per annum. The story* about censuring an officer for cutting off his pig-tail refers not to Canada, but to another period of his life. He lived rather retired; a select few only were admitted to his intimacy; his habits were here, as elsewhere, regular; his punctuality, proverbial; his stay amongst us, marked by several acts of kindness, of which we find traces in the addresses presented on several occasions, thanking him for his own personal exertions and the assistance rendered by his gallant men at several fires which had occurred.† He left behind some warm admirers, with whom he corresponded regularly. We have now before us a package of his letters dated "Kensington Palace." Here is one out of twenty; but no, the records of private friendship must remain inviolate.

* The anecdote of the officer, who, on being ordered on foreign service, cut off his queue and buried it with military honors, is humorously related by Erskine Neale, in the Duke's Biography, p. 325.

† *Christie's History of Canada.*

The main portion of the "Mansion House," at Montmorenci, is just as he left it. The room in which he used to write is yet shown; a table and chair—part of his furniture—are to this day religiously preserved. The Lodge is now the residence of G. B. Hall, Esquire, the proprietor of the extensive saw-mills at the foot of the falls.

Marchmont.

> "Oh! give me a home on that bold classic height,
> Where in sweet contemplation in age's dark night,
> I may tread o'er the plain where as histories tell
> Britain's stout-hearted Wolfe—in his victory fell."

Adjoining the expanse of table land, now known as the Plains of Abraham, and divided from it to the east by a high fence, lies with a southern exposure a level and well-cultivated farm—Marchmont—tastefully laid out some sixty summers ago by Sir John Harvey, next occupied for several years by Sir Thomas Noel Hill, subsequently owned by Hon. John Stewart, and for a long time past, the permanent residence of John Gilmour, Esquire, of the well-known Glasgow house of Pollock, Gilmour & Co. To the west, Marchmont farm is bounded by Wolfesfield; to the south by the river heights, having a valuable timber cove (Wolfe's cove,) attached to it. The dwelling, a cheerful and sunny residence, decks a sloping lawn, not far from the high bank, embedded as it were in a clump of fir, ash, maple and pine trees, which conceal it from the St. Lewis road, and afford, on the opposite side, a variety of charming glimpses of our noble estuary, the main artery of Western commerce. A spacious and richly-stocked conservatory opens on the drawing-room to the west of the house. This embellishment was erected by the present proprietor.

In the the summer months, visitors travelling past Marchmont cannot fail to notice the magnificent hawthorn hedge, interspersed here and there with young maple, which encloses it on the St. Lewis road.

Marchmont, even shorn of its historical memories, would much interest an observer who had an eye to agricultural pursuits carried to a high state of perfection. The outhouses and arrangements for raising cattle, poultry, &c., are on a truly comprehensive scale.

Connected with Marchmont, there are incidents of the past, which will ever impress it on the mind of the visitor. A century back, over this same locality, the tide of battle surged for several hours when Wolfe's army had ascended the cliff. No later than 1860, the crumbling bones of fallen warriors were discovered whilst laying the foundation of the flag-staff to the east of the house. They were buried again carefully under the same flag-staff—erected to salute the Prince of Wales when passing Marchmont. Let us hear one of the actors on that eventful September morning of 1759—Capt. John Knox :—

"Before day break," says he, "this morning we made a descent upon the North shore, about half a mile to the eastward of Sillery; and the light troops were fortunately, by the rapidity of the current, carried lower down, between us and Cape Diamond. We had in this detachment thirty flat bottomed boats, containing about 1600 men. This was a great surprise on the enemy, who, from the natural strength of the place, did not suspect, and consequently were not prepared against, so bold an attempt. The chain of sentries which they had posted along the summit of the heights, galled us a little and picked off several men (in the boat where I was, one man was killed; one seaman, with four soldiers, were slightly, and two mortally wounded, and some officers), before our light infantry got up to dislodge them. This grand enterprise was conducted and executed with great good order and discretion; as fast as we landed the boats were put off for reinforcements, and the troops formed with much regularity; the General with Brigadier Monckton and Murray, were ashore with the first division. We lost no time, but clambered up one of the steepest precipices that can be conceived, being almost a perpendicular and of an incredible length; as soon as we gained the summit all was quiet, and not a shot was heard, owing to the excellent conduct of the infantry under Colonel Howe. It was by this time clear day-light. Here we formed again, the river and the south country in our rear, our right extending to the town, our left to Sillery, and halted a few moments. The general then detached the light troops to our left to route the enemy from their battery, and to disable their guns, except they could be rendered serviceable to the party who were to remain there; and this service was soon performed. We then faced to the right and marched towards the town by files, till we came to the Plains of Abraham, an even piece of ground which Wolfe had made choice of, while we stood forming upon the hill. Weather showery; about six o'clock the enemy first made their appearance upon the heights, between us and the town; whereupon we halted and wheeled to the right forming the line of battle."

Belvidere Lodge.

On a prettily wooded corner lot, bounded to the west by the Belvidère road, to the south by the Grande Allée or St. Lewis road, and crowning a rising ground surrounded on three sides by tall fir trees, you notice, from a distance, the glittering roof of Belvidère Lodge, exactly opposite to Marchmont. From the veranda and drawing-room windows, your glance lights on the very spot opposite, where, at day-break, on the 13th of September, 1759, were deployed the English battalions until they wheeled to the right and took a position one mile closer to the city to meet the French on their way from the Beauport camp.

The accompanying sketch, copied from a rough old drawing made either from the English fleet or from Sillery, on the day of the battle, gives the position of the English about seven o'clock in the morning, and seems to relate to what Capt. Knox states in his *Journal* to have occurred in front of the spot on which Belvidère Lodge now stands.

"What galled us most," says Knox, "was a body of Indians and other marksmen they had concealed in the corn opposite to the front of our right wing and a coppice that stood opposite to our centre, inclining towards our left, but Colonel Hale, by Brigadier Monckton's orders, advanced some platoons, alternately, from the forty-seventh regiment, which, after a few rounds, obliged their skulkers to retire; we were now ordered to lie down, and remained some time in this position. About eight o'clock we had two pieces of short brass six-pounders playing on the enemy which threw them into some confusion and obliged them to alter their disposition, and Montcalm formed them into three large columns; about nine the two armies moved a little nearer to each other. The light cavalry made a first attempt upon our parties at the battery of Sillery, but were soon beat off, and Monsieur de Bouganville, with his troops from Cap Rouge, came down to attack the flanks of our second line, hoping to penetrate there, but, by a masterly disposition of Brigadier Townshend, they were forced to desist, and the first battalion of Royal Americans was then detached to the first ground we had formed on after we gained the heights, to preserve the communication between the bank and our boats."

The second drawing is taken from the St. Lewis road, and shows the flower garden and lawn with a tall fir tree in the centre.

Belvidère Lodge, the residence of Mr. William Drum, is a pleasant and handsomely-situated country seat wherein to enjoy his honestly-made fortune. In addition to the commodious dwelling and pretty grove of pine trees, there are, with the usual adjuncts of our country residence, a well-stocked fruit garden, a large vegetable field, fine meadows, ice-house, &c.

Wolfesfield.

" The hill they climb'd, and halted at its top, of more than mortal size."

The successful landing at this spot of the English forces, who, in 1759, invaded Quebec, no less than its scenery, lends to Wolfesfield peculiar interest. Major, afterwards General, John Hale, later on conspicuous for gallantry during the long and trying siege of Quebec, in 1775–6, was one of the first men who, in 1759, put his foot on the heights in front of the locality where now stands the dwelling, having climbed up the hill by the *ruisseau St. Denis*, heading the flank Company of the Lascelles or 47th Regiment. General Wolfe made the main body of the army march up, Indian file, by a pathway which then existed where the high road is at present. At the head of this path may yet be seen the remains of the French entrenchments, occupied on that day by a militia guard of 100 men, chiefly Lorette militiamen, a portion of whom had that very night obtained leave to go and work on their farms,*

* " Ce capitaine avait avec lui beaucoup d'habitants de Lorette, dont le lieu était à portée de ce poste ; ils lui demanderent permission d'aller travailler la nuit chez eux ; il l'a leur accorda: (on pretend que ce faut a condition d'aller aussi travailler pour lui, sur une terre qu'il avait dans cette paroisse."—*Memoire sur les affaires du Canada*, 1749–'60, p. 114.

who fired at Major Hale's party, and then, says an old manuscript, thinking they had to deal with the whole English army, they surrendered, with their officer, Capt. De Vergor, who being wounded, could not escape, and exclaimed, "Sauvez vous." This was shortly after midnight, and Wolfe, notwithstanding the grievous indisposition he was then laboring under, organized a plan to get up supplies and ammunition from the *bateaux;* this he had accomplished by four in the morning, when he drew up his men on Marchmont field. The sailors of the *bateaux* were the men employed in carrying up the provisions and ammunition. Wolfe had grog served out to them as they reached, tired and panting, the top of the hill with their loads, using to each kind and encouraging words. The crowning success which followed is lengthily described elsewhere. The first house built at Wolfesfield was by a Captain Chandler; David Munro, Esquire, was the next proprietor. The occupant for the last thirty-eight years has been an old and respected Quebec merchant, well known as "the King of the Saguenay," on account of the extensive mills he owns in that region—William Price, Esq., the aged father of the Hon. David Price, Legislative Councillor. Mr. Price has added much to the beauty of the place, which enjoys a most picturesque river view. In front of the dwelling there is a fine lawn, shaded by some old thorn trees, with comfortable rustic seats close by the ravine St. Denis. This ravine is a favorite locality for botanizing excursions. Wolfesfield, without being as extensive as some of the surrounding estates, is one of the most charming rural homes Quebec can boast of.

Elm Grove.

An eccentric writer has asserted that the surroundings and belongings of a man furnish a fair index to his character. If this theory is to hold good, persons passing along the Grande Allée road and noticing on the north side a lofty new dwelling, ambitiously looking down from its lofty roof on the surrounding grove of trees facing Wolfesfield, would not inaptly conclude it must be the mansion of the Chief Magistrate, the Mayor of the Parish, and so it is: An important event connected with Elm Grove, finds its place in our annals under date of the 18th August, 1860. The Mayor of Sillery, in the name of the citizens and burgesses was called on to welcome, within the limits of the municipality, on his way to Spencer Wood, our Sovereign's first-born, Albert Edward, of the United Kingdom of Great Britain and Ireland, Prince of Wales, Duke of Saxony, Prince of Cobourg and Gotha, Great Steward of Scotland, Duke of Cornwall and Rothesay, Earl of Chester, Carrick and Dublin, Baron of Renfrew and Lord of the Isles, K. G.* On this auspicious occasion a high platform, close to Elm Grove, bore His Worship, his Councillors and Aldermen; therefrom he spoke out the sentiments of Canada and of Sillery.

The plantation of elms from which this seat takes its name, together with other trees, conceal the dwelling so entirely from the road, that unless by entering the grounds no idea can be formed of their beauty and extent; amidst the group of trees there is one of lordly dimensions, in the centre of the garden. The new dwelling at Elm Grove is a stately, substantial structure; its internal arrangements, and heating apparatus, indicate comfort and that *bien-être* for which Lower Canada homes are proverbial. A winding, well-wooded approach leads up to the house from the Porter's Lodge and main road. From the upper windows an extensive view of Charlesbourg, Lorette, Beauport, Point Levi, and surrounding parishes, may be obtained.

Elm Grove, owned for many years by John Saxton Campbell, Esq., was purchased in 1856 by J. K. Boswell, Esq., the proprietor of the Ste. Anne and Jacques Cartier salmon rivers. It is but just to note as we pass this gentleman's energetic efforts to protect the fish and game of the country. Mr. Boswell was one of the originators of the "Quebec Fish and Game Protection Club," an institution which of late has branched off in every important Canadian city. The view here given is from the flower garden in rear.

---

* We read in Mr. Morgan's *Tour of the Prince of Wales*, page 16, of the paroxisms of loyalty this visit threw Canada in. DeCordova's humorous pen thus depicts the occurrence;—

" ....As for the Canadas, loyalty 's run
Into madness almost for Victoria's son;
They have dined him and wined him in manner most royal,
Addressed and harangued him to prove they were loyal,
* * * * * *
Feasted him, toasted him, ball'd him, and preached him."

Thornhill.

> " ....let us pierce into the midnight depth
> Of yonder grove, of wildest, largest growth,
> That, forming high in air a woodland quire,
> Nods o'er the mount beneath."

There is a peculiar feature noticeable about Quebec country seats which speaks volumes for their attractiveness as healthy and pleasant retreats; not only have they been at all times sought after by wealthy and permanent residenters, but also by men of European birth holding for the time being the highest position in the country, both under the French and under the English monarchs. Thus the celebrated Intendant Talon was the first owner of Belmont; Intendant Bigot had his luxurious chateau at Charlesbourg; Attorney General Ruette D'Auteuil used, near two centuries back, to spend his summer months at Sillery, where, later on, Bishop Dosquet, a French ecclesiastic, had his pretty villa at Samos (Woodfield). Vaudreuil was also a Canadian land-owner. Later on Governor Murray purchased extensively on the St. Foy road, amongst others, Belmont and the "Sans Bruit" farm; Governor Haldimand must have his lodge at Montmorenci Falls, subsequently occupied by the father of our august Queen; Hector Theophilus Cramahe, (afterwards Lieut.-Governor), in 1762, had his estate—some 500 acres of cornfield, and meadows—at Cap Rouge, now Meadowbank, owned by J. Porter, Esq. The Prime Minister of Canada, and present Governor of British Guiana, Hon. Francis Hincks, following in the footsteps of Sir Dominick Daly, must needs locate himself on the St. Lewis road, and in order to be close to his chief, the late Earl of Elgin, then residing at Spencer Wood, the Premier selected and purchased Thornhill, across the road, one of the most picturesque country seats in the neighborhood. You barely, as you pass, catch a glimpse of its outline as it rests under tall, cone-like firs on the summit of a hillock, to which access is had through a handsomely laid-out circuitous approach between two hills. An extensive fruit and vegetable garden lies to the east of the house; a hawthorn hedge dotted here and there with some graceful young maple and birch trees, fringes the roadside; a thorn shrubbery of luxuriant growth encircles the plantation of evergreens along the sides of the mound which slopes down to the road, furnishing a splendid croquet lawn. One of the chief beauties of the landscape, is the occasional glimpses of the Grande Allée and Spencer Wood, obtained from the house The dwelling was erected many years ago by Alexander Simpson, Esq., then manager of the Bank of Montreal, at Quebec. Forming portion of it, to the west, and looking towards Charlesbourg, there is a snug English-looking little nest, "Woodside," with the prettiest of thorn and willow hedges: in its young days it was so often chosen as a retreat for newly married people, that it was playfully called "Honeymoon," now, in its mature years, it has degenerated into "Bachelordom." Until May last, it was occupied by Messrs. Dobell and Becket, extensive Liverpool merchants; a sketch is here given. The view of Thornhill shows the front of the house. Thornhill has recently exchanged hands, and become the seat of Archibald Campbell, Esq., Barrister, of Quebec.

Spencer Wood.

High on the frowning cliffs of Sillery, one mile from the city limits, may be seen from the deck of the Montreal steamers, on their passage up or down, General Powell's superb old domain (Powell Place)—now known as Spencer Wood—as such well remembered when owned by the late Henry Atkinson, Esquire, by visitors from every corner of the continent of America. Shall we describe it at present, in its period of decay and blight ever since, in 1850, the seal of the province and the sign-manual of the Commissioner of the Board of Works to the deed of purchase made it provincial property? Shall memory go and shed a tributary tear over what survives of its past beauty—re-visit the spot where once was a gushing jet d'eau, fed by an elfish stream, now converted into a receptacle for rubbish—where formerly stood the princely dwelling of a man of taste, to view a large barn-looking shed, some two hundred feet in length? Shall we seek for a grapery, second to none in Canada, to find a broken-down ruin, through which the winds of heaven whistle a mournful dirge to departed years? Shall we accept, in lieu of the former pretty terraced flower garden in rear of the dwelling, a dull, silent court-yard, surrounding the *new* entrance? Nothing, then, remains of the primitive splendor of Spencer Wood. Pardon: its unrivalled scenery, its winding shady approaches, its pavillions, its ancestral oaks, still remain; it is beautiful still, notwithstanding man's neglect; a right royal demesne, fit even for the proudest nobleman England may send to rule this important dependency. Individually, we have much respect for several of the men who have occupied the high position of Commissioner of Public Works in this Province; collectively, we much incline to that legal fiction which would refuse to this as to other corporations "a soul to be saved;" or * * .

Let us, however, live in hope. Possibly for Spencer Wood and for the rest of Canada a good time is coming. In the meantime, let us introduce the reader to it, such as we well remember it, when it was the cheerful home of one of the leading merchants of Quebec; as such a subject of unfeigned interest to all visitors. Imagine, then, "a noble old seat, comprising once a couple of hundred acres, enclosed east and west between two streamlets—the '*ruisseau St. Denis* and Belle Borne,' who make themselves scarce, so scarce, the tiny rogues, in summer, that they nearly disappear from view,—clothed in a dense growth of primeval forest trees, shutting out here and there the light of heaven from its labyrinthian avenues,—with a most extensive and varied river landscape, blending the sombre verdure of its old trees with the vivid tints of its velvetty, sloping lawn, fit for a ducal palace; add a large flower and fruit garden, ornamented with a lovely little fount, supplied with the crystal element from the Belle Borne rill by a concealed aqueduct; conservatories, graperies, peach and forcing houses for pine-apples and tropical fruit, in all about three hundred and fifty feet of glass, chiefly on the portion known as Spencer Grange; pavillions picturesquely hung over the yawning precipice on two capes, one looking towards Sillery, the other towards the Island of Orleans; bowling greens; archery grounds; a well-selected library of rare or standard works; a collection of medals; illuminated missals; statuettes, *objets de vertu*, purchased, during a long residence of the owner, in Italy, France, Germany and England: such was, for many years, the elegant mansion of Henry Atkinson, Esquire.* The accompanying engraving shows the house, which was completely burnt on the 12th March, 1860. How often, in strolling over the grounds, have we not been inclined to ask whether the designer had not before him *Hervey's Dialogues*, slightly modifying them to suit some

*As we are penning these lines, the mail brings us the news of the death of Hy. Atkinson, who expired at Paris, on the 14th May last, at the age of 73 years, after spending the winter at Nice, in hopes of restoring his health.

of the leading features of Spencer Wood. "Nature had sunk the lawn into a gentle *decline*, on whose ample sides were oxen browsing and lambs frisking. The lusty droves lowed as they passed, and the thriving flocks bleated welcome music in their master's ear. Along the edge of this verdant slope was stretched a spacious and extensive walk, which, coated with gravel and enclosed with iron fencing, looked like a plain stripe of brown intersecting a carpet of the brightest green. Shady bowers and rustic chairs to rest the promenaders along the main avenues encircling the property, nearly five miles round. The redundancy of the neighboring rill, gurgling amidst a group of nayades; the rest leaping over the cliff and straggling down—a silver thread, resplendent with the glories of the rainbow." Was it not from Hervey that was taken the idea of the fairy flower garden, with its terraces and southern, sunny exposure? "A *parterre*, planted with an assemblage of flowers, which advanced, one above another, in regular gradation of height, of dignity and of beauty; first, a row of daisies, gay as the smile of youth, and fair as the virgin snows; next, a range of crocusses, like a long stripe of yellow satin, quilted with threads, or diversified with sprigs of green; a superior order of ranunculuses, each resembling the cap of an earl's coronet, replenished the third story with full-blown tufts of glossy scarlet; beyond this a more elevated line of tulips raised their flourished heads and opened their enamelled cups, not bedecked with a single tint only, but glowing with an intermingled variety of radiant hues; the whole viewed from the house looked like a rainbow painted upon the ground, and wanted nothing to rival that resplendent arch only the boldness of its sweep and the advantage of its ornamental curve."* It became, in 1850, the residence of the Earl of Elgin; his *fêtes champêtres* and pleasant entertainments—who has forgotten them? A grievious family bereavement, the loss of an only son, made seclusion desirable for Sir Edmund W. Head during his residence at Spencer Wood. His Excellency Viscount Monck has now resided for two years at Spencer Wood; thus exchanging, for a time, the lovely scenery of his own ancestral halls, Charleville, on the banks of the Dargle, for the leafy bowers of Sillery. Several tasty improvements have marked his sojourn there; a spacious conservatory, amongst others, and a small plantation of evergreens, to the east of the house. About the beginning of the century, Powell Place was called

* Spencer Wood garden is described in *Loudon's Encyclopædia of Gardening*, page 341, and also in the *Gardeners' Magazine* for 1837, at p. 467.

Spencer Wood, after the Right Honorable Spencer Percival, the patron of Honorable Michael Percival, the owner. It had previously been the summer dwelling of Sir James Craig, when Governor General of Canada. Eminently adapted for the residence of a Governor General, from its size, beauty, and proximity to the city, being merely twelve minutes drive therefrom, it is likely long to remain Government property; its projecting highlands pointing out favorable spots for round towers, redoubts, &c.*

Spencer Grange.

"Retirement, rural quiet, friendship, books:"—*Thomson.*

When Spencer Wood became the gubernatorial residence, its owner reserved the smaller half, Spencer Grange, some forty acres, divided off by a high brick wall and fence, and terminating to the east in a river frontage of one acre. A small rustic bower facing the St. Lawrence overhangs the cliff, close to where the Belle Borne rill tumbles down the bank to Spencer Cove—in spring and autumn, a ribbon of fleecy whiteness. To the south it is bounded by Woodfield, and reaches to the north a

* Mr. P. Lowe, during many years in charge of the conservatory, furnished us with the following note :—"The hot-houses belonging to Henry Atkinson, while in my charge, consisted of pinery, stove and orchid house. In the pinery were grown specimens of the Providence, Enville, Montserrat and Queen pines—a plant of the latter variety, in fruit, being exhibited at the Horticultural Exhibition, Montreal, in September, 1852, the fruit of which weighed between five and six pounds, being the first pine-apple exhibited of Canadian growth, but not the first grown at Spencer Wood; it was noticed in the *Illustrated London News* of the same year. The following are the names of a few of the plants grown in the stove-house :—*Ardisia; Alamanda; Amaryllis, Achimenes; Aschynanthus, Asclepias, Begonias, Crinums, Centradinias; Calumnias, Drymonias; Euphorbias, Franciscia; Goldfussia; Gesneras,* in twelve varieties; *Gloxinias,* in twenty-four varieties; *Gloriosa; Gardenias; Hibiscus; Inga; Ipomœa; Justicia; Lasiandra; Legastrema; Musa-Cavendishii,* which we fruited—the only one fruited in the province to this day, to my knowledge—the bunch of fruit weighed ninety pounds; *Maranta; Melastomas, Mennetties; Nymphies; Osbeckias, Pentees, Passiflora; Psideum: Stephenotus, Strelitzias; Russellca; Ruellea; Rondilitia, Tabernaemonana; Tradiscantia; Vinca; Clerodendrons,* &c., &c. In the orchid house, the following are a portion of the names of plants grown by me :—*Bletia; Bolbophyllum; Cyppripedium; Cymbedium; Catasetum; Cattleya; Brassavoleas, Dendrobiums, Epidendrons, Ærides; Gongora; Gomezia; Maxillaria; Oncidium, Plurathalis; Pholidota; Physosiphon; Plurathalles; Peristerias, Ripsalis, Stanhopeas; Zygopetalum,* &c., &c. The houses containing the above were heated by hot-water pipes for atmospheric heat and open tanks for bottom heat; they were the most complete of the kind I have seen either in Canada or Great Britain—so much so, that, during my stay with Mr. Atkinson, we used to produce for Christmas and New-Year's Day pine-apples, cucumbers, rhubarb, asparagus, and mushroons, all in the same house."

point opposite the road called Stuart's road which intersects Holland's farm, leading from the St. Lewis to the St. Foy highway. The English landscape style was adopted in the laying out of the flower garden and grounds: some fine old trees were left here and there through the lawns; three clumps of maple and red oak in the centre of the meadows to the west of the house grouped for effect; fences, carefully hidden away in the surrounding copses; hedges, buildings, walks, and trees brought in here and there to harmonize with the eye and furnish on a few acres a perfect epitome of a woodland scene. The whole place is girt round by a zone of tall pine, beach, maple and red oaks, whose deep green foliage, when lit up by the rays of the setting or rising sun, assume tints of most dazzling brightness,—emerald wreaths dipped into molten gold and overhanging under a leafy arcade, a walk which zigzags round the property, following to the southwest the many windings of the Belle Borne streamlet. This sylvan region, most congenial to the tastes of a naturalist, echoes in spring and summer with the ever-varying and wild minstrelsy of the robin, the songsparrow, the red-start, the thrush, the red-eyed fly-catcher and other feather choristers, while the golden-winged woodpecker heralds at dawn the coming rain of the morrow, and some crows, rendered saucy by protection, strut through the sprouting corn, in their sable costume, like worldly clergymen computing their tythes. On the aforesaid walk, once trodden over by the prince of American naturalists, the great Audubon, whilst on a visit to Mr. Atkinson at Spencer Wood, was conferred the name of *Audubon avenue*, by his Sillery disciple, the author of the *Birds of Canada*. The grand river views of Spencer Wood, are replaced here by a woodland scenery, ever sure to please the eye of any man of cultivated taste, accustomed to the park-like appearance of the south of England. In front of the mansion, close to the lawn, stands the noblest Elm tree of Sillery (*Ulmus Americanus*), leafy to its very roots. Here amidst literature and flowers after leaving Spencer Wood, lived for several years, Henry Atkinson, a name in those regions once synonimous with ornamental gardens and flowers. Graperies, conservatories, an orchid house, soon sprung up under his hand at this spot, larger than Spencer Wood had ever boasted of in its palmiest days.

The present owner has added an aviary—a small museum of the Canadian *fauna*, and collection of works and plates on Canadian subjects. On the western corner of the Spencer Grange property, and depending of it, can be seen from the road, *Bagatelle*—a long, straggling, picturesque cottage, with trees, rustic seats, walks and a miniature flower-garden round it: a small prospect pavillion opens on the St. Lewis road, furnishing a pretty view of the blue range of mountains to the north; in summer it peeps from under clusters of the green or purple leaves of some luxuriant *Virginian* creepers — our American ivy — which climb round it. *Bagatelle* is generally occupied by an *attaché* of Spencer Wood. The ex-military aide-de-camp, Captain Retallack, lived there several years, and was succeeded by His Excellency's secretary, Denis Godley, Esquire: the accompanying sketch was taken when occupied by the latter. It is now the residence of an English clergyman, Rev. S. Vial, who succeeded the Rev. M. Fothergill, at present incumbent of St. Peter's Chapel, Quebec.

Two views of Spencer Grange are given:—one, of the house and new grapery from the rear; on the lawn is visible, the vigilant guardian of the grounds, the Italian mastif "Wolfe," a *molossus* in size; the second exhibits a full view of the house and both graperies, with a family group.

Spencer Grange for several years past has been the seat of the author.

Woodfield.

"Deambulatio per loca amœna."—*Frascatorius.*

Unquestionably the most ornate and richly laid-out estate around Quebec is Woodfield, formerly the elegant mansion of the Honorable Wm. Sheppard, at present of Fairymead, Drummondville. For many years past it has become the permanent residence of the Gibb family. The horticultural department and conservatory are under the immediate charge of Andrew Torrance, Esq., Mrs. Gibb's brother. His taste is too well known to require any praise, and truly may it be said that the lovers of sweet flowers, trim hedges, and fairy scenery, can easily beguile several hours together in exploring the broad acres of Woodfield, equal in extent to Spencer Wood itself. But let us hear on this subject one who knows how to describe and embellish a country seat:—

"In the early part of the last century," says the Honorable Wm. Sheppard, "this estate was in the possession of Monseigneur Dosquet, titular Bishop of Samos *in partibus infidelium,* and he gave it that name after his Episcopal title. He built a substantial stone residence near the brow of the hill, overlooking the St. Lawrence—a one story house—with a high peaked roof, long and narrow, after the mode of building in those days, something in the style of the manor house of Beauport. The name of Samos is now superseded by that of Woodfield, yet it is still in use as applied to the high road passing on its western side, commencing at the termination of the road leading from Quebec in that direction, called the Grand Allée, where it forks into the Samos road and the Chémin Gomin at Spencer Wood. It is not known how long Bishop Dosquet occupied his estate.

"Soon after the cession of Canada to the British Crown, this property passed into the hands of Judge Mabane,* by purchase, from the reverend proprietors of the seigniory. Mr. Mabane changed the name to Woodfield, and made extensive alterations to the house, adding to it a second story, giving it by other additions a more imposing appearance from the river, and adding two pavillion wings, connected with the house by corridors.

"About the year 1807, the late Honorable Matthew Bell purchased Woodfield from Miss Mabane, the judge's sister. Mr. Bell occupied the house as a summer dwelling only, and it is not known that he improved the estate to any extent, unless it were the garden, which he enlarged and stocked with choice fruit trees. Previous to the purchase of Mr. Bell, Woodfield was occupied as a dwelling during several years by Bishop Mountain, the first Protestant Bishop of Quebec. During his occupation he removed a bridge which spanned Belle Borne Brook, with the intention of cutting off communication with Powell Place (Spencer Wood), the neighboring estate, for reasons which it is not now necessary to enter into. The bridge was subsequently restored by the sons of Sir R. S. Milnes, Governor General, and was known by the name of Pont Bonvoisin.

---

*Judge Adam Mabane died in 1792.

"In 1816 Woodfield passed into the possession of Mr. William Sheppard, by purchase, from Mr. Bell. Mr. Sheppard improved the house and grounds greatly, erecting vineries and a large conservatory; changing the front of the house so as to look upon a rising lawn of good extent, interspersed with venerable oaks and pine, giving the whole a striking and pleasing aspect. The alteration in the house gave it a very picturesque appearance, as viewed from the foot of the old avenue, backed by sombre pines. Mr. Sheppard added to the estate about sixty acres of land on its southern side, it being now bounded by the road leading to St. Michael's Cove. During the alterations made in the house, a leaden foundation plate was discovered, stating that the house was built in 1732, by Bishop Dosquet. This plate was deposited for safe keeping in the Museum of the Literary and Historical Society, where (if still extant) it may be consulted.

"In December, 1842, the house was unfortunately destroyed by fire, and with it a valuable library of some three thousand volumes, many of them costly illustrated works on Natural History and other sciences. Shortly afterwards a new house was built on a more desirable and commanding site, in the midst of splendid old oaks and pines, looking down upon an extensive lawn, with the St. Lawrence in the middle distance, the view terminated by the South Shore, studded with cheerful-looking cottages. To suit the new site, Mr. Sheppard laid out a new approach, placing the entrance somewhat nearer Quebec than the old avenue, following the roundings of Belle Borne Brook, and leaving it with a striking sweep, among groups of trees, to the house. This approach is one of the greatest attractions of the place. He also built a large conservatory in connection with the house.

"Woodfield changed hands in 1847, having been purchased by Thos. Gibb, Esq., who exchanged it with his brother, Jas. Gibb, Esq., a wealthy merchant of Quebec, president of the Quebec Bank, who added much to the beauty of the estate.* Woodfield, with the improvements and embellishments made by the preceding proprietor is one of the most imposing and showy places in Canada, well worthy the encomiums passed upon it by J.

---

* A fairy plot of a flower garden was laid out near the edge of the cliff to the north-east, with a Chinese Pagoda enclosing the trunk of a large tree at one side, and a tiny Grecian temple at the other.

Jay Smith, Esq., of Philadelphia, editor of the *Horticulturist*, who, with a party of friends, visited it in 1857. He says, in that work: 'James Gibb, Esq., at Woodfield, possesses one of the most charming places on the American continent. Thoroughly English in its appurtenances, and leaving out its views of the St. Lawrence, its lawns, trees, and superb garden, are together, a model of what may be accomplished. The whole scene was enchanting. The traveller felt as if he was transported to the best parts of England, and our whole party uniting in an exclamation of pleasure and gratification. Here is everything in the way of well-kept lawns, graperies and greenhouses, outhouses for every possible contingency of weather, gardens, redolent of the finest flowers, in which bulbs of the best lilies make a conspicuous figure, and every species of fruit that can be grown. The traveller who does not see Woodfield has not seen Canada in its best trim.'

"The remains of one redoubt are visible near Belle Borne Brook, just above Pont Bonvoisin, or Bridge of Friendship, no doubt intended to guard the approach to Quebec by the footpath from Pointe à Puiseaux.* Another larger one was on the west side of Samos road, nearly opposite to the entrance gate of the new approach to Woodfield; it commanded the Samos road.

"Woodfield once could boast of a well-stocked aviary. The garden, of large extent, has always been celebrated for its fruit and flowers; for the taste for which it was laid out, and for the beautiful prospect obtained from it of the Citadel of Quebec, of the intervening portion of the St. Lawrence, with the numerous shipping in the harbor busily engaged in taking in their return cargoes of the staple article of exportation."

Sous les Bois.

This country seat, two miles from the city limits, stands in view of Pointe à Puiseaux, at Sillery, exactly fronting the mouth of the Etchemin

* Probably the four-gun battery mentioned in the account of the Battle of the Plains. We also find in a diary of the siege operations on the same day, "A mortar and some 18-pounders were carried to Samos, three-quarters of a league from the town. Batteries were erected there, which fired before night on the man-of-war that had come to anchor opposite *L'Ance du Foulon*, which was forced to sheer off."

River. Imagine a roomy, substantial, one-story cottage, equally well protected in winter against the piercing north, east and west winds, surrounded by large oaks and pines to temper the rays of an August sun, and through whose foliage the cool river breeze murmurs in the vernal season, wafting pleasure and health to the inmates. Add one of those unrivalled river landscapes peculiar to Sillery, well-cultivated fruit gardens, pastures, meadows, and lawns intersected by a long curving avenue, fringed with single trees at times, at others tastefully concealed in a clump of evergreens, and leading to the house by a circuitous approach, which hides the mansion until you are a few feet of it. Place in it, a toiling professional man, eager, after a dusty summer day's duty in St. Peter street, to breathe the coolness and fragrance of his rustic homestead, and enjoy the presence of his household gods; again add to it, the conviction in his heart that country life has increased the span of his existence by twenty years, and you have a faint idea of one of our many Canadian homes, of *Sous les Bois*, the residence of Errol Boyd Lindsay, Esq., one of the few remaining Quebecers who can recall the festivities of Powell Place, when Sir James Craig flourished there in 1807.

Benmore.

It will not be one of the least glories of "Our Parish," even when the provinces will have expanded into an empire, with Sillery as the seat of Vice-Royalty, to be able to boast of possessing the Canadian, the adopted home of a British officer of wealth and intelligence, known to the sporting world as the Great Northern Hunter. Who has not heard of the *battues* of Col. Rhodes on the snow-clad peaks of Cape Tourment, on the Western Prairies, and all along the Laurentian chain of mountains? One man alone through the boundless territory extending from Quebec to the North Pole, can dispute the belt with the Sillery Nimrod; but then, a mighty hunter is he; by name, in the St. Joachim settlement, Olivier Cauchon; to Canadian sportsmen known as *Le Roi des Bois*. It is said—but we cannot vouch for the fact—that, Cauchon, in order to acquire the scent, swiftness, and sagacity of the cariboo, has lived on cariboo milk, with an infusion of moss and bark, ever since his babyhood; but that this very winter he killed, with slugs, four cariboo at one shot, we can vouch for.

A few weeks since, a *habitant* with a loaded sleigh passed our gate; on the top of his load was visible a noble pair of antlers. "Qui à tué—ces cariboo?" we asked. Honest Jean Baptiste replied, "Le Colonel Rhodes, Monsieur." Then followed a second—then a third. Same question asked, to which for reply—"Le Colonel Rhodes, Monsieur." Then another sleigh-load of cariboo,—in all twelve cariboo; two sleighs of hare, grouse, and ptarmigan; then a man carrying a dead carcajou; then, in the distance, the soldier-like phiz of the Nimrod himself, nimbly following on foot the cavalcade. This was too much; we stopped and threatened the Colonel to apply to Parliament for an Act to protect the game of Canada against his unerring rifle. Were we not fully aware of the gratifying fact that, under recent legislative enactments, the fish and game of Canada have much increased, we might be inclined to fancy that the Colonel will never rest until he has bagged the last moose, the last cariboo in the country.

Benmore nestles cosily in a pine grove on the banks of the great river, the type of an English country gentleman's homestead. In front of the house, a spacious piazza, from which you can watch the river craft; in the vast surrounding meadows, a goodly array of fat Durhams and Ayrshires; in the farm-yard, short-legged Berkshires squeaking merrily in the distance; rosy-checked English boys romping on the lawn, surrounded by pointers and setters; such were the grateful sights which greeted our eyes one lovely June morning round Benmore, the residence of the President of the Quebec Game Club, and late Member of Parliament for Megantic.

Kirk Ella.

"The merchant has his snug retreat in the vicinity of the metropolis, where he often displays as much pride and zeal in the cultivation of his flower garden, and the maturing of his fruits, as he does in the conduct of his business, and the success of a commercial enterprise.—*Rural life in England— Washington Irvine.*

This villa, erected in 1850 on the north side of the St. Lewis road, facing Cataracoui, affords a striking exemplification of how soon taste and capital can transform a wilderness into a habitation combining every appliance of modern refinement and rustic adornment. It covers about eighty acres, two-thirds of which are green meadows, wheat fields, &c.,

the remainder, plantations, gardens and lawn. The cottage itself is a plain, unpretending structure, made more roomy by the recent addition of a dining room, &c., in rear. On emerging from the leafy avenue, the visitor notices two *parterres* of wild flowers—kalmias, trilliums, etc.,—transplanted from the neighboring wood, with the rank, moist soil of the Gomin marsh to derive nourishment from; they appear to thrive. In rear of these *parterres* a granite rockery, festooned with ferns, wild violets, &c., raises its gritty, rugged outline. This pretty European embellishment we would much like to see more generally introduced in our Canadian landscape; it is strikingly picturesque. The next object which catches the eye is the conservatory in which are displayed not only the most extensive collection of exotics in Sillery, but also, we venture to say, in the whole of Canada. In the centre of some fifty large camellia shrubs there is a magnificent specimen of the fimbriata variety—white leaves with a fringed border; it stands twelve feet high with corresponding breadth. When it is loaded with blossoms in the winter the spectacle is exquisitely beautiful. In rear of the conservatory is a vinery, a peach and apricot house, like the conservatory, all span-roofed and divided off in several compartments, heated by steam-pipes and furnaces, with stop-cocks to retard or accelerate vegetation at will. On the 31st May, when we visited the establishment, we found the *black* Hamburg grapes the size of cherries; the peaches and apricots correspondingly advanced; the cherries under glass quite over. One of the latest improvements is a second flower garden to the west of the house, in the English landscape style. In rear of this garden, to the north, there existed formerly a cedar swamp, which deep sub-soil draining with tiles has converted into a grass meadow of great beauty; a belt of white pine, spruce, tamarack, and some deciduous trees, thinned towards the south-west, let in a glimpse of the St. Lawrence and the high-wooded Point Levi shores, shutting out the view of the St. Lewis road, and completely overshadowing the porter's lodge; out-houses, stables, root-house, paddocks and barns are all on a correspondingly extensive scale. We have here another instance of the love of country life which our successful Canadian merchant likes to indulge in; and we can fancy, judging from our own case, with what zest the portly laird of Kirk Ella, after a toilsome day in his St. Peter street counting-house, hurries home to revel in the rustic beauty which surrounds his dwelling on all sides.

Kirk Ella, named from the paternal mansion in Yorkshire, is the seat of Ed. Burstall, Esquire, one of our most wealthy merchants.

Cataracoui.

The conflagration of Spencer Wood, on the 12th March, 1860, made it incumbent on the Provincial Government to provide for His Excellency Sir Edmund Head a suitable residence. After examining several places, Cataracoui, the residence of Henry Burstall, Esquire, opposite to Kirk Ella, was selected, and extensive additions made, and still greater improvements and decorations ordered when it became known that the First Gentleman of England, our Sovereign's eldest son, was soon to pay a flying visit to Her Majesty's Canadian lieges. Cataracoui can boast of having harbored two princes of the blood royal, the Prince of Wales, and the sailor boy, his youthful brother Alfred; a circumstance which no doubt much enhances its prestige in the eyes of its present owner—in wealth, one of our "Merchant Princes." It was laid out about 1836 by Jas. B. Forsyth, Esq., the first proprietor, and reflects credit on his taste.

This seat, without possessing the extensive grounds, vast river frontage, and long shady walks of Spencer Wood, or Woodfield, is an eminently picturesque residence. A new grapery with a lean-too roof, about ninety feet in length, has just been completed: the choicest* varieties of the grape vine are here cultivated. Several tasty additions have also recently been made to the conservatory, under the superintendence of a Scotch landscape gardener, Mr. P. Lowe, formerly in charge of the Spencer Wood conservatories, &c. We had the pleasure on one occasion to view, on a piercing winter day, from the drawing room of Cataracoui, through the glass door which opens on the conservatory, the rare collections of exotics it contains,—a perfect grove of verdure and blossoms,—the whole lit up by the mellow light of the setting sun, whose rays scintillated in

* The vinery contains the following new varieties, etc.:—Black Alicante, Foster's Seedling White, Muscat Hamburg, Lady Downs, Golden Hamburg; also the common Black Hamburg (which there is none to surpass), Joslyn St. Albans, Muscat of Alexandria, Sweet Water, Black St. Peter's, &c., &c. The conservatory is stocked with seventy Camellia Japonica of the newest varieties, twenty varieties of choice Azelias; Chorozemas, Heaths, Epacris, Dillwynia, Eriostemon, Acacias, Geraniuums, Fuchias, with a large collection of creeping plants, &c., &c.

every fantastic form amongst this gorgeous tropical vegetation, whilst the snow-wreathed evergreens surrounding the conservatory waived their palms to the orb of day in our clear, bracing Canadian atmosphere—summer and winter combined in the one landscape; the tropics and their luxuriant magnolias, divided by an inch of glass from the realms of old king frost and his hardy familiars, the pine and the maple. Charming was the contrast, furnishing a fresh proof of the comfort and luxury with which the European merchant, once settled in Canada, surrounds his home. What, indeed, can be more gratifying, during the Arctic, though healthy, temperature of our winter, than to step from a warm drawing-room, with its cheerful grate-fire, into a green, floral bower, and inhale the aroma of the orange and the rose, whilst the eye is charmed by the blossoming camellia of virgin whiteness; the wisteria, spireâ, azalea, rhododendron, and odorous daphne, all blending their perfume or exquisite tints. Cataracoui has been recently decorated, we may say, with regal magnificience, and Sillery is justly proud of this fairy abode, at present, the country seat of Charles E. Levey, Esq.

Beauvoir.

Crowning a sloping lawn, intersected by a small stream, and facing the Etchemin Mills, you notice on the south side of the St. Lewis road, next to Clermont, a neat dwelling hid amongst huge pines and other forest trees; that is one of our oldest English country seats. Family memories of three generations consecrate the spot. Would you like a glimpse of domestic life as enjoyed at Sillery? then follow that bevy of noisy, rosy-cheeked boys in Lennoxville caps, with gun and rod in hand, hurrying down those steep, narrow steps leading from the bank to the Cove below. How they scamper along, eager to walk the deck of that trim little craft, the *Falcon*, anchored in the stream, and sitting like a bird on the bosom of the famed river. Wait a minute and you will see the mainsail flutter in the breeze. Now our rollicking young friends have marched past ruins of "chapel, convent, hospital," &c., on the beach; you surely for all that did not expect them to look glum and melancholy. Of course they know all about "Monsieur Puiseaux," "le

12

Chevalier de Sillery," "the house where dwelt Emily Montague"; but do not, if you have any respect for that thrice happy age, the halcyon days of jackets and frills, befog their brains with the musty records of departed years. Let the lads enjoy their summer vacation, radiant, happy, heedless of the future. Alas! it may yet overtake them soon enough. What care could contract their brow? Have they not fed for the day their rabbits, their pigeons, their guinea-pigs? Is not that faithful fellow-boatswain, who saved from drowning one of their schoolmates, is he not as usual their companion on ship-board and ashore? There now, they drop down the stream for a long day's cruise round the Island of Orleans. Next week, peradventure, you may hear of the *Falcon* and its jolly crew having sailed for Portneuf, Murray Bay, the Saguenay or Betsimis, to throw a cast for salmon, sea-trout or mackerel, in some sequestered pool or sheltered bay.

> "There we'll drop our lines, and gather
> Old Ocean's treasures in."

Are they not glorious, handsome, manly fellows, our Sillery boys? No wonder we are all proud of them, of the twins as much as the rest, and more so perhaps. "Our Parish" you must know, is renowned for the proportion in which it contributes to the census: twins—a common occurrence; occasionally, triplets.

And who then owns this happy Canadian home? Ask the first person you may meet in the parish.

Sillery House.

The illustration exhibits a front view of this handsome dwelling, situated at the foot of the Cape, close to the Jesuits' old house, on a line with the river: it stands in the centre of an extensive garden, with here and there some large forest trees interspersed. This residence was built a few years back by John Sharples, Esquire, of the firm of C. & J. Sharples & Co., whose vast timber coves are in view from Sillery house. The plate shows also a family group.

Bardfield.

Pleasant the memories of our rustic homes! 'Tis pleasant, after December's murky nights, or January and February's inexorable chills, to go and bask on the sunny banks of our great river, under the shade of trees, in the balmy spring, and amidst the gifts of a bountiful nature, to inhale fragrance and health and joy. Pleasant, also, to wander during September in our solemn woods, "with footsteps inaudible on the soft yellow floor, composed of the autumnal sheddings of countless years." Yes, soothing to us are these memories of home—of home amusements, home pleasures, and even of home sorrows. Sweeter still, even though tinged with melancholy, the remembrance of the departed friends,—those guardian spirits we once saw moving in some of our Canadian homes in the legitimate pride of hospitality—surrounded by young and loving hearts—enshrined in the respect of their fellow-men.

Oft has it been our privilege at that festive season of our year, when a hallowed custom brings Canada's sons and daughters together with words of greeting and good-fellowship, to wend our way to Bardfield, high on the breezy hills of Sillery, and exchange a cordial welcome with the venerable man who had dwelled in our midst for many long years. Seldom has it been our lot to approach one who, as a scholar, a gentleman, a prelate, or what is more than all those titles put together, a truly good man, impressed himself more agreeably on our mind.

Another revolution of the circling year and the good pastor, the courteous gentleman, the learned divine, our literary* friend and neighbor, the master of Bardfield, had been snatched from among us and from an admiring public.

Where is the Quebecer who has not noticed the neat cottage on the north of the St. Lewis road, where lived and died the Lord Bishop Mountain? As you pass you see, as formerly, its lovely river view, gravelled walks, curving avenue, and turfy lawns traced by a hand now cold unto death. Bardfield continues to be occupied by Miss Mountain and other members of the late Bishop's family. A schoolhouse, in the rural Gothic style, quite an ornament for Sillery, has

---

* The late Bishop is the author of a collection of poems known as the *Songs of the Wilderness*, many of the subjects therein furnished in the course of his apostolic labors in the Red River settlement.

been erected by His Lordship's family, as a memorial of the sojourn at this spot of this true friend of suffering humanity and patron of education.

Clermont.

> " A house amid the quiet country's shades,
> With length'ning vistas, ever sunny glades,
> Beauty and fragrance clustering o'er the wall,
> A porch inviting, and an ample hall."

It ought to be a pleasant subject of reflection for several of our political chiefs, after staunchly asserting the rights of a down-trodden nationality, to obtain from a grateful country the full recognition of the talents enlisted in her cause. The satisfaction must be two-fold, when wealth accompanies honors, when the smiles of fortune light up each step of her favorite in his upward course.

The proprietor of Clermont, thirty odd years back, was a friendless, unknown, unprotected law student of Quebec. A very few years more and you find him a leading Barrister, Mayor of his city, Member of Parliament, Cabinet Minister, Speaker of the Legislative Council, a Justice of our Supreme Court of Appeals, and lastly, Chairman of the High Commissioners selected to give a Code of Laws to Canada—a gigantic task, already successfully achieved.

All these traits and more we find concentrated in the owner of yonder pleasant country seat, basking in the sunbeams of a May morning.

The Laird of Clermont descends from an old French family, settled two centuries back at *Ste. Anne du Nord*, County of Montmorency. History* has recorded how one of his maternal ancestors, " Marie Caron, épouse de Jean Picard," was carried off with her four infants, on the 4th June, 1660, from Ste. Anne, by a party of Indians—how the Marquis D'Argenson, Governor of Quebec, sent another party of Indians to rescue the captives—how the relief party concealed themselves on the shore opposite to Quebec, on a point where the enemies' canoes were expected to pass—how a volley, poured in *à propos*, killed

* *Ferland's Histoire du Canada*, vol. I, p. 454, and note.

two and wounded three of the marauders, unfortunately the heroic mother receiving in the fight a ball, from the effects of which she died shortly afterwards, one of her children being also wounded to death : the rest were saved.

Clermont* is indicated by one of the most reliable of our historians, the Abbé Ferland, as the spot where one of the first Sillery missionaries met with his end at the hands of some hostile Indians. This occurred in the spring of 1655. The missionary at the time was helping the colonist to build a small redoubt to protect their maize and wheat fields from the inroads of their enemies. On viewing, at Sillery, in 1865, Clermont the country seat of an eminent gentleman of the long robe, memory reverts to the same locality two centuries back, when another eminent gentleman of the long robe, the Attorney General Ruette d'Auteuil, had his country residence at Sillery.

Clermont stands about two acres from the main road, three miles from Quebec, a handsome, comfortable and substantial villa. The umbraceous grove of trees which encloses it from view, is a second growth, planted by the present occupant some fifteen years ago: its progress has been truly wonderful. The view from the veranda and back of the house is magnificent in the extreme.

It was built by the Hon. Mr. Justice Caron, and has been his family mansion ever since he left Spencer Grange. We find in it combined the taste and comfort which presides in Canadian homes, and in the fortunes of its owner, an illustration of the fact, that under the sway of Great Britain, the road to the highest honors has ever been open to colonists, irrespective of creed or nationality.

* "En 1655, les Iroquois furieux d'avoir vu manquer l'effet de leurs propositions faites aux Hurons, firent des incursions dans la colonie et jusqu'au bas de Québec. Au mois de mai, on plantait le ble-d'Inde dans les environs de Québec : un frère Jesuite avait voulu engager les algonquins à faire la garde chacun leur tour et, pour leur donner l'exemple, le bon Frère avait voulu être la première sentinelle. Il s'était donc avancé en explorant dans les bois (c'était dans le voisinage de la propriété actuelle de M. le Juge Caron, sur le chemin du Cap Rouge), tout à coup le Frère reçut deux coups de feu qui l'étendirent à terre grièvement blessé, et en même temps deux Iroquois, sortant d'un taillis, l'assommèrent et lui enlevèrent la chevelure. (Cours d'histoire de de l'abbé Ferland à l'Université Laval). Page 4 du *Journal de l'Instruction Publique*, pour Janvier, 1865."

*In the last century, the late Chancellor Livingstone owned a noble country seat on the banks of the Hudson, also called Clermont.

Ravenswood.

> " Near some fair town I'd have a private seat,
> Built uniform, nor little, nor too great;
> Better if on a rising ground it stood,—
> On this side fields, on that a neighboring wood;
> A little garden, grateful to the eye,
> Where a cool rivulet runs murmuring by."

In the year 1848, Samuel Wright, Esq., of Quebec, purchased from John Porter, Esq., that upper portion of Meadowbank (the old estate of Lieutenant Governor Cramahe in 1762), which lies to the north of the Cap Rouge or St. Lewis road, and built a dwelling thereon. In 1849 Mr. Wright's property was put in the market, and Ravenswood acquired by the present owner, William Herring, Esq., of the firm of Charles E. Levey & Co. No sylvan spot could have been procured, had all the woods around Quebec been ransacked, of wilder beauty. In the centre a pretty cottage; to the east, trees; to the west, trees; to the north and south, trees—stately trees all around you. Within a few rods from the hall door a limpid little brook oozes from under an old plantation, and forms, under a thorn tree of extraordinary size and most fantastically shaped limbs, a reservoir of clear water, round which, from a rustic seat, you notice speckled trout roaming fearlessly. Here was, for a man familiar with the park-like scenery of England, a store of materials to work into shape. That dense forest must be thinned; that indispensable adjunct of every Sillery home, a velvety lawn, must be had; a peep through the trees, on the surrounding country obtained; the stream dammed up so as to produce a sheet of water, on which a birch canoe will be launched; more air let in round the house; more of the forest cut away; and some fine, beach, birch, maple, and pine trees grouped. The lawn would look better with a graceful and leafy elm in the centre, and a few smaller ones added to the perspective. By dint of care, elms of a goodly size are removed from the mountain brow. The efforts of the proprietor to plant large trees at Ravenswood have been eminently successful, and ought to stimulate others to add such valuable, such permanent elements of beauty, to their country seats. One plantation, by its size and luxuriance, pleased us more than any other, that which shades both sides of the avenue. Few of our places can boast of possesng a more beautifully-wooded and gracefully-curved approach to the ouse than Ravenswood. You see nothing of the dwelling until you merge from this neat plantation of evergreens. We once viewed it under s most fascinating aspect: 'tis pretty in the bright effulgent radiance of ay, but when the queen of night sends forth her soft rays, and allows hem to slumber silently on the rustling bows of the green pines and rs, with the dark gravelled avenue, visible here and there at every urve, no sounds heard except the distant murmur of the *Chaudière* iver, the effect is very pleasing.

The accompanying sketch of Ravenswood was taken from under the horn tree, close to the pond.

The Highlands.

The range of heights which extend from Spencer Wood, west, to the black bridge over the stream at Kilmarnock, gradually recedes from the road, leaving at its foot a spacious area interspersed with green pastures, lawns, ploughed fields and plantations. On the most elevated plateau of this range stands "The Highlands," a large substantial fire-brick dwelling, with an ample veranda, erected a few years back by Michael Stevenson, Esquire, merchant, of Quebec. The site is recommended by a fine view of the River St. Lawrence, an airy and healthy position, and the luxuriant foliage of the spruce, pine and maple in the back grounds. The internal arrangements of the dwelling, whether regard be had to ventilation in summer or heating in winter, are on the most modern and improved plan. "The Highlands" lie close to St. Michael's Cove, teaming with historical recollections, a little to the west thereof, in front of St. Lewis road of historic renown, over which pranced, in 1663, the Marquis of Tracy's gaudy equipage and splendid body-guard wearing, as history tells, the uniform of the *Gardes de la Reine*. In Sept., 1759,* The Rochbeaucourt Cavalry, with their "blue uniforms and neat light horses of different

* "7th September, 1759.—Fine warm weather; Admiral Holmes's squadron weighed early this morning. At six o'clock we doubled the mouth of the Chaudiére, which is near half a mile over; and at eight we came to anchor off Cap Rouge. Here is a spacious cove, into which the river St. Michael disembogues, and within the mouth of it are the enemy's floating batteries. A large body of the enemy are well entrenched round the cove, (which is of circular form) as if jealous of a descent in those parts; they appear very

colours," scoured the heights in all directions, watching the motions of the English fleet, which you see in the plate of the Seige Operations, lying at anchor at Sillery, ready, the huge black leviathans, to hurl destruction on the devoted city. In 1837, we remember right well seeing the Earl of Elgin's magnificent equipage, thundering daily over this same road: the Earl being a particular admirer of the Cap Rouge scenery. This seat has just passed over, by purchase, to Chas. Temple, Esq., son of our respected fellow-townsman, Major Temple, who for a series of years served in that same 15th Regiment, to whose prowess the Plains of Abraham bore witness during the war of the conquest.

Rosewood.

" Along their blushing borders, bright with dew,
And in yon mingled wilderness of flowers,
Fair-handed Spring unbosoms every grace;
Throws out the snow-drop and the crocus first;
The daisy, primrose, violet darkly blue,
And polyanthus of unnumber'd dyes;
The yellow wall-flower, stain'd with iron-brown;
And lavish stock that scents the garden round;
From the soft wing of vernal breezes shed,
Anemonies; auriculas, enrich'd
With shining meal o'er all their velvet leaves;
And full ranunculas, of glowing red.
Then comes the tulip race, where beauty plays
Her idle freaks; from family diffus'd
To family, as flies the father dust,
The varied colors run; and while they break
On the charm'd eye th' exulting florist marks,
With sweet pride, the wonders of his hand.
No gradual bloom is wanting; from the bud,
First-born of spring, to summer's musky tribes
Nor hyacinths, of purest virgin white,
Low bent, and blushing inward; nor jonquils

---

numerous, and may amount to about one thousand six hundred men, besides their cavalry, who are cloathed in blue, and mounted on neat light horses of different colours: they seem very alert, parading and counter marching between the woods on the heights in their rear, and their breastworks, in order to make their numbers show to greater advantage. The lands all round us are high and commanding, which gave the enemy an opportunity of popping at our ships, this morning, as we tacked in working up."—*Knox's Journal*, Vol. ii., page 56.

Of potent fragrance; nor narcissus fair,
As o'er the fabled fountain hanging still;
Nor broad carnations, nor gay spotted pink;
Nor, shower'd from every bush, the damask rose."

A tiny and unostentatious cottage buried amongst trees. All around it, first, flowers; secondly, flowers; thirdly, flowers. The garden, a network of walks, and spruce hedges of rare beauty; occasionally you stumble unexpectedly on a rustic bower, tenanted by Apollos or Greek slaves in marble, or else you find yourself on turning an angle on the shady bank of a sequestered pond, in which lively trout disport themselves as merrily as those gold-fish you just noticed in the aquarium in the hall hung round with Kriegkoff's exquisite "Canadian scenery." You can also, as you pass along, catch the loud notes issuing from the house aviary and blending with the soft, wild melody of the wood warblers and robin; but the prominent feature of the place are flowers, sweet flowers, to charm the eye and perfume the air. Do not wonder at that; this is the summer residence of a gentleman whose name stands high on the Montreal and Quebec exhibition prize list, and who has been as successful in his commercial ventures as he has been in the culture of carnations, zenias, gladiolus, roses and dahlias. We remember seeing six hundred dahlias in bloom at Rosewood at the same time; the *coup d'œil* and contrasts between the varieties were striking in the extreme.

Several views of Rosewood are given. This rustic cottage is the summer residence of Jas. Gibb, Esq., of the old firm of Lane, Gibb & Co.

Cap Rouge Cottage.

With its rear facing St. Augustin parish, eight miles from the city, a commodious dwelling graces the summit of the lofty cape or promontory, which terminates westward the elevated *plateau*, on the eastern extremity of which, Champlain, in 1608, raised the lily-spangled banner of the Bourbons. Unquestionably the environs of Quebec are rich in scenery, revelling one half of the year in rural loveliness, the other half enjoying that solid comfort, which successful enterprise, taste and free institutions communicate to whatever they touch; but no where, not even at Spencer Wood, or Woodfield, has nature lavished such beautiful landscapes, such enchanting views. Three centuries ago, Europeans had struck here their tents, until the return of spring, attracted by the charms of the spot; three hundred years after that, a man of taste—to whom we may now without fear, give his due, as he is where neither praise nor censure can be suspected,—an English merchant had selected this site for its rare attractiveness; here he resided for many summers. In 1833 he removed to Spencer Wood. We allude to the late Henry Atkinson, who was succeeded at the Cap Rouge Cottage by William Atkinson, Esq., merchant of London, England. Mr. William Atkinson lived in affluence and happiness at Cap Rouge, several years. There are yet at Quebec those who remember the kind-heartedness and hospitality of this old English gentleman.

Geo. Usborne, Esq., was the next occupant of the cottage. The estate consisted formerly of close on one hundred acres of land, extending north across the king's highway, with a river frontage of about twenty acres; the lot on the south side of the road is laid out, one half in a park, the remainder in two or three fruit and flower gardens, divided by brick walls to trail vines and ripen fruit. It lies quite sheltered with a southerly exposure, bounded by the lofty, perpendicular river banks; the base, some two or three hundred feet below, skirted by a narrow road, washed by the waves of the St. Lawrence. A magnificent avenue glides along the high bank under centennial, ever-verdant pines, whose far outspreading branches, under the influence of winds, sigh a plaintive but soothing music, blending their soft rustle to the roar of the Etchemin or the Chaudière rivers before easterly gales; how well Pickering has it:—

> "The overshadowing pines alone, through which I roam,
> Their verdure keep, although it darker looks;
> And hark! as it comes sighing through the grove,
> The exhausted gale, a spirit there awakens
> That wild and melancholy music makes."

From the house veranda, the eye plunges westward down the high cape, following the capricious windings of the Cape Rouge stream far to the north, or else scans the green uplands of St. Augustin, its white cottages rising in soft undulations as far as the sight can reach. Over the extreme point of the southwestern cape hangs a fairy pavillion, like an eagle's eyre amongst alpine crags, just a degree more secure than that pensile old fir tree which you notice at your feet stretching over the chasm; beneath you, the majestic flood, Canada's pride, with a hundred merchantmen sleeping on its placid waters, and the orb of day dancing blythely over every ripple. Oh! for a few hours to roam with those we love under these old pines—listen to the voices of other years, and cull a fragrant wreath of those wild flowers which everywhere strew our path.

Is there not enough of nature's charms around this sunny, truly Canadian home? And how much of the precious metal would many an English duke give to possess, in his own famed isle, a site of such exquisite beauty? We confess, we denizens of Quebec, we do feel proud of our Quebec scenery; not that on comparison we think the less of other localities, but that on looking round we get to think the more of our own.

Cap Rouge, from its having been the location of Europeans, early in the sixteenth century, must claim the attention of every man of cultivated mind who takes a pleasure in scrutinizing the past, and in tracing the advent on our shores of the various races of European descent, now identified with this land of the West, yearning for the bright destinies the future has in store.

At the foot of the Cape, on which the Cap Rouge Cottage now stands, Jacques Cartier and Roberval wintered, the first in 1541-2; the second in 1543-4. Recent discoveries have merely added to the interest which these historical incidents awaken. The new *Historical Picture of Quebec*, published in 1834, thus alludes to these circumstances:—

"We now come to another highly interesting portion of local history. It has been stated that the old historians were apparently ignorant of this last voyage of Cartier. Some place the establishment of the fort at Cape Breton, and confound his proceedings with those of Roberval. The exact spot where Cartier passed his second winter in Canada is not mentioned in any publication that we have seen. The following is the description given of the station in Hakluyt: 'After which things the said captain went, with two of his boats, up the river, beyond Canada'—the promontory of Quebec is meant—'and the port of St. Croix, to view a haven and a small river which is about four leagues higher, which he found better and more commodious to ride in, and lay his ships, than the former. * * * The said river is small, not passing fifty paces broad, and ships drawing three fathoms water may enter in at full sea; and at low water there is nothing but a channel of a foot deep or thereabouts. * * * The mouth of the river is towards the south, and it windeth northward like a snake; and at the mouth of it, towards the east, there is a high and steep cliff, where we made a way in manner of a pair of stairs, and aloft we made a fort to keep the nether fort and the ships, and all things that might pass as well by the great as by this small river.' Who that reads the above accurate description will doubt that the mouth of the little river Cap Rouge was the station chosen by Jacques Cartier for his second wintering place in Canada? The original description of the grounds and scenery on both sides of the river Cap Rouge is equally faithful with that which we have extracted above. The precise spot on which the upper fort of Jacques Cartier was built, afterwards enlarged by Roberval, has been fixed by an ingenious gentleman of Quebec, at the top of Cap Rouge height, a short distance from the handsome villa and establishment of H. Atkinson (now of Jos. B. Forsyth). There is, at the distance of about an acre to the north of Mr. Atkinson's house, a hillock of artificial construction, upon which are trees indicating great antiquity; and as it does not appear that any fortifications were erected on this spot, either in the war of 1759, or during the attack of Quebec by the Americans in 1775, it is extremely probable that here are to be found the interesting site and remains of the ancient fort in question.

"On his return to the fort of Charlesbourg Royal, the suspicions of Cartier as to the unfriendly disposition of the Indians were confirmed. He was informed that the natives now kept aloof from the fort, and had ceased to bring them fish and provisions as before. He also learned from some of the men who had been at Stadacona, that an unusual number of Indians had assembled there—and associating, as he always seems to have done, the idea of danger with any concourse of the natives, he resolved to take all necessary precautions, causing everything in the fortress to be set in order.

"At this crisis, to the regret of all who feel an interest in the local history of the time, the relation of Cartier's third voyage abruptly breaks off. Of the proceedings during the winter which he spent at Cap Rouge, nothing is known. It is probable that it passed over without any collision with the natives, although the position of the French, from their numerical weakness, must have been attended with great anxiety.

"It has been seen that Roberval, notwithstanding his lofty titles, and really enterprising character, did not fulfil his engagement to follow Cartier with supplies sufficient for the setttlement of a colony, until the year following. By that time the Lieutenant General had furnished three large vessels chiefly at the King's cost, having on board two hundred persons, several gentlemen of quality, and settlers, both men and women. He sailed from La Rochelle on the 16th of April, 1542, under the direction of an experienced pilot, by name John Alphonse, of Xaintonge. The prevalence of westerly winds prevented their reaching Newfoundland until the 7th June. On the 8th they entered the road of St. John, where they found seventeen vessels engaged in the fisheries. During his stay in this road, he was surprised and disappointed by the appearance of Jacques Cartier, on his return from Canada, whither he had been sent the year before with five ships. Cartier had passed the winter at the fortress described above; and gave as a reason for the abandonment of the settlement, 'that he could not with his small company withstand the savages which went about daily to annoy him.' He continued, nevertheless, to speak of the country as very rich and fruitful. Cartier is said, in the relation of Roberval's voyage in Hakluyt, to have produced some gold ore found in the country, which on being tried in a furnace, proved to be good. He had with him also some *diamonds*, the natural production of the promontory of Quebec, from which the Cape derived its name. The Lieutenant General having brought so strong a reinforcement of men and necessaries for the settlement, was extremely urgent with Cartier to go back again to Cap Rouge, but without success. It is most probable that the French, who had recently passed a winter of hardship in Canada, would not permit their Captain to attach himself to the fortunes and particular views of Roberval. Perhaps, the fond regret of home prevailed over the love of adventure; and like men who conceived that they had performed their part of the contract into which they had entered, they were not disposed to encounter new hardships under a new leader. In order, therefore, to prevent any open disagreement, Cartier weighed anchor in the course of the night, and without taking leave of Roberval, made all sail for France. It is impossible not to regret this somewhat inglorious termination of a distinguished career. Had he returned to his fort, with the additional strength of Roberval, guided by his own skill and experience, it is most probable that the colony would have been destined to a permanent existence. Cartier undertook no other voyage to Canada; but he afterwards completed a sea chart, drawn by his own hand, which was extant in the possession of one of his nephews, Jacques Noël, of St. Malo, in 1587, who seems to have taken great interest in the further development of the vast country discovered by his deceased uncle. Two letters of his have been preserved, relating to the maps and writings of Cartier: the first written in 1587, and the other a year or two later, in which he mentions that his two sons, Michael and John Noël, were then in Canada, and that he was in expectation of their return. Cartier himself died soon after his return to France, having sacrificed his fortune in the cause of discovery. As an indemnification for the losses their uncle had sustained, this Jacques Noël and another nephew, De la Launay Chaton, received in 1588, an exclusive privilege to trade to Canada during twelve years; but this was revoked four months after it was granted.

"Roberval, notwithstanding his mortification at the loss of Cartier's experience and aid in his undertaking, determined to proceed; and sailing from Newfoundland about the end of June, 1543, he arrived at Cap Rouge, 'four leagues westward of the Isle of Orleans,' towards the end of July. Here the French immediately fortified themselves, 'in a place fit to command the main river, and of strong situation against all manner of enemies.' The position was, no doubt, that chosen by Jacques Cartier the year previous. The following is the description given in Hakluyt of the buildings erected by Roberval: 'The said General on his first arrival built a fair fort, near and somewhat westward above Canada, which is very beautiful to behold, and of great force, situated upon a high mountain, wherein there were two courts of buildings, a great tower, and another of forty or fifty feet long, wherein there were divers chambers, a hall, a kitchen, cellars high and low, and near unto it were an oven and mills, and a stove to warm men in, and a well before the house. And the building was situated upon the great River of Canada called *France-Prime* by Monsieur Roberval. There was also at the foot of the mountain another lodging, where at the first all our victuals, and whatsoever was brought with us, were sent to be kept, and near unto that tower there is another small river. In these two places above and beneath, all the meaner sort was lodged.' This fort was called *France-Roy*; but of these extensive buildings, erected most probably in a hasty and inartificial manner, no traces now remain, unless we consider as such the mound above mentioned, near the residence of Mr. Atkinson, at Cap Rouge.

"On the 14th September, Roberval sent back to France two of his vessels, with two gentlemen, bearers of letters to the King; who had instructions to return the following year with supplies for the settlement. The natives do not appear, by the relation given, to have evinced any hostility to the new settlers. Unfortunately, the scurvy again made its appearance among the French, and carried off no less than fifty during the winter. The morality of this little colony was not very rigid—perhaps they were pressed by hunger, and induced to plunder from each other—at all events the severity of the Viceroy towards his handful of subjects appears not to have been restricted to the male sex. The method adopted by the Governor to secure a quiet life will raise a smile: 'Monsieur Roberval used very good justice, and punished every man according to his offence. One whose name was Michael Gaillon, was hanged for his theft. John of Nantes was laid in irons, and kept prisoner for his offence; and others also were put in irons, and divers were whipped, as well men as women, by] which means they lived in quiet.'

"We have no record extant of the other proceedings of Roberval during the winter of 1543. The ice broke up in the month of April; and on the 5th June, the Lieutenant General departed from the winter quarters on an exploring expedition to the Province of Saguenay, as Cartier had done on a former occasion. Thirty persons were left behind in the fort under the command of an officer, with instructions to return to France, if he had not returned by the 1st July. There are no particulars of this expedition, on which, however, Roberval employed a considerable time. For we find that on the 14th June, four of the gentlemen belonging to the expedition returned to the fort, having left Roberval on the way to Saguenay; and on the 19th, some others came back, bringing with them some six score weight of Indian corn; and directions for the rest to wait for the return of the Viceroy, until the 22nd

July. An incident happened in this expedition, which seems to have escaped the notice of the author of the treaties on the *Canon de bronze* (A. Barthelot), which we have noticed in a former chapter. It certainly gives an authentic account of a shipwreck having been suffered in the St. Lawrence, to which, perhaps, the finding of the cannon, and the tradition about Jacques Cartier, may with some probability be referred. The following is the extract in question : 'Eight men and one bark were drowned and lost, among whom were Monsieur de Noire Fontaine, and one named La Vasseur of Constance.' The error as to the name might easily arise, Jacques Cartier having been there so short a time before, and his celebrity in the country being so much greater than that of Roberval, or of any of his companions."

Cap Rouge Cottage is now owned by Joseph Bell Forsyth, Esq., of the firm of Forsyth, Pemberton & Co.

Beausejour.

About one mile beyond the St. Foy Church, there is a magnificent farm of one hundred acres, lying chiefly on the north side of the road. The dwelling, a roomy, one-story cottage, stands about two acres from the highway, from which a copse of trees interrupts the view.

There are at present in process of completion at this spot, several embellishments which bid fair to render it worthy of the notice of every man of taste. It is merely necessary to assist nature in order to obtain here most gratifying results. Between the road fence and the dwelling, a small brook has worn its bed, at the bottom of a deep ravine, sweeping past the house lawn westward, and then changing its course to due north-west : the boundary in that direction between that and the adjoining property. The banks of the ravine are enclosed in a belt of every imaginable forest shrub, wild cherry, mountain ash, raspberry, blueberry, interspersed here and there with superb specimens of oak, spruce, fir and pine. Recently a second avenue has been laid out amongst the trees between the road fence and the brook, to connect with the lawn at the west of the house, by a neat little bridge, resting on two square piers about twenty-five feet high : on either side of the bridge, a solid dam is being constructed of the boulders and stones removed from the lower portion of the property, intended to form two trout ponds of a couple of acres in length each; a passage in the dam is left for the water-fall, which will be in full view of the bridge. On the edge of the bank, overhanging the ravine, nature seems to have pointed out the spot for a pavillion, from which the disciple of Isaac Walton will throw a cast below. The green fringe of mountain shrubs in bud, blossom or fruit, encircling the farm, materially enhances the beauty of this sylvan landscape,—the eye resting with particular pleasure on the vast expanse of meadow of a vivid green, clothed in most luxuriant grass, some 10,000 bundles of hay for the mower, in due time. About two acres from the house, to the west, is placed a rustic seat, under two weather-beaten, though still verdant oaks, which stretch their boughs across the river: closer again to the cottage, the eye meets two pavillions. The new avenue, rustic bridges, ponds and pavillions, are all due to the good taste of the present owner, Louis Bilodeau, Esq. This rural home was for several years occupied in summer by the Rev. Edmund Sewell, and does not belie its name—Beauséjour.

Belmont.

Owners—Intendant Talon, 1670; General James Murray, 1765; Sir John Caldwell, 1810; J. W. Dunscomb, Esquire, 1854.

That genial old joker, Sir John Barrington, in his *Sketches*, has invested the Irish homes and Irish gentry of his day with features certainly very original—at times so singular as to be difficult of acceptance. True, he lived in an age and amongst a people proverbial for generous hospitality and for conviviality carried to its extreme limit. Gargantuan banquets he describes, pending which the jorums of punch and claret imbibed appear to us something fabulous. Irish squires, roystering Irish barristers, toddling home in pairs after having stowed away under their belts as many as twelve bottles of claret a piece, during a prolonged sitting, *i. e.*, from 6 P.M. to 6 A.M. Such intrepid diners-out were known as "Twelve bottle men;" and, verily, if the old Judge is to be credited, they might have been advantageously pitted even against such a Homeric guzzler as history depicts Aurora Konïgsmark's sturdy son, Marechal Saxe, who, in his youth, 'tis said, tossed off, at one draught, and without experiencing any ill effects, one whole gallon of wine.

The first time our eye scanned the silent and deserted banquetting-halls of Belmont, with their lofty ceilings, and recalling the traditional accounts of the hospitable gentlemen, whose joviality had once lit up the scene, visions of social Ireland of Barrington's day floated uppermost in our mind. We could fancy we saw the gay roysterers of times by-gone—first a *fête champêtre* of lively French officers from Quebec, making merry over their Bordeaux or Burgundy, and celebrating the news of their recent victories over the English at Fontenoy,* Lauffeld or Carillon, to the jocund sound of *Vive la France! Vive le Marechal Saxe! à la Claire Fontaine*, &c.; then Governor Murray, surrounded by his veterans, Guy Carleton, Col. Caldwell, Majors Hale, Holland, and some of the new subjects, such as the brave Chs. DeLanaudière,† complimenting one another all round over the feats of the respective armies at the two memorable battles of the Plains, and all joining loyally in repeating the favorite toast in Wolfe's fleet, *British colors on every French fort, port and garrison in America.* Later on, at the beginning of the present century, a gathering of those Canadian Barons, so graphically delineated by J. Lambert in his *Travels in Canada, in* 1808—one week surrounding the festive board of this jolly Receiver General of Canada at Belmont; the next at Charlesbourg, making the romantic echoes of the Hermitage ring again with old English cheer and loyal toasts to "George the King," or else installing a "Baron" at the Union Hotel, *Place d'Armes*,—possibly in the

* The sanguinary battle of Fontenoy was fought on the 11th May, 1745. The Duke of Cumberland, subsequently surnamed "the butcher," for his brutality at Culloden, commanding the English, &c.; the French led by Marechal de Saxe. This defeat, which took place under the eye of Louis XV., cost the British 4041, their allies the Hanoverians, 1762, and the Dutch 1544 men. Success continued to attend the French arms at Ghent, Bruges, Oudenarde, and Dendermond, which were captured.—(*Lord Mahon.*) Wolfe, Murray and Townshend were at Fontenoy. The battle of Lauffeld took place on the 2nd July, 1747, the English commanded by Cumberland, the French by Saxe, the chief of the English Cavalry, Sir John Ligonier, being taken prisoner.—(*Lord Mahon.*) The French victory of Carillon, in which the Militia of Canada bore a conspicuous part, was won near Lake George, 8th July, 1758. The English army, under General Abercrombie, though more numerous, was repulsed with slaughter.

† Chs. Tarieu De Lanaudière, Knight of St. Louis, commanded a portion of the Canadian Militia at Carillon, and also during the campaign of 1759. Under English rule, he was Aide de Camp to Sir Guy Carleton—served in 1775, and accompanied the General to England, where Geo. III. rewarded him handsomely. He was called to the Legislative Council, and appointed Deputy Postmaster General of Canada.

very council-room in which the State secrets of Canada are now daily canvassed—and flinging down to the landlord, as Lambert says, "250 guineas for the entertainment." Ah! where are now the choice spirits of that comparatively modern day, the rank and fashion who used to go and sip claret or eat ice-cream with Sir James Craig, at Powell Place? Where gone the Muirs, Painters, Munros, Matthew Bells, De Lanaudières, Lymburners, Smiths, Finlays, Caldwells, Percevals, Jonathan Sewells? Alas! like the glories of Belmont, departed, or living in the chambers of memory only.

This estate, which, until lately, consisted of four hundred and fifty acres, extending from the line of the Grande Allée down to the Bijou wood, was *conceded* in 1649 by the Jesuit Fathers to M. Godfroy. It passed over, in 1670, to the celebrated Intendant Talon, by deed of sale executed on the 28th September, 1670, before Romain Becquet, Notaire Royal. Messire Jean Talon is described in that instrument as "Conseiller du roi en ses conseils d'etat et premier intendant de justice, police et finance de la Nouvelle France, Isle de Terre Neuve, Acadie et pays de l'Amerique Septentrionale." Shortly after the conquest it was occupied by Chief Justice Wm. Gregory. In 1765 it was sold for £500 by David Alves of Montreal, to General James Murray, who, after the first battle of the Plains, had remained Governor of Quebec, whilst his immediate superior, Brigadier Geo. Townshend, had hurried to England to cull the laurels of victory. In 1775, we find that one of the first operations of the American General Montgomery was to take possession of "General Murray's house, on the St. Foy road." General Murray also, probably, then owned the property subsequently known as Holland's Farm, where Montgomery had his headquarters. All through our history the incidents, actors and results of battles are tolerably well indicated, but the domestic history of individuals and exact descriptions of localities are scarcely ever furnished, so that the reader will not be surprised should several *lacunæ* occur in the sketch of Belmont, one of the most interesting Canadian country seats in the neighbourhood of Quebec. The history of Holland House might, of itself, furnish quite a small epic; and, doubtless, from the exalted position of many of the past owners of Belmont, its old walls, could they obtain utterance, might reveal interesting incidents of our past history, which will otherwise ever be buried in oblivion.

In the memory of Quebecers, Belmont must always remain more particularly connected with the name of the Caldwells, three generations of whom occupied its spacious halls. The founder of this old family, who played a conspicuous part in Canadian politics for half a century, was the Hon. Col. Henry Caldwell, for many years Receiver General of the Province, by royal appointment, and member of the Legislative Council. He came first to Canada in 1759, says Knox,* as Assistant Quartermaster General to Wolfe, under whom he served. When appointed Receiver General, the salary attached to that high office† was £400 per annum, with the understanding that he might *account* at his convenience to the Imperial Government provided he honored the drafts on the treasury. He did *account* at his convenience, or rather he never accounted at all, probably as it was anything but *convenient* to do so, having followed the traditional policy of high officials under French rule, and speculated largely in mills, &c. The fault was more the consequences of the system than that of the individual, and had his ventures turned out well, no doubt the high-minded Colonel and Receiver General would have made matters straight before dying. In 1801 Col. Caldwell was returned member for Dorchester, where he owned the rich Seigniory of Lauzon, and a most extensive mill at the Etchemin river, the same subsequently owned by J. Thomson, Esq., and now by Hy. Atkinson, Esq., late of Spencer Wood. The Colonel was re-elected by the same constituency in 1805, and again in 1809; lived in splendor at Belmont, as a polished gentleman of that age knew how to live, and died there in 1810. Belmont is situated on the St. Foy road, on its north side, at the end of a long avenue of trees, distant three miles from Quebec. The original mansion, which was burnt down in 1798, was rebuilt by the Colonel in 1800 on plans furnished by an Engineer Officer of the name of Brabazon. It stood in the garden between the present house and main or St. Foy road. The cellar forms the spacious root-house, at present in the garden. Col. Caldwell's exquisite entertainments soon drew around his table some of the best men of Quebec, of the time, such as the gallant Gen. Brock, John Coltman, William Coltman, the Hales, Foy, Haldimand, Dr. Beeby of Powell Place, J. Lester, John Blackwood. In 1810 Mr. John Caldwell, son of

* *Knox's Journal.* Vol. 1, p. 179.

† The Bureau was at the foot of Mountain Hill, next to (the Old Neptune) *Chronicle* Office.

the Colonel, accepted the succession, with its liabilities, not then known He made the Lauzon manor his permanent residence in summer, and was also appointed Receiver General. In 1817 Belmont was sold to the Hon. J. Irvine, M.P.P., the grandfather of the present member for Megantic, George J. Irvine, Esq. Hon. Mr. Irvine resided there until 1833. The beautiful row of trees which line the house avenue and other embellishments, are due to his good taste. In 1833 the property reverted to the late Sir Henry Caldwell, the son of Sir John Caldwell, who, in 1827, had inherited the title by the death of an Irish relative, Sir James Caldwell, the third Baronet (who was made a Count of Milan by the Empress Maria Theresa, and descended by his mother's side from the 20th Lord Kerry). John Caldwell of Lauzon, having become Sir John Caldwell, *menait un grain train,* the old peasants of Etchemin repeat to this day. His house, stud and amusements were those of a baron of old and of a hospitable Irish gentleman, spreading money and progress over the length and breadth of the land. At his death, which happened at Boston in 1845, the insignificent Etchemin settlement, through his efforts, had materially increased in wealth, size and population. There was, however, at his demise, an *error* in his Government balance sheet of £100,000 on the debit side!

Belmont lines the St. Foy heights, in a most picturesque situation. The view from the east and north-western windows is magnificently grand; probably one might count more than a dozen church spires glittering in the distance—peeping out of every happy village which dots the base of the blue mountains to the north. In 1854 this fine property was purchased by J. W. Dunscomb, Esq., Collector of Customs, Quebec, who resided there several years, and recently sold the mansion and garden to the Roman Catholic Church authorities of Quebec, reserving 400 acres for himself. The old house, within a few months back, was purchased by Mr. Wakeham, for many years the manager of the Beauport Asylum. His successful treatment of diseases of the mind induced him to open, at this healthy and secluded spot, under the name of the "Belmont Retreat," a private *Maison de Santé,* where wealthy patients are treated with that delicate care which they could not expect in a crowded asylum. The same success will, doubtless, attend Mr. Wakeham's enterprise at Belmont which crowned it in Beauport.

Holland Farm.

This estate, which formerly comprised two hundred acres of ground, extending from the brow of the St. Foy heights to St. Michael's Chapel on the Samos or St. Lewis road, possesses considerable interest for the student of Canadian history, both under French and under English rule. The original dwelling, a long high-peaked French structure, stood on an eminence closer to the St. Foy road than does the present house. It was built about the year 1740, by a rich Lower Town merchant, Monsieur Jean Taché,* who resided there after his marriage in 1742 with Mademoiselle Marie Anne Jolliet de Mingan, grand-daughter to the celebrated discoverer of the Mississippi, Louis Jolliet. Monsieur Jean Taché was also *Syndic des Marchands*, member of the Supreme Council of Quebec, and ancestor to the present Premier, Sir E. P. Taché. He at one time owned several vessels, but his floating wealth having, during the war of the conquest, become the prize of English cruisers, the St. Peter street Nabob of 1740, as it has since happened to some of his successors in that *romantic* neighborhood,—lost his money. Loss of fortune did not, however, imply loss of honor, as old memoirs of that day describe him, "Homme integrè et d'esprit." He had been selected, in the last years of French rule, to go and lay at the foot of the French Throne the grievances of the Canadians. About this time, the St. Foy road was becoming a fashionable resort, *Hawkin's Picture of Quebec* calls it "The favorite drive of the Canadian Belle before the conquest." The person meant is probably the beautiful Madame Hughes Pean, *née* De Meloises, the consort of the Town Major of Quebec, who doubtless occasionally dropped a card on the lady of the wealthy Canadian merchant. This is an interesting period in colonial life, but imperfectly known,—nor will a passage from Jeffery, an old and valued English writer, illustrative of men, manners and amusements in the Colony, when it passed over to the English monarch, be out of place:—

"The number of inhabitants being considerably increased, they pass their time very aggreeably. The Governor General, with his household; several of the *noblesse* of exceeding good families; the officers of the army, who in France are all gentlemen; the Intendant, with a Supreme Council,

---

* Mr. Jean Taché was the first owner of the "Old Neptune Inn" at the foot of Mountain Hill, and of a poetical turn, having written the first Canadian poem, intituled *Tableau de la Mer*.

and the inferior magistrates; tho Commissary of the Marine; the Grand Provost; the Grand Hunter (if the office should be revived under the Confederation, it must necessarily fall to the lot of the Sillery Nimrod); the Grand Master of the Woods and Forests, who has the most extensive jurisdiction in the world; rich merchants, or such as live as if they were so; the Bishops and a numerous Seminary; two colleges of Recollets, as many of Jesuits; with three Nunneries; amongst all these you are at no loss to find agreeable company and the most entertaining conversation. Add to this the diversions of the place, such as the assemblies at the Lady Governess's and Lady Intendant's; parties at cards, or of pleasure, such as in the winter on the ice, in sledges, or in skating; and in the summer in chaises or canoes; also hunting, which it is impossible not to be fond of in a country abounding with plenty of game of all kinds.

"It is remarked of the Canadians that their conversation is enlivened by an air of freedom which is natural and peculiar to them, and that they speak the French in the greatest purity and without the least false accent. There are few rich people in that Colony, though they all live well, are extremely generous and hospitable, keep very good tables, and love to dress very finely. * * * * * The Canadians have carried the love of arms and glory, so natural to their mother-country, along with them. * * * * * War is not only welcome to them but coveted with extreme ardor." *

During the fall of 1775, the old mansion sheltered Brigadier Richard Montgomery, the leader of the American forlorn hope, who fell on the 31st December of that year, at Près-de-Ville, Champlain street, fighting against those same British whom it had previously been his pride to lead to victory. The husband of Miss Livingstone, now in arms against his late Sovereign, was dealt with summarily as he had dealt with the St. Joachim Canadian peasantry in 1759, whose dwellings he was instructed to burn and did burn. "There were," says Fraser's manuscript, † "several of the enemy killed and wounded, and a few prisoners taken, all of whom the barbarous Captain Montgomery, who commanded us, ordered to be butchered in a most inhuman and cruel manner, particularly two

* *History of French Dominion in North and South America.*—Jeffery, London, 1760, page 9.

† The war in the valley of the St. Lawrence in 1759, seems to have been like the war in the valley of Shenandoah in 1864.

who I sent prisoners by a sergeant after giving them quarters, and engaged that they should not be killed, were one shot and the other knocked down with a tomahawk, and both scalped in my absence. After the skirmish we set about burning the houses with great success, setting all in flames." About the year 1780, we find this residence tenanted by a worthy British officer, who had been a great favorite with the hero of the Plains of Abraham. Major Samuel Holland had fought bravely that day under General Wolfe, and stood, it is said, after the battle, close by the expiring warrior. His dwelling took the name of Holland's House: he added to it, a cupola, which served in lieu of a *prospect tower*, wherefrom could be had a most extensive view of the surrounding country. The important appointment of Surveyor General of the Province, which was bestowed on Major Holland, together with his social qualities, abilities and education, soon gathered round him the *élite* of the English Society in Quebec at that time. Amongst the distinguished guests who frequented Holland House in 1791, we find Edward, afterwards Duke of Kent. The numerous letters still extant addressed by His Royal Highness from Kensington Palace, as late as 1814, to the many warm friends he had left on the banks of the St. Lawrence, contain pleasant reminiscences of his sojourn amongst his royal father's Canadian lieges. Amongst other frequenters of Holland House, may also be noted a handsome stranger, who after attending—the gayest of the gay—the Quebec *Chateau* balls, Regimental mess dinners, Barons' Club, tandem drives, as the male friend of one of the young Hollands was, to the amazement of all, convicted at a mess dinner, of being a lady in disguise. A *fracas* of course ensued. The lady-like guest soon vamosed to England, where *he* became the lawful spouse of the Hon. Mr. C———, the brother to Lord F———d. One remnant of the Hollands yet endures; the old fir tree on that portion of the property purchased by James Creighton, farmer. Holland tree is still sacred to the memory of the five slumberers, who have reposed for more than a century beneath its hoary branches. Nor has the recollection of the "fatal duel"* faded away. Holland farm, for many years, belonged to Mr. Wilson of the Customs Department, Quebec; in 1843 it passed by purchase to George Okill Stuart, Esq., of Quebec; Mr. Stuart improved the place, removed the old house and built a handsome new one on a rising ground in rear, which he occupied

* The reader is referred to First Series of *Maple Leaves*, for an account of the duel.

for several summers. It again became renowned for gaiety and festivity when subsequently owned by Robert Cassels, Esquire, for many years Manager of the Bank of British North America at Quebec. Col. Lysons had leased it in 1862, for his residence, when the unexpected vote of the House of Assembly on the Militia Bill broke through his arrangements. Holland House, still the property of Mr. Cassels, is now occupied by the present Manager of the Bank of British North America, Farquharson Smith, Esquire.*

Morton Lodge.

The extensive green pastures which General James Murray owned, in 1768, on the St. Foy road, under the name of *Sans bruit*,† form at present several minor estates. One of the handsomest residences of this well-wooded region is Morton Lodge, on the south side of the highway, and bounded by the Belvidère road,—about thirty-two acres in extent. It was honored with this name by one of its former owners, the originator of the lodge, some fifty years ago—the late James Black, Esquire. Morton Lodge is built in the cottage style, with a *suite* of roomy apartments forming a spacious wing in rear; the lawns in front of the house, with a grove of trees, add much to its beauty; a handsome conservatory to the east opens on the drawing-room; it is located in the centre of a flower garden. The additional attraction of this residence is an extensive collection of paintings, purchased at various times by the owner both in Canada and in Europe: the French, Flemish and Italian schools are well represented, and Kreigkoff's *Winter Scenery in Canada* is very worthy of attention.

Morton Lodge, for many years past, has been the residence of David

* Montgomery Place, on the Hudson, the residence of Mrs. Ed. Livingston, a country seat of unrivalled beauty.—"It is," says *Downing*, "one of our oldest improved country seats, having been originally the residence of General Montgomery, the hero of Quebec. On the death of his widow, it passed into the hands of her brother, Edward Livingston, Esq., the late Minister to France."—page 31.

† "John King, living on General Murray's farm, at *Sans bruit*, having the best pasturage for cattle in the neighborhood during the summer, well watered by several runs, informs all those who may choose to send him their cows that they will be well taken care of, and that he will send them cow-herds to town every morning at six o'clock, who will bring them home every evening between five and six. The price will be two dollars for the summer, to be paid said King on St. Michael's day."—*Quebec Gazette, 14th April*, 1768.

Douglass Young, Esquire, President of the Quebec Bank, and formerly a partner of the late G. B. Symes, Esquire. Mr. Young claims, on the maternal side, as ancestor, Donald Fraser, one of Fraser's (78th) Highlanders, a regiment which distinguished itself at the taking of Quebec, whilst fighting under Wolfe, on these same grounds.

Forming a portion of this estate, to the west, may be noticed a cosy little nest, *Bruce's Cottage*, as it was formerly called—now Bannockburn—surrounded on all sides by trees, lawns, flowers; in rear, a small grapery brings in its annual tribute of enjoyment.

Bannockburn is now occupied by Wm. Himsworth, Esq., Assistant Clerk, Executive Council of Canada.

Hamwood.

How many vicissitudes in the destinies of places, men, families, nations! See yonder mansion, its verdant lawns, with the leafy honors of incipient spring encircling it like a garland, perfumed with the aroma of countless buds and blossoms, embellished by conservatory, grapery, avenues of fruit and forest trees. Does not every object bespeak comfort, commercial success?

When you enter that snug billiard-room, so cosily fitted up with fireplace, ottomans, etc.; or when, on a balmy summer evening, you are seated on the ample veranda, close by the kind host, do you not, my legal friend, feel inclined to repeat to yourself—"Commerce, commerce is the turnpike to wealth, to affluence, the path to consideration?"

But was the scene always so smiling, so redolent of rustic enjoyment? If so, why have erected yon stately column, with a fat, helmetted Bellona on the top, mysteriously looking round as if pregnant with a mighty, unfathomable future? Why! ask history why. Open *Knox's Journal of the Siege of Quebec*, and therein read how, in front of that very spot where now you stand, along that identical road, over which you emerged from the city, war once threw her pall. Darken the picture; make it, for the sake of contrast, a winter scene, with the howling blast sighing mournfully through the few remaining gnarled pines and oaks spared by the soldiers; add to it, tired teams of English troops, laboriously drawing, yoked eight by eight, long sledges of firewood for Murray's depressed, harassed garrison, and you have something like John Knox's *tableau* of St. Foy Road on the 7th December, 1759:—

"Our garrison, now undergo incredible fatigue, not only within but also without the walls, being obliged to load and sleigh home firewood from the forest of St. Foy, which is near four miles distant, and through snow of a surpassing depth; eight men are allowed to each sleigh, who are yoked to it in couples by a set of regular harness, besides one man who guides it behind with a long stout pole, to keep it clear of ruts and other obstructions. We are told that M. de Lévis is making great preparations for the long-meditated assaults on this place (Quebec) with which we are menaced. Christmas is said to be the time fixed for this enterprise, and *Monsieur* says, 'if he succeed he shall be promoted to be *Marechal de France*, and if he fail, Canada will be lost, for he will give it up.'" *

Do not, dear reader, however, fear for the old rock; it is tolerably secure so long as Fraser's Highlanders and British Grenadiers garrison it.

We have here endeavored to contrast the smiling present with the dreary past; peace, progress, wealth, as we find it to-day in this important appendage of the British Crown, ready to expand into an empire, with the dismal appearance of things when it was scantily settled, and in those dark days when war stalked through our land. Hamwood takes its name from that of the paternal estate of the Hamiltons, county of Meath, Ireland, and without pretending to architectural excellence, it is one of the loveliest spots on the St. Foy road. It belongs to Robert Hamilton, Esquire, a leading merchant of Quebec.

The illustration shows a front view of the house.

Bijou.

We confess that we ever had a fancy for historical contrasts—it is our weakness, perhaps our besetting sin—and when, on a balmy June day, at the hour when the king of day is drinking the dew-drops from the flowers, we ride past this unadorned but charming little Canadian home, next to Westfield, on the St. Foy heights, as it were, sunning itself amidst emerald fields, fanned by the breath of the flagrant morn, en-

* Vol. ii., p. 224.

livened by the gambols of merry childhood; memory, in spite of us, brings back the ghastly sights, the sickening Indian horrors, witnessed here on the 28th April, 1760. There can be no doubt on this point; the mute but eloquent witnesses of the past are dug up every day: shot, shell, bullets, old bayonets, decayed military buttons, all in the greatest profusion.

"The savages," says Garneau, "who were nearly all in the woods behind during the fight, spread over the battle-field when the French were pursuing the enemy, and killed many of the wounded British, whose scalps were afterwards found upon the neighboring bushes. As soon as De Lévis was apprised of the massacre, he took vigorous measures for putting a stop to it. Within a comparatively narrow space nearly 2,500 men had been struck by bullets. The patches of snow and icy puddles on the ground were so reddened with the blood shed, that the frozen ground refused to absorb, and the wounded survivors of the battle, and of the savages, were immersed in pools of gore and filth, ankle deep."

Such *was* the deadly strife in April, 1760, on the identical spot on which, reader, you and we now stand on the St. Foy heights. Such is *now* the smiling aspect of things as you now see them at Bijou, which crowns the heights over the great Bijou marsh, the dwelling of Andrew Thomson, Esq., merchant, of Quebec. Some natural springs in the flower garden, in rear of the dwelling, and the slopes of the ground, when turned to advantage, in the way of terraces and fountains, bid fair to enhance materially the beauty of this rustic spot.

Appended is an excellent view of Bijou.

Westfield.

At Mount Pleasant, about one mile from St. John's gate, a number of agreeable suburban residences have sprung up, as if by enchantment, within a very few years. This locality, from the splendid view it affords of the valley of the St. Charles, the basin of the St. Lawrence and surrounding country, has ever been appreciated. The most noticeable residence is a commodious cut-stone structure, inside of the toll, erected there a few years back by G. H. Simard, Esq., ex-member for Quebec, and now owned by Fred. Vannovous, Esq., Barrister. Its mate in size and appearance a few acres to the west, on the St. Foy road, is owned by Eugene Chinic, Esq., the President of the *Banque Nationale.* In the vicinity, under the veil of a dense grove of trees, your eye gathers as you drive past, the outlines of a massive, roomy homestead, on the north side of the heights, on a site which slopes off considerably; groups of birch, maple, and some mountain ash and chesnut trees, flourish in the garden which surrounds the house; in rear, flower beds slope down in an enclosure, whose surface is ornamented with two tiny reservoirs of chrystal water, which gushes from some perennial streams, susceptible of great embellishment at little cost, by adding *Jets d'eau.* The declivities in rear seem as if intended by nature to be laid out into lovely terraces, with flowers or verdure to fringe their summits. In the eastern portion stands the gigantic hawthorn tree, the pride of Westfield. To us, an old denizen of the country, a stately tree has ever been a companionable, in fact, a reverential object. In our eyes, 'tis not only rich in its own native beauty: it may perchance also borrow interest from associations and become a part of our home—of ourselves: it may have overshadowed the rustic seat, where, in our infant years, one dear to us and now departed, read the Sunday hymn or taught us with a mother's sanctifying love, to become a good citizen, —in every respect worthy of our sire. Perchance it may have been planted on the day of our birth; it may also commemorate the natal hour of our first-born, and may it not like ourselves, in our early days, have required the fostering care of a guardian spirit,—the dews from heaven to refresh it and encourage its growth. Yes, like the proprietor of Westfield, we dearly love the old trees of our home.

We were invited to ascend to the loftiest point of this dwelling, and contemplate from the platform on the roof the majestic spectacle at our feet. Far below us waived the nodding pinnacles of countless forest trees; beyond and around us, the site of the old battle-fields of 1759 and 1760; to the east, the white expanse of the St. Lawrence sleeping between the Beauport, Orleans and Point Levi shores; to the northwest, the snake-like course of the St. Charles, stealing through fertile meadows, copses of evergreens—until, by a supreme effort, it veers round the compass at the Marine Hospital; there, at sunset, it appears as if gamboling in the light of the departing luminary, whose rays anon linger in fitful glances on the spires of Lorette, Charlesbourg and St. Sauveur, until they fade away, far away, in the blue distance, over the sublime crags of *Tsonoathouan*, or else gild in amber tints the wooded slopes of the mountainous ridges to the west. In describing this old family mansion, erected more than forty years ago, by the late Charles Grey Stewart, Esq., we would be failing in the duty we have imposed on ourselves, were we to omit noticing the magnificent stabling accommodation erected here. This building, about one hundred feet in length, fronts on the St. Foy road. Westfield has, since 1846, been the permanent residence of John Thomson, Esquire. It is surrounded by the residences of those near and dear to his heart: Hamwood, Bijou, Ettrick House and Teviot House, the latter two, named after spots, familiar to Mr. Thomson in his youth.

Teviot House.

"24th July, 1759.—A great number had gone from it (the army) to hunt, who, having found considerable game towards St. Foy, kept up such a continual fire that the Indians, supposing we were attacked at Sillerie, proceeded thither. On their return they represented that some inconvenience might result from such practice. M. de Vaudreuil perceived it, and forbid the army to hunt any more."*

We will be forgiven for prefacing our sketch of the home of a keen sportsman, as shown in the accompanying photographic picture, by the above scrap of sporting intelligence, and we also take occasion to invite our Canadian Nimrods to discuss the problem therein involved. What species of game the St. Foy woods could contain in such abundance on the 24th of July, 1759? It could neither be grouse, spruce partridge, woodcock, nor snipe, this being the breeding time of all these birds. We can think of no other game frequenting the environs of Quebec in July, in such abundance, except the passenger pigeon (*ectopistes migratorius*), which, until thirty years back, used to spread in clouds all over the surrounding country, and were shot as late as 1814 in the gardens and enclosures within the city itself. Woodcock were abundant on the St. Foy heights every fall, and snipe formerly were bagged by hundreds in the Bijou marsh, at the foot of the heights. Teviot House stands on an elevated *plateau* on the south side of St. Foy road, half a mile from

* *Paris Documents.* Vol. x., p. 1026.

the city limits. It affords, from its drawing-room windows, a remarkable view of the surrounding country, and occupies a portion of the old battle-field of 1760. Tons of cannon balls, shot and shell, and rusty bayonets have been dug up there. Recently a quantity of old metallic buttons, with the figure XV., were picked up, showing that they once ornamented the scarlet uniforms of many gallant fellows of that XVth Regiment, who, "at eight in the morning on the 28th April, 1760,"* had issued triumphantly from St. John Gate—*never to return.*

Teviot House is the residence of Richard Cassel, Esq., manager of the Bank of Upper Canada, Quebec.

Castor Ville.

"In woods or glens I love to roam,
* * * * *
Or by the woodland pool to rest."

In the deepest recesses of the Lorette woods, amongst the most shady meanders of the sinuous Cabire Coubat, some five miles due north from Castel-Coucy, we know a bank, not precisely where

"The wild thyme grows,"

but where you are sure, in spring and summer, to pluck handfuls of trilliums, wild violets, ferns of rare beauty, columbines, kalmias, ladies' slippers, ladies' tresses (we mean of course the floral subjects). In this beautious region, sacred to Pan, the Nayades, Dryades, and the daughters of Mnemosyne, you might possibly, dear reader, were you privileged with a pass from one of our most respected friends, be allowed to wander; or perchance in your downward voyage from Lake Charles to the Lorette Falls, in that *vade mecum* of a forester's existence—a birch canoe—(a voyage, by the by, compared to which Captain Cook, Bougainville, Lapeyrouse and Anson's sea wanderings dwindle into airy nothings), you might, we repeat, possibly be allowed to pitch your camp on one of the mossy headlands of Castor Ville, and enjoy your luncheon, in this sylvan spot; that is, always supposing you were deemed competent to fully appreciate nature's wildest charms, and dally, like a true lover, in her coyest and most furtive glances.

Castor Ville, a forest wild, where many generations of beavers, otters, cariboo, bears, foxes and hares once roamed, loved and died, covers an area of

* *Fraser's Manuscripts.*

more than one hundred acres. Through it glides the placid course of the St.Charles—overhung by hoary fir trees—from the parent lake to the pretty Indian Lorette Falls, a distance of about eight miles of fairy navigation which every man of taste, visiting Lake St. Charles, ought to enjoy at least once in his life. It is completely mantled over by a dense second growth of spruce and fir trees, intersected by a maze of avenues. The lodge sits gracefully, with its veranda and cannon, on a peninsula formed by the *Grand Desert* and St. Charles streams. You cross over in a canoe to that portion of the domain beyond the river: along the banks a number of resting places—little bowers of birch bark—boats and canoes anchored all round—here and there a *portage*—close by a veritable Indian wigwam, *Oda 8io** by name. On some bright morning in early spring, you may chance meet, in one of the paths, or in his canoe, a venerable hunter, the Master of Castor Ville, returning home after visiting his hare, fox, or otter traps, proudly bearing Renard in his game bag, next to which you may discover a volume of *Moliere, Montaigne,* or *Montesquieu.* On selling Castel-Coucy, its loyal-hearted old proprietor, taking with him the guns of the fort, retired to the present wild demesne, in which occasionally he passes, with his family, many pleasant hours, amidst books and rural amusements, far from city noises and city dust.

Castor Ville belongs to the Hon. Louis Panet, member of the Legislative Council of Canada.

The Manor House, Beauport.

Let us view one of the remnants of feudal times. On the Beauport road, four miles from the city, and a little to the east of Colonel Gugy's present habitation, stands an antiquated high-gabled French stone dwelling, very substantially put together. About thirty years back there was still existing close to and connected with it, a pavillion or tower, used in early days as a fort to protect the inmates against Indians. It contained the boudoir and sleeping apartments of some of the fair *seignieuresses* of Beauport. Although it is not likely to be the original house which Robert Giffard, the first seignior, built there more than two centuries ago, it is probably the oldest seigniorial manor in Canada. Robert Giffard's house—or, more properly, his shooting box—is thought

* *The Great River.* Such was the name the Lorette Huron Indians pressed Hon. Mr. Panet to take when they elected him their honorary chief.

to have stood closer to the little stream in the neighborhood. The first seignior of Beauport had two daughters who married two brothers, Juchereau, the ancestors of the Duchesnays; and the manor has been in the possession of, and occupied by the Duchesnays for more than two hundred years.

Robert Giffard had visited Canada, for the first time, in 1627, in the capacity of a surgeon; and being a great sportsman, he built himself a small house on the banks of the Beauport stream, to enjoy in perfection his favorite amusements—shooting and fishing. No authentic data exist of the capacity of Beauport for game in former days; we merely read in the *Relations des Jésuites* that in the year 1648, 1200 ptarmigan were shot there; we also know that the quantities of ducks congregating on the adjoining *flats* caused the place to be called *La Canardière.* There is a curious old record in connection with this manor, exhumed by the Abbé Ferland; it is the exact formula used by one of the tenants or *censitaires* in rendering *foi et hommage* to the Lord of the Manor. Guion (Dion?), a tenant, had by sentence of the Governor, Montmagny, been condemned on the 30th July, 1646, to fulfil this feudal custom. The document recites that, after knocking at the door of the chief manorial entrance, and in the absence of the master, addressing the farmer, the said Guion, having knelt down bare headed without his sword or spurs, repeated three times the words,—"Monsieur de Beauport, Monsieur de Beauport, Monsieur de Beauport, je vous fais et porte la foy et hommage que je suis tenu de vous porter, a cause de mon fief du Buisson, duquel je suis homme de foy relevant de votre seigneurie de Beauport, lequel m'appartient au moyen du contrat que nous avons passé ensemble par devant Roussel à Mortagne, le 14 Mars, 1634, vous declarant que je vous offre payer les droits seigneuriaux et feodaux quand dûs seront, vous requerant me recevoir à la dite foy et hommage." Lord of Beauport, Lord of Beauport, Lord of Beauport, I render you the fealty and hommage due to you on account of my land du Buisson * * which belongs to me by virtue of the title-deed executed between us in presence of Roussel at Mortagne, the 14th March, 1634, avowing my readiness to acquit the seigniorial and feudal rents whenever they shall be due, beseeching you to admit me to the said fealty and homage." This Guion, a mason by trade, observes the Abbé Ferland, was the man of letters and scribe of the parish. There is still

16

extant a marriage contract, drafted by him, for two parishioners; it is one of the earliest on record in Canada, bearing date the 16th July, 1636. It is signed by the worthy Robert Giffard, the seignior, and by Francis Bellanger and Noël Langlois; the other parties affixed their mark. It possesses interest as serving to illustrate the status and education of the early French settlers. In 1628, Robert Giffard had been taken a prisoner of war by the English, on board of Rocmont's fleet. On his return, and in acknowledgment of the services rendered by him to the colonial authorities, he obtained a grant of the seigniory of Beauport, together with a large tract of land on the River St. Charles. For many long years the ancestral halls of the Duchesnays at Beauport rang with the achievements of their warlike seigneurs. One of them, Nicholas Juchereau de St. Denys, distinguished himself at the siege of Quebec in 1690. "Le sieur de St. Denys, seigneur de Beauport," says Charlevoix, "commandait ses habitants; il avait plus de soixante ans et combattait avec beaucoup de valeur, jusqu'a ce qu'il eut un bras cassé d'un coup de feu. Le Roi recompensa peu de temps après son zêle en lui accordant des lettres de noblesse." His son distinguished himself in Louisiana. Two other members of the family won laurels at Chateauguay. A descendant, Lieut.-Colonel Philip Duchesnay, is at present Extra Provincial Aide de Camp to His Excellency the Governor General, whilst another, Lieutenant Théodore Duchesnay, has just exchanged his commission in Her Majesty's 100th Regiment of Foot for a provincial appointment as Brigade Major; two other scions of this old family are Legislative Councillors.

The present owner of the manor, Col. Gugy, has built himself, close to it, a comfortable modern dwelling, wherein, amidst rural retirement, he divides his existence between literature, briefs and his stud, noted all over Canada. He has recently added to his domain, by purchase, a large tract of land from the adjoining property. The broad acres which in 1759 resounded to the tread of Montcalm's heavy squadrons, now the quiet home of a barrister of note, bear the name of Darnoc. *Cedant arma togæ.*

Ringfield.

FRANCISCUS PRIMUS, DEI GRATIA, FRANCORUM REX REGNAT.
Inscription on cross erected 3rd May, 1536, by Jacques Cartier.

We will be pardoned for devoting a larger space than for other country seats, in describing Ringfield, on accoun tof the important events of which it was the theatre.

Close to the Dorchester Bridge to the west, on the Charlesbourg road, there was once an extensive estate known as Smithville—five or six hundred acres of table land owned by the late Charles Smith, Esq., who for many years resided in the substantial large stone dwelling subsequently occupied by A. Laurie, Esq., at present by W. McKay, shipbuilder, opposite the Marine Hospital. Some hundred acres, comprising the land on the west of the *ruisseau* Lairet, known as *Ferme des Anges*,* were detached from it and now form Ringfield, whose handsome villa is scarcely visible from the Charlesbourg road in summer on account of the plantation of evergreens and other forest trees which, with a white-thorn hedge, line its semicircular avenue on both sides. One might be inclined to regret that this plantation has grown up so luxuriantly, as it interferes in the summer months with the striking view of the Island of Orleans, St. Lawrence, and surrounding parishes. Before the trees assume their vernal honors there can be counted, irrespective of the city spires, no less than thirteen steeples of churches in so many parishes. Ringfield takes its name from its circular meadow (Montcalm's hornwork). In rear it is bounded to the west by the little stream called Lairet, with the *ruisseau* St. Michel in view; to the south its natural boundary is the meandering Cabire-Coubat.†

Ringfield has even more to recommend it than the rural beauty common to the majority of our country seats: here were enacted scenes calculated to awaken the deepest interest in every student of Canadian history. On the banks of the River St. Charles, more than three centuries back, it is now generally supposed, wintered, in 1535–6, during his second voyage of discovery, Jacques Cartier, the intrepid navigator of St. Malo. We have

---

* Emery de Caen dined here with the Jesuits, 6th August, 1632.—*Relations des Jesuites.*

† Cabire-Coubat (expressive of windings, says Sagard,) called by Jacques Cartier, the River Ste. Croix (of the Holy Cross), and subsequently denominated the River St. Charles, in compliment, says La Potherie, to Charles de Boües, Grand Vicar of Pontoise, founder of the first mission of Recollets in New France.

Champlain's* authority for this historical fact, though Charlevoix erroneously asserts that the great discoverer wintered on the banks of the River Jacques Cartier, twenty-seven miles higher up than Quebec. A careful examination of *Lescarbot's Journal of Cartier's Second Voyage*, and the investigations of subsequent historians leave little room to doubt Champlain's statement.† Jacques Cartier in his journal, written in the quaint old style of that day, furnishes us curious descriptions of the locality where he wintered, and of the adjoining Indian town, *Stadaconé*, the residence of the Chief Donacona. The Abbé Ferland and other contemporary writers have assigned as the probable site of Stadacona that part of Quebec which is now covered by a portion of the suburbs of St. John, and by that of St. Roch looking towards the St. Charles. How graphically Jacques Cartier writes of that portion of the River St. Lawrence opposite the Lower Town, less than a mile in width, "deep and swift running," and also of the "goodly, fair and delectable bay or creek convenient and fit to harbor ships," the St. Charles (St. Croix or Holy Cross) river; and again of the spot wherein, he says, "we stayed from the 15th September, 1535, to the 6th May, 1536, and there our ships remained dry." Cartier mentions the area of ground adjoining to where he wintered "as goodly a plot of ground as possible may be seen, and, wherewithal, very fruitful, full of goodly trees even as in France, such as oak, elm, ash, walnut trees, white-thorns and vines that bring forth fruit as big as any damsons, and many other sort of trees; tall hemp as any in France, without any seed or any man's work or labor at all." There are yet some noble specimens of elm, the survivors of a thick clump

---

* "Champlain a certainement jeté un grand jour sur cette question, en prouvant aussi bien qu'il était possible de le faire, que Jacques Cartier avait hiverné dans la rivière Saint Charles, et en faisant lui-même des investigations sur les lieux. Seulement il pourrait bien sefaire qu'on eût pris trop à la lettre un mot de son édition de 1632, où il dit que les vaisseaux de Cartier hivernèrent là où était de son temps la demeure des Jésuites. Quant à Charlevoix, non seulement il n'a pas éclairci la question, mais il n'a fait que l'embrouiller. Tout ce qu'il dit la dessus, à trés peu d'exception près, est plein d'erreurs, et inconciliable avec la situation et la conformation des lieux décrits par le capitaine Malouin."

† The late Amable Berthelot, one of our antequarians, in reviewing the papers published by Mr. Jos. Hamel, in 1843, on the recent discovery of the wreck of the *Petite Hermine*, on the *Ferme des Anges*, at the mouth of the Lairet stream, thus expresses himself, p. 3:—"Il ne me fut pas difficile, en suivant attentivement le texte du second voyage de Jacques Cartier, tel que nous le donne Lescarbot, de prouver, jusqu'à l'évidence, que ce navigateur malouin avait réellement passé l'hiver à la rivière St. Charles, et non à celle qui porte aujourd'hui le nom de Jacques Cartier; et je crois que depuis ma dissertation, il n'est resté en ce pays aucun doute sur ce sujet."

that once stood on the edge of the hornwork. As to vines, they thrive amazingly in the open air at Ringfield, and some vines of the sweet water variety were loaded last year with splendid fruit. The precise spot in the St. Charles where Cartier moored his vessels and where his people built the fort* in which they wintered may have been, for aught that could be advanced to the contrary, where the French Government in 1759 built the hornwork or earth redoubt, so plainly visible to this day, on the Lairet stream. It may also have been at the mouth of the St. Michel stream which here empties itself into the St. Charles, on the Jesuits' farm. The hornwork or circular meadow, as the peasantry call it, is in a line with the General Hospital, Mount Pleasant, St. Bridget's Asylum and the corporation lots recently acquired by the Quebec Seminary for a botanical garden and seminary, adjoining Abraham's Plains. Jacques Cartier's fort, we know to a certainty, must have been on the north bank of the river,† from the fact that the natives coming from Stadacona to visit their French guests had to cross the river, and did so frequently. However strange it may seem that Champlain does not appear to have known the exact locality where, seventy years previously, Stadacona had stood, the cause may exist in the exterminating wars carried on between the several savage tribes, leaving, occasionally, no vestige of once powerful nations or villages. Have we not seen in our day a once warlike and princely race—the Hurons—dwindle down, through successive decay, to what *now* remains of them?

* "Le lundi, onzième jour d'octobre, nous arrivasmes au Hâble de Sainte Croix, où estaient nos navires, et trouvasmes que les maistres et mariniers qui estaient demeurés avaient fait un fort devant lesdits navires, tout clos de grosses pièces de bois plantées debout, joignant les unes aux autres, et tout à l'entour garni d'artillerie, et bien en ordre pour se défendre contre tout le pays."—(*Second voyage de Jacques Cartier*, p. 48.) Republished by Literary and Historical Society of Quebec, in 1843. At the foot, we read, "On pense que ce fort a dû être bâti à l'endroit où la Petite Rivière Lairet se decharge dans la Rivière St. Charles." "The exact spot in the River St. Charles, where Cartier moored his vessel, is supposed on good authority to have been the site of the old bridge (a little higher up than the present), called Dorchester Bridge, where there is a ford at low water, close to the Marine Hospital. That it was on the east bank, not far from the residence of Charles Smith, Esq., is evident from the river having been frequently crossed by the natives coming from Stadacona, to visit their French guests." (*Hawkin's Picture of Quebec, p.* 47.) The Abbé Faillon in his elaborate work—*Histoire de la Colonie Française au Canada*, 1865—in some valuable notes on Jacques Cartier, p. 496, discusses the erroneous views of Charlevoix and Father Leclerc, and corroborates the accepted belief about the River St. Charles and not the Jacques Cartier River, as being the spot where the great discoverer wintered in 1535–6.

† Would this river be the Lairet or the St. Charles? We like to give every circumstance calculated to throw light thereon: writers seem to agree that Jacques Cartier wintered in the St. Charles, as Champlain says, in his edition of 1632, on the Jesuits' property—it may, however, have been a few acres to the east or west of the spot generally indicated.

A drawing accompanies this sketch, copied from an engraving executed at Paris, the subject of which was furnished by G. B. Faribault, Esquire, retracing the departure of the St. Malo mariner for France on the 6th May, 1536. To the right may be seen Jacques Cartier's fort,* built with stockades, mounted with artillery, and subsequently made stronger still, we are told, with ditches and solid timber, with drawbridge, and fifty men to watch night and day.

Next comes the *Grande Hermine*, his largest vessel, of about one hundred and twenty tons, in which Donacona, the interpreter, and two other Indians of note, treacherously seized, are to be conveyed to France, to be presented to the French monarch, Francis I. Close by, the reader will observe *L'Emerillon*, of about forty tons in size, the third of his ships; and higher up, the hull of a stranded and dismantled vessel, the *Petite Hermine*, of about sixty tons, intended to represent the one whose timbers were dug up at the mouth of the St. Michel stream in 1843, and created such excitement amongst the antiquarians of that day. On the opposite side of the river, at Hare Point, the reader will notice on the plate a cross, intended to represent the one erected by Cartier's party on the 3rd May, 1536, in honor of the festival of the Holy Cross; at the foot a number of Indians and some French in the old costume of the time of Francis I. So much for Jacques Cartier and his winter quarters, in 1535–6.

Two hundred and twenty-three years after this date we find this locality again the arena of memorable events. In the disorderly retreat of the French army on the 13th September, 1759, from the heights of Abraham, the panic-stricken squadrons came pouring down Côte d'Abraham and Côte à Cotton, hotly pursued by the Highlanders and the 58th Regiment, hurrying towards the bridge of boats and following the shores of the River St. Charles, until the fire of the hulks anchored in that river stopped the pursuit. On the north side of the bridge of boats was a *tête de pont*, redoubt or hornwork, a strong work of a pentagonal shape, well portrayed in the accompanying plan of the Siege Operations before Quebec. This hornwork was partly wood, defended by palisades, and towards Beauport an earthwork—covering about twelve acres; the remains (the round or

* "Le Capitaine fit renforcer le Fort tout à l'entour de gros fossés, larges, et profonds avec porte à pont-levis et renfort de rangs ou pans de bois au contraire des premiers. Et fut ordonné pour le guet de la nuit......cinquante hommes à quartre quarts, et à chacun changement des dits quarts les trompettes sonnantes; ce qui fut fait selon la dite ordonnance."—*Voyage de Jacques Cartier*, page 52.

ring field), standing more than fifteen feet above ground, may be seen to this day surrounded by a ditch; three thousand* men at least must have been required to construct, in a few weeks, this extensive entrenchment. In the centre stood a house, still visible on an old plan, in which, about noon on that memorable day, a pretty lively debate was taking place. Vaudreuil and some of the chief French officers were at that moment and in this spot debating the surrender of the whole colony. Let us hear an eye-witness, Chevalier Johnstone, General de Lévis' aide-de-camp, one of the Scotchmen fighting in Canada for the French king, against some of his own countrymen under Wolfe, after the disaster of Culloden. It was our good fortune to publish the recently-discovered journal of this Scotch officer for the first time last winter. Chevalier Johnstone's description will strike every one from its singular accuracy:—

"The French army in flight, scattered and entirely dispersed, rushed towards the town. Few of them entered Quebec; they went down the heights of Abraham, opposite to the Intendant's Palace (past St. John's gate), directing their course to the hornwork, and following the borders of the River St. Charles. Seeing the impossibility of rallying our troops, I determined myself to go down the hill at the windmill, near the bake-house,† and from thence across over the meadows to the hornwork, resolved not to approach Quebec, from my apprehension of being shut up there with a part of our army, which might have been the case if the victors had drawn all the advantage they could have reaped from our defeat. It is true the death of the general-in-chief—an event which never fails to create the greatest disorder and confusion in an army—may plead as an excuse for the English neglecting so easy an operation as to take all our army prisoners.

"The hornwork had the River St. Charles before it, about seventy

* It is evident that the Beauport entrenchments were to be on a vast scale. In those days of *corvées* and forced labor, when it was merely necessary to command *de par le roi*, it was easy to bring together large bodies of men. "M. de Montcalm, arrivé à Québec (from Montréal), commanda tout le monde pour travailler à des retrenchements qui furent tracés vers une paroisse nommée Beauport. Comme il pensa que ces ouvrages ne seraient pas en état avant l'arrivée des vaisseaux anglais, ce qui pouvait être d'un jour à l'autre, il envoya un ordre à M. de Lévis, qui était à Montréal, de commander, généralement, tous les hommes de ce gouvernement de descendre à Québec, et qu'on avait besoin d'un coup de main. Il envoya à cet égard des ordres précis et conformes, dans toutes les paroisses, qui mirent tout le monde en mouvement."—*Mémoires sur les affaires du Canada*, 1749–1760. Finally, Vaudreuil decided that Montreal would furnish 1,500 men only for this service.

† This bakehouse appears to have been some where at the foot of Abraham's hill.

paces broad, which served it better than an artificial ditch; its front facing the river and the heights, was composed of strong, thick, and high palisades, planted perpendicularly, with gunholes pierced for several pieces of large cannon in it; the river is deep and only fordable at low water, at a musket shot before the fort; this made it more difficult to be forced on that side than on its other side of earthworks facing Beauport, which had a more formidable appearance; and the hornwork certainly on that side was not in the least danger of being taken by the English, by an assault from the other side of the river. On the appearance of the English troops on the plain of the bake-house, Montguet and La Motte, two old captains in the Regiment of Bearn, cried out with vehemence to M. de Vaudreuil, 'that the hornwork would be taken in an instant, by an assault, sword in hand; that we would be all cut to pieces without quarter, and that nothing else would save us but an immediate and general capitulation of Canada, giving it up to the English.'

"Montreuil told them that 'a fortification such as the hornwork was not to be taken so easily.' In short, there arose a general cry in the hornwork to cut the bridge of boats.* It is worthy of remark, that not a fourth part of our army had yet arrived at it, and the remainder, by cutting the bridge, would have been left on the other side of the river as victims to the victors. The regiment 'Royal Roussillon,' was at that moment at the distance of a musket shot from the hornwork, approaching to pass the bridge. As I had already been in such adventures, I did not lose my presence of mind, and having still a shadow remaining of that regard, which the army accorded me on account of the esteem and confidence which M. De Lévis and M. De Montcalm had always shewn me publicly, I called to M. Hugon, who commanded, for a pass in the hornwork, and begged of him to accompany me to the bridge. We ran there, and without asking who had given the order to cut it, we chased away the soldiers with their uplifted axes ready to execute that extravagant and wicked operation.

"M. Vaudreuil was closetted in a house in the inside of the hornwork with the Intendant and with some other persons. I suspected they

* It crossed the St. Charles a little higher up than the Marine Hospital, exactly at the foot of Crown street.

were busy drafting the articles for a general capitulation, and I entered the house, where I had only time to see the Intendant with a pen in his hand writing upon a sheet of paper, when M. Vaudreuil told me I had no business there. Having answered him that what he said was true, I retired immediately, in wrath, to see them intent on giving up so scandalously a dependency for the preservation of which so much blood and treasure had been expended. On leaving the house, I met M. Dalquier, an old, brave, downright honest man, commander of the regiment of Bearn, with the true character of a good officer—the marks of Mars all over his body. I told him it was being debated within the house, to give up Canada to the English by a capitulation, and I hurried him in to stand up for the King's cause, and advocate the welfare of his country. I then quitted the hornwork to join Poularies at the Ravine* of Beauport, but having met him about three or four hundred paces from the hornwork, on his way to it, I told him what was being discussed there. He answered me, that sooner than consent to a capitulation, he would shed the last drop of his blood. He told me to look on his table and house as my own, advised me to go there directly to repose myself, and clapping spurs to his horse, he flew like lightning to the hornwork."

Want of space precludes us from adding more from this very interesting journal of the Chevalier Johnstone, replete with curious particulars of the disorderly retreat of the French regiments from their Beauport camp, after dark, on that eventful day; how they assembled first at the hornwork, and then filed off by detachments up the Charlesbourg road, then to Indian and Ancient Lorette, until they arrived, worn out and disheartened without commanders, at day break at Cap Rouge.

On viewing the memorable scenes witnessed at Ringfield,—the spot where the first French discoverers wintered in 1535-6, and also the locality, where it was decided to surrender the colony to England in 1759—are we not justified in considering it as both the *cradle* and the *tomb* of French dominion in the new world?

Ringfield has, for many years, been the family mansion of George Holmes Parke, Esquire.

* A small bridge supported on masonry has since been built at this spot, exactly across the main road at Brown's mills.

17

Coucy le Castel.

"Sol Canadien, terre chérie
Par des braves tu fus peuplé,
Ils cherchaient, loin de leur patrie,
Une terre de liberté,
Qu'elles sont belles, nos campagnes,
Au Canada qu'on vit content!"

About the year 1830 that portion of the environs of Quebec watered by the River St. Charles, in the vicinity of Scott's bridge, had especially attracted the attention of several of our leading citizens as pleasant and healthy abodes for their families. Two well known gentlemen in particular, the bearers of old and respected names, the late Honorable Mr. Justice Philippe Panet, and his brother, the Honorable Louis Panet, Legislative Councillor, selected two adjoining lots covering close on eighty acres, on the banks of the St. Charles, the Cabire-Coubat of ancient days. The main road to the east intervenes between the Hon. Judge Panet's seat and the mossy old dwelling in which General Arnold had his head-quarters during the winter of 1775-6, now the residence of the Langlois family. Judge Panet built there an elegant villa, on an Italian design, brought home after returning from the sunny clime of Naples; the rooms are lofty and all are oval. Several hundred sombre old pines surround the house on all sides.

The neighboring villa, to the west, was planned by the Honorable Louis Panet, about 1830; also the grounds tastefully laid out in meadows, plantations and gardens, symmetrically divided off by neat spruce, thorn, and snowberry hedges, which improve very much their aspect. One fir hedge, in particular, is of uncommon beauty. To the west an ancient pine, a veritable monarch of the forest, rears his hoary trunk, and amidst most luxuriant foliage looks down proudly on the young plantation beneath him, lending his hospitable shades to a semi-circular rustic seat—a grateful retreat during the heat of a summer's day. Next to this old tree, runs a small rill, once dammed up for a fish-pond, but a colony of muskrats having "unduly elected domicile thereat," the finny denizens disappeared as if by magic; and next, the voracious *rodores* made so many raids into the vegetable garden that the legal gentleman, who was lord of the manor, served on them a *notice to quit* by removing the dam. Thus ejected the amphibii crossed the river in a body and "elected domicile" in the roots of an elm tree at Poplar Grove, opposite and in full view of the castle, probably by way of a threat. On the high river banks a twelve-pounder, used formerly to crown a miniature fort erected there. We remember on certain occasions hearing at a distance its loud *boom*. Coucy le Castel is surrounded on two sides by a spacious piazza, and stands in an elevated position close to the river bank. From the drawing-room windows is visible the even course of the fairy Cabire-Coubat, hurrying past in dark eddies, under the pendulous foliage of some graceful elms which overhang the bank at Poplar Grove, the mansion of L. T. McPherson, Esquire. Now and again from the small fort, amidst the murmur of rapids not far distant, you may catch the shrill note of the king-fisher in his hasty flight over the limpid stream, or see a lively fish leap in yonder deep pool; or else, in the midsummer vacation, see a birch canoe lazily floating down from *la mer Pacifique*, impelled by the arm of a pensive law student, dreaming perchance of Pothier or Blackstone,—perchance of his lady love, whilst paddling to the air:—

> "Il y a longtemps que je t'aime
> Jamais je ne t'oublierai."

The neighborhood of running water; the warbling of birds; the distant lowing of kine in the green meadows; the variety and beauty of the landscape, especially when the descending orb of day gilds the dark woods to the west, furnish a strikingly rural spectacle at Coucy le Castel, thus named from a French estate in Picardy, owned by the Badelarts, ancestors on the maternal side of the Panets.

In 1861 Coucy le Castel was purchased by Judge Taschereau, of Quebec, under whose care it is acquiring each year new charms. A plantation of of deciduous trees and evergreens has taken the place of the row of poplars which formerly lined the avenue. The Judge's *Chateau* stands conspicuous amongst the pretty but less extensive surrounding country seats, such as the old mansion of Fred. Andrews, Esq., Q. C., the neat cottage of Fred. W. Andrews, Esq., Barrister, festooned with wild vines, together with a tasty lodge erected by Dr. Marsden on the Little River road.

Crane Island.

"Sweet memory, wafted by thy gentle gale,
Oft up the stream of time I turn my sail,
To view the fairy haunts of long-lost hours,
Blest with far greener shades—far richer flowers."

It has frequently been our pleasant task, in the pages of "*Les Oiseaux du Canada*" and "*Les Poissons du Canada*," to point out to the sportsman and to the naturalist the beautiful island of which a sketch is here given as a locality well suited for the exercise of their respective crafts

"In the *season* of the year."

Before considering Crane Island in relation to its capacity for sport, let us view it in its utilitarian aspect. It lies in the St. Lawrence thirty-six miles lower down than Quebec; extreme length, six miles, with one and a half mile as extreme breadth. The soil on the ridge which runs along the middle of the island is light, though fertile, and well adapted to the culture of maize and potatoes; the lower, or wheat lands, are amongst the finest in America, being the result of alluvial deposits of many ages—a loam of great depth, inexhaustible richness, much similar to the renowned "bottoms" along the banks of the Mississippi. Its fertility may arise from its insulated position; the sun's rays being reflected from the surrounding waters, and the early frosts, so pernicious to wheat harvests in other localities, nearly unknown on the island. From time immemorial, Crane Island has been famous for the delicious produce of its dairies and the bountiful harvests of hay its meadows and beaches yield, with no other manuring than the alluvial richness which the high tides of spring and fall communicate to them, like the overflowing of the Nile to Egyptian rice fields. A highway, as level as a bowling-green, extends from one end of the island to the other; from the peculiar nature of the soil, it requires no repairs, and is ever pleasant to ride or drive over. Population, about one thousand souls.

Crane Island is united to the next island (Goose Island), not shown in the sketch, by a belt of low land, four and a half miles long by one and a half broad, covered with most luxuriant hay, forming artificial meadows, from which the inhabitants draw their annual supply of winter fodder, without the slightest tillage.

Goose Island appears to have been thus called from the myriads of geese, ducks and teal which it formerly and still harbors. The *Relations des*

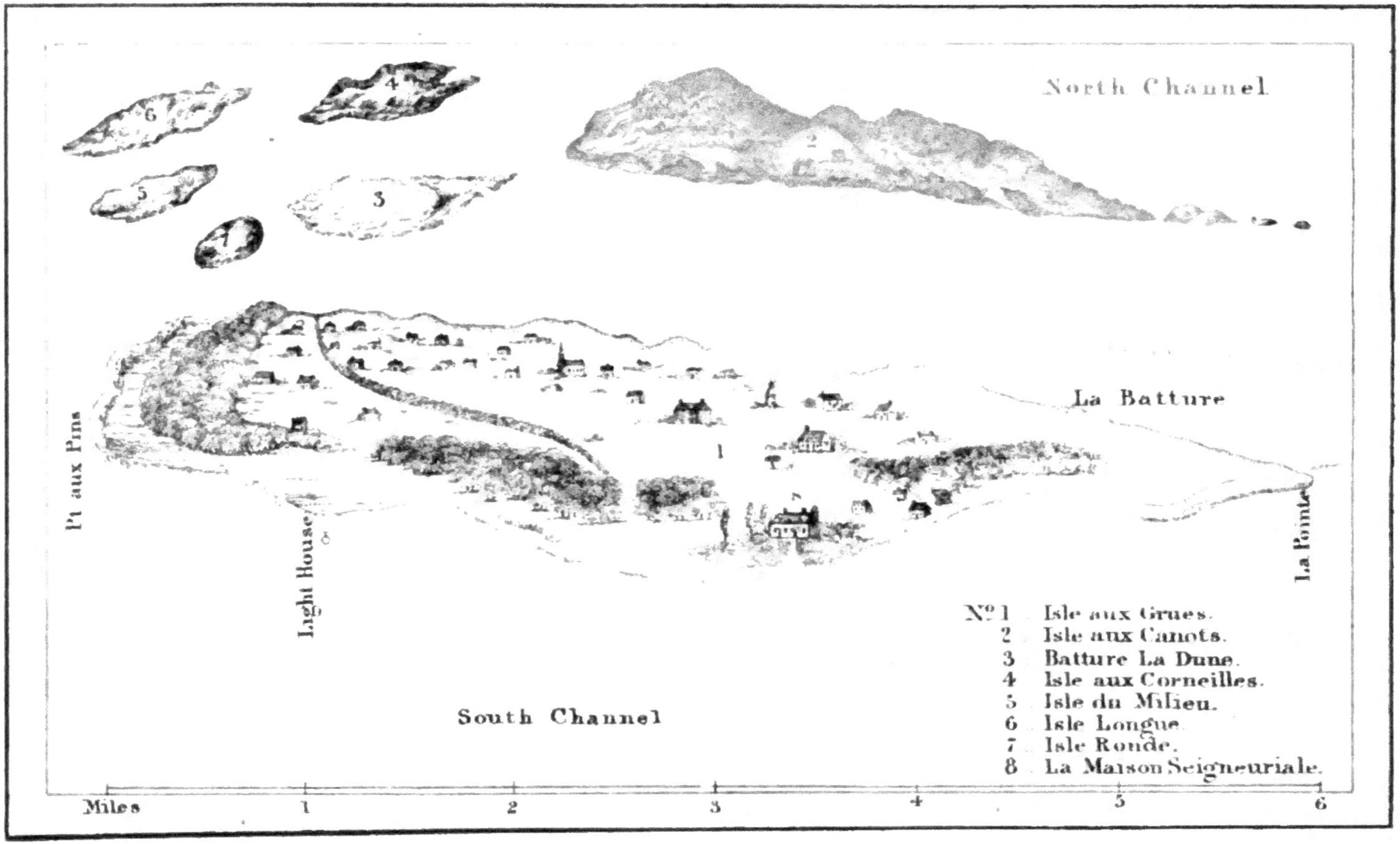
North Channel
Pt aux Pins
Light House
La Batture
La Pointe
South Channel
Nº 1 Isle aux Grues.
2 Isle aux Canots.
3 Batture La Dune.
4 Isle aux Corneilles.
5 Isle du Milieu.
6 Isle Longue.
7 Isle Ronde.
8 La Maison Seigneuriale.
Miles
1
2
3
4
5
6

Jesuits for 1663 graphically describe it as the inviolate sanctum and breeding-grounds of ducks and teal, "whose loud voices made the whole place resound in the summer season, but who kept a profound silence during the spring and summer of 1663, owing to the frightful and continuous earthquakes which caused the soil to roll and heave to such a degree that church steeples would bend to the earth and rise up again;" a feat which, from its novelty, would be particularly attractive to witness from a baloon, for instance—from the deck of a ship—from anywhere—in fact, except from old mother earth.

The Iroquois or Five Nations, in 1653, made a descent on Goose Island, at the lower extremity of the island, now a farm in possession of the Hôtel Dieu nuns of Quebec, and known as "Conti;" they murdered M. Moyen* and his wife; his children were carried away as prisoners. One of his daughters married the brave Lambert Close, whose courage shed lustre on the early times of Montreal.

Crane Island is the most conspicuous and valuable of a group of islands, *Ile aux Canots, Ile aux Corneilles, Ile Ste. Marguerite*, &c., conceded, in 1646, by the Company of New France to the Chevalier de Montmagny, then Governor of the colony. The sporting knight was in the habit of spending the shooting season here; whether his lodge stood where M. de Longueuil subsequently built his manor, on the east end of the island, must be a mere matter of conjecture. The extraordinary abundance of game which the island harbored then may be conceived, judging from the sport the place still affords in these degenerate days of pot hunting. An English millionaire who became the purchaser of Crane Island, out and out, might, with the assistance of a few game keepers, soon be in a position to boast of owning one of the greatest game preserves in the world; not only do the ducks come there in the fall and spring in myriads, but they also, as previously stated, make it their breeding-place. A few years back it was a common thing to see a pot-hunter scouring the beaches with a Newfound-

* "Les Iroquois s'accagèrent l'Isle aux Oyes, à douze lieues de Québec; tuent toutes les familles de Moyen et de Macart, emmènent les enfans dont Mlle. Dugué était; repassent à Montréal, y donnent quelques attaques. * * * Les dits Iroquois tuent un nommé D'aubigeon, puis veulent pourparler. M. LeMoine venait d'escorter un ambassadeur Iroquois, raconte le sac de l'Isle aux Oyes; on fait dessein de surprendre les pourparleurs. M. LeMoine les prend, allant seul à eux avec ses pistolets. Le capitaine de la troupe des pourparleurs Iroquois, nommé La Plaine, vint le lendemain pour délivrer ses gens, et est encore pris par M. LeMoine avec quatre autres".—(*Histoire du Canada.*—L'Abbé Belmont.)

land dog and capturing the young ducks before they could fly. At present the islanders insist on their right of property* and prosecute all trespassers indiscriminately, thereby not only protecting the game, but also preserving their beach hay from the destruction which trespassers committed by tramping it down and making holes on the swamp to secrete themselves while watching for geese and ducks on the wing, in which holes the cattle used to fall and perish.

Towards the Eastern (McPherson's) Point, as it is called, may be seen the old manor, *La Maison Seigneuriale*, built on the spot where stood, at the end of the last century, the residence of one of the first *seigneurs*, Daniel Lienard de Beaujeu. Behind it, to the north, is visible the old wind mill, and a cluster of pretty white cottages, chiefly occupied by well-to-do river pilots, extending to the extreme west end of the island, crowned

* It is really curious to note the care taken, both under French and English rule, to protect the game in these *preserves*. No less than two Ordnances were passed, one in 1731 and the other in 1769, to assure to the Seigneurs of Crane Island the exclusive privilege and right of shooting, granted them by their original title-deed by ——— Gilles Hocquart.

"Sur les plaintes qui nous ont été portées par le Sieur de Touville aide Major des Troupes, Seigneur des Isles aux Oyes, aux Grues, au Canot, Ste. Marguerite et la Grosse Isle, que plusieurs particuliers tant de cette ville, que des isle et des côtes voisines s'ingerent de chasser dans les d; isle, quoique qu'il n'y ait que le *Seigneur qui ait le privilege a lui accordé par ses titres*, à quoi il nous aurait requis de pourvoir, nous faisons très expresses defenses à toutes personnes de chasser dans l'étendue des d; isles et Seigneuries sous quelque pretexte que ce soit, sans la permission du Sieur de Touville et à peine de 10 livres d'amende contre les contreventants, et de confiscation de leurs armes et canots au profit du dit Seigneur; et sera la presente Ordonnance lue, publiée et affichée en la manière accoutumée. Mandons, &c.

"Fait à Québec, le 20 mars, 1731.

"(Signé) HOQUART.

"(*Archives de la Province—Registre des Ordonnances*, Folio 70 Recto."

"By His Excellency, Guy Carleton, Captain General and Governor in Chief of the Province of Quebec, Brigadier General of His Majesty's armies, &c., &c., &c.

"Taking into consideration the representations which have been made to us by the Sieur De Longueil, Seigneur of Crane and Goose Islands, Canoe and Ste. Marguerite Islands, and also Grosse Isle, that by his title he has the exclusive right to shoot on these said Islands—that notwithstanding several persons both from the city and neighboring parishes, and even the inhabitants of these islands, attempt to shoot there without leave, destroying the hay on the beaches, and catching the young ducks that they find there, thereby deminishing the numbers considerably for the next hunting season, and also removing each year a quantity of thatching grass; also using as fire-wood the timber on those islands, we hereby expressly forbid that any person either from Quebec or from the neighboring seigneuries, and likewise, that any of the inhabitants of these islands, under whatever pretence, do shoot on these islands or any portion thereof, without the express permission of the Sieur de Longueil, under pain of legal punishment. We also forbid them to remove the young ducks, to carry away the thatching grass, to destroy the meadow hay, or burn the timber on the said islands, without the leave of the said Sieur de Longueil, and the said Sieur de Longueil may have this ordenance published in the neighboring parishes.

"Done at Quebec, 28th July, 1769.

"(Signed) GUY CARLETON.

"*Reg I. Foi et 'Hommages*, Folio 226."

by a maple wood called "Le Domaine;" the parish church, of course, as in all Canadian scenery, looms out in the centre—*the parent watching over the welfare of her offspring.* As a river view, nothing can surpass in grandeur the panorama which the broad St. Lawrence here unfolds on a radiant summer morning, when, with the rising tide, a fleet of swan-winged merchantmen emerge from the *Traverse*, far below, in the direction of the church of *St. Roch des Aulnets:* at first imperceptible white specks on the horizon, gradually growing larger and larger, on the bosom of the glad waters, until they each in succession crowd on you, top-sails, top gallant-sails and royals all set, a moving tower of canvass advancing straight to where you stand—so close, when an island pilot,* perchance, is in charge, and takes the inshore channel, the deepest though the narrowest, that you can distinctly hear the voices of all on board.

The high tides of spring and fall wash the foot of the rising ground on which the manor stands; the game, such as ring-plovers, curlews, sea-snipe, sand-pipers, then light within a few rods of the house. To the north of Crane Island, and separated by a narrow pass, you notice a small island (No. 3), which the tide covers each day; that is the celebrated *Dune*, well known to Canadian *chasseurs* as abounding with Canada geese (outardes), snow-geese, ducks and small game. Every day in May and September you may see a flock of snow-geese and outardes feeding there, some three thousand, beyond a rifle's range, or winging their rapid, noisy, wedge-like, flight towards the muddy St. Joachim flats opposite.

Home of our early days, thrice blessed isle, the congenial abode of many feathered denizens, the seat of plenty and of domestic peace, how oft, a youthful fowler, have we, gun in hand, trudged knee-deep through thy reedy, boundless marshes. Fatigue! pooh! there was in those days no such word in our vocabulary. How many sunny, blissful hours, during the long mid-summer vacation, have we beguiled away on thy grassy lawn or in thy well-stocked orchard, dreaming away life's May dreams, or waiting impatiently until the increasing murmur of the swelling, bursting tide should indicate high water, the auspicious moment when we sallied forth to pour destruction among the serried squadrons of beach-birds cooped up on thy pebbly shores! Haunts of our early days, accept this tribute of our youth!

* An island pilot, when in charge of a ship, always salutes his island home, when sailing past, with the Union Jack.

These fertile islands constituting the *Seigneurie de l'Isle aux Grues, Isle aux Oies*, &c., have belonged for near seventy years to the McPherson family, the descendants of which, *Les Dames Seigneuresses*, as their simple and contented tenants style them, still inhabit the old manor.

Ladies' Protestant Home.

This charitable institution originated in a society which was formed in 1855, under the name of the "Ladies' Quebec Protestant Relief Society." It was begun on a very humble scale, by the following ladies:—Mrs. Carden, Mrs. W. Newton, Mrs. S. Newton, Mrs. Knight, Mrs. Puffer, Mrs. Maxfield Sheppard, Mrs. Archibald Campbell, Mrs. James Bankier, and Miss H. Newton. These, with the help of the Rev. Mr. Carden, Mrs. Bradshaw, Miss Oldacre, and others, associated themselves together for visiting and relieving the wants of the Protestant poor of the city, but they soon found that without some home or house of refuge, much of the charity was misapplied; they, therefore, in 1858, made an appeal to the public for means to hire a house and provide a shelter for those cases that were utterly homeless and destitute. This appeal was most favorably received, and such was the encouragement they met with that the ladies soon after solicited an Act of Incorporation, which was granted in the spring of 1859; and thus, under the name of the "Ladies' Protestant Home," was founded the present institution, which claims to receive and help "destitute and unprotected women and female children of all Protestant denominations, in the city of Quebec." To this, the original design, has been added the maintenance of two infirmary wards for the treatment of non-infectious diseases.

The building which forms our illustration, is situated on the left-hand side of the St. Lewis road, just within the turnpike. It is a handsome, spacious house, admirably suited to the purpose for which it was erected, and the site is one of the healthiest and finest in the city. The Home was built by Mr. Hugh Hatch, contractor, Mr. Lecourt being the architect, under the direction of the following gentlemen—John Gilmour, Esq., Dr. Blatherwick, Mr. Sheriff Sewell, O. L. Richardson, Esq., A. C.

Buchanan, Esq., George Veasey, Esq., McLean Stewart, Esq., Joseph Bowles, Esq., and John Musson, Esq., who voluntarily undertook to collect and solicit the funds necessary for the work. So successful were they, and so generously were subscriptions bestowed by all the leading members of the Protestant community, that the large sum of sixteen thousand dollars was soon at their disposal, and in May, 1863, the Home was completed and occupied; it now forms one of the most popular and useful of the many charitable institutions of the city of Quebec.

OFFICERS OF THE SOCIETY, FOR 1865.

PRESIDENT—Mrs. John Gilmour. VICE-PRESIDENT—Mrs. William Walker.

SECRETARY—Miss Griffin. ASSISTANT-SECRETARY—Miss Isabel Sewell.

TREASURER—Mrs. Bankier.

COMMITTEE OF MANAGEMENT:

Mrs. W. Newton,	Mrs. Bowles,	Miss Gibb,
" W. Poston,	" Oakes,	" McCallum,
" C. Wurtele.	" Richardson,	" Shaw,
" W. H. Jeffery,	" Wiley,	" Clark,
" Vannovous,	" Austin,	" B. Clark,
" D. R. Stewart,	" Powis,	" E. Stewart,
" W. W. Scott,	" C. Holt,	" S. Sewell,
" James Douglas,	" Barton,	" Prior.
" J. Dinning,	" Bouchette,	" McLean,
" Robarts,	Miss Racey,	" Newton.
" W. White,	" E. McKenzie,	

MATRON—Miss McKellop.

PHYSICIANS:

J. S. Sewell, M.D., John Racey, M.D., W. Boswell, M.D., A. Rowand, M.D.

ADVISORY COMMITTEE:

John Gilmour, Sheriff Sewell, John Musson, James Dinning, Geo. Veasey, A. C. Buchanan, J. G. Ross, H. Fry.

SECRETARY—Wm. Hossack.

ERRATA.

PAGE 18—Instead of "the famous Royal Roussillon Regiment, commanded by Poularies," read "the famous Royal Roussillon Regiment." Poularies was not present at the first battle of the Plains, being at the Beauport camp, in charge of the Montreal Regiments.

" 96—4th line, instead of "the Earl of Elgin," read "the Earl of Durham," in 1838.

" 98—Instead of "struck their tents," read "pitched their tents."

OPINIONS OF THE PRESS.

(From the Quebec *Morning Chronicle*.)

MAPLE LEAVES. Third Series. Canadian History and Quebec Scenery, by J. M. LeMoine, Esq., Quebec. Hunter, Rose & Co., St. Ursule street, 1865.—pp. 143, (with photographic views.)

The author of "Maple Leaves" is without exception the most industrious of all our Canadian *littérateurs*. Combining in his own person the blood of the two great races who have made Canada their home, he is characterized by a most noble quality. His works, as a national writer, are singularly free from the blemish of sectional prejudice. The spirit by which he is actuated is Canadian in the true sense of the word; and whether his pen describes the triumph of the flag bearing upon its snow-white field the golden lilies, in the wooded gorges of Carrilon; the gallant achievement of the heroes who followed Wolfe to victory on the Plains of Abraham; the glorious though expiring feat of French power on the heights of St. Foy, in April 1760, or the valiant defence of the fortress-city in the winter of 1775-76, with its small quota of regular troops and its few thousand inhabitants, against Richard Montgomery and his continentals—he is never unjust but always impartial. This excellent quality arises from that true patriotism which desires to do becoming honor to the glories of our common ancestry, and we congratulate the writer upon its possession. In the series of "Maple Leaves"—of which, through the kindness of the author, we have been favoured with an advance copy—the author devotes his pen to a subject to which he is qualified to do ample justice. Eschewing the role of historian so little understood and so often prostituted to base purposes, Mr. LeMoine has applied himself to the task of preserving from oblivion those themes which may be called the unwritten chapters of our history, inasmuch as they are outside the legitimate scope of the narrator of great events though not less interesting to the present age, as affording an insight into the inner-life of our ancestors. The author of

OPINIONS OF THE PRESS.

"Maple Leaves" is at present doing for Lower Canada what John Timbs and the author of "Haunted London" have done for the antiquities of England's metropolis; what Jules Janin has done for Brittany, that land hallowed by the legends of Arthur and Merlin; what the antiquarian societies of all Christendom have done for their respective countries. In the third issue of "Maple Leaves," Mr. LeMoine has, however, managed to strike upon a new and comparatively untrodden path of literature, albeit it is with the *genre* we have already defined, "Canadian Homes" for his text, and he has done ample justice to the beautiful theme. It is true he has confined himself to the country-seats in the immediate vicinity of Quebec; but he cannot be blamed for doing so inasmuch as they are beyond all others most fruitful of historical reminiscences. The volume now before us may therefore be said to be made up almost wholly of historical and descriptive sketches of the domains around the ancient capital. There are over thirty of these sketches, and we must say that they are all in excellent style. The author has had the good sense not to overlay his work with heavy chronological details. On the contrary, there is a judicious commingling of light and shade—of history and legend—of the stern records of time and the bloom of autumnal landscapes; and the result is that the volume is at once rich in historical lore and interesting as a handbook of accurate and pleasing descriptions. Commencing with the Mansion House, Montmorency—with its reminiscences of the Duke of Kent, and General Haldimand (one of the best papers in the volume by the way)—the author relates in a lively, sketchy manner, the story of every domain of note in the environs of Quebec. Stately Elm Grove and beautiful Thornhill; lordly Spencer Wood with its every luxury which can make home attractive, its magnificent site on the high grounds overlooking the great river, its conservatories, its gardens, its thousand beauties; Woodfield, with its ancient recollections and its present magnificence; beautiful Benmore—Kirkella, Bardfield and Cataqui; splendid Clermont, on Sillery heights; dainty Rosewood; Cap Rouge or Redclyffe, standing amid the ancient pine of its rocky promontory, like a giant sentinel overlooking river and valley; Holland Farm, with its tragic recollections; Beauport Manner House, redolent of the *ancien régime*; Ringfield the, old battle-ground, consecrated by the blood of heroes; Morton Lodge, Hamwood and a dozen other noted residences—all these receive full justice from Mr. LeMoine's pen. Graceful and facile in style, his pages contain a vivid idea of the green lawns and the shady woods, the sleeping pools, the meandering streams and the flowery slopes of the old mansion grounds in which he has found such a congenial topic. There are other papers in the volume now before us, but the theme we have alluded to forms the *pièce de résistance*. The other subjects, however, deserve some mention. There is an admirable sketch of the campaign of 1759, containing many interesting facts drawn from almost forgotten sources. The portion devoted to the history of Sillery—its woods and its wild flowers is beautiful in the extreme. We may even say more for the paper on 'Literary Gossip on Olden Times" with its selections from the pages of "Emily Montague," and its quaint *souvenirs* of the early colonial days of British rule, and garrison life in its infancy. In closing our notice we may say that Mr. LeMoine has given to the Canadian public a volume racy of the soil and full of interest, for which they have reason to be truly grateful. We are glad to learn that the leading merchants—the present proprietors of many of our oldest domains—have liberally patronized the book, and we sincerely hope all friends of our national literature will do likewise. One of its most attractive features consists of a series of photographic views of the principal country-seats, by Mr. Livernois, of St. John street, in that artist's best style. Altogether, the volume is a credit to Canadian bookmaking.

CANADIAN FISHERIES.

THE Deep-Sea, Lake and River Fisheries of Canada are very extensive, and of yearly increasing importance. From both are derived great quantities of fish-food, which, fresh and cured, forms a staple product for export and home consumption. In Lower Canada are found nearly all the varieties known to British waters. The deep-sea fisheries yield an abundance of such of the edible fishes as cod, mackarel, herrings, halibut, hake, etc. The fresh-water fisheries afford ample supplies of salmon, trout, striped-bass, black-bass, pickerel, white-fish, herrings, perch, shad, pike, sturgeon, eels, maskinongé, haddock, flounders, smelts, caplin, sardines, etc. The fishes are caught at various seasons throughout the year.

Angling for salmon and white-trout has been very successfully practised during the last three seasons upon the several tributaries of the River and Gulf of St. Lawrence. These streams being now under strict protection are fast becoming replenished with salmon. Many of them have latterly afforded excellent sport to fly-fishermen.

In Upper Canada the lakes and rivers abound with white-fish, salmon, salmon-trout, lake-trout, speckled-trout, herrings, bass, pickerel, maskinongé, sturgeon, siskawitz, and many other inferior kinds. Most of those species inhabit the clear, cold and deep waters of the Great Lakes, and are in fine condition, large and numerous. The trout and black-bass found in Lake Superior, and in almost every stream emptying into it, are heavy and game fish, rising greedily at artificial flies, and giving rare delight to anglers.

For full particulars, reference to be made to the Commissioner of Crown Lands.

QUEBEC, 1865.

CPSIA information can be obtained
at www.ICGtesting.com
Printed in the USA
LVHW100423110522
718424LV00003B/70

9 783375 005955